He's kinda tall

He's kinda tall

Julian's Sophomore Year, Part 2

Winter 1962-63

a romantic comedy

by

Eldot

First Edition

ΔΙΦΡΑ

In memory of HMMH

Publisher's Note:

This book is intended for a mature audience. It is not written to serve or encourage prurient interest; it contains no pornography or graphic language, but there are several intimate passages, including male/male. Readers who are offended by that should not read this book. All the characters in the story would have been 68 years of age or older when the story was written in late 2019. Any similarities or references to actual persons have been systematically modified to eliminate any basis for recognition.

Library of Congress Control Number: 2020911590

ISBN: Hardcover   978-1-7328805-5-9

        Softcover   978-1-7328805-6-6

        ePub, Kindle   978-1-7328805-7-3

By the same author:

You're in *high school* now: Julian's Sophomore year, Part 1

The Julian's Private Scrapbook novels:

Barr's Meadow
The Poker Club
The Shooting Gallery
Thunder and Lightning
The Champions

eBook only: Inside the World of Eldot
The Little J and Roger series

Authors Note:

Set in the early 1960s, this novel presumes background knowledge that many contemporary and international readers may not have. To offset that, an illustrated glossary provides explanatory information. There are more characters to keep track of than most novels; who everyone is and how they fit in is supported by an Index of Names and Places. It provides a short description as well as noting the chapters in which the character or name appears.

These are not necessary or required to understand or enjoy the novel— they are there merely to satisfy curiosity tweaked by details in the text and to free the reader to focus on the story.

This novel is unconventional; the subject of sexual orientation and activity is central and is dealt with honestly, with a comical approach. Readers who are uncomfortable with the subject should be prepared to skip over a few passages.

Julian's Sophomore Year is a work of fiction, though elements of it originate in true life experience. Any similarity to real persons is coincidental and unintended; some of the places exist, but are used fictitiously.

Prefatory note on the use of words referring to African Americans or Blacks.

The author is unprepared to expound authoritatively on the proper terminology to use when referring to this segment of the population. Since this book is fiction and both time and place specific, erroneous assumptions could be made when racial references are made. This is to clarify the author's intent, lest that issue get in the way as you read the story. Race is a political issue of major proportion currently, and that is not where this story is intended to land: this is for fun and entertainment, and for making a contribution to the progress and well being of our society generally; it is not intended to be a part of the political dialog of the 2020s. Though the author is a strong supporter of the Black Lives Matter movement, this book is not written to express that view nor be a part of the discussion. That issue exploded into the news after this segment of Julian's story was written. It is a welcome coincidence.

As a result, instead of using the racial terminology of the sixties, an attempt has been made to lessen or sidestep the offense inflicted by many of those words. In the early sixties, the term Black was rarely if ever used in most of the country; it was coming soon, but would have been the least likely word to use as it is on eighteen pages of this story.

However, this is being read by mixed generations of readers, many that could take offense—serious offense—at historical authenticity when employing racial terminology. Witness the occasional attempt to censor or ban Mark Twain, one of the earliest advocates for equality and fairness. Jim in Huckleberry Finn is one of literature's most powerful testimonies on their behalf. So, be it cowardly or naïve or good guessing, I have departed from authenticity—I do not feel comfortable using those terms, so I don't. I see no need to list them either.

This issue was unanticipated, caused unintentionally by the decision to place the story in 1962 North Carolina. The author has never been there: one reason it was chosen. But that's another subject, and is discussed elsewhere. See below, page 664, **Inside Eldot's World: a literary gazetteer** (2012).

A few reader comments

…imbued with positive, canny eroticism

The author goes inside the heads of the characters, so that we understand their bashfulness, their longing or curiosity. There is a nonchalant, playful tone that removes the stigma of queer intimacy.

…a wonderful look at boys transitioning between childhood and adulthood.

Previous books in the Julian story

Julian's Private Scrapbook

Barr's Meadow

The Poker Club

The Shooting Gallery

Thunder and Lightning

The Champions

viii

Preface to *Julian's Sophomore Year*

After a few months of nagging, I began to pay attention and the Muse got her way at last. That, and a few very nice prods from readers of the *Julian's Private Scrapbook* series, convinced me that it was time to write more about Julian. I'm not sure how long this "phase" of his story will run, since I'm not in charge, really. I have come to understand that it isn't over until the Muse decides it's over. Julian's life, like most, has many chapters—even chapters within chapters. This book is one of those—the first year of high school is special for most of us; it certainly was for Julian.

The grand social purpose that motivated the *Julian's Private Scrapbook* series lurks in the background, unsolved as always: social change is never as rapid as one would like. There are still bullies, there are still boys who don't know what to do about their life. Laws and institutions remain inadequate and clumsy, sometimes indifferent or cruel. So it's worth the effort to add a positive chapter or two.

About all I can do is insist that it remain fun and interesting. I hope that you are able to enjoy the ride as well. It's not supposed to be more work.

Eldot, June, 2015

July-August 2020:

Five years have zoomed by since I wrote the preface to **You're in *high school* now,** Part 1 of Julian's Sophomore Year. It seems more like ten. Demand for social change has proven to be far more rapid and widespread than I had thought possible. It's still early days in dealing openly with the issue that confronts Julian and Mark, but that too has begun at last. If the effect of social media on LGBT issues continues at the current pace, it could be old news before the decade is finished. This author will do what he can to provide sunlight—the best protection available to truth and fairness. Prejudice and misunderstanding depend on darkness and ignorance: those are not allowed in Julian's story.

The emergence of the BLM movement onto the front page is coincidental, making this part of Julian's story timely. I hope this modest effort helps that movement as well.

If you are new to Julian's story, welcome: you have entered partway. A few words of explanation should put you at ease—you don't have to read the earlier parts of the story first—though you may want to after you finish this segment. It is a love story, but a complex and controversial one. Not a "quick read," it relies on comedy and other literary devices to make it fun and interesting. The special "backgrounder" that follows this preface explains this more fully should you be interested.

The plan to complete Julian's first year of high school in one book was not allowed by the Muse. Readers need to be alerted: this Muse is demanding. She insists on detail and employs both direct and indirect methods to tell Julian and Mark's story. Contemporary romance novels rarely require keeping track of more than one or two characters. Generally its work is finished in less than two hundred pages. This Muse is just getting into high gear at that point. She insists on employing the deductive capability of the reader as a way to engage participation.

The pace has picked up: the timeline in Julian's Private Scrapbook was two weeks, and took five parts. The fist part of the Sophomore Year covered four months.

Part 2 had to wait while the author dealt with other matters. There are only so many hours in a day, and it was necessary to hold the Muse at bay. This book had been percolating all the while, eager to emerge. Thanks for your understanding, patience, and support.

Have fun with this, please: there is no hurry. Most stories are about what went wrong—this one is about what went right and how; this is a happily ever after story. There are important steps along the way—they aren't always dramatic—but they are profound nonetheless.

Part 3 is underway; when the Muse is back on duty, I will try to encourage more brevity. It would be nice to know her name.

Julian's Sophomore Year part 2: backgrounder

Telling this story began fourteen years ago as a letter to the editor. I was outraged by yet another sensationalist news item on local television. Some time ago television stations adopted the practice of accusing and convicting people of "improper" behavior without stopping to find out the facts. Truth and fact rarely have priority in those stories. Being the first to report a scandal is what they prize. Too often the accusations are without merit, and an innocent person has their career and livelihood taken from them without recourse or compensation. Especially vulnerable are youth workers of all varieties—coaches, teachers, scoutmasters—any whose work places them in proximity with their charges for any extended period of time are in harm's way; often, they don't realize it.

Professional training does not include preparation on how to deal with an adolescent that develops a crush or a desire for intimacy of one kind or another. Teachers, coaches, scout leaders, especially if they are relatively young, can be particularly attractive to younger people, and they tend to be vulnerable for several reasons. First of all, they want to be generous, patient and understanding—they don't want to say anything hurtful or offensive. Some are misunderstood and appear to be open to a personal relationship. It doesn't take much or very long for some young people to move into high gear. A sharp rejection is unwise—it can and does trigger denials, protestations and accusations, even anger at being caught or rejected—that can lead to exaggerations, more accusations and falsehoods. That's when the media sniffs it out— soon, it spins out of control. There is no way to defend against these forces, and a career and more is destroyed beyond repair.

That's not to say there are not predators, bad actors, and stupid mistakes—those exist and need to be dealt with appropriately. But in far too many cases a news flash is not what it seems; a miscarriage of justice is underway. There seems to be no safeguard against this kind of exploitation. The First Amendment is taken advantage of just as often as the Second, and it's unlikely that will change any time soon. So the only remedy is education and proper training.

When the letter to the editor exceeded the length newspapers accept, it was back to the drawing board. There is a reason newspapers have a word count limit: most readers don't want a lengthy Op Ed article either. Fictionalizing the subject was the solution—people will stay with a story if it is well told, or if its subject is an area of interest. I took a couple of years to find a pathway—aside from a college class in short story writing many, many years ago, I had never dabbled in writing fiction. I'm sorry it took so long for me to get around to it. It's fun and challenging, and I discover something new frequently. I recommend it as a good use of "retirement" time.

I chose to do something different: a comedy—another story of exploitation and heartbreak was not needed, and I wasn't much interested in playing in that world anyway. I abandoned the original objective of scolding the TV news and focused on the core issue. Like a coin, there are two sides: what is going on in the young person's head on one side; on the other, what can or should the target of the youth's misplaced or ill-timed affection do about it? Mark and Julian provide a peek at that, as well as a few laughs. The Julian story begins when he is in the seventh grade. On the verge of becoming a teen-ager, he joins a scout troop. The five part Scrapbook series deals with his discovery of sex and how to handle his new urges. The Sophomore Year focuses on setting life and career goals, so the tenor changes accordingly. Employing comparison and contrast with other boys is again the major narrative device. Though it compounds the length, it provides credibility and authenticity, and allows a wider range of behaviors and a little spice. Market demand, convention, and technology have shaped the material: those rules have to be followed; aside from word count, they have prevailed. Why hurry? Let's have fun with this.

If you are new to the Julian story, you might benefit from reading the style explanation at the end of the book before starting.

Table of Contents

Visual and Supplementary Material   615

Key to symbols

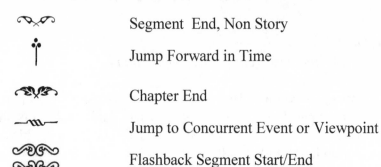

⤫	Segment End, Non Story
⸙	Jump Forward in Time
	Chapter End
	Jump to Concurrent Event or Viewpoint
	Flashback Segment Start/End

Fonts employed in *He's kinda tall*:

Times New Roman: all narrative and character content, all third person point of view is in standard Times, sentences are capitalized; all first person is in *italics*, sentences are not capitalized with one exception: **Inside Guy's** sentences are capitalized in order to distinguish them from the other 'half' of Julian's brain.

Optima: sound effects, noise, anything heard that isn't spoken by a character or can't be identified by quotation marks; these are placed between arrow brackets:

> > squipp-squipp… < < and > > **whack!** < <

Optima is also used for telephone conversations, radio, and song lyrics.

American Typewriter: Hand printed or quoted from typewritten copy

Bradley Hand Bold: Handwritten notes and conscious fantasizing

Apple Chancery indicates handwritten calligraphy

1 *Friday, November 16, 1962*

Bernard Withers glanced at the clock—half an hour remained in the school day. His students were on task completing their worksheets, freeing him to indulge in his favorite end of the week diversion: predicting what the weather prophet would say on the evening news. *so far, it's a tossup. the 64 dollar question is whether or not it will be stormy this weekend... and if so, how much rain will come with it.* Withers scratched his chin thoughtfully as he gazed out the window.

The branches of the great white oak were his secret ally—surprisingly, quite reliable as a weather gauge. Over the years Withers had made an informal study of the phenomenon. The vantage point was ideal: the three hundred year old tree dominated the view from his third floor window.

A lifelong interest in meteorology had led him to stake a claim on this room; offers to occupy a more convenient location—one of the privileges of seniority at Jackson High School—were gratefully declined. No matter what they said, he always elected to stay put. From here he could see all—or enough, thanks to the tree—to predict what was coming. In fifteen years he'd only been wrong once. After it survived the freak windstorm in 1950, Withers named the tree after his favorite mathematician—like Pythagoras, the tree had withstood the test of time. The Farmer's Almanac wasn't nearly as reliable.

It had been an ordinary November day—a brisk southeast wind had prevailed all morning, indicating that the tropical low was moving north. All the signs were there: it would be raining before nightfall—or so it had seemed. Last period a second possibility entered the picture: the wind had calmed suddenly. *easy enough to explain: the cold front from the Great Lakes has reached the western slope of the Appalachian range*. The classic struggle between weather fronts: southeast versus northwest. Withers nodded… the choice was one he'd faced before. Somewhat tricky, 50-50 on its face, but his special "consultant" would provide the clue he needed.

After checking to see if any students needed attention, his gaze returned to the tree.

Two rows back, another of the oak tree's fans appeared to be concentrating on his Geometry worksheet—Julian Forrest had spent almost two weeks in October sitting between its massive roots during his lunch hour—the perfect place to make a series of drawings depicting the school's fascinating architecture. One of them included the very window his teacher was gazing from. The arrival of the autumn winds and temperature had forced him and his new friend Randall to move inside.

He had completed the daily assignment. As usual, when he had time on his hands and nothing else to do, he kept busy by doodling or drawing pictures, ruminating about one thing or another—whatever crossed his mind. Today, like his Geometry teacher, a glance at the wall clock had triggered his train of thought: the end of class bell would ring in twenty minutes, and the weekend would begin.

Friday was one of his favorite days of the week—Friday meant no school for the next two days, guaranteed. Julian liked school, but he also liked a couple of days to do other things—**especially** after going through a week like this had been.

what I'd really like to do is to go camping—I'd go every weekend if I could.

Going on trips with the scout troop was one of his favorite things. Unfortunately, it was the wrong time of year. With a shrug, his train of thought focused on weekends in general.

whoever thought of having weekends off did the world a big favor. they should have a special day to honor him—or her… come to think about it, it could have been invented by a lady… why not? maybe she wanted her man to be around the house to do the heavy stuff once in a while… at least one day out of the week. yeah… that's only fair. then, after doing the chores, he could go camping with his buddies. He gave a nod, quite pleased with himself.

either way, man or woman, the day of honor should be on a Friday, not a Monday—when you start the week on Tuesday it seems like you're a day behind. that was sure true this week. Friday is better; that way, instead of trying to catch up, you work hard to get finished in time.

Julian nodded again, with conviction: he couldn't remember ever having a more complicated week—he could use a time out. *that's for sure!* He glanced to the right, checking the boy next to him... good—still working on his study sheet; He had caught himself just in time—*almost said that out loud.*

Sometimes he forgot to remember where he was, which could be a problem. At home he was likely to talk to himself out loud; in school he knew better: *talking to yourself looks pretty weird.* Conversing with himself was automatic; an only child, it was an easy way to entertain himself. Over time it had evolved to become his way of sorting things out.

He drew another example in the margin of his worksheet... this one exactly three times taller than wide. Head tilted, he gave it a second look... *no matter how different these appear, they all have the same definition. that's kinda neat, actually.* He drew one that leaned to the left.

Discovering a mathematical paradox had no philosophical importance for Julian—it was just a coincidence as far as he was concerned. Its appeal was aesthetic; visually elegant, he proceeded to fill the blank areas on the worksheet with a variety of these intriguing boxes called parallelograms.

The worksheet wasn't difficult; he beat the clock by over ten minutes today. It wasn't because he was especially smart. No—he gave Mr. Withers credit for designing the assignments properly: he made the subject interesting; he made sure you had enough time to understand it—and, enough time to do the exercises.

His attention returned to the subject of Fridays. At the bottom of the sheet he drew an oversize Friday. The round dot on the top of the i sat atop an embedded parallelogram.

Friday

neato... makes it look more like the word sounds. come to think about it, why don't they spell it Fryday? Lately, one thing about Friday really annoyed him: the T.G.I.F. fad.

every Friday you hear somebody say that in the hallway— sometimes you hear it a lot. stupid. they're not actually thanking God it's Friday. it's just a clever saying, not a prayer. personally, I don't think God had anything to do with inventing Friday; he has more important things to do. I've been to Sunday school, I've heard all the Bible stories and TGIF wasn't one of them. they're fables meant to teach important things like don't steal, don't kill, things like that. being thankful it's Friday seems a little silly next to those; anyway, it's not one of the "Thou Shalts."

Julian wasn't the religious type, actually. The best thing about Sunday school was the coloring books. The classroom had lots of those—they were fun. After he finished filling them all in, there wasn't anything to do. It got too boring in there, just listening to Bible stories. His mom was smart; she knew it was silly to make him stay in there; so he got to join Cub Scouts instead. They met right next door.

*I know: I'm gonna say T.W.I.F: Thank **Whoever** It's Friday; TWIF for short.* The whimsical sound appealed: *twif makes it sound like you're gonna have fun for a couple of days. if you try to say tgif, it sounds like you're choking on something... tgif has to go.*

Just as the last day of the week was popular, the last period of the day was popular too. Mostly, that's because everyone was about to start the fun part of the week—the **twific** part. Today that was coming up real quick—he checked the clock again: in fourteen minutes and twenty seconds.

His attention returned to the worksheet. Freehand parallelograms nearly filled the open space: tall skinny ones, short squatty ones... acute angled ones—

that's another thing: why are they called acute? why not pointed? or sharp? The way things got named was one of his pet peeves. Nothing was cute about a sharp angle.

hey: can this shape be used in a drawing? He opened one of his sketchbooks—*maybe I have one or two...*

The very first drawing he made at Jackson High filled the page: the stairs going from the atrium up to the third floor—*this ought to have a long wide one or a tall one... hmm... nope. how about upside down... sometimes that helps you see composition elements... hum.*

He squinted, expecting a parallelogram to pop into view...

"Why're you looking at it upside down?" Harvey enjoyed sitting next to Julian—sometimes they worked together in class. Julian was always so cheerful about things.

"Trying to see if I had any parallelo thingys in here by accident." Julian slid the tablet between them.

Harvey looked close. He didn't understand. He turned it right side up; the drawing showed the skylight in the atrium along with one of the staircases. Julian's sketches were amazing; watching him draw was interesting... sometimes he did that when time was left at the end of the period.

"I thought with all those straight lines I might have a few."

"Oh, yeah..." Harvey turned the tablet ninety degrees to the right. They studied it for a minute.

"Oh, **now** I see why..." Julian grinned wide.

"Why what?"

"When you show distance, you can't have parallel lines!" *I can be so stupid at times.* "A parallelogram is two dimensional!"

He tested that by holding the tablet face out right in front of them; he held one side firm as if it was hinged and pushed the other edge away... sure enough. The sides were still parallel, but the top and bottom pointed toward each other as if they were going to meet somewhere.

"Oh, yeah. You're right." Harvey understood, sort of. But what difference did it make?

Neither boy paid attention when the door to Mr. Withers' room opened. A student aide entered quietly, delivered a folded slip of paper to the teacher and discreetly left the room. That sort of thing happened routinely, no matter what class or teacher. Even if they had noticed her, neither boy would have suspected that it had anything to do with him—or that it was a sign that something important was going to happen.

Julian played with his idea, trying to create a 3-D parallelogram; he swiveled the tablet in the air every which way... showing depth perspective was easy enough... his drawings did have that—lots of that... *I see some parallel lines, but no parallelograms.* He looked more closely—*wait a minute! those lines aren't parallel either. huh.* His eyes blurred as he concentrated on what he had just grasped—a drawing couldn't have **any** parallel lines if it was drawn accurately— *every line in the drawing that isn't straight ahead of my eyes is headed away from me or behind me! that's why I can see it!* One of Mr. van Horn's drawing lessons several weeks ago came to mind... He was good at drawing, but not so good at remembering words—especially exact words. *hmm...*

Harvey's eye caught some movement off to the right.

"I think Mr. Withers is signaling you."

Julian looked over— *gosh. me?* He pointed to himself.

Mr. Withers nodded.

Julian got up at once; he didn't think he was in trouble or anything—several other kids were talking quietly. Mr. Withers was never a hard-nose about that anyway. He grabbed his worksheet.

Withers held out his hand. "Is that your worksheet?" At a glance he could tell that Julian had mastered the material. The precision of his work always impressed. The wide variety of shapes demonstrated mastery just as well as the formulas, if not better. As usual, there was nothing to mark; he initialed the upper right corner and added a plus sign before returning it. "I like your examples," he pointed to the doodles. "Keep this with the others. I've just received a note from Mr. Barnes. He wants you to come to his office right away."

Julian didn't know that name.

"He's the Dean of Boys. He gets around to talking to every boy in the school, eventually. It must be your turn. The office aide is waiting outside—she'll take you there. You don't need a hall pass."

oh... The puzzled expression turned into a smile and a nod. "Thanks."

"Have a nice weekend." Julian's smile always charmed... a sunny face, no matter the weather. Withers looked outside... November is rarely sunny—*busy wind this morning... made sure more branches were picked clean.* The telltale signs had returned, just as he had expected: southeast would prevail. He made his prediction—*storm on the way; could be a big one; winter is in a hurry to get here this year.* He hadn't developed a way to forecast the strength and duration of a storm system yet; that was a tough one.

"What's the matter?" Harvey wondered if Julian was in trouble.

"Nothing, I hope." He put his papers away and assembled his books. "I'm supposed to go see Mr. Barnes. Do you know him?"

"Sure!" He'd been called to see Mr. Barnes a few weeks ago. "Prob'ly wants to talk to you about careers an' stuff."

"Ah," Julian nodded. That was something he wanted to talk about, actually. Geraldine made a comment about that the other day— "...you need to learn something besides drawing if you expect to earn a living." Geraldine was usually right about that kind of thing, unfortunately. She was his mom's boss. Working on her yard crew last summer was fun.

"See ya," he tucked the Geometry textbook under his left arm along with his sketchbooks and three ring binder.

"See ya," Harvey waved and checked the clock. Ten minutes— *what do I do with ten minutes? maybe I should take up doodling.* He hunched over his worksheet and drew a parallelogram. *wish I could draw as good as Julian... dang.* The right side of Harvey's parallelogram had a dent. *drawing freehand isn't as easy as it looks.*

Julian closed Mr. Withers' door and smiled at the office aide. "Hi. I'm Julian... what's your name?" It was the polite thing to do, ask their name. His mom taught him that a long time ago: *they aren't robots, they're people.*

"Sh-Sherri," she stammered.

"Hi Sherri." He gave her a polite grin; she was a new face. He gestured to the right as a gentleman was supposed to, expecting her to lead the way. He promised his mom that he'd practice that kind of thing whenever he got the chance. She and Geraldine had given him a crash course in etiquette a few weeks ago. "You're in high school now," they kept saying. He didn't count how many times they reminded him... it ran into the hundreds. *the thing is, you don't get a chance to practice this stuff very often.*

It took Sherri a minute to recover—she never dreamed she would be chosen to escort **this** boy to the office. She certainly never expected he would ask her name. "Uh... we're supposed to go to your locker. Whatever you will need over the weekend, you know, you should get now."

"Oh... that makes sense. That way I won't have to come back up here!" He grinned. His opinion of Mr. Barnes was favorable already; no one wanted to make an extra trip up three floors. "It's down at the other end." He started off. It was nice not to be fighting end of the day traffic for a change—especially on Friday. Walking down the vacant hallway felt strange—kind of special.

Sherri followed as closely as she dared, her heart beating with excitement. The thought that she would ever be walking down the hall with this particular boy was... well, she never imagined such a thing; there were no words in her vocabulary. Unexpectedly, something else caught her eye: his backside. Until now she hadn't noticed how cute a boy's rear end could be—so tantalizing in those suntan pants. She wanted to touch, see how it felt... she blushed— *Sherri Lynne, what is the matter with you?!* She scurried to catch up— *what must I look like?* She smoothed her hair, just in case.

Julian Forrest was oblivious to the effect he'd had on the office aide. He had dismissed as irrelevant the fact that he had Choice Buns. He had studied about that at Camp Walker last summer and concluded that as long as he could use them to sit on, he was satisfied—he couldn't do anything about what they looked like anyway, so why worry about it?

He saw no point in looking at buns anyway: faces and eyes were what he looked at: people were interesting to look at, that's all. They didn't have to look sexy or pretty or any of that.

He had no idea that the girl following behind thought he was famous, extremely popular, or special. To be fair, it was a very recently acquired status, one he had not sought—never would have sought. He thought of himself as just an ordinary kid, a lowly sophomore—nobody special. Little did he know that after last Saturday night, everything at Jackson High had changed—for him, at least. He had been awarded a special prize at the annual Sadie Hawkins' Day Dance: **Best Li'l Abner.** It was an accident as far as he was concerned. He didn't even know there was a contest. His only concern was not messing things up on his first ever dance date. Having that dance over and done with was a huge relief. He wasn't aware of the impact he'd made when he accepted the award—his perfect costume, his bright happy smile, his unique light blond hair… the pool of light created by the 2500 watt follow spot made him look like a movie star—the intense beam of light sparkled excitedly—as if a trail of magical diamond dust followed wherever he went. The light followed him across the dance floor as he returned to his date, merrily waving the certificate. The spotlight remained fixed on the couple as he showed her the award—just then, her name blared from the loudspeakers: she was winner of the best **Daisy Mae** award. Hurriedly, she grabbed the certificate, thrust it onto their bale of hay, and grabbed his arm. Surprised, Julian was forced to run alongside as she scurried across the dance floor to the judges' stand.

He grinned proudly as the extravagant floral necklace was lowered around her neck, partially covering what the jaw-dropping low-cut Daisy Mae blouse had showcased so well. In a flash, she swiveled on the spot, wrapped her left arm around his neck and pulled him close. Her right hand held the back of his head in place as she planted a spectacular kiss squarely on his lips—all in that pool of intense white light. She made him look like the most handsome most exotic creature imaginable; for days he was all the buzz. No one knew who he was; he wasn't active in school activities—his only social interest, boy scouts, was outside of school. That, and perfecting his drawing skills, was all that interested him. So when he appeared in that pool of light, it was as if he had materialized magically from a wonderful dream.

9

>> *ch-klanck!* <<

whoa… The sound of the locker being opened was a surprise. *so loud*— Usually it was absorbed into the mix—hundreds of lockers being opened and slammed shut at the same time; a churning roar always filled the hallway at day's end. This time, the abrupt sound was a reminder that he was out of class, and for a reason. He knelt on one knee and began his end-of-the-day book sort. Serious homework had been assigned: English and History in particular— *they'll cut into the twific time, for sure.*

He plopped the Geometry book onto the Biology.

these stay here.   I think I can get everything else done on Sunday... have to: Saturday is all set... Randall and I are gonna develop and print pictures in his photo lab. I'm supposed to help him take pictures of the football game tonight... his first assignment for the school paper!

ohmygosh! Randall! we always meet at my locker after school. I won't be here… I'll be in the office! what am I gonna do?!

Sherri was **so** glad they had gone to his locker first—it provided an opportunity to look closely at his hair and face. *he's even better looking up close… oh dear… something's wrong.* "What's the matter?"

"I hafta leave someone a note." He sat cross-legged on the spot and opened his three ring binder to the section with blank paper and scrawled:

Randall:

See you downstairs—they called me to the office.

—Julian

He tore it out and folded it in half. "I hafta drop this off on the way." It meant backtracking the full length of the hall, but they could take the other stairway. He gathered everything he needed and stood— *too much to carry… hmm.* Since he wasn't leaving the building, he didn't need to wear his jacket—but with all these books… it made things easier just to put it on.

"We should hurry." She didn't know that, but it was probably important not to waste any time. She still hadn't adjusted to the fact that she had been given this privilege—*wait until I tell Janet... she'll be so jealous! best of all, now I know his name... and I get to walk all the way to the office with him.*

"You want to run?" Julian grinned.

She froze for a minute—*his smile! Janet will die!* She recovered quickly and put on her scolding maiden-aunt frown: running in the hall was against the rules. "We'll walk fast."

Julian giggled merrily and started one of the fast walk routines he picked up last summer from Barney, one of Geraldine's yard crew. Why not? No one else was in the hallway. He did the one that kept his upper torso and hips frozen while his lower legs moved in long gliding steps. He gave Sherri his Cheshire cat grin and walked as fast as he could—*oop!* his books almost slipped out from under his arm. He grabbed tight and sped on, pumping his right arm in time with his left leg.

Spontaneous fun was typical Julian. Wherever he could, he usually found something to amuse himself—especially fun if he had never done it before.

you don't get the chance to do a Barney comical walk every day. besides, playing around in the hallway when everyone else is sitting behind a desk watching the clock is really fun—I wouldn't do this if anybody was looking.

By the time they reached Mr. Frankel's room he'd about run out of steam. *that kind of walking isn't smart if you have very far to go.* He stopped to catch his breath; opening the door carefully, he peeked in—*it's my lucky day!* Mr. Frankel was close by—at the end of class sometimes he collected assignments at the door.

"Hi," Julian whispered. "Can you give this to Randall?"

Mr. Frankel was surprised at the intrusion, but he knew Julian. "Glad to," he took the note.

"Thanks… gotta hurry!" He closed the door quietly and hustled toward Sherri who was waiting patiently a few steps away. "Thanks. I really appreciate you letting me do that."

11

Sherri was unable to find the right words. She doubted that she'd ever get another opportunity like this. It wasn't just that he was so handsome, so *sexy*: that wonderful shirt made his face glow... perfect with those suntans— *the saddle shoes go so well with his jacket; it's like he stepped out of an article in Seventeen... he makes it feel like springtime.* Not only was he well dressed, she couldn't believe how **nice** he was. *he's different from other boys... playful...* That was a total surprise. *he's not stuck up at all!*

Frankel stepped out to see what was going on—Julian was hurrying away with a girl... most unusual. He took the liberty and opened the note— *oh, of course: an office girl. that explains it. I hope nothing is wrong.*

Julian was a favorite in fourth period.

—⁓—

Roy Barnes closed the manila folder and tucked it into the vertical file behind his desk. He had just briefed Kirk Fox, the Student Body President, on its contents—what little it had to say was positive, in a generic sort of way. The boy they were about to meet was a B plus student who had a perfect attendance record and no negative comments. In Junior high he had not been active in any sports or involved in any school activities. A brief note from a counselor mentioned that he was fond of the outdoors and scouting... otherwise, he was an unknown quantity.

They waited with the door standing open—time was running short. He needed to talk with the Forrest boy before taking him to the Principal's conference room; it would be Kirk's role to make the introduction.

"So you've seen his drawings?" He kept an eye on the doorway.

"Just the one he drew of Theresa on Wednesday. That's all Trish talks about. She wants me to pull rank somehow and get her in line for the next one," he shook his head. "I have first lunch, so I haven't seen him draw. I have to admit, though, it is good. **Really** good."

"Well, we're about to meet him. I'm interested to know your opinion. The three of us are about to join the Principal in his conference room. You need to pay very close attention. If I'm right, you and he will get to know each other very well before long."

It had been a whirlwind week for Barnes—short because Monday was Veteran's Day, which meant no school. In this town, other than the parade, not much happened—especially with the Cuban blockade still in place. He had discovered Julian by chance the next day. He had done a drawing in the cafeteria—a portrait of a girl. Impromptu, evidently. Why, Barnes didn't know. But it set off a flurry of activity, particularly among the junior class girls. That was the most amazing part of this: the effect on the Country Club set, the tightest clique in the school—to call them exclusive was being generous. Yet this sophomore boy, from out of the blue, had them mesmerized—desperate to have him draw their portrait. That was three days ago. Every day since, the crowd around him had doubled. Barnes was still in the dark about the cause of all this, but he had an on the spot inspiration: this boy might provide a way to deal with the most worrisome block of students—the ones who determined much of what was "in" and what was not. Getting their cooperation was essential. Up to now the prospects for that remained uncertain if not doubtful. His hunch was a long shot, but— *so far it's looking pretty good; we'll know before long.* He checked his watch again.

—⚡—

With his escort in tow, Julian hurried down the stairway, scolding himself for not being ready. He had not spent one minute thinking about what questions to ask, what information he needed to gather. He had recently completed the first quarter of his sophomore year, so it was time to deal with that seriously. He'd only had one job his whole life, and that was last summer doing yard work. The only other thing he had ever done was scouting. Up to now, that was the most important thing in his life—*still is; that's where Mark is.*

The one decision he **had** made about his life was Mark: someday he and Mark would be a couple and live together for the rest of their lives. The problem with that—well, there were lots of problems,

13

probably—but the biggest one right now was that it had to be kept a secret. Even from Mark... **especially** from Mark.

Mark talked some about career goals during summer camp. The troop spent two weeks at Camp Walker—everyone was there except for Frankie: he had to work. That camp was so important! That's when Julian first realized he should probably be an artist. Up to then art had been like a hobby, mostly. Something new happened at camp—especially when he drew people.

the large size paper probably... when you draw someone on a large piece of paper, you can show so much more—you almost have to.

Camp is also when he found out that he had to wait for Mark. He needed to grow more, be more **qualified**—or something. He'd gone to camp thinking that he could trick Mark into "messing around" in the woods somewhere; that would get his long planned romance started at last—their future life would be underway by the time they got back home—*boy oh boy, was that ever a stupid idea.* Thanks to the example of his friends Tom and Nick, he figured out that he had a lot of work to do before he could expect Mark to think of him as a **man**, as even being **eligible**. He was still a little **kid**, practically—hardly worth Mark's time. Inside Guy had revised the schedule: when he could look Mark straight in the eye without having to stand on his toes—that's when he could come up with a plan.

boy oh boy was I lucky... I could have ruined everything so easy. Inside Guy stopped me just in time.

Julian had a special way of problem solving. From early childhood he talked to himself when he was alone. Doing that made it easy to have fun when he had to be by himself. By the time he entered his teens, it was standard procedure to confer with his inner voice. "Inside Guy" tended to be cautious and careful, which was a good thing. When he was in a tight spot it made a big difference to have a helper along, even if he was imaginary.

Julian counted on him to be there today; they faced a major challenge: plan a career that won't get in the way of the main goal—*the secret main goal: Mark and me. I think I can do that... I have to do that.*

—◊◊◊—

Dr. Stanley Middleton, Principal of Jackson High School, was enormously encouraged. The two people he and his committee were interviewing exceeded his expectations. From what he had seen so far, there would be no problem from either of them down the road. That meant a great deal, because he was facing the biggest challenge of his career, and he needed all the help he could get. His task was to take the lead in the district's plan to implement the Brown Decision. Two weeks ago, without warning, Civil Rights and all that entailed had been dumped in his lap. Instead of having the summer to prepare along with the other schools in the district, the plan had changed. Now the high school had to implement its program at the start of the next semester— seven weeks from now. At least they didn't have to deal with the busing issue until next year—the only positive note so far.

He and his administrative team had been brainstorming in secret, trying to come up with a solution. It was essential to achieve the goal without a lot of publicity and controversy—one that would avoid protests and demonstrations and the like. This was key to maintaining stability in student discipline and conduct. Several districts had been successful in making the transition, so it was possible. He wanted to ease Jackson High into the future with as little disruption as possible. The district did not need another court case. Until three days ago, a way forward had eluded them.

On Tuesday his Dean of Boys discovered a lad that just might be the key to success. At first glance the idea seemed like an act of desperation, not a plan—but they had been unable to come up with anything else. The simplicity appealed, certainly—but it was very hasty; there was no time to devise a backup, no provision for contingencies: it was all or nothing, because the meeting was **today**. They had about two hours, do or die. The boy's mother, a remarkably likeable woman, sat directly across from him.

"You see, I'm from Illinois, originally," Francine continued. "For us there was never a problem; we lived in west Joliet. Industrial area, working class people... segregation didn't exist in our part of town. A lovely family lived just a few houses away. One of Julian's favorite playmates was their fourth child, as I remember... maybe fifth. It was a

15

large family. The boys spent hours together at our house and at theirs." She thought back... "The two people Julian missed most when we moved here were his grandfather and Little Joe," she smiled. "He was so cheerful and musical. Well, it was natural; his father was a musician—Big Joe Biggs was his professional name."

"I understand completely," the principal nodded. "I'm from northeast Ohio: settled by abolitionists from New England... attempts to segregate never took hold to begin with." Here the population balance was about the same, but that's all. There hadn't been any unrest, but that was good luck more than good planning—there was plenty of open conflict not far away. Never comfortable with the norms here, he didn't want to be the one that woke up a sleeping dragon. He turned to the scoutmaster; his support would be important.

"Well, I'm a local, pretty much. My father was a District Ranger in the Nantahala National Forest. We had several at the station working on one crew or another year round—right alongside a couple of Cherokees. So I grew up with them. Whites were a minority—we didn't rate any special consideration, though. Everyone was treated the same; my father insisted on that. Right after he retired we moved here—I was just starting high school. I lost touch with Blacks for the most part, since Jackson didn't have any. When I went to college I can't say it changed that much. There were a few, but I rarely ran across them—exchange students from Africa, I think. I always thought they got a bad deal, actually. I wanted to get a few into the scout troop but the brass nixed it—they were worried it might undermine the all Black troop. That's what they said, at any rate..."

While Mark gave his input to the Principal, Francine took the opportunity to look around the table again. They had been introduced very rapidly; obviously, these were the people in charge. A sizeable group—the only familiar face was the counselor from Wallace Junior High. She had no reason to be concerned, but as Julian's mother she was alert nonetheless. Each had a briefing packet of some kind; what it contained she could only guess—*maybe I should have let Geraldine come along after all... she's at home in this kind of meeting.*

She took a sip from a small Dixie water cup... the office secretary had distributed the prefilled cups while introductions were being made. Festive colors, the decorative ring around the top resembled

16

a string of music notes. Four matching six-inch plates were spaced a few inches apart in the center of the table. Atop each sat a modest supply of sugar cookies; these had remained untouched—a well-intentioned courtesy that Francine presumed would probably remain a decoration. They seemed out of place on the handsome walnut conference table, and didn't appear to be very appetizing. But this wasn't a birthday party. When Mark paused, she leaned forward.

"Excuse me, but I still don't understand what this is about." She had been assured that her son was in no trouble, but what did his opinions about Negroes have to do with anything? *all these people here…*

"I apologize, Mrs. Forrest. I needed to get an idea of where you stood before going into that. I'm pleased to say you have set my mind at rest—both of you. What I needed to know was whether you would have any problem with what we plan to ask of your son… I needed to know that before approaching him." He cleared his throat. "I've been handed a tough assignment, and I'm hoping that Julian will help me meet the challenge everyone at Jackson High will be facing in a few weeks."

Francine felt somewhat comforted, but still didn't know what was expected; she couldn't imagine how or why they had singled out her boy.

"Last year, the school board adopted a resolution to proceed with implementation of the Brown Decision. They put it off for as long as they could; now we're under the gun: no more federal money unless we get off the dime. The schools will be integrated next year, period. No more delays." Half the textbook budget and thirty teaching positions were at stake.

Mark approved; *about time…* he listened carefully.

"But I got a big surprise three weeks ago from the Superintendent: we are going to have a "test run" of sorts here at the high school at the start of the semester.

"Test?" Mark didn't see how that could be… *you either do it or you don't.*

"Poor word choice… early start might be a better way to phrase it. Next semester we will be enrolling a boy from Boston. His father is taking a post at the University. It seems they're not about to allow their son to be enrolled at Joseph Rainey. They put pressure on the Superintendent, and he agreed to their request."

"Is there something wrong with that school?" Francine knew of it, but it was in the other part of town—*Geraldine never has a listing over there.*

"Not as far as I know. But it's a long way from where they plan to be living, and the boy has never been in a segregated all Black school. He's accustomed to being surrounded by whites. In any case, it is the law now, so there isn't any choice, really."

"So the problem is going to be with the whites," Mark could see that at once.

"Possibly. We're hoping to head off any trouble before it starts. There are several success stories in other districts—we're not what you could call pioneers, but we still have to plan it carefully. Some people are always opposed to change. But I need to consider the boy: he'll be the **only** Black here until next year—so he'll be all by himself." He turned to Francine. "That's where your son comes into the picture: we think Julian would be perfect to serve as his guide and helper—his "Buddy," if you will."

Francine didn't know what to say. "Why Julian?"

Mark wanted to know that as well. Julian was not particularly ambitious.

"You may not be aware of this, but your boy has become very popular—and not just among the sophomores."

Francine was caught by surprise. "He hasn't mentioned anything. What's going on?"

"He's been entertaining students in the cafeteria by drawing portraits. Girls in particular are desperate to be captured by his pencil. It seems he gives them the drawing."

Mark and Francine looked at each other, surprised.

"I knew he was having lunch there," Francine and Eloise had been collaborating on that—*come to think about it, yesterday she mentioned something about two girls...*

18

"I'm not surprised about the drawings," Mark grinned. "He did that at scout camp last summer—giving the drawing to its subject delights him, for some reason."

"Our hope is that Julian will agree to let the new boy be a "sidekick" of sorts; we want him to be accepted without any fuss. Having to wander through the school all alone is not a good start for anyone—especially in mid-year. It's likely some students will not like the idea of him being here at all. If he's accepted at the start by someone as popular as Julian, our hope is that others will join in and make the boy feel welcome—or at least safe." He awaited a reaction.

"Well, there shouldn't be a problem," Francine was certain of that. "His summer job involved working with Negroes. Three of them, to be exact. They got along just fine."

"We know a little about that," Middleton continued. "His art teacher mentioned it. Evidently Julian was very friendly with at least one of them. That's another reason we think he can help us. I daresay that few Jackson students have had much experience working with Blacks. The unknown can be the source of misunderstanding—it can strengthen prejudice. That's why we have to assume there will be a bump or two along the way. What we ask of you, what we **need**, is for you to stand behind Julian—be there if he needs you. I can see that I don't need to worry about that."

She appreciated his words, but the big question hadn't been answered. "When will he find out about all this?"

"In a few minutes, as a matter of fact. He should be in the Dean of Boys office by now."

"So he doesn't know about this yet?" Mark wasn't happy with how this was being handled. Ambushes, whatever the cause, were a fundamental violation of fairness; it was fortunate that he had been included today—he would have preferred an opportunity to prepare Julian, but this would have to do.

"No, he doesn't. This will come as a surprise. He will be able to refuse, of course. But to be frank, I have loaded the scales on purpose. That's one reason I wanted you two here—I'm hoping your presence will make it easier for him to understand, and to accept. I **need** him to say yes." Middleton had learned long ago that surprise was an excellent

19

tool—he tended to get what he needed more often if he didn't allow the object of his exercise enough time to think of a reason to say no.

Mark nodded. *at least the man is honest about it.   still, manipulating people is a smelly thing to do.*   He didn't have another suggestion... too late anyway.

—⁂—

Julian had never been to the office, so he followed Sherri. A rather stern lady was behind the counter—very skinny, wearing clear plastic framed glasses with sharp cat eye points projecting from the upper corners. Her hair was pulled back tight into a bun: she was someone he didn't want to get on the wrong side of, he could tell that right off. She looked like the lady that made the PA announcements sounded: this had to be her. He smiled anyway, because that's what he always did. She didn't smile back, but raised an eyebrow as if she was surprised. The phone on her desk rang just then and she shifted her attention. Her voice confirmed his hunch. A picture formed in his head: the witch flying the broom in the Wizard of Oz— *she must be a relative.* An oversize painting behind her caught his eye: the school when it was brand new— *wow... only two floors back then...*

"It's this way," Sherri prompted. Her charge had gotten sidetracked.

"Oh... sorry!" He hastened to join her at the entrance to an inside passageway. A few doors stood open— *must be offices.* "In there?"

"The first door."

"Thanks, Sherri," he gave a parting smile.

She watched him step toward Mr. Barnes' office—right hand raised to cover the blush she felt spreading across her face— *he remembered my name!*

As instructed, Julian stopped opposite the open door. A laminated plastic sign mounted at eye level confirmed that he was in the right place:

Roy Barnes
Dean of Boys

The man was seated at his desk talking to a student—a senior. Julian had seen him before, somewhere. Smiling wide, he mimed tapping the invisible door with his right hand: "knock, knock."

"And here he is!" Barnes stood at once and stepped around his desk to shake hands. "You can put your books down here, if you like." He pointed to the two-drawer file cabinet next to his desk—the top was bare.

Kirk recognized Julian at once, but it took a moment to adjust to his shirt— *is that a **Strad?!**...* a coral color he hadn't seen before.

"I'm Mr. Barnes, and I'm sure you know who this is: Kirk is your Student Body President."

wow... Julian was not expecting to meet anyone important— *maybe he's about to leave...*

"Hi," Kirk grinned. "I didn't expect to see Li'l Abner!" He reached out and shook Julian's hand. His eyes focused on the unique slant topped shirt pockets— *yeah... it's a Strad, all right... pockets are* ***so*** *cool...*

Julian blushed. He didn't know what to say— *why is everyone shaking my hand?* Being recognized by the Student Body President? *yow.*

"Julian here was named Best Li'l Abner at the Sadie Hawkins dance," Kirk explained.

"Oh..." Barnes was taken by surprise—he hadn't been on duty that night "Well, congratulations!" *I didn't know there was a girlfriend... let's hope that won't be a problem.* "Please, sit down."

Something told Julian that this wasn't about careers.

"I wanted to talk a little about your drawings in the cafeteria," Barnes said, returning to his chair.

"Oh." Julian grinned. "That's lots of fun." *so that's what this is about.*

I don't think so, said Inside Guy.

Julian was glad Inside Guy had showed up this soon. Something was up, for sure. All of a sudden it seemed very warm; he was sorry he'd put on his jacket— *should I ask to take it off, or...*

To help set the boy at ease, Barnes leaned back in his chair. "I saw you drawing in the cafeteria on Tuesday, and I was curious about how you came to be doing that."

"Oh. It was by accident, really." *I have to figure a way to tell about this...*

Start at the end and go backwards—otherwise you'll have to tell about the dance and Rita and all that. Inside Guy came in handy at times like this.

"Y'see, Marcie, this girl who I was sitting next to, asked about my sketchbook." He shrugged. "No big deal; I told her to go ahead and look through it. I was still eating my apple; besides, I wasn't planning to do any drawing anyway. After she looked through it, she passed it over to Theresa—it was Theresa that invited me to have lunch with her and her friends. Anyway, they asked some questions about the drawings; I thought I could answer best by showing them. So I did a quick sketch of Marcie's face." He shrugged. "I didn't think it would be such a big deal. Now lots of kids want me to draw their face. I hope it's okay... I didn't get permission or anything."

"So Marcie isn't your girlfriend?"

Julian laughed. "No. I just met her that day. She's a **junior**." *sophomore boys didn't have junior girlfriends.* Of course, he didn't plan to have a girlfriend at all. But he was smart enough to keep that to himself.

"Ah, I see..." Actually, Barnes didn't see at all. He waited for clarification. A girlfriend was not in the game plan. Incredibly, no one on the committee had thought about that.

Julian sat forward and pulled the sketchbooks from his stack. He had all three along because Randall planned to photograph them after school. He selected the one with the decorative numeral three on the cover and flipped through, searching for the portrait that had started all this. He handed it to Mr. Barnes. "I drew that one in the atrium a while ago. Theresa was all worked up about it. That's what made me think of drawing Marcie." He looked at the Student Body President and shrugged, "it was the first time I ever ate lunch in the cafeteria, actually." *boy, would I like to take off this jacket!*

Kirk didn't know what to make of this. He watched Mr. Barnes go through the sketchbook, looking very closely at the other pages. From the expression on his face, Kirk could tell that they must be as good as the drawing of Theresa. He was curious to see what was in there himself. He checked out Julian again. "Where did you get that shirt?" Kirk had several Stradivari shirts in his wardrobe; he intended to add one of these if it was still available. Strads were notorious for selling out—*when they're gone, that's it… not available by special order—I learned that the hard way. this one is like a summer party in Palm Beach.*

"This?" Julian pointed at his chest. "At Oglivy's." He didn't explain that Geraldine had insisted that he get it or why she wanted him to wear it on Fridays—that would take hours. He was happy to let her make all his fashion decisions; he was completely indifferent about that stuff. What he liked best about this shirt was the open top pockets; most shirts only had only one, if any. *super handy as pencil holders.* He didn't care much what he wore, actually. Except when it was too warm, like it was this minute. Then all he wanted to do was take things off. He decided to do just that—*why not?!* Obviously, he was stuck here for a while. He took off his jacket and folded it across his lap— *that's a **lot** better*.

Kirk stared at the shirt, now fully exposed. He was consumed with envy—*I **have** to get one of those. after school today?* Biting his lip unconsciously, he was worried—*probably too late. I need to find out how long ago he got that…*

Barnes refrained from making any verbal comment about the drawings… he had never seen anything like this. The quality was extraordinary: now the giant split leaf philodendron in the atrium presented itself. He had walked by this a thousand times, but somehow he was seeing it for the first time. Now he understood what Ralph was talking about. If anything, the art teacher had understated the boy's talent. He turned to the next drawing—*a shoe! why a shoe?! yet, it's interesting…* It took a moment to remember that he was supposed to be interviewing the boy, not studying his drawings; fortunately, he had been listening… "uhh… first time?"

"Yeah… I always sit where I can draw something interesting. I like to draw… that's why I have a sack lunch."

"You drew these during **lunch?!**"

"Mostly; there's lots of time, so it makes sense." *oh, I remember what started it now…* "Marcie saw the number on the cover and wanted to know why it was so fancy. She thought it was for my third period class. So I explained that it was the third sketchbook." *silly to have a notebook for P.E., which is what I have third period.* "I always have it along so if I see something interesting, I can do a sketch."

Barnes wanted to spend some time with this—that would have to come later. He passed the sketchbook over to the Student Body President, and turned his attention to Julian. "Well, you are a gifted artist; I can see why the girls want you to draw them. Is it true that you let them keep the drawings?"

"Sure. Why not?"

"I don't know, I thought you'd like to keep what you draw."

"Nah… I can always draw another one if I want. I just like to improve—the more I do the better I can do. Besides, it's fun—best of all is that it makes them happy. I like that. I like to show people how interesting they are to look at."

Barnes was sorry the others had not heard this remarkable exchange; he was uncertain where to go next. "So a crowd watching you draw is something new?"

"Gosh yes. I didn't know what to think, at first." He still didn't; he didn't mention that he'd noticed a girl or two staring at him ever since that day—*I don't understand that either, actually.* "I figure they'll get bored after a while. One nice thing is now I get to draw stuff in the cafeteria. I needed a new place."

"Julian is being a little too modest." Kirk had made up his mind about this kid: anyone that wore a Stradivari shirt was **in**. "It's because of the Sadie Hawkins dance. He made a big hit when he won that award." The picture of Rita and her bulging topside giving Julian an embrace with lips locked together was impossible to forget—they were frozen in the bright spotlight for what seemed like **forever**. All the boys were envious, and all the girls wanted to be where Rita was. She left prints on his face that could be seen clear across the gym.

>> *blaaaaaaaz!* <<

The end of class buzzer! Julian sat up, shock registered on his face— *I almost forgot... Randall! he doesn't know where I am!*

"Is something the matter?" Barnes could see that Julian was worried.

"Umm, yeah. I'm supposed to meet someone after school. He doesn't know where I am."

"Oh." Barnes wasn't expecting a snag like this. "We're supposed to go to a meeting in the conference room now." He stood. "I hope they can wait a few minutes." He realized that Julian must be referring to the Hallstrom boy; it was safe to assume he would be willing to wait. He gestured to Kirk to lead the way.

meeting? in the conference room? uh-oh... what's going on? Julian didn't know how to react. From Mr. Barnes tone of voice he didn't sense any danger, but...

The Student Body President crossed in front of him and stepped to the doorway; when he turned right, Julian knew instantly that he was in trouble: that led **away** from the hallway, deeper into the office complex. He didn't move.

"You can leave your coat here." Barnes gestured to the chair. "Your mother will be waiting, so we should get going."

Mom?! The **last** thing he expected to hear—*I must be in trouble after all.*

Take it easy, take it easy. Something is up, but you didn't do anything wrong. Inside Guy was still on duty.

He stepped forward with reluctance, craning his neck on the off chance he could see Randall— *darn! he hasn't had time to get down here. what am I gonna do...*

Ask when we get there. Mom will help. Inside Guy made sense at times like this.

Kirk led the way and stopped by an open door a few feet down the corridor. He smiled at whoever was inside and stood back, ushering Julian in.

Julian did not like this. Nobody said what was going on, for one thing... and what about Randall? He entered and looked around to see where his mother was— *my gosh... so many people! there's Mark!*

"Julian, I'd like you to meet Dr. Middleton, the Principal." Kirk raised his eyebrows to indicate how important this was.

Middleton stood and turned to greet the boy, but was startled somewhat. The colorful shirt aside, it was obvious that the boy was distressed. He reached out his hand, nonetheless. "I am pleased to meet you, Julian."

Julian shook his hand, but was unable to give his usual smile.

Both Francine and Mark realized something was wrong... Julian was never cold like this. Neither knew for sure what to do—they were guests here too. Mark took the initiative.

"What's the problem, Julian?"

He was so relieved Mark had asked that.

"The thing is, Randall's expecting to meet me right now. I don't know how to let him know where I am."

"And you don't want him to worry."

"Well, yeah. He's **counting** on me!" *Mark practically read my mind.*

Wisely, The Principal and the Dean of Boys deferred—it was clear that Mark could fix this; obviously, the boy was very distressed.

Mark proceeded without seeking permission; he stepped around the table and looked Julian in the face. "Where is he supposed to meet you?" He had lots of experience at this, and he knew Julian as well or better than anyone.

"I gave a note to Mr. Frankel. I told him I was called to the office. He's prob'ly out there by now. Can I go and explain?" What he needed to explain he didn't know, but that didn't matter.

"Well, why don't you let me do that? That way you can get started; all these people shouldn't be kept waiting."

"Oh." That made sense. "Okay. Just tell him I'll be along as soon as I can."

"What's so special about today?" Julian's intensity meant that something else was going on.

"Today is his first assignment for the school paper! He's gonna photograph the football game!"

"And he's counting on you to help with that."

"Well, not help, exactly. I don't know that much about cameras and stuff. But he's **new** here; he's counting on me to be there. I **promised**."

"Excuse me, but maybe I can help," Barnes interrupted. "The school paper office is close by—would he go there?"

"Yeah! That's right! We were in there yesterday!" He looked at Mark. "Andy was there. He writes all the sports stories."

"Got it." Mark knew exactly what to do. He held Julian by the shoulders and looked him in the eye. "I'll take care of this. I want you to set your mind at rest. You are needed in here right now. Okay?" He didn't need to tack on any scout phrases… they went without saying.

Julian relaxed. He had absolute trust in Mark. He gave his best happy face and nodded.

Mark gave Julian's shoulder a small pinch and winked for good measure. He turned to the Principal. "I shouldn't be long; please go ahead… Julian can catch me up later—I take it **The Cardinal** is still in room 120?"

"Why, yes…"

Mark left at once. He had been on the school paper staff—he knew exactly where to go.

Mark's **incredible** shoulder pinch—Julian's **favorite** thing. It did the trick. The sunshine was back in his smile. He extended his hand to the Principal again. "I'm sorry. Y'see, Randall is new here... he's from Washington, the state. He's kind of shy, so I try to make him feel welcome," he shrugged, and smiled apologetically.

"I see." The Principal was amazed by the change in the boy's countenance. "Well, I'm glad that's been solved. Please, be seated. I have a few things I'd like to discuss." He glanced at the Dean of Boys. *Roy's instinct about this boy was absolutely correct: he is beyond what I expected.*

Julian gave his mother a happy wave—he was glad to see her here—*looks like I'm not in trouble, at least.*

That's what I've been telling you. Inside Guy was impatient at times.

Julian was **very** glad Inside Guy was paying attention; he glanced at the Student Body President who was taking the chair at his left—*I don't know what I'm supposed to do... why are all these people here?* He sat down in the only empty chair—*oh... I'm right next to the Principal...*

"I can see, Julian, that you are experienced in doing the very thing I need help with."

Julian did not expect to hear that at all: "Help?"

2 *lateral pass: Andy is handy*

As Mark opened the conference room door, an unexpected roar of sound poured in—he stepped into the passageway and closed the door quickly. *wow.* He gave the door a gentle pat of approval, surprised at how effective it was as a sound barrier—*impressive... good thing, too. they don't need the distraction of whatever's going on out here.* He didn't want to miss anything but he was confident that Julian could handle what was coming, especially with Francine present.

Only one way led out; he headed toward the hubbub. The office lobby was packed with agitated students.

"We'll have none of that!" screeched the Principal's Secretary. **"How would you like to go to the back of the line?!"**

Mark winced at the sound; he recognized the voice at once—gratefully, he was at a safe distance. He couldn't see the student being scolded; jockeying for position to sign up for something or other had caused the problem—*special rally bus probably...* The effect of her voice was remarkable—the horde quieted down at once. However, finding a path to the main hallway was still going to be interesting.

"S'cuse me..." he inched forward, hands formed into a prow. Grateful that Miss Watkins was otherwise occupied, his smirk turned into a grin— *Gladys Watkins—still here, still running the ship of state.* She was an institution; he wondered how many Principals she'd gone through— *she's one of a kind, thankfully.*

The hallway was busy, but not impossible. Friday after school hadn't changed much since he was a student. *we were a happy bunch, in a hurry to leave the hallowed halls, off to party or a dance—anything non-academic; worries were put on the shelf.   clothes are more interesting these days...* Several items were familiar—might well have come from Oglivy's. As purchasing agent, he ought to know. Across the hall a shirt caught his eye. The dark green long-sleeve was wool or suede, he couldn't be sure from this distance—*where did that come from? looks terrific—something Oglivy's should offer. mental note: do some catalog checking Monday.* Winter inventory was on the floor already, but room could be made— *Pendleton maybe... Woolrich or Levi...*

"Hey, Mark!"

"Whoops!" he stopped quickly. "Hey, Les!" Bumping into his old friend was a pleasant surprise: "Sorry, I need to watch where I'm going!"

A mischievous grin connected the two. Glancing to the left Les Switcher cupped his hand: "Off limits."

Mark wasn't checking out the buxom brunette passing by just then, of course, Les knew that—but he had always enjoyed teasing Mark, the least girl crazy guy he knew. They had been wrestlers on the championship team in '54. A friendly punch to the left shoulder: "What brings you aboard this fine November day?"

"Top secret, actually." Mark tugged at the whistle chain around the wrestling coach's neck. "No practice today?"

"Oh yeah, even on game days. They can start without me—" he held up a file folder; "have to turn this in first."

"Good luck with that! They're full up in there," Mark gestured to the office door with his thumb.

"I'll give it a few minutes," he shrugged. "So, how's Patty?" Les had always wanted Patty for himself, but Mark was the only boy she ever considered seriously. It took her years, but she finally landed him. 'The Artful Dodger' was too great a challenge to resist, evidently.

"Don't let her hear you call her that... it's Pat or Dr. Schaefer, if you please."

"Oo... I'll try to keep it in mind; she and I go back to the third grade y'know—she'll always be Patty to me. I'll compromise: how's about Doctor Pat?"

"Worth a try. Uhmm…" Mark didn't want to give his old pal the brush-off, but he was in a hurry…

Les stood back a step and gave Mark a careful head-to-toe assessment. "Pretty classy these days… you must have been promoted."

Mark nodded with a shrug "Yeah… I have to dress up now—assistant manager. I'm on the floor mornings."

"Well!" Switcher was impressed. "Bravo! Always knew you'd get ahead." Actually, he was surprised that Mark had stayed in town—another of Patty's accomplishments. "That means you're here to stay! All right! So, when will I get to coach Mark Junior, then?"

oh boy… no Mark Juniors were likely—that also was top secret, Very Top Secret. "Still on hold—the Doctor-in-training is in charge of that department." Pat's professional life was real handy at times. "Sorry. So how's your tribe coming along?"

"Still at three, but number four is in the oven. Doris is determined to have a daughter. Say! Any chance Doctor Pat could help out with that?"

"Dunno," Mark laughed. "Maybe she could prescribe a pill."

"Don't I wish!" Les had mixed feelings—a daughter would be nice, but would require another bedroom: Major Problem.

Mark checked his watch. "Les, I'm in a bind for time right now—"

"That's right: you said Secret Mission." Switcher gave Mark a likely story grin. "Any hints?"

Mark had not been cautioned, but it was safe to presume that he was expected to keep the matter confidential. Besides, he didn't want to miss any more of that meeting than he had to. "I don't know too much myself, actually—but you'll find out fairly soon, probably at your next faculty meeting."

That was not what Switcher had expected to hear—he gave his old pal a sober what's-going-on look.

"Listen, it's nothing to worry about, okay?" Mark hadn't meant to cause any problems. He gave Les a friendly tap on the shoulder.

"Gotta get a move on. Drop by the store one of these days—I'll give you a special rate if you keep it under your hat."

"Scout's Honor?" Les pretended to be satisfied.

"Scout's Honor." He raised his right hand. "Thanks, Les. Catch you later." He headed toward the school paper room two doors down.

Les watched him go to the Cardinal classroom, head tilted. What could this be about? Faculty meeting? And why would Mark be here? He was mildly disappointed at being put off, but he knew Mark well enough not to be offended. With a shrug he proceeded to the office.

—m—

The Cardinal room hadn't changed: through the window in the door Mark could see Randall and Andy at the far end talking with the Advisor. Three others were banging away on typewriters. No one was working at the paste-up table. The Advisor was new—not a surprise. *old Baldy Henderson was overdue for retirement before I graduated.* He tapped on the door and opened it enough to poke in his head. "May I come in?"

Ernest Ladendorff stood at once. "Please do." *who do you suppose—*

"Mark!" Andy turned to Mr. L enthusiastically. "He's my Scoutmaster." *what's he doing here? wow... out of uniform, he looks different. cool sports jacket...*

Randall turned around quickly— *wow, this is a surprise.* Without thinking, his eyes automatically checked out Mark's slacks— *yes.* A few weeks ago he was a guest at the Boy Scout Troop meeting. Mark looked just as sexy as he did that night. He wore the same kind of slacks—today they were a light blue, but they fit exactly the same. He compared what he saw now with the images in his memory. Checking guys out had been a habit for some time; unfortunately, he didn't always realize what he was doing. Luckily, he'd never been caught. He forced himself to look up.

"I hope I'm not interrupting." Mark strode to the front of the room.

32

"Not at all." *so, this is the scoutmaster Ralph talked about.*

"I'm on a mission to see Randall, actually—but I think both of you might as well be in on this." He patted Randall on the shoulder and offered his hand to the teacher. "I'm Mark Schaefer. I'm here to explain why Julian isn't."

"Ladendorff... Ernie to my friends. Pleased to meet you. No trouble, I hope?" Ladendorff knew what was going on, but was under instructions to keep it secret. The man wasn't what he had expected to see at all—*looks like he stepped out of a full page ad in GQ.*

"No, no—quite the opposite. He's in a meeting in the Principal's office, and he'll be tied up there for a while." He turned to Randall. "He wanted you to know where he was."

"Oh..." Randall was concerned. "What happened?"

Mark looked over his shoulder to see if any of the other students were listening— *no problem.* The newspaper staff was fully engaged— the noise of their typewriters served as an effective sound barrier. He sat on the corner of a small student desk—an automatic perch, one he'd used countless times when he was a student here.

"Nothing has happened; Julian is fine." He spoke quietly. "I'm not at liberty to tell you any particulars. The Principal has a special assignment for Julian to take on. You'll find out about it from him."

"Wow... umm, when?"

"I don't know. The meeting has just begun. I need to get back in there. But Julian was upset about leaving you in the lurch. He says you need him to help out tonight."

Randall looked at Andy to see what he thought.

"Well, I'll be there the whole time." Andy was sports editor as well as a member of Mark's scout troop.

"That's good to know; I don't know if Julian will be late or not. He doesn't know that himself yet. Can I count on you to do whatever Julian would do?"

"No sweat. Andy is handy," he bounced on his toes.

"Super. That helps a lot." Andy was his new Tiger Patrol Leader—a scout he could rely on. He looked at Randall. "So, you're going to photograph the game."

"Yes." He didn't want to admit that he was a little nervous; he'd never photographed a football game before.

"If they're half as good as your mountain photographs, they'll want to use them all." He gave him a friendly tap on the shoulder. "I take it you have seen what he can do?"

Ladendorff shook his head. "Not yet. Tonight is his first assignment. His equipment is top drawer."

"Well, he knows how to use it." Mark had spent over an hour enjoying his photographs several weeks ago—a most enjoyable experience. Randall's parents were as engaging as could be, and outdoor enthusiasts to boot. The wall clock emitted a familiar click. "Okay, then." He waved to the teacher. "Sorry, but I need to get back to the conference room." He stood.

"Umm…" Randall was still concerned—he and Julian had plans for the afternoon. "How long will the meeting last?" *I'm supposed to photograph the sketchbooks; we didn't have time yesterday.*

Mark frowned, unable to answer. "I don't know. When is the game?"

"At seven," Andy answered. "We're gonna do some pre-game interviews, so the plan is to be here at six."

"Shouldn't be a problem then." He checked his watch: two and a half hours or so from now. "But you asked how long the meeting would last, didn't you?

Randall nodded.

"I can't say." Mark pondered for a second. "It could be over in ten minutes as far as I know." A glimpse of the teacher's facial reaction made him consider that again. "But it could be an hour, too." *obviously, he knows what's going on.*

"You need to go ahead with your assignment. Andy can fill in for Julian nicely. I'm sure he'll join you as soon as he can, but it might

34

not be for a while. I plan to stick around for as long as I'm needed—if his mother can't bring him I will."

He tried not to let his disappointment show. *Dad is expecting to see the sketchbooks too...*

"Tell you what: if you don't hear from me in another ten minutes, you can figure that Julian will be tied up for a while, and you should go ahead without him." He reconsidered: "Better make that fifteen minutes. What do you think?"

Randall nodded, reluctantly. Not much else he could do.

"Sorry about this, but it will work out, you'll see." Mark waited for a positive expression. "By the way—say hello to your parents for me, will you?" A nod and a smile at last. He tapped Randall on the shoulder and gave Andy a thumbs up. "Nice meeting you," he reached out to shake the teacher's hand.

"Indeed," Ladendorff shook hands gladly. He planned to find out more about this man from his Sports Editor—obviously a person he should know.

Mark walked to the door, paused to wave, and left the room. *too bad I'm in a hurry... would have been fun to spend a little time getting caught up at* **The Cardinal**. Memories... good memories, connected him to that room. *the new Advisor is a plus.* Mark was impressed by his informal appearance: no tie.

'double time, Mark!' he walked fast... *hope I haven't missed too much... Julian is being handed a huge assignment.* Mark assumed that he would be needed for more than "standing behind" his scout, to use the principal's words. *he was smart to include me... being on the ground floor could make a huge difference. rough waters are ahead... could be very rough if the TV and newspaper get wind of this. and they will. Julian is so honest and unsuspecting—he has no defenses.*

As Mark closed the door, Andy directed his question to Mr. L: "What's going on?!"

Ladendorff dodged the question. "Scoutmaster, you say?"

"Yeah... he's terrific." Andy frowned, confused. *why would Julian and Mark be in the Principal's office?* Maybe Randall knows.

"Don't ask me," Randall shrugged. "Special assignment? Julian hasn't said a thing." *whatever it is, it must be a surprise. Mark said his mom is there, too...*

"Looks kind of young to be a scoutmaster..." Ladendorff scratched his chin, thoughtful.

"Yeah." *at camp that really stood out.* "Mark went to school here himself. I don't know when he graduated."

"Mark Schaefer... I'll check a few yearbooks. Can't be too far back—from the look of him, he can't be thirty... probably twenty five or six... barely out of college. That would put him in the class of... what, '53? Thereabouts." He stepped over to the yearbook archive. The Journalism Advisor had the only **complete** set in the district. It was under lock and key.

Randall's eyes returned to the door Mark had just closed. Suddenly he felt strange... like he had been cut adrift. An odd sensation... unused to surprises, he was at a loss how to react. He hadn't expected to be 'on his own,' so to speak. For a second it felt like he was on a raft—alone, lost somewhere in the middle of the ocean... *that's nonsense.* He glanced at Andy. *I'm **not** alone... I'm in good hands... I can do fine without Julian, actually—as long as Andy is there. I don't **want** to, exactly... but I **can**.*

What an unpleasant realization: *Julian is the only friend I've made since I moved here last summer.* He had become so used to Julian's presence, he took it for granted. He didn't just rely on Julian, he had become dependent. *not very smart, Randall.* That, and a high estimation of his own intellect, had led him to feel confident and secure. This surprise splash of reality, like a basin of cold water, forced him to wake up—he was vulnerable... unsure of himself. Yet... he glanced at Andy again... something clicked. He felt reassured... his feet were back on solid ground... *I feel very lucky. odd how Julian seems to cause insights like this from time to time.*

He looked around at the clock— *3:42... fifteen minutes; what can I do for fifteen minutes?* He faced Andy, hoping he would suggest something. He had no reason to mistrust Andy, but he was still counting on Julian to be at his side at the game.

Andy puzzled over this development… he didn't know Julian very well—other than the troop scrapbook, nothing about him came to mind. He doubted the Principal would be interested in that… and again, why would Mark be involved? He turned to ask Mr. L, but he had gone over to the glass cabinet… checking out an old yearbook. With a shrug, he pointed to a filing cabinet. "Why not look at some back issues? You can see the kind of shots we usually use." *that's a good way to kill fifteen minutes.*

"Yeah! Good idea!" **great** *idea*… He had never looked at sports photos closely— *not as a photographer. admittedly, some tended to draw his eye… track and field certainly… swimming… wrestling and basketball could be nice.* He thought of them as 'secret treats.' Football? Not until now. *I do need to know where to use a flash… that is a weak spot. I've used a flash all of three or four times in my life!* He followed Andy over to a bank of filing cabinets. *they must have them organized. yes… this will help a lot.*

3   *Kassa: the object of the exercise*

The music in the background was unfamiliar, but interesting. Kasey wasn't particularly fond of brass instruments—*certainly not a trumpet—but this music is okay...engaging in its own way.* He tried to imagine it being played on a clarinet. *Benny Goodman would be perfect for this... he'd make this really intense...* Kasey's right arm gestured gracefully, following the melody line. When it came to popular music, smooth jazz was near the top of his preferred list; he hadn't heard this piece... *probably Harry James... maybe Miles Davis.* The music coming from the built in sound system in the adjoining room helped; *better than silence.* It served to offset the suspense, the uncertainty about what he was facing. He did not know precisely what was happening, but it had to be fairly important, or he wouldn't be here. His parents weren't in the habit of using him as window dressing of some kind—he was here for a reason, for a purpose.

Unusual was their not explaining what that was. No, not unusual—that term implied that this sort of thing happened often... **unprecedented** was the word he needed. Being held in suspense was new, **that's** unusual. Common sense told him that something was about to happen, something that he might not like. Observation had shown that what one liked and wanted and what reality required were never alternatives—they were rarely friends. Not that he had experienced anything personally, but he was privy to a variety of parental 'behaviors,' to phrase it politely; his peers at Belmont represented a small body of knowledge on the subject. If it weren't for that, he probably wouldn't be on the alert—and this trip was **very** strange. Presumably, what he wanted would taken into account—with any luck, this wouldn't be a total disaster. But above all, Kasey was a realist, not a dreamer; he realized that taking things for granted was stupid. Meanwhile, he had learned from his mother how to be patient and how to mask his feelings... *keep my powder dry, to use Professor Marchbank's terminology.* His history teacher was one smart cookie—and his mother's inscrutability was legendary.

when will they get back? they've been gone long enough... The minute hand on his wristwatch had barely moved since he last checked. Waiting was so annoying. He'd brought a book along, but it didn't appeal—too complex... required full attention, like any serious schoolwork tome. This one he enjoyed—once into it he hated to be interrupted. He'd read half of it on the train, since there wasn't anything else to do—his parents weren't acting like tourists and had their own reading material.

So, his mind wandered, thinking about this and that. *they couldn't have gone very far...* His parents had been called away unexpectedly—why and what for was not explained; his presence was not required for whatever it was about, evidently. His attention returned to the music—preferable to studying the furnishings in this posh hotel suite. The armchair he occupied was comfortable enough; it was either new or neglected; expensive—meant to satisfy visiting high-class guests and dignitaries, not for living with. He crossed his right foot over his left knee and settled in for the duration. The armrest was a good support, just the right height for his elbow. Head resting on his left palm, his eyes blurred—the music re-occupied his attention. *I wonder if places like this ever have a piano...*

Kasey wanted to play clarinet like his idol Benny Goodman—Benny Goodman could do it all; instead, he played the oboe. Reason: the only slots in the Belmont Hill music program that needed filling were trombone and oboe. Piano, his first choice, always had a surplus, so was never a consideration. He was good at the keyboard, but so was everyone else. He had learned long ago that competitions—when he was allowed to enter—were pointless, usually. Since oboe players were scarce, it was the obvious route—they were rare, so they usually found work. *at least that's what Mr. Samuelson says.* If his career path was to be music instead of writing, it was smart to have the necessary grounding. He played the clarinet anyway of course, when he could. It wasn't as fussy… *has a wider range… and it's what Benny Goodman plays. 'nuff said.*

So how do you find work as an oboe player? First, you learn to play the thing. That takes practice… **lots** *of practice… every day kind of practice.* **Except** today: "No, Kass," his mother said. "It's important to be with your father for this trip." So, he came along as required; *it isn't every day that you get sprung from school to travel out of state with your parents.* The fact that it meant extending his Thanksgiving break by several days was particularly awkward—he would have to make up three exams and who knew what else when he got back. He wasn't used to that kind of thing—it was typical for the yacht club types who went on trips to Bermuda or wherever, but they had ways to compensate the powers that be—i.e., lots of money.

Kasey presumed that he was at the bottom of the list when it came to annual family income. His dad wasn't poor, but he had to go to work every day like any other professor. His mother was independently endowed, but that was never talked about—her "dowry" was one of those hush-hush areas he would be told about when the time came—the never specified time. He presumed it was a traditional coming of age thing, probably when he turned 21.

The problem about this trip was no explanation; **why** was it important? *all I did today was tag along, smile politely and shake a hand now and then; I was there for show, I guess… no one asked me anything. all I got was a lot of odd looks and hesitant grins.* **Important** was not what came to mind as a word to describe the past five hours—or was it six?

I could have used the time to learn the Saint-Saëns I brought along… that's what I'll be doing when I get back to my room at Belmont. But, no: instead of getting a head start on that, he had to spend the day trying to appear interested… in what, exactly? another science lab? Science labs were not of any interest to Kasey. *if you've seen one centrifuge, you've seen them all.* That's one area where he and his father parted company. His father was impressed by what they saw: glass tubing, racks of test tubes, microscopes, elaborate instruments and gauges, scales of all sorts… *not my thing. I suppose I was needed for some other reason—moral support?* That didn't make sense either… *Dad doesn't need my moral support; he knows what he's doing.*

Obviously that was the committee's opinion too. *we were treated like royalty—pretty strange. I was dressed royally, at least.* The deep green Belmont Hill Academy Blazer took care of that. *makes a better costume than a white lab coat.* The coat of arms on the breast pocket was very classy.

The sound of the door opening interrupted his train of thought. *finally.* He just realized that he was hungry. Supper was next on the schedule, more than likely. For that, he was ready.

—m—

Julian had not sat in this **particular** location before—it was wonderful but it was awkward—a little scary, actually. To his left was Mark, the most important man in his life. To his right was his mother—coincidentally, the most important woman in his life—always had been, always would be. They were in the front seat of the scoutmaster's new station wagon. It was the natural thing… *there's plenty of room for three people, so it makes sense. it's more friendly.* Putting either him or his mom in the back seat would seem very odd, very **un**friendly. *so how do you sit there calmly when your insides are churning with excitement because your left thigh is touching the man who always turns you on, whose scent drives you crazy, and who nearly always causes you to get a stiffy?* If either one of these people found out how he felt, his entire life would be ruined, that's all.

Figure out something to talk about that gets your mind off that. Inside Guy was on duty, which was a good thing.

"Do you have any idea why they chose you for this?" Francine still puzzled about the Principal's choice. Her boy had never shown any interest in social or political activity.

"Beats me," Julian kept his hands folded in his lap, just in case.

"They found the perfect person, that's what surprises me." Mark wondered how many students they had considered before they discovered Julian.

"Perfect?!!" Julian looked at Mark in amazement.

"What do you mean?" Francine had not expected Mark's observation.

"Julian is always open to new things, he's bright, he's fun, and he has no problems when it comes to Black people—gets along with them just fine, from what he's told me."

Julian agreed. *it's true... I got a kick out of those guys last summer. I wonder if this kid will be like them.* Picturing them at Jackson High School, though... *I don't think so.*

"You remember Little Joe?"

"Sorta." Julian tilted his head and grimaced. He hadn't thought about his kindergarten pal for as long as he could remember. He squeezed his eyes shut... a vague picture was all that formed. "He played on a drum all the time."

"That's surprising. You used to go over to their house a lot."

"Dunno why, but I don't remember that much." *maybe it will come back to me. when Grandpa died I sort of stopped thinking about stuff... then we moved here with Geraldine and everything, I didn't spend a lot of time thinking about who we knew in Joliet. I was only 5.* He thought for a minute... he remembered the street they lived on, a little... lots of litter along the sidewalk...

Her boy's school clothes were less formal than Francine would have preferred; the blazer he wore on Sundays would have made a better impression. He could have added that easily when they stopped by the house to get his scrapbook. But the committee thought it best for him to go as is, just as he dressed at school. They were of the view that the new boy would be less intimidated; they thought he'd feel more welcome if he met Julian as he was at school—seeing what a typical Jackson High student looked like might help him feel more at ease. *just as well, probably. Julian is never comfortable when he's dressed up.* She was a little concerned about his ability to take on this task. The news often had stories about problems and protests around school integration. Could her boy deal with that? An image formed in her mind of him facing a picket line of angry adults shaking signs and hurling ugly insults... not a pretty picture. She doubted if that would happen here, but she couldn't rule it out as a possibility.

Julian tried to form an image of the boy they were on the way to meet. Not a lot to go on... *how tall is he? is he big and burly like Jake? or gangly like Zeke? those guys were as different as could be except for being Black. maybe he's short and delicate like Justin.* Besides Little Joe, he had only known three Blacks in his life, all of them last summer. They were in Geraldine's landscape crew... *a lot of fun, actually. a different way of talking... I don't think they finished high school.*

"If this works out, you could make it your community service project."

"Yeah! I never thought of that. I need one too." *perfect.* Julian liked it when he could do that—combined goals were always more satisfying somehow. What with Geraldine and his mom fussing about him getting a girlfriend, finding a good project for his Life rank had been sidelined. This would be a lot easier as a part of scouts; made good sense. *besides, it will take less time that way.* That's one thing he had learned about high school—things take more time—lots more. *especially now that I'm helping Randall in his photo lab... life is getting* **busy**.

Society's problems were an area that had never drawn Julian's interest or attention. Aside from lessons about the Pilgrims seeking freedom from the King of England, General Washington and Thomas Jefferson and those other guys forming a democracy, contemporary social issues had not been a subject of classroom study. They talked a little about slavery in the sixth grade—some in the eighth grade, but mostly that class was about the Indians being kicked out. Julian never got why they forced the Indians to move to Oklahoma. The only Indian he remembered seeing was Ed, a guy that worked on Geraldine's crew—and he wasn't a pure blood—half Cherokee; he didn't look much different. The Civil War was saved for high school.

It hadn't occurred to him to ask why he had never seen a Black student in his school. Since they all lived on the other side of town, they went to school over there. Inquiry and discussion about the phenomenon of segregation had not yet been a part of his curriculum, or of his life, for that matter. He couldn't recall if it had ever come up. He had always paid attention to his hobbies or scouts, and lately, to drawing. American history wouldn't occupy one of the required slots in his school schedule until next year. It just dawned on him: *I don't know what to do... I don't know anything about this stuff.*

His eyes focused on the car they were following—the principal and Mr. Barnes were leading the way to the meeting on the university campus. Julian's eyes were busily noting all the interesting buildings along the way, but instead of looking for a subject to draw as usual, they were looking for something, anything, that was familiar, something to hang on to. Nothing was there.... awareness that he was uninformed, uneducated, and unprepared had taken root. Aside from Mark and his mother, he was alone. This was something he had never experienced. *what if I foul it up?*

Hold on, now... Inside Guy applied the brakes on that line of thought. *You can handle this... this won't be half as hard as facing Rita and her friends.*

I hope you're right. Actually, now that he thought about it, Inside Guy probably **was** right. The only reason he was scared, and he wasn't really **scared**, was the same as always, like in that campout. *why do they always keep you in the dark until the last minute?*

Julian just decided that he was looking forward to meeting the new boy—whatever his color. *he's the one that has an excuse to be afraid. my job is to fix that. I can do that. he doesn't have to be afraid of me. that's a start, isn't it?*

Atta boy. One of Inside Guy's limitations was not being able to pat Julian on the back.

—⚏—

"Penny for your thoughts," Lewis Wood asked quietly. His son's silence was, as usual, impossible to interpret. This trip was organized primarily for his benefit, though he did not know that.

"Hum? Sorry, Dad; I was daydreaming." Actually, he was wondering where they were going for supper. His parents had parked on the sofa, obviously awaiting a call or something—whatever was next.

"I'm curious about what's going on in your head. You must have had a rather dull time today. Did anything you saw or anyone we met make any sort of impression?"

Kasey shrugged with a grin, pleased that his father was aware of his feelings. "Not really. They seemed like competent people, but you'd expect that." He ran through a few images in his memory. He hadn't been as attentive as he could have been... *half a dozen or so people in white lab coats...* he hadn't focused on any of them in particular. *one was very tall, very muscular... massive nose. another had odd glasses...* "The one with the goatee seemed a little stuffy, but..."

"Good observation." *he's one that I'll need to watch... a go-by-the-book type for sure. he may not like my approach.*

"The other man, the one in the expensive suit: what's the story about him?"

Lewis winked at his son, pleased by his keen observation. "He's the reason for all this; he's the man with the money." Not only that: he would be giving everyone in that tour today guaranteed employment for a year or more—potentially, for several years. "He's the man who brought us down here. He thinks—or hopes—that my work will save his life." He watched his son closely.

"His **life?!**"

"Yep. He has a rare blood disorder. If a cure or a treatment can't be found, he has a year, maybe two left. He thinks I'm the one who will find the answer."

Kasey looked at his father, amazed. "Is he right?"

"I don't know; I hope so. It would be stupid to make any promises, but I think I have a good shot. My experiments have been very encouraging. I don't know how he knew about my work, but he did. He plans to make me part of a special research team to study his condition. He has the money to pay for it. This is his alma mater; as a thank you he plans to give them a new building for their School of Pharmacy."

"Wow." *that explains why we're in this super fancy hotel.* His friends at school were used to this kind of thing, but this was his first stay at a Hilton. Impressive as it was, it didn't explain why he was here. *what do they need me for?* He glanced at his mother again for a clue.

46

Nothing… she's doing another needlepoint. In other words, she's not going to spill the beans. Suddenly it dawned on him: *are we going to move here?*

A tap on the door signaled that the chauffeur had arrived. Before he had a chance to ask anything, his parents had risen and headed for the door. In a daze, he followed.

4   *a ride in the faded '48*

It seemed somewhat daring to be riding home in Andy's car, but it was the smart thing to do, considering the time it would save. *very thoughtful of him—we spent a lot longer than I expected looking at back issues: way more than fifteen minutes. good thing, too: I know almost nothing about sports—**especially** football.* That used to be a source of pride. Now he saw how stupid that was. Since he had no athletic ability, no potential, he didn't even try. He told himself it was a waste of time. *a person with my brains had more important things to do.* A couple of days ago, Julian had set him straight on that.

I tried to compliment him—I said being an artist was a lot more important than being on any old sports team. "That's just silly," he said. Then he told about Tom—how he had come to the rescue after the dance. He told about what it meant to him to be on the football team, and what his being on the team meant to his friend Nick and to the school. Obviously, it was a good thing all around for him to be a football player. Then he said, "it's a good thing I'm **not** a football player, because I wouldn't be any good at it at all. Same goes for you. We're doing everyone a favor by not being on the football team."

Julian had an original way of viewing the world—it's seemed too simple, but somehow he usually got things right. *I am so lucky to be his friend. I have lucked out so many times since moving here!*

Sometimes Randall worried about that—the scales were bound to tilt back the other way sooner or later. He was used to being pushed around and bullied, used to staying out of sight. Deep down he feared that eventually something would happen… things could slip back to normal any time. Thanks to Julian, he had stopped worrying about it day in and day out.

He didn't know it at the time of course, but from the first **day** at this school, his luck had changed. Radically changed. He was always pinching himself to be sure he wasn't dreaming. It was all due to Julian. *the moment I first saw him **everything** changed. second period will always be special because of that... he was all I could think about—for weeks.*

He reached up and touched his forehead—that's the part of him that had actually met Julian first: they collided head-on in the hallway one morning. *instead of dashing all my hopes and dreams, my clumsiness brought good fortune. now that's my lucky spot.*

That's why, when Mark stopped by to tell them that Julian wasn't going to make it after all, he was afraid his luck had run out finally. But no—Andy stepped in. *kind of interesting, actually. Andy is more like me—sort of average looking. well, no one is as beautiful as Julian.*

Randall had mixed feelings right now—he didn't want to be disloyal. On the other hand, he was intrigued. The fact that Andy was a senior didn't affect him as much as he expected. Usually he steered clear of the older kids; in Pullman, where he used to live, they were always a threat. Avoiding their attention was about the only survival strategy he had. So far that had not been true here—especially after the campout at Hayden Park he and Julian had been invited to. *that was run by two seniors and it was... well, it was wonderful. wild, but wonderful.* It had proven that just because they were a little older didn't mean they were bad or dangerous. Still, it seemed somewhat daring to be riding home in Andy's car like this.

he's in Julian's scout troop; it has lots of seniors. they all seem to be great guys. maybe I don't need to worry about that any more. age difference doesn't mean as much once you're in high school, I suppose. he's been super friendly—treated me like an equal from the start. The trouble was self-confidence. *how do I talk about anything without sounding stupid?* Nothing was more obnoxious than a bubbling greenhorn trying to sound impressive.

It would never have occurred to Andy that he could appear formidable or hard to approach; he was unaware of Randall's internal struggle. Partly, that was due to the fact that he was a senior, and seniors tend to forget what it was like to be a sophomore. Besides, he was in a terrific mood. His life was going great: he was a Patrol Leader in his scout troop, he was Sports Editor of **The Cardinal,** and he was still in the academic top ten at school. The only areas in his life that needed fixing were his car—*it's 15 years old, muffler is shot*—and his sex life. Ever since summer camp that had been neglected... Tony, his regular playmate, had fallen madly in love with Danny, and was no longer available... and Tom, the one he really wanted, had done the same thing: *now he's Nick's private property.*

So, for the last five months all he'd had to play with were his memories and his right hand—*finding someone who likes to mess around isn't so easy.   if you're not careful, word gets out that you're queer—then you're in all kinds of trouble.   they'd never let me in the locker room if they knew what I liked about the place.*

The dividing line between being careful and being a chicken isn't very clear—especially when you're hungry. That's why he was having a little trouble right now... he was getting horny. His gut told him that Randall was available... but his brain wanted him to be careful. So far, his brain was in charge. But the faint glow in his lap was a sign that it wouldn't take much to change that. So far, he'd seen nothing encouraging in the lap to his right... but he had a very good idea of what was sleeping down there. Randall had been Julian's guest at a troop meeting and he had trouble not showing off what he had. **Very** nice; Andy had an excellent recollection of the occasion.

What was not clear was whether they were more than good friends. *Julian is always a tough one to figure... he's friendly with everyone.   he is so in with the brass that you have to be careful.   if you stepped over the line, you'd probably get your medicine super quick.   I don't know if he ever goofs around.   if he does, he sure is cool about it. he looks so pure—someone you'd expect to see on Leave it to Beaver, only better: in Living Color.*

For now, Andy thought it wise to bide his time. *with any luck, I'll see an opening, a hint.   if only I had some of Tony's talent—and instinct.   he can spot a friendly reaction before it happens... doesn't wait around, either.* Andy was able to imitate Tony's outgoing style in lots of ways—it helped in his newspaper reporting, for sure. But when it came to getting into someone's pants... well...

His thoughts were interrupted— "Thanks for giving me a ride."

"Sure. I figure it will save time. It won't be that long before I have to come and get you for the game." As they drew closer to Randall's house, Andy became a little self-conscious about his car—it didn't belong in this neighborhood. Several nicknames for his motorized chariot had been proposed: *Tony calls it the "Fun-time Four-door;" Tom calls it the "Faded '48," a tribute to its advanced state of oxidation.* Forest green had become sort of a dull Necco lime green. Andy was inclined to call it Granny's Guzzler—a tribute to its original owner, Grandmother Ashbaugh, and to its appetite for gasoline. His paper route took care of that. Since it was a hand-me-down, he had no complaints.

"Sorry about the muffler." *at least you can't see the exhaust.*

Randall gave a short laugh. "It's not as loud as a motorcycle." *I hate those things...*

"Yeah, that's true... more like a hot rod." He laughed, "Frankie asked when I got a Smitty."

Randall didn't know what that was.

"I guess that's what you do if you want your car to impress everyone: put on a Smitty—a muffler that doesn't muffle." *that and a set of baby moon hubcaps.* He shook his head; he wasn't interested in customizing cars or hot rods. Reliable transport was all he required.

Frankie... name sounded familiar... *oh, I remember* "You mean the bugler?"

"The very man. He's the troop hot rod expert. Says fixing my muffler will run me 50 or 60 bucks," he grimaced. That kind of money was hard to come by. Andy's plan was to allow the problem to annoy his father until he couldn't stand it any longer; technically, it was **his** mother's car.

Randall didn't know anything about hot rods. He knew quite a lot about his parents' cars—not because he was interested in cars per se, but because it seemed good policy. He had yet to take Driver's Education, so he'd never driven a car. Except for the time his father let

52

him move the Rover a few feet on one of their climbing trips, he'd never been behind a wheel. Car maintenance wasn't a subject he knew much about either—if one of the cars needed attention, his father simply had it taken care of.

Riding in this car was definitely a new experience—not an adventure, exactly, but it did heighten an awareness: this was not at all like his mother's Continental. He presumed another comment about the muffler would be a bad idea. The bugler, on the other hand was fair game—and of some interest.

"Frankie's in Concert Band—plays a cornet. He's good." A good bugler, too: Randall had visited a troop meeting with Julian, and Frankie was in top form. The question in his mind that night was whether he was at all like the other guys in that Flaming Arrow Patrol. Every one of them was of a like mind when it came to sexual preference. That was the other major piece of luck in his life: discovering that he was not alone in that, and that several of Julian's scout friends were of the same mind. That wasn't luck, it was more in the line of a miracle.

It just occurred to him: could Andy be one of that group as well? Not likely... he'd never been mentioned. *when he came up to me in woodshop class two days ago, I had no idea who he was...*

Unconsciously, Andy scratched himself and made a small adjustment to relieve a slight pinch in his groin. It was noticed at once by his passenger. It added to Randall's underlying question about Andy: could he be like some of the other guys in Julian's troop? Tony and Danny especially. The entire leadership patrol were 'brothers,' so to speak. He was tempted to do a similar adjustment to see if it would be noticed. He was about to do that when he saw the 48th street sign. *too late.* "It's a left turn here."

Andy checked out the neighborhood... *wow.* He kept a straight face... in this part of town, his car stood out like a wadded up lunch sack that had bounced off the side of the trashcan instead of going in. This was the country club part of town. Now he understood why Randall had such fancy photography gear. He remembered the directions from yesterday: third house on the right. *man alive... they could put two more houses in the front yard.* He drove up to the end of the driveway: a **three** car garage... *yikes.*

The trunk wasn't shut completely—the bicycle was too large. But it was secure. He'd carried his own bicycle like this more than once. He lifted it free and set it down in front of Randall. "There ya go!" At least the bicycle was standard, not a thin tire racer. Andy had one of these at home—most of the delivery guys at The Times had one of these: heavy duty. *good old Schwinn. mine's a Hornet. the Jaguar is a little fancier.*

"Thanks." Randall wheeled it over to the bike hutch and slid in into its slot. When he turned he saw the expression on Andy's face. "We all have bicycles; my dad likes to go on bike rides as a family sometimes."

nothing wrong with that. Andy scratched his head… one thing he could not imagine, was seeing his parents astride bicycles. *strange how something like this could show you instantly how lucky you are.* Being without a family set of bicycles suited him just fine.

Randall jogged over to the garage doors and peeked in the first window: his mom's car was there. That meant they needed to go in the house first. "I have to check in." He grabbed his books and the camera bag. "We can go through the mudroom. It's quicker."

Andy had been in a mudroom before—a fad in all the better new places. Sandy Rayburn's place had one. They seemed sort of odd in town, actually; horses weren't allowed in the city limits. Although, this place looked like it could have stables out back somewhere.

"Hi Mom," Randall chimed as he opened the door. "I'd like you to meet Andy. He's the sports writer I told you about. I brought him home so he could see the photo lab."

"Why, how nice. It's good to meet you, Andy." Eloise Hallstrom was taking a break from a leisurely afternoon read to fix a cup of tea. "I'm sorry I don't have anything special for you to try out. But I do have ice cream on hand." After school snacks were **de rigueur** for growing boys. She noted that Andy was considerably taller—probably by five or six inches. *yes… Randall mentioned that he was an upperclassman.*

Randall glanced at Andy with a 'sorry about this' expression, but Andy was obviously ready for a treat.

54

A dish of ice cream, it so happened, was the perfect solution for Andy, whose after school tummy had been nagging for some time now. He checked his watch... a rapid calculation told him that he could spend about thirty minutes without a problem.

Randall peeled off his coat as he did an about face. "Plenty of extra hooks on the inside wall," he headed back into the mudroom.

After hanging up their coats, the boys took a seat at the table.

Eloise had just removed the ice cream from the freezer when she remembered. "I take that back!" Sharples had suggested that she add icebox cookies to Randall's sack lunches. "I **do** have something special!" She had intended them to be a surprise next week, but today is better... *they're worth considering for the Bridge Club: this will be the perfect test.* Rule One was never serve a dessert to the bridge ladies that hadn't been pre-tested. She detoured to the counter on the far side... "dessert central," as her husband referred to it; she had picked up a couple of dozen this morning.

While Randall's mother fussed, Andy checked the place out—it was a lot classier than the kitchen he had grown up with. He'd been in fancy houses before, so it wasn't a total shock. What did strike him was that Randall didn't exactly fit in—he looked like a plain ordinary middle class kid. All the other rich kids he knew sort of showed off what they had—couldn't help it. His mom was high society, for sure.

The mudroom door opened suddenly. "Great Scott!" exclaimed the grinning giant that emerged. Brandishing a fully packed Strand double strap briefcase, Helgar Hallstrom grinned eagerly at the boy sitting at the kitchen table with his son. "You must be the lucky man!"

Andy was at a complete loss for words: he had just been addressed by the most unique person he had ever seen... *must be six four!* A Norse god trying to disguise himself as Sherlock Holmes— deerstalker cap, Ulster coat and all, lunged forward. Straight blond hair, bright blue eyes...

Eloise turned from the counter with the special cookie box in her right hand; she gave her husband a disapproving sound: "**ahem**!" Her eyes lowered to his feet.

"Oops... sorry, dear," he chuckled. He winked at Randall and his friend and disappeared into the mudroom.

"My dad," Randall shrugged. It was rare, but not unknown for his father to violate mom's rules about stepping on her immaculately waxed kitchen floor while in his street shoes. It was fun when she caught him in the act. Since he walked almost a mile to and from the university campus every day, his shoes often left evidence of their most recent service.

Eloise fetched three dessert bowls; she didn't need to ask whether Helgar wanted to join in. *he's just another hungry boy: the biggest one.* Why he never gained weight was a constant source of amazement and envy.

"Let's start over," Helgar said cheerfully, reappearing without his street shoes and outer wrappings; the loafers didn't diminish his height. "I'm Randall's father, and a man who is consumed by envy: I presume you are the proud owner of that 1948 Dodge?" He reached out to shake Andy's hand.

"Er..." Andy took the man's hand—he was not at all surprised at the iron grip. Thankfully, he didn't hold it very long. He was at a loss for words. How could this man be Randall's father? On second glance, the nose... that verified a connection; otherwise, Randall looked like his mother.

"My best friend in the world had a car just like yours—at first I thought he was paying a surprise visit." Helgar seated himself at the end of the table opposite his son. "Some of the best times in my life were spent in that car." He sat back and grinned. "Those were the days." He winked, "Secrets, lots of secrets... not for mixed company," he nodded in his wife's direction. "Yes... high school days are special," he grinned. "Especially if you have a '48 Dodge." He winked at Andy. "Don't worry—your secrets are safe." *you could stash a case of beer in the trunk and cover it fast... no one ever caught on. Lester was so good at that.*

"Now, don't give these boys any ideas from your misspent youth." Eloise delivered three servings of Rocky Road ice cream. Helgar's was healthy—nearly twice the size she served the boys. She knew how to head off his inclination to go for seconds and leave a mess behind.

Helgar winked at the boys. "She's right, of course. You need to discover those things on your own. That's what makes them special." He helped himself to a large spoonful. When Eloise placed a plate of cookies in the center of the table his eyes lit up.

"Only **two**," she spoke to her husband pointedly. "It's not long until supper." She smiled at Andy. "Are you staying for supper?"

"Oh… no; thanks, but…"

"No matter. Some other time, perhaps. Randall's friends are always welcome." She was glad he had deferred… a glance at the clock told her that fixing something for him might be difficult. She had enough set aside for Randall and Marietta, but… she caught a glimpse of Helgar taking a bite of cookie… his silent reaction was positive. *perfect.* She would leave the boys to their own devices; it was time to start dressing for the banquet.

"I take it that you're the newspaper writer Randall spoke of."

"Yes, sir. Andy Ashbaugh."

"Randall tells me that you're in that scout troop he visited."

"Yes, sir." Andy grinned proudly.

"Well I must say, I was impressed by your scoutmaster. He brought Randall home afterward; we had a wonderful time getting acquainted."

"Mark is the best," Andy agreed enthusiastically.

"So, what is your duty in the troop?" Helgar didn't know much about the organization.

"I'm Patrol Leader of the Tigers; we have six patrols."

"Congratulations. I'm not surprised. I suspect your scoutmaster is a good judge of who can do a proper job. Picking good leaders is the key to success."

Andy blushed slightly; it was nice to be flattered.

"Say, it just occurred to me—I neglected to find out how to contact him. I have a question or two that could use his expertise."

"I think he's in the phone book; his last name is Schaefer. But don't call him tonight—he is in charge of Oglivy's on Friday nights. They stay open until nine on Friday. He's the Assistant Manager."

"Ah, I see. That's good to know. Thanks." Helgar took another bite of cookie. *Oglivy's. I've heard that mentioned somewhere… a department store, if memory serves.*

Consuming the dessert occupied their attention for a while—there was little need for conversation—the introductory essentials had been satisfied. Randall noticed the time on the wall clock and glanced at Andy.

Andy had almost finished his ice cream when Randall touched his wrist. He checked the wall clock. "We better get a move on, if you're going to show me that photo lab.

"You're right. Are we late?" He knew they were okay.

"Not yet; finish your ice cream." One of Andy's strong points was managing his time.

"If it's okay, Dad, we'd like to develop the film after the game." Since it was Friday, he had some slack about his bedtime.

"Of course—I couldn't wait if it was me," Helgar related to that instantly. "I'm not sure when we'll be returning." He turned to Andy: "Just park over on the right side. That way if we're late coming in, you won't block our car."

Andy stood; time to get a move on.

"Try not to go **too** late out there," he gave the standard parental cautions, with a thumb up. "Just be quiet when you come in… you know what goes." He followed them out. "Good luck with the weather," he waved as they trotted up to the garage. "You'd better go prepared." The forecast was for rain. The sky was overcast: an on-the-way feel to the air. *they could get lucky… one never knows for sure when the rain will start.*

"Your folks are really nice," Andy remarked as he followed him to the side door entrance.

58

"Thanks." Randall was happy with his parents, generally. He for sure wouldn't swap them for any others he'd seen. "The photo lab is on the far side." He led Andy through the garage.

Andy checked out the Lincoln... *matches the house*. The Rover was a surprise at first—until he remembered seeing it in one of the mountain snapshots. The dark green Washington license plates were cool.

Randall flipped the safety alert switch that showed the darkroom was in use. "Have you been in a darkroom before?"

"Yeah—at the newspaper downtown I got a tour once. So I know the rules."

"Good. This is probably the same thing. The entry is a little bigger than average, I guess. Just hold onto the railing; it will lead you in."

Andy put his hand on the guide bar and went ahead. The darkroom's yellow safelight soon replaced the darkness. "Whoa..." He was amazed, to put it mildly. This was almost as big as the darkroom at the **Times-Herald**, and they had a crew of four.

Randall led the way at that point. "This is the drying closet." He opened the door so Andy could see in. "That's the roll I took yesterday in the cafeteria."

"Can I take a peek?"

"Umm... sure." He'd never had anyone ask that, but...

Andy detached the clip from the hanging line and removed the long strip of film; he knew how to handle 35mm negatives properly. He held the clip up high—with the help of the safelight he could see the frames easily. "Looks good."

Andy's treatment of the negatives was reassuring. "You want to make a print?"

"Well, sure—only I've never done that myself, before... I've only watched."

"Oh... how much time do you have? If you have to come back here at six to pick me up—"

Andy checked his wristwatch and did a quick calculation. Assuming there were no surprises at home, he had about 45 minutes. "Half an hour plus." He was eager to see how Randall worked—and maybe see if he was right about this kid.

"Okay—pick a frame you want to see; I'll get the trays ready."

While Andy stood to the side and held the negatives up to the safelight, Randall uncovered the chemical trays and turned on the rinse tank. He went to the supply cupboard and pulled out his scissors.

"Found one." He didn't know for sure what it was, but it looked interesting—a kid sitting on a bench in the cafeteria.

"Lay the strip flat on the counter, curl side up. Keep track of the frame you want. I need to cut it into archive lengths." He proceeded to cut the negative strip into 6-frame lengths. "Hold that by the edge and bring it over to the enlarger; be careful not to get any fingerprints on the film—they're the devil to get rid of, and they show." He left the other strips on the counter. He could put them away later.

"Second frame from the left—number 17."

Randall took the strip carefully and fit it into the film carrier; he slid it in place and turned on the enlarger.

"Cool!" Andy was impressed.

"You want to print the full frame, or enlarge part of it?" There was a lot of information in this frame—it could be cropped. He remembered taking the shot; a boy sitting alone in the crowded lunchroom had intrigued him—he seemed uninterested in Julian and his fans. Sometimes a zoom in provided a nice surprise.

Andy stooped to look carefully. He could see what Randall might be implying. *a closer view would be nice.*

A predictable phenomenon was underway: circumstance had put two warm bodies together in a cool dark room. That these two bodies belonged to adolescent boys, ready—if not overdue—to do what adolescent boys almost always needed to do after school when no one was around—was also a coincidence. When their warm bare arms touched, accidentally of course, their sensory system responded automatically. Signals were sent to their respective automatic startup

60

centers. Both felt a sudden warm pulse in their groin—an entirely pleasant sensation, one they knew well. Neither suspected that it was a mutual experience. They accepted it as an accident—best not to jump away or flinch. No need—why risk offending someone who intended no offense? The contact was brief; nothing to worry about.

Randall moved the enlarger head upward until the image of the seated figure filled the 4 by 5 print area, and focused. The Nikon lens had done what it was designed to do—he could see that at once. He was accustomed to working with a negative image.

Andy saw the same thing a minute later as he watched the print come up in the developer tray.

It wasn't long before they realized that they were both interested in the same area. They exchanged a subtle grin.

"How big can you enlarge that?" Andy was up halfway and not trying to hide the fact. He rather hoped that it would be noticed—it was.

Randall knew at once what Andy wanted to see, and what that implied; he was eager to demonstrate the possibilities. His first thought was to turn the enlarger to the side and project the image on the wall. That seemed a bit rash—if this were a 120 negative, he would have. Instead, he raised the head all the way to the end of the rail, and refocused. Some clarity was lost, but not much. He adjusted himself. He didn't try to hide his condition either: he was up full.

Andy stepped close to see. Randall waited ever so briefly before going to fetch another 4 by 5... his hope that Andy would touch him— by accident, of course—was rewarded.

The wonderful thing about this sequence was not so much the fulfilled expectation of what the camera had captured; that was very nice. But, **O Happy Day,** the boys had reached an agreement about what they wanted to do without either one having to say a word. Neither was imposing or requesting—they had made a mutual discovery. When that happens, much of the awkwardness of a first time vanishes.

They still didn't need to talk. Andy simply put his arm on Randall's shoulder and stood close as he completed developing the print.

Randall felt a wonderful glow run up his spine. He was too shy to look at Andy in the face, but he leaned close—as if they were

61

sweethearts waiting in line. His face was flushed and he felt fabulous. This was a new thing entirely. It was a little scary, but it was heavenly. He wanted the print to take forever to process so that he could extend this moment—but he also wanted to get out of these pants as fast as possible. He had already determined that they needed to go upstairs to take care of this.

Randall had never had a "quickie" before. He was still slightly numb in the brain. He watched Andy turn his car around and drive away. When it was out of sight, it dawned on him that he needed to get a move on. He returned to the darkroom to finish putting the negative strips into the contact sheet sleeves. Andy planned to return after the game to help develop the game film. He was planning to come over tomorrow and assist making the prints. He left the trays ready to process a print or two, just in case.

Oddly enough, he had forgotten that Julian planned to be here tonight. That was just as well… he had to sort out what had happened in the last half hour. He had no experience to reference. He glanced down… *good*; he had receded enough. He was very hungry.

5   *arrival at the university*

"Drat it!" *couldn't quite make it*—the light had turned red by the time Mark reached the intersection. The Principal's car was the last one to get through the yellow warning light. *hope he doesn't get too far ahead...* He wasn't sure exactly where they were going, other than to the university.

Julian considered using his demerit-free cussword, but with his mom right beside... *not a very good idea.*

whoa. "Look at that!" Julian had never seen such a ritzy car.

The glossy black limousine turning left did seem out of place—Mark hadn't seen one like that before—*after the light changes I'll catch up and check it out... have to anyway...* he needed to get behind Middleton again. He could take a closer look when he passed it. "Movie stars and big name athletes, mostly, use those. I saw a rig like that in Atlantic City once." *I wonder if they're going to shoot a movie in town.* The tinted windows prevented the passengers from being visible.

Francine had never seen one like this either; *maybe in a newsreel.* "I'll check with Geraldine—she has an inside line to the Chamber of Commerce. They'll know if something special is going on." *a movie crew in town would be very good for business; make the hotels happy.* Some of her clients had expensive cars, but they didn't look as long; this one was more like a chauffeur service.

A mid thirties classic Packard 12 Cabriolet was the last car though the light; it also turned left. The pale beige body and matching cloth top was complimented by milk chocolate fenders and trim. The outboard Rosewood Steamer Trunk appeared to be scratch free. Immaculate, it looked like it had just left a museum.

"Maybe there's an auto show this weekend." Mark hadn't heard about one. *strange time of the year...could be a private event, not open to the public.*

Julian nodded. "That's prob'ly it." Two super fancy cars... he looked to the left to see if there were more in the line forming at the stop light—the traffic was fairly heavy this time of day—the rush hour had a while to go. *maybe they'll have one of those old timers, the ones with cranks in front and spoke wheels.*

Francine wasn't particularly impressed; automobiles were of little interest to her—she barely noticed; her concern about the evening had returned. The impending meeting at the university was largely an unknown. They had indicated that it would include dinner—a relief of sorts, since it meant that she wouldn't have to worry about that. But it gave a dimension to the evening that she hadn't anticipated. Having Mark along was an enormous relief. *Geraldine will probably pout about not being included... she might have been helpful... she's used to dealing with complex issues—but it would have been very awkward to arrange...* This time she was on her own—and that was for the best. She didn't want to **need** Geraldine. This was Francine's job, her role. Once in a while, she paid attention to that. Her primary uncertainty was about her boy. This was a huge responsibility, and they had not had time to talk about it. That was unfair; but she could manage... *not much choice, in any case.* She was being railroaded and knew it. But it was for a worthy cause.

Julian's attention was divided: partly, he was feeling guilty about Randall. He had been expecting to help out at the football game. He felt duty bound: he'd not been to even one of the games. He owed it to Tom to go at least one time, and this was the last game of the season. Then, there was tonight: he was at a loss. *what should I be doing or thinking about for this new... what do I call it? assignment? project? job?* Nothing seemed to fit. It sounded interesting enough; he could understand, sort of, the new kid's problem: being new, like Randall. That had turned out to be fun—a lot of fun; and it was great to have a pal like Randall. It meant a lot to Randall, for sure. *so maybe this will go the same way. no reason to think it won't is there? besides, meeting a Black my own age will be interesting. Jake and Zack are more than twice as old as I am... dunno about Zeke. could be even older.*

Guessing people's age accurately was not one of his talents. And his knowledge of Blacks was almost zero. He'd never paid them any mind until he joined Geraldine's crew last summer.

Mark gunned it the second the light changed: he had to get back behind the principal's car.

When the surf green Olds re-entered traffic in front of him, Mark was greatly relieved; the principal had pulled to the side when he realized that Mark had not made the light. The mini-caravan continued—their destination was another half mile distant, far enough to get separated again.

The university had several access points; the one they turned into was not where Mark expected to be going. The private entrance to the Administration Building was for the President and his staff only. Unmarked, the drive led to a relatively small parking area out of sight at the rear of the building. He had never been here, didn't know of its existence. His familiarity with this part of the campus was minimal—the School of Business where he had studied was separate, closer to downtown.

A brief delay—the principal's car had slowed to a stop. A small group of people was crossing in front of him: several men in suits, one lady, very well dressed, and a tall, rather thin boy wearing a green blazer. Three in the group, including the boy, were dark skinned.

it's them! Julian's jaw dropped: *tall! wow... **super** tall.* His first thought was of the new Wolf Patrol Leader: a basketball player, also very tall and slender. He grinned wide and turned to Mark. "Norman!"

Mark nodded. *if the boy's an athlete, Norman would be a big help.* He had no reason to think Norman would have a problem. Admittedly, racial issues had not been an area of attention for Troop 9, an oversight that was unfortunate, and his fault. That would be remedied, and pronto. Knowing now that the schools were about to go through this transition, his boys needed to be properly trained and prepared to assist. The Troop was going to be a part of the solution, not otherwise. He had to admit that he couldn't say for sure if he would have any problems.

The parking area was nearly full. He pulled into the only open space he could see—it was next to a black limousine—the very vehicle that they had seen earlier; on the other side of it, the Packard. *well... that explains that.*

This was a much bigger event than Francine had expected: *look at all these cars...* she didn't stop to count them, little point in that—but **two** catering vans from Sharples, one on each side of the entrance? It would seem that they were about to attend a banquet. A frown formed— had she known, she would have dressed accordingly. Her attire would serve, but it would have been nice to know about this—she had better formal wear. She had been expecting more of a cafeteria setting. Unconsciously, she smoothed her hair; it was prone to stray when exposed to the wind. It was growing dark out; the approaching storm was being ushered in by an erratic breeze. Fortunately, she had worn her long coat this afternoon. *would have been nice to have my Sunday hat.*

Mark went around the front of his car to assist Francine—that enabled him to look closely at the limo: *Chrysler... should have known.* He had not seen a Ghia Imperial Crown sedan up close—he recalled seeing a magazine ad about it a year or so ago. *more daring than a Cadillac or Lincoln, for sure. snazzier than the one Eric and I saw in Atlantic city—looks new.* About a yard longer than his station wagon, he felt an instant moment of sympathy for the driver of this land yacht. The need for a chauffeur license was obvious.

Julian slid out on his mother's side of the car; he kept his eye on the other group, just now going into the entrance at the top of the steps. He didn't have time to see much more before the green blazer disappeared from view. *oo...* He just remembered the lessons in etiquette that Geraldine had given him before the dance. *am I supposed to help my mom, or is Mark supposed to?* She and his mom hadn't gone into it with that much detail. He kept an eye on him... *prob'ly him... he's oldest... he knows what to do...* He guessed correctly: Mark had stepped into place at her side as an escort. *that's a relief... now I can think about other stuff—like what I'm supposed to do.* Not only that, it would make it easier to tell Geraldine how this all went. *she can be real crabby if she wants... she'll want to know all about this.* He opened the rear door to fetch his books. He was told to bring them along to show to the new boy. Adding the scrapbook to the stack sure didn't help any... they were spilled across the back seat. He checked the sky... *boy. wish I had my backpack... looks like it could start raining any time.* He needed to keep these from getting rained on; his backpack would have been perfect. *oh well, too late... gosh...* He didn't want to fumble...

He hurried to catch up. He was used to following behind, but didn't want them to get too far ahead... using both arms helped. Mr. Barnes and the principal were going inside already... it wasn't very far to the building. *huh...* For a back door, this was pretty classy. Mark was holding it open for his mom; he followed her in. The Principal, Dean of Boys and Student Body President were being greeted by someone he couldn't see. The pause gave him a chance to catch his breath and look around. It seemed familiar for some reason. *must be the lights.* Overhead, the round globes providing the light were like the lights in the hallways at Jackson. Everything else was fancier, including the carpeted floor.

"Greetings! Mrs. Forrest, I presume?" a cheerful voice inquired. The President's Executive Secretary took her hand.

Francine was surprised to hear her name—too surprised to form a verbal response. The woman was very engaging, and genuine. She felt at ease at once—*what a nice surprise.*

"And you must be Julian!" she chirped happily. "We are so looking forward to meeting you!" She turned to Mark and offered her hand for a courteous shake. "Welcome to the University, Mr. Schaefer." She stood in the center of the hallway to brief them about the dining arrangements.

"Dinner will be served after President Selfridge gives his welcome and introductions are made. Seating is prearranged—I will lead you to your chairs. I'd be happy to take your coat now, if you like."

Julian wondered if that included him—he had a school jacket that need to go somewhere. *maybe there's a coat stand or something in there...*

"You can put your jacket on the back of your chair, Julian, if you don't mind." She had been instructed to say that—the school jacket needed to be seen by the other boy. "There's a small table for your books. You'll see it when we're there."

Her manner was so smooth and cheerful, Julian felt at ease... almost like he'd been here before. He followed behind his mom as they followed the nice lady down the hall to a set of double doors. An attendant was standing by the far side. *looks like a butler or a waiter. gosh... I didn't expect this to be such a big deal...*

—ɱ—

When the boy he was supposed to meet came into view behind his parents, Kasey couldn't believe his eyes—they opened very wide in shock. What they saw was impossible: *he looks just like **Alexander!** I just read about him on the train!* It was an effort to not shake his head to check whether or not he was awake. His World History seminar assignment to write a five to ten page profile on Alexander the Great was very much on his mind, and this kid looked **exactly** like the description in the book he was reading. The illustration showed him and a few others being tutored by Aristotle. *unbelievable!* That illustration had come alive, and the central character had walked off the page. *am I in the Twilight Zone?* Suddenly, what he was facing had transformed into an entirely different world than he had expected or even imagined. His preconceptions had just been flushed away. *if only Professor Marchbank was here!*

The formal U shaped banquet arrangement was a total surprise—a new experience in every respect. Visually, what confronted Julian was marvelous; the flower arrangements were beyond anything he had seen anywhere... every few feet a cluster, each different and special. He wasn't able to stop and look at any of them like he would have liked. The lady was leading them in too fast. *man, look at all these people... too many to count! maybe we're late or something...*

When the boy he was supposed to meet came into view twenty feet or so away, Julian smiled wide automatically—that's what he always did. This time it was on purpose. He noticed three things all at once: how tall he was, even sitting at the table; his ears poked out—*not as much as Arnie's...* reminded him of Sid a little—and his eyes: *they're **blue!*** He didn't have time to look very long, because the nice lady needed to tell where to put his books. The table was against the wall next to a huge painting, right behind where he was supposed to sit. The wall was super fancy, but he didn't have time to look at it either. *boy,* *sure glad to unload those!* He shucked his jacket and hung it on the chair back that the lady had pulled out from the table. *whoa...* a white place card stood in front of the plate:

Julian Forrest

His name, clear as day, right next to the Black boy. *wow.. fancy!* He just realized that he didn't know the boy's name. He checked: *yep.* He'd moved his place card to the other side of his plate:

Kasey Wood

He glanced at the other tables—everyone had a name card! *wow... this is so neat...*

The lady made him feel welcome. She even helped him scoot forward as he sat, which he thought was very courteous... it gave him a sense of importance. It didn't register in his mind that the evening had been carefully orchestrated, that he was being directed, that nothing was being left to chance.

Don't forget to say thank you... Inside Guy whispered... he was very much present for this.

He smiled at the lady gratefully as he settled in. "Thanks." He gave a couple of Groucho eyebrow raises to the Student Body President who had been seated across from him on the other side of the U corner. He turned to his left and smiled politely. "Hi. I'm Julian."

Kasey was very surprised and turned to return the unexpected greeting: "Umm... hello. I'm Kassa. But most people call me Kasey..." *everyone does.* The intense coral shirt had startled him. It had been concealed under the school jacket. But the eyes were what startled him the most: *brown! how can they be brown? Alexander's eyes were blue, weren't they? no: wait a minute... the book said he had one blue eye and one brown eye. this is really strange.*

Julian didn't want to stare, but the bright blue eyes totally amazed him. He extended his hand: "Glad to meet you. Excuse me for staring, but I didn't expect you to have blue eyes." He shrugged. *shows what I know...*

Cheerful candor was the last thing Kasey expected. It put him at ease at once. Hesitant, he shook Julian's hand. "Yes, they usually surprise people. I inherited them from my mother. They run in her family." He paused, then smiled in return. "I didn't expect you to have brown eyes."

Julian laughed. "I got mine from my mother too!" Actually, he wasn't sure about his father's eyes, since he had never seen them. *Geraldine says they were blue.*

Laughter was infectious… Kasey grinned, completely relieved of his residual misgivings. *what should I say back?* He hadn't expected to meet anyone his own age, let alone an Alexander look-alike… a cheerful Alexander at that.

Julian's attention shifted to the room and the people at the expansive table setup. He counted 17 seated around the U; white linen tablecloths made it appear to be one unit. Two large trays occupied the space between the floral arrangements—one a variety of vegetables— mini carrots, celery sticks, olives, pickles, cherry tomatoes, mini peppers, baby pickles. The other tray featured fruit wedges—melon, pineapple, dates, three kinds of cheese squares and little square crackers. There was enough to stuff himself pretty good if he wanted. None of those appealed to him right now, surprisingly. A good thing, since he'd have to ask someone to pass him the tray—it was out of reach: he was at the end of the table. *whatever this is, it's interesting, for sure. maybe somebody is getting an award.* Mr. Barnes and the Principal were conferring about something as they munched on baby carrots. They were right at home—this couldn't be bad or anything to worry about. Obviously he wasn't very important, sitting in the corner; Julian was relieved—glad, in a way.

Fortunately, Julian had no idea how important he was—that in itself was an asset. His character and native abilities were very much a major concern of the man at the far end of the other arm of the U: the eyes of Frederick Swann, the man paying for all this, were focused on him. The two boys were the only uncertain factors in his plan—everyone and everything else was in place. By the end of the evening, he would know, as well as he could expect, his prospect for success.

Kasey was still adjusting to this new situation—his assumptions about what was coming had been completely wrong. That was unusual in the extreme—he usually had things figured out ahead of time. The banquet setting was unexpected to begin with—rather overdone, actually. But what was this boy doing here? His gaudy shirt aside, he had appeared in an oversized leather sleeved school jacket, carrying a stack of books—clearly, he had just come here from his school. The implication seemed obvious... *that could become my school at some point.* When would that be? It couldn't possibly be on the same level as Belmont. *what about my music?* At once, he realized that he had been taking a lot for granted. He had not been this unsettled ever, as far as he could recall. He was being tested—without warning, he was being tested. He was uncertain what, if anything, he could or should do about it. Now he understood something for the first time: he was still a child, for all practical purposes. He was not in charge—he never was, and he was just now becoming aware of where he fit in or didn't. This was territory he had never visited. Why wasn't he afraid, or angry about any of this?

Kasey had just been the latest person to experience the unique impact of meeting Julian Forrest—a force that he would come to appreciate in time. His infectious smile and demeanor, a phenomenon that varied in strength and impact was not purposeful or conscious; an aura as much as anything, and Julian was totally unaware of it—one reason it was so powerful. Totally honest, and like Pig-pen's dust cloud, it surrounded him everywhere he went. It always had an impact—always positive, as if an odorless spray had cleansed the air.

Usually Julian was ready for a snack after school, but not today: he needed to get used to all this—all these people. Mr. Middleton hadn't told them about this part. He glanced around to see if anyone else seemed as confused as he was. He waited for Inside Guy to help out, but he was just as puzzled. The trouble was, they'd put Mark at the other end of the table, the worst place possible. *wouldn't you know!* Julian could hardly see him.

Directly in front of him a huge plate with a whole bunch of silverware on each side awaited; a fancy napkin was folded so that it stood like a small pup tent—it sat on the far side of his plate. In front of it was a fancy menu card along with a small scorecard pencil.

> > *tink-tink-tink...* < < Someone had tapped the side of an empty wine glass. The nice lady that had helped them get seated was at the speaker's stand in the open end of the U.

"Good evening, everyone." She paused to allow conversations to finish. "On behalf of the University it is my honor and pleasure to thank you for being here this evening. Now that we are all seated, I have a few announcements before introducing our host, Dr. Selfridge. I am Mary Henderson, his Executive Assistant. The menu for this occasion is in front of you..." she held one up for everyone to see. "Please take a few minutes to look it over; the servers will begin to collect orders shortly. Simply mark inside the box by the items you wish. If you need to modify anything or need any information, circle the item, and the server will attend to your concerns. In a few minutes I will introduce everyone by name. You need not stand, but a nod would be nice. Once that is completed, I will present President Selfridge. If you have any questions or needs, don't hesitate to ask. Simply signal me or one of the attendants. Should you need to visit a rest room, you'll find them at the far end of the hall, on the other side of the stairway. Again, thank you all for being here." She returned to her chair on the right side of the U formation.

ooo... Julian reached for the menu. He replaced it with his place card like Kasey had. Printed on cardstock, it was six inches wide and twelve inches long—a boxed border enclosed a long list; each item had a small open square at its left. *fancy! wow! the lettering...* he turned to Kasey and grinned wide. "Boy, look at this!" *it even has my name printed on it!* He examined the hand printed name closely—he had never seen it hand written in calligraphy. *maroon ink... I didn't know they had maroon ink...*

6 *before the big game*

Andy pulled into the driveway right on time, but he was uncertain how to proceed: was it proper to knock at the back door? This was one detail they had not arranged. He stepped up to the door. *is there a doorbell? nope.* He couldn't see anyone through the window—not a surprise: *no one sits in their mudroom waiting to greet visitors... better go around front. shouldn't be a problem; I'm expected.* The front was very nice—not as grand and showy as it could be, considering the neighborhood. He pushed the doorbell button—the knocker was a bit too fancy. He didn't have to wait long.

"Why, greetings," Helgar Hallstrom boomed. "Do come in." He checked his watch—he was running late. *cutting it a little close...*

The bow tie still waiting for his wife's expertise told Andy that they were about to go somewhere. "Thank you, sir." He shook the hand that had been extended. *what a grip! I forgot about that. man... this guy does not look like Randall at all.*

"No Julian? I thought he was coming with you."

"Something came up I guess—he'll probably join us at the stadium." He shrugged. Secretly, he wasn't disappointed; he hoped whatever the Principal had going would occupy Julian for the entire evening. Developing the film after the game without Julian present would be ideal—he needed to follow through with Randall without Julian around. He had to make sure that he hadn't spooked him—that what they had experienced this afternoon was real. They didn't have time to talk about anything—his mother called him to supper before they had time to zip up. He had been confused and up in the air ever since he left. He didn't even know Randall; yet, what they did seemed automatic, required almost. That had never happened before.

"Randall's in the photolab. He practically lives out there these days," he laughed. "Come along and we'll give him a buzz." He led Andy down the hallway to the kitchen.

Andy unzipped his coat and followed. *warm in here.*

"It's too bad there isn't time for a visit," Helgar commented, indicating that he should sit at the small table nonetheless. About to leave himself, he was simply being courteous.

"We don't have a lot of time, but we're okay." Actually, he was a hair early, but he didn't especially want to hang around. As Randall's father stepped over to press a button on the wall, the glass covered cookie platter on the counter caught his eye. Randall's mother had provided a couple of those after school... *yum yum...*

"Yo, Randall!" Helgar spoke cheerfully. The small box mounted next to the phone was an intercom.

> > hi Dad < < the voice came through, clear and strong.

"Your ride is here." He winked at Andy. The expression on his face was fun. "This little box saves a lot of time and trouble." He sat at the table. "Tell me a little about your scout troop." *might as well get a little background...* Helgar fully intended to explore the possibilities... that scoutmaster had inspired a fantasy worth pursuing.

Andy hadn't expected the subject to come up, but he was proud of the troop. "Sure..." *what to say?* "We meet every other Wednesday at St. Bartholomew's. He shrugged. "We march in parades and go camping..." *what else...* "oh: we do food drives and community projects...you know, litter cleanup sweeps, things like that."

"Camping! Well, now...right up my alley; tell me more... where do you go?"

"Depends on the weather; in the summer I like Mount Mitchell the best." Andy pondered... "the Patrol campouts begin in March. We don't do much in the winter."

Randall came in via the mudroom, out of breath. "Sorry, I lost track of the time, I guess. I had to finish loading cartridges. Are we late?"

"Hey, no sweat. We're good." Andy stood and extended his hand. "Nice to see you. We should get going."

"Just park over on the right side when you come back."

Andy held up a thumb as he followed Randall to the mudroom.

Helgar followed them out; he wanted to see that Dodge again. That brought back good memories. He waved as they trotted to the car… that wonderful car. *made more than one beer run in that Dodge… a hot car in its day—and reliable.*

He rechecked the sky—yep: rain all right, just like the man said on the news. He wasn't worried—Randall had grabbed his parka on the way out. Everything he needed was in that case. He returned to the kitchen. *hmm…* He just had a thought… *we'd better take an umbrella…*

"Helgar!"

oops… Eloise calling from the bedroom made him hop to. They were running late again. A glance at the wall clock made him grimace. *very late…* Well, rainy nights were usually good for an after dinner "snuggle." That would take care of things.

Being escorted hurriedly through the vacant gymnasium was unexpected. *maybe we're late after all…* Andy hadn't said exactly where they were headed. The press hat felt funny; Randall rarely wore anything on his head. Evidently it served as a pass of some kind. Hey… *isn't this the Girl's gym? this is where Julian went to that dance!* He remembered now: this is where he and his mother had registered just after they arrived from Pullman. The sound of athletes razzing one another in the distant dressing rooms indicated their destination.

"Rule one: touch base with the coaches **first**. You don't want to tick them off, or you're dead. If they know you're here, and if you understand how to be 'invisible,' they'll let you do anything and go anywhere. If they think of you as one of their assistants, you're allowed incredible freedom. You want them to **expect** to see you—they begin to want you there—it's amazing. He stopped to look Randall in the eye:

"That's **top** secret, by the way. No one is to know that but you and me. Okay?"

"Uh, yeah…" Andy's sudden intensity was a surprise.

Andy tapped his temple. "It's just being smart. Don't let anyone know the tricks of the trade unless you have to. You lose your advantage if they know what you're up to."

Competition was a new thing to Randall. He had never worried about having an advantage; the concept was totally foreign. But he was intelligent enough to realize that it would be useful to learn these things from Andy.

"After we get squared away with the coaches, I'll give you a walk through of where we need to be to get the best shots. That way you can sort of anticipate what to use, what to do—you know, whether to use a flash or to change a lens." Andy had worked with photographers before and knew some of that. He led the way into the dressing area. "After that, we'll go out to the field." He was fairly confident they were early enough; the stands would still be half empty.

"Umm…" Randall hesitated. The sign indicated that they were in the **wrong** place.

Andy saw Randall's expression.

"The visiting team always uses the girl's showers and locker area," he grinned. "That way they don't get a peek at what we're up to. It's part of the Home Team Advantage. C'mon. There are no girls in there now, I guarantee."

Randall had never expected to go through these doors. He didn't know what to make of that, exactly. It was a privilege he didn't really want—though he knew several in his P.E. class that would do almost anything to get a peek in here—with girls running around in the nude, of course. Luckily, he was being spared **that** fate. He followed, amazed at Andy's confidence. *look at him! he marches through the area as if he owned the place.*

Andy headed straight for the office. He could see the visiting team coaches in the window; there were two, and one player—probably the team captain. *perfect.* He stood at the door waiting to be seen and invited in. He put on his best boy scout on duty face. He was spotted and the door opened.

"Yes, may I help you?" asked Scott Spenser, coach of the Coyotes varsity team.

"Hello; I hope I'm not interrupting. I'm Andy. I'm here from **The Cardinal**, our school paper. This is Randall, my photographer. If you have the time, it would be nice to have a short interview—with you and any of your players—your choice, of course—and get a few snapshots. We'll be happy to send you copies of any pictures we take— if you have any shots in particular that you'd like us to take, we'd be happy to oblige."

It took Spenser a minute to react. This was unexpected—a new twist. He was cautious, but impressed all the same. "Step in for a moment." He glanced at his assistant coach to see if he had any objection.

"I'll be honest with you—I've never had a host school send a reporter before."

"Well, to be honest with you, I wasn't sent. It's my idea—I'm trying to learn how to be a good reporter. I see it as my job to give equal access to both sides. A good reporter shouldn't be a cheerleader—he should be objective; that's what our Advisor says at least, and I think he's right."

Spenser was impressed and inclined to go along with this, but he wanted a little reassurance; he turned to his colleague.

Roscoe winked his approval. He admired the boy's initiative; besides, he might let something slip about the host team... *they're ahead in the rankings.*

"Okay—we can take a couple of minutes right now. Later might not be so convenient." He gestured to an empty chair.

"Thank you, sir, I appreciate this. I take it you don't object if Randall takes a few snapshots?"

Spenser wasn't worried about the cameraman—*just another kid...obviously a sophomore—hardly a threat.* "Sure... as long as you make me look good," he laughed.

Randall cleared his throat. "I'll do my best." He could tell the man was only kidding. Andy had won these guys over. *amazing.* He opened his case and pulled out his Nikon and light meter. *wow. now I have to prove I can do this.* This wasn't like a hike in the mountains.

"So, what would you like to ask?"

Andy flipped open his steno pad. "First off I want to know what you would like me to see and observe as I report the game. Second, I'd like to know what the most rewarding thing about being a coach is—besides the fame and fortune, of course."

The coaches had a good laugh.

Randall was impressed. Andy had these guys laughing and eating out of his hand. He stepped back and took a reading. The light in this office was marginal… better go with a slow shutter speed; 1/60 should work. He took a few shots at 1/60—and just as a test, retook them at 1/125. Indoor shots were not his strong suit. Comparing these afterward would be very important. *if I get to do any other games, I want to know more going in.* He didn't pay attention to the conversation, but tried to capture a good image of the coaches together and separately. He moved to the other end of the office carefully; a few shots from there, just in case the lighting was better. A good close-up candid of the player would be nice.

"So, are there any photos you'd like us to take? Anything of the team or the first string? Randall here is good at this, believe me. Maybe your yearbook would like a few special shots."

"Say, now that is a **great** idea. You'd be amazed at how hard it is to get good shots into the yearbook."

Andy's watch was his guide. "I reckon we can spend a few minutes here. Do you want to round anyone up, or should we just wander around? Maybe you have a manager that could help us with the names. We don't want to be in the way…

Spenser looked out of the window. "The boys are suiting up. Why don't you ease your way in and take a few shots while Jack here rounds up a couple of guys for a quick pose." He nodded to the player to go ahead.

"Right. I can't promise yet, but maybe during halftime or after the game we can grab some follow-up shots. I really want to do a good job for you as well as the home team."

"Say, I just thought of something—I don't want the boys to be worried that anything will get photographed that shouldn't be…"

Randall was ready: "don't worry about that, sir. I'll use a depth of field setting that blurs everything but the subject's face and upper chest. That way, no accidental background information can sneak in."

"Oh… well, then. That sounds okay. I'll let the boys know that."

"I'm going to do without a flash as much as possible. The only area I'm worried about is this room and maybe around the lockers. Until I take a reading, I don't know how much I can grab. The shower area is out anyway—too dark without a flash."

"Thank you, sir, for your cooperation. Do I have your name spelled correctly?" Andy turned the steno pad around.

"Perfect. I'll let the manager do the fact check whenever you'd like. We need to get a move on." He gestured toward the door.

"How many shots do you have on those rolls, anyway?" Andy picked up the pace… *we might have had spent too much time in here.*

"I loaded forty shots per roll this time—I assumed that we'd be able to use that many—and I don't have to change rolls as often."

"You load your own film?"

"Sure. It's a lot less expensive that way—you can reuse the cartridges.

"Why don't you go for fifty?"

"Won't fit in the cartridge—I tried it once. Forty is a tight squeeze." *the cartridge end comes off if you're not careful; say goodbye to the whole roll if that happens.*

Andy wondered whether Randall had any questions... *seems to know what he's doing...* "Say, was that true, what you said about the background being out of focus?"

"Sure. What I didn't say was that I'd take them **all** with a shallow depth of field. I took some just to be safe, you know. There wasn't much 'going on' anyway."

Andy patted him on the back. "I can see we will do just fine, you and I. There will be lots more of the home team... they're in the middle of dressing down by now." He led the way to the boy's gym. He thought a minute... "How many rolls do you have, by the way?"

"A dozen. I emptied my bulk roll," he grinned. "Hot damn!" Andy slapped his palm. "That's a lot of pictures."

"Around four hundred and eighty."

"Wow!" Andy laughed. *what a terrible fate, having to spend tomorrow reviewing at all those pictures of half dressed football players... I won't be able to get anything else done this weekend.*

Randall was startled by the change in the air—the boy's locker room **smelled** like the boys locker room. He didn't take note at the time, but the girl's locker area had not smelled like this. It was sort of neutral; at least it didn't reek of perfume. That's one thing he and Julian had in common: an aversion to perfume. The other difference was the long row of urinals. The girls didn't have those—just a lot more booths.

"Andy!" shouted Coach Brodie, beckoning with impatience. He wanted to see this high-end photographer. *Ladendorff told me about him. appears to be a typical sophomore... he totes a fancy enough case.*

"Coach, this is Randall." Andy bounced on his toes happily. "He's going to shoot some great pictures tonight!"

Randall was not accustomed to being presented in such a manner... *am I supposed to say anything, shake hands, or...*

"Mr. L tells me you know your stuff."

"Thank you, sir... I've been photographing for a number of years. My grandfather was a professional photographer. He trained me well."

80

Andy whispered loud in a mock secret voice: "He has his own darkroom. A **real** darkroom. I've seen it."

That impressed the coach. "So, what's your turnaround time?"

"I'll have the contact sheets ready for you to mark on Monday. You and Mr. L can go over those and decide what I should print."

"You can't print them all?" Brodie expected to see some prints.

"I could, I suppose—but I don't have a print processing machine. I have to do each print by hand. I doubt that you'll want more than a few dozen; I expect to have several hundred shots."

"Several **hundred**?!"

"Well, yes... there are two teams, and special things like interviews and player profiles, plus the cheerleaders and pep band. I have to allow for missed shots, unforeseen problems... I don't have a motor drive, but I can advance film rapidly enough for most conditions." He opened the case and pointed to the pouch. "I have 12 rolls of film on board. I plan to take some long lens shots of the crowd, and a few of the game from up high in the stands. I expect that most game shots will be from the sideline. I assume you'd like to see shots from various angles around the field. You probably want to see some things in particular, so I'm counting on Andy to pass along special instructions during the game."

Brodie was blown away. The grin on Andy's face told him that in spite of how young and green he looked, this boy was the real thing.

Andy broke in: "I thought we could get a pregame interview with Terry and Tom, and get a few shots of you talking with various players informally," he gestured enthusiastically. "I'd like to assemble a variety of shots for a special insert in **The Cardinal**. The yearbook will be able to use some good shots too."

"I like the sound of that..." Brodie paused. "Let me talk to the guys first... I don't want them freaking out because someone's loose in here with a camera." He made a point of looking at Randall to see if he understood the implication.

"That's a very good idea: you can tell them that I will not take any pictures that could be embarrassing. I'll set my camera lens so that only the main subject will be in focus. My depth of field will be very narrow—that way, everything in the background is a blur—no accidents are possible."

too bad Steve isn't here to hear this—he's out with the JV team. I'll fill him in later. "Okay—time's a-wastin." Brodie turned and stepped into the middle of the dressing area and roared, "All right you guys, listen up!"

His piercing baritone voice filled the dressing area. In seconds there was silence; the team turned to pay attention. "Special orders for this game." He gestured to Andy and Randall. "School paper is here to do a special feature. You all know Andy. They have a new photo man who knows his stuff. I've given them clearance to go anywhere and everywhere to get their story—so be careful what you say—it could be quoted. The cameraman tells me that he can get what he needs without getting any you-know-whats by accident, so you don't need to worry. Just keep the horsing around to a minimum. Terry—you're up." He gestured to Andy to go ahead.

Andy stepped over to Terry Marshall, the captain, undressing at his locker. "Hey." He didn't know Terry well, but he had always seemed friendly enough.

Terry pulled off his T-shirt and tossed it into the locker. He'd been interviewed by the reporter from the **Times-Herald** last week, so he had a good idea about what he was supposed to do; the school paper wouldn't be much different. "So, what do you want to know?"

While Andy took notes his steno pad, Randall stood back and took a reading. *ooo… marginal in here.* He opened the f stop to 1.4, the max. He focused and took a shot. He moved around slowly and tried several angles, one from behind. The disrobing continued—it was a ritual as much as anything, and the background noise covered the clicking sound of his shutter almost completely. He moved around and focused on other players; some grinned wide and struck a pose just for fun. He moved toward the coach and snapped a few of him talking one on one with a player. Before long he had a couple of shots of each player singly or in a pair. He had a wide range of shots—a few very nice ones that violated the conditions—but plenty that would cover his tracks.

One player caught Randall's eye... he was sitting alone on the bench in front of his locker, all dressed and ready to play. Obviously a fellow sophomore, he sat listening to his teammates with a complex expression—admiration, maybe a little hero worship... but something else too. Randall took a candid shot, then approached. "Hi."

Wally snapped out of his reverie. "Oh... hi."

"I couldn't help but notice... you seem to be ready before anyone else."

Wally shrugged. "Yeah, I usually get ready as fast as I can, just in case."

"In case of what?"

"That the coach will notice me and..." he crossed his fingers, "put me in the opening lineup."

The kid's face told Randall that he was nursing a wish that maybe he didn't believe was gonna happen. "Does he ever pick you?"

"Not yet." His expression showed determination, resolve. "So far all I've done is ride the pines. My day will come—I am on the team."

Randall blushed. "I don't know what that means."

"Really?" Was this kid a dummy, or what? "It's another way to say bench warmer.

Randall didn't know that one either. But it had a negative connotation.

"Just because you're on the team doesn't guarantee that you'll get to play."

"Then how do you get any experience?"

"You don't. That's why I try to be seen. Coach has a lot to worry about. And the other guys are real good. There's always the chance someone will get injured. My turn will come." *it **has** to.*

Randall was moved. *ridin' the pines... a new metaphor... clever.* "Well, good luck. Say, what's your name? I'm Randall."

"Wally. Wally Hughes." He grinned. "Nice talkin'."

"Yeah, real nice." *if I get a chance, I'll put in a word for him.* He moved off and took another snapshot of Wally's face.

7 *dumplings, roast beef or salmon?*

Julian was in a quandary—he had never been at a formal dinner like this, and wasn't sure what he should do: *do I pick what I really want, or should I pick what*... he checked the name on the place card again: *Kasey Wood ...what Kasey picks?* Did it matter, even? It was obvious that Kasey was at ease—apparently this was not a first time for him. One look at the blazer revealed that this was nothing unusual... *he's not a landscape crew Black, that's for sure. too bad I couldn't bring Randall along—he and his folks would fit right in around here.*

He took a closer look at the menu. *whoah*... He skipped down the list rapidly... *gosh.* He'd never heard of some of these things... *maybe there's something... what's a potsticker?* The other ones in the first section were easy enough to figure. *Hors D'oeuvres* ?? Julian had not run across that one before...

Why not ask Kasey? Inside guy suggested.

good idea. He turned to the left: "y'know, I'm sorta new at this..." he held up the card and put his fingertip below the word. "I bet you can help. What does this mean?" *I don't want to foul up here.*

That told Kasey a lot. He refrained from letting his disbelief show. This was the opening he had hoped for. "Um... it means the same as appetizer. Sort of a pre meal snack." He took the opportunity to look at Julian directly—he'd been wondering how he could do that. It was still hard to believe what he was seeing: not only were the eyes a rich deep brown, they were framed by long black eyelashes unlike any he had ever seen—combined with the open and cheerful face and the random waves and tufts of light blond hair, he felt an infectious positivity—he was forced to smile.

"Oh, I get it! Sort of like chips-n-dip!" he laughed. *must be French; Hors... weird.* Sid's folks always had chips-n-dip ahead of supper. His mom never served those as far as he remembered. "Thanks!" he grinned; it was good to know that Kasey didn't mind sitting next to a dummy like he was. Randall came to mind again... *I bet he knows all these things.* He had recognized the name on the trucks on the way in: *his mom goes there all the time... they put out top quality stuff.*

Kasey was puzzled somewhat by Julian's... he couldn't put his finger on the right word: ignorance didn't fit. *naïveté?* Hard to believe, but that was close. Aside from his evident social rawness, how could a boy this well dressed and good looking be so... well, **friendly**? *yes: friendly!*

What Kasey had not realized, yet, that for the first time in his life, a white boy had talked to him **directly**—as if they had known each other for years. That had never happened to him before. His defenses were unnecessary. It would take some time to comprehend that and to accept it as genuine.

Frederick Swann was suffering an attack of self recrimination for failing to make it possible to see for certain what was happening between the boys—it appeared to be positive, certainly... they were going through the menu together. That was a good sign at least. If only there were a way to get a camera surveillance in place, to see and hear them close up. *why didn't I think of that...* He was accustomed to having whatever he needed taken care of with dispatch. *not tonight.* He had an unobstructed view, but they were at the other end of the room. *well, perhaps the after meal meeting will be sufficient. most of the others will have left by then.* He would be within earshot. What he needed tonight was not something he could get with a cashier's check. All he could do was wait... and hope. Humbling, that was—and he was grateful for being aware of it. His eye moved to the right to focus on Lewis Wood. The expression on his face was the most important one: Lewis had made it clear that his son could make this go the wrong way. His unshakeable requirement was that his son accept, as his own, the decision to locate here, to forego his plan to finish his high school education in Massachusetts. It was a very tall order. Wood did not want his son to have any regrets, any sense that he was doing as he was told.

It was a long shot on its face. Only he and Lewis understood how fixed this position was, and Swann was worried.

Julian picked up the pencil stub and regarded it with a frown: he'd never seen such a stupid thing as this—clearly brand new. *hmm.* He put it down and took one out of his shirt pocket—one thing he always had on hand was a freshly sharpened No. 2 pencil—although, this one could use a fresh visit to the sharpener; it had been employed drawing parallelograms a little while ago... he checked the tip. *looks okay... now then: do I pick one of each?* An empty box by everything on the menu indicated as much. *boy oh boy: no way could I eat one of everything.*

Kasey watched Julian study the menu. He was beginning to wonder if the Alexander look-alike was a little slow upstairs. Unlikely, but a possibility. He was used to the private school attitudes that accompanied the best and the brightest, as they liked to call themselves at Belmont. He was guilty of that himself, he had to admit. He cautioned himself to not make any hasty judgments. He picked up his pencil. The Hors D'doeuvres were predictable. "The meatballs are probably a good bet," he offered.

Julian smiled wide: exactly what he had thought. "Good choice," he liked meatballs. "Wait: are you s'posed to tell how many, or can you only have one?" He looked at Kasey directly—partly to get another look at those eyes. They were special, those eyes. A color of blue he had never seen before.

Kasey paused before answering—taken aback at the expression on Julian's face. It was at once reassuring and ingenuous: he was unused to seeing that. It required processing. "Well, now that you mention it... I suppose you write a number in the box." *hmm...* That was a valid question. *chalk one up for the local.* He wrote in a 2 and showed it to Julian with a subtle grin.

Julian bounced with delight. *this is gonna be easy...* "Me too." He put a 1 in the Deviled egg box. *should I get a strawberry?* He'd never had one dipped in chocolate.

Careful, you gotta save room for the other stuff. You don't want to have any leftovers. Inside Guy was paying attention, as usual.

He moved to the main course group. *Entrees* This one required some thought. The ham was familiar... he wasn't especially fond of it; *makes a good sandwich once in a while.* He glanced to the side to see what Kasey was going to have. *say !!!!* He just figured out something: *what a great idea!* "How about this: you order one thing and I order a different one—that way we can exchange bites and find out what two of these taste like!" He grinned and did a Groucho eyebrow raise.

Kasey grinned back without thinking: having fun at a banquet table was so out of step, so unusual it had immediate appeal—unconsciously, he was suddenly a twelve year old: "Why not?!" he laughed. *what an idea!* He looked at Julian eagerly. "Which one do you want?"

Julian responded in kind with a giggle. "Okay..." although he had sort of hoped Kasey would pick first. He looked at the list again. It was between the chicken and the roast beef... he didn't like fish especially, except for his mother's tuna sandwiches. The dumplings sounded good... He pointed to the chicken and showed it to Kasey to see if he approved.

perfect! that meant he could pick the Prime Rib, one of his favorites. He held his menu up for Julian to see his finger on the Prime Rib box.

They looked at each other with a big grin. They were on the same wavelength.

Kasey's parents exchanged surprised looks and looked at Julian's family, to whom they had not yet been introduced. Slowly, they leaned back so Francine and Mark could get a glimpse of the interaction. All four felt a warmth, a glow—the unknown dread and fear about what could go wrong had evaporated. The sighs were almost but not quite audible. Francine was amazed; Mark had expected this, but thought it would take longer. What Julian had done last summer to the ogre of Camp Walker was just as amazing.

Frederick Swann was beyond happy. The positive chemistry between the boys was clearly evident even from this distance. He hadn't felt a rush like this since... he couldn't remember when, in fact. He

88

wasn't aware of the tear that had run down his right cheek until it started to itch. He ignored it for as long as he could. He had to calm down… he could feel his blood pressure raging. He took a deep breath and relaxed. Who had planned the seating arrangement? They were due a reward. Swann's rewards were usually very generous. His eye moved to the opposite side of the U table: the party at the end closest to the blond boy was likely from the high school. They were in for a nice surprise or two as well. It may have been as much luck as skill that they chose this boy, but that made no difference. His gaze returned to the blond. *remarkable… unusually good looking.* That too was unexpected.

Mason Davis—Swann's especially alert butler and aide de camp—took note of his employer's rare show of emotion. He wasn't quite an Alfred Pennyworth, but he was of that caliber. His 15 years of service had been a source of pride and satisfaction. He was privy to his employer's condition and needs as much as anyone, so his response was one of intense gratitude as well as happiness for his employer. It meant that his employment stood a chance of lasting a few years longer. He wasn't ready to retire; he knew he'd never find another position like this one. Nonetheless, he was enormously fond of Frederick Swann—he stood ready to be of assistance certainly, but his well-mannered and controlled relationship was quite emotional.

Principal Middleton and Roy Barnes had paid attention as well; Middleton in particular felt a sense of glee—if he were alone he would be shouting something aloud to release the tension that had plagued him for the past three months. He exchanged a glance with Barnes. Simultaneously, they helped themselves to a sip of water. Barnes helped himself to a Wheat Thin and square of cheese. The tray was directly in front of him. Suddenly, he was starved; his eye rapidly surveyed the other items on the tray.

Another person alert to what was underway was Eloise. She and Helgar had arrived late and were seated halfway down the U on the same side as the Principal. She elbowed her husband whose attention was on the menu. He was about to inquire what she wanted when he was cut off by the President's Executive Secretary tapping the side of her empty crystal goblet.

> > *tink-tink-tink-tink* < <

"I see that most of us are ready to proceed. The servers will now begin to collect the menu cards. Again, it is my pleasure and privilege to represent the University and to introduce everyone. I will begin at this end on my left with the Dean of the School of Pharmacy, Dr. Elliott Freeman and his lovely wife Elizabeth…."

The introductions underway, Julian and Kasey returned to their menus; they didn't know all these people anyway. They were past ready to satisfy their empty growing-boy tummies! In no time, they decided that sharing side dishes might be fun too. Why not? It was a big table, after all, lots of room… They enjoyed themselves enormously, joking about the items on the menu, scolding the catering service for not including this or that—mostly just to have fun. It was a wonderful regression into playground ritual behavior common with new kids moving into the neighborhood. They were careful, just barely, not to make a lot of noise and annoy the adults in the room. They remained absorbed, unaware that they were the object of several amazed and delighted people's attention.

Though oblivious to the introductions being made, the Executive Secretary's voice was crisp and clear—a pause in their jolly banter allowed a familiar name to capture Julian's attention—

"… Doctor Helgar Hallstrom, Associate Professor of Microbiology, and his wife Eloise." She gestured with the same polite expression she had been employing for everyone.

Julian's jaw dropped and his head snapped up. *!! wow!! Randall's parents!!* He turned and exclaimed in a hushed voice: "I know them!" *what are **they** doing here?* He waved at them merrily. "Wow!" He grinned at Kasey.

He looked down the long table to see whom Julian meant. The tall blond man stood out immediately: *he was on the tour today with father!* He faced Julian with a concerned expression. He didn't much like coincidences.

"Hey, don't worry: they are really nice people. They just moved here from the State of Washington. Randall is one of my best friends! He's their son." The nod endorsing Randall was genuine, and honest.

90

That helped, but he needed to know more. It was likely a coincidence after all. He paused to think a bit. The seriousness of the occasion was back on his radar. Julian's openness and instant likeability prevailed... but he was tuned in to what was going on again. He was grateful to Julian for that as well as the sunny feeling—something he very much needed.

Eloise had recognized Julian's amazing blond hair the minute she and Helgar entered. She didn't draw his attention to it right away, but planned to once they were settled. Embarrassed by arriving late— that always mortified her, but Helgar, not so much. She had smiled demurely: fortunately, their chairs were not far from the door. This was not the first time they were "fashionably" late, to use Helgar's rationalization. A quick glance around the room sufficed to reassure her that none of those gathered here knew who they were socially, so no harm done. When Julian waved at them she gave her husband a gentle nudge under the table. After considering it a moment, she had deduced the reason he was here. He was the perfect choice. Somehow, she found that comforting.

"Hm?" He looked up from the menu.

She leaned slightly and spoke softly, "Return Julian's wave. He's at the end table."

Helgar saw him instantly, of course—that distinctive head of hair made him impossible to miss. *what a pleasant surprise...* He gave a mini salute. *no wonder he wasn't with the reporter, the one with the Dodge. he'll miss the game. why would he be here?* He thought for a moment... *of course! to welcome Lewis' boy.* He nodded. *good choice... yes indeed. hats off to whoever thought of that. now then...* His attention returned to the Bill of Fare. He was pleased to see several items, but hadn't landed on anything specific yet. He turned the sheet over to see if there was a wine list. *no... not a surprise. would have been nice... house wine will have to do.*

As he was folding his napkin, Roy Barnes felt a gentle tap on his shoulder. He turned to his right.

"Excuse me, sir. It is time, I believe." Mason said softly, his head tilting leftward toward Julian.

"Yes, it is. Thank you." He scooted his chair back. They had planned a tentative program for the three boys—Kirk in particular was briefed thoroughly on what he needed to do; every indication was more than positive. He stood and stepped around behind Julian and Kasey, alerting Kirk as he passed by. Swann's man stood in place, ready to lead the way.

His timing was indeed perfect—the boys had run out of things to talk about, now that the desert dishes had been removed. "Excuse me, boys, if you don't mind."

They turned to see what he wanted.

"Assuming that you'd just as soon not have to sit through a slide show and a series of speeches, we have arranged for a place to wait." He paused while they thought about sitting here as opposed to getting up and moving around.

Kasey and Julian looked at each other—silently, they came to the same conclusion at once: *lead the way!* Simultaneously, they scooted their chairs back.

The gathering would be seeing a presentation about the proposed School of Pharmacy Center. A pair of AV technicians were setting up a screen; prop tables had been put in place in the open area of the U for the displays. It was the perfect opening; a few people were taking the opportunity to make a restroom visit.

Julian followed Kirk as he followed Mr. Barnes; he gave a cheerful greeting to Helgar and Eloise as he passed by. They were walking too fast for him to say anything—he could always do that later. Instead, he gave his typical Cheshire Cat grin. Helgar gave him a thumbs up. When Kasey stepped beside him at the end of the table, the difference in their height drew was a surprise. *wow.* He couldn't think of anything to say, so he just grinned happily.

This was one of those occasions when altitude was an advantage—his view over the top of Julian and Kirk had enabled him to see what they saw at the same time they did. He was used to that, and took it for granted. The interaction between Julian and the professor he had seen earlier today on the lab visits reminded him that he should ask about him when he got a chance. He'd enjoyed the dinner so much, it had slipped his mind. He needed to get more information about him and this whole thing. His glance at the display being set up as he passed by confirmed what his father had said earlier at the hotel. This was a much bigger operation than he had envisioned. He wanted to learn more about what he would be facing—a lot more. Julian's smile was reassuring—comforting, actually. That was something he had never experienced; it was so genuine.

It was too soon for Kasey to appreciate how important Julian's openness and positive attitude was to his thinking; it had eliminated most of the fear and insecurity that might have led to him resist this change in his life—he was conscious of the significance of that from the start. The built in emotional roadblocks had been pushed to the side, replaced by desire to secure the friendship that was luring him. **Or**... was it a Siren's song, drawing him into perilous waters? Dr. Marchbank's lecture about that had just flashed into place.

Barnes and the three boys followed the butler to a spacious room across the hall. "Thank you Mason," Barnes said, taking the lead into the room. He and Mason had been in touch frequently the last few weeks. He stopped to introduce himself to Kasey, and then explained briefly that they were about to miss a few speeches about a new building at the university. "My guess is that that will take an hour or more. Am I correct in assuming that you aren't especially interested in that?"

The boys nodded at once. Barnes wasn't surprised, "me too, but..." he shrugged, "I get to hear the whole thing." Then, beginning with a gesture to the sidebar, he went on: "if you're thirsty, help yourselves to a glass of water." Several drinking glasses and a pitcher of ice water occupied the center. A small tray of cookies of various kinds awaited there as well, next to a small sink; on the right, a small refrigerator with soft drinks inside. At the other end of the room, half a dozen easy chairs were arranged around a small coffee table. A grand piano sat in an alcove on the right, surrounded by bookshelves—it appeared to be a setting rather than a functional library, but the books were real, not props. This was a multipurpose room that served many needs—a place to have a small informal visit, a small conference or committee meeting, even an intimate presentation ceremony. Behind them, left of the entrance, a folding screen concealed a sizeable area; what was behind was not visible. "If you need anything, all you have to do is call Mason—he will be right outside." Mason gave a short bow. His tunic's double row of decorative buttons and leather gloves put the stamp of elite upper class on the proceedings.

Julian approved of this arrangement: this was ideal for getting to know his new Buddy. "Fancy enough," he said happily. He glanced at Kirk— *oo... I need to introduce him first of all.* As they walked to the circle of chairs, he began: "Kasey this is Kirk, our Student Body President!" He wowed his eyes to indicate that meeting him was special.

Kirk had almost sat, but reached for a handshake. "Hi. Kirk Fox is the name," he was surprised at how friendly things were. "Glad to meet you."

"Kassa Wood. Most people call me Kasey," he settled into the middle chair.

Julian gave his chair a good test—he bounced up and down a few times and punched the armrests. "Not bad, not bad..." Grandma's winged armchair was about the same fit... he could spend an hour here, no problem.

Kasey was startled by Julian's absolute inhibition-free behavior. Before he could think about it, his train of thought was upstaged.

"Kasey," Kirk continued, remembering the place card. "I've never seen it spelled that way." He had been prepped; his job was to be SB President, a position he took seriously. The committee believed that he and Julian could do a better job without any faculty present.

"It's a nickname for Kassa, spelled with a K. I'm named after my great-great grandfather. Most people like Kasey better. I don't mind, but my mother is a little stiff in the neck about it. I promised her I would always introduce myself as Kassa." He tipped his head sideways, indicating he didn't have any choice, really.

Julian and Kirk understood how that went. *no big deal*, Julian said to himself; but he was glad that there wasn't a nickname version of Julian.

Kirk's pronunciation differed slightly from Julian's... *a slightly Southern quality*. Julian's was more like the north and center part of the country—network radio and television came to mind. Kasey was aware that his own was regional—the boys at Belmont had fun with that once in a while.

Kirk was still adjusting to the Boston accent—something he should have expected. "So, it looks like you will be going to Jackson High," he began. The blue eyes were fascinating. Unlike Julian, he didn't feel comfortable about asking—hopefully, an explanation would come along at some point. He made an effort to avoid staring.

This was a familiar situation—Kasey had learned long ago that it was smart to explain a few things up front. "If you're wondering about my eyes, they run in my mother's family. She's from England, but was born in Ethiopia—that's in east Africa, south of Egypt. About half her family is born with blue eyes." He didn't go into her royal heritage. That was to be avoided if possible, even though she carried herself regally in both demeanor and appearance. He had been trained to be as low profile about that as possible.

He wanted the focus to be on the school he would be attending. When the Dean of Boys introduced himself, he concluded that it had been decided, as he had guessed earlier. He assumed that the decision to move here had been made as well. The impact of meeting Julian had removed any negative feelings about that. Without thinking about it, he realized that this boy was more interesting and personable than anyone he had ever met—none of his classmates at Belmont came close. They were friendly, but not personal—he had never had a true personal friend and didn't know what that was like—in fact, he didn't understand his visceral reaction to Julian, either. He knew that it was something he wanted and needed, and unconsciously, he meant to keep it.

Kasey's statement freed Kirk to look more closely. *such a bright blue...* he had never seen anyone with eyes that bright. *interesting.* He took the liberty of looking at the rest of his features more closely. Kasey did not look like any Black he had ever seen—didn't look Negroid at all—yet he was as dark as most of the ones he had seen—which was not a huge number, now that he thought about it. One was a lot darker— very black. That was just as rare. He had been told the population numbers, but didn't remember precisely—it was around twenty percent, lower than the state average. He had no idea how many would be attending Jackson next year, but he doubted if any of them would look like Kasey. It didn't matter to him personally—he'd be in college anyway.

Julian was stuck on yet another new word. *where's Ethiopia? I bet Randall knows... too bad he isn't here...* His eyes had landed on Kasey's hands. They looked a little like Zack's, only very delicate. Obviously he hadn't spent any time doing yard maintenance.

Mason interrupted the chat. "I'll leave your books here, if that's satisfactory," he said as he placed them on the coffee table. "I'll put your jacket over one of these chairs." He pointed to one at the side.

"Oh!" Julian had forgotten about those. "Thanks! Thanks a **lot**." That meant they wouldn't be going back to the big room. That suited him fine. Luckily, he had thought to snag the place card with his name in fancy maroon lettering.

perfect! Kirk thought to himself. While they were eating, Mr. Barnes had suggested using Julian's sketchbooks to show what the school looked like. The atrium drawings in particular showed the school off very nicely—the front entrance as well. The question was whether or not to do that now. *maybe we ought to get better acquainted first.* He wasn't exactly sure how to go about doing this, actually.

Julian had a thought—seeing his sketchbooks on the table gave him an idea: "What do you like to do?" School could come later. The blank look told him he needed to say more. "I mean, do you have any hobbies, anything besides school? I belong to a scout troop. You don't happen to be a scout or anything..."

Kasey smiled regretfully, "no... I was almost a Cub once, but we moved at just the wrong time," he grimaced. *I wanted to do that, too... almost forgot about that...* "I spend most of my time practicing, I guess. I play the oboe," he added apologetically, taking a glance at the Piano in the corner. He wouldn't mind limbering up his fingers on that for a while. That always cleared his brain and made him feel worth something.

there's another one: what's an oboe?! maybe Kirk knows... This was a night full of new words. *man, am I stupid sometimes.*

Take it easy, take it easy...   Inside Guy didn't know what an oboe was either, but he didn't want Julian to screw this up. So far everything had gone great.

"That's excellent!" Kirk said enthusiastically. "We have a Concert Band. I'll bet they'll like having you. It's a class, too!"

"Yeah!" *Randall plays a clarinet in that... should I...*

Inside Guy thought it best to save that for later.

Julian agreed. *anyhow, I can ask Randall what an oboe is.*

The boys didn't take notice of Mason placing Julian's Cardinal Jacket across one of the chairs, nor the silent entrance of Frederick Swann earlier as he slipped behind the screens about twelve feet away. Mason had already placed a small table there alongside a captain's chair. The split between the second and third panels was wide enough to view the boys without difficulty. Mason had thought to bring a seat cushion along—he'd fetched it from the Packard's outboard trunk.

Kirk needed a way to get to the nitty-gritty: they had a job to do. He was uncertain about how to do it best. He'd never been in this position. He didn't want to foul anything up—no second tries were possible; it was do or die...

"Do you play an instrument?" Kasey hoped so... he sought a link of some kind, something they had in common—some reason to... He didn't know how to articulate what he wanted because he had never felt this need before. What he didn't realize was the simplicity of that need: he needed a Pal, a Buddy, like he had back in the third grade. He sensed that Julian was perfect for the part.

"Gosh no. I spend all my time drawing." Julian liked music, sort of, some music... but he could do without it. He was always turning it down or off, it seemed. *I better not say that out loud.*

Inside Guy agreed; he didn't need to comment. Sometimes he was impressed by Julian's ability to figure some things out without being told or nagged at.

Kirk was quick to jump into the opening: "Boy, do you ever!" He had been hoping for a way to bring that up, and here it was! He looked at Kasey wide-eyed: "You should see what he does with a pencil!" He shook his head in disbelief. He wasn't consciously trying to hook Kasey, though he had been hoping to find a way to do just that. He couldn't have done it better if he had planned it. This was his honest opinion, and that was stronger than any artifice would have been, no matter how skilled or practiced.

Intended or not, it got Kasey's attention and fit the need he had to engage with Julian. The praise was clearly genuine, and he was interested to see why.

Julian blushed slightly. He never knew how to handle compliments like that. He was too aware of how much he needed to improve, to learn. He needed to earn that kind of praise—he had a way to go, too.

"Show him, Julian." Kirk knew the sketch books were right in front of them—the guy in the butler outfit had just put them there a couple of minutes ago.

Kasey looked him straight in the eye: "Would you mind? I'd like to see what you do." That was spontaneous—he had surprised himself. He was used to being slightly removed and sarcastic about things—that was sort of how things were done at Belmont. He had shed that without realizing it. It felt **very** good.

"Sure… I don't mind. He grabbed the one on top. Luckily, it was the first of the three. "I started these on the first day of school, actually. I'm better at it now, some." He handed it to Kasey. "The number on the front tells that it was first," he shrugged. "Doing the fancy cover was kinda fun."

When Kasey opened it, Kirk scooted his chair close—he wanted to look at it too. He didn't get the chance at school.

Julian followed suit and scooted his chair close on the other side; he figured he might need to tell about a few things as he thumbed through the sketchbook.

Kasey's jaw dropped in disbelief. He looked at Julian, then at Kirk; his affirmative slow nod was loud and clear: these were the real

98

thing. "Wow." That was out of his mouth before he realized it. These removed any question he had about this boy's ability or talent. These required his full attention.

The three boys huddling together was wonderful to behold—Swann was beyond pleased. It confirmed what he had seen in the other room; this was up close. It was premature of course, but it seemed almost as if his cure was in the mail. He could feel it in his gut. *Lewis Wood has to see this.* When he had calmed down, he stood, about to summon Mason.

Mason, of course, was watching all the while—he stood where the boys could see him, should they need his service. This position also put him in Swann's line of sight to the door. He stepped over so that he could hear his employer whisper the order he knew was coming.

8   *ridin' the pines no more*

Field lights, Randall soon discovered, were a photographer's best friend at a football game—none of the shots on the last 3 rolls would need any pushing. In some ways, it was better than daylight—shadows were not a problem—huge banks of floodlights on both sides of the playing area wiped them away automatically. Even the stands were fully lit—excepting the very top rows—but even they were visible. His long lens was very happy; he zoomed in on the home team bench again—this lens made it seem like he was ten feet away. The boy who said he was "riding the pines" fascinated him—he had been intensely following the action on the field the entire game. Randall admired his persistence; he was rooting for him to get the break he— *oh!* He had just leapt out of view.

terrific! Wally had just been summoned by the coach. He followed along through his lens... *I can capture him being put into the game!* He got a great shot of the coach giving him one-on-one instructions about something; his gestures were a little convoluted... Randall knew nothing about the game—he relied on Andy to write the captions, since he didn't know what anyone was doing—but he was confident it was being captured on film. *interesting how they can ignore rain splashing on their faces.* He was surprised that the player benches were out in the open, and not in a dugout like baseball players enjoyed.

The heavy rain was a factor that he hadn't expected. He was used to dealing with drizzle and snow—he and his father had faced that more than once on a climb or long hike in the Cascades. But this was different—heavy and intense, this kind of weather would have ended a mountain trip long ago. Here it seemed to be a common thing—all the fans had come in rain gear. Umbrellas of many colors and sizes protected those that weren't under the canopy—over half the crowd.

Mud had become a problem—damage to the turf was considerable; the rain had begun fifteen minutes into the game and aside from a couple of light spells, had not let up. Some areas of the field could be beyond repair. He got a great shot of a player sliding face down as he came to a stop. From the way the crowd cheered, it must have meant he had made a "first down." He'd heard that term used frequently.

It was somewhat tricky to deal with the incessant rain, especially when it got a little breezy. The rubber lens hood was deep enough to block the rain as long as he didn't need to aim in the wrong direction— then the only solution was turning his parka into a temporary tent he could peer out of—in this weather, that was iffy—the wind might catch hold and blow it back over his head. *baptism by storm, not fire, this assignment.* But he was invigorated in a way he had not expected: the adrenalin rush was fabulous. He was in his element doing this.

The game clock was as confusing as ever, but he could tell that the game was getting close to the end. The Cardinals were ahead, but there was probably time enough remaining for that to change. That was one factor that he didn't fully grasp—the clock stopping so often confused him. At least it was immense, and there was one on both ends of the field—he was always glancing over and discovering it had stopped: game time and real time were very different. He was aware that he was probably the only one here that didn't know that; he chose to keep that to himself. The idea was to do as Andy had demonstrated before the game—appear to know what you're doing and look like you belong there doing it.

It was time to change his location—they were approaching the home team's goal line again—he had learned that he needed to get there ahead of time if he expected to get a shot from the end zone. That was one aspect of this game that helped considerably, being able to anticipate what was coming. That had enabled him to get several excellent action images. If his light meter was accurate, his shutter speed was fast enough to get almost everything. Andy's tips sure helped. It didn't take long to get the hang of this assignment after all. That allowed Andy to go where he usually did when he was reporting. He didn't have to babysit his greenhorn photographer.

Andy had stopped taking notes after the first quarter—the rain had nearly ruined his steno tablet—at least he was able to stash it in Randall's camera case, conveniently placed next to him for safekeeping. He hoped the interviews weren't ruined. What he needed was a way to record those as well as a game description. No such animal existed. The game wasn't being broadcast, or he'd ask them to tape it. He had to pay super close attention so he could recreate this later. *maybe I'll get a chance to touch base with the **Times-Herald** reporter... he might share something.* Luckily, he had a good memory. *I'll go over it with Tom and Coach Brodie before I turn it in...* He concentrated on the coach talking to the manager... *darn rain! can't hear a word they're saying.* He didn't recognize the hand signals either. The only out of the ordinary thing he'd seen was the player at the end of the bench being sent in to replace number 14. Probably seeing to it that he got to play in at least one game. *Coach is a good guy...*

A few key people knew that for two weeks Wally had been preparing to pull off this surprise. He had a special job—looking like a greenhorn was part of the plan. With luck, his "clumsiness" would be completely misconstrued, and the hidden pass off would succeed. Even the team was in the dark—the coach didn't want any leaks or accidental talk about it—anything that could alert the other team.

Tom was ready; Wally joining the line meant the surprise play was imminent—brand new, it had never been used before. Play was now on the 50 yard line, an ideal location and time to put it into action. The trick had two parts: first, a quick handoff to Stan, whose rapid handoff to Ted would be hidden from sight by Wally, allowing him to belly run into the opening that had been set up by the blockers. He would fake having the ball and go through like a bullet and be protected as if he had the ball. Meanwhile, while they were chasing Wally, Tom would move the other way; the Coyotes would be expecting him to fall back to make a pass—instead, Sandy had done that. Tom's job was to be super fast and get around the end before the other team realized what he was up to. He would catch the pass as soon as he was clear. It depended on Ted's accuracy and his being clear to make the pass. They took it for granted that Tom would be in place in plenty of time, and that Ted's pass wouldn't be blocked.

The Cardinal team would know the new play had been called by another trick: the center would use the Coyote team's last play call instead of their own—which should make the Coyotes confused at least, and possibly follow the play their call triggered—this would put them at a disadvantage because they would be expecting to employ the wrong defense, not an offensive play. It was a very risky trick, depending on a lot of good luck as well as skill. They were confident about the skill part. It was a one shot device, but would give them a 14 point lead; the other team could never catch up, let alone win. Coach Brodie had explained it in detail at the pregame briefing so that everyone knew what to do when the time came.

"71-3, 454, 71-3, **HUT!**" The center's hard count began, loud and clear; several players did the last minute shift of position, then he snapped the ball as usual.

The play worked as planned. The crowd jumped up instantly.

> > *BLAAAAAAAT!! BLAAAAT!! BLAAAAT!!* < <

Trumpets, trombones and tubas blasted full volume. The fans hopped up and down roaring and cheering at the top of their lungs and the band began another rousing performance of the Jackson High Fight Song.

Dancing and hugging uncontrolled, it took some time for the fans to realize that the game was going again; most had assumed that it was over. In effect it was—but three minutes remained on the clock.

Tom's speed was one of the Cardinal's major assets. The opposition should have anticipated that he would try something—his running ability was widely known and usually prepared for. But they were in a world of hurt anyway, and the chances that they could make another touchdown were slim to none. Their awareness of this had caused them to make their kickoff more for form's sake than anything. So they didn't pay proper attention to how the Cardinals defensive line went into action. Specific pairs ran toward the opponents' goal line instead of blocking—so when the Coyotes charged, they couldn't be caught and stopped.

Tom caught the ball as planned, and at the right moment did a lateral pass to the quarterback, who started the run to the home goal. As he did that, Tom dodged the blockers sent after him and ran back up center field, which was wide open by then. He arrived ahead of time—catching the pass was easy—he ran full speed and made **another** touchdown.

The stands erupted again. The field goal gave them another 7 points. Score: 34-20. 1:40 remained on the clock. The game was over, for all practical purposes, but the teams resumed their positions. The bell went off 12 seconds after the kickoff. The field filled with a joyful crowd.

Mud? What mud? Once the fans got onto the field, they threw caution to the wind. Well over a hundred people would have a load of laundry to do on Saturday. Randall got some wonderful shots of the aftermath.

Two rolls remained in his case. *I should have made a couple more—I need to get more cartridges—a **lot** more. I used too many during halftime...* He made a mental note to see about an over the shoulder carrying case for this long lens. Running back and forth to his big case to swap lenses was a real pain.

"Just stick as close to me as you can. It gets pretty wild after a winning game—tonight will be **crazy**," Andy said as he and Randall followed the team toward the school. "See if you can get a shot of the coach being splashed..." he grinned slyly. "But keep back a ways... you don't want your camera to get what the team has saved for Coach Brodie!" Eventually, Randall would be able to circulate as he had before the game.

To their right, the other team was way ahead and would get to the Girl's gym before they could catch up. He tapped Andy's arm and pointed.

Andy grimaced. He hadn't figured a way to deal with them post game. A trip to their school next week was in the cards if he followed through on what he had promised their coach. Covering the home team came first—and it would require his full attention for a while. The Coyotes would be on the way home before he would be able to touch base with their coach. Next week would be better anyway—he could take along some of Randall's camera work. He owed them that.

Fortunately, the fans were being stopped from following them into the building. Just as they approached the door, the rain stopped. It was as if the weather god had been trying to stop the game and had given up at last.

In the parking lot, a doubly satisfied Cardinal fan paused to observe the sky as he approached his car. Bernard Withers was at the wrong end of the school, or he would express his appreciation directly to the great white oak tree. Thanks to Pythagoras, he had dressed appropriately for the game.

9   *white ones and black ones*

The roar outside the window had been annoying Julian for several minutes—made it hard to concentrate; he was trying to explain these drawings—Kasey and Kirk had never been to a scout camp. His frustration level was full up: "**What** is going **on** out there, anyway?!" He got up to see.

The large floor length window was heavy grade glass, but not soundproof; the downpour was audible even though it wasn't hitting the window directly. "Wow! Look at it rain!" He didn't think it was going to be such a big storm.

"Want to look?" Kirk started to get up…

Kasey took a second to react—being asked was unexpected; he was the one who always had to ask. "Oh… Yes! sure…" he stood. He still had not adjusted to being treated so… he looked for a word or expression that identified how it felt to be treated as if he was a cousin from out of town, someone who belonged—as opposed to being polite to a visitor.

Kirk had forgotten he was so tall. When Kasey gestured for him to go first, he peeled around his chair and stepped over to join Julian. He stood to the right so Kasey could stand in the middle. What he saw out the window triggered a small conscience attack: he should be at the game. He wasn't needed, but as SB President he felt a duty to attend all home games—appearances mattered. But the Principal wanted him to be here. He understood the need for that and didn't disagree. Now that he had spent the evening here, he was very glad—not because he wasn't getting soaked to the skin at Jackson Stadium, but because now he had a better idea of what would be needed down the road. Plus, he really liked the new kid. That surprised him. He was eager now to be a part of the program, an active part. He honestly did not know if there would be any problems… the subject never came up, that he knew of. Everyone was so worried about the Cold War and the Draft, the subject of Integration never came up.

Kasey was ready for a break. The scout drawings were not as interesting. He was pleased when Kirk made room for him. It felt good to stand between these two. Before looking out, he looked down at Julian, then at Kirk. He felt strange… no—he felt **good**, and **that** was strange. *sometimes I wish I wasn't so tall…* His head turned outward.

"Boy, check out the puddles! Hoo-hoo," Julian chuckled. "This keeps up, and we may have a few clogged street drains to worry about on the way back." He pictured Mark driving his station wagon through a lake in the street… on tiptoe, he cupped his hands around his face—the reflection of the room made it hard to see very well. "The building is plenty high. I don't see any puddles close up."

Kirk cupped his hands on either side of his face. "Wow." The dense rain blurred the view almost like fog.

Kasey paused a moment then joined the other two—sure enough, cupping his hands removed the reflection. No one was out there— understandable. His concern about how odd the three of them must look with their faces pressed against the glass made no difference whatever. "Does it rain like this often?" Kasey didn't know anything about the weather down here.

"Not for this long," Kirk observed, "unless it's a major storm. They didn't predict anything unusual, I don't think." He hadn't heard today's forecast, actually. *a lot of puddles, all right…* the lighting along the campus walkways did a good job showing what was going on out there. Not being at the game was a lucky thing, for sure. Didn't seem to be any wind.

"Yeah. This is more than usual," Julian agreed. *not much wind… angle is almost straight down.* He had seen enough; he stood back and turned to Kasey. "So, then," he gave a soft poke into the tummy conveniently located an inch away—right below the tip of the wine red necktie. He looked up with a grin. "What do **you** do for fun? I draw stuff. What about you?" He opened his eyes wide and gave his signature Cheshire Cat grin.

108

Magic moment: the familiarity was not only unexpected, but his response to it was instant. He felt a sudden glow quite unlike anything he remembered. Kasey did not realize, and wouldn't until much later, that it had sealed the deal. He had never had a friendly poke like that— the gesture of a real friend, a pal. He also did not realize that he was grinning from ear to ear. He didn't remember anyone ever asking him that question. It took a minute to focus on it... "I spend my free time practicing, I guess." The oboe required a lot of that. "For fun I like to play the piano." He glanced again at the one a few feet away. **That's** when he felt the best, actually. The piano was able to take him away...

Julian was fascinated by Kasey's big grin. He wanted to draw that somehow.

"Why not play something?" Kirk suggested. As long as it was raining, why not? He gestured toward the Steinway.

"Yeah! Would you? I'd like to hear that. I don't know anything about music." He usually turned it off when he could. This would be different than those radio songs his mom listened to.

The invitation was genuine—Kasey could tell that, and it fit perfectly what he felt a need to do: free himself for a while from the pressure he had been under the last three days. The door was open... *hmm*... "Should we get permission?"

"I'm on my way!" Kirk hurried to ask the servant... *or is he a butler? more like a chauffeur. I thought they had to stay with their cars...*

Julian got a kick out of the way Kasey pronounced some words: permission was the latest—sounded like pahmission.

You'll get used to it, Inside Guy commented lazily.

"C'mon," he tugged at Kasey's belt and led the way over to the piano. He figured it would be okay to play the piano... "they can always shut the door."

Kasey giggled involuntarily... being towed by his own belt was so novel, so... fun was the only word that came to mind. *nice... very nice...* Being accepted at face value was a new experience. He knew it was honest and real... how he knew that was also a mystery. There was no time to stop and think and analyze any of this—ordinarily that would

109

cause him to pause and step back for a second look. Not tonight. He felt totally accepted. He would come to realize later how liberating that had been. It was the force of that that governed his thinking, his decision to leave Belmont.

That it would please so many other people would probably remain unknown; his father would not reveal how key he had been for several years, if ever.

The Steinway was as handsome an instrument as he had ever seen... had that rarely-played look—*hope it's in tune*... he sat on the bench, adjusted its position and opened the keyboard.

wow... Julian had never looked closely at a concert grand keyboard. *white ones and black ones... I remember that*... he stood back a ways so he didn't distract.

Kasey placed his right hand on the keyboard and played a basic C Major chord. *yes! tuning is perfect... oh! jumped the gun...* he turned to see if Kirk had secured an okay.

Rushing back, Kirk was gesturing an okay signal. Mason had closed the open half of the double doors. Just as well—the room was acoustically bright—wall paneling and hardwood floors reflected sound rather than absorbed it—and with the top closed, the piano's sound was rich and full; proximity to the wall seemed to amplify it.

Kasey searched for something he knew from memory. The only candidates that jumped out were old, ones he learned for the recital after he finished his first year lessons. *ah, this is simple...*

He broke into a rousing, fast paced Scott Joplin piece. A wide smile covered his face: this felt so good!

Kirk exchanged a delighted look with Julian. His first thought was the piano in the cafeteria. Somehow, that had to be preset and ready—when they hear him play this... *man! wait until I tell Mr. Middleton!* He was sorry they had closed the door.

Julian was fascinated. It was amazing to see the elegant long fingers create this amazing sound just by touching those keys—Kasey wasn't hitting the keys hard at all; it sounded so professional. He wondered what it felt like, what it would sound like if he touched the keys. It didn't appear to need any force, any strength. He didn't recognize the song at all, but it was tuneful and happy—much more interesting than anything they played on the radio. *and he knows it **by heart**... how does he do that?*

Kasey had not played this for a long time—it was such fun. It didn't surprise him that it came into his active memory so easily—he had excellent recall. It was reassuring to have this so accessible... it had been a long time.

Julian studied the hands and how deftly, how confidently they moved—almost as if they belonged there. Several images were preserved automatically in his image bank—the inside camera was always on; once in a while he concentrated on that, making recall at the sketchpad relatively easy. He wanted to get a good look from a distance—a clear idea of the drawing he was going to make was forming as usual–it would be horizontal... from the side, slightly above eye level... the entire piano had to be shown. He liked the way it curved around the far side.

The Entertainer, it so happened, was an old favorite of Swann's. A wide smile spread across his face. He turned to Mason, glowing. Mason felt so proud suddenly. His employer rarely shared his feelings directly. That doubled the pleasure seeing Swann happy usually provided. Ten years younger, in many ways he was a surrogate younger brother.

Kirk led the enthusiastic applause at the end; Julian joined in—then did a most unexpected thing: unplanned and unlike his usual response, he sat on the bench at Kasey's left. Wide open, since Kasey was so tall and long legged, he was able to slip in with ease. "Scoot over a little," he nudged with his whole right side. The body contact didn't phase him of course, but Kasey was startled, to say the least.

He was not offended, but it was so unexpected and unconventional he was surprised. Julian's spontaneity had been so consistent, it wasn't a shock; it didn't occur to him to be offended—it was instantaneous proof of being accepted as a friend: impossible to be anything but delighted.

"Show me something simple—I want to know how that feels, to play those keys." He was concerned: "I wouldn't want to do anything wrong—you know, break or wreck anything."

Julian's happy open-mouthed grin was contagious. Kasey had an instant thought: *chopsticks!*

Swann beckoned to Mason hastily.

"Sir?'

"Bring Lewis Wood here as soon as you can: I want him to see this. If it means leaving the presentation, so be it. I want him here, now." He didn't need to say or do anything more. Mason was completely reliable. As he slipped out quietly, Swann stood behind the screen to watch. This was fun as much as anything.

"Two fingers… see?" Kasey pointed his two forefingers out, placed his left on the E, and his right on the G key and played the first triple note sequence.

> > *plink-plink-plink!* < <

"See?" He played it a second time.

"Neato!"

"Okay, now you do it."

Julian reached out with his right hand… *let's see… I think it was that one. why don't they have a number or something on these?*

"One more to the right," he chuckled. He glanced at Julian briefly, a whimsical thought had flashed in front: here he was, of all people, teaching Alexander the Great to play **chopsticks**. The comical irony was so preposterous he was inclined to laugh aloud—he restrained himself. Probably one of those things he couldn't share—*Professor Marchbanks, maybe.*

> > *plink-plink-plink!* < <

"Perfect! Now let's do the rest of it—it's pretty simple, all you need is those two fingers." He played the rest of the first bar.

Gradually, one step at a time, he took Julian through the first stanza. On the fourth run through, Julian had learned it.

—ᴍ—

The special underground features of the proposed building included a special tunnel connecting the new facility to two other buildings—the audience was eager to hear the details of this innovation—connecting R&D to practical operations meant a great deal in terms of inter-departmental operations. A fourth tunnel to the Physical Plant would be added later. It would mean a significant increase in speed and efficiency. The speaker paused for the technician to change in a third rotary tray of slides to the carousel projector. The faint sound of a piano could be heard. Lewis and his wife exchanged a glance: they knew at once who was at the keyboard. They had heard Kasey play this dozens of times when he was a small boy. As the presentation resumed, it remained barely discernable, providing a welcome nostalgic background.

A few minutes after the Joplin, which Lewis had been following more closely than he should have been, he felt a light tap on his left shoulder.

—ᴍ—

Just as Julian finished the second run through of chopsticks, Mason silently opened the door at the far end of the room. Swann beckoned to Kasey's father; he stood to the side and allowed him to watch from the makeshift blind. The expression on his face confirmed the wisdom of his decision to get him here quickly.

"Okay!" Kasey exclaimed. "You've got it. Now, let's trade places: you sit where I am. When you play it again, I'll do the special second player's part."

"Cool!" Julian scooted right as Kasey peeled off and circled around.

"All Set?"

113

"I think so…" Julian put his two fingers above the keys. Kasey's nod told him they were in the right place. When he started, Kasey added the lower note harmony—it was a success first time!

"Neato!!"

Kirk burst into applause.

"That is so **cool**!" Julian gushed. "Thanks a lot. I always wanted to know what that was like. Now I do, thanks to you!" *he didn't have to do that…* He gave Kasey's right shoulder a Troop 9 fist tap. He wanted to show that it mattered—he slid off the bench.

"Lots of time left, can you play another one?" Kirk wanted this to continue for several reasons—he really wanted to hear some more, but he wanted somehow to get Mr. Middleton in here. Maybe they could be doing this when that meeting was over.

Kasey couldn't believe what was happening, but wanted so badly for it to be real he didn't stop to think—he pressed on. He took a deep breath, sat back and thought a minute… a couple of others came to mind: he had it! He paused a second, then began a gentle **Somewhere Over the Rainbow**—the very first piece he had memorized.

He was in a nice warm place… a childhood place, a happy and secure place. What a pleasure…

Julian paused for a minute, amazed. *I know that one…* He shook his head and did a beeline back to his chair. He turned it around, grabbed a tablet and hopped up: he had to get that drawing underway. The expression on Kasey's face was wonderful—he had to remember that above all.

Kirk knew that music—who didn't? Instead of taking a chair close by, he joined Julian and turned Kasey's chair around—he was about to see the artist that had produced those three sketchbooks do a new one, live.

A faint burst of applause from across the hall told Swann and Wood that the presentation had ended. The banquet attendees would be dismissed very soon.

114

Things were moving ahead so rapidly that Swann was slightly giddy. Naturally cautious, he forced himself to reset. Some quick calculations about the next two or three days was indicated. An opportunity that had not been in the picture emerged. Lewis and his family were scheduled to catch the train back to Boston tomorrow. That needed to be dealt with. He stood back and pondered a moment.

Notation in his pocket notebook: "Instruct Samuels to do a thorough review of the High School and any personnel that seem key." He thought a moment and added, "try to have it ready by December 15. My eyes only." Swann's gifts were always carefully chosen and researched as well as generous.

Mason was on standby—he recognized the signs. New orders were about to be given.

—ɯ—

Mason approached the University President with haste. He had to insure that he not issue any instructions to the special guests. As he spoke quietly to Selfridge, he gave a hand signal to Barnes and then to Helgar. They needed to stay in place until he finished with the President.

Mark expected the Principal to give an indication of what they should do. "Let's wait a minute," he cautioned Francine. "Something is going on…" he had seen the Chauffeur's hand signal to Barnes.

Francine turned to Candace Wood, whom she still had not met. "I think we're supposed to wait," she said quietly. When Candace turned to face her, she got a good glimpse of her blue eyes for the first time. "Hello, I'm Francine, Julian's mother."

Candace was grateful that Francine had taken the initiative. "Hello, Francine. I had deduced that, but I am so pleased to meet you at last." Her demeanor warmed slightly. "As you probably know, I am Kassa's mother." She was eager to speak with her—the response of her son to Francine's boy was unprecedented—Kassa had never been able to form a friendship like this—and that's what it was: of that she was certain.

The British accent was unexpected—Francine thought it fit her elegant demeanor perfectly.

Mark waited to catch Helgar's eye; he gave a thumbs up signal to show that he had been recognized. The Thumb signal was returned at once.

Eloise touched Helgar's arm. "Why don't we move down the table to sit with the others? I think they'll ask us to do that anyway." She had been watching for a signal of some kind. Clearly the man in the chauffeur's tunic was in charge at this point.

"Good idea…" he wanted to move to the now empty chairs next to Mark, but thought it best to escort Eloise to sit by Candace first— Lewis had been called away for some reason. They had just sat when Mason and the University President walked directly to the group.

—m—

As the other guests departed and Mason was organizing the parents in the banquet room, Kasey opened the piano bench to see if any music scores were handy—he had nothing else memorized well enough to play properly. He was in luck: Beethoven's Waldstein Sonata, and Rachmaninoff's Paganini Rhapsody. He pondered briefly—he had played the Rachmaninoff a year or so ago. *rather long though…* Still, it was more welcoming than the Beethoven—the Waldstein was plenty long too.

While Kasey prepared himself and the piano, Julian continued to sketch; fortunately, the easy chair was a low backed modern design; he could sit on the back with his feet on the seat without tipping over. This provided the slight downward view he wanted—it enabled showing the graceful curve of the piano's long side. It also gave a more friendly angle to Kasey's head and arms—almost straight ahead was better than from slightly below—this compensated for his unusual height perfectly.

"This is a little long—I don't know if you'll like it. I do, actually. I guess I can play this until they come to get us… I doubt if I'll get through it though—it takes about 20 minutes…" He wasn't positive about that... *might be slightly longer.* He hoped Kirk would approve—he didn't want to make them listen to something they disliked.

"That's okay by me," Julian was delighted: the longer the better... this sketch would take a while. He had the important composition dots in place already. He had figured those out in advance. *this is so **neat**! too bad I don't have my large paper*... This had to be a full figure, not just a head: the arms, the fingers...

Kirk settled in. He wasn't a Classical music fan, but that didn't matter. His hope was that Mr. Middleton and Mr. Barnes would come in before he was finished playing. He checked his wristwatch. *man, it's getting on... they have to be ending that meeting before long.*

Kasey was pleased with himself; it had been a while since he had played this. He did spend time at the upright in the dorm's common room a few times a week, so he was not rusty at the keyboard. He was able to compensate for the missing string quartet with little difficulty.

Mason opened the double doors quietly—the boys remained unaware of anything in the back of the room—the piano masked other sound in the building. The tongue pointing out of the corner of Julian's mouth evoked a chuckle; Mason had organized and planned the arrival carefully—everyone carried in a straight-backed chair—Mark and Helgar had two. Mason indicated where they needed to be placed. Mark placed the chair he was carrying for Francine. Next to him, Mason had a chair for Kasey's mother—he seated her next to Francine. Bringing a few chairs from the banquet room enabled them to sit without disrupting the mini recital—the boys were totally engaged; Kirk watched Julian draw, completely absorbed and awestruck. Julian was in his element, more intense than usual—the music was a new force, and he was intent on getting as much done as possible so that when he did the big version he would remember everything.

In minutes, the impromptu audience was in place; the boys were none the wiser. Mason joined Swann at the back; he and Lewis had stepped out from behind his makeshift vantage point.

Still formulating what he planned to say when he assumed control of the gathering, Swann wanted the boy's performance to proceed for as long as he chose to play. Remarkably, their arrival was quiet enough; the boys didn't notice—Kasey's performance had them captured completely. A concert grand in use can fill a very large space. A Steinway can fill Carnegie Hall with ease—this room was like a closet, comparatively.

In spite of its impromptu beginning, the dynamics of a recital concert soon fell into place. Each listener's brain followed its natural inclination and need. Personal requirements and priorities vary widely, and the Rachmaninoff was as good as any music for providing an environment suited perfectly for some mental sorting, cleanup, and resting. For several of the gathered, immediate cares and concerns were set to one side. Francine took the opportunity to reset her feelings about Julian—her boy was now her son. She hadn't realized that fully. It was fulfilling and rewarding, but it came with a mild trace of regret. Mark too was reassessing his connection to Julian—it was far more complex and intimate than he realized, and would remain substantially subconscious for a while yet. For the present, he felt like a big brother as much as a scoutmaster, and that disturbed as much as rewarded. Introspection was an unpleasant process that he avoided unless it was urgent—this issue was nascent; it needed to remain on the shelf in his very crowded closet—some aging was required.

Lewis and Candace were more skilled and practiced in meditation and self analytic thinking than most, and were keenly aware of their son's state of mind and the hazards he was likely to encounter as he approached adulthood. This trip had been planned with his state of mind the top priority. They knew what they needed to watch for: his readiness to take ownership of a major decision. They had never seen him look so happy, so engaged. His playing was far more polished than they remembered—they didn't have an opportunity to hear it very often. Seeing him concertizing was a complete surprise. The only handicap they felt was not sitting next to each other to witness this.

Helgar and Eloise were less in need to resolve personal issues than any in the room. Eloise was ready and able to assist wherever needed. Her son's issues were in process, and proceeding well, thanks to Julian. Helgar had settled into his new position at the university, and was staged to join the new research project. His need to play wanted some attention, and that's where his mind drifted. He was alert, hoping to find an opportunity to connect with Mark.

Middleton and Barnes were busily considering the best way to plan an academic program and schedule for the first Black to be enrolled at Jackson High School—and what contingencies needed to be prepared for. That was much more doable than they had ever thought possible now that the remarkable Julian had hopped into the saddle. This was new territory for both—exciting and invigorating as well as scary. The boy's unique physical characteristics were unexpected—a potential complication.

Swann was in a life or death race, and his challenge was complex. He needed to be the planner and director of the effort, and maintaining objectivity and patience was going to be as difficult to manage as anything in his life. His good fortune was to have Mason at his side. Uncanny prescience was Mason's special gift, and his devotion and affection made all the difference.

President Selfridge had planned to leave as soon as it was gracefully possible, but his curiosity had led him into the gathering. He and his administrative assistant stood at the back, unable to tear themselves away. His first thought was his Music Department. He doubted if it was a likely goal—this boy was probably headed to a conservatory like Juilliard. Just as well—he was in no hurry to integrate. There was no Supreme Court mandate requiring it—he doubted if he'd have to deal with the issue. In the final analysis, he knew better than to leave too soon: one of the largest donors in the University's history was throwing this party.

When the Rachmaninoff came to its finish, the applause was instantaneous. The startled boys turned and saw the adults. They looked at each other as the applause continued. It was genuine and hearty. After adjusting, to the surprise at seeing the impromptu audience, Kasey searched for his father—he had noted the gentle smile on his mother's face—unusual, she rarely smiled. It indicated praise and approval, and it meant a lot. He was enormously grateful that she was there. Concerned that she wasn't next to his father, he searched—he was always at his

119

mother's side. *there! in the back....* Kasey' eyes found his father's at last and locked in place: his plea was seen and understood.

Lewis had never seen such a complex expression on his son's face: it was at once a combination of joy and a plea of desperation. Had his eyes the power of speech, they would be crying aloud what Kasey was shouting in his mind: *"can I stay?! please, can I stay?!! I have to stay!!!"*

That's what his mother heard, loud and clear.

Lewis' studied, deliberate nod told Kasey what he desperately needed to know: they could stay. He turned to Swann and extended his hand. "I am happy to verify what we have just seen. I presume we will meet in the morning to discuss the arrangement that need to be made."

"Thank you, Lewis. We can talk about tomorrow's schedule after everyone has departed, if that is acceptable." Swann nudged Mason and moved back a few feet. He had formulated is plan; Mason needed to be briefed. His euphoria was in check for the moment.

Something about the way his father nodded told Kasey that the decision to stay had been agreed to. He assumed that five months would be adequate to tie up his affairs at Belmont. The widest grin he had ever displayed drew a tear from his mother.

He would soon discover that he had less than two months: the change would be at the end of the semester, not the end of the year.

How could any of this happen so quickly, so easily? For Julian, skin color was just like hair color—no big deal. A little over fourteen years ago, When Julian was a year old, he made his first friend: Little Joe. For four years, his world consisted of his mother, her parents, and Little Joe. Those were happy days; when he wasn't being entertained by his grandfather, he was playing with Little Joe, who spent as much time at Julian's house as Julian spent at his. The fact that Little Joe and his family were as dark skinned as any Blacks in Joliet was of no consequence to Julian or his family. For over two years, the playmates often took their naps cuddled together like puppies. Skin color was not an issue for anyone, child or adult.

120

He was a few weeks away from his fifth birthday when his grandmother died suddenly. Within a month his grandfather followed. It was his friend Little Joe that helped him get through the day while his mother settled her parents' estate. Before he knew what was going on, Geraldine had convinced his mother to restart their lives in North Carolina. Thus within a few months, he had lost everyone he knew and loved but his mother.

When chance brought him to Frederick Swann's special banquet, the emptiness created by losing Little Joe as well as his grandparents had faded by and large, but it was still there: Kasey was ready made to fill the vacant place. No one understood this, including Julian. It had been repressed by a very thoughtful and attentive Geraldine, who had adopted both he and his mother as a way to fill her own need for companionship and sense of purpose.

10 *cornmeal, ketchup and Karo syrup*

"Man, you are a mess!" Randall laughed. "I hope that doesn't happen after every game."

"The last game of the season is always super special if we win." Andy had never seen it quite this extreme, but the double touchdown **was** super **super** special, for sure. "I hope you don't mind, but I need to swing by my house on the way—I don't want to mess up your place any." He glanced over to his passenger. "Did anything get on you or your camera?"

"No, I was far enough back," he was grateful for having a great lens—he was able to get a few closeups before he ran out of film. "I just hope the shutter speed was fast enough. I might have a blurry one or two, but think I got a couple of good ones." Randall had used all twelve cartridges. "What about you? Your notepad get hit?"

"I tucked it under my arm just in time—that's why I got it right in the face," he shook his head. He knew what was coming, but he was surrounded by players, and couldn't get out of the way. Anyone within three feet got hit pretty good. "I didn't know they were going to come in from three sides—they didn't want him to slip away, I guess." His post game interview had to be held over to Monday, which meant he couldn't finish his write-up until Tuesday at the earliest.

"What was that goop, anyway?" *it looked so **gross**.*

"Cornmeal and ketchup, mostly." *probably some syrup to help make it stick and stop the cornmeal from settling out...* That worried him a little—if it wouldn't wash out he was less one shirt, and maybe his coat. His pants and shoes got a few dribbles and drops too. *they must have mixed up at least three gallons.* He was glad he didn't know the details—that let him off the hook when he wrote about it.

Randall just realized that Andy was right about cleaning up. *Mom would have a fit if he tracked anything into the house.* He could see that Andy's car seat would get a stain or two. *I don't need any of that in the darkroom either.* He was lucky—his pant cuffs as well as his socks were soaked from the rain, but everything else had been well protected. Aside from a summer thunderstorm in the Wallowas or Cascades, he had never seen rain just stop cold like that; that was a new one—it was as if someone had turned off a faucet.

"Gotta warn you—my house is different than yours." That was an understatement. "They'll probably be watching TV. My folks are big movie fans, and the Friday Night Movie is sort of sacred. They might ignore us—unless we arrive during a commercial break." He hoped that the movie was on—that reduced the need to stop and introduce Randall and explain what caused his gooey rose-colored hair and all the rest. *Billy will be happy, for sure.* "We might get lucky and jet straight to my room." Asking him to wait in the car would send the wrong message—his mind had started to focus on what had happened before the game and what he needed to do to follow up. So far, everything seemed okay.

The failing muffler in the 1948 Dodge made it impossible to arrive quietly. They had to enter through the front door—the back porch was in a state that he didn't want to explain or apologize for. If he weren't such a mess he would probably not bring Randall here at all. He opened the door slowly and peeked in.

As luck would have it, the entire family was glued to the TV set: tonight was the first local showing of **The Alamo**. The movie was approaching the end—the last battle was underway. Everyone in the room was hoping that a miracle would happen and Sam Houston would arrive with reinforcements. Not being students of Texas history, they didn't realize it was as hopeless as it looked.

The TV set was on the east side of the living room; the route to the bedrooms and bathroom took the boys behind the rapt family. The familiar sound of the muffler had announced Andy's arrival, eliminating any curiosity about who had opened the front door—barely audible, it had enhanced the gunfire, cannons, and Tiomkin soundtrack. Beyond loud, the TV volume was usually up high to accommodate his hard of hearing Grandmother. Andy put his finger on his lips to give a silent shh, and led the way to his room.

Randall had used his rain slicker to cover his camera case on the back seat, allowing him to be soundless as he passed by. He followed quietly, glancing to his left; seeing so many people was a surprise. He didn't know that Andy came from such a large family. The color TV set was new—a step up from the one in the den at home. For the most part, television was an occasional item in his family. The color was certainly appealing... *I should ask Mom if we plan to get a color set.* He didn't stop to look closely; Andy had turned right—his room was up the stairway the end of the hallway. He hurried to catch up.

"Go ahead and sit at my desk," Andy gestured to the chair as he slipped off his coat. "Sorry, but I have to take a quick shower." He pointed to his matted and sticky hair.

Tempted to laugh, Randall sat. *boy, am I lucky...* He was one of the few that didn't get hit by some of that goop. The sticky garments shed crumbs as they were being removed. It took a minute for him to realize that Andy was **undressing**. Suddenly, his attention focused on that fact—their "quickie" above the garage had not included disrobing— it was too hurried, too desperate. The entire boy was about to be on display. Aside from P.E., the only person he had seen nude was Julian. Uncertainty about what to do took hold. He was enormously curious and interested, of that there was no question. There had been no time to think about this, which was always discomforting; he felt a need not to do anything that might offend—he had an underlying attraction to Andy. He wanted to be his friend and maybe more. Once again, he was in a new place... his eyes had glazed over, revealing that his thoughts were internal for the time being.

Andy had been hoping for an opportunity to talk about what they had done—he fully intended to pursue the possibilities he had discovered. He didn't want to do that here, of all places... his sex life was a secret at home. He had not come up with a way to deal with that. He was fortunate to have his own bedroom—he and his sister shared that privilege. The three other boys had to share one bedroom, and it was **very** crowded. Billy was chomping at the bit to inherit, presuming that Andy would go off to college somewhere as soon as he graduated. That

125

problem had to be dealt with, since he planned to live at home for a couple of years at least. He glanced at Randall as he removed his pants—what he saw startled somewhat.

"Are you okay?" The glazed eyes were ambiguous.

"Hm?" Randall looked up. "Oh—sorry, my mind was on something else, he shrugged. "I'm fine."

Andy slipped into his do-what-Tony-would-do mode: "that's good. I didn't want you to miss my striptease:" he took his skivvies off with a flourish and tossed them onto his bed. "Ta-daa!" he wagged his hips a couple of times.

Randall blushed instantly, and grinned wide. *thank you, Andy,* he said to himself. Andy had just solved the problem he had been wrestling with: how to talk about it. He looked at Andy's waving boytoy. His began its auto response. He borrowed Julian's Groucho Marx flashing eyebrows. Flirting was new and unfamiliar territory, a place that he hadn't known about; he didn't know where he was, precisely just yet, but he was drawn to whatever it was.

"That's better," he put his hands on his hips proudly. "Hold that thought—I shall return a changed man!" He bounced out of the room and skipped straight to the bathroom—he left both doors open, as usual. He didn't expect anyone to come upstairs; closed doors were the exception in this house, not the rule.

A wave of gratitude ran down Randall's spine and ended with a tingle in his crotch. He stood and adjusted Little R, already on his way up. He exhaled and mouthed a silent WOW! While Andy showered, he surveyed the room and its décor: *time to learn who Andy is...* he could learn a good deal by just being observant—removed the need to ask a lot of questions.

"Onward, Men!" Andy gave the Faded 48 dashboard a healthy pat and shifted into first gear. Like several boys in Troop 9, he found Mark's standard phrases fun and useful. He had showered as fast as he could; he and Randall were able to escape the Alamo's tragic end without being noticed. "How long does it take to develop film?" He had never done any lab work and hadn't watched much either.

"I was just thinking about that," Randall grimaced. "The good news is it takes about 20 minutes. The bad news is I can only develop three rolls at a time; then the film has to rinse in running water for at least half an hour before being hung the drying closet—that takes about two hours. So if we work as fast as we can, we'll get them developed by about 11:30, but it will be about 1:30 in the morning before we can print anything." He looked at Andy sadly. "We can develop tonight if you can stay that long—but we have to do all the printing tomorrow."

"Too bad—I was hoping to see something tonight." Andy tilted his head... "The **Times-Herald** has faster turnaround—a lot faster."

"They probably have a crew full time, all 24 hours. I don't know if the overnight photo places use any special machines or not; I suppose I could probably have prints inside a couple of hours if I had the right setup. Got a few thousand bucks handy?" *they must have a way to rinse and dry faster...* He had never looked into it, actually. Most of those places used the same process he did, as far as he knew. His grandfather did not do any consumer processing—his work was mostly portraits and weddings.

Andy parked on the far right side of the driveway behind Hallstrom's three-car garage as Randall's father had instructed. He checked his watch: almost 10:15. *well, at least we can get the developing done tonight.*

Randall hopped out and ran over to peek: the Continental was not there. "They haven't come back yet. They had some kind of dinner at the University, I think." *probably having cocktails or something about now... we probably have an hour or so before they'll get back.* Since it was Friday night, he figured they would let him stay up an extra hour or so—enough time to finish developing. He ran back to get his camera case.

Andy led the way through the dark "tunnel" again. His tour this afternoon had taught him all the basics of entering the darkroom. This was **very** cool. *I wonder if we'll ever have a darkroom at Jackson High.*

"The problem is," Randall continued as he followed Andy around the bend, "I can only do three rolls at a time." He strode over to the counter by the sink and pulled the developing tanks off the rack he had built at the Jackson High woodshop.

"Aha!" Andy grinned. "I recognize that!" He gave Randall a pat on the back. "Excellent craftsmanship. I know the lad that made that!" He rocked his head back and forth importantly.

Randall blushed slightly. "As you can see, this one is for a single reel; this one holds two." He shrugged, popping the reels into their tanks. "Three into 12 rolls is four developing sequences. At twenty minutes each, you get the picture. Add another 5 to ten minutes to load these, what time will we be done?" He grinned mischievously. He grabbed the lids and walked back to the main work counter.

Andy held up his left hand and used his fingers to do the numbers while Randall pulled the film cartridges from the case and lined them up in sequence. Numbering them was a habit his grandfather had taught him; it simplified identifying the negatives later on. He had been careful to expose them in order.

"We can do this faster if you can help load the reels," he tipped the reel out of the one reel tank. "The trouble is, it has to be done in complete darkness. Even a **tiny** bit of light will ruin the film."

"Can't be that hard," Andy took it in hand.

"It isn't, once you learn to do it in the dark." Randall opened a drawer and pulled out a scrap of film he kept on hand just in case. Now he was glad he hadn't tossed it. "See if you can thread this onto that reel with your eyes closed."

Andy took the scrap and closed his eyes. The first time was a disaster—it crinkled almost at once. He pulled it out and tried again. He failed again. "This is harder than I thought!" He tried again.

Randall wasn't surprised. "Open your eyes and try it."

After another try he did it slowly, watching closely. "Oh, so **that's** it!"

"Yep. Once it's aligned properly, it will slide right in. However: the longer the strip is, the harder it is to do—you can't force it, or it will dislodge—then you have to pull it out and start over. And you have to be careful not to touch the front or back. You do that, and your fingerprint will be preserved forever—they can't be removed. You have to handle it by the edge only." He looked at the scrap closely. "Thought so... take a look."

"Ooo!" he grimaced. "I don't want to foul up any of your photos, that's for darn sure. How long does it take you to do a roll?"

Randall considered that. "Not long, really, maybe two or three minutes." *still, with twelve rolls, that will add up... maybe I have a longer practice strip...* Randall thought a second. *nope.* He opened another drawer and pulled out his change bag. "You can practice doing it in this while I load the first three reels in the change booth." He flopped it onto the counter by the empty reel. "Maybe you can get the hang of it. You put both hands into these sleeves after tucking in the reel and film."

change booth? That was a new thing. He looked around the room.

Randall grabbed the first three rolls and stepped to the end of the counter. The small recess in the rotary door was almost invisible in the dim yellowish light. He slid it to the left and set the first three rolls on the work counter. "Bring the cans and lids," he pointed to the drying rack. The nearly soundless door revealed a tall narrow cylindrical closet with a small work counter; the shelf above held a small tray with another three empty reels.

"OH! I didn't notice that." *it's only in plain sight, Andy.* He handed Randall the tanks and lids. A bit embarrassing... he shook his head and looked closely at the ingenious closet. Andy didn't mind being corrected when he was hasty or wrong—it helped from time to time, especially when his Senioritis had led him off track—one reason he was a good reporter: no assumptions or presumptions were allowed. Fetching the cans and lids was easy enough.

While Randall threaded the film onto the three reels, Andy leaned against the counter; the opportunity to consider his plans and hopes for the evening was welcome—he had not done that yet, really. He took a deep breath and started afresh: what was his personal goal tonight? A chance to consider that carefully was nice—**very** nice. He turned around and picked up the black changing bag. *might as well give this a shot while I think about what to do later...* he tucked the empty reel into the right sleeve opening. He pulled the sleeve up with his left hand and gabbed the film scrap; he wiggled into in the other opening. *this is hard... I need another hand!* The tight elastic around the sleeve opening was good at keeping out the light—it was also good at being nearly impossible to enter one side without having a hand free to pull up the other sleeve.

Andy did not know what the developing process required. The fact that it had to have close personal attention the entire time was disappointing at first; he had expected to find time to at least talk about where they were going—or not—if there wasn't time to do some real "playing around." He preferred to use euphemistic terms for having any actual sex activity. They were able to dance around the issues a little, but he was growing a bit frustrated. He wanted to have a good idea of where this was going before the night was over. Evidently that wasn't in the cards after all.

As Randall was loading the second set of cartridges in the booth, Andy had a new job: he had been assigned to run cold water into the developing tanks of the first set. Every 5 minutes he was supposed to swap the tanks. They were supposed to sit under running water for half an hour before being hung to dry. He wasn't making much progress in the planning department—he had to pay attention to this. At least there was a good timer in front of him. The sound of running water was interrupted:

>> *Yo, Randall!* << The intercom speaker blared. Helgar's deep voice was all the little speaker could handle.

>> *We're home at last. How goes it?* <<

Andy jumped in surprise. "Hi Mr. Hallstrom... this is Andy. He's in the booth loading another set of film rolls. We still have six to go after that."

>> *Well, I can't say I'm surprised,* << Helgar laughed. >> *No problem. Just tell him we're home. It's later than we thought, but this is special—tell him to keep at it... No pressure, but any idea of how long he'll need to work? His mother wants to know if you boys need anything.* <<

say, now... Andy remembered those cookies. *a few of those and a coke would be nice...* "I'll ask the boss," he stepped toward the booth.

"I heard," Randall was halfway finished with the third roll. "I don't generally allow any food or drink in the darkroom..." he paused. "Sorry, but if you want a snack, we have to go to the house. You decide if we want to take the time." He'd just as soon not, but realized that Andy might want to. He could go either way.

Andy went to the intercom—*that's right: no button... it's always on.* "He says not now, thanks." *no cookies after all...*

>> *Understood...* << Helgar knew his son's work ethic well.

>> *Okay; we'll be going to bed soon. He knows the routine* <<

Helgar was just as happy—he had a little romping in mind. Eloise was fun, especially after a few glasses of rosé. They kept serving it all through the presentation. They were primed to play, and overdue.

Randall emerged from the booth. "I heard. Maybe there'll be time after we're finished," he kept a straight face. "I happen to have a few goodies upstairs." He gave Andy the Groucho eyebrow bit.

Andy found that **most** reassuring. He handed Randall the D-76 jug; he had learned the procedure.

After they had begun the developer agitation, Randall ventured a comment—he had been wondering how he could make some sort of headway—he was hoping to spend a little time upstairs when all the film was in the drying closet—something besides his mom's lemonade and cookies. He was unsure about how to start. He hoped that just talking about things in general would lead to something. "I'm sorry I don't have a couple of stools to sit on. I've never had to do this many reels before— if this assignment is what we're in for, that would help." *I could use one in the changing closet too...*

"Good idea. We've been on our feet quite a while. This floor is getting harder."

"You're right! Padded rubber floor mats! I need a couple of those too. Thanks for mentioning that." He'd seen those in the supply catalog. A couple more developing tanks was already on his list.

On the third rest in the developing sequence, Andy was ready. "You know, I need to talk a little about..." he looked at Randall carefully, some hesitation visible in his expression. "I need to be sure that you aren't bothered by me being a little older..."

Randall was enormously relieved that he didn't need to bring that up. He was ready. He shook his head slightly. "No, I'm not, actually. A few months ago I would have been spooked probably, but not now." The Hayden Park overnight had fixed that, permanently. *Andy is the same age as Louis and Chuck.* He looked Andy straight in the eye: "I have discovered that age difference means less every year. In five years it will be meaningless for all practical purposes. My father works with a large faculty in the Physics department—I doubt if any two are the same age; if they are, it's a coincidence. I can't tell the difference, and I doubt if any of them can either."

>> *zzzzz!* <<

The timer went off. They stepped over to the sink and emptied the tanks. Randall nudged the rinse tray to one side as Andy reached for the stop bath jug. They had formed a teamwork approach—Andy was a fast learner.

As this was underway, Andy processed Randall's reply—it was welcome, certainly, but unexpected and somewhat startling. It revealed a maturity and higher intellectual level than he was used to. It had not occurred to him that Randall was so intelligent—*a true egghead type. I should have seen that.* He didn't know if it would be a problem or not. It was something entirely new; he was used to being the bright one in the room.

Fortunately, Andy was open-minded and not at all egocentric; he didn't need to compete or be in charge. He was grateful for the heads up, however. He had a hunch that Randall was a whole bunch smarter than he was. That was a good thing to be aware of. As he poured fixer into Randall's two reel tank, he delivered a calculated nudge with his left hip.

As Andy poured fixer into his one reel tank, Randall returned the nudge. It seemed unnecessary to verbalize. They were both blushing— and developing a familiar sensation directly below their belt buckles. As soon as they could free both hands, they would need to need to make an

132

adjustment. Tempting as it was, Andy kept his mouth shut: a Tony phrase would not sound right. This was not a laughing matter. On the other hand, silence didn't seem right either. It came to him: "so… what kind of cookies do you have in the cupboard up there?" he couldn't help smirking.

Randall thought for a minute. He caught a glimpse of Andy's face. He grinned wide. "Lots of kinds." He knew a package of peanut butter was there, and probably chocolate chips. Sometimes his mother left a surprise, so there could be more. He hadn't checked for quite a while—He didn't go up there very often. But he guessed that Andy was probably using the word metaphorically anyway. He kept a straight face. Little did Andy know that he was a graduate of Julian's special scout camp lessons—as well as being a Level One Initiate of a certain Secret Society. Andy was in for a big surprise. He felt a familiar sensation below. That was always welcome, but the wait to satisfy was a lot longer than Little R was used to.

One consolation: they were about to have a peek at the first three rolls before being hung in the drying closet—those were the rolls taken in the two dressing rooms before the game. Randall was expecting at least three very nice surprises, maybe more. Those frames would be mysteriously missing from the contact sheets.

He's kinda tall

11   *a packed weekend*

As the applause faded, Swann handed Mason a handwritten memo and walked briskly around the group. He headed directly toward Kasey. Clearly, he was the man in charge, even though many of the assembled had never met or even seen him—Helgar, Lewis and President Selfridge were the only people in the room who had actually had a conversation with him. He reached out to shake Kasey's hand.

"You are well on the way, young man, to a career in music, if that is your goal. The Rachmaninoff demonstrated that easily—but you had me sold when you played Scott Joplin. Thank you for that—I had not heard that in a long time." His handshake was firm, his eye contact intense.

Kasey was at a loss for the correct words—he had deduced who the man was from the way he carried himself. He had seen that before at Belmont—a few boys' fathers were multi millionaires. They always behaved like they owned the place, no matter where they were. He had been in the background on the lab tour the first day; his father had explained who he was. He was able to smile and nod his head. He took an instant liking to the man. The fact that he was well over a foot shorter didn't seem to matter. "Thank you…" he was able to get that out, at least.

Everyone remained in place—even though they did not know him, it was obviously a good idea to stay put.

"I've been looking forward to meeting you all evening," he said as he reached Julian with his outstretched hand. "Julian, am I correct?"

Julian sat up eagerly with his typical smiling eyes and face. He had no idea who the man was, but the way he treated Kasey was so nice, he liked him at once. He wasn't like anyone he had ever met. He didn't know how to answer his question without sounding stupid or silly, so he just grinned.

"I am Frederick Swann, Julian. I appreciate your being here. As you may have guessed, this is my party, in a way. I hope you enjoyed your dinner," he paused for a moment to adjust to the boy's smile, his sunny smile—it was quite unique; almost disarming, for want of a better word. "I am curious about your drawing—am I allowed to see it before you have it finished?"

The fact that he had asked was all Julian needed to verify his first impression of the man. "Oh, sure. I don't mind. But you're right—I need to work on it more. I got a pretty good start though…" he handed his sketchbook to the very nice man.

Swann was unable to prevent his double take from showing. He looked at Julian briefly to verify that he was, indeed, so young—then returned his eye to the new drawing. It took a while to register. The skill and talent was at a level he had rarely seen—and he had spent a small fortune on art. If the boy were a minimalist, this was a gallery ready cameo now. It reminded him of Picasso—he did work sketches much like this—throwaways once the full size piece was completed. This was more complete than a work sketch would be. Part of his mind shifted into planning mode: at minimum, a commission from this boy was inevitable. He returned the tablet. "Thank you. If you don't mind, at some point I'd like to talk with you about your drawings. Do you think you could make room for that in your busy schedule?"

"Gosh, yes." He thought a second. "I usually have time after school, unless I'm helping my friend Randall…" he gestured to the other end of the room. "He's Mr. Hallstroms's son. He has his own **darkroom**!" he nodded proudly. "You oughtta see his pictures sometime. He is really good at taking pictures."

Swann was grateful for the information—he had not known that. It went onto the next list he was formulating for Mason. He turned to the other boy and extended his hand. "Hello. I confess that I don't know your name."

Kirk shook his hand like a good politician. "I'm Kirk Fox. I'm Student Body President at Jackson High School. Thanks for the dinner," he flashed his eyes.

"My pleasure," Swann was glad the boy in Kirk was still in charge of the politician. He turned to the adults: "If you don't mind, I need to have a short discussion before you leave—I know it's late, but this will greatly simplify things. It won't take very long, I assure you." He gestured with both arms. "Will you join the boys and me over here? A few of you may need to bring a chair, but there are enough here for almost everyone." He nodded to Mason to stand ready to assist. "Why don't you three sit where you were before," he gestured to Kasey to join the other two boys.

Mark slowed to a crawl… a small lake occupied the intersection ahead. Cars were getting through, but caution was in order. The rain had stopped over an hour ago, but it had created a few problems. He nudged Julian, "Let's hope this gunboat actually floats."

Julian giggled. Mark was so cool. He grinned at his mother.

Francine had been thinking about the new weekend schedule that Frederick Swann had put into place. She needed to contact Geraldine. She checked her watch. She'll still be up—*she's a night owl anyway— usually reads in bed for hours.* "Thanks, Mark, for staying with us for this—I hope you won't be in trouble at the store." She knew that Friday nights were part of his assignment.

"No problem; I get to make up for it tomorrow—double shift." It would be an effort—ordinarily he would be using that time to prepare for Sunday—it was Troop 9 Sunday at St. Bartholomew's. *that reminds me…* He nudged Julian again. "Have you done one of the Troop doing the Sunday procession?" *the Scrapbook could use that.*

"OO!" he had to shift gears. "Man, I forgot all about that!" He frowned. *that's right…* he was hoping to get caught up with Randall. He felt guilty about not helping out at the football game. And now tomorrow was gobbled up—he had to help Kasey get his schedule all organized at school; he had no idea how long that would take. *man… things are getting busier all the time!* He turned to Mark. "You think Andy will be able to help Randall tomorrow too?"

"Tomorrow?"

"Yeah—we were gonna develop the football game pictures tomorrow. Now I hafta be at school helping Kasey." *this is bad...*

"Well, he said he could fill in for you—knowing Andy, he will do his best." Mark was certain of that. "I'm sorry you're missing out on that. But what you are doing is really important, Julian. And **no one** could fill in for you there!" *there is only **one** Julian...* Mark was beginning to appreciate that in new ways—Julian was more than just one of his scouts—that was becoming clearer all the time. It didn't concern him at all; it was fascinating in a way. He didn't dwell on things like that.

Julian thought Mark's remark over... it was against his nature to think of himself as special. He knew he was different, naturally. Keeping a low profile about that was standard procedure; so far that had worked out. This was different though. "Yeah...you're right," he paused for a minute... *it was that way with Randall too, in a way... but this isn't the same*. He didn't have the word he needed to describe it; *this is **trickier** or something...* He trusted Mark. "Do you think it will be hard for Kasey?" He was worried a little. Kasey would stand out, that's for sure.

Mark paused before answering; it was important to be precise. "Yes. I expect it will. But with our entire Troop pitching in, he'll be okay. You won't have to do it all." He had already decided to take it on as a Troop Project.

Julian snuck a peek at Mark's face—the light from the dashboard was enough to see that Mark meant this with all his heart. This was the secret Mark that he talked to every night almost... this fresh picture in his mind reinforced that perfectly.

He faced the street ahead, enjoying a momentary sensation of gratitude mixed with purpose. Things were getting very interesting lately. The banquet and the evening had opened his mind some—the world was more interesting and complicated than he realized. He felt very, very fortunate. He resolved to have another talk with his mother about things.

Francine was able to observe her boy without being detected. She was enormously proud of him... she had not realized how capable and mature he had become. It was logical and she probably should have suspected it. She had indulged herself by keeping him a child in her mind—he was such a comfort. She needed to get smart and catch up. He would need a great deal more than motherly approval in the coming months.

—m—

Kasey was doing his standard review of the day's events a bit earlier than usual—a sense of urgency had taken charge. His decision had been almost entirely emotional, not rational. That was fundamentally unsettling. He needed to talk with his parents this time. He didn't usually do that until he'd prepared. There wasn't time—he sensed that he needed to sort this out tonight—tomorrow was too late. He tipped his head back and forth unconsciously as if to shake everything into line.

Lewis and Candace knew their boy well—they preferred for him to break the silence. They didn't need to look at him directly, but the dark interior of the limousine was a good place to do this sorting out.

"I need to talk about things…" He couldn't wait until they got to the hotel. He liked it being dark right now… he didn't know why. In some ways, he felt like a five year old… that was uncomfortable.

"I know the feeling," Lewis offered. "How can we help?"

"I've never done that before, I don't think—you know what I mean?"

Lewis paused. "You need to help me a little… what exactly are you referring to?

"Make a snap decision like that. He looked at his father. "Have you ever met anyone like Julian?"

Lewis chuckled. "No, that boy is special." That was an understatement.

"I have never experienced anything like that: I felt **instantly** that he was my **friend**…" he was grateful his mother and father were here. "I realized all at once that I have never had a **real friend**. I had to grab him before he got away. Nothing else mattered." He thought a minute. He was just now articulating this phenomenon. He needed to know if it was a blessing or a warning.

"Kassa," his mother touched his arm gently, but firmly. "You are blessed, my son. This is a trait of your lineage... My father had this ability, as did his before him. It is what a great leader needs: the ability to see instantly what is true." She remembered hearing her father talk about it once when she secretly sat in on a conversation of his when she was a child. She looked at him directly. "He had fine tuned his ability. You also are from the line of Solomon. It always comes out." *especially in the men...* If her son were in line to rule, he would have been in training long ago—that included integrating the ability into the executive tool chest—it was treasured, and kept secret.

Kasey was more than a little skeptical about his mother's cryptic references to their lineage. One day he planned to study up on it; it was all very hush-hush. It didn't really have any utility here in America. Still, her words rang true—he seemed to know that too. He gazed out the window, grateful that it was a blur not requiring his attention. Oddly, he felt reassured. He did not understand why; that itself was annoying more than anything. He gazed out the window, his eyes unfocused. He was ready for tomorrow. He **felt** ready, that is. He had no way to justify that. A sea change had taken place tonight. He was grateful that he would have a few weeks in Boston to deal with that. That realization removed what would otherwise have been a state of panic about what he was about to face. He would be ready to return and face whatever was in store.

His mother's eyes twinkled; her son had handled this challenge as easily as she had expected—a bit faster. The local boy had been enormously helpful. That was a complete surprise. Her husband was smiling back at her; the bridge had been crossed. Her thoughts turned to the coming months. Top on the list was getting acquainted with Francine Forrest. The news that they went to the same church was enormously helpful. She had been worried about that. Her image of Christianity in the American South was anything but positive. The Church was her link to the ancient family. Having a local portal made all the difference.

—ɯ—

Middleton's mind was going gangbusters. "Do you anticipate any problems tomorrow?" There were a few unknowns—the unforeseen complication potential was very high.

"The only problem I foresee is getting all the staff required to build his schedule. I may not be able to set that up tonight—not at this hour."

"How early should we be there? The Wood family will arrive at 10."

"No later than 8." Barnes thought for a minute. "I can double check the Forrest boy's schedule tonight and plan my phone calls. With two of us, we should be able to connect with all of them." *if anyone is out of town, we're cooked...*

"Do you need me there?" Kirk was willing, but he didn't know what he might do.

Barnes had not considered that. "I don't know. Let me think about that. What do you have planned for tomorrow morning?"

"Nothing special—maybe talking with Stan or someone about the game." He sympathized with the two men in the front seat. This was a major job, for sure. "I hope we won, naturally." *we were favored to...*

"That's right!" Barnes, like Middleton, was unable to hide his guilty as charged grimace. "I'll call Brodie when we get to the school." *he should be at home by now unless he's out on the town.*

"What about Monday?" The plan to break the news to the staff had been modified significantly by Swann. Now they would meet the boy and his family as well as hear the news about his enrolling for second semester.

"Mason assures me that it can be handled smoothly. He will be on standby for a signal. They will be introduced when we have the staff ready." He had an afterthought. "Should we have a piano on hand?"

"That's a great idea!" Kirk exclaimed. He leaned forward. "Where do you have the faculty meeting?"

"That varies," Middleton replied. "Cafeteria or Auditorium, usually."

"Ever use the choir room?" Kirk knew a piano was ready and waiting there.

"Ooo…" Middleton was slightly hesitant about that—it would affect the meeting dynamic in awkward ways.

"I'll wager Mason would like that—that way they wouldn't have to come into the main building," Barnes saw the advantage at once. *the walk from the front parking lot is long… they'll be seen. the rumor mill will run with it.* "Mason could have them safely tucked away in the Limo until the last minute." *he could drive around to the rear of the building and park right by the annex door.* "That's a great idea, Kirk."

"Any after school activity there on Mondays?" Middleton was skeptical.

Barnes wasn't sure. "I'll check the calendar when we get back to school. We can always cancel or postpone whatever it might be—this has top priority."

"How many people can that room handle?"

Barnes thought about that a minute… "We've had as many as 80 in the choir, so…"

Middleton nodded his approval. Overall, it was a good way to handle this. "Better call Joe Rosso tomorrow. He deserves a heads up."

memo to Mason

<u>Top priority:</u> arrange a meeting with the Rector of St. Bartholomew's. I need to meet with him privately ASAP about Sunday morning. I have never met him, so I need you to brief me in advance. We need to make Lewis' wife and son's visit on Sunday morning smooth and positive. That element has not been part of my planning, and it is probably very important.

2: Remind me to call Lucian in the morning about Sunday evening at the Hallstroms. I'll need accommodations for 11; I don't how many they can handle. I may decide to join the party.

3: Find out what you can about the Hallstrom boy; he is an unknown at this point. It would be helpful if he and Lewis' son were on good terms as we proceed. Julian may be of value there.

3: Find out who the Hallstroms' Real Estate Agent was. It would help if we could find a property before they leave Boston. We may need to make the guest house available for a period.

4: Have Sawyer contact me about doing a rapid workup of the High School—I need enough information by Monday to secure the support of that staff, regardless. I'll need a carrot or two.

5: Identify the upper management of Oglivy's. I need to know more about the scoutmaster. He is likely behind much of that boy's uncanny ability. We may have use for him in the organization.

6: I need to know more about the boy's mother. Is she a widow? A family background is needed. No hurry—discretion essential.

He's kinda tall

144

12   *catching up at last*

Julian's conscience had been screaming at him for months—but something always got in the way, somehow. He couldn't stand it any longer—besides, after all that had happened in the last couple of weeks, he just had to share his enthusiasm and excitement with someone **else**— it felt like he was starting to bore everyone around here. Since it was Saturday afternoon and it was too late to do much else anyway, and since it was pouring down rain again, he leapt at the chance to get caught up with his special friend at Camp Walker. *I might finish it in time to mail on Monday...* He inserted a sheet of paper into his mom's typewriter.

boy... where should I start...

> > clack-clack-clack... < <

Dear Uncle Max,

The typewriter drowned out the kitchen radio—his mom was reading a book in the living room with the radio blaring away as usual; and he needed a break from Kasey's drawing—it had been transferred to the last large sheet that Uncle Max gave him at Camp. *boy, it's sure lucky I had that, too.* That's one drawing that had to be done on a large sheet. *I hafta get more of those... maybe Mr. van Horn can spare a few...* he continued typing:

> I'm sorry I haven't written to you before
> now—I have a million excuses, I've been so
> busy with school and scouts and everything.
> I was going to tell you all about my Summer
> Job—boy, was that fun. I got to do hedges and
> lawns and dandelion patrol all over town

> practically. You wouldn't believe how much
> stuff we had to haul to the dump every day.
> We had a special trailer hitched to the tool
> pickup. Some days we had two loads!

He withdrew the sheet and scooted his chair to the left; a cartoon of the crew members using a rake, hedge clippers and garden hand tools took shape; he added hoses, lawnmowers and a wheelbarrow. At the far right, a small one of him being hosed down by Zack. At the bottom of the page he showed the pickup truck and trailer with Ed waving happily from the driver's seat. He threaded the sheet back into the typewriter.

> As you can see, we were busy. I had to
> quit that job when school started,
> unfortunately. Maybe I can do that again
> after camp next summer. I miss stopping by
> for a milkshake on the way home. At the end
> of a hot day, those really help. They had lots
> of flavors to try, and that made it fun too.
> (they were all good except licorice.)

I don't know what anyone sees in that flavor. I was lucky, though—Zack polished if off for me. He paused to think of a way to change to a new subject—otherwise he would end up writing so much about last summer he wouldn't have time to tell about Kasey, which is what he wanted to do the most of all. But it was important to say something about school first—otherwise, he wouldn't be able to tell about Art Class. *man, was it stupid to put this off for so long!*

Better late than never, observed Inside Guy.

yeah, yeah, I know. He shook his head. *didn't rub it in, at least. onward, men...* Quoting Mark helped him refocus.

> The classes I have at school: wow. High
> school is way different that I thought it would
> be. I take World History, Typing, (that's why
> I am typing this letter—I need the practice.) I
> take English, Biology (ugg! I like the teacher,
> but what we have to learn in there sometimes
> is not... I don't know how to describe it in a
> nice way. It's one of those things that's

supposed to be good to know, I guess. I'll be
glad when it's over). Everybody takes P.E.
naturally, and my last class every day is
Geometry. I like that class—the teacher, Mr.
Withers, is funny a lot of the time, and you'd
be surprised at how that class has helped me
draw better.

He paused to insert a selection of geometric shapes, each with a
label and formula.

Last Friday we learned all about
Parallelograms—(that's the one on the left. Do
you know, it's one shape that can be skinny or
fat, tall or short, big or small? Kind of neat,
really.

I saved my favorite class for last: Art.
What a great teacher I have now: his name is
Mr. van Horn. You'd like him—

He started a new page with a cartoon of Mr. van Horn standing at
an easel drawing a horse with a stick of charcoal. It occupied the lower
left half of the next page; he put the sheet in the typewriter and
continued:

He really knows a lot. I'm getting better
all the time thanks to him. There's so much to
learn! Next semester we will learn all about
color and how to paint. We will start with
water colors then the last quarter will be how
to oil paint like the famous artists do. I'd
never learn about these things by myself. I
am one lucky kid, that's all there is to it!

Julian paused again—there was so much to tell about—about his
new friends at Jackson High School, about Randall from the state of
Washington—*boy, Uncle Max wouldn't believe the camera stuff he
has—and the darkroom! and then what about Rita and that crazy
dance!*

>> chuckle <<

He grinned, picturing himself in that ridiculous yellow rain slicker and straw hat. No wonder they looked at him strangely when he arrived at the dance. *maybe I should draw a sketch of Rita and that blouse!* He shook his head. *better not. man. I still don't know why those boobs didn't pop out.* He laughed out loud, thinking about Sammy's shoe whacking the car heater. *P.U! and what about the school clothes I bought? boy... lots to write about.* He checked the clock at the table by his bed. *how am I gonna get time...*

oop: potty break. He needed to answer another call from Mother Nature; she wasn't exactly happy about stuffing himself at that fancy dinner last night.

Francine looked up from her book when Julian passed into view on his 'errand.' She was so proud of him. She still hadn't shared what happened on Friday night with Geraldine... she wanted to savor it a bit longer. She was due to arrive any minute... the clock on the mantle verified that. Her phone call was a good yardstick... obviously, she had been talking with either Frederick Swann or his assistant. Francine wasn't entirely confident about Geraldine and her views on segregation. The issue had never come up at the office. She pondered briefly— Geraldine's tendency to assume command wasn't needed here... but Francine knew her well—enough to know that she could adapt when it was required. Business always came first with Geraldine.

The sound of Julian humming to himself in the bathroom evoked a nostalgic response. *I wonder what he was laughing about...* She rolled her eyes and shook her head. His habit of talking to himself worried her for a while, but Doctor Overstreet had put her mind to rest about it. Evidently it was a common trait among single children. She had expected him to grow out of it, but it was just as prevalent as ever. *presumably when he's on his own, he'll have outgrown the need.* She doubted if a wife would put up with it for very long. *if there is to be a wife.* She was not at all sure of that, now. Geraldine was itching to make the arrangements, but it was likely years away—after college at least. Francine was content with that prospect—no, she was **glad** about it. She wasn't ready for him to leave. Indeed, she wondered about that: would she ever be ready, really? Julian opening the bathroom door interrupted her train of thought. As usual, he gave her a happy smile on the way back to his room.

"What was so funny a minute ago?" Sometimes he shared things like that.

"Oh," Julian giggled. "I'm writing a letter to Uncle Max," he smiled happily and crossed over to sit a minute with his mom. The ottoman was a handy place to park temporarily. "I was thinking about how to tell about the dance, and how Sammy's shoe sort of spoiled things." He shrugged. "I prob'ly won't write about that... I doubt if he would be interested, actually. There's lots of other things to tell about."

"You're right about that, although you'd be surprised at what Uncle Max might enjoy hearing about. After all, you did win Best Li'l Abner!"

Julian shrugged. "Yeah... I was gonna tell about Rita's blouse and everything, but that might not be a good idea." He was curious about her view on that, now that he thought about it.

Francine restrained herself, but was unable to prevent an automatic grin. That was one event that still broke her up. Every once in a while, Geraldine would chuckle quietly to herself at the office, remembering Julian's description of his dance experience opposite a strapless double D cup. It wasn't very long ago. So much had happened since, it seemed like old news. Two weeks! It seemed more like two months.

"Anyway, I'm trying to tell him what's been going on—I know he'd like to know." He was certain of that. Sarge didn't have any family now, except the camp. Julian felt a responsibility to make up for that, somehow. Sarge was important. He was a good man, and fun to be with, period.

Francine's attention shifted to last night. "Tummy upset? Something wrong about what you had to eat?" The menu had a long list of things she never prepared. Julian was inclined to try new things.

"Not what, but how much. I never ate so many good things before. That place sure makes good stuff to eat." He had been trained to clean his plate—leaving anything behind made him feel guilty. "Like you always say, my eyes were bigger than my stomach."

"Well, it served a good purpose. I suppose Kasey has more room in his tummy than you do—it looked like you were trying to eat identical meals." The way the two boys had hit it off was marvelous to witness. She had never seen anything quite like it.

"I didn't think of that... but you might be right. He sure was interested in what I thought about things. I never expected to have so much fun—it was almost a contest—not to see how much we could eat, but how things went together, stuff like that... everything was good, no matter what we tried. Kasey wanted to leave some things behind, but I wouldn't let him. I told him that if he put something on his plate, he had to eat it all. You taught me about that a long time ago." That was one reason he had eaten too much—*helping Kasey finish his baked potato, prob'ly.*

Francine was pleasantly surprised. "How did he react? Was he annoyed or angry?" A boy from a family like his was probably not bothered by a few leftovers, let alone put up with being scolded about it.

"No. He looked a me a second, and said Thank You." Julian shrugged. It proved that he had figured right. For some reason he knew right away that Kasey was an honest and smart kid. Just looking him in the eye told him that. He nodded to himself... *yep;* the look on his face made him feel good. *real good.*

One of Julian's traits was trusting people. Until they proved or behaved differently, he had no reason not to. Francine and Geraldine used to worry about that, and it still concerned them—the episode after the Sadie Hawkins dance proved their concern was justified. Fortunately, he was rescued in time—but she wasn't confident he had learned what he needed to. He was still incredibly vulnerable.

"I better get back to that letter. I'm typing it... I never did that before." *taking the page out to put in a drawing slowed everything down.*

"That's a good idea. Before you go, what about supper? You didn't have much lunch."

"I dunno. I'm fine now..." he considered the question. "Yeah. I'll be hungry by then. Any leftovers? The macaroni and cheese was sure tasty." Actually, he'd like a hot dog. But she didn't have those very often—she didn't think they were very good for him—too many preservatives. She was kind of fussy about things like that.

"No, we finished that off. Don't worry—I have lots of things I can make up." She checked her watch: *three hours. plenty of time.*

"Whatever you want to do as long as it's easy. Besides, we have another big one tomorrow night. Mr. Swann made a special request for us to be there, remember?" That's when he planned to give Kasey the drawing.

"Yes. I'm supposed to invite Geraldine."

Julian wondered when she would enter the picture. *maybe she can find a good house for them like she did for Randall's parents.* That's one thing Geraldine was good at, for sure. "Good. I want her to meet Kasey in person." He figured that would help in the long run. He stood: "back to that letter I go," he skipped toward his room.

She waved back as he returned to his bedroom. She glanced out the window... still raining. *hmm. I sure hope that's over with by tomorrow—* The Wood family planned to attend Church in the morning. *that will be very interesting. Mr. Swann is handling that.* She needed to find a way to get better acquainted with her as a person, mother to mother. She remembered what it was like to get restarted in a strange town—even with Geraldine doing so much for her and Julian, getting settled in in a completely strange town was not easy. Candace has a rough time coming. Francine had resolved to be her helpmate in every way possible. Once they were settled in, she would be there, ready. She would not wait to be asked. Julian's example would be her guide.

Back in his room, Julian opened the drawer to check the time—he kept Uncle Max's watch there to keep it safe—he used it more than the alarm clock by his bed. It made him feel good. *almost 3:00... boy... I gotta get to work! I still have a lot to do on the drawing.*

Skip the dance for now. If you have any time left over tonight, you can add it to the end. Inside guy was good to have on hand when Julian had trouble making up his mind.

good plan. I'll tell about Randall first—then about Kasey.

> > *clack-clack-clack…* < <

Julian wasn't sure if typing was any faster than writing by hand. *Prob'ly easier to read tho…*

Inside guy did not offer an opinion on that one.

Julian did not hear Geraldine arrive—the typewriter effectively masked nearly all sound outside his room. He had no idea how long she had been there, but a familiar burst of laughter from the kitchen revealed she was there. He was glad his mom had the job of filling her in about Kasey. He wanted to get this letter finished before supper. *a lot left to do on the drawing.* He wanted it to be ready to give to him tomorrow night after supper. That was standard practice, but he realized that no one there understood that. So he expected to enjoy a few surprised faces. He was confident this would be a good one—somehow, he seemed to know that. Drawing was becoming a more conscious, more refined activity, especially when it was on large paper: it didn't talk back, exactly… but he seemed to know when the drawing was satisfied, when it was done. *practice makes perfect…*

Unconsciously, he was humming the first thing Kasey played on the piano—for some reason it had stuck in his memory. That was unusual—the only song he knew by heart was the falling star one—everything else was mostly noise.

Julian was due to revise his thinking about many things, of course, not just music: that's part of growing up. Being in high school had already changed him more than he understood, or suspected: after four months he was already well on his way: the fun had just begun.

13 *at last, the bonus shots*

"How long have we got?" Andy was almost ready to make his pitch. After these were done, he would know if his hunch was right. All the contact sheets and key game shots had been printed plus a few extras, so he was ready for Monday. They could do the prints for the other school later. Now they were started on the "special" frames, the ones that had been pulled; only he and Randall would ever see these. *boy oh boy…*

The wall clock was right above them. "About an hour—my mom is very fussy about everyone being at the table on time." He did a rough calculation. "We've got time to do four or five, I think. Remember, they have to be tucked out of sight before we leave." There was always a possibility that someone else could enter—the dark room wasn't locked. *Mom said I might need to show it to somebody from the campus tomorrow.* Thanks to Julian, he had a secure hiding place upstairs. Plenty of room to add these to his special library. Of course, Andy would never see those—no one but he and Julian would even know they existed. He moved the enlarger head upward and focused. "I thought so!" He stepped back so Andy could get a better look.

"Oh, my g…." he stared in shock—his wide dropped jaw turned into a grin of delight. "Who is **this**?! how… did he see you take this?"

"No—this is a guy on the other team. I don't know what he was doing—checking for something… maybe he had a pimple down there or something…" *or maybe it was on the way up.*

"Gotta be an 8 incher, at least…" Andy licked his lips unconsciously.

Randall was experiencing a similar buzz below the waist. He was very proud—his new 70mm lens was perfect for this, just as he had expected. It didn't need extra light or a flash unless the subject was seriously underlit. *better than the 50, I think...* he zipped over to the cupboard for a 4x5.

Andy bent down close. The detail was **amazing**.

"You can do the honors," Randall slipped the paper into the easel and pressed the exposure switch. One second was enough for this one. He opened the easel and stood back.

"This is **Choice**! really choice..." He removed the paper and took it over to the developer tray while Randall secured the negative. They had established a standard two man routine—made things move efficiently.

Randall had put each strip into a single sleeve—some were an isolated frame, others a small set, depending. A few were taken surreptitiously, at arms length—those were guesswork, since he couldn't stoop down low without getting caught. Fortunately, the sound level was so high the camera couldn't be heard unless you were right next to it. The only downside was not being able to correct the focus—the only way that could be done was by looking through the lens while making the adjustment. *someday, maybe they'll come up with a camera that can focus itself.* He was eager to see how well he had guessed. He pulled up another strip and held it up to the light... "Oh boy: the show-off!" he chuckled. *this one is next...*

Andy was so impressed with the first one he was at a loss for words. He slipped it into the Stop Bath. "You have to look at this! It's incredible!"

Randall inserted the next strip into the carrier. "On my way..." He skipped over next to Andy and took the tongs. After a good swish he lifted it out of the tray for a close look. *whoah...* "I didn't expect it to be this good—this is blown up quite a ways... usually they get a little fuzzy zoomed this large." If it were fine grain film like 120, it would be even better. *a little too furry for me...* excess body hair did not fit Randall's aesthetic standard. He returned it to the tray. "Wait until the next one!" he giggled. "The guy thought I was pretending to take these shots. Remember the guy that did the showoff dance? He didn't know it, but I

154

was actually taking the pictures—I made it look like I was joking around. I got three or four really good ones!"

"No, I didn't see that. I must have been talking to the captain—I paid close attention to what he had to say."

The first frame was blurred, but the second had been exposed at just the right moment. The player had thrust his hips forward and was about to pull back when Randall zoomed in. This and the third frame were perfect close-ups of a wagging pride-and-joy being swung from side to side. It was about the third swing, and the effect was an exaggerated length, though it might also have captured early signs of becoming enlarged; it had been frozen in perfect focus—first one side, then the other.

Andy was speechless—he looked at Randall in awe.

Randall blushed and shrugged modestly; he was very pleased, and a little surprised. He was certain his depth of field setting had blurred many, many otherwise superb specimens. *I wonder how fast I can change that setting... mmm...* He needed to do some practice sessions. He glanced at Andy... maybe, just maybe, they could do a little testing upstairs one day next week. He owed the janitor or whoever was responsible for installing the 250 watt bulbs in the overhead light fixtures; in the locker rooms, that made all the difference.

"How many of these are there, anyway?"

Randall grimaced sheepishly and pointed to the counter. They were lined up in order.

"I didn't see you do **this**," Andy stepped over quickly. He did a count. "Man alive!" he grinned. It just occurred to him: "Did you get one of Tom?"

"I don't think so..." he thought back the after game celebration. "I might have got something accidentally after the splash party..." Tom got hit as hard as the coach—the double touchdowns deserved special recognition.

Andy counted the strips in the lineup. "Can we do contact sheets for these?"

"Sure... makes perfect sense." That would simplify finding the good ones. They got to work at once... there was just enough time to do that before they had to stop for the day.

Six 8x10's later, they watched the sheets circulate in the washing tub. Andy checked the wall clock and shook his head. Casually, he extended his left hand and gave Randall's left bun a friendly stroke. It seemed automatic and expected, but it was a step forward. He enjoyed the warmth; the contour was pleasant as well, even though Randall's suntans were not a tight fit.

Randall had looked at the clock as well. "Not enough time..." He realized he was blushing. Andy's hand felt wonderful... no one had ever done that... it seemed so natural. A small hum, almost a coo revealed that it was appreciated and enjoyed.

"I figured as much." Thanks to Mark, Andy rarely used a four letter word, so he didn't have one handy.

A period of silence followed as each searched for a when and where; they were in need now. They still had not talked about their newfound romance, if that's what it was. That could have been problematic, but oddly it didn't seem to be critical.

Randall took a chance and looked at Andy directly. It was a silent search... for both boys, an open discussion was overdue. This start was reassuring, if temporary. Too bad after supper wasn't available: schoolwork required his attention—tomorrow was already booked by his parents. He didn't know the details yet, but his mom had made it a point: make sure he was not in his darkroom hideaway tonight. She was one smart lady—seemed to know when he had required work to do. Something else was afoot. She had not gone into detail, but tonight was a non photolab night, like it or not.

"Maybe after we show these to Coach Brodie on Monday..." Randall offered. *unless Julian will be here, that is.* Somehow, Randall didn't see him as a part of this now. That in itself was very significant; he needed to sort that out. A week ago, that question did not exist. Friday, everything changed. Rapid change was not something he had ever had to deal with. Oddly, he was not terribly worried about it... that too was atypical. He glanced at Andy again briefly... *what is it about him that puts me at ease?*

156

"Perfect. Mr. L too." With any luck, in addition to what the coach and school paper needed done after school, they could work in a few more 'special' prints... and Andy could make his sales pitch upstairs in the Studio. Now that he had seen what Randall could do, he had plans... **big** plans. Besides, he had a hunch that boxy sofa up there was a hide-a-bed. If Randall didn't know how to operate it, no problem: among other things, Andy was an experienced hide-a-bed operator. Tonight his thoughts were about more pragmatic issues—one of the advantages of being two years older was having had his identity questions settled already. The prospect of accompanying a younger "brother" into the fold was welcome and something he could do well... very well.

Andy, of course, did not know that Randall was already there, really. Before long, that would be cleared up... wouldn't take long at all.

He's kinda tall

14 *plenty of room*

Swann need not have worried about the Hallstrom's facilities. Other than the monthly bridge club meeting Eloise hosted, they had not yet had an occasion to use the spacious entertainment and reception area that faced the vast back yard. They had purchased this property from a family that routinely hosted upward of a hundred guests at a time. It had its own wet bar and restrooms. The Baldwin grand piano was an unexpected bonus that Eloise enjoyed playing from time to time. Out of sight from the front, special access from the driveway allowed service vehicles to provide convenient and efficient staging. The only thing it didn't have was a special parking lot. Instead, the previous owner had put in a swimming pool. That and a croquet field shared half of the remaining lawn. Large maple trees and rhododendron provided privacy from the neighboring properties.

Far more than the Hallstroms needed or would likely ever use, the price was right; Eloise knew a good investment when she saw one. She planned to double their money when the time came. She was able to take advantage of the tax waivers the previous owners had enjoyed for making the area available to host a variety of fundraisers for charity and nonprofit organizations. The driveway from the street widened at the top of the slope; when it approached the three car garage, 24 cars could park off street with an experienced valet on duty. With the Airstream motorhome and 30 foot Sea Girl walk-around no longer occupying the space, it was just an oversize driveway.

Conveniently enough, Sharples' Delicatessen had catered many events for the previous owners, and had everything needed ready to go—a party of eleven was small. If it were for anyone but Eloise, they would have dispatched a few steam tables and called it a day as they did routinely when serving fewer than 50. That, and the name Frederick

Swann were an exception. Either meant an on-site chef and at least two servers. They knew well how to keep those accounts satisfied and secure. And it had to be said that they took pride in their work and always strove for excellence. Lucian Sharples was a well known gourmet chef before he retired—he always thought of himself as a just a good cook. Once in a while, he supervised in person—but he was getting along in years now—his legs had limits that had to be respected. But he had a private line that he always answered in person—when Frederick called he was expecting a pat on the back for the University event. Frederick was one of his favorite people—he and Frederick's father went way back.

"It goes without saying, your crew was in top form Friday," Swann started his call in mid-sentence as usual; Lucian was like a favorite Uncle—niceties were pointless.

"Thanks, m'boy," Lucian leaned back pleased at the sound of the voice. He was glad to have his mind taken off the temptation that had been nagging at him for the past hour. Another Altesas Reales awaited in his humidor. He was supposed to limit himself. He'd already had one this week—three left. He enjoyed teasing himself. These were hard to come by, so he tried to earn the privilege.

"Something has come up—I need a small favor."

Those words were especially welcome. "Ask away—'your wish is my command,'" Lucian quoted his father's old line for the umpteenth time.

Eloise was in her element. She and the Sharples' Maître de l'Occasion had arranged three tables for four in the center of the room in perfect proximity—everyone could see and hear everyone else as well as have a more intimate individual table of four conversation. It encouraged an informal relaxed experience.

A table for twelve would have created a primary head-of-the-table position, which didn't suit Swann's purpose. He sought to establish personal connections to undergird the professional respect—Wood and Hallstrom were to be the core of his research team. He wanted their

160

dedication as well as their genius—their families were part of the support system, pure and simple. There was little time—the opportunity to lay this foundation was an unexpected surprise. That and the discovery of the Forrest boy had given Swann enormous encouragement. He now had reason to be optimistic for the first time in many months. It made him feel like being social again. The life of a recluse had become heavy, tedious. This was fresh air at last. Sitting with the three boys was a genuine treat. Remembering what it was like to be fifteen was more engaging than nostalgic, another bonus.

"What amazed me most of all was how impervious those guys were to the rain: through my telephoto lens I could see it splashing off their cheeks and they didn't even blink. Now, that is concentrating." Randall enjoyed the irony of reporting about a football game—a sport about which he knew nothing. As it happened, the other two boys weren't football fans either. He didn't know about Mr. Swann. He was only now adjusting to his presence. He remained an unknown, by and large.

"Wow... we saw that out of the window, didn't we?" Julian nudged Kasey under the table with his right knee. He didn't know the word Randall used, but...

Kasey nodded fervently. "Yes! They just kept playing?" No football at Belmont—soccer and polo were their sports. He had gone to a few matches with his housemates. He could take it or leave it. Watching it in the rain—or snow, this time of year—is something he would never do. What he found most interesting was Randall's vocabulary and accent. That shouldn't have come as a surprise, considering that their fathers were colleagues, but he had become accustomed to Julian and Kirk's more colloquial usage.

"Non stop. The fans were dressed for it, too—must be part of the fun, staying dry was part of the challenge I guess."

Now that he thought about it, Julian was glad he missed the game after all. The only thing he had was the awful yellow rubber thing Geraldine made him wear to that dance; he really didn't want to put it on again, ever. He turned to Mr. Swann: "Are you a football fan?" He thought it important to include him in the conversation. Julian had taken a liking to him automatically last night—he was glad to see him again.

161

The direct question took Swann off guard. He had not expected to be active in the conversation. The blond boy's question was so obviously honest it took a moment to frame a response. "I suppose not," he began. "I seem to always have something else to do. Thanks for asking."

"Sure. Me too. I was always busy with scouts I guess. We hike and camp instead." He didn't mean to be critical or anything. "But a couple of the players are in my Troop. It means a lot to them."

"Well, Tom made two touchdowns at the very end of the game! He's the best player on the team from what I could see." Randall took another sip of lemonade.

"Neato!" Julian turned to Kasey: "You'll like him, I know. He and his friend Nick are my best friends, really. We're in the same patrol! Mark put me in with them last summer." He didn't go into detail. His attention turned to the menu. It was simpler than the one on Friday—no little boxes.

Swann complimented himself for deciding to sit here—he had lost touch with the younger generation. These weren't typical teenagers, probably, but that made no difference. Remembering what it was like to be new, to be unfettered from social and political protocols was wonderful—it provided a freshness, a sense of youth. And somehow, this boy made him belong. That was astounding and preposterous, but that's how he felt. He began to see what had captured Lewis' boy. Clearly, Randall was another fortunate. *I have selected the perfect place to spend the evening.* He had a few questions when the opportunity arose, but being included was unusual, and that added an unfamiliar aspect— chance. It provided an element of adventure… enjoyable. Absolutely, utterly enjoyable.

Helgar was intrigued and mixed in his feelings. He had not known about Mark's wife before tonight. He wasn't sure what to make of her—clearly a bright woman—about to be a bona fide M.D., she would have to be. The question in his mind was whether, like himself, Mark was a switch hitter when it came to romping between the sheets. It was likely going to be difficult to determine. For some reason, Helgar had assumed he was a bachelor. *I may have been headed the wrong way up a one-way alley.* Fortunately, he had not made any moves. Still, the man was a perfect specimen. It was still well worth his time to sniff around. No one else had come into view.

Pat was thrilled to be included, and to be seated with professionals of this caliber. She felt right at home. She would have benefitted more from being with the other ladies perhaps, but attending a social event with Mark was always special. The call from Swann's private secretary came out of the blue—fortunately, she wasn't on call. Lewis reminded her of Dr. Janus. The blond giant sitting across from her was fascinating in the extreme. His deep voice and hearty laugh alone put him in charge. Mark's description of him a few months ago was understated. She had almost forgotten about it.

Lewis was grateful for the opportunity to meet the scoutmaster—the man clearly had a great deal to do with the extraordinary boy that captured his son's fancy. Their presence had modified his expectations about what they were facing in this town. He had never studied the state or any of its cities, never had a need. It had not attracted any special attention other than having a couple of outstanding universities. He had known several Duke graduates and read a few academic papers over the years. But the same could be said for Alabama, and he would never consider raising a family down there. This man was a local, born and raised. That was enormously encouraging, as was the boy. He had known Helgar professionally for a few years and had no concerns whatever about him or his family. They were probably more accepting than people at home in Boston.

Geraldine was fascinated by Candace Wood. The explanation of how she came to be called Candace was useful—fully Anglicized spellings were rare—transposing the letters C and K was a Latin phonetic artifact; rarely corrected, they were easily overlooked and forgotten. Kandake fit the lady's exotic appearance and Queen of Sheba demeanor perfectly. She was surprisingly adept at socializing, and her British accent was so unexpected it evoked a polite smile and a readiness to hear more. "So you have a daughter as well?"

"Yes. Zeyla is almost four." She paused then amplified. "She looks more like her father, whereas Kassa reflects my heritage—that's where his blue eyes and unusual height originate."

163

Geraldine was enormously grateful to get this information without having to probe. She realized early on that she would need as much information as she could get to deal with the Chamber and Real Estate Board. Finding a property anywhere on this side of town was going to be very revolutionary. For almost a century, 28th Avenue had served as a de facto color line; it had never been crossed. A law wasn't necessary; practice was almost stronger than a statute. That was about to change, but she didn't fancy being the leader of a civil rights movement.

Francine wondered if they were planning to have more children, but hesitated to raise the question. She had expected to see them in the Parish Hall after the service this morning. "I missed you this morning— it was very crowded. It always is on Boy Scout Sundays. Julian is all wrapped up in the ceremony, of course. His patrol leads the procession."

"I'm sorry, we attended the early Eucharist. Mr. Swann thought Father Wilson would be able to spend a few more minutes with us. I think it was his suggestion." The service is much shorter, and attendance tends to be low—that was true in Boston as well. "Remarkably, he knew our Rector at Christ Church—they were classmates at Seminary, I believe."

Francine understood—*just as well… the 9 o'clock was very full this morning.*

"When did you come to this country?" Eloise was delighted by the woman's speech. It was very polished, very high—somehow, she wanted to show her off to the Bridge girls. She was uncertain about their segregation notions—it had not come up. But being new to the area herself, she didn't have a feeling for what was allowed and what was never spoken of. The ladies here had a stash of codes and traditions for which no written manual existed. Established order was like an antique—polished and kept in a locked cabinet, safe from the dust of the real world. Some questions dare not be asked—to do so would disqualify the person asking.

"Shortly after the War." A private memory lingered for a moment. She turned to Francine. "Lewis was seconded by the army to oversee our security. We were sent there early on by my family when the Italians invaded our home country. Lewis is my 'war hero,' so to speak."

164

Eloise was thrilled to hear this. *a war bride! I've never known one…*

Mason had located himself at the end of the counter facing the wet bar—it had fixed stools with swivel seats; the short backs were well designed and enabled him to observe the group with ease. Swann had a direct line of sight for sending signals or cues. Thus, he was able to have a meal with the party, a nice bonus. This particular string of activities had been very rewarding—far more engaging than many of Swann's associations—unusual because of the large number of people it involved. So far, it was manageable—and it was nice to take a load off for minute.

"Ribs!" Julian nudged Kasey's elbow with his. He didn't see a stubby pencil this time. "How do we order this time, anyway?" No boxes to check.

Kasey's eyes brightened; a big grin appeared— "You want to do what we did before?" He turned to Randall. "We had so much fun! Julian picked one thing, I picked another and we split our orders! Ever tried that?"

Randall was still adjusting to Kasey's uniqueness—the mannerisms and accent were arresting. He could see at once why Julian liked him so much—it was hard not to, really. The notion of having fun was so typical of Julian, he assumed the idea was his. Randall had no experience with Blacks whatever; aside from a few foreign students from Africa, they were unknown in Pullman.

Julian continued to focus on Mr. Swann; merrily, he related what they did: "I ordered chicken and dumplings and he got the steak and baked potato." He rubbed his stomach. "Ate too much, but it was fun. Trouble is, I liked everything." He leaned close and added confidentially, "If you ever need to order out, you should use these guys." He reinforced his high opinion of the outfit that had been making their outstanding lunch sandwiches: "Randall's mom does all the time. They have really good desserts too!" He expected Randall to confirm his endorsement.

"Thank you for the advice." Swann had trouble keeping a straight face. He could hardly wait to make his next call to Lucian. "I'm

165

sure you are right." He examined the menu as if he had not seen it before. He and Eloise had finalized the bill of fare yesterday.

Randall hadn't looked at the menu yet—he was familiar with Sharples' cooking—his mother bought her main dishes there regularly. *beef or pork?...* They have both... *Chicken Cacciatore and baked ham*—his mom ordered those fairly often. He wasn't used to seeing choices. The ribs were new, and so was the Game Hen. Italian Meatball and Linguini was another she had not ordered. He glanced over to her table, puzzled. Deciding what to order was not something he had to do very often. It was not the way she did things. Someone else had a hand in this. He shrugged and took another look. There were more: salmon, halibut... *what's going on here?*

Swann noticed the confused look. "It might help if you look at the very top," he pointed to the title: *Sharples' Sampler*. All three looked at the title and then to Swann. "The waiter will bring a small sample of everything on the list, I believe. That's why there are no hors d'oeuvres. He will take your order after you have had an opportunity to try them all." That was his idea, and Lucian wanted to test the concept. This was the perfect trial run.

"Brilliant!" Julian exclaimed, rechecking the list. This changed everything. Julian loved his mother's cooking, no mistake about that— but she never made dishes like these.

Kasey tilted his head and scanned the list. "mmm..." *this is going to be more interesting than I expected.* He looked directly at Swann. "What if you like more than one of these?"

Swann was delighted to be addressed directly by Kasey at last. "I'm sure they will provide whatever you wish. The only limitation is how much you can eat."

"Whoah!" Julian giggled. "Isn't this great?" He beamed. "Even better than Friday!" He gave Randall the Groucho eyebrow lift. He leaned toward Swann, as if sharing a discovery. "See what I mean? These guys are smart! This way, you know what to order next time as well!"

The hard part is going to be not ordering too much, Inside Guy offered.

166

oo. you are right. Julian remembered the super full tummy—
took all day yesterday to settle everything.

Swann looked over at the always attentive Mason and winked;
his pleasure was impossible to hide. It helped to express that to his
confederate—which is how he regarded Mason. Sharing private
moments added depth and humanity like nothing else.

Julian shook his head happily: "Boy. My mom is right again."
He rubbed his tummy; Mr. Swann might wonder what that meant. "She
always says my eyes are bigger than my stomach." He took a sip of
lemonade. "That always happens whenever we go to a restaurant with
Geraldine," he squirmed and did a few mini wing flaps with both arms,
hands tight against his chest… sometimes that helped settle things. "At
home she always knows how to leave room for dessert."

Kasey exchanged glances with Randall without thinking—
Julian's uninhibited movements and gestures hadn't drawn any special
reaction. Spontaneous ebullience was a trait he had never encountered
before—it was unconscious and completely disarming. Randall returned
a knowing smile—he felt connected with Kasey, having had his unique
friendship for almost three months was special. He sensed that Mr.
Swann was equally delighted by it.

Swann was, as a matter of fact, taking delight that that very
quality. "Perhaps we should wait a little before ordering that—you don't
want to miss the experience of biting into one of Lucian's Chocolate
Hazelnut Truffle cakes."

The sound of that drew the boys' attention.

Swann winked confidentially: "I know the cook." The
expressions on the boy's faces were justification for letting that slip out.
"In five or ten minutes, you'll have room," he nodded, taking another sip
of coffee. Dining with this trio had been most entertaining.

Julian tilted his head and regarded Swann directly: he was
suddenly very interesting. He didn't have anything to say, really, but he
was grateful for being reminded—he didn't know anything about this

man. Like Geraldine, he ate like a bird. People that age were always worried about putting on weight; he thought it would be rude to say anything. *maybe I can ask about his car...* He waited for advice on that from Inside Guy.

"Meanwhile, maybe you could tell me a little about your drawing skill. How long have you been taking lessons?" He was always interested in who was doing quality work. This boy was something he had not expected.

"Wow! That's my very favorite class. Mr. van Horn is really a good teacher!" he bounced in his chair automatically. "That's the best thing about High School. You get to learn lots more. I always liked school, but now..." he looked at Swann again. "I bet you had some good teachers. You prob'ly know what I mean." *I must sound a little silly... better shut up.*

Swann pursued the hunch: "who did you have before?"

Julian was confused. *who?* He paused to think. "Nobody, really. My fifth grade teacher was real good—she used to take us on field trips to draw stuff," he nodded. "She taught me a lot. Mrs. Connor. Yep," he added. "Good teacher."

Everyone at the table was astounded: by and large, this boy was self-taught. Until now, Swann had not had the pleasure of making a discovery—clearly this boy was that, by any measure. He turned to Randall. "Tell me something about your photography. Does your school have a good photography teacher as well?"

Randall laughed. "Hardly. No, my grandfather taught me everything I know," his tone revealed that it was an emotional endorsement as well. "That was my only disappointment about this school. They don't even have a darkroom," he shook his head. "Even Pullman had one of those." *bare bones probably; never got to use it...*

Swann now had two things to go with: excellent. His attention moved to Kasey.

Kasey was still adjusting to the revelation about Julian. "I've been very fortunate. My parents began my piano lessons when I was five. I had five years. When I turned twelve, they started me on the clarinet. Now I'm learning oboe."

168

"So you are planning a career in music?" That seemed obvious to Swann, but direct input was likely to be of value—this boy's father was a vital component in his plan.

"I like it well enough," Kasey acknowledged. The concept of having a Life Career Goal was never a comfort zone component.

Swann gave him an explanation-expected expression.

"I like to write," he shrugged. "Realistically, I can't expect my parents to subsidize me… I need to support myself, eventually. Hence, I am learning how to play the oboe." He shrugged. "I like it well enough. I don't need to be a virtuoso."

Swann found this very useful. This would get some attention.

Julian piped in. "He's just a little shy," he turned to Kasey. "I know how you feel. I can't stand it when people go on and on about how good I can draw." He shook his head.

Randall looked at Swann and rolled his eyes. *hopeless…*

Swann realized how wise it was to be sitting here. Like most adults, he tended to forget that adolescent boys were more than adults-in-training. He began to recall his own youth. This was a very real, visceral reminder. This opportunity might be a windfall; he was not about to dismiss its value.

Julian brightened. "What do you like to do for fun?" He was just being polite, actually; he didn't mean to be nosey. But he figured everyone had something interesting to do. Old people usually did. Mr. Swann wasn't old, not like Uncle Max. *more like Geraldine, prob'ly.*

Swann was not ready for that question. A glance at Mason was automatic, but he knew he was on his own here. The smirk told him that Mason was tuned in, as always. This was one he couldn't delegate. Fortunately, he was given a pause by the timely arrival of Lucian's Chocolate Hazelnut Truffle Cake. The whipped cream topping was spectacular.

Eloise stood on cue from Swann. As hostess, she needed to direct the events they had planned. "Please, everyone, don't feel rushed—finish your dessert while I say a little. There is no hurry; the dessert tray will be open for as long as we are here," she gestured to the servers who responded with a slight bow. "I am so pleased to have you in our home." Eloise was an experienced hostess, and it showed. "Since we all know one another, I will dispense with introductions. But I must thank our host and benefactor," she beamed and gestured toward Swann and added "and to the Sharples' staff, of course." She moved forward rapidly to head off any urge to applaud. "I do have a surprise of course: the time has come to show off the talented musicians in our company." She gestured to Randall and Kasey. "They were not expecting this, but I think we all would like to hear an after dinner sample from Randall and Kasey—both are very talented, and perfect for the occasion."

She was unable to prevent an enthusiastic applause.

Julian beamed and sent a wink to Swann; he leaned over with cupped hand and whispered: "Mothers!" he giggled. "They get to do things like this all the time." He knew what Randall and Kasey must be going through.

Swann was delighted by the confidence. A boy's perspective was another unexpected treat. He remembered that perception from his own boyhood. He returned a boyhood nod. Goosebumps ran down his back.

Randall had been alerted yesterday, but it had slipped his mind; she had not been very specific. Mason handing him his clarinet was a complete surprise.

Kasey saw the clarinet and his eyes went wide: "You play a **clarinet**?!"

Randall was surprised by his interest. "I'm in Concert Band at school." A guilty-as-charged expression was all he could provide by way of explanation.

Julian was delighted. *oh boy!* Finally he would get to hear Randall play that. He gave Swann his Cheshire Cat grin. He had found considerable pleasure in Swann's presence. Julian's ability to relate to older men was an attribute that he did not think unusual. That's why he liked Uncle Max and Camp Director Jorgenson—and his teachers at school. Old guys were interesting, that's all.

170

There was little choice. Kasey stood and gestured for Randall to accompany him to the Baldwin. He had noticed it just after they arrived. He wasn't expecting to test it out, but he was curious to see what it sounded like—the low ceiling in this room was worrisome. When he approached the piano, a big surprise. Some time during the dinner, a score had been placed on the rack above the keyboard: **Piano Sonata in C Major, K. 545 - I. Allegro.** He and Randall provided a pro forma smile to a very pleased Eloise. Kasey's mother was smiling wide, very unusual for her.

Swann noticed Julian's reaction. He had seen them too—one of the advantages of the seating arrangement was being able to see everyone at any time.

"They're in cahoots." He looked at Swann solemn as stone: "My mom and Geraldine do that all the time." What he didn't know but should have suspected: his turn was coming.

Swann was having the time of his life with this boy! Fun was the last thing he expected to dominate his evening.

Only the first movement of the Mozart was on the rack. That was by design as well. Eloise didn't want an extended performance. Her goal had been achieved. Randall's ability had gone unappreciated for too long.

No one expected what came next. After the applause, Kasey did something bold and out of character—somehow, he felt the freedom as well as the urge. "You play very well, Randall. May I?" he looked at Randall hopefully.

Confused, but seeking to be open and friendly, he handed his clarinet to Kasey.

Softly, Kasey confided: "I do this whenever I can." He grinned wide and stood in place. He chose not to do a test; he leaned forward and put the clarinet to his pursed lips.

The opening bars of Gershwin's **Rhapsody in Blue** replaced the surprised quiet. His model was Benny Goodman—he had heard a recording at school, and practiced it whenever he could. The oboe player in him came out anyway, adding something special.

Swann was stunned, as was everyone else. This had replaced the Joplin.

Kasey handed the clarinet back to an awed Randall. "Thanks." He avoided looking at his parents. He had taken a risk, but it was worth it. He assumed it would come up on the way to Boston, if not before. Randall's performance had prepped the instrument perfectly, which helped.

Another burst of applause covered Randall's amazed expression: Kasey had not cracked a single note. Randall knew the significance of that better than anyone else in the room. Concert Band was going to get a huge surprise.

Geraldine stood before the musicians could return to their table—Francine had insisted she do the honors. "Stay put, boys." She grinned at Julian: "You have something to show everyone too, Julian." She strode over to Mason, who had slipped out to the station wagon during supper. He held out a roll of paper. She took it over to Julian. "Now is the right time, I think." Julian had asked her opinion on the way here.

He was planning to do it just before leaving for home if nothing else seemed right. He half figured he'd have to wait until tomorrow after school. This was better—a lot better. Even so, he couldn't resist sharing this with Mr. Swann, who seemed to enjoy hearing his viewpoint. "See what I mean?" He tipped his head to indicate his smiling mother. He walked over to Kasey. "Thanks. You were fun to draw." He handed Kasey the roll of paper.

Kasey was dumbfounded. He hadn't forgotten about Julian making a sketch on Friday—but this wasn't the sketchbook. He had to sit down. Fortunately, the piano bench was right behind him.

Francine and Mark knew he planned to give Kasey the drawing—he always did. Mark was the only one who had had the experience. It came back to him instantly. Julian's mother and Geraldine had never seen him present a drawing to its subject, nor had Eloise, but they had heard about it more than once, so they weren't surprised.

Kasey removed the rubber band carefully as if it protected a fragile piece of glass. He passed the rubber band to a grinning Randall.

172

Randall was so pleased—having posed for Julian, he knew what was about to unroll. This one could be seen publicly. He had longed for Julian to get credit for doing this. He never quite understood why Julian took it so matter-of-factly at school, as if he were passing on any old piece of paper.

Kasey unrolled the portrait slowly... he stared at it in disbelief. It was so magnificent! Beyond anything he had expected. The sketchbook had impressed him greatly, but this was a different order of art entirely. He stared at it open mouthed for what seemed an eternity. He looked at Julian in awe—he could find no words to express his feeling—he had seen himself—inside, who he was—as sure as he was sitting here. This drawing made him feel glorified and naked all at once. He could hear the Rachmaninoff playing, it was as if he were playing it this very minute... he was reliving how he felt. It was the most complex emotional sensation he had ever experienced.

Mark recognized what Kasey was experiencing. Julian had done the same thing to him. Powerful didn't begin to describe its impact.

Swann and Kasey's parents, seeing what the portrait had evoked, needed to know what was going on. "Can you share a view with us?" Swann turned his chair to face it directly. He had a hunch, having seen the boy's preliminary sketch on Friday.

He too was awed—everyone was. Discovery was an understatement.

Julian rolled his eyes. *I was afraid of something like this...* he remembered how Leonard had reacted to his drawing last summer. Uncle Max and Mr. Jorgenson didn't make a big deal out of it though... Mark had, but that was different. He was special. He shrugged. *he'll get over it eventually.*

Inside Guy wasn't sure about that, but he didn't say anything; he nudged silently. Julian was aware he was holding back. He shrugged again. *shoulda waited til tomorrow. not much I can do now, anyway.* He sat back and twiddled his thumbs. The smile on Kasey's face was all he needed to see.

"Randall, can you hold one side? That way the curl on the bottom will disappear." Swann stared at it intently. This merited serious attention.

Everyone in the room was captivated. Francine was amazed at the response and looked at it more closely. She thought she knew Julian's work as well as anyone… she began to see that she had not paid very close attention after all. *I've been taking these for granted…* Having studied art at college long ago and spending over a year married to Julian's father, she was inclined to skim and summarize. That memory remained a source of pain and regret. Julian was able to eclipse it most of the time, but the blemish was permanent, to put it mildly.

Swann had an inspiration. The dinnertime conversation gave him a shortcut to what he had in mind. "Randall, are you in a position to photograph this?"

"Sure," he didn't hesitate—he was all set up as a matter of fact. "Whenever you want."

"Excellent." Swann stood. This was more than opportune: he took over. He glanced at Mason as if to confirm something was in the works. "Lead the way." He faced the adults in the room. "Shall we?" It wasn't a request, though he intended it to be. Sometimes his natural ability to lead took over. In this instance, it was welcomed. Everyone needed to stretch a leg after that meal. Perfect timing.

While the group followed Randall out the sliding door, Eloise stepped over to the Maître d'. "If you can, keep the dessert tray in service? Coffee and tea, you understand. I'm not sure what or when, but we won't be away terribly long." She knew Helgar would require another piece of cake and a scoop of ice cream.

The patio was modest in size; the Sharples' service truck sat unobtrusively at the far end—it had been here many times. The power terminal was built in to the small hutch at the edge of the concrete pad. The sidewalk was actually a narrow service drive that ran to the main driveway between the bicycle hutch and the side door to the 3-car garage. It was cleverly masked, running between two large maple trees before going around to the north end of the house, where it ended near the swimming pool. Artfully positioned azaleas and knee high shrubbery along both sides made the area around the side and back appear residential and park-like instead of commercial. The border lights every four feet lent a festive quality—the rain had stopped last night late; the patio and walkway were already dry.

174

Julian hopped over to walk with Mark. "Wait until you see this," he grinned. He was hoping to spend a little time with him, at least. He wanted to meet his wife, actually, but hadn't figured a way to pull it off. The chance that Mark might introduce her was Inside Guy's idea. He was good at thinking of things like that. He'd been pretty quiet tonight. He usually was when a lot of people were around. Otherwise, he might slip up and get caught talking to himself. That all this fuss was over his drawing did not register—he was happy to see Randall take over the spotlight.

Randall stuck with Mr. Swann. "I used all my black and white film at the football game. I haven't had time to pick any up. I plan to do that tomorrow after school. But I have color in both formats, so we should be okay—but I have to send that out for processing," he added apologetically.

Swann gestured for Mason to walk with them. There was a chance Mason could remedy that problem in short order. Swann didn't have to wait for Monday. "What is your film of choice?"

"Depends on the occasion," he was pleasantly surprised. Apparently Mr. Swann knew something about film. "Generally, I use Tri-X for my 35mm camera and Verichrome for my 120. I prefer Kodacolor over Kodachrome..." he hesitated about going into any specialized films. He had not done any microscopic work yet, so he wasn't much use to his father... but he planned to take that on eventually. "I find that Tri-X is more versatile than Plus-X—especially in low light situations."

Swann checked to see if Mason was listening. "Where do you get your film?"

"Camera World has everything in stock, usually. I dislike ordering by mail—it inconveniences my parents and takes too long. If Camera World doesn't have it in stock, they can order it faster than I can anyway. But they aren't open on Sundays."

"Tri-X?" Mason asked.

"Yes. I buy it in bulk and load my own cartridges." He liked Mason. "I usually have a few single rolls for emergencies, but I used everything I had for that football game." He shook his head, "got carried away, I guess. He looked at Swann sheepishly. "It was my first game."

Swann's nod to Mason had been taken as understanding and sympathetic politeness by most. However, Mason was on his way to meet Sawyer, car telephone in hand. The 1936 Packard was not the antique it appeared to be. Its special upgrades were unobtrusive, but state of the art or better. He was unsure if he could make it back in time—but Sunday traffic was in his favor. Fortunately, of those present, only Swann and his lieutenant knew what his back channels were and how effectively they functioned: Swann had a small photo lab of his own, and Sawyer was always on call.

Once in the upstairs apartment, now his studio, Randall had to think briefly... *how to go about this*... he didn't have a cart full of folding chairs, for one thing. "Julian, my cameras are in the darkroom. Can you go fetch them?" As Julian reached the door he added, "pick up a couple of rolls of film from the drawer... one of each." He focused on Mr. Swann, but realized everyone was paying attention to his first group tour of his operation. "He's my right hand man down there." *until Andy came along, that is*... he just realized that Julian had not seen what they did yesterday. *is he ever going to be surprised...*

Eloise was enjoying a minor deja-vu. She spoke softly to the other mothers: "My father was a photographer. He relied on Randall his last few years. Randall was devoted to him." This setup was a minor tribute as well as a functional studio.

Helgar beamed, bursting with pride... he could see that Swann was impressed. Not that it mattered, but he was pleased to see his son's ability appreciated. One thing that Randall would never do is toot his own horn. Fortunately, his ego wasn't in need; he was self assured as well as self directed. What more could a father want?

Randall had moved an easel into position and carefully estimated the angle of his diffusion panels. The floods were in place and ready to turn on. He put a large medium gray panel on the horizontal mounting board and stepped over to the set of drawers for a roll of tape. He gestured to Kasey. "Bring that over to the counter." He made a small loop. "Lay it flat, face down."

With reverence and hesitation, Kasey did as he was asked.

"It's all right. I've done this dozens of times. The tape peels off easily—it won't damage the paper or leave a trace. It's made for this purpose."

Kasey was reassured. *I need to have this framed somehow...* He glanced at his father. This would be in his care until the move. He didn't want to take it to Belmont. *too valuable...*

Photographing the drawing took very little time. Swann's suggestion that Randall give the group a tour of the darkroom was welcome—everyone was curious.

The tour took a while—there were a lot of people, and everyone wanted to see it. Once there, they indulged themselves reviewing the football contact sheets and prints. Randall stopped short of doing a print, but it was necessary to let everyone get a good look at what a negative looked like being projected. Just for fun, he found a 120 negative of a campus scene and projected it onto the wall. He could do a poster size print if he had larger trays.

As Swann had planned, Mason was waiting for them in the garage, package in hand. "Can you indulge me one more time, Randall?"

There was only one answer. The entourage returned to the studio and watched Randall carefully empty the cameras and reload them with black and white film. Randall, it turned out, was an excellent narrator. He described what he was doing each step of the way.

Mark's frown puzzled Helgar. "Problem?" he asked quietly.

"Yes and no, I suppose. I've been trying to figure a way for my boys to see what Randall does. They ask about his mountain pictures often." He scratched his head. "I considered asking him to put together a merit badge program, but… the problem is, this is far too costly for most of them." He shook his head.

Swann checked to see if Mason was listening—he gave a silent signal. In a few weeks he expected to see a plan. Mark Schaefer was already on the active list. This was useful—very useful. An action item was always helpful.

"How long does it take you to do the entire process? Lewis was hoping that somehow, they would have a print of this drawing to take home with them.

Swann had the same question.

"Between two and three hours if I'm in a hurry," Randall said confidently. "About 20 minutes or so to develop the film. The problem is drying it. The negatives have to be air dried for two hours in the dust free cabinet I showed you downstairs. Prints are faster; they dry rapidly if I use glossy paper. Matte paper takes longer—they require pressure— those can take hours. I don't have a drying drum. Those take about two minutes."

"What do the pros do? To speed that up?" Swann inquired.

"I don't really know. They may have a machine that does it all automatically. I don't know how they can speed up the drying process—a fan would draw in dust and ruin the film. Once it dries, dust particles can't be removed—they become embedded in the emulsion." He shook his head. "That happens, you're up the creek." He checked his watch. "I can develop these tonight, no problem. Can't print until tomorrow after school."

Swann did some calculating. The flight to Boston would take two hours, roughly—maybe three. Maybe this could be put together. He wanted Randall to do this himself—taking to Sawyer's lab would not be fair to the boy. He turned to Helgar. "What's bedtime?"

Mason had put the drying drum on his list. He added film dryer. If one existed, it too would be acquired.

"I know," Randall beamed. "I can get up early and make the prints before school!" He looked at his mother—she was the alarm clock backup.

Eloise stepped forward. "I'm sure we can do what's needed." She knew Randall would insist anyway—and it was not anything unusual. She played hostess momentarily: "there's coffee, tea and whatever waiting for us in the house," she clapped her hands together gently to indicate they were on a new page. "Ice cream and cookies anyone?"

does a bear... Helgar stopped himself in time. "Maybe a brandy?" he invited Lewis to precede him as the group turned to leave.

Swann reached out to Randall. He wanted to talk to the boys who had given him the most pleasurable evening he had experienced in a very long time. "Thank you, Randall. You are a gifted young man." He turned to the other boys. "All of you are. I appreciate your contribution to the evening—and to what you will bring to the world. I feel privileged. I hope to see you again." He looked at each separately. "All of you." He gestured to the door. "Allow me, please." He wanted them to leave first. He had a word or two for Mason. He checked his Rolex: *just past 9:30. seems later...* he was pleasantly surprised. The early start had been wise. Eloise was to be thanked for that.

Julian just realized something: *I almost forgot!* He grabbed Kasey by the elbow. "You gotta meet Mark." he pulled him over quickly before they got back to the house. "Wait up!" Mark and his mom were about to join Geraldine. He looked at them, glowing. "I want you to meet my new friend in person." He knew they didn't have a chance to do anything but look at him.

"Thank you, Julian," Mark was very proud of Julian for not forgetting. He deferred to Francine.

"I am so happy for you, Kassa," she reached out both hands to hold his extended right hand. "You are welcome here, and so is your sister, who I hope to meet soon."

"Thank you... thank you very much." Hearing her use that name was a nice surprise. He turned to Mark: "Julian showed me the Troop Scrapbook. I am pleased to meet you in person."

"I'm sure we will get to know each other soon—you are hereby invited to meet the Troop in person. They will want to do everything they can to make you welcome at Jackson High."

Julian was going to get Geraldine in on this, but she was talking to Kasey's mom about houses. Kasey's dad was talking to Randall's dad... so...

You did right; time for one of those cookies Randall's mom has on hand. Inside Guy knew how to wrap things up.

Julian reached for the belt and tugged. "C'mon… you gotta grab one of Randall's mom's cookies to take along. She gets 'em by the dozen; real good, too. Take a couple—they're kinda small."

15   *the faculty meeting*

Lucian was delighted when the private line's ring broke the silence; it was likely one of three people, all favorites. And it was time to let the cat out for the rest of the afternoon. He needed to move around anyway. He was fishing for a clever way to respond but was startled by the burst of laughter that erupted from the handset. It sounded like Frederick, which was a pleasant surprise. He expected to hear from him tomorrow.

"… cahoots!" Swann had to catch his breath before greeting his old friend. The phrase wouldn't leave him alone 'They're in cahoots.' The solemn expression on Julian's face was what made it so indelible.

"Frederick?" Sharples was inclined to chuckle himself—the laughter was infectious.

"I'm sorry, Lucian, truly. I've been unable to control myself. I have to share this—I had the time of my life last evening. I'm calling to report on our little menu pilot. It was quite a hit I'm pleased to say…" he took a deep breath. "How long has it been since you had dinner with three teenage boys?"

That was unexpected. He paused, but knew the answer. "Since forever." He saw no reason. "What have I been missing, my boy?" He found the proposition diverting.

"I haven't long—I'm about to go to a meeting. But this keeps interrupting my concentration. I'm hoping sharing it with you will help me move on." As they approached the school district central office, he told Lucian about the artist's unique perspective of having to cope with parental overseers—mothers in particular.

—〰—

Julian felt very strange—out of place: walking down the hall alongside Mr. Barnes? *wow*. At least most of the kids had left for the day. Besides, in the Senior Hall, no one knew who he was anyway, so no big deal. Anyway, Kirk was on his other side, so all he had to do was smile—Kirk was probably going to do all the talking. Julian wasn't shy, but talking to the entire faculty at their meeting wasn't something he was expecting to do, ever. Getting it over with was what he looked forward to. Keeping quiet about what went on last Friday and the weekend wasn't so hard after all. They told him to keep quiet until this meeting was over with. He glanced up at Kirk happily—he never saw him at school usually—he was a senior and had first lunch, so that wasn't unusual. It reminded him that there were lots of kids he never got to see or know. He had a better idea of what a big job Mr. Barnes had.

To be honest, he had mixed feelings about all this. One side of him wanted Kasey and his folks to forget about going back to Boston—he really liked Kasey. But the other side wanted things to slow back down for a while. The amazing thing was he got his homework done and finished his letter to Uncle Max. He didn't expect to get either one finished. He was even ready for all his classes today.

They were on the way to the Music Annex at the back of the school. That and the Industrial Arts wing were at the far end of the school. Other than the orientation tour at the end of summer, he had not been out there. His Art class was on the second floor above the woodshop, so he had looked out the window over the area—once in a while, the marching band practiced down there—he enjoyed seeing them do what Troop 9 did before parades. He had always wondered why the Annex wasn't connected with a hallway—it had a breezeway instead.

He looked forward to seeing Kasey one last time. They were about to fly back in Mr. Swann's private airplane. Secretly, Julian was slightly envious—he'd never been on an airplane—or in one either. One time the Troop had an event at the airport, but he was still a Tenderfoot. They didn't get to go close to any planes though. They didn't have any of the ones he had made models of. Well, that figured, since the airport here wasn't a military base. It wasn't a very big airport, actually. He hadn't studied up on it.

"I have to ask you to be patient—you'll need to wait in the hall for a while," Barnes explained. "I don't know when Mr. Middleton will be ready for you to join the meeting. He has a few things to clear up first. Kasey and his parents aren't here yet; you'll be invited in as a group. Kirk will do the honors and introduce everyone."

good, Julian was perfectly happy to wait. He had no idea what he would say to a room full of teachers, anyway… *I'll probably look silly, more than anything.*

Don't be so sure about that—somebody might ask a question or something. Inside Guy had checked in finally.

maybe… but they'll want to hear from Kasey more, prob'ly.

That's why you need to be on your toes… he might need some help. Inside guy was worried about the Boston accent. Julian might have to translate or whatever it was called.

As they entered the Annex, Barnes gestured to the small row of chairs against the wall. "Sorry, boys," he apologized. "It shouldn't be too long." He pointed to the outside door. "Mason, Mr. Swann's driver, will be here soon. He plans to park right outside. He'll know what to do. Any questions?"

Julian shook his head. He was glad they didn't have to wait in the breezeway. Kirk seemed to know what was going on, anyway. The only thing bothering him was not having Randall along. He was used to meeting him after school. He still felt bad about not helping out with the game and all the work afterward. But yesterday was proof that Andy had followed through just as Mark said he would. The photos of the game were as good as he figured they'd be. Seeing those was a big relief to his conscience.

He and Kirk sat down to wait.

"Blue shirt today," Kirk commented. He'd expected to see the Strad again.

"Yeah—Monday is Blue day." He leaned back. "Geraldine and Mom decide what I wear to school." He shrugged. "It's a big deal to them. I never understood why," he shrugged. "Saves me the trouble, I guess. I never paid attention to that before," he grinned guiltily and admitted—"still don't, really."

"Geraldine? You have a big sister?"

Julian laughed. "No way! That would be awful! No, she's my mom's boss." He tilted his head. "She's kinda like my mom's big sister, though. Huh. I never thought of that before." He nodded. *yeah. that fits.* "That's right—you weren't there last night. We had another fancy dinner at Randall's place. She was there. I think she knows Mr. Swann." *Geraldine knows everybody.*

He was about to ask Kirk what he liked about being Student Body President when Andy and Randall poked their heads out of the band room next door. "Hey, you guys, come on in here to wait." They had been sent by Mr. L to cover this for the school paper. Randall had his camera along—thanks to Mason, he had plenty of film. They might use one of these for the yearbook.

Without a thought, Julian jumped up and walked over to join the smiling faces. It happened so fast, he nearly missed it. He was transported back to Camp Walker suddenly—he recalled Nick and Tom working at the stove in the Flaming Arrow camp. A space had opened between the two, but he had felt the energy as well as seen it. He glanced at Randall quickly, but he was looking at Kirk. Andy was being very cool... maybe too cool.

Don't jump to conclusions, now. Inside guy was probably right about that, as usual.

In any case, Julian hoped his impression was right; it would simplify things greatly. He had been hoping to find a way to redirect Randall's affections. This could be it. *good timing...*

"Hey-hey," Andy chimed and offered a friendly fist bump to Kirk—one of those macho senior boys' customs. It was supposed to confirm that you were one of the 'guys.' Translation: you liked girls, not boys. Andy was a survivor.

"Sorry," Julian shook his head; he had been summoned out of class again, and couldn't meet Randall after class as usual. He looked around at the room—full of chairs and music stands—nobody else was here. *thought so...*

Randall shrugged, trying to appear sweet and innocent. "Yeah, I got cornered again too," he pointed his thumb at Andy. "We got drafted to cover this for the school paper."

—w—

Middleton hoped he wasn't mistaken about this; moving the meeting to the choir room worried him—it felt confined, crowded. He had not detected any overt negative responses; the duration was likely to go longer than his meeting usually ran, so he wasn't convinced yet. The Athletic Director was almost finished. He checked his watch again. The Superintendent would be here any time now—he was counting on that— he didn't have anything else that needed attention. The Winter break was only a few weeks away—aside from the new leak in the roof thanks to Friday's deluge, everything was ready. He was most conscious of what would be taking place shortly **after** the break. Having the Superintendent present the news in person was enormously helpful.

Art Frankel had chosen to sit by Julian's English teacher instead of his usual place among the other members of the Science Department. He was impressed by her perspective. Ever since they had been drafted by the Principal to observe Julian's lunchtime portrait session, or demonstration, or performance—he wasn't sure what to call it—and Saturday's early registration, they had been on the next page. He kept a straight face and said quietly, "Are we ready, everyone?"

Lillian St. John smirked, "I can hardly wait." She didn't see the history teacher. "I'm a little worried about Alistair."

"Yes." He had seen Quimby find a seat in the back row; there was no point in drawing attention by turning around to look. "He's behind us, in the back." Not a good sign. "The blue eyes spooked him, I think." *admittedly, they are arresting, to say the least... hard not to stare at him.*

"I think everyone else is eager to work with the boy." She certainly was; he had already read much of what the class would be assigned next semester. She was eager to read some of his stories. Her proposed literary magazine might have gained an edge because of this. Getting it into the Department budget was the only real barrier. She was not the Head and nowhere close to becoming in charge.

Frankel remembered Archie's poorly disguised reaction. *took one look at his height and nearly filled his shorts*. The boy was already taller than anyone on the basketball team—by several inches.

The door opened. Surprise Number One: it was the Superintendent. With him was a distinguished gentleman they did not know. Something about him stood out. Frankel was not familiar with such things, but the man's attire was a major clue. It had the sweet smell of wealth and power.

No one noticed Ladendorff leave the room. He had a photographer and reporter to fetch.

"Stay seated, please," the Superintendent said, as he walked directly to the rostrum. No introductions were necessary, since everyone knew who he was. He always began with the same line at staff meetings. The straight faces in the front row didn't show any particular reaction other than sitting up attentively. Robert Thompson wasn't disliked by the staff, but he wasn't regarded as being anything unusual. He'd been in place for eleven years, wasn't going up a career ladder—in another ten years, give or take a few, he was expected to retire and move to Florida. That is, if everything didn't blow up in his face in a few months.

"You all know why were are meeting, so I need not go into detail. If you will recall, during the Fall Inservice, I laid out what the Board had ordered for next summer and next year. There has been a minor 'revision.'" He made quotation marks in the air. He paused for effect. He looked around, as if checking to see whether everyone was listening.

His action effectively masked the door being opened quietly to allow four people to enter: Ladendorff led the way, shepherding in two students, obviously from **The Cardinal**. Andy stepped to the far right and stood by the piano, and Randall stood at his right. Behind them was a well dressed man, holding a supply of multi-paged handouts. He remained by the closed door.

The Superintendent cleared his throat; the eyes that had been distracted returned to see him gesture to the gentleman standing slightly behind at his right. "Allow me to introduce you to Frederick Swann," he extended his hand politely. "The floor is yours," he gestured deferentially to the rostrum. It was courteous and controlled. He was skilled at masking any personal or political attitude. He took the empty seat in the front row next to the Principal.

The staff was amazed by his brevity—that was a first.

"Thank you, Robert," Swann said politely, stepping to the rostrum. The use of the Superintendent's first name was unusual to faculty ears—but given his carriage and attire, fitting. It placed him at the top—about which there was no doubt from the moment he stepped into the room.

"My apologies for keeping you from your usual activities this afternoon. It is an inconvenience I intend to reward you for undergoing. I will be as brief as possible; in the coming months, you will learn much more—there is no need to be complete at this stage. It is my fault that your schedule to meet the Board of Education's mandate has been advanced six months, and that you have not had an opportunity to make the appropriate preparations. It is a challenge I am confident you are able to meet; I intend to be of assistance wherever possible.

Lillian looked at her colleague with wide eyes; her mouth was closed, but her jaw was dropped in surprise. Her expression was reflected back: Frankel had the same reaction, as did several others in the room. His delivery and language matched his attire.

"Allow me to introduce Mason, my aide-de camp, so to speak." He turned and extended his right arm.

Mason stepped forward and gave a small bow, stack of paper handouts held between his hands.

"As he distributes my information and questionnaire packet, I will expand."

Mason stepped to the first row. He had pre-counted the number of seats; the end person in each row was given the correct number. This was standard—the teachers knew what was expected, they did this themselves, many of them every day in their classroom.

Swann reached under the rostrum for the glass of water that had been placed there in advance. He was a man of great confidence and self-assurance. Not at all nervous, he was aware that this meeting was enormously important. He had to have these people on his team. That was more than a slogan: his life depended on it. That's why he was doing this in person. He allowed the attention to loosen—he knew better than to compete with himself, so he waited until everyone had a copy. He noticed Randall standing politely, camera in hand—a sudden change in the order of his presentation was required.

"There is plenty of time for you to deal with this material, so there is no need to look at it now. It includes my background and what my needs are. At the end is a questionnaire or input sheet for you to turn in if you wish. There is no due date. Your Principal will inform me when any have been submitted." He paused to verify that everyone was paying attention. "This is your personal copy—I must ask you to make it your eyes only. I will explain that in a moment."

Here he went impromptu: "Before continuing, I'd like to recognize someone whom some of you know already." He gestured to the right side of the room. "Last evening, it was my pleasure to meet Randall and see his work." He gestured for him to approach. "What you may not know, this young man is an accomplished photographer. I have seen his work and can vouch for his ability and skill." The expression on his face was a nice treat. He didn't get to do things like this often.

"He brought it to my attention that you don't have a darkroom at this school. I was surprised, and I confess, disappointed. This will come as a surprise to everyone here: I am going to provide whatever is necessary. As soon as it is possible, you will have a darkroom of your own. It will be fully equipped and funded to meet your needs. Randall will serve as the Architect's primary consultant. That will assure that it will be state of the art. In addition, whatever staff needs follow will also be fully funded." He paused for another sip of water. The silence was deafening, as he expected.

"I see that he is accompanied by another student; I presume he is the reporter from the school paper I was told of. I hope to make his acquaintance soon as well." He paused to let things calm down. His announcement had been more of a jolt than he had expected.

"Which leads me back to one of the issues I planned to address— the matter of the press and publicity. That is an area I need everyone to

188

be careful about. What we are doing and what my contributions to your school and program will be depend on confidentiality. That is why you have not been informed of this until now. The newspaper and television people must be thought of as a threat as well as an opportunity. What we are doing could be exploited as well as employed. Interviews and access must be with my knowledge and permission. If you get inquiries, you need to deflect or delay automatically. Report them immediately to your Principal. I need to know if there is interest. I may provide training and advice and allow access, but it has to be controlled. Freedom of the Press is something I treasure, but I respect its dangers." He stared at the Superintendent: "This condition underlies everything." He turned to Randall. "Please, feel free to cover this event as you wish, Randall. I will meet with you and your reporter later to discuss how and what will be used." He faced the group. "Don't let the sound of his camera distract you from what else I have to say. The darkroom is the first item on what I expect to be a healthy list." He paused. "I have just added proper seating in this room. Sitting captive in those austere Spartan deskchairs can't be very comfortable. Remember that last page in your handout: use it." He added, "and remember, please, the document you have is yours and only yours. Do not share or lend it out, or leave it somewhere carelessly, or copy it. If you need to replace it, the Principal will provide a copy."

Another sip of water. He was on a roll... it seemed to be going well. He nodded to Barnes. It was time to bring in the two boys he had waiting in the wings. He could see that several had noticed their copy was numbered. He didn't need to bring that to their attention.

—ɯ—

Lewis chose not to put his son on the spot; he was processing things in his head, as usual. They had not been parked behind the school for long. The Packard was cozy and warm—more comfortable than the limousine. He didn't feel like waiting in silence; he spoke to his wife. "What did you think of Father Wilson?" They hadn't spent any time on that, what with all the other activity yesterday.

She turned to him, unusually animated. "He knew the Abbey! He'd been there for some kind of event—I think when he was a Seminarian."

"Small world, as they say. I didn't hear your conversation. Kasey and I were discussing the architecture." *laminated beams fascinate him.* "I'm trying to remember the Rector's name…" he recalled the vast cavernous gothic structure. During the war, Bath was filled with activity… a lot of hustle and bustle… they nearly overflowed the place. Somehow, the Abbey never got a direct hit. It had not been a monastery since the sixteenth century when Henry VIII banished the Benedictines and absorbed all their property.

"Neville." She gave him a look of disbelief. "How could you forget him, of all people?!"

"He insisted that I call him Charlie." He patted her arm: "No, I haven't forgotten him. That man could keep a secret. His sacristy sure came in handy." *his support was personal, not ecclesiastic.*

Kasey was tuned in—this was a topic he knew nothing about. His parent's romance in England was never talked about. That whole thing was a puzzle. One day he was going to get in on what their secret was. The conversation had interrupted his frustrated ruminations about the situation he faced. Conflicted, he did not want to go back to Boston, but realized he must. This kind of inner conflict was new. He didn't know how to address it with his parents.

The door to the school opened just then, and he saw Mason heading their way. "We're about to be introduced." *or shown…* Sometimes he had a cynical take on things like this. *one of the facts of life as a Black in this country. could be worse.* He had met a new group of adults before and knew what to expect when they saw what a freak he was. He had learned to avoid eye contact in these situations.

—◊—

Swann turned to greet Julian and Kirk as Barnes showed them in. "Welcome, boys; thanks for being so patient." He turned to the faculty as Barnes returned to his seat by the Principal. "I'm sure most of you know these outstanding individuals. I am pleased to turn this over to your Student Body President, who will do the honors." He reached out to shake Kirk's hand.

This was one of those occasions where being prepared was not quite enough. The rapt attention of the entire faculty was a new experience, far more daunting than he had imagined. But he persevered, took a deep breath and faced the teachers.

"Thanks, Mr. Swann." He swallowed and began—not easy, because his mouth had suddenly become very dry. "Last Friday I had the privilege to meet our new student and his family. I don't know how to describe him, but he was not what I expected." He needed to choose these words carefully. "I know you will like him." His mind went blank. He had this memorized, but it was **gone**! He played for time... "I almost wish I was going to be here next year." *nothing...* Turning to Julian, he cut to the chase: "this is the person you need to meet first." He realized this was actually the smart thing to do. He beamed at the teachers. "Julian Forrest has volunteered to be Kasey's guide and help him fit in at Jackson," he paused. "He is the **perfect** person, believe me!"

Frankel and St. John nodded simultaneously.

Julian hated 'aw shucks' moments like this. He smiled, shrugged, and almost said 'no big deal,' but Inside Guy caught him just in time.

He was not aware that the door was open just a crack, and that Mason was waiting for the right moment to bring in the Wood family. This had not been rehearsed or planned closely. However, Swann had taken precautions; Mason was waiting for him to give the usual signal. Julian stepped forward to the rostrum and began with a simple shrug. He hadn't anything special planned.

"The thing is, Kasey's just like you and me, really, only a little smarter, probably. I'm really glad to know him. It's my plan to make him my Buddy and to be his, just like we do in scouts," he stated proudly. "Y'see, whenever we go swimming or on a hike or anything, we have a Buddy—it's fun, and if you get into trouble or anything, your Buddy can lend a hand, or go for help if you need it," he pointed to his head. "Smart as well as fun," he looked at the Principal pointedly. "Sometimes, you are the buddy who helps out—or, you just have fun together. Why not? I think we ought to do that every time we have

191

somebody new, to be honest. Figure it out: nobody likes to be alone, especially in school. That isn't any fun, being all by yourself all the time. You learn a lot more when it's fun, that's all." He gave his no-big-deal shrug.

Swann nearly felt the light bulb flash in his head; he could see the Principal had the same thought. Both he and Barnes—he could see it in their faces. Once again, this boy had done his magic. Keeping quiet and straight faced was not easy.

"Besides, everybody is a little different. Sometimes you need to take that into account." He paused a minute—this had not been thought out. "Me, for example. I have a one-track mind. I need a poke sometimes to get my attention. Kasey, now, has a different problem— he's kind of tall." He thought about it. "When you think about it you realize that's not his fault. Another friend of mine was born on Halloween—people always want to come to his birthday party dressed as witches or ghosts or skeletons. It isn't fair. It isn't his fault, but he's stuck with it anyway, for life."

Get back to Kasey… Inside Guy was on duty, thank goodness.

right… "Anyway, he's a good kid, and I'm lucky to be his friend. And boy, is he ever good at playing the piano!"

Swan nodded, and Mason opened the door.

"Neato!" Julian exclaimed. "They're here!" He jumped and opened his arms in greeting, "come on in—everybody's waiting to meet you," he turned back to the teachers. "I forgot to mention something: they're from Boston, way up north." He shrugged, "it takes a minute sometimes to figure out what he says—but you get used to it. This is Kasey, and his mom and dad!" He skipped over and gave a friendly poke in the tummy.

Kasey blushed in spite of his planned aloofness—Julian had erased that altogether. He was grinning from ear to ear, unable to think straight. Julian had disarmed him completely.

Julian tugged him to the center of the room by the belt: "Told ya he was tall. You don't notice it that much when he's sitting down." He looked at Kasey expectantly—he was expected to say hello at least.

The room was completely silent. They felt empathy at once—the blond boy was a delight, but he had certainly put his friend—or Buddy—on the spot.

Kasey chuckled, resigned to his fate. He gestured to Julian with his left hand as he faced the teachers: "The irresistible force meets the unmovable object." He pointed to himself and shrugged. "Guess who won."

The staff laughed at once. It was the perfect tension release. When they had calmed a bit, he continued. "Thank you, Julian." He looked at the teachers smiling back. He was at ease and in control now. "I am glad to meet you." He looked at Julian fondly and spoke slowly. "I will try to speak clearly." He and his parents had heard Julian's preparation remarks in the hallway thanks to Mason having opened the door a few inches.

His 'cleahly' evoked another laugh. 'Foace' for force had illustrated Julian's point first thing. "I think it appropriate for me to introduce my parents. This is my father, Dr. Lewis Wood, and my mother." He looked at his father proudly, and gestured for him to take the floor.

Father and mother had been pronounced 'fahthah' and 'muhthah,' which placed him instantly in the Kennedy neighborhood. It added a charm—Julian's alert had been right on; his smile was infectious—it echoed Julian's. Most of the faculty felt included.

Lewis hooked arms with his wife and stepped forward to speak. "Thank you, son." He surveyed the group. Speaking to an assembled staff was not an unusual task. "We are pleased to be here. We enjoyed meeting with several of you on Saturday to work out Kasey's schedule for next semester. We are pleased and looking forward to being a part of the Jackson High School community." He gestured to Swann. "Thanks are due to this gentleman for being so thoughtful and thorough in his preparations. Little happens by coincidence, but he succeeds in obscuring that fact. I advise you to follow his suggestions. He is always a chapter ahead of the rest of us." He paused. "I am fortunate to have been added to his team." He continued. "My wife Candace prefers not to speak publicly, but I can say on her behalf that we are looking forward to finding a place here. We don't expect it to be bump free, but it is worth our effort." He referred to Swann. "This is a good man. We need to keep him around."

The staff was rapt—even the ones who had met them were wowed. Unused to being addressed by a Black, this one was a college professor with a Boston accent whose flawless syntax earned their respect instantly. His tone and demeanor matched his son's, and his wife's exotic elegance made them feel privileged. At last they were free to talk about it. Lillian St. Johns desperately wanted to see Alistair Quimby's response to all this. Surely he could see how important he was to this. How could she not break into applause and cheer?! She had to clench her fists and force herself to sit still. Thank goodness Art was here—his restraining hand helped.

Three rows back, Archie Snead was absorbed in thought—the boy's first day in PE had to be carefully planned... *a few group activities were the way to go... then a few free throws... alphabetically, of course... having Julian in the class helped... hmm... Forrest and Wood aren't sequential. hmm...*

Julian cupped his hand and gestured to Kasey, who bent down to listen. "I like your folks." He didn't have anything to add; that covered it. He elbowed Kasey to emphasize his sentiment. Kasey was one lucky kid, that's all. His father was super.

The faculty saw Kasey's smile. The friendship was obvious. The ones who didn't know Julian looked at him again. He was unique, no doubt about it. The two together couldn't have looked more unalike, or unlikely.

Swann took the floor again—he knew when to take charge. "Thank you Lewis, thank you very much." He turned to the teachers. "Now I must ask your indulgence. Before we adjourn, I feel impelled to congratulate you for the work you have done and do every day. These boys are evidence of that. They are important, and so are you. But I wonder if you are fully aware, really, of their capabilities—the way an outsider sees them. I want you to see a little of what I saw last Friday." He turned to Kasey. "Have you got something short? Say, two or three minutes?"

Julian looked at Kasey hopefully, with a big grin, "Yeah!" *brilliant!*

194

Without hesitation, Kasey thought of a good one. *they'll probably recognize this...* He stepped around the piano he'd been standing next to—a baby grand; it would serve nicely. He pulled out the bench and opened the keyboard lid. An older instrument, it had been cared for properly. He assumed it was in tune—testing that would be pointless, in any case.

"Neato!" Julian exclaimed, with a minor jump. He grinned at Kasey's parents and at Mr. Swann. *too bad mom and Mark aren't here...*

Swann signaled Mason. His final surprise was next.

Kasey concentrated briefly, extended his arms and leaned back. He played the first three and a half minutes of Beethoven's **Fur Elise**. He stopped at the first natural break—he sensed that was sufficient. He was uncertain about parts of it, and didn't have the score here. He gave Julian a wide grin and stood.

The faculty's applause was spontaneous—there was no way to contain what had been building up. Swann let it run its course.

Julian ran over to give a friendly hug. "Thanks, Kasey. That was a **new** one!"

"Thank you once again Kasey," Swann echoed. With raised eyebrows he looked at Julian. "Now it's your turn." He held out his hand for Julian to approach.

Ever clueless, he skipped over happily. He liked this man.

"I have a little surprise for you." He turned to the staff. "I am told that this young man provides a lunchtime diversion with his pencil. To emphasize my point about the importance of what you do, and how well you perform it, I point to this extraordinary boy. I am certain there are others. Your role in their lives is enormous. I applaud you as well as them. I intend to do what I can to support your enterprise. Last night this young man gave a very special present to his friend. I am sure he won't mind if Kasey and his family share it for a moment with everyone here." He gestured for Mason to enter, and took several steps back.

Mason entered with the recently framed portrait. It had been mounted on high quality mat board in a thin metal frame, as if destined to hang in a gallery—Swann's spare time territory. This had been done earlier in the day by a professional.

"Whoah…" Julian was amazed to see it like this. He had never seen his work framed. Swann, head tipped to the right, was in thought; Julian broke in: "Thank you. This is nicer. Kasey deserves this." he approved. *yep… Mr. Swann is a good man.* It did not occur to him that the artist and the quality of his work were being honored by the way it was presented just as much as the subject of the drawing.

Swann placed his approving hand on Julian's back. "Thank you, Julian." He looked at the faculty and to the Administrators for a signal or sign of some kind. They were fully absorbed, looking at the portrait— with the subject standing beside it, it was impossible not to marvel at Julian's uncanny ability to capture a moment in time. He gave them a few minutes and then decided to adjourn.

"Thank you again for giving me this time. I'm sure you all have things to get back to. Oh—I'd like the Journalism and Art teachers to stay for a moment, if they could spare another minute. Unless there is another reason to remain, you can get up out of those dreadful chairs at last." He presumed the Principal or Superintendent would have informed him if they had anything. He stepped over to Lewis to discuss the drive to the airport. It had not been decided whether or not to make a stop anywhere to refresh or have a snack. The plane was well provisioned. A two and half hour flight was ahead of them.

Middleton couldn't believe the clock: almost 4:30. *how can that be?!* He looked at the Superintendent in disbelief. *how could anyone cover that much ground in under an hour?!* Less, because he had used up ten minutes before the man arrived. He was grateful for not having to follow him to dismiss the staff.

The Superintendent's only concern was failing to have someone from the Board here. He hoped that was not a mistake. Fortunately, his ego wasn't troubled by Swann's well disguised imperial nature. It delivered what was required and then some. It was nice to watch for a change. Unlike many of his peers, he was not a vain person. He whispered to Middleton, "Harold's?" A cocktail was in order.

Middleton nodded. *perfect.*

"I'll drive." He needed to say something to Swann first.

it's only Monday… Stanley usually waited until Friday to wet his whistle. His eye fell on Julian. *thank you, Roy Barnes!* He nudged his Dean of Boys' elbow: "We're going to Harold's. You can ride with us— Bob is driving."

The strong 'invitation' was not a surprise. He needed to touch base with the Student Body President first; he stood. "Be right back." Kirk was standing perilously close to the door.

It took an unusually long time for the staff to leave the room; instead of hurrying to leave, they lingered, many browsing through the handout, many simply in thought about the unusual meeting. They felt elevated, they felt honored, challenged, and energized. No faculty meeting had provided that kind of an experience. They felt ready, yet grateful they had a few weeks.

Art Frankel nudged his colleague: "let's pay our respects to the parents before they are whisked away."

Miss St. Johns nodded instantly. "Thanks, Art," she looked at him gratefully, impressed by his thoughtfulness. "What an excellent idea." She wanted to connect with the boy's mother, especially.

16   *a ride in the Packard*

After asking Lewis to remain for a moment, Swann walked directly to the Superintendent. "I'll be leaving with Mason, Robert, so you need not wait." He turned to Middleton. "I appreciate your facilitating this meeting—this was an ideal location—I couldn't have asked for more." he extended his hand to give a thank you. He included Barnes with an approving nod. "I need to have a word or two with a few of your staff, if you don't mind." He interrupted himself: "—oh: I hope my extempore announcements about the darkroom and these seats were acceptable—usually, I plan ahead. I dislike surprises. If my promises are problematic, I'm sure we can sort it out. I am quite serious about them." He looked directly at the Superintendent. "My research and development man will be in touch about meeting with you in the coming weeks to deal with any other improvement opportunities you have been aiming for—I hope to be of some value in that regard."

"If all your surprises are like today's, be my guest!" Swann's courtesy was genuine, of that he was certain. He bounced on his toes slightly, restraining himself as much as he could. His mind was already at work dismantling the bond issue the Board was planning to put up for a vote in the spring. With Swann's resources, they might not need that for another two years.

Swann noticed that several teachers were reading his packet; a few were writing. "I trust it was acceptable for me to adjourn," he explained. That had been deliberate—he wanted to head off a forced applause.

"Not a problem, I assure you." Swann was one act he did not want to follow.

Randall had taken all the shots he thought were likely to be needed; he went to his case to retrieve three special envelopes. He had brought the 8x10s he had made for Mr. Swann. He'd made a few extras—one for Julian and another for Kasey. The electric dryer that Mason delivered this morning was a miracle. He had not known they even existed; he planned to get a box of large paper like his grandfather used to go with it. As he turned, he saw Swann approach: this was a much different man than the one he had supper with last night. Watching him handle the faculty and administration was eye opening indeed.

"Good afternoon, Randall, good to see you again." He accepted the envelope—he knew what it contained. "Thank you." Randall's expression verified that he was pleased with them. He would look at them closely later. He spoke the man standing to his left: "am I correct to conclude that you are the Journalism teacher?" Obviously so—he looked the part, corduroy sports jacket with leather arm patches—a tinted green visor was the only missing component.

"Earnest Ladendorff at your disposal," he reached out, eager to shake this man's hand. "The students call me Mr. L."

"I like that!" he paused. "I know it's early, but I do need to know what your plans are—when is your next paper published?"

"Next week—we should be able to have the copy and photographs ready by then. If we go to press on Monday, we should be able to distribute by Wednesday," he smiled proudly.

Swann nodded slowly. "I see." He looked at him directly: "I want you to rethink that." He let it sink in. "Let's pull up a chair."

The corner seats in the front row were open.

"Here's what I would prefer: nothing at all about this until the first day of the next semester." He waited for that to settle in as well. "By then you and Randall and your staff—I assume this is your reporter?"

Andy had taken the liberty to remain close. "I'm Sports editor, but I do other stories sometimes…" he added: I'm Andy… Andy Ashbaugh."

"Double A," Swann reached out. "Good to know you, Andy." He shook his hand.

200

Andy blushed slightly—no one had ever been so quick or clever to reply... *Double A... nifty.* He would use that. The handshake made him feel important somehow.

"What I would like is for you to plan a special issue—a mini magazine, if you will. In addition to your regular material, special feature articles on Kasey—who he is and what he can do, where he is from and so forth. I have people who can meet with you and your staff to plan it." He let that sink in. He noted a frown on Andy's face. He had a hunch. "In the meantime, you can do a special issue on your school's recent victory on the football field." He gestured to Andy's partner. "You must have seen Randall's outstanding photographs by now." Andy's frown vanished instantly.

Ladendorff was at a loss momentarily—this man was in a different world. *we're small change here...* He could see at once that Swann's concept was vastly superior. The only matter was advertising.

"May I ask what causes your hestitation?"

"Not hesitation, exactly... I see the advantages and no disadvantages..."

"But?'

"I'm not sure if I have enough ad sales to cover the cost."

"I am delighted to hear that. That problem no longer exists, you see. I have a PR director that will meet with you and your team to plan your advertising strategy." He tried to keep a straight face. "I realize how important community and merchant support is. There are ways to enlighten them with regard to the advantages of being visible in your school publications. You advise the yearbook as well?"

Ladendorff nodded.

"That helps. Coordination will be much easier. So—" he paused. "Are we on the same page about print dates?" He disliked having to press, but he needed to get to the airport with the Wood family. He did not need to mention that he would underwrite any expense requirements that arose.

"Well, that goes without saying..."

"Please: I do not want to coerce your cooperation—I am in a time squeeze just now. If you have any hesitation, any at all, I need you to be open and clear about your needs. If you need some time, I can meet with you next week."

Ladendorff could tell that was an accurate and honest statement. "I'm serious. I look forward to working with you every step of the way," he grinned apologetically. "I'm not used to your level of efficiency." He planned to get used to it. Public schools rarely travelled in the fast lane.

"Thank you. Mr. L." He was pleased by how quickly the man understood. He stood and shook his hand again before stepping toward the front of the room; he'd had an eye on the staff member studying Julian's drawing—it had been parked on a chair by the piano.

Mr. L and Andy stared at each other, speechless. Ladendorff snapped his fingers. *drat! I forgot to bring up the darkroom!* He had no idea where to put it. He was short on space already.

"Remarkable, isn't it?" Swann didn't introduce himself. The art teacher's concentration was professional.

"Oh—yes, it is." He needed to be careful—Julian was paying attention. This drawing was on a level far above anything he had done in class. That was not a complete surprise—no one knew better than he how limited and confining working in class was.

"Julian speaks highly of you as a teacher; it is a pleasure to meet you. I fancy myself as a connoisseur, of sorts. I'm not an artist myself, but I value it highly. I have a modest gallery of my own."

"As much as I would like to, I can't claim credit for this." Ralph van Horn was not surprised to learn that Swann had a gallery of his own, given what the man had been saying; the framing provided for this drawing was additional evidence. He was not a "connoisseur," himself. That required more than his teacher salary could support.

Swann turned to Julian. "What is troubling you?"

He frowned at Mr. Swann. "Elbows." He shook his head. "It's always elbows." He gestured. *looks like a stick figure from a game of hangman...*

Swann looked closely. He didn't see the problem. He waited for a clarification.

Julian pointed to the left elbow tip. Kasey had taken off his Blazer after they played chopsticks last night. He was wearing a short sleeve shirt.

Swann saw it immediately; the knob appeared to be rather large. Only Julian could see it as a flaw. "Well, you have spotted a problem that's easy to remedy, Julian, for someone with your gift." He happened to know a little about this. "Sometimes the eye tricks you. Attempting to be literal, this can happen. Have you studied Michelangelo at all?"

Julian shook his head. He knew the name. "The guy that painted that famous ceiling?"

"Yes—those very figures show what I'm talking about. If you look at those elbows closely, you will see that they don't look realistic at all. But if you stand back, they look fine."

"Really?"

Swann winked at the art teacher. "Yes, really. You see, they look right because they aren't, oddly enough. The eye takes everything in the picture at once and adjusts it to look as it is supposed to look. From down on the floor of the Sistine Chapel, they look perfect. Up close they are strange, almost grotesque. The artist learns how to exaggerate or diminish, where to lengthen or shorten. You have to see it from a distance in your artist's eye while you are up close drawing it."

Julian's eyes opened wide—he knew instantly what Swann was talking about. He leaned close: sure enough, up close was the problem. If he squinted he could imagine seeing it from several feet away. "Huh." He turned with a huge grin. He knew exactly how to fix it. He looked at Mr. van Horn, thrilled.

"Michelangelo was a genius at this. If you look at his famous David sculpture, up close, the head looks way too large, because it is. When you see it high above on a six foot high pedestal where he expected people to see it, it looks perfect; the statue itself is 17 feet tall."

"Wow!" Julian hopped up and down and smiled at van Horn. "You **told** us about that! I remember! It's **perspective!**" He realized at

203

once that over twenty feet away, his head would look way too small if it was actual size.

van Horn felt a buzz—Julian's enthusiasm was infectious—it was rewarding to know that he'd gained something from his class. Swann's wink was extremely gratifying.

"Some time I want to talk with you about doing a drawing for me. Would that be possible?"

"Gosh yes. I'd like that."

"But first, I have a favor to ask: would you ride with us to the airport? I think Kasey would like that. Mason can take you home afterward."

"Can I?!" he grinned at Mr. van Horn as if to share the good feeling with his favorite teacher. "Neato!" He did a couple of typical Julian hops.

"Thank you, Julian. We'll be leaving in a few minutes—do you have everything you'll need?

"OH! My jacket and books! They're in Mr. Barnes' office!"

It was not a coincidence that Barnes was tuned in to the conversation. He had told the Principal that he'd catch up with them later—he had thought better about leaving with them. "Did I hear my name?" He approached.

"Umm, I left my jacket and books in your office." He grimaced.

"That's my fault." He turned to Swann. "Have I time to go retrieve those? The office is probably locked by now."

"Thank you. That would certainly help." Swann didn't want to send Mason.

"I'm on the way…" Barnes left at once.

Andy kept a straight face—he had been afraid that Julian was counting on going home with him and Randall. *this is perfect.*

"Randall, I need a favor." Swann reached out.

Randall leapt forward. Swann had interrupted his train of thought.

"Do you have a few exposures remaining on your roll?"

204

Randall nodded. He had several—half a dozen or so.

"Lewis?" He gestured to Wood. "If I may presume, I'd like you and your wife to pose for a photograph with the artist and his portrait... you too, Kasey."

The surprised faces clearly approved, telling Swann he had a green light. Randall returned to his case for the Nikon.

The Choir teacher and basketball coach exchanged glances: it didn't look like they would get a chance to talk to Swann after all.

Randall the Photographer took charge. He had several shots in mind, including one of Swann. He wouldn't take no for an answer.

Julian had forgotten how far it was to the airport; he was glad, actually, because it gave him time to admire this unique car. It was comfy enough; there was plenty of room, what with Mr. Swann sitting up front with Mason. It was a big surprise when Mason rolled down the privacy window the rest of the way. He'd never seen one of those. Now everyone could talk together. He liked sitting across from Kasey and his parents on this little jump seat. It felt a little weird to be facing them while the car was going the other way, so he sat sideways as much as he could—that way he could see forward if he turned his head. He smiled at Kasey's mom: "Kasey says you're from England! I've never met anyone from there. Do you miss it?" He couldn't figure out anything else to ask.

Candace was surprised by the question—she had not expected to talk with this interesting boy, but was delighted he had made that possible so easily. "Why, no, actually. It was a long time ago. I've lived here in America most of my life, now." She found this boy unique, to say the least. She had begun to see why her son had responded to him so favorably.

"I'm glad. Being homesick is awful." He took the opportunity to look at her eyes; they were just as bright as Kasey's. "Same for me: we moved here when I was only five years old. I forget what it was like in Joliet, mostly." He shook his head slightly. "Messy streets is about all— except for my grandpa and grandma, I don't miss anything." He shrugged. "We came here when they died." He paused. "Well, they were real old." he gave her a big grin: "My mom knew Geraldine—thanks to her, we had a place to go!"

"Do you like it here?"

"Gosh yes! Who wouldn't? We get to go camping in the summer and everything." He nudged Kasey's left knee with his right. "I forgot to mention that before. You're gonna like that!"

Kasey was surprised by his mother's reaction—he was a mix of amused and confused. He had never been camping.

Candace was entertained and reassured: this boy accepted her son without reservation. She caught Swann—he was listening closely. She sent him a reassuring smile. She was open to him going camping—it would do him some good to get out of the house once in a while.

"Boy… I've never been in an airplane…" They had just passed another sign pointing to the airport. Julian stared out the window eagerly. He giggled and bumped Kasey's leg again. "I s'pose you do it all the time… is it fun?" He imagined what he would see out of a plane window. Nothing clear appeared. "Must be interesting, all those teeny people and cars way down below." It didn't sound like it would make a good drawing though… He just had a thought. He bent forward to grab tablet number 4 from his stack of books—it had lots of blank pages. He opened to one and wrote down his name and address. He tore it out and passed it to Kasey. He handed him the sketchbook and pencil. "Tell ya what: write down your address—I'll send you a note. I know I'll think of something I forgot to ask. Besides, I might think of stuff that will come in handy when you come. If you think of something you forgot about, you can send me a note, okay?"

Swann exchanged glances with Mason. *how could I be this fortunate?*

Lewis wanted to see his son's face but couldn't. The flight was long—that would have to do. He studied the headliner instead. Remaining silent was extremely difficult.

Kasey had never been asked to jot down his address—correspondence with a friend was something he had never experienced or contemplated. It took a long minute to remember the Belmont address: after his name he wrote down the Road, city and state, but he could not remember the numbers. He passed the tablet and pencil to his mother—she sent him mail from time to time. He had no occasion to write that information down. His embarrassed blush faded when he noticed that Julian's attention had moved to something out the widow.

"OO, look!" Julian pointed: in the distance a single airplane stood by itself on the apron. That had to be it! It had an open door and stairway.

Mason turned the Packard toward the new Lockheed Jetstar. Swann had acquired one of the first models almost a year ago. It was proven and reliable.

"I'm sorry you can't come along Julian—it will be past your bedtime before I get back, or I'd invite you to join us."

"Gosh." He had never even considered such a thing. He tapped Kasey on the knee. "Lucky you. I bet it's fun."

faster than the train, for sure. Kasey noted the jet engines; they were a surprise. He wasn't sure about the fun part though. The fact that Mr. Swann would be flying with them was reassuring. It did appear to be brand new.

Swann continued, "But you can get a peek inside, how's that?" He turned around. "On the way home, you can ride up front with Mason, if you'd like."

"Wow…" he whispered. He couldn't think of anything to say… it reminded him of taking that ride with Uncle Max last summer. No other scout had done that before. This was the same thing: Special. *how do I say thank you without sounding stupid or something?*

Sometimes it's best not to say anything, Inside Guy advised.

yeah, I guess you're right…   Still, he didn't want to seem ungrateful.

Mr. Swann is a real smart man… he'll understand. He'll know.

Julian got it: *Mr. Swann will be glad I didn't say the same old thing he gets a hundred times a day.* Inside guy had come through again.

He touched Kasey's arm: "Hey! I know!" he turned to Mr. Swann: "Can you stop here a second?" He grinned at Kasey: "You wanna race?"

Kasey couldn't help himself: he grinned at his father, wondering if he'd jump off a cliff if Julian asked. "Why not!" He did not recognize himself. Racing was something he never did—never thought about.

The merry expression on their son's face was so unusual and wonderful, so unlike him they were thrilled. Mason had slowed to a stop. Julian's giggle nearly masked Kasey's—that was a sound they had almost forgotten about.

"No fair starting early," Julian cautioned as Kasey opened the door—waiting for Mason to come around the car was silly—he scooted out quickly.

Grinning wide, Kasey awaited Julian's instructions.

"Tom and Nick do this all the time at camp—easy as pie: we count to three. On three, we take off." He looked at Kasey eagerly. "Ready?" He assumed a starter's crouch.

Kasey stood next to him and aligned his left foot.

"One... two... THREE!" They took off.

Neither boy was athletic, so it was a comical display more than a contest. Swann glanced at the rear view mirror. What he saw reflected in their faces was worth a million dollars. For Swann, that was not a metaphor.

"He has given Kasey back his childhood," Candace said softly as she squeezed her husband's hand. The awkward gangly boy with the hair waving wildly in the breeze was the personification of boyhood joy.

A tear escaped Swann's eye as he signaled Mason to drive slowly toward the plane. He marveled at how that boy was able to trigger such a visceral emotional response—he had not felt anything quite like it before. It seemed so basic, so elemental. He saw the same effect in the rear view mirror.

Kasey heard Julian catching up; he glanced to the side and saw his cheerful determination. It forced him to put on the steam—head down, he renewed his effort—they were nearly there.

Julian was a few steps behind, panting hard. He stopped awkwardly—a pair of shoes had appeared in front of him suddenly, having just stepped off the ladder. He stopped just in time. At his right, Kasey was happily catching his breath—another new sensation.

"Sorry..." he brushed his hair to the side.

"What for?!" Julian exclaimed. "You won, fair and square!" He gave Kasey a friendly hug.

Kasey didn't know what to say—he had never felt like this before.

The pilot was his own height, a little shorter than he expected. "Hi! I'm Julian. I almost bumped into you!" He giggled. "Are you the pilot?"

"Steward, Sir. Franklin. At your service, sir." He had been called and was expecting the party. The footrace was an unexpected novelty. "You run well, sir."

"Thanks." He knew the man was just being nice.

Swann wished he could have brought Randall along to capture this on film. "This young man is here to get a brief tour, Franklin. Lead the way, please."

"Neato!" Julian exclaimed and reached for Kasey's always handy belt. He hopped over happily and tugged. "You get to go up first: you won the race!" Skipping around, he pushed from behind: "We gotta get a move on!"

Swann waited until they were at the top. At the foot of the ladder he addressed Candace directly "I hope the small delay won't matter... we can make up for it once we're airborne."

"I don't know how to thank you for what you have done, Mr. Swann." She looked at him more directly than was her custom. "Thanks to that boy, our son has had his boyhood restored. Probably just in time." She held her husband around the waist. "We had not realized it had been pushed aside. He will be a better man. A happier man."

Lewis' arm around her shoulder enabled him to show that he agreed strongly. His wife was very good at expressing insights in a nutshell.

After the mini-tour, Swann accompanied Julian to the Packard. "Thank you, Julian." He looked at him seriously. "I don't know if you realize how much you have done for Kasey already." He studied Julian's face closely. This was a young man, not a boy. The perception was as humbling as it was instructive: why were adults so apt to be so dismissive of and about teens? The drawing was one of insight and perception as well as skill and craft—it could have been done by a mature, experienced, well-weathered in his mid-forties artist. But it was created by a fifteen year old that hopped up and down with glee at the slightest provocation as if he were a six year old. To what extent was his attention to Kasey purposeful?

"Thanks, Mr. Swann." He mulled it over. "I try to put myself in his place is all—try to feel what he does, in a way. Moving here must be kinda scary, considering. What would **I** want? No big deal, really. I do that when I draw people—I try to see through their eyes, feel what they are feeling. Helps me do a better job—helps it mean something." He tipped his head. "I don't actually think about it much until later—that's when I want to see if what I have on the paper is what I see in my head, not just my eyes." Somehow, he knew that Mr. Swann understood what he was talking about.

"Did you let him win your little race?" It was obvious that Kasey was not used to running. A scout in good condition, as Julian was, would have an edge.

"No." He gave Swann a rare direct eye to eye statement: "I forced him to try. With his long legs, I figured he could," he shrugged. "I know what you mean, but I wanted him to **try** to win. It had to be honest. Otherwise, it wouldn't mean anything, really—it wouldn't be a big deal. Besides, if it isn't fun, why do it?" He noticed the grinning face and waving hand in the window. He waved back with a typical Julian bounce. "See what I mean?"

Indeed… the proof was right there, purposeful or not. Swann took the liberty of holding Julian by the shoulders. "We must leave. I will be in touch soon. Please say hello to your mother for me, will you?"

"Thanks, Mr. Swann. You're a nice man. I like you a lot." Julian didn't usually say that out loud. This time he thought it was important.

210

He could tell it made Mr. Swann feel good. He watched him return up the ladder. He turned to Mason; his eyes betrayed how eager he was: *it's not every day you get to ride up front in a Packard!*

He's kinda tall

17   *Flaming Arrows to the rescue*

"I've got a problem," Julian announced the second Randall appeared.

The school day had ended minutes earlier, and the abrupt greeting as he was coming out of Mr. Frankel's door was unexpected. Yesterday, Julian had stayed after school with Mr. van Horn—something special about his pencil technique. Randall thought he would do that again today. The expression on Julian's face told him that this was something else. He pulled him to the side—the Friday rush to get out of the building made hearing difficult. "What's going on?"

"Give you one guess—" he didn't wait for Randall's response. "It's Geraldine again." He rolled his eyes.

Randall frowned. This didn't make sense yet. He tilted his head, expecting clarification. He knew who Geraldine was, but he was unaware that she was a source of problems. This was one of those occasions where Julian had brought him into a conversation he had started three pages ago; it took a while to catch up.

"She's back at it again to get me a 'girlfriend.'

Randall's eyes went wide: "That's right! I forgot all about Rita!" It was Geraldine that outfitted him for that dance several weeks ago. "Not another dance!"

"Almost as bad: a movie!"

"Movie?! What movie?"

"Dunno—I get to pick one, I think. Anyway, I'm hoping Nick and Tom will help me figure out what to do. I'm gonna go to Sparky's. They always go there after school."

Randall paused—Julian didn't know that his after school schedule had undergone a revision—along with his morning transport. There had been no way to bring Julian 'up to date' on that—or the way things were with him and Andy. But Julian remained at the top of his priority list, so it was Andy that would have to make allowances. Still, he was now riding to and from school with Andy—his bicycle was in its hutch at home—on the inactive list for now. "Um… is it okay if Andy comes along?"

"Yeah! He and Tom are friends—they're both in the Troop!" He thought about that. "Maybe he has an idea or two—he's a senior, he probably had to face this too." Most kids did, as far as he knew.

"Good—he'll be in the Cardinal Room—he always touches base with Mr. L after school."

They headed for Randall's locker as they usually did when school was out for the day.

—∿—

Andy was waiting for Coach Switcher to finish talking to one of the wrestlers; he'd been told to hang around in his office—it was near the entrance to the Boy's P.E. locker area—all the coaches and P.E. staff had a cubicle they called an office. Room enough for a teacher desk and chair, filing cabinet and single student conference chair, it was cramped and stuffy—not made for spending a lot of time in, Andy didn't think. Not where he wanted to end up working, that's for sure.

The door opened—true to his word, he had returned in two minutes, not five. "So, what can I do ya for?" he chimed happily, leaving the door open—unless it was confidential, he liked the air to circulate as much as possible.

Andy was ready: he plopped a set of prints that he and Randall had made of last Friday's game, including a few of the pre-game shots taken in the locker area. "We have a new photographer on the Cardinal staff. I wanted you to see what he can do—it's time we did a better job of covering the wrestling team." He sat back and waited for the reaction he knew he'd get—the only people who had seen these were Mr. L and the football coach.

It took a minute to sink in. Photography was not an area of interest particularly, but there was something about these... *I know these boys!* He looked more closely. "When were these taken?"

"Last Friday, just before the game." Andy was pleased at the reaction he saw—it was what he expected. Randall's work was way beyond the usual; these could have been taken by a Life Magazine photographer. He waited for the coach to take a second look at them all. "Anyway, I thought it would be good to have a shot or two of the wresting team in action. Might raise interest, especially now that football season is over. Basketball doesn't kick in for a few weeks, so…"

The possibilities of this were impossible to ignore—but he didn't have a home match until week after next.

"Mr. L showed me the wresting article in the '54 yearbook. You and my scoutmaster looked great."

"You're in Mark's Troop?" he grinned.

"Sure am!" He could see it in the coach's eyes: *they were friends in high school.* That gave Andy the reporter a special connection—just what he was after.

"Well: what do you have in mind?" Any kid that worked under Mark would be reliable.

"I thought we could sit in on a practice or two next week to get an idea of what kind of things to look for, let the guys get to know us, you know—so that when we cover a match it wouldn't cause any problems—they'll be expecting us, and we'll have an idea of what kind of shots to take. Randall will give you a contact sheet—all you need to do is mark the ones you'd like to see in The Cardinal—and in the Yearbook. He can also take the team picture—save you some money, actually."

That got Les Switcher's attention. "These are **free**?"

"Yep." Andy could see the green light flashing already; in a week or two, he could make his "special project" pitch.

215

"Has Coach Brodie seen these?!" *stupid question… of course he has*. Les could picture him seeing these for the first time—he would like to have been there to see that—he was forever bellyaching about the pictures in the **Times-Herald**.

—ᴍ—

Mr. L was delighted to see Julian show up with Randall—he wanted to sound him out. This boy's work was outstanding, and his connections were perfect. *he'll be at the center of things next semester*. Having him aboard would likely be very handy all the way around. In fact, from what little the Black boy had said on Monday, he too might become an asset: the school paper could well be a safe haven and part of his support system. This room would be perfect for serving as a "Home Base," and that's what he hoped to make it—if the Student Body office didn't have the inside track on that.

"Andy should be back pretty soon; he's down talking to the wrestling coach." He nodded, "good to see you again, Julian."

"Thanks." Julian liked this teacher—he was different… kinda laid back. "What did you think of Randall's photos?" Not that there was any doubt, but he felt obliged to ask.

"Very pleased, yes indeed!" *perfect…* "Your recommendation was right on. He certainly knows what he is doing." Lest the subject get changed, he continued: "which reminds me: my compliments on the portrait you drew of our 'new student.' You know what you're doing too. Tell me: have you done any kind of cartoon drawing?"

cartoon? Julian drew a blank. "You mean like the funnies?"

"Not exactly. Those strips usually have a story—which is okay, of course. Recurring characters are fun too."

"Yeah, I like Pogo a lot, and Peanuts, naturally." He liked the realistic ones too. "I like Prince Valiant and Tarzan in the Sunday paper. Rip Kirby has good drawings… I don't care much about the story though." He shrugged. He liked the car in that most of all—and Rip's glasses and pipe were kinda neat.

216

Ladendorff opened his top drawer and pulled out last week's **New Yorker**. "I was thinking more about single frame cartoons." He flipped through the magazine and found one. He handed it over. "Something like this." While Julian flipped through the magazine, he reached for yesterday's **Times-Herald**. The editorial page usually had one or two.

what the... Julian was taken by surprise. He had not seen anything like this before. Cartoon had an entirely new definition suddenly. He stepped over to a desk and pulled out a chair. He needed to look at this more closely.

"Flip through—there are several—all are very different. People compete to have their cartoons printed in there—the artist is allowed to do whatever he wants, pretty much." Now that he thought about it, giving Julian some time to think about this was a very good idea. Clearly, this boy had a brain as well as an eye. It would be a mistake to rush him into this. Ladendorff was a good teacher as well as an opportunist. Opening doors was as important as anything—allowing his students to explore and discover made all the difference in the world. He had a hunch that Julian's potential was significant—he would have something very special. Watching him in the cafeteria came back to him—*he works very fast, and rarely uses an eraser*. This boy saw it in his head before his pencil hit the paper. That was very unique—he had never seen that before.

"My mom takes that magazine," Randall commented. He didn't care for it much. High society material... the Bridge Club ladies like it. He shrugged. "Julian has some good cartoons in the Troop 9 Scrapbook." Mr. L should have a look at those.

Andy popped in, smiling wide; he gave Mr. L a thumbs up signal. "We're expected at practice on Monday!"

Ladendorff would have been surprised to hear otherwise.

Julian was concentrating on another cartoon and missed what had been said. He did that sometimes—got so involved in what he was looking at, the rest of the world vanished temporarily. Sometimes Inside Guy gave him a poke, but not always.

weird—this one was weird. *I don't get this one at all. huh.* He shook his head. *I guess they don't have to be funny...* he didn't see the point: *if it isn't funny, why bother?*

Maybe it's funny to other people, Inside Guy theorized.

I s'pose you're right... still, he couldn't imagine who would like this one, actually. It wasn't even very well drawn... *kinda ugly, really.*

The frown on Julian's face caught Ladendorff's attention; he waited for an explanation. He was surprised that the boy had gotten so absorbed. This was proof positive that he was giving serious attention to this—New Yorker cartoons were often very oblique. He didn't always understand them himself—but he didn't admit that openly.

Randall's comment to Andy about going to Sparky's had gone unnoticed; he knocked on the desk: "Hello?"

Julian's head popped up: "Huh?"

"Sparky's?"

"Ohmygosh—sorry." Julian stood up quickly. He turned to Mr. L. "Umm... could I borrow this for the weekend?" He wanted to take his time with this. He needed to figure these things out. He didn't know why, exactly, but he felt strongly about it. "I can give it back first thing on Monday—"

"Of course. You can have it for as long as you need... no hurry." The telltale signs of a challenged student were there: this had made his day. Sometimes the best days were an accident. *good thing to keep in mind.*

"Thanks." He didn't know what else to add, so he shrugged instead and turned to Andy with a big grin: "Now I get to ride in your car! I've been wanting to do that."

"After you, Assistant Troop Scribe!" Andy nudged with his elbow. "Did you know you were in the presence of a Flying Arrow Patrol member?" He kept a straight face.

Randall tilted his head. *that's right—I remember that, actually.* "How could I forget?" He pushed Julian to get him started. "This is your party, lead the way."

Julian had never seen his bicycle put into a car trunk before; it didn't matter whether or not the "lid" would close. He thought calling it a lid was stupid: it was more of a door. Calling the luggage compartment a trunk was the problem: trunks had lids. Mr. Swann's Packard had a real trunk in back. No way would his bicycle fit in that. He could have just met them at Sparky's, but Andy seemed to want to give him a ride; no big deal.

The back seat of Andy's car was a new experience for sure. He had been in the back seat of several cars in his life, but this one was different. It was more 'broken in,' to put it nicely. He had hopped in back automatically without thinking—he didn't have to be told that the front seat was Randall's space now. The fact that he hadn't been invited to sit up front confirmed that he was probably right about where Randall's affections had landed.

"Sorry about the muffler," Andy always said that for form's sake. He wasn't sorry, especially, but he was embarrassed.

Julian checked out the headliner—a couple of tears. Something with a sharp corner had been shoved into it. Lots of stains on the back seat... yep, this was a true used car. Nothing smelled bad. They didn't have far to go, only a few blocks. He couldn't think of anything to say, so he just looked ahead. Randall was almost in the center of the seat, not next to the door. Andy was driving with his left hand on the steering wheel. No telling where his right hand was or what it might be doing. Julian had to smile—he wished there was a way to tell Randall that he approved. Maybe a chance would come along. *oop! we're here already.*

Andy pulled into the drive-in and parked about halfway out. It was customary to leave the first few slots empty in case somebody wanted car-hop service. Even this time of year, some kids wanted that— especially ones on a date. Sometimes it was so full inside it was the fastest way to get served. There was no drive thru service at Sparky's.

"Is it okay to leave my books in the car?" The booths in there were kind of cozy.

"Might as well," Andy replied. "Just leave 'em next to mine or Randall's." Made sense… he planned on taking Julian home anyway.

Randall could see Tom and Nick—Julian was right: they had a booth by the window—the same one as the last time he and Julian were here. *they must have it reserved.* Julian had just run over waving at them with one of his sketchbooks.

"Hey, we have company today!" The Cheshire Cat grin suddenly appearing in the window evoked a fond memory or two—Nick had seen that more than once last summer. No one else ever did that.

Tom waved a greeting. It was always fun to have Julian around. He beckoned him to hurry inside. He pointed at him then swung his finger around to the empty space next to him in the booth.

Nick couldn't help noticing Randall and Andy going toward the door—something about the way they were walking made his antenna hum a familiar tune—he saw himself and Tom briefly. *what do you know…* He liked what he saw—he liked it a lot.

Julian was right behind them and did a beeline for the booth; he scooted in next to Tom. Andy and Randall sat opposite, next to Nick.

"Hey, Ace," Tom gave Julian's shoulder a gentle fist bump.

"I was hopin' you were here—I need to apologize for missing the game on Friday—I hear you were great!" Randall's account had been very detailed.

"No sweat—with all the rain, it was hard to see what was going on half the time."

"Yeah, but I really wanted to go. I'm glad we won, anyway."

Tom expected to hear a why—instead he saw a frown.

"I had to go to a special meeting. Mark was there too. But I'm not s'posed to tell about it yet." He put his finger to his lips.

Andy and Randall put their hands over their mouths—they were surprised Julian had brought it up. Everybody had to promise Mr. Swann to keep it secret.

220

Nick was curious, but he knew Julian well: he could keep a secret as well as anyone he knew. The fact that the scoutmaster was there meant that they would know about it at some point. They had been well trained by Mark to respect the need to keep some things confidential. He noted that Andy and Randall appeared to be in on it.

"So, what else is new?" Tom had concluded that these guys were here on purpose.

"It's silly, maybe, but kind of important: I'm s'posed to find someone to go with on a double date to the movies." His face was borderline terror and panic. "I don't know what to do." He was supposed to have this figured out by now—he'd been postponing it for a long time, since before that dance.

"What's so hard about that?" Tom wanted to laugh, but he knew Julian was serious.

Nick didn't understand the reason Julian was being forced. "So, who says you have to?"

"My mom—and Geraldine. Geraldine mostly, but my mom is going along with it." He shrugged. You have to do what your mom says, that's all. He didn't say that out loud, of course. "I heard them talking in the kitchen on Saturday... they plan to make a big deal out of it tomorrow after Thanksgiving dinner."

Nick allowed Tom to take the lead.

"Like I said, what's so hard?"

Julian cleared his throat and extended his left hand: "One. I don't know any girls. Two, I don't know anybody who wants to go on a double date; three: I've never gone on a double date. Four: I've never asked anyone to go on a date to begin with. Five," he looked at Tom in desperation, "I don't know what movie to pick." He shrugged. "I figured you had to do something like this once and could help me out a little..." Tom the hero could do almost anything, really.

The look on Julian's face was genuine, although keeping a straight face was about all he could do. Anyway, a fellow Flaming Arrow was in trouble: there was only one thing to do. "This is top priority: this is an official Flaming Arrow Project as of this minute!" He swung around and gave a loud summons across to the counter: "Yo! **Frankie!**"

Frankie, the Troop 9 bugler heard his name called; he turned and saw Tom and Julian in the booth with three other guys. He waved back.

Tom beckoned: "Bring your coke over here." he pointed to the space next to Julian.

"Later," Frankie said to the kid next to him; the Assistant Scoutmaster tone of voice was unmistakable. He grabbed his coke and half finished bag of chips and trotted over.

His stool was grabbed at once by one of the kids standing near the door—a small waiting line had formed—after all, it was Friday, one of the busiest of the week: you had to be seated to be served. Frankie almost bumped into the waitress on her way to the same booth. Fortunately, she wasn't delivering an order.

After putting his glass down, he extended his left hand to Julian for the official Troop 9 handshake. "Hey, how's it hangin." The standard boy greeting was meaningless, essentially. It filled the blank space and was safe to use in public. He nodded at Randall—he knew him from Concert Band Class.

Georgia rolled her eyes and put her left hand on her hip. "Are we ready to order now?" Her sarcasm was thinly disguised. She was glad to see the blond one again—he always left a tip.

"OO!" Julian grabbed the plastic menu stand—he always got a milkshake after checking for new flavors.

"Burger and Fries, Cherry coke for me," Andy chimed. He turned to Randall.

"Cherry coke and a couple of chocolate chip cookies, please." He didn't want much—supper was not far off.

"Maplenut!" Julian had never tried one of those.

"What size?"

"Oh… regular size. I don't have room for a big one. Thanks, Georgia" He always used her name; he could tell she liked that. She was kind of top heavy like Rita, but didn't stink of perfume.

Frankie held up his nearly empty glass, indicating he needed a refill. "So," he turned to Tom: "What's up?"

"This one's right up your alley: our Troop 9 Assistant Scribe needs a double date to the movies.

"What movie?"

Julian gave him a 'How do I know?' face.

Nick stepped in: "Julian doesn't have a girlfriend. He's following orders from headquarters here." He made quote marks in the air. "We're hoping you have a quick fix. Any ideas?"

"Are you kidding?" he looked at Julian straight in the eye. "Get real: you can pick any girl in the school! Li'l Abner?" He shook his head at Andy. "I was there—I saw that famous kiss happen."

I'll never live that down....

"Appearances can be deceiving... Julian was drafted to go that dance—he didn't have any choice. He spent weeks taking dance lessons to get ready. I know what he feels like—I've never asked a girl to go to a movie either—or anything else." Nick didn't need to mention that he didn't much mind that. Neither he nor Julian were "into girls." That's one thing you didn't announce to the world if you had any sense.

could have fooled me! Frankie paused to think... he got it finally. *I should have figured that out, come to think about it.* He mulled it over briefly. *odd request, but doable.* Actually, now that he thought about it, it should be easy enough—all the girls in second lunch were waiting in line to have Julian draw their picture. Finding a safe one was the trick. "Sounds like a job for Rhonda—she knows practically everyone."

Julian was paying full attention—he didn't know Rhonda, of course. He waited expectantly... so did everyone else at the table: they all had the same "handicap" when it came to girls. Fortunately, they didn't have a troublesome mother complicating their life.

"Rhonda and I go way back," Frankie explained. "We're buddies—**mostly**," he added. "She's not out to corral me or anything. We just have fun," he shrugged. "I'll get her to find the right one..." the humor of Julian's predicament appealed to his better nature. "This is a one-time thing? You're not trying to get a girlfriend or anything, I hope."

Randall laughed at that one. Julian shook his head slowly, dead serious. Tom and Nick glanced at each other, laughs successfully suppressed.

"Right. So when do you need to take care of this?" Mothers usually had deadlines.

"She didn't give me an exact date..." Julian thought about what he had overheard. "Any time before the end of the semester. They want to be sure I do it before Kasey gets back. They figure I won't have the time after that."

They're right, too, Inside Guy observed. He was tuned in.

"Casey? Did he go somewhere?" Norman's assistant patrol leader Casey Snyder was his best prospect to be the next Bugler.

"No, no: different guy. This one is new. He's moving here from Boston. I'm gonna be his special Buddy." He grimaced—he wasn't supposed to talk about that yet. He could see the worried look on Andy and Randall's faces. "You'll find out about it at the next Troop meeting."

"Oh, I get it." *so he's a scout; cool.* "So—back to the movie. Before Christmas—they always have a new movie coming out around then." He nodded vigorously. "That will help too. Tell you what: I'll give Rhonda a buzz tonight—maybe take her out tomorrow or Friday. I don't think it will take her long to come up with a name or two."

Julian sat back, relieved at last. "Boy. This is great, Frankie. I owe ya big for this." He could almost see the expression on Geraldine's face. That was gonna be **sweet**.

"One more detail," Frankie nudged. "Who is the other couple? Might make a difference."

Details like that would never have entered Julian's mind. A back to the starting line expression formed. "I'm s'posed to decide that too. I was gonna ask Sid, but I don't think he would go through with it, to be honest."

Frankie grinned wide. "Don't sweat it: Rhonda and I will do it. She'll jump at the chance to go on a double date with Li'l Abner!" He laughed. *she'll brag about that for months.*

Tom sealed the deal: "We need an official Flaming Arrow Victory cheer." This was Nick's assignment.

yikes...   He improvised: "Make a fist..." he grabbed Julian's hand and pulled it upward above the middle of the table. "Okay, men: hands in the center!" Tom, Julian and Frankie reached up and grabbed as well, forming an irregular triangle. "All for one..." he grinned at Tom.

"One for all!" Tom responded. *perfect.*   He punched Julian on the right shoulder.

Julian beamed wide... he was the luckiest kid in town, no doubt about it. "Thanks, you guys."

Tom nudged him silently. This was a very special guy in his life. There wasn't anything he wouldn't do for Julian.

"As long as we're gathered together, I have a couple of questions about the game." Frankie wanted to know about the secret play—with all the rain, he could not figure out how they pulled that off.

While they talked about the game, Julian relaxed and let his mind wander—he wasn't much interested in football, to be honest. Unconsciously, his train of thought returned to an unfinished piece of business: the cartoon. He had a sudden flash—sometimes that happened. He opened his trusty sketchbook to a blank page and drew a square. One would need a ruler to detect any flaw. He proceeded to draw a caricature of himself on the right half of the space. He gave himself a goofy expression, and showed the eyes looking to the right. His right hand was raised at the elbow, with his thumb pointing away to the right. He made a few wrinkles in the shirt, and exaggerated the belt sagging loosely—he was going for an after school end of the day look. Just for fun, he showed the zipper down an inch or so. He exaggerated the size of the zipper pull.

Randall and Andy paid close attention to this—the game details were easy to follow at the same time. The speed at which Julian drew was absolutely amazing.

After checking it closely, Julian drew a second figure standing in the left side of the square. Very different: the figure was wearing a perfectly pressed blazer, and a necktie. The shoulder line was at the top of the box, the head not visible. The person was too tall to fit into the frame. A few detail lines indicating pockets, the long necktie, and a shiny belt buckle. Under the box, he wrote the caption for his first cartoon:

'He's kinda tall.'

Aware that Randall was watching, he turned the tablet around and pushed it across the table.

Instantly, they burst into laughter.

Julian, it seems, had been discovered by a second Muse. He reached for the maplenut milkshake—he was not aware it had been delivered. *mmm... tasty...*

18 *November wrapup*

a turkey and dumplings

Julian helped himself to another blob of mashed potatoes. They were perfect for what he really wanted: more of his mom's gravy. He liked nearly everything she cooked, but there were extra good things that she only did on Thanksgiving: turkey gravy and her own cranberry sauce, especially. Those she learned from Grandma Mattson. Super tasty, full of chunks of gizzard and liver and mushrooms. He made a crater and filled it with gravy; after mixing it all together he filled his spoon; he took his time to swallow. "Y'know, those fancy dinners were good, but this is better, Mom. Maybe Sharples' ought to hire you to show 'em how to make a really good gravy." He helped himself to another spoonful. "Yep."

Geraldine agreed, but didn't want to encourage the idea of Francine working for anyone else: she had become a key component in her real estate business—she was arguably the most prestigious realtor in town, and she wanted that to remain the case.

"Why, thank you, Julian." Her boy's enthusiasm and cheerfulness always made her feel good—now, after the events of the last few days, she had a new appreciation of his abilities as well. She didn't deserve all the credit for that, but she had been a good parent and was entitled to some of it.

The time was right: Julian sprang his surprise. "Aunt Geraldine, I have a question for you." He said this matter-of-factly, as if it was an everyday kind of question. "What movie do you think I should pick for my double date?"

Fortunately, Geraldine had finished swallowing the sip of water she had just taken—otherwise she would have sprayed everyone at the table. She was unable to answer for a number of reasons—first of all, she didn't pay attention to what movies were showing unless she was planning to go to one, which was almost never. Second of all, she was planning to ask Julian that very question after dessert—she had that all planned. Her goal of getting that accomplished by the end of the year was Item One on her agenda. Now, instead of leading the charge, she was on the other end—that **never** happened. She stared at Julian wide-eyed and speechless.

"I mean, I never took a girl to a movie before. I want to pick one we both will like." Only made sense to keep that in mind. He always sought a way to make it fun. *nobody wants to sit through a movie they don't like.*

Geraldine expected Francine to assist but all she saw was much like what she felt herself. Obviously, she wasn't expecting this either.

By accident, Julian had just discovered something very important: when one knows an attack is imminent, make the first move. He waited for Inside Guy to pat him on the back for a change.

Took you long enough to figure that out. Inside Guy always saw the negative element.

"Be right back," Julian scooted his chair back. He had the movie page in this morning's **Times-Herald** all ready. It had been lying in plain sight on his drawing table all day.

Geraldine hoped Francine had an explanation. She was expecting to pry this out of him, and here he was, on the next page!

"I had no idea he was even thinking about this," she said, getting up to exchange the turkey platter for the pumpkin pie. "He hasn't said a thing." She stopped in mid-step: "Did he overhear us talking the other day?"

"I don't see how—you had the radio turned up as usual." *he was practicing typing—made an awful din.*

Her boy was full of surprises these days. Francine was enormously pleased.

Geraldine was conflicted. This was where she wanted Julian to be going, but she had planned to be in charge, so she was disappointed as well. That was new and she didn't much like it. It had been a while since she had done any self-analysis. Reluctantly, she had to recognize that she had an imperfection that needed attention.

Julian stopped off to empty his tank—made it easier to have dessert: Hazel from across the street had made one of her famous pies. Those were really good too—almost as good as her cookies. He stepped over to wash his hands—when his mom was around, that was required. It gave him a chance to look in the mirror. He winked at the blond dummy who smirked back.

The nifty part of this was getting that out of the way so he could get the letter to Kasey finished by bedtime. Letting Geraldine pick the movie was perfect.

—〰—

b   a rainy day at Belmont

This comfy chair was the best thing at Belmont. So 'at home'— and so conducive for just thinking and reading... Kasey wondered if there was any way he could take it with him. He'd like to keep it forever: his unusual physical requirements were difficult to satisfy.

He had paused briefly to reflect on the passage he had just read—it might be useful as a reference in the paper that was due on Tuesday. A dreary rainy day out—surprisingly warm for this time of year—usually it was snowing by now. Even so, the fire in the common room fireplace was welcome. He took another moment to reflect on his circumstances. Doing a routine assignment seemed strange, all things considered. He had not had competing priorities before now—it was different from playing the piano, which required managing two different sets of fingers. Here he had to finish up the old and plan the new simultaneously.

This place had its good points, he had to admit; but aside from this chair and the cozy fireplace, the list of what he would really miss was likely to be fairly short. Understandably, the about to happen change in his life had preoccupied him for days. He didn't have any doubts or second thoughts, but he wasn't eager to leave. The contradiction confused him; shouldn't he be at home helping out? His parents faced a huge task—moving an entire household was a major job. They assured him that Mr. Swann had taken care of that. All he needed to worry about was wrapping up his affairs here. First on that list was when—or if—he should tell his housemates. He was leery about that— the kind of farewell party they were capable of throwing did not appeal: he was not a party boy. Those things tended to be at someone's expense—usually the "guest of honor's." *boys will be boys...*

will I miss any of them? Probably, a little; he didn't have any ill feelings or grudges. He wasn't especially close to them personally— their families were not connected in any sense, professional or social. But he had spent four and a half years here with two of them. Edison was the only new one this year. That didn't make them a second family—more like a special boys club. No, it was the suddenness of this that made it difficult. On the other hand, would knowing about it for months have been of any value?

This was all speculation, since he had never had this experience. Presumably his dedication to the task, so to speak, his commitment, might have been reduced if he had been planning to leave all along. Perhaps it was better this way after all.

Having to sort this out by himself was a mix too—he didn't need any extended farewells, or any 'oh, are you still here?' wisecracks from Hayden, well intended as they might be. He didn't know of any other mid-year departures. Unusual, certainly, but he doubted if it was completely unique.

what about my teachers? do they know? They must have been told by the administration. Would it make a difference? His English and History professors were going to be hard to replace. He doubted if any of the teachers at Jackson were PhDs. Did that matter? He had met them, but that was hardly a basis for assessing their excellence. He was going to miss Professor Marchbank, that was certain. *I wonder if I could stay in touch with him...*

230

The career implications remained an unknown. The only concern was whether or not he would need the Belmont pedigree. He had all but mastered the oboe—about all he needed there was a repertoire for auditions; or should he reconsider his career options? That was not particularly attractive, though he wasn't a dedicated oboe enthusiast. He had learned The Swan as if he was going to stay—he enjoyed playing it; he hadn't seriously explored any other career path. And then there was the social issues: what will it be like—not only to be in a public school, but one where he was likely to be regarded with suspicion and hostility? He'd been sheltered from that all his life, by and large. He was aware that aside from the dark pigment he didn't look like most Blacks—in fact, he tended to forget that he was anything different. He knew he wasn't, really, but there were a lot of uninformed people out there. But what he needed to be prepared for was an unknown. Was he correctly informed about the South to begin with? He had no specific authority to base any opinions on; assumptions were always a bad idea, always led to trouble. Preconceptions were just as dangerous. On the other hand, never having to deal with these issues was not very wise either—he couldn't hide in a private school north of Boston all his life. *you have to learn how to swim if you expect to get across deep water...*

Indeed: there was the matter of what kind of home life he wanted once his education had been completed. Did he want a wife and children? If so, shouldn't he be getting ready? He had been deprived of any opportunity to prepare for building a family of his own. His hormones were not a problem at this point, but he couldn't expect that to remain the case indefinitely. One of the secret attractions of this whole thing was the built in factor of having girls his own age around asking the same questions—an area no one had addressed. Belmont was an all boys' school—the annual mixer was a decades old tradition, but it was a token event and nothing more. Perhaps the Health class he would be taking will deal with these questions.

His ruminations were interrupted:

"Mail Call," Hayden announced, entering the room with his typical swagger. An ongoing need to be important always determined his manner of delivery—subtlety and finesse were not in his nature, nor a part of his program. He was unable to simply hand a letter to its recipient: he needed the public thank you for having troubled to collect it from the in box on their behalf. Besides, he enjoyed keeping track of who was getting mail—where it had come from, who had sent it—these tidbits were handy at times. He was able to retain that information indefinitely. Why he had a need to know wasn't a question asked openly; most presumed he was hungering to receive one himself. Kasey didn't recall that ever happening, but it could have—the mailbox was out of sight downstairs.

Bemused, he watched the familiar ritual—today everyone was getting something—not surprising, since the holiday break was right around the corner. He wasn't expecting anything himself, of course. Spending most weekends at home removed the need to send him a letter. He had no correspondents, and both his magazines had been delivered for the month. He was content to watch—who knows, Hayden might manage to say something new or amusing—sometimes, his barbs were well aimed. Even so, this ritual was unlikely to be on his nostalgia list.

"So… today we begin with Sir Lawrence! 3 items, sir." He held up a 5x5. "Perfumed as usual—we all know who that's from!" He delivered it delicately, as if it was fragile. "Insufficient postage on this one… must be from Grandpa. And, the one from mom and dad."

"Next, it's Big Dubbya, wunnerful, wunnerful Wyatt." He held one up to the light. "Heavy this time, Dub! Must have a letter with the card… or a few photos." He looked at the postmark. "Ah, they're still in Bermuda. That explains it." He stepped to the next chair.

"King Leo the Lionhearted has a letter from Queens for starters, and…" he counted the others, dramatically fanned out like a poker hand. "Five Season's Greetings." He presented them with a mini bow of obeisance. "All is well in the realm."

"Saint Joseph," he held up an oversize envelope and peered at it closely, as if he had x-ray vision. "Of course: plane tickets for the flight to Florida…" he held up two 4x6 envelopes, one red, the other white. "Seasons Greetings."

At this point Kasey's attention drifted inward. He opened the flyleaf of the book he was reading to peek at the 8x10 Randall had given him after the Jackson High faculty meeting. Having that had turned out to be more than comforting. It affirmed, it verified… and it triggered reliving the moment—he heard the Rachmaninoff in the background. It

232

didn't make sense, but he seemed to know exactly where he was in the score when this moment was preserved—it seemed to be almost a live recording—it made him feel just as he had at that moment.

Indulging himself for long was not going to be allowed: Hayden had stepped close and broken through—

"Can I have a drum roll and a fanfare, please? We have a first!"

Edison was a good mimic; he did a passable mouth imitation of this—he had a sense of humor—Kasey liked him a lot.

"It's Kasey at the Bat Day! A day all will celebrate for years to come!" He held up a large 9x12 envelope for all to see. The size alone was a surprise—but what made it very special was the drawing on the back—it depicted a cartoon face peeking out of a split, waving a hand at the viewer—the tousled hair a parody of Julian's wavy locks. Hayden did a slow parade around the room and showed it to everyone long enough for them to get a good look. The wide-eyed grins that followed seeing it built suspense as Hayden had intended. After each had seen it, he held it flat in his hands and slowly stepped in front of Kasey. With a bow, he presented it. "From your surprise-to-us-friend in North Carolina."

Kasey didn't need to see the mischievous grin and twinkle in Hayden's eye. The blush that he knew must be revealing how embarrassed—and how **thrilled** he was, could not be prevented. He felt exposed suddenly. He had never felt that before. The question about whether or not to tell his housemates had just been taken out of his hands; he didn't control this any more than he controlled anything else in his life. He took the envelope gently, as if it was fragile. Hanging wide open in shock, his mouth morphed into a wide grin and he issued a short laugh. The cartoon was wonderful—he could see Julian at once—it reminded him of the expression on his face when they were filling out the menu cards at the banquet. He looked at Hayden in disbelief—he was at a complete loss, unable to say a word.

Hayden was prepared for this—he had stopped by his room to fetch the letter opener off his desk. He presented it to Kasey, again with a bow. He had never seen Kasey nonplussed before. That was a treat.

Kasey was expected to use it **now! and here!** He didn't see any alternative. Curiosity wouldn't allow him to wait—the instinct to rush

233

madly to his room with this was blocked. On purpose, Hayden was standing squarely in the way.

Kasey was a realist. Everyone was staring at him, waiting. Once he recovered from the shock, he was able to proceed. The letter opener was perfect; he returned it to Hayden and peeked inside: three sheets of paper and a page size piece of lightweight card stock. He pulled the contents out: three typewritten pages sprinkled with hand drawn illustrations; a large cartoon was mounted on the card. Depicted on the right side was the same tousle haired character, pointing his thumb at a well dressed person standing next to him with a Belmont Coat of Arms patch on the breast pocket—the necktie knot was at the very top of the cartoon box, no head visible. The caption forced him to burst into robust, hearty laughter.

The boys were amazed and delighted—they had never heard or seen Kasey respond like this to anything—they had to see this! They jumped out of their chairs and hurried over.

Kasey glanced at it again, grinned wide, and handed it to Hayden.

A ring of very curious housemates surrounded his comfy chair. They huddled close to get a good look. "Take it easy, take it easy," Hayden raised it high. "I'll pass it around." The cardboard panel was ideal for this.

Kasey was worried for a minute—he was grateful to Hayden for keeping it out of harm's way. While they were distracted, he read the letter:

> Hiya Kasey!
>
> Happy Thanksgiving! I just had dinner with my Mom and Geraldine (she's my Mom's boss). I don't know if you remember her or not—she was at the special Sunday Supper at Randall's place.

{ a cartoon figure of Geraldine is plugged in at the right }

> Sometime I wish you could taste my Mom's special turkey gravy—it's even better than the gravy Sharples' makes. It was nice to have a simple supper for a change, after

those fancy ones we had last weekend!
Anyway, since I have a couple of free days
extra, I figured it would be a good idea to
send you the cartoon I drew at Sparky's after
school on Wednesday. Mr. L thinks I ought to
try my hand at that—so, here it is, my very
first cartoon. Tell me if I should show it
around or not.

Kasey glanced up—the expressions on his housemates faces was
proof enough: they were as amused and impressed as he had been. The
courtesy of asking permission reinforced his judgment about Julian. He
read on.

Back to Geraldine: I didn't tell you
about her before. She's the one who always
tries to get me hooked up with a girlfriend.
Actually, she'd like me to have lots of them,
one for every day of the week, probably. I
learned a long time ago to just keep my
mouth shut and smile and let her do her
thing. What else can I do? Anyway, I faked
her out by asking for her help to pick a movie
to go to on the double date she has been
pushing me to go on. That shut her up for a
while.

What I didn't tell her was that my
Patrol has decided to help me out and find a
girl that wants to see a movie. That's what I
was doing at Sparky's: getting their help.
That's a secret, by the way: I want her to
think I'm doing that by myself.

{ insert at beginning of second sheet: large page wide drawing of
the restaurant booth with the six attendees packed in: Randall, Andy,
and Nick on one side, Frankie, Julian and Tom on the other, with their
cokes and milkshakes; the waitress was depicted separately below on the
right, looking impatient. A separate caption identified Georgia and her
oversized top }

> Truth is, I don't have time for that stuff. That's one thing that makes scouts so important—they can give you a hand at almost anything, since somebody usually knows what to do. Frankie, the Troop Bugler, is an expert on girls, and he's in the Flaming Arrow Patrol. So while I'm drawing stuff or whatever else, he and his girlfriend are taking care of things. I'll let you know how it goes—I'm supposed to have that date before Christmas. Frankie has this snazzy hot rod and he'll take all 4 of us. What a relief that will be! Once that's over with, we can go on that special campout before vacation ends. Which reminds me: let me know when you and your folks plan to be here—maybe you can go with us! It isn't decided yet who is going and where...

"Ahem!" Punctuated with a strong stomp by his left foot, Hayden made a dramatic call for Kasey's attention.

Kasey looked up. He didn't need to ask: clearly, he was expected to read the letter aloud. He didn't have time to think—that it was presumptuous and a violation of his privacy didn't occur to him until much later. Hayden had clearly taken control of the situation from the start. To refuse would have been petulant and anti-social. But Kasey was uncertain about his ability to speak for long to begin with—it was not his long suit. He handed Hayden the letter with a nod indicating that he was being given the assignment. He was nearly at the end of page two.

As Hayden began, Kasey realized how fortunate it was to have him read it—he was an accomplished speaker already, and intelligent and creative enough to do it with a flair—Kasey had no trouble putting Julian in his minds eye as he heard the words he had just read a second time—it was enjoyable. He sat back and listened, as happy as he ever remembered being.

His closed eyes and smile was noticed by everyone; they were happy for him, and could hardly wait to hear him explain what was going on.

236

The letter continued:

> Mark probably won't be able to go on
> this one, since he has to be at the store—it's
> one of the busiest times of the year. You'll get
> to know him soon enough, I guarantee.
>
> Last of all, I want to brag about my
> ride home—I got to ride up front with Mason!
> That is some car. Did you know it was made
> in 1936? It's just like new. Mason says it has
> been restored and has special stuff added,
> including a telephone! It's in a special
> compartment you hardly even notice. It's the
> same color as the car! The top opens up and
> makes the front seat into a convertible.
> Luckily, he didn't have it open—too cold out,
> of course. The seat was super comfortable,
> and covered with real leather, just like the
> back seat. A second phone connects with the
> one in the back. That one is in plain sight, on
> the dashboard. There's special set of controls
> for the back seat: an air conditioner, a heater,
> and a switch to turn on the special heater
> inside the back seat! There's a fancy radio
> that has extra stations—the driver can tune
> in to the taxi and police anytime he wants.
> Lots of dials, so many I can't remember them
> all. I don't know anything about cars, but I
> know this one is really loaded with extra
> stuff.

{ a page wide drawing of the dashboard was inserted; a caption
apologizing for being partly guesswork, with a little arrow pointing to
the woven leather cover on the steering wheel. }

> So anyway, I hope everything's going
> okay—and if you get a chance, say hello to
> everyone—your Mom and Dad and sister
> especially, and all your roommates. Even
> though I probably won't ever meet them, say

hi anyway. It never hurts to be friendly,
that's my motto!

'Bye for now,

Julian

A silence unlike any Kasey remembered followed. He accepted the pages back and carefully tucked them into the envelope. He took a deep breath and sat back. "Well, now you have met Julian. I met him myself on the Friday before Thanksgiving. That's less than two weeks ago." He let that sink in.

"I have some news for you—I have been wondering about how I was going to break this—" he smiled at Hayden. "Thanks for taking care of that, actually." He paused. "I didn't know anything about this before it happened: my father has been recruited to join a special research program. His work at the Medical School has drawn the attention of a person that needs his work to succeed. He expects it to take over a year—too long to live out of a suitcase. He insists on having the entire family along—so we have to move to North Carolina. There is no other choice."

He waited for a question, but none followed. "They have gone to great lengths, including recruiting Julian to be my guide and..." he didn't know any other way to express this: "my friend." He took another deep breath. "I have never met anyone like him. I doubt if anyone has. This letter is only a hint. He is a bundle of positive energy, a force of nature. And an incredible artist. These cartoons don't tell you about that at all—he showed me three sketchbooks of drawings that he has made at school this year. He's **my** age, but draws like a professional." He opened his book and took out the 8x10. "He drew this last Saturday—it's an enlarged version of the sketch he made the night before after the banquet where I was introduced to him. We were seated together purposely." He held it out for Hayden, assuming that he would circulate it like he had the letter pages.

He watched as Hayden took it around—they had returned to their comfy chairs as he was reading the letter. They looked at it, amazed, and at him, expecting him to amplify his remarks. He couldn't think of anything to say—so he stood and crossed over to the piano. He played the Joplin piece first. They could talk more later.

He had a new problem: he had not expected to feel an emotional tug like this—it was clear that his housemates cared, cared deeply about him. Their well-tuned facades had obscured that far better than he had imagined possible—something else he had not expected.

He's kinda tall

19 *Andy makes his pitch*

Randall was glad to be leaving that din behind—basketball practice was underway big time, and they had to walk around a dozen or so players practicing one skill or another—dribbling, shooting baskets, various drills, all very loud. He didn't see how these guys could do that without some kind of protection. One basketball being slammed down was bad enough, but a bunch of them at the same time was really awful. He needed to get some good earplugs: next week he would have to begin photographing these guys in action. Hearing was too important—Concert Band was challenge enough. As a musician, he needed to protect his ability to hear.

Today they were meeting with Coach Switcher to show the shots he had taken on Tuesday's wrestling match. He was pleased, by and large; he expected the coach to approve what he had done. He had a few experimental enlargements that would surprise.

Andy and Randall had been photographing the wresting team for a couple of weeks now; they had covered several practices and one match. After the coach had seen the proof sheets and a few prints, his enthusiasm was at a peak for Randall's work as well as Andy's article for the school paper. He had familiarized himself with the coach's habits, and caught him as he was about to pack up and go home. He'd timed it just right—aside from the basketball practice, the area was deserted.

Andy tapped at the doorframe: "Got a minute?"

"Ah, yes!" Les Switcher was eager to see to what this pair had in hand. Getting attention from the school paper was a windfall—he was tired of his boys being an afterthought in the Jackson Athletic Department. "Let's meet in the conference area." The office cubicles were too small—he wanted a table so he could spread the pictures out—marking the contact sheets was better than guessing, but just barely.

The PE department had carved out a small space where the staff could meet when needed—it was helpful for a number of things; the regular classrooms were too far away.

Randall was well organized. He put the marked contact sheet directly in front of the coach, then spread the twelve 4x6 prints in two rows of six. He had made one 8x10—it was placed above. Andy, who had sat on the opposite side of the small conference table, seemed impressed.

"Lordy!" These were beyond anything Switcher had hoped for. He looked at the boy, amazed; he would never have associated him with these. For still photographs, they seemed so alive, so dynamic. The boys were working very hard, and these photos showed just how hard.

Andy let the coach take his time. When he had examined each carefully, he cleared his throat and began. "Now comes the hard part: I can use up to three in the next issue. You get to decide which ones make the cut," he grinned.

"Oh…" Switcher was both disappointed and pleased. He wanted to use them all, of course—but three was fantastic—a 300% increase in coverage! He set one aside immediately—"Lanny won his match, so this one should go in…" He liked Lanny's determined grimace, especially. The long shot showing the team watching Ronnie's match was nice… hmm… He held one up close and frowned slightly.

perfect… Andy was pleased he had chosen that one: the coach had focused on the frayed jersey—Randall's enlargement had highlighted it perfectly.

"Is there any way you can doctor these?" He wasn't thrilled at the idea of having one of his top wrestlers looking like a flock of moths had invaded the locker bay… although this was obviously wear and tear.

Randall frowned. He hated to mess with a negative—that was abuse of a sacred trust. "I could ink it in, but I hate to wreck a negative—I doubt if I could repair it afterward."

Andy held his powder a little longer while the coach found another print. "You could sure use new uniforms…"

"Tell me about it!" He'd all but been told the boys would have to buy their own from now on. Some of the guys didn't have the money—pure and simple. He selected the last print and looked for signs of wear or damage. "Seems like I recall something about a special insert." Andy had made that offer several weeks ago—Switcher didn't think it was serious, but it was a great idea.

"I'm glad you brought that up. I have a qualified approval. My problem is finding a way to pay for it. If I can do that, it's guaranteed. The Cardinal can't spare any money—it will cost anywhere from five to eight hundred—double that if we want any color." Ads weren't enough.

Resigned, the coach understood. "Figures."

The time had arrived: "I have an idea, if you have a minute."

"Sure."

Andy opened his notebook and pulled out a manila envelope. From it he extracted the colorful 9x12 calendar that he had picked up several weeks earlier. "The Fire Department is doing a fundraiser—I think we could do the same thing." He pushed the calendar over for the coach to examine. Randall kept his cool.

what's this?! The bright glossy group shot of the fire department was bold: A cheerful banner across the top read, "Hall of Flame, 1963." Below, a group of bare chested well-oiled firemen perched flirtatiously on a fire truck. In the lower right corner in small print, "Special Fundraising Calendar, $10." Switcher flipped the cover page open to January. The top page featured a single firefighter in three poses: in the largest one, taken from behind, he was standing nude. One foot on an oxygen cylinder, his head turned to the left. Left hand on his waist, his right hung at his side holding a helmet. The other views were meant to tease and titillate the ladies, but had something blocking the genitals. It was daring, but not pornographic.

"Wow!" the coach laughed. The idea was more amusing than anything. He could never get the boys to go along with this, let alone the Administration. He looked at each month carefully, nonetheless. As Andy had hoped, as the coach went through the months, his response mellowed somewhat, and the shock element diminished considerably.

"My idea was to have a group shot of the team as a cover, then each month feature one or two team members, in various poses—no full nudes of course... a bare chest or two here and there..." He paused to let the coach catch up with him. "There are at least 500 sure customers walking the halls every day..." The Girl's League had at least that many members. He let the coach do the math. "We could do one every year."

After hearing that, it was a no brainer. The coach was not only sold, but was a solid advocate. Before he and Randall left, they had developed a rough project calendar. There was no way to get it out before the winter break, but Valentine's Day might be possible. The group shot was scheduled for the end of the week, and a photo session for the first wrestler on Wednesday. The goal was to get the cover and four months done before the semester break.

Randall wondered if that was realistic, but kept quiet. He was fascinated with Andy's skill at this kind of thing. He needed to make sure his parents hadn't scheduled anything next Wednesday that would complicate a photo session in the upstairs studio.

Wednesday: the faded '48 pulled into the long driveway at 4875 Alton Circle with three occupants. Andy had dealt with the muffler at long last, so it was possible to arrive "unannounced." This was helpful—Randall's mother was hosting her bridge club today, and she didn't appreciate the sound effects his dusty green four door chariot's failing muffler had provided before he got it fixed. Finding an open space to park wasn't a problem, since the Hallstrom driveway could accommodate many more than the dozen bridge players now in the 'party room.' As it happened, the upper end was wide open. He was able to park in front of the far bay, his usual spot.

"You guys want ice cream and cookies before we get started?"

Andy extended his arm across Randall's lap. "Only if you twist."

Randall grinned at Lanny, the wrestler that occupied the shotgun position at his right, as he gave Andy's forearm a token twist. "My mom always has plenty, especially on Bridge days. We can help ourselves before we go up." About an hour and a half of Bridge remained before supper—his mom liked to have that at five o'clock, rain or shine. Sometimes, like today, it was catered; the family ate in the dining room as usual while she played hostess in the big room.

Lanny greeted that news enthusiastically—after school treats were special—ordinarily, he'd be at practice. Coach wanted him to do this today instead. He was very curious, especially now that he had gotten a glimpse of Randall's house. *so, this is how the other half lives...* Lanny came from a different part of town; he had never been inside any of these posh homes. He had no idea that Randall was a rich kid—he sure didn't act like one.

They hurried across the driveway to the mudroom entrance—a cold penetrating rain was just getting underway.

Randall plopped his books on the bench and shed his coat, his usual ritual when coming home. "Do you want to take off your coats now, or when we go upstairs?" he hung his on the assigned peg.

Andy knew the routines here—the opportunity to take a cookie or two for the road when he and Lanny had to leave made the choice easy. "Might as well do it now." That meant they would have to come back to the house. Randall's mom never let him leave empty-handed. She was super in his book—both his parents were.

He and Lanny took off their coats. The opposite wall had several open pegs; the Bridge club had used a dozen or so—plenty were left.

Lanny hadn't thought about it at first—he'd never been in a mudroom before. The fact that this one could accommodate thirty coats meant that this place was a lot bigger than he thought. The huge parking lot of a driveway should have made that obvious.

Randall opened the kitchen door. "Thought so," he remarked quietly as they entered. The dessert counter had a variety of items: an apple pie with only one piece taken, half a chocolate cake, and a box of icebox cookies. He opened one of the built in freezer doors and gestured, "come over and pick your flavor." Because the previous owners did so much entertaining, the kitchen was equipped with a separate industrial sized freezer as well as a double-wide refrigerator. Lime sherbet, strawberry, vanilla, and Rocky Road ice cream were the choices today.

man alive. Andy was amazed—before, Randall's mom always served them—he didn't realize she had all this to choose from.

Wide eyed, Lanny licked his lips and pulled his head back. *cookies and ice cream? I guess!*

"She has lots to pick from today because of all the bridge players," he shrugged apologetically. "We need to dish up and carry our plates over to the studio," he spoke softly. His mother would not like to hear anything. He had permission, but keeping quiet was rule number one. He opened the regular everyday flatware drawer; needless to say, the ladies were using the fancy china and silver service. The ice cream scoop and other serving tools were already on the counter—no need to fetch those.

Andy and Lanny didn't need to be waited on—they each grabbed a large flat bowl and took a little of this and some of that—as much as they thought polite, but less than they might have. Randall wasn't very hungry—a scoop of lime sherbet and a couple of cookies would be plenty. He knew to save room for supper—his mother's usual catering service would be here at five o'clock. He and his sister would have the dining room all to themselves—his dad was out for the evening.

Bowls filled and ice cream tubs safely back in the freezer, Andy led the trio to the mudroom door; Randall closed it quietly as they departed the kitchen. The nasty weather had settled in—serious rain was hitting the window. "Help yourself to an umbrella—make sure it's a red one." His dad had bought those special so that they wouldn't grab a guest's by mistake. The large combination shoe and umbrella stand was full, thanks to all the bridge players. The red ones at one end stood out.

"Is it gonna snow?" The size of the raindrops was worrisome. Lanny was concerned about Friday's match—the highway up there was not where you wanted to be if it was snowing.

"I don't think so." Andy was right behind. "They said it would be nasty, but snow isn't in the cards until after Christmas." Either way, the paper route would be miserable for a while, for sure.

Randall let them duck inside while he held the door open.

"Thanks…"

246

"Just leave the umbrellas open at the foot of the stairway." Randall parked his to the left and led the way up.

Lanny did a quick glance around before following. He was totally amazed by all this. This garage was twice as big as any he had been in. It was like being in a movie or something. The classy Lincoln and Land Rover had lots of room. He hurried to catch up.

The kitchenette at the far end included a 4x6 table where the three could deal properly with their after school treat.

"Boy, you weren't kidding." Lanny was impressed "This is all yours?" He'd never been in a photographer's studio. Like everything else, the place was bigger than it looked from the outside. The bank of windows overlooking the driveway suggested a garret, not a full size room. He had been expecting to be in an extra bedroom or something. It was real cozy up here. You'd never guess it was so cold and miserable out.

"Wait 'til you see the darkroom," Andy took another bite of cake.

"I inherited most of the gear from my grandfather. I used to help out in his studio before he retired. Not here—in California; this used to be an apartment for a live-in handyman; my dad lets me use it for a studio."

*this kid **is** the real deal... wow.* Lanny figured Randall's grandfather must have been rich and famous out west.

"Here's the plan: I'll do a dozen or so frontal shots of you in various wrestler type poses—then another dozen from various angles— low, high. I'll finish the roll with close-ups. We're supposed to take one in color—I use a different camera for that." He gestured to the two tripods. The cameras were preset—he had done that before school.

"Where's the dressing room?" The one door opposite the windows looked like an outside entrance, not a room.

"You're in it," Andy quipped. "This is your all-in-one photo studio." He pointed to the hide-a-bed sofa as a likely place. "You're among friends."

Lanny didn't blush, but he felt a little silly. It was a stupid question.

Randall pointed to his right: "the back of the bathroom door is a full length mirror if you need one."

might as well get on with it... Lanny felt somewhat self-conscious, but he was eager to see the photos nonetheless. He had spent some time doing practice poses at home.

Randall went over to check the cameras.

Andy leaned back and watched Lanny change into his wrestling singlet. Mildly curious, he had never witnessed this particular process—did he wear anything underneath? He doubted it, but never knew for sure. He'd never had the courage to inquire. Lanny was pretty well endowed, so he couldn't hide much, no matter what—one of the aspects of wrestling that guaranteed a fan base.

Lanny did not wear anything under his singlet—some guys wore a jockstrap, but most didn't because it looked awful and was uncomfortable. Besides, sometimes they pinched or slipped halfway off during a match—that was **not** fun. Regular underwear was too warm—made him sweat a lot. He figured if somebody wanted to see what he had down there, why worry about it. He liked the freedom, he liked how it felt. Coach let guys do what they wanted.

Andy opened his steno pad to a blank page and wrote Lanny's name at the top—he needed to document this and be ready to jot down what came to mind.

Lanny finished tying his split sole shoelaces and stepped over to the staging area—it was easy to tell where to go—both cameras were aimed at where to stand.

"We'll do the color first—I'm taking these with the high resolution color film. Later, you can order your own copies. They can be enlarged as big as you want at Camera World. Two poses: first, Coach Switcher wants a formal at attention, facing the camera. Second, he wants you to stand however you want—an informal look. In that one you can clown around or whatever—just smile at the camera; you can let the shoulder straps hang loose."

248

The first shot was easy enough. For the second, Lanny pulled the shoulder straps forward as if they were suspenders and stood at a three quarters turn, with a smirk; his right knee was bent, his left holding his full weight. At home, this had looked real good—his mom had a full-length mirror he could use. The pose inferred that he was inviting the viewer to peek at what he was carrying in his special red basket.

The Cardinal Red spandex jersey with a tasteful half-inch wide white strip around the edges stood out favorably when being properly lit by floodlights. The slightly warm grey background panels complimented a wide range of subjects—that's why Randall had chosen it—his grandfather had favored it. It was especially nice for enhancing facial skin tones.

Andy was delighted—*we have a natural actor: excellent!* It was obvious that Lanny had been getting ready for this project. *if the rest of the team is this good, these calendars will sell out in a couple of weeks.* It just occurred to him to jot down a reminder: 'check into what a second run costs.' *might be smarter to put in a larger order to begin with.*

Randall stepped over to the Nikon. "Okay—now for the frontal poses. Do you know what you want to do?"

"You don't have a list?" Lanny thought Coach would have that figured out.

"No, I don't know that much about wrestling. It shouldn't be hard." He turned to Andy. "Why don't you keep track as we go—I just want to have 12 or so to choose from. We'll probably only end up using three or four at the most."

Andy grabbed for his steno pad. "Ready."

This wouldn't be hard—Lanny had been practicing for days. He had several in mind.

"The camera is fixed—so when you hear it click, that means the picture has been taken and you can go to the next pose—just hold good and still until you hear the click of the shutter—I'm using a fairly slow exposure time, 1/60. That way I get better detail."

These went rather smoothly—Lanny had indeed been practicing. He went through a ritual of sorts—first positioning his feet, then his stance—whether in a crouch or not, where to hold his arms, whether to twist his torso. He was facing a camera instead of a mirror this time, so it took a minute to visualize what he looked like. But he required no prompting. It seemed like he had done this before.

Andy watched this carefully—he realized that this session was likely to come in handy as the project moved forward—others might need a suggestion or two; not all of them were likely to be so well prepared.

Before long, however, Andy had a problem—a growing problem: he had been too interested in how spandex behaved. Under a couple of photo studio floodlights less than 20 feet away it appeared to be very different indeed. It succeeded in providing cover, but so well it showed off what was being covered—even better, it showcased how it moved. In an odd way, it was more revealing than remaining nude would have been. Nothing was left to the imagination, nothing was blurred or obscured—instead, it was enhanced. It took a while to realize that what he saw occurring slowly was, in part, the effect on the wearer: the various shifts in position and repeated tensing of muscle groups compounded the stimulus considerably, making the slow alternating stretch-release, tense-then-relax of the fibers seem massage-like. This stimulus was subtle, but significantly different from the same motion in a fast wrestling match. Lycra's unique ability to stretch in any direction without creating ridges or folds made it particularly welcome to an appreciative eye like Andy's. It virtually caressed the body underneath—probably the main reason Lanny liked how it felt to wear his singlet.

Lanny was well endowed—he always pointed himself down to appear as small as possible—a general, generic sort of appearance. This was fine when he was standing for a portrait. But any motion or change in position made his considerable package shift and move wherever the force of gravity and the minimal rules of spandex allowed. Since he was circumcised, a lot of detail was there to be showcased; from the very start, the fine weave molded itself lovingly around everything. Rather than pressing the flaccid three-inch treasure flat, it held it in place, enabling it to be viewed critically—or, on this occasion, appreciatively.

Andy had failed to pay attention to his own response in time—it had been keeping pace with the area under close scrutiny. At last, a pleasurable pulse against his upper thigh forced him to realize what had been going on. *oop…* He was in trouble: he had been so fascinated he didn't notice what had been gradually happening—finally, the resistance of his trouser fabric was too much to permit any more gradual engorgement—the pulse was automatic. At this point, there was no way to stop what was underway in his crotch. He was seated in full view of the performer who had inspired this approving response: not very smart. Andy presumed that Lanny was not a person of his "persuasion" when it came to sexual matters. Alerting him would wreck the entire project—worse, lead to his being unwelcome anywhere near the boys dressing area again. All he could do was turn slightly, cross his legs, and hope that it didn't go all the way—difficult when it had gotten such a strong and pleasurable start. Unfortunately, the show was far from over… he was unable to divert his attention to an area less interesting for very long. It was a private viewing in more than one sense, and it was only twenty feet away. He could not leave without disturbing Randall's work; besides, the minute he moved his condition had to be visible.

Andy was not the only one with a problem: Lanny didn't realize what this activity could lead to when he wasn't concentrating on winning a match. The sensation of the fabric rubbing up and down and back and forth had a mildly pleasurable feeling as it always had; it had never led to anything before. Now, it was subtle enough, gradual enough to go unnoticed until well after becoming visible—spandex was extremely flexible to begin with, and his singlet was over five years old. Before the pressure of the material was sufficient to draw his attention, he had become considerably enlarged. He had seen other wrestlers develop a problem, but it had never happened to him. His fondness for wearing the singlet was not coincidental: he liked how it felt. He also liked how it felt to be nudged and pressed by another wrestler in competition—but he had never given that any thought. That was in an area of his brain that wasn't quite ready to deal with questions along that line.

He was not an analytic individual—like most guys, he took body contact for granted—a part of the assignment. Since the first days of civilization in ancient Greece, it had been regarded as mankind's honorable alternative to combat—a sacred gift from the gods. Lanny had probably read that or heard that somewhere, but it wasn't something he ever thought about—if anything, it legitimized participating in the sport. Of course, other aspects of Greek heritage no longer applied: clothing was rarely worn by boys in those days, and same sex activity not being taboo no longer applied. He probably did not know these things—probably wouldn't unless he went on to college.

It certainly didn't come to mind when he too realized that he was in trouble. It wasn't until the pleasurable aspect of striking these poses began to transform into something very different. The time of day had contributed to the problem—after school was always an ideal time to satisfy the adolescent hormonal prompt to 'take a break' when conditions allowed—for many, it was part of the daily routine programmed by mother nature for adolescent boys. The familiar after school invitation to his right hand from his 'best friend' was usually welcome.

Finally, the spandex resisted further expansion—it forced the same sensation Andy had felt a short time earlier. Stopping to make a manual adjustment seemed like a bad idea: two guys were watching. There was no fly entrance, no way to access the problem directly—making any adjustment was impossible without an external grab and push combination that would make it worse. He decided to carry on as if nothing was happening; stopping to fix the problem would only make them see what was going on down there. The best thing to do was try to get this done as quickly as possible.

Both Lanny and Andy puzzled about their condition, but were unable to decide what to do. After he had taken several pictures—he didn't know how many—Randall noticed what had happened: *Lanny has a raging hard on!* He took his finger off the shutter button.

"Um…" he felt a little awkward. "You guys, I think we have a little problem." Oddly enough, he was not in the same condition; attending to the technical requirements and an underlying but controlling awareness that these guys were seniors had served to keep him entirely limp; he had not been paying attention to any special area—he had been avoiding that on purpose.

Randall's words broke the silence: it was more than enough to get their attention—it was a relief. Lanny stood upright and looked down at himself. Sure enough: he pulsed it a couple of times to verify what he knew to be true. He looked up and shrugged. "Sorry." He didn't know what else to say.

Andy was quick to act—instinctively, he knew it was essential to put Lanny at ease—he had to erase the inevitable fear that this would be talked about. He stood and spread his arms wide. It was risky, but he had a hunch. "Don't worry—it happens. Blame Mother Nature." He did a quick pirouette—borrowed from Tony, like many of his on-the-spot inspirations. He wasn't as well endowed, but he was a close second. "Power of suggestion," he shrugged. "What's a guy gonna do?"

They had a good laugh all around. That relieved one of the problems. They were comfortable with each other and their condition at least. The erections remained as hard as ever—demanding priority attention.

"What are we going to do?" Lanny asked, flexing himself naughtily.

Andy's watch read 4:20. They were supposed to leave at 5.

Awkward pauses aren't usually fun, but this one was diverting: Lanny needed a way to get a minute or five in the restroom—he could take care of this quick. That was a bit too daring to suggest out loud.

Andy was tempted to suggest doing a circle jerk—he knew Randall could join in and they would have a great time.

Randall offered a surprise suggestion. "What about doing a special photo set? A nude snapshot or two might be interesting." He could do a set like the one he and Julian did a few weeks ago. "Would you like to have a special set, just for yourself?" *might be perfect—he obviously admires himself.* Randall wouldn't mind making a secret set for himself when he got the chance.

Lanny and Andy looked at each other in surprise. For different reasons, they liked the idea. The fact that Randall had suggested it was ideal: it made him responsible in a key way—it made such a set possible—more important, made it permissible. He opened his arms wide: "Why not?"

Andy reinforced the idea. "Yeah… might as well. Nobody but us would know. My lips are sealed—scout's honor." He raised his right hand, showing the traditional three finger honor sign.

That was enough to set Lanny's mind at ease. Secretly, he had thought about having a set like that; he was enthusiastic about the idea.

Randall unlocked the Nikon from the tripod. This kind of set would allow a lot of variety and flexibility. He changed the shutter speed to 1/125—a faster response would assure nothing would be blurred or out of focus. There was more than enough light.

Having the gift of total recall, Randall proceeded to recreate the series of poses Julian and he had performed. The first step was turning off the left flood—he had learned that correct use of shadow made these far more engaging, artful, and sexy; he fetched the small step unit and put it where it would be the most helpful. "Let's start with a few low angle shots—put your right foot on that box. I'll move around and get you from two or three sides." He moved close and got down on one knee. What the light did was wonderful; Lanny's nearly hairless body, unmarred by skin blemishes that afflicted many in his age group, was like a live sculpture. His muscles were defined, not grotesque and disproportional. Barely seventeen, he had spent many hours admiring his physique in the mirror—he seemed to know precisely how to stand, how much to flex, how to focus on various muscle groups. He was a photographer's dream—the sharp shadows highlighted even the smallest, most subtle muscle definition.

After the low shots and a series of straight on views, Randall fetched the small stepladder and took a few high angle views. He checked the counter—a couple of shots remained. "Do you have anything in mind?

Lanny had felt it a couple of times—he was almost running a stream down there. "Uh, what about…" he wasn't sure how to put it.

"Spread it around!" Andy chimed. He had been watching closely and was in similar condition.

"Yeah!" Lanny nodded eagerly at Randall. *a shiny, glossy, ready for action magic wand!* He had imagined that—he wanted to see what that would look like.

Randall had not expected to be fulfilling three different fantasies; he stepped close and got down on one knee. "I'll take as many as I can and finish the roll." He was about three feet away—the light was perfect, the depth of field left everything else in a blur. When Randall took the second shot, he felt the telltale end of roll resistance. "One more: give it a good pulse."

Just as a surge appeared at the tip, Randall took the final shot.

An awkward pause. They looked at each other, hesitating to suggest what was on their minds.

Andy broke the silence: "Okay you guys, let's face it: we need to do a circle jerk. No one but us will know."

"Perfect!" Lanny had done that in the seventh grade. It was fun then and it would be fun now. It was a standard 'boys-will-be-boys' ritual, safe from the dreaded accusation that he was "into boys." The fact that these guys were willing to join in was special—he wasn't worried that it might be found out.

Andy gave Randall a wink, and turned toward the hide-a-bed sofa. "This way, men!" Mark quotations were always handy, and fun.

Randall fetched the box of Kleenex from the bathroom. They had started without him and left the center open. This suited him just fine—that gave him two to watch while he satisfied Little R. This was something very new—he had never associated sex with having fun. His only regret was not being able to preserve it on film.

Soon Randall found that watching another person enjoying himself while he was doing the same thing made it an entirely different experience. Two others at the same time made it complex. It didn't occur to him to just shut his eyes and fantasize as usual. Right off he discovered that they did it differently—that had never occurred to him either. He was playing catch-up or fill in or something: his experience was limited—Andy was special, but they'd only played around three or four times, and never found time to talk about it. Julian's 'special education' series and the Initiation in Hayden Woods were akin to a graduate seminar by comparison. A very odd life experience gap remained. He was accustomed to attending to Little R in solitary, that practice had itself acquired a status of sorts—he was glad to have that put aside: he was becoming "one of the boys" at last! This was more basic, more fundamental somehow than recognizing his sexual preference had been.

He focused on Lanny's technique first—aside from size, their equipment was the same: Lanny was uncircumcised but a size bigger—maybe two sizes. He used both hands. Randall tried to approximate the same techniques to see how they felt. This was fun! He grinned and without thinking, glanced at Lanny. Lanny grinned back, acknowledging his approval.

Lanny had not realized until that minute that he was showing this kid how to do this. It gave him a big brother sensation—he liked how that felt.

Andy was an experienced practitioner of this rite, and was able to enjoy it on a different level. In some ways it was an aesthetic experience as well as a physical relief; it was always pleasurable. As a connoisseur he was able to focus on the visual aspect; he had played with a lot of boy toys—since the fifth grade, scouts had made that easy if not automatic. Lanny's technique was familiar—Tom had a similar way of holding the shaft at the base while doing a circular rim rub. Number seven did something like that at Freddy's Shooting Gallery last summer. He used it himself when he was in a hurry. Usually, he preferred a slow pump— that enabled him to activate sensors along the entire shaft. Unfortunately, his tube of joy jelly was in the glove compartment of the Dodge—too late for this session. Saliva would have to do.

It didn't take long to get on third base; Lanny was first to approach home. His pleasure grew intense... he did not hold back—the showman in him was given full control. His legs stretched straight as if trying to push the sofa back a few feet—

"NNNNN... **Yah!!**"

The first shot grazed his right earlobe on its way to the floor behind the sofa. The next three landed at the top of his chest.

Andy had been keeping pace and his came next. Less dramatic, he uttered a low sound, sort of hybrid moan-grunt; it was a nice one, but half his attention was on Lanny's after stroke squeezes; he licked his lips. *if only*...

Randall had been too busy watching and had a way to go. He closed his eyes and concentrated.

Andy exchanged glances with Lanny—inadvertently, they had become fraternal partners in Randall's rite of passage to the world of big boys. Unexpected, it felt good to have a little brother, and to share the experience. They would probably never talk about this, but it would become a part of their sense of being healthy, strong men. Their eyes returned to Randall's approaching moment of achievement; unconsciously they stroked themselves in concert, becoming hard again. As Randall bucked involuntarily they watched appreciatively, curious to see the quantity and how far the force of its departure took it.

It shot straight upward a modest 8 or 9 inches; his three shots landed conveniently on his lower torso. Cleanup would be easy. He relaxed and exhaled. He didn't feel anything special—his mind had been distracted by more mundane matters—specifically, what they would do next. They had gone way off script and he knew that time had become a problem.

"Whoo!" Randall exhaled. "Sorry I took so long…" He couldn't stop to check how late it was.

"Good job!" Lanny patted him on the thigh.

"Well done!" Andy added a pat on the back. He sensed that would be read by Lanny as proof that he and Randall were not as well acquainted as in fact they were.

Randall moved his head to the right to see across the room—the clock on the wall was directly behind the Yashica, still on its tripod. He had been thinking during the pleasure session and come up with another idea.

"You guys want to develop the photos now?" It was 10 minutes to five.

"I thought we had to leave at 5." Andy would love to get it finished.

Lanny didn't have any objection—in fact, he thought it was a good idea.

"Well, if you can stay for supper, we can do it right afterward. I'm sure my mom wouldn't mind."

They looked at him, expecting more information.

"She has Sharples' Catering tonight—they serve her bridge tournaments. They always have plenty to go around. Two more plates is no problem. If you need to get permission from home, there's a phone on the desk." He pointed to the small desk near the back door.

For a school night, it turned into quite an evening. Mr. Swann's gifts had made lots possible—the power washer, electric film dryer and print dryer had revolutionized his turnaround time; his operation was now up to date. With two assistants he was finished well before 9 o'clock. Lanny had his special prints safely tucked into a manila envelope.

The need to relieve the pressure that viewing the prints had caused was best taken care of later, in their respective bedrooms. It was a little too soon for a second round. Doing a second round had implications that Andy didn't want to become problematic—he was certain that Lanny had gone as far as he was likely to.

Randall hid the negatives with a pledge to put them where no one else would be able to find them. Only he knew the exact location and how to fetch them. That was his ironclad rule: negatives were sacred, not to be seen or touched by anyone to whom he hadn't given permission. The only alternative would have been to destroy them—Lanny did not want that to happen. Over time, he hoped to find a way to get Randall to let him have them.

Unfortunately, the number of frames suitable for use in the calendar was far short of the original plan—a follow-up session would have to be scheduled to fill in the gaps. No problem… they could bear up under the inconvenience. It offered a challenge that was too intriguing to ignore.

20   *the blind double date*

Julian checked Uncle Max's watch again—he still had another half hour of boring to go before Frankie would be here to pick him up. The long awaited movie date was about to happen—at this point, he was looking forward to it, if only to get a break from reading any more of his Biology textbook, the most boring book he had ever had to deal with in his life.

He raised his head and yelled "**Bor-ing!**" at the wall. He did that every 15 minutes… helped him stay awake.

Semester exams were a new thing for Julian, and he didn't much like the idea, to be honest. Jackson High would be going on a special exam schedule because the tests went two periods long. Since he was so busy, he had reserved this weekend to get ready—next weekend was too busy with scouts. He had spent all day yesterday studying History, English and Geometry—he had saved Biology for last—that was what he worked on today—except for Church and the movie, that was all he had left to work on. He didn't have to study for P.E., Typing or Art. So he was confident he would pass everything, but he wanted to get as many A grades as he could—those made his mom super happy, or he wouldn't be working this hard. Well, that wasn't true—he wanted to please Mark, actually. But that was secret.

Anyway—there were special things about this movie date: it was Sunday afternoon, not Saturday night, the way Geraldine wanted. That was amusing, really, because she had to go along with the movie Frankie chose, namely, **Lawrence of Arabia**. The only tickets Frankie could get were for the first showing on Sunday—everything else was sold out. Julian didn't know all the details, only that it was the hardest movie to get tickets for—everybody wanted to see it—all the seats were reserved!

259

So he figured it would be a good movie, which was all he cared about anyway. It was fun to see Geraldine coming to grips with this—she had to agree that it was a good movie. She couldn't come right out and argue for a movie that was an excuse to do a bunch of necking.

That's the last thing Julian wanted to do of course. He assumed Frankie would do some of that anyway—he was supposedly a famous Ladies Man. But he messed around with boys too—Danny and he had that bet last summer about getting the best tanned buns. Danny had let it slip that the winner of the bet got to choose who went first in a suck-a-thon. That was Julian's substitute word for a blowjob—fit better. But that was something you didn't do at the movies.

The other unusual thing about this movie was who his date would be. Her name was Brenda, that's all Julian knew. She had dark hair and was on the dance team—he didn't remember her last name: forgot to write it down when Frankie called. She had second lunch, but he had never met her. She seemed to know who he was, Frankie was sure about that. Both Frankie and his girlfriend were seniors—another strange thing about this date; but his girlfriend was the true expert. She knew Brenda, and said she was perfect. Rhonda was on the Dance Team too. He hoped Brenda wasn't a senior, but it didn't matter, since he figured this would be a one-time thing. Once Kasey moved here, there wouldn't be a bunch of extra time for movie dates. He doubted if Kasey would be interested in going to the movies a lot—and getting him a date was probably not going to happen until next year at the earliest...

Get back to work, Julian. Inside Guy was on duty early, just in case.

His eyes returned to the page—he was about to finish the chapter. *might as well get on with it...*

Geraldine opened the third binder—keeping busy while they awaited the arrival of Julian's date partner was more than helpful... a godsend, this idea. Francine had come up with it at the office yesterday. As she had anticipated, they had run out of things to talk about. Getting these property profiles up to date was a good use of the time. "I take it there is nothing in the news that I need to worry about—I'd have heard if we were about to go to war." Francine had been reading the Sunday **Times** for the last hour.

"All is quiet on that score. There's an editorial about the movie Julian is going to—it complains about being sidelined by the distributors—big cities don't have to worry about limited engagement clauses, evidently. In Raleigh, it will run for as long as it's selling tickets."

"Limited engagement?"

"Yes—it has only two weeks here, and they are all sold out— have been for some time. It's expected to take Best Picture at the Oscars." Francine had read the review—Julian was one of the fortunate few.

"Well, **that's** a consolation, I suppose." Geraldine planned to read up on that—*might be a marketing factor.*

"Bor-ing! Troooly Borrr-ing!!" echoed from Julian's room.

Francine chuckled. It was good to know he was on task.

Geraldine was amused: "How many of those protests have there been? I haven't been keeping track."

"Half a dozen, at least." She glanced at the clock. "I expect at least one more before his ride is here." Hopefully, he'll have finished studying before the movie—she didn't expect him to be up to anything academic after the epic 4 hour movie and inevitable pizza afterwards. She doubted if they were planning to make a trip up to the viewpoint. Julian wasn't likely to fall for that one again.

> > *ding-dong!* < < The doorbell interrupted their separate trains of thought.

Geraldine was out of her chair and halfway to the door before Francine could put down the newspaper. She was going to meet this boy at last: he was the only information source. The fact that he was early didn't register—though it was a good thing. She beat Julian to the door with ease.

Frankie was about to ring a second time when the door opened abruptly. The woman standing before him was not Julian's mother—he knew that right off, since he had seen Mrs. Forrest with Julian several times since he joined the Troop. He recovered rapidly. "Hello, I'm Frankie." He didn't need to say more—Julian had just stepped to her side, wide smile as usual.

"Hiya Frankie! This is Geraldine, my mom's friend. C'mon in!" He stepped back.

"Pleased to meet you," Frankie wished Julian had said more—he didn't think it was good manners to call her by her first name. "I'm Frank Ferris, but everyone calls me Frankie." He bowed slightly and stepped inside so she could close the door—it was very chilly out— snow was expected in the mountains.

The boy's good manners impressed Geraldine—she had forgotten that he was one of Mark's scouts. That was reassuring. That explained the early arrival, more than likely. "Why, thank you, Frankie. Julian's mother and I have been looking forward to meeting you. Please come in," she gestured to the nearby chair. He behaved quite gentlemanly—his medium length wool coat was dark—a blue, green and black plaid with a narrow deep orange highlight band. He had taken off the matching cap when he introduced himself. Geraldine hadn't considered Julian's outerwear—his leather sleeved jacket was attractive, but very schoolboy. Eventually, he would need something like this... next year, perhaps.

Frankie knew the way to handle this one—he'd had lots of experience being 'interviewed' by curious parents—usually they belonged to a girl he was taking out for the first time. It helped to know that Julian had to deal with a protective screen—helped explain why he was so clueless most of the time. He took a seat—Julian's mother had parked on the oversize ottoman, leaving the other chair open for Geraldine. *interesting...* Geraldine was in charge, evidently. *playing the suspicious father part... no problem...* He had his script ready, as usual—he'd probably be using again it in a few minutes when they picked Brenda up.

"Hello, Mrs. Forrest! Good to see you again—I don't remember if we have been introduced or not, actually. I hope you don't mind my coming a little early—it's on purpose," he grinned, pointing to his temple. "Be Prepared, that's the scout motto! My job is to make sure our lad is properly prepared for the occasion—he tells me this is his first double date. It's going to be a lot of fun—more so if he's all squared away," he winked, indicating that he expected them to agree. Since they didn't leap in at the pause he had provided, he continued. "This one is special because it's almost like going to a double feature—there's an intermission half way through." He turned to Julian: "I hope you had a good lunch!"

Julian nodded automatically—they did have a nice after Church lunch; but he didn't know about the super long part. He was hoping to get home halfway early.

"The review in the paper certainly praises it highly—you were very fortunate to get tickets!" Francine wondered about that. Tickets were almost double the usual price.

With a sly grin Frankie winked at Geraldine. "Top secret: I have an inside connection at that theater—I didn't have to wait in line." He didn't go into detail about that. He put his finger to his lips to reinforce the point about confidentiality. "By the way—if you ever get into a jam about tickets there, be sure to give me a call—I might be able to help."

Geraldine was growing more impressed by the minute. This young man was bright and resourceful. She was reconsidering her view about high school students and boy scouts. Clearly, Mark deserved some credit for this as well. She had taken him for granted—Francine was wise to depend on him. He was more than a neighbor and big brother, wasn't he?

"So anyway, four hours of popcorn and coke is going to require a good pizza party afterward. Sundays are usually light at Shakey's. I figure a healthy hour or so, maybe two, we should be getting him home by bedtime or a little before," he nodded confidently. "It is a school night, after all." Frankie thought that would put their minds at ease. It left some time for a little playing around—he didn't want too much of that himself—there was plenty of room for that during the movie. He took a deep breath, almost inviting a question.

It didn't come, so he turned to Julian: "I am here to make sure you are properly dressed for the occasion, first of all. There are some dos and don'ts—and four plus hours is a big deal." He was pleased to see the expression on Geraldine's face.

263

Francine was curious about the girl—nothing had been said. She was reluctant to inquire, fearing it would imply mistrust. She was counting on Geraldine to pin him down on that.

Geraldine no longer had any doubts about this boy or the girl. That it was a girl rather than another scout pal was what counted.

Frankie knew when to move—he was satisfied that they were satisfied. "Well, let's have a peek at your wardrobe, Julian," he stood. "Time's a wastin'." He winked at Geraldine again, just for good measure—giving her status as inside partner was usually a good move. "Lead the way!"

Geraldine and Francine watched Frankie escort Julian to his room. They looked at each other, a mix of being quite pleased and amazed. It was time to have a fresh cup. They headed back into the kitchen.

Frankie let Julian get well into the room before he paused to turn around—he needed to see if the ladies were watching. *good.* They had gone into the kitchen and were out of sight. He carefully and quietly closed the door. *time to talk turkey.*

Julian was so wowed by Frankie's performance he was at a loss to say anything. He didn't really know him at all—he wasn't at camp last summer, so other than Troop and Patrol meetings, he had no experience with him. But both Tom and Danny liked and trusted him, so he did too. He figured it was smart to just pay attention.

"There." Frankie spoke softly. "They don't need to hear all the details!" Translation: 'we don't **want** them to hear all the details.' He did a cursory glance around the room. "Cool room!" he checked out the bulletin board. Actually, it seemed a little plain... too tidy. After meeting the ladies, he understood at once. He was looking for clues as much as anything—he didn't really know Julian at all. He seemed like a Total Purity, but both Danny and Tom had assured him that he was a Total Expert. They didn't explain—result: Frankie was Totally Curious. *no pinups...* Well, the kid wasn't stupid—he wasn't about to have anything visible, not with those two sniffing around. The drawings were expected... *he's sure good at that...* the model airplanes were leftovers

264

from boyhood more than likely. *nothing incriminating: well done Julian!*

Julian didn't know if he was supposed to sit down or not. He had showered and cleaned up—as far as he knew, he was ready to go...

"Okay—lets take a second look at what you're wearing. Did you pick these on purpose? Your shirt and pants?"

Julian shrugged. Geraldine always handled that area. Today she hadn't said a word—so he put on his Monday outfit. No big deal.

"Let me see your shirts first." Frankie stepped over to the closet and pulled the sliding door wide open. He didn't have to look very long—he pulled out the coral pink Strad. "Perfect!" He looked close: *a Strad, of all things!* That was a huge surprise. "Where did you get this?!"

"At Ogly's. I get everything there, naturally." *that's where Mark works.*

Frankie was impressed; he didn't know they handled Strads. *good to know.* "What about pants: are these all you've got?" he pointed at the suntans.

Julian stepped around and pulled his Levis out of the closet. "I have some Bermuda shorts too." He doubted if those would be a good idea this time of the year.

"How tight a fit are these?" Frankie checked the suntans again. *a little loose...* "You have an older pair? One a little more lived in?"

"No—I have a pair that's bigger is all." He was ready to start wearing those next Semester, actually.

"Hmm. I want to see how these fit." He held up the Levis. *hanging in a closet is pretty weird... nobody hangs their jeans in the closet!*

Julian kicked off his shoes and took off the suntans.

Frankie took the opportunity to check him out—average. *oh well...* The Jockey briefs had to go; he would deal with that next. He watched Julian pull on the Levis... promising. He stepped over to the door. "Walk back and forth a couple of times." He needed to see if he could see anything besides a fold in the denim. *not with those Jockeys...* nope. "Okay—this is gonna seem strange, but trust me on this, okay? I want you to repeat that, but without the Jockeys on."

?!!? no underpants? "I have boxers—a bikini pair too—"

"No, nothing. I need to see how things hang—sometimes that's important."

Julian thought this was kind of weird. He hated underwear, so it didn't bother him at all. He shucked the Levis and the Jockeys, gave his hips a good couple of twists to loosen everything, then slipped the denim back on.

Frankie was pleased by the brief performance; he wouldn't mind spending some time playing with that. *not much hair down there... at least it's dark*—blond pubic hair had never attracted his eye. "Leave the bottom button open."

?? why do that? Julian was amused more than anything. He still didn't see what Frankie was trying to accomplish. "Do I tuck my shirt in?"

"Good question! Not now—take it off for now... T-shirt only. Go ahead—strut your stuff."

Julian performed the mini parade—playfully this time, ending with a sideway thrust of his hips.

This was what Frankie wanted to see. *with a few more washings these will be perfect... finished shrinking—broken in at least.* Hanging in the closet didn't seem to hurt them any. "Okay! now put on the orange shirt—or is it pink? Whatever it is—and tuck it in." Next week he planned to stop by and see if Oglivy's still had these in stock.

Julian complied. "How's that?" He was getting a kick out of this.

"One more thing..." he stepped forward and pulled the pants front down below the belly button. "The idea is to show a little more of that torso—turns 'em on to see that."

Julian wasn't especially interested in doing that, but he went along with it for now; he figured he could pull them up later on. They were tight enough to stay on at least. He did the demonstration walk again.

266

"You pass the test—good work! Now the final touches," he stepped close. "Lift your arm."

Julian complied.

"Good—the shirt doesn't pull loose—that's important, keeping that tight." He leaned close and sniffed. *nothing...* "What deodorant do you use?"

"Deodorant?"

"Yeah, pit stick or spray? I don't smell anything."

"Eew... I never use that stuff. Too stinky." He rubbed his nose. That reminded him. "I hope Brenda doesn't use a lot of perfume—I really hate that."

"Don't you ever get the pits?" Frankie was a little worried about Brenda—that's one thing he didn't know.

"Only if I work super hard, or run a lot, like in P.E. I always take a shower afterwards. No big deal." He wasn't about to use any of that stinky stuff.

Frankie looked closely: "You don't shave yet, do you?"

"Sorry. I keep hopin'." He shrugged.

"Well, don't be in a hurry—it's mostly a hassle. So one thing left: you have a pocket comb?"

"Somewhere, yeah." He wasn't sure where it was. He stepped over to the suntans to check. *nope.* "Must be in the bathroom."

Frankie opened the door. "Lead the way," he gestured for Julian to go first. He paid close attention to details as he passed by—aroma and all. *interesting...* He had not thought about this: Boy smell. He liked that... yes indeed.

The ladies perked up: the sound of Julian's door opening surprised them slightly; they glanced at the clock. No problems, evidently.

Julian grabbed the comb from behind the faucet handles and handed it to Frankie. "Sometimes I forget to put it in my pocket."

"Be smart to have spare, just in case. Now, then." He proceeded to tinker with how the hair fell in front—he wanted less forehead. *nice*... he liked the way Julian's hair behaved. "turn around." The back was perfect. This was one lucky guy—he sniffed—no hair oil, all natural. *very lucky*. "Take a look at yourself." He stood back.

"Huh." Julian was surprised.

"You okay with that?"

Julian shrugged. "Yeah, I guess. What's the big deal?" He always combed it back.

"Trust me—the ladies will faint at the sight of you coming in the door."

Julian looked again. *weird*... he made a mental note to be sure he kept it combed back, entering a room or otherwise, whenever girls were around. This was good information. Nick and Tom were sure right about this guy. He knew his stuff all right. He grinned and turned around. "Are we ready?"

"Yes we are—grab your jacket and hang it over your shoulder. Time to show off." He followed Julian out—he had not closed the door. He half expected to see the ladies, but they were still in the kitchen.

The ladies, it so happened, were listening intently, nonetheless. They were expecting to see a presentation. And here it came.

Feeling slightly sheepish, Julian stepped into the kitchen with his jacket slung over his left shoulder—something he rarely did. Usually, he let it hang by his side or tucked it under an arm. He did a bow and turned around.

Geraldine was thrilled: Julian was transformed! A couple of details had made all the difference. She controlled herself just in time. "I approve. I certainly do approve." She clasped her hands gleefully and beamed at Frankie. He had become her ally, her helpmate in this endeavor. She stood and opened her arms for the obligatory hug. She tucked a ten dollar bill discreetly into Julian's shirt pocket and turned him over to Francine.

"Have a wonderful time, Julian." She gave him a motherly kiss on the cheek and tucked and extra five dollars into the other shirt pocket.

"I remembered my wallet this time," Julian bragged—he had grabbed it off the table when he took his coat off the back of his chair.

Frankie smiled proudly. This had gone nicely; very nicely. "Onward, men," he gave Julian a pat on the backside and winked at the ladies. "My wheels are rarin' to go fetch our dates!" He turned to Geraldine, who was following them to the door. "I'm glad it's early in the day—you can get a good look at my pride and joy. I like to show it off whenever I can."

Geraldine was very pleased indeed. "Here's a little for the gas tank," she said quietly, tucking a five dollar bill into his hand.

Genuinely surprised, Frankie was very grateful. That's one problem he couldn't fix: his '57 Bel Air 4-door loved ethyl gasoline—lots of it.

Even though Frankie had the tickets in hand, they still had to wait in line—the house was sold out, and even with two lines, it took a while to admit 2250 people. The largest in town, Julian had never gone to a movie here. He'd only gone to the Rex—it was in the older section of downtown. This one was in the newer area, closer to the University. He didn't know this part of town too well.

Picking up the girls had taken a little longer than he expected. Rhonda, Frankie's girlfriend, was kind of pokey. That's why they were this far back. He and Frankie had to sit through part of a basketball game on TV—her dad was practically glued to the set. Her mom was busy in the kitchen. So they didn't go in to meet Brenda's folks. That was ok, she said—her dad was taking a nap and waking him up would have been a bad idea. Her mom seemed nice enough—she came to the door. He figured they weren't used to having company.

He still didn't know her last name. He wasn't sure how to ask—or if he should. He thought he ought to say something nice at least—just standing out in the cold wasn't a whole lot of fun.

"Sorry it's so cold out..." Julian huddled as close as he could, considering—Brenda was wearing a big fluffy coat—some kind of imitation fur thing with a hood—long, like a bathrobe; it almost touched the sidewalk it was so long. From a distance she probably resembled a medium sized polar bear. It was super nice of her to come to this—

269

technically, it was his fault she had to stand out here in the cold. He was glad she was about the same height as he was—at least he didn't have stoop down to talk to her like he had to with Rita.

"My father says it's supposed to be snowing in the hills tomorrow or Tuesday." She enjoyed seeing the steam her breath caused. She was well protected—and well padded by Mother Nature.

The line moved forward another few steps. That was encouraging.

She sounded cheerful, which gave him a little confidence. "Frankie says we have the best seats in the balcony!"

"Yes, I know," she winked knowingly.

Julian didn't get the significance of the wink, though he couldn't help noticing her tone of voice was a little odd. That happened from time to time—He was rarely in tune with social trends or fads, or closely held secrets. He was called clueless for good reason. Some guys in the Troop called him Charlie Brown; he took it as a compliment, mostly—well, it fit: he was like Charlie Brown—always figuring things out afterward. At least he caught it this time, so he was getting better—or smarter. He shrugged, assuming that he would find out later if that wink was important. Subtleties and subtexts were not interesting in the least. He was not a gossip nor did he approve of secrets as a rule. He had **one**, of course—and that was enough. Otherwise, he wanted things in the open— that way he didn't have to keep track of what was supposed to be secret and what was okay to talk about.

He was getting cold—for the first time in his life, he was sorry he had agreed to take off his skivvies: his school jacket didn't go below the waist, and these Levis didn't have any extra anti cold features. *how long will it take to get inside?* At least it wasn't windy. He stood on tiptoe: they were almost at the corner—half a block more.

"I wonder if they have hot chocolate in there." That would be a lot better than a cold drink, that's for sure.

"Ooo, I like that idea!" Brenda was fond of chocolate—she planned to get a large Snickers bar and a couple of boxes of Milk Duds to go with her popcorn. *movie size packages! always jumbos!* "I love hot buttered popcorn, don't you?" She was ready to get started on that.

270

Popcorn and milk duds were what made movies worth going to. "I'll probably want a second tub after the intermission," she confided. She assumed Julian was capable of keeping her supplied... mentioning it up front, her sister Jeannette had advised, usually made it happen. Asking for it later was always awkward. Double features were a special treat, mostly because of the second tub. A cup or two of hot cocoa on top of that would make her day, for sure.

Julian stole glance at her face. He had not seen her without that coat—her face was a little chubby, at that.

It would be, after two tubs of popcorn, Inside Guy remarked.

Julian was glad he was on board. He just remembered that dance with Rita: the girl might have something on her mind besides watching the movie. He was glad he would be in a seat the whole time, in case she was interested in rubbing his buns. He didn't know Rita was until it was too late. Figuring out what girls were interested in was not an area he wanted to spend any time on, actually. Anyway, Little J was hiding as far back in as possible thanks to the cold—Julian was planning on him to stay that way until he got home. As long as no one massaged his buns, Little J would stay asleep. *never did figure out why that happens...*

The line had reached the corner at last; large wall posters lined the sidewalk—Julian squeezed his way over for a peek. "Neato!" He grinned at Brenda, inviting her to look with him. "Huh..." there was a huge picture of this guy dressed in a white robe with a special white thingy on his head, waving a pistol—he was leading an attack in the desert. "Wow..." he looked at Brenda wide eyed: "This is a True Story!" He did not know that. It looked spectacular... no wonder everyone wanted to see it. *maybe it'll have the Sphinx and pyramids in it...* He always wanted to see those.

"Oop!" Brenda had grabbed him by the elbow—the line was moving again, only faster. *that's a relief...* They scooted close to Frankie—he had the tickets.

The first thing Julian did once they were inside was spend that extra five dollars: a fancy souvenir booklet was on sale at a special table. Not only was he interested in it—it was perfect for showing to Geraldine and his mom. Of course, he had to get one for Brenda too, so it took all five dollars. She was thrilled as well as surprised. He could tell that she didn't expect him to do that.

She was indeed impressed, but didn't spend any time with it—she had to make sure no one got in front of them at the concession center—she could read it later after they were settled in upstairs. Getting the necessaries was her first priority.

Julian had expected her to open that bulky coat, but all she did was flip back the fluffy hood. He was pleasantly surprised—she was a little chubby faced, but her brunette hair was very attractive, and she wasn't all painted up like Rita had been—no lipstick, no pink cheeks and eyeliner—she looked like a real person.

Inside Guy thought they might have told her what not to do, but Julian decided to give her the benefit of the doubt.

Fortunately, the line to get refreshments was reasonably fast—plenty of cashiers. Julian tucked the fancy program into his open jacket and secured the bottom two snaps so it wouldn't fall out: both hands were fully occupied. He blew a silent puff of relief after paying for everything; he didn't know that theater prices were jumbo sized and then some—matched their corresponding oversized treats. As the person who had invited Brenda, he got to pay for hers as well as his own. The ten dollars that Geraldine had given him was enough to pay for both—which was a good thing, because he'd need what was in his wallet for the pizza party afterwards. The funny part was the tubs—he was going to get a large rather than a giant, but she made him get a giant, saying "it will save you money—I'll finish what you don't want." Julian couldn't think of anything to say; he was in for a lot of popcorn sound effects. This was the most expensive date he had ever had. Actually, it was the only date, other than the Sadie Hawkins dance. He understood now why Frankie had to have that job after school and Saturdays—he went on these dates all the time.

The balcony still had a lot of empty seats when they arrived; getting to their assigned seats was the easy part—the usher, Frankie's friend Rodney, helped by carrying the cups of hot chocolate and showing them where to sit. Julian had one of the popcorn tubs, Brenda's humongous sized Snickers bar—*must be double size at least*—and her giant Pepsi. Brenda's right hand grasped a large tub by the lip; in her left,

272

the fancy program and two oversize boxes of Milk Duds—thanks to the fur lined mittens, her coat pockets were full. She dribbled a trail of popcorn half the way up the ramp. He was so busy paying attention to his cargo, he didn't have a chance to look around—it was a lot newer than the Rex—none of the fancy ornate decorations, just huge movie posters everywhere. The Orpheum was twice as big, easy.

Brenda was on his right, Frankie on his left. That was okay, but no one was about to provide an extra seat for her bear rug of a coat—as a result Julian had a considerable amount of fluffy white spilling almost halfway across his lap. She had to sit on it, since it was too big to go anywhere else; it served as a cushion, which was one of the reasons she had worn it—ten years old, the balcony seats were no longer plush. Julian had to contend with the left sleeve—he tucked as much as he could alongside his right leg. This was about as cozy a fit as he had ever had in a movie theater—or anywhere else. There wasn't a lot of extra legroom either. When she finally got squared away, he handed her the huge Pepsi. It vanished from view between her feet. The thought of her kicking it over nagged at him for a while—eventually he realized that she was practiced at this. All he could do was roll his eyes. But he was grateful: this girl would be fully occupied—she wouldn't have time to worry about his buns, or anything else. He glanced at Frankie and got a wink back. *hmm...* these winks were getting annoying.

Inside Guy didn't like them either, but he didn't have any advice.

Finally, Julian looked down to the screen: a fancy crimson curtain was pulled across it: it was twice as wide as the Rex—he couldn't remember if it had a curtain or not. He was glad they had arrived early after all—this way they could get settled in. He didn't see a clock anywhere, but there was music playing in the background. He turned to Brenda—she had a wristwatch. "Well, we're all set, I guess. How long do you suppose 'til the movie starts?"

Brenda held up a finger to indicate he had to wait a sec—she needed to take a swig of Pepsi to wash down that last handful of popcorn. Fortunately, she had it in her right hand—evidently she had finished the cup of cocoa already or tucked it between her legs—he didn't want to check and see, but it seemed logical; her legs didn't have much space between them, if any. Like most girls, she was a lot wider than he was.

"Real soon, I think." Brenda didn't check her watch since it would have required putting her Pepsi down. "When the lights start to dim, that means it will start—usually they have the previews and newsreel first. I doubt if they will have a cartoon—not with this movie," she shook her head and helped herself to another handful of popcorn.

"Thanks," Julian was glad she was knowledgeable, because he sure wasn't. The last movie he had seen was Swiss Family Robinson, and that was over a year ago. He parked the tub of popcorn on his right leg and reached for the booklet. He wanted to glance through it before he touched the popcorn—he figured greasy fingers would spoil the book—no sense in that. The light was good, but not bright enough to read the text without holding it up close to his eyes. Lots of photos from the movie, of course. One page about the director and other movies he had made; a page about Lawrence, a page about making the movie in the desert... man, this was as fancy a book as he had seen. He was real glad he had picked this up. That's when the lights started to dim.

"Ooo-ee!" the movie was about to start. The music in the background grew louder. While he was reading the booklet, the rest of the balcony had filled. Sure enough, it was a full house. He was glad he had taken his jacket off—it was very warm to begin with, and all these people seemed to add to that—what with the bear coat spillover, he was a little worried that it might get too warm. So he folded his jacket up and tucked it under his seat. Other than rolling up his sleeves, there wasn't much else he could do. He took another sip of hot chocolate. *tasty.* It ought to be: cost twice as much as it did at Amanda and June's.

About those winks—what Julian, along with most people, didn't know was how Rodney had turned the Orpheum's balcony into a very special playground that only a few knew about: Rodney's friends and friends of those friends, for the most part. Predictably, the number had grown slightly over time as word spread, and others took advantage of the opportunity, but it was still a relatively closely held secret. The management of the theater was not in on the secret enterprise, though it was responsible for its genesis. A staff cutback three years earlier had an unintentional effect: the balcony personnel had been reduced to a single usher. The workload up there was so light they would have cut both positions, but their liability policy required them to have at least one person on duty. The result was to grant that person a unique role—it had become a mini domain of sorts—whatever that usher allowed was, in fact, allowed.

It was not long before the possibilities were explored by the enterprising Rodney. He had an arrangement with the box office to reserve a small block of six seats in the balcony; whenever he needed, these were held until the very last. Rodney could buy any or all of them right up to show time, or not, for any showing on his shift. The manager had a similar standing arrangement on the main floor that was used for accommodating his special guests—that's what had given Rodney the idea.

Rodney's seats were known as "the best seats in the balcony," because the occupants knew they would have the best view of the screen as well as the freedom to play around without having to worry about being asked to leave. As long as there were no complaints from other patrons, anything could happen, and sometimes did—especially if there wasn't anyone else in the balcony. The usher had a blind eye. Sometimes, Rodney got a special treat himself, or a folded banknote in the shirt pocket as a satisfied viewer left the balcony. Smart enough not to have a standard fee, he was not subject to any complaints. Over time, it became rumored that the Orpheum balcony was a good place to go if you wanted to do a little necking or "petting" while you watched a movie—so not all the patrons were "friends of Rodney." He had little or no control over them, and had to give them the same freedoms, lest he get a complaint. So far, he had not had a problem.

Julian was the only one in the party of four that knew nothing about this.

The music came to an end, and the house lights dimmed rapidly. When it was completely dark, the crimson curtain opened slowly; simultaneously a long wide black rectangle opened on the wide white screen. An entirely different piece of music began. It was jarring to begin with, then became grand and sweeping, quite lyrical—even romantic. Julian was confused: had something gone wrong? Nothing was showing down there—only that black space—then suddenly, as the music ended, the Columbia Pictures Logo appeared, remained a short while, and faded when another piece of music started. Immediately an image appeared—a very odd image. The camera was aimed straight down at a paved area; a motorcycle was at the far left. The audience had a bird's eye view from about twenty five feet above. Soon, a figure entered from the lower right and walked over to the motorcycle. He fussed with something, then walked back where he had come from. He reappeared as the credits began. At first this was confusing—he was being expected to watch what the man was doing, read the credits, and listen to the music, all at once. But he thought it was clever that the credits were arranged so that they occupied the empty pavement in the right half of the screen.

Then everything changed: the music stopped and the camera was looking at the side of the motorcycle from about three feet away: it filled the entire screen. As he stomped on the kick-starter, the man sat on the motorcycle. The music had stopped—all the audience could hear was the roar of the motorcycle; it sped away.

Julian had not gone to many movies, and he was not used to what they could do—he was awestruck and open mouthed with suspense— soon he was gripping the left seat arm as if trying to stay on that motorcycle—when it careened off the road and crashed he held his arm across his face as if to protect himself from crashing with the guy on the cycle. It all went so fast!

Suddenly, they were in front of a huge stone cathedral with a hundred foot wide staircase. The credits continued as the camera paused to eavesdrop on various people leaving what was obviously the funeral of the motorcyclist. He listened carefully to what they said, but it took a while to make any sense. Julian had never heard of Lawrence or any of these other people. The only thing he recognized was their English accent.

Somehow, he knew better than to ask either Frankie or Brenda what was going on. He decided to figure it out by himself and hope that it would get easier as it went along. It was too early to decide if he would like this movie or not—but it was supposed to be the best movie this year. He didn't much like the thought that he was too stupid to figure it out.

The scene jumped to a workroom somewhere—the motorcyclist was coloring in something on a map with a water color brush. At last.

276

Julian was at home here, and things were starting to make sense. Then everything changed again! When Lawrence blew out the match, the scene jumped to the desert just as the sun was rising over the horizon.

"Whoa!" Julian whispered. From that point on, he was rapt with wonder at what he was seeing—it was wonderful, it was exotic—and he wanted it to stop for a minute so he could do a sketch. He couldn't believe that they would hold the view for so long—it made him feel like he was there. "Whoah," he whispered: all of a sudden, he spotted a teeny dot moving... slowly, ever so slowly, the camera moved and zoomed in closer: it was someone on a camel! must be a mile away—maybe more!

Visually, this movie was beyond anything he had expected. That alone kept him glued. The soundtrack was surround stereo—hearing it from all directions was a new thing as well—especially with the volume so high. Now this was hands down the best movie he had ever seen! His physical discomfort soon faded, and he was swallowed up. Much of the story line might have troubled him—he had no knowledge of the time or characters or events being depicted—but the visual treatment was so masterful, that alone had him captivated. Every other scene he could see a drawing he wanted to do. The only objection Julian had so far was the distance from the screen: he wished he were in the front row.

"Wow! Did you see that?!" he asked Brenda. The bi-plane had just flown out from behind a big cliff—it was teeny, like an insect. *maybe the Red Baron is in this!* He tried at first to share the experience with her—he felt an obligation to do that. She usually nodded and took another handful of popcorn—she was a slow eater—almost a machine like pace. Evidently she knew how to make the bucket last a while, no matter if the movie was exciting or suspenseful. Once she had shed the coat, he was able to form a more accurate opinion about her weight: not as heavy as he expected, but she had a few extra pounds. She didn't have a double chin yet, but that would likely develop in a few years. Thanks to the movie soundtrack, he couldn't hear her popcorn being consumed; it was so heavily buttered it didn't have any crunch to speak of anyway.

After a few mouthfuls, he went light on the popcorn—he liked the plain kind better; she would end up eating most of his. Besides, he had finished his hot chocolate; he didn't have anything to wash it down with—popcorn almost requires a companion drink—he always got a lemonade if he could, since it didn't fizz up and make him full and have to burp. He didn't have enough hands to carry anything more when they were at the counter, and he didn't want to make two trips. So, he made do with a single cup of hot cocoa—it had cooled by the time they were seated.

It soon became clear that Brenda didn't want to talk during the movie, which was fine with him—he didn't want to talk anyway. Before long, he was completely absorbed by this incredible, spectacular film. He didn't understand a lot of it at first, but it was starting to make sense. He wished Randall was here—he probably knew something about this. He decided early on that he wanted to see this movie a second time.

All of a sudden, the picture dimmed slightly, and froze: a gigantic INTERMISSION appeared—real impressive lettering—and the music began to repeat themes from the early part of the film. Julian leaned back, disappointed that it had been interrupted. He took a minute to adjust. As the house lights came on he was trying to sort out the story. He wanted more of those epic views of the desert especially. He hadn't heard about this super wide film before—adjusting to the composition elements had his imagination going. He wondered if it was something he should explore in his drawing. He wanted to talk with Mr. van Horn about that first thing.

He shook his head to get back to the here and now—Geraldine and his mother had spent time brushing him up on what a gentleman was expected to do on occasions like this. He turned to Brenda: "Boy, that was something! You sure know how to pick a good movie!" He couldn't think of anything else to compliment her on. It was sort of awkward, because he hadn't had much of a chance to get acquainted with her—it was too cold, too hurried and too complicated all around before the movie. He couldn't even see what she looked like, all swallowed up in that white fluff.

Brenda giggled lightly, her usual response in awkward situations—she had nothing to do with selecting the movie—but she couldn't very well explain that she was what had been selected. Last week her friend Rhonda had called saying she was about to give her the surprise of the year. She wasn't kidding: here she sat, right next to the one and only. She wasn't about to pass this up! Rhonda was sort of like her third older sister, only a **lot** smarter.

"What a nice thing to say." She batted her eyes, waiting for him to continue the conversation. She hadn't completely adjusted to the fact that she had actually been sitting next to him for two hours. She had watched him from afar in the cafeteria for the last few weeks, but she couldn't imagine him drawing her portrait. She wasn't a great beauty and knew it—she thought of herself as being in the 'less said the better' category. Saved her a lot of unnecessary pain and suffering and a lot of money. Having a couple of older sisters was more than good luck—she didn't need to go through what they had.

"Frankie says you have second lunch, like I do." Now that he could see her, he thought it only right to get to know her a little. "I don't remember seeing you in the cafeteria—'course, I just started going there lately—I useta eat my lunch in the Atrium or outside."

That was news. "Why did you do that?" She never understood why some kids did that.

"I like to draw things—lunch is perfect 'cause there's lots of extra time. Now I'm drawing in the cafeteria—only it's just faces now. Eventually I'll draw other things, probably." He was about to ask her what her favorite class was, but he was interrupted.

"Time to stretch our legs!" Frankie announced as he stood, shaking his legs to get the blood circulating again. The inference was clear: time to hit the boy's room. The sooner they got in line the better. A full theater meant a wait—maybe a long one—the major disadvantage of sitting in the balcony.

"Oh!" Julian remembered at once: Geraldine had refreshed his memory on what the boy was supposed to do at intermission. He turned to Brenda and smiled, "Would you like to move around a little, go down to refresh yourself?" Geraldine had told him to ask that—it was girl code for going to the restroom.

"Yes, that would be nice," Brenda held up her empty Pepsi cup and tipped her head politely.

"Oh, yeah—you prob'ly need another one for part 2… silly me."

279

"Thank you, yes…" she held out the popcorn tub that Julian had given her when hers went empty. "I might need another one of these. You need one too, I expect," she blinked her eyes demurely. She couldn't believe how nice he was. She didn't expect that.

Julian was too polite to see the ironic element—the cute little butterfly smile on the well-fed face would have evoked a roll of the eyes from Geraldine. Julian was just as glad, however, that she was a regular person, not just a couple of huge boobs waiting for him to do whatever—he interrupted himself: *as a matter of fact, what do guys do with those, anyway?* He'd never asked anyone about that, of course; he wasn't as stupid as **that**.

Well, whatever they did, he wasn't after any helpful tips. Brenda wasn't exactly what he would call fat, but she outweighed him by a bunch—*maybe that's why her top part doesn't poke out as much*. One thing he had never done was compare girls' boobs—some were almost as flat as boys. He thought they were the lucky ones. Anyway, it didn't matter, since showing Brenda off to his mom and Geraldine was not part of Frankie's plan. Geraldine had given up on the idea of taking them to Amanda's for dessert, since they were going to Shakey's.

"We can leave our coats here," Frankie announced. "Rodney's on duty—but take your purses along." They always did, but he thought it best to suggest it anyway.

As he was supposed to, Julian stood and let Brenda pass in front of him before following Frankie to the aisle. After she had gone by he reflected a minute—she didn't smell of perfume, at least. She smelled like buttered popcorn. He found that amusing, but refrained from saying anything. Rhonda was right: she was the perfect date. He'd have to finish getting acquainted later. He felt a responsibility to do that. He checked to make sure his souvenir program was safely tucked under his seat with his jacket. He grabbed all the empty cups and tubs—provided she didn't need more candy, he had enough to pay for everything.

Don't forget, you'll have to tell Geraldine and Mom all about her. Good old Inside Guy was still on duty.

Julian was glad to get a reminder—that was a fact if anything was. He had to make this date satisfy them for a while. That had to be kept in mind above everything. It seemed clear that she wasn't going to be like Rita, at least—so he had to figure some other angle. *we need to work that out.* Sometimes, like right then, he pointed things out **to** Inside Guy.

This was one of those times when being a lowly sophomore was visible: Frankie was considerably taller; he had shiny dark hair, so he didn't look like his big brother. Not as muscular as Tom, he was well developed. Julian figured he went to the gym a lot—seemed to be concerned about his looks. Well, what with the fancy hot rod and all, that was understandable. He took pride in being known as a ladies man.

As one would expect, the girls headed for the girls restroom. Julian wasn't under pressure, particularly—all he'd had was a cup of cocoa and a few handfuls of popcorn. He stuck to Frankie anyway. Getting better acquainted with him was a good idea too.

"So, what'd ya think?" Frankie asked quietly—he'd let the girls get a few feet ahead.

"Man! This is about the best movie ever. I didn't want it to stop." He could hardly wait to see the rest of it.

"Not that—what about Brenda?" Frankie hadn't paid them or the movie any attention—he was busy with Rhonda. That was the main advantage of all those long scenic parts—made it easy for her to play around a lot.

Julian checked to see if it was okay to talk—he didn't want them to hear anything. They were chatting up a storm just like Rita and Theresa did at the dance—must be a girl thing—it was safe if he was careful. "Well, she sure likes popcorn." He shook his head. "Rhonda was right—so far she's perfect." He didn't bother to explain what Geraldine was after—that was obvious. Besides, they had covered that at Sparky's.

As they walked down the ramp, Julian wondered if he should get a spot in the refreshment line—the lobby was jammed full already.

"Better stick with me—too easy to get separated with this many people. The intermission is twenty minutes, so we have plenty of time." Julian would be hard to find in a crowd this thick, even if his hair did stand out.

Julian shrugged. Frankie knew best.

281

Frankie had spent the first half "playing" with Rhonda—or letting her play with him—same difference. She was ready to take a break, and Frankie was ready to focus on Julian. He wanted to see if Tom and Danny knew what they were talking about. If his hunch was accurate, about half the balcony would be empty after the intermission. A lot of people would have had their fill of this movie—too highbrow. That would make lots more possible. In theory, Rhonda was working on that. She knew he played on both sides of the street, but she was under orders to not suppose the same was true of Julian. Frankie was not about to betray a fellow Flaming Arrow. His problem at this point was location—some things could not be talked about in a line of guys waiting to take a whiz. *we'll be there in 5 minutes, maybe, if we're lucky.* He'd have to find out more later.

The girl's line was considerably longer; Rhonda and Brenda were focused on the latest "boy news" while they waited. Her lips pursed, as if tasting something slightly tart, Rhonda got to the point at once: "Well, I'm dying to know: what's it like to be sitting next to the sexiest boy in the Sophomore Class?" Her head was hunched low with gleeful eagerness.

"I didn't expect him to be so nice—he's really quite sweet and thoughtful. But you were right—he's interested in the movie, not me." That was what she was told to expect.

Rhonda was mixed in her mind about the best way to deal with part 2 of the movie. Frankie wanted to "pay attention" to Julian after the intermission. It was too crowded tonight to do very much, in any case. *should I have Brenda sit where she is, or move around next to me?* Frankie had been vague about that. She had a hunch that he needed to be more careful than usual with this one. There was no buzz about him— Rita was not about to say anything—that was made very clear when she tried. In any case, Rita was just using him to control Stacey to begin with—everyone knew that. Something happened after the dance, but she was unable to find out a thing—even Barbara's lips were sealed. *very odd.*

The fact that Julian didn't have a steady girlfriend was odd too, though. He was a hard one to figure—all he seemed interested in was drawing. He didn't come across as a churchified goody goody type—he seemed to like girls, but… maybe he was just a slow developer. He wasn't promiscuous in the least. She had known other boys that seemed to be "immune" to those typical boy urges. Some of the brainy types came to mind there—they were slow developers for sure.

"You want to stay next to him, or move around next to me?"

Brenda thought about that. The implication was clear—but somehow, it didn't seem right. The boy didn't seem to mind her at all. She felt welcome, strangely enough. She didn't want to hurt his feelings by disappearing from his side without an explanation. He was interested in the movie. She knew that some people sat up in the balcony for other reasons, but she doubted if Julian was the type. "Only if you think I should." She didn't want to, really, but this was Rhonda's call to make.

Rhonda gave it some thought. "How's this: as the movie goes on, if it seems right for any reason, you can make a move—either to come around by me, or maybe flirt with him a little—see if he needs an 'invitation.' He might just be following the rules because he's a good scout. Test him out if you want… you never know, lots of boys are too chicken to start, but play just fine if they can find a way to get started. He could be one of those."

The second round of refreshments was less cumbersome—Brenda was able to handle her giant tub and jumbo Pepsi easily; she had saved half the Snickers bar and one of the Milk Duds boxes—both were safely tucked under the coat. Julian had a large lemonade and large tub of popcorn. They didn't have plain, but he didn't have them add the extra butter to his this time. He had paid attention to how the popcorn was prepared while they waited in line. They didn't have a popcorn kettle at all—it was delivered in huge bags, already popped. He watched them pour a bag into the large wide bin where sunlamps heated it. It seemed freshly popped. Extra butter was poured over it after it was scooped into its tub. They added however many dippers full you wanted. Made sense, considering how much they sold: it took time to make popcorn.

Getting back to their seats was easy, since the balcony was slow to fill up. Brenda's coat stood out like a furry iceberg in the dark blue ocean of seats. The lemonade hit the spot—Julian took a big gulp, then helped himself to a handful of popcorn—the lightly buttered flavor was okay. Not as greasy, the large size tub fit nicely between his legs—he didn't get a giant this time. He was all set for part two.

Thinking about some of the scenes that had impressed him the most, he turned to Brenda: "Did you know they had quicksand in the desert?" The part where the boy got swallowed up continued to haunt him.

Brenda was pleased he had asked. "I never thought about it before," she admitted. "I thought it was something in the swampy areas. Don't they have that in the Everglades?"

"Yeah—they warned us about it in scouts—sometimes you run across it on a hike." He had never actually seen any himself. The idea of being swallowed up like that was horrible. What had impressed him even more was how Lawrence stopped the other boy from getting caught in it. The expression on Lawrence's face had hit him just as hard—he immediately thought of Mark protecting a scout like that—maybe even himself. In an odd way, Lawrence made him think of Mark. Silly, maybe, but he did. Especially when he made them serve the boy lemonade in that bar—that's something Mark would do for sure.

"Do you go on a lot of hikes?" Brenda didn't know anything about scouting or hikes, but she rather enjoyed talking with Julian. He was different from anything she had expected. Somehow, she thought Rhonda was wrong about him—he wasn't at all like Frankie. Not that she didn't like Frankie. Maybe it was because he was a sophomore. Being a junior, she felt different about him—kind of sisterly. He would make an ideal little brother.

Music from the movie began—Julian liked that theme a lot—it reminded him of those incredible desert landscapes. The crimson drape was still closed. The music must be a warning to everybody to get back to their seats—a good thing to do, because more than half the balcony was still empty. "I sure hope they all get back in time," he remarked, helping himself to some popcorn. He didn't like the idea of people blocking the screen while they found their seats in the dark.

Brenda could see that was an honest concern—that cinched it for her—he wasn't interested in playing: he wanted to watch the movie. Well, that suited her too. She decided to pay closer attention to the rest of it herself. It was an unusual movie. She couldn't say she liked it—war

284

movies were not on her favorite list. It might come in handy in a history class, from what she had heard; next year she would be taking Modern Problems—this war might be one of the things they covered.

The lights dimmed and the drapes opened below—she noticed how Julian had already prepared for this: he wasn't about to miss a second. Well, she didn't especially want to sit next to Rhonda anyway. She took another fistful of popcorn—*mmm. delicious...* Buttered popcorn was one thing she never got at home. A bit of heaven, this was.

The second part had a long music prelude just like the first part, only this time it started with drums being pounded hard. Then the theme music played. Julian figured that must be the way they made some movies. Getting people's attention first, then into the right mood was a good idea, actually. He was beginning to feel like he was back in it already. The music stopped abruptly—*oboy...* Julian was absorbed by the big screen almost at once.

Frankie's attention was divided—he needed to familiarize himself with the couples still present. As he had expected, half the seats, maybe slightly more, were empty. Some would be watching the movie, but some would only appear to be. His plan required knowing which to watch and keeping track of what was developing—or not. This was essential: he needed a way to get started—a direct approach was likely to go badly—that he did **not** need. A good example was the best way—that's what he was on the lookout for—there were three couples located just right—with any luck, one of them would provide what he was looking for. In the meantime, he made the usual preparations—he was experienced and expert at this. First, he adjusted his coat slightly; it was spread across his lap as it had been in the first half of the film. Open like a blanket and dark colored, it was perfect for masking what he was up to. Everything was hidden from view. Fluffed up, it was better than a blanket; it held a peak: any movement underneath was invisible as well. Unlike many balcony regulars, he preferred a high degree of privacy.

He wasn't terribly horny—Rhonda had taken the edge off there very nicely; it was the challenge of this: irresistible. He had claimed possession of the armrest again. Julian didn't rely on it anyway—his left arm was employed holding his lemonade, his right was free to dip into his popcorn tub. Frankie glanced at the screen occasionally, but he wasn't paying close attention—only enough to avoid making his move at the wrong moment—distracting Julian would be a bad idea if the timing was wrong.

It took a little longer than he expected—five was the usual. About ten, maybe 15 minutes in, one of the couples he'd been watching provided what he had been waiting for. The action in the film wasn't particularly essential at this point, so he gave Julian a slight nudge with his elbow.

Julian was engrossed completely; the nudge was intentional, so he turned to see what he wanted. Frankie raised his eyebrows and carefully pointed down to the right. Julian looked down where he had pointed; he was surprised to discover that so many seats were still empty. Evidently a lot of people had left at the intermission. Then he saw what Frankie was pointing at—he couldn't believe his eyes! This guy was slouched back, his legs spread wide: a girl's hand was holding his cock, slowly jacking him off while they were kissing. His jaw dropped open wide in shock.

Julian was not only shocked, but he was instantly confronted with a complex mixture of responses: first, the sight had sent an instant flash to Little J. Second, his concern for Brenda: she was uppermost in his conscious mind. Without turning his head, he glanced to see if she was looking down there. As it happened, she was preoccupied with the box of Milk Duds—the top didn't want to open. She needed one hand to hold her popcorn bucket... she hadn't seen anything. Maybe the angle wasn't as good from her seat. He looked at Frankie, wide eyed.

Frankie gave Julian the Groucho double eyebrow raise. Meant to invite, he didn't push it. He needed to wait a minute or two to see if Julian's auto response had kicked in. He watched where Julian's eyes went next: Yes! They went back to the sideshow. It wouldn't take very long.

Julian was in a jam here—he truly wanted to pay attention to the movie—he glanced at the screen; the lap activity down there was in the same direction: there was no way to not see that as well as the lower right side of the movie. The other factor, also unexpected, was the fact that Little J was overdue for his regular standard exercise—final exam studies had blocked that completely for several days. It took absolutely no time for Little J to awaken and get ready to perform. Julian felt a very strong tingle beneath his scrotum—one of his favorite sensations. It was always followed by another favorite sensation, Little J filling up to salute position.

At first Julian didn't realize that Frankie's hand had reached over—he was being checked on. The trouble was, Little J liked that—he liked it a lot. Instinctively, Julian shifted the tub of popcorn slightly—he needed to do what he could to prevent Brenda from noticing anything. There wasn't much else he could do—his left hand was holding a large lemonade cup; he'd hardly made a dent in it.

Frankie was very pleased: Julian was about a third up already. He went into action at once. He withdrew his hand and pulled it under his coat about six inches. He pinched the inner lining in the usual place and slowly drew the coat over Julian's lap. He had done this many times before and knew precisely how to do it without anyone seeing a thing. He had never tried it with an unsuspecting girl in the next seat. He wasn't worried, because Brenda was savvy to what went on here, but he wanted to see if he could do it without her catching on. He could feel the growing treasure under his hand as he reached for his access point. The cover in place, he turned his hand over. As he had planned, the bottom button of the 501 fly was still open. He tucked his middle finger in and gave a gentle lift to the scrotum, insuring that it was completely free. He located the next button up and opened it. He opened two more. By that time, Julian's boytoy was up full—ready and eager to be massaged, no annoying skivvies in the way.

One of Frankie's specialties, this maneuver; it had been fine-tuned for a while—over two years. This was the second with an unsuspecting companion in the adjoining seat. Julian was average size, and circumcised. That made it super easy. The only thing Frankie couldn't do was lubricate. That was okay too—took longer to get there, which was preferable anyway. A bonus! He felt a familiar hand approaching from the left: Rhonda was testing to see if he was up and ready again. He slid forward slowly and spread his legs wide. This was nice… a second time always took longer. He'd never had a three way quite like this. He gave her an approving grin and turned his head forward. Anyone looking his way would swear he was watching the movie.

Julian troubled about his situation briefly, uncertain about what to do. On the one hand, he wanted badly to watch the movie—and he didn't want Brenda to know what was going on. On the other hand, Frankie knew how to please Little J—it felt **wonderful**. Suddenly it hit him: *those winks!* Did Brenda know this was going to happen? Was she in on this? The very idea seemed outrageous.

Could be, Inside Guy opined. *Remember what Rita did. Remember, she winked when you said we had the best seats.* He didn't need to explain further.

Julian might be clueless, but he wasn't stupid. He had to assume that there was a fifty-fifty chance that she knew—*but what if she is planning to do something like Rita was? what then!??!*

Inside Guy had no opinion on that, but thought it would be smart to keep it in mind.

Julian checked as carefully as he could to see what Brenda was doing. She had solved the Milk Dud problem and was carefully fishing in the box for another one—she was busy chewing, obviously savoring every moment. She glanced briefly at the screen, then closed her eyes. It was clear that her taste buds were in charge. There was no sign that she had seen what was still going on about three rows down. For the time being, that's what had Julian's immediate attention; it had upstaged the Arabian desert.

His mind at rest about her as a potential lap explorer, the remaining question was whether she would figure out what Frankie was doing; she couldn't see a thing; as long as he sat still, she wouldn't be any the wiser. He shifted the popcorn tub slightly—he didn't want it to slip and fall off his lap. He helped himself to a couple of kernels… it did taste good, at that. Gradually, he relaxed and paid attention to what Frankie was doing—it was different, new—and **very** pleasurable. Julian was always interested in something new when it came to Little J. He wasn't in a constant search like he had been at camp last summer, but he wanted to have as good a background as he could so that when the time came, Mark would be pleased. He took the scout motto seriously: he would Be Prepared. Besides, he planned on seeing this movie again. Next time he would go with Randall—or maybe Kasey. Better yet, both of them. Slowly he slid his rear end forward and opened his legs a little

288

wider. Might as well make it easier for Frankie. He needed to pay attention to how he did this—it was a totally new approach. He doubted if he would ever need to do it personally, but... *you never know*...

The time had come—Julian had not thought about it until this very minute: how was he going to shoot without making a huge mess? Little J was likely to have a huge load—almost 5 days worth, at least. *how will Frankie know when I'm ready?*

Frankie had perfected a way to deal with this. He could tell it was close—the pre-cum was regular and plentiful, intensifying the sensations, and Julian had tensed. He rotated his grip. Doing this one handed was tricky, but he knew what to do. His thumb on top at the center of the head, his forefinger directly opposite, he had formed a cup ready to be filled. The trick was holding the shaft at the right angle—it had to be precise, and tight—he dare not let it slip. He knew just when to squeeze. Hopefully, Julian's involuntary spasm wouldn't be noticed by Brenda. If it was, she wouldn't be a problem.

Instinctively, Julian knew how to help: he had carefully shifted the popcorn tub toward the back. He slid his right hand down under the coat and grasped the base of Little J's shaft and held it tight... this enhanced the pleasure considerably—the pulsing was especially thrilling—he could feel the ejaculate move through the channel as he had expected—it made controlling things easier, although it couldn't stop his thighs from quivering erratically. Frankie's coat took care of hiding that. All he needed to focus on was holding his head in place. He grimaced as it reached the peak. It was all he could do to control the urge to groan ecstatically and keep from pumping like crazy.

It was the strangest shoot he'd ever had. But boy, did Frankie know how to make it feel good.

Frankie held his hand in place for a while, lest a late spasm undo his careful work. After Julian had flexed the shaft three times, he knew it was safe to withdraw his hand. Slowly, carefully, he delivered the payload to his mouth. *mmm... sweet, very sweet.* Julian was a number two on his 5 point scale. *nice.*

Julian was very mellow for a time—Frankie had re-buttoned his fly and gone away by the time he returned to the here and now. He scooted back and finished his lemonade. Below, Lawrence was being helped up out of a mud puddle or something. He had lost track of what had been going on. His attention returned to Arabia—or wherever they were.

21   *Grandma Molly*

>> ***beep-beepety-beep-beep!*** <<

"They're here!" Julian finished his orange juice and hopped up from the kitchen table: Tom and Nick were outside. Troop 9 was on the way to Fernbrook Manor for the annual holiday decoration party. He could hardly wait: a whole building full of Grandmas and Grandpas! *what could be more fun than that?!* He grabbed his sketchbook. He already had his jacket on.

Francine went to the door to see him off. "Say hello to Mark for me," she leaned forward for his hug. She no longer leaned down—by spring, he would probably be leaning down. He was growing so much faster than she had expected.

He skipped merrily down the steps. "See ya later," he waved goodbye and hopped in—Nick had opened the door for him. *oo goody! I get to sit up front...*

>> ***beep-beep!*** <<

Tom gave the horn a bye-bye tap, and they were off.

Julian wiggled—*a little tighter than usual.* It had been a while since he got a lift from Tom. *I just love Saturdays!* On Saturdays he got to sleep in, he got to have a late breakfast with his Mom...

"So what's new?" Nick couldn't help thinking of Julian as his little brother—he wasn't so little any more, though; the front seat was really full now with him on board—didn't used to be. He was curious about how the double date went last weekend, but thought it best to wait for Julian to mention it. With Frankie involved, it might have been "unusual," as dates go. The movie was supposed to be worth seeing more than once.

"Spent some time helping Geraldine decorate her office for Christmas," he laughed. Working with the guys again was fun—he hadn't seen them since last summer. They were sure different from Kasey. "Her crew is fun to work with." He turned to Tom: "You ever had to decorate a roof?"

"Roof?" Tom hadn't done that, but he had helped his brothers to run a string of lights along the gutters one year. *no thanks* His mother had put an end to that—she hated seeing any of them on a stepladder. Anyway, outdoor decorations were too much work.

"Yeah—she has a Santa Claus landing on the roof. My job was to make sure Rudolf couldn't get loose and pull everything down." Julian had given Geraldine a good scare. He was just as glad that she made him come down, actually—it was cold and windy that day.

"Cool." Tom had seen that. "Looks nifty at night. The nose blinks."

Nick couldn't resist: "So, how was Lawrence of Arabia?"

Julian turned to him wide eyed: "That's the best movie ever! You hafta go see it when you can! I sure want to see it again." He nodded eagerly, and grabbed his arm: "did you know they had quicksand in the desert? This kid got sucked down, right out of sight—they couldn't save him." He wondered how they made that look so real.

Nick had not heard about that. The long article in Life Magazine had not mentioned that scene. Julian's answer set his mind at rest about Frankie and the date—he didn't even mention the girl.

Julian sat forward, concerned: Tom had missed the turn.

"We're going to drive straight there, I hope that's okay with you—or did you want to ride on the bus with the Troop?" Nick was afraid the bus had already left; he and Tom were going shopping afterward—Christmas wasn't far off.

Julian shrugged. "I can stick with you guys, if it's okay—unless you think Mark would mind."

292

"I told him we would be picking you up, so we're okay there." Tom knew they couldn't make it to the Church in time anyway—he was late on purpose so Danny could do the organizing; that was Mark's idea.

Julian nodded; he planned to ride back on the bus. His mom and Geraldine were planning to pick him up at the Church parking lot to go Christmas shopping.

When they entered the retirement home parking area, the bus was already there; Mark was talking to Mr. Swann. He was here along with a delivery van from Newberry's. Julian figured he was pitching in on this project. *that's the kind of thing he would do, for sure.* He liked Mr. Swann a lot.

"We're a little late," Nick gave Tom a 'told you so' look.

Tom wasn't worried: Danny would do the organizing just fine. He could use the experience; Tom was working with Mark on that as well as a new super secret project for next year. *hmmm…* Finding an open parking slot was going to take a little time; there were a lot of cars. *must be a lot of visitors today.* "Get out here, you guys—I need to find a place to park."

"Good idea." He hopped out, skipped around the front of Tom's car and ran up to Mark, saluting: "Sorry we're late; Mom says hi."

"We just finished unloading; you're okay," he returned Julian's salute. "Danny and Frankie are getting things underway in the lunchroom."

Julian was delighted to see Mr. Swann… he didn't see the Packard though. "Hi, Mr. Swann. I want you to meet Nick—he's training me to take over as Troop Scribe. Nick, this is Mr. Swann." He gave the Groucho eyebrow signal that this man was really important.

Swann offered his hand. "Pleased to meet you, Nick."

"Thank you, sir." Nick could tell the man was special—his clothing and manner of speech made that obvious. Maybe he owned Fernbrook.

Julian glanced at Nick—they needed to join the Troop. "Is it okay to go inside now?" He was afraid Danny needed them already.

293

"Yes, you should. Thanks, boys." Mark gave a salute.

"See ya," Julian waved at Mr. Swann. He ran alongside Nick. They'd be there in a flash. "I wonder if it's like last year… do we help the same people?"

"I don't know. There's always new residents. Ask Danny—he probably knows all that." What he didn't know was why they were starting an hour earlier. It clicked in his head suddenly: Julian said they would find something out at the next Troop meeting. That man must be a part of it.

"Can you tell me who Mr. Swann is?"

"Gosh!" He stopped in his tracks "I forgot! You guys don't know yet!" *what to do?* He could trust Nick. "Once we get things squared away, I'll fill you in. But you have to zip your lips about it until the Troop meeting, okay?"

Julian's word was enough. Intriguing, that was certain: something was afoot. He thought back to the meeting at Sparky's. Andy and that photographer Randall were in on it too: something about Casey. He was fond of puzzles. He would spend the day trying to see how much he could guess correctly.

Swann turned to Mark: "Unless you need me, I'll just wander around and watch for a while."

"Please, feel free." He was delighted to support and encourage Swann's interest. "Thanks for helping us out here—the additional decorations will help considerably. The residents will be pleased, for sure—some of their decorations have become a little tired over the years."

"How long have you been doing this?"

"The Troop, over ten years, at least. I just kept it going when I assumed the job five years ago—it's been an annual Troop project for a long time. It means a lot to the boys—and to the residents. We'll come back in January to take everything down," he looked around. "I'm hoping the Church has some storage space—they don't have much here, I'm afraid."

"I'll see what I can do about that. Thanks for the tip." He had already arranged for the residents to enjoy January rent-free. A storage room would be easy to arrange.

Danny stood at a table at one end of the cafeteria, officiating. The Flaming Arrow flag alerted the scouts that it was the head table for the operation. He had names and assignments on his clipboard. Several scouts were seated at tables waiting to be told where to go—some were waiting for their assigned senior citizens to rise and shine. Others were still bringing in cases of ornaments and artificial trees. Residents were expected to come in person or call in to signal they were ready to have their room decorations put in place. The Zebra Patrol had started decorating the main room with a string of lights—they would start the big tree next—this year's was nine feet high; decorating the outside had been assigned to the Tigers.

"How goes it?" Tom inquired. He was pleased with what he saw: he had been late on purpose so that Danny would get his feet wet in the job he would have next year when he became Assistant Scoutmaster. Tom didn't want to "retire," but it wasn't a matter of choice.

"Oh, hi. Goin' good. Some guys are waiting—the people they are supposed to help aren't up yet. We're starting a little early this year, thanks to Mr. Swann: he bought a truckload of new decorations: this year we get to do the outside as well as this this room. He has a bunch of artificial trees too. The rooms are supposed to use those now if we can talk them into it."

This place was about to look very festive. Julian felt something poking him in the rear.

"Here's a job for ya," Frankie quipped. He had snagged one out of the last case they unloaded. "We have two sizes to choose from."

Julian turned: he had just been poked by an artificial Christmas tree box. "So you hafta put these together?" He thought they came ready-made.

"It's easy—they just unfold." Frankie was in charge of distributing the new trees. "We have two sizes: small and smaller." He opened the box; he planned to display one on the main table.

"Hey, Julian—" Danny cupped his hand and turned to face him. "You have a fan here—Mr. Sanderson is at the table over by the fireplace." He pointed a thumb over his shoulder.

"Oo, yeah—Sid and I did their room last year! Neat old guy!" *Grandpa Jim...* he peeked over Danny's shoulder. He and Sid had fun with them. "What should I do? I'm not a Wolf any more—everyone has a new Buddy." Maybe Tom knew; Tom was his new patrol leader as well as the Assistant Scoutmaster.

Tom looked at the clipboard. "Sid and Kurt need a job—why not take them along? We have plenty of teams." He tried to honor Buddy requests when they were made. They didn't have to be in the same patrol. Each resident was assigned a pair of scouts to help decorate their apartment. A team of two could usually take care of a room in 15 to 30 minutes.

Julian looked at Mr. Sanderson again—he was by himself... *that's strange* "Where's Grandma?" *oh-oh...* He had a hunch. "Can you guys reserve Sid and Kurt for them? Let me go over there first." He needed to see if anything was wrong.

Rather than going to his car, Swann wanted to witness how this Troop functioned; and now, how Julian fit into the operation. The scoutmaster didn't know it, but he was on Swann's acquisition list. An executive talent like his didn't happen by every day. He entered the dining hall and turned left. He had spent enough time here to know the layout. Practiced at finding good "perches," he had pre-selected a likely spot from which to begin his observation. Next to a pillar along the north wall, he had a good view of the entire room. A resident was sitting by himself by the fireplace about twenty feet farther along. He chose not to join him. He needed to observe, not socialize. Julian and the boys he came with were doing something at the head table—the leadership team, obviously. Schaefer's skill at developing leaders was on display: they didn't need him present to function. *excellent.* He still hadn't adjusted to seeing Julian and Mark in scout uniforms; they gave the event an interesting, unique quality. He had not been in scouts.

He had arrived at an opportune moment, evidently: Julian did one of his signature hops and began waving merrily at the man seated near the fireplace. In no time at all, he had scurried across the room. Interestingly, Julian didn't see him sitting this close by—he was focused on the old man... probably in his 80s.

"Hiya Grandpa Jim!" Julian's voice carried well—he had called from the center of the room as he skipped over, grinning wide. "Too bad I couldn't sneak up behind and surprise you with a hug, but you had your eye on me," he giggled. "Can I hug you anyway?" His smile showed a genuine affection for the old man.

"You're a sight for sore eyes, Boy, that's for sure!" he opened his arms wide.

Julian put his sketchbook on the table and leaned close to give him a big hug. "I guess you can tell I grew a lot since last year—I'm way too big to sit on your lap now!" He pulled a chair over and sat next to the old man. He grabbed his left hand and asked brightly: "Where's Grandma?"

"Infirmary." He tried to appear hopeful, but the boy probably saw through it.

"Oo-ee! Well, we better get over there! I need her Holiday Hug!" He looked closely to see if he could guess how bad she was—last year he had been a little worried; she was kind of frail.

"Bless your heart, Boy—she could use your Holiday Hug too." he squeezed Julian's hand and stood. He was fully ambulatory and in fine shape. Julian's cheer was infectious.

Julian decided not to ask any questions. He'd figure out for himself how bad it was when he saw her. When the old man opened his arms, he hugged him again. Suddenly, he felt very needed. That was a new feeling—a good feeling. "Wait 'til I tell you about summer camp at Lake Walker! Have you ever been to Lake Walker?" He wanted to tell all about Uncle Max. He grabbed the sketchbook and they set out for the Infirmary.

"Years ago. Nice up there in the summer." *too far to drive for a picnic, but good for camping.* The boy's energy gave him such a lift. *maybe he can perk Molly up.*

Julian snagged a handful of candy kisses from a small bowl on one of the tables as they left.

Swann waited to follow—he doubted that Julian had seen him... he was focused on the old man. He didn't want to interfere—but he wanted to witness as much as he could. The way Julian related to this old man was remarkable, but not a total surprise.

Julian wrinkled his nose: this room smelled funny—like medicine or something. *they need some air wick in here* At the far end, Grandma Molly was propped up in bed, reading a magazine. He jumped right in without pausing: "There she is!" he exclaimed and hurried over to the far side of her bed. "I just found out you were here!" He reached out—"I need a big hug first, then we can talk."

Swan had hurried to catch up: he wanted to see this. The bright acoustics of the hallway had enabled him to hear the conversation. If nothing else, the boy was a natural born caregiver: another trait to research. He peeked around the corner just in time to hear her expression of surprise and joy as Julian hurried across the room.

"Sorry, I grew a bunch since last Christmas." He plopped the sketchbook on the foot of the bed and took both her hands in his. "Can you sit up? I don't want to do anything wrong or make anything worse."

"My, Julian—how you've grown! What has your mother been feeding you?"

Julian laughed. "That's better," he grinned at her big smile. "I do eat a lot more—takes longer to get full. She doesn't like leftovers, so I help out there." He squeezed her hands. "I snatched you a treat." He pulled a candy kiss out of his shirt pocket and peeled it partway open for her.

Her eyes lit up.

"I hope you're allowed to have these."

"My, yes."

"Good." he pulled the others out of his shirt pocket and put them on the bedside table. "Can you get out of bed? Maybe you can go for a walk with Grandpa Jim and me," he grinned.

The surprise on her face was evidence that she was not expecting to do anything like that.

"That's a wonderful idea, Molly." Nurse Jensen had just swept into the room. The voices had drawn her attention. Unannounced visitors were unusual. Molly was not used to receiving anyone other than her husband. Visitors were always welcome here. She went to the wardrobe closet for the robe.

"This room sure needs some flowers," Julian wrinkled his nose. *who should I talk to about that...* "Smells like the janitor's closet in here... a bunch of flowers would make it stink a lot sweeter."

Grandma Molly chuckled. "I've gotten used to it, but you're right." *roses would be nice...*

Swann added that to his growing list. This entire facility needed a major redecoration effort: carpets, art works, paint... He paused a moment to look at Julian. The boy continued to surprise: the bubbly innocent persona combined with a rather mature thoughtfulness was unexpected and unique—neither one was artifice. Thinking ahead to take a few candy kisses along was not what he would have predicted. *interesting...* his footrace at the airport had a similar quality.

Julian and Grandpa Jim took the silent instruction from the nurse and stepped away while she prepared Molly for leaving the room. They ran into Mr. Swann, who was standing just outside jotting something in his pocket notepad.

"Oh, Hi, Mr. Swann!" Julian turned to his Grandpa for the day: "This is Mr. Swann, Grandpa Jim; he's helping the Troop out this year—he bought a whole bunch of new decorations for everyone, including a new tree for your apartment! Think of that!"

"Mighty nice of you." Sanderson looked close, then shook his head. "Thought for a minute I recognized you from somewhere. Reckon not." He smiled at Julian and shook his head. "Used to have a sharper memory."

"My grandpa used to say his head was too full up to hold any more," Julian giggled. "Said he was allowed to toss things out now and then to make room."

"There it is… yessir, I reckon he had it right. Thanks, Lad." Sanderson planned to use that one. He nodded gratefully.

Just then Sid and Kurt appeared at the far end of the corridor. Danny had sent them to find Julian for their assignment. They scurried quickly up: "Reporting for duty, Chief Inspector!" Sid quipped, saluting.

"Perfect! Grandpa Jim, you remember Sid from last year. Can he and Kurt go ahead and put up the decorations in your apartment, or do they need to wait until we can go there?" He turned to Sid: "Grandma is in the Infirmary for a while, so she won't be able to help out."

Sid remembered last year. "We can do the door and window and put up one of the new trees real easy. Then you can add things later."

Sanderson saw the wisdom. "I hate to miss out—Molly misses it more." He pondered briefly. "Makes sense, I reckon." He looked at Julian gratefully. "That way it will be ready for her when she gets sprung from here," he nodded. "Much obliged… room's open, go on ahead." He remembered Sid's face: "Appears you grew an inch or two yourself—still could use more meat on your bones," he would have patted the boy's arm, but he was too far away. He pointed at Kurt. "This fella's plenty fit though. What's your name, son?"

"Kurt, sir," he bowed slightly, and pointed to Sid. "I'm workin' on it. Ain't easy, either."

Julian added his support: "Kurt's the best thing that ever happened to Sid—keeps him in line most of the time." He turned to Sid: "When you're done in the apartment, round up some help so we can decorate the Infirmary too." Julian looked at Mr. Swann. "This place could use a little cheer, y'know?" He checked the doorway to see if Grandma Molly had appeared. A frown appeared briefly.

"Problem?" Swann inquired.

Julian stepped close so that Grandpa Jim couldn't hear: "Not exactly. I was just wondering how I could draw a picture of them together. I think it would make them feel good, y'know? But they don't know about me drawing stuff, to begin with." He felt so powerless. "I still don't know why she's in here, either." Mr. Swann was still standing by. "Any ideas?"

Swann was a fast thinker. "Take your walk, then sit down for a visit with them and show them your sketchbook. I'll see what I can do. Will that work for the time being?"

Julian nodded eagerly: something told him that Mr. Swann had something in mind. Knowing him, it would work out. He remembered the photography session at Randall's. The only problem here was not having Mason around to help. Maybe he could fix things anyway.

Seeing the clouds lift from Julian's face was an experience in itself—one he would treasure. "I'm on my way." He stepped over to the old man and extended his hand: "Pleased to have met you. I'll be seeing you again, I'm sure." He turned to watch the nurse help her patient step into the hallway. Swann felt a rush—being part of the crew was fulfilling: a sensation he had not felt for years. *a call to the florist first; Brian can take care of the problem in no time.*

"I must look a fright!" Molly complained as the nurse helped her get past the door. "I'm a little stiff in the knees today," she smiled apologetically.

"You look a lot better on your feet," Julian quipped, stepping to her side to hook his left arm under her right. "How about letting me steady you for a little while."

"That would be nice." She looked up at him. "How many inches did you grow?!" *at least his face is the same…*

"Almost four. Drives my mom crazy," He grinned at Grandpa Jim. "So anyway: how long are you gonna be stuck here? Can they fix what ails you?"

Grandma frowned. "I'm under observation. I've been in that bed for almost a week." She gave him a very frustrated grandmotherly face. "I'm a puzzle."

Julian wasn't satisfied. He looked at Grandpa Jim—maybe he knew more. He didn't seem to. "Well, can't you give 'em a deadline? You're not gonna fix it just laying in that bed all day. Tell 'em to give you a bottle of get better pills."

That tickled Grandma Molly—she giggled. "I might just do that!" She looked at her husband, delighted.

Milton Witherspoon was relatively new to Fernbrook Manor, having settled into his rooms only last Spring. The opportunity to offer art classes had figured into his decision to spend his declining years here. He was delighted to respond to the gentleman's request to lend a hand—hopefully, it would boost interest in his weekly water color class. Fortunately, he had everything the boy needed. He was doubly grateful to have this opportunity. When Swann invited him to watch, he very nearly declined. What a mistake that would have been: if he hadn't seen the boy do this drawing himself, he would never have believed it. Drawing a live subject was extremely difficult to begin with, and this boy was drawing a couple of subjects who were barely sitting still. They certainly weren't posing.

He didn't know Jim and Molly well, but they were nice people. Most residents were—another reason he chose to live here. He was eager to see them react to this work of art—and that's what it was. That and watching Swann watch the boy artist was fascinating. He seemed to be studying the lad as if he was writing a book about him. He hadn't had time to learn anything about the man, but the manager certainly held him in high regard.

The young artist's narrative about Lake Walker had held everyone's attention; along with the couple's responses to the Christmas ornaments that the boy named Sid kept passing them for approval, the time sped by. Some of those evoked a memory that they needed to share. They were choosing which ones to hang on their new tree. Witherspoon's wristwatch revealed that they'd been watching the artist nearly 40 minutes, and it seemed like ten.

The boy's technique was unlike anything he had seen—he began by placing what appeared to be random dots in key places—evidently this was his way of locking in the composition. Once the bed and settee were firm, he roughed in the figures, then stopped to study them closely—he squinted for a time, immobile—then sprung into action, drawing both figures in place without looking at them at all, other than a brief glance to verify a detail now and then. It became clear that their motion was not a problem at all—he seemed to have a fixed position in his head. Their likeness was uncanny—beyond photographic. He had certainly mastered the standard number two pencil.

"Grandma Molly," Julian had a problem. "Could you hold your left hand still for a minute? I need to be sure about something." He was finishing the detail on her wedding ring—it needed to be accurate. He squinted; the glare made it too difficult to see clearly. He stood and handed the drawing board to Mr. Swann. "Can you hold this a second? I need to look up close."

He was only ten feet away, so it took no time. "Hold it still a sec: ah… thought so," he nodded. "The glare made it confusing. Now I know what to do. Thanks. I'm almost done." He stepped back to his chair.

Swann had looked closely at the drawing: her hand looked perfect as it was. He watched closely to see Julian make a final touch—clarifying the mounting that held the diamond in place. Fractions of an inch, a miniscule revision that hardly anyone would notice. The perfectionist at work. He exchanged glances with the other artist in the room. Clearly, they had the same response to this.

Part of the composition included a few round ornaments resting on the small table next to the box they had been in. Julian had placed them carefully: instead of signing the drawing as usual, he inscribed his signature and dedication carefully as if it was painted on three of the orbs: *"for Grandma Molly and Grandpa Jim"*, *"Happy Holidays 1962"* and *"from Julian."* He did not include his last name. The inscription was so small it was easy to miss from more than three feet away.

"There! All done." Julian stood and took it over, still taped to the drawing board. "Thanks for letting me draw you." he stood back a minute to look at their faces, then returned to his chair. This part was fun—seeing how happy they were had made his day. He gave Mr. Swann a grateful smile: he had made this happen. "And thank you for letting me use your drawing board! It was perfect." He had forgotten the man's name.

"My pleasure, lad. Any time." He extended his hand. What a thrill it was to have seen this—*this boy will be a name in the art world one day.*

Julian paid attention to Swann and the Nurse; they couldn't get their eyes off the couple. He had achieved his goal; they were sniffing the flowers Mr. Swann had delivered while he was drawing. When they were delivered Grandpa took a sprig and gave it to her to smell. Mr. Swann really liked that. They sure improved the air in the room. She kept it in her lap, so he had drawn it in as well—Inside Guy had the idea originally.

He turned around: "how you guys doin'? Need any help?" The room was a lot more cheerful with the Christmas decorations. The Nurse had worked with them closely. The blinking lights around the doorway were super.

"We're all done. What do you want us to do next?" Sid gave Kurt a poke in the ribs.

The wall clock said it was time to get a move on; Julian stood. He needed to get back to the dining room. "We have about an hour before lunch. I need to get back to the Troop, Grandma Molly. Can you have lunch with us, or do you hafta stay here?"

Molly looked at her husband hopefully. He held out his arm at once: "If you feel up to it…"

The Nurse was listening in. "I think you should, Molly. That will tell us a lot. Your strength and stamina are what we need to know more about. We can use a wheelchair if you want, but I think you should try on your own." She spoke to the visitors. "You can go finish what you need to—I can take it from here. We'll see you at lunch."

"Yay!" Julian hopped. "Gimme another hug first!" He opened his arms wide.

"Bless you, Julian." she was about to tear up. She reached for the Kleenex in her sweater pocket.

Grandpa stood. He needed a hug too. He didn't have any words handy.

"Great! We'll see ya later." He turned to Mr. Witherspoon. "Can you let them keep the drawing board a while? Later on we can figure a way to take care of it."

"How about I mat it for them? I have everything in the classroom—we mount sheets this size routinely; I may have one already cut."

"If we can do it after lunch, I'd like to help you with that." Swann intended to look after this drawing and preserve it for his collection. He wanted it handled properly. Until he could have it professionally done, this would have to do.

"Fine with me." He turned to Sanderson: "Bring it along to lunch to show to everyone, Jim. We can go up there afterward."

Swann stepped forward and extended his hand to Grandpa Jim. "I am Frederick Swann. Thanks for allowing me to observe. I will be in touch with you later." He turned to Molly. "You seem fit to join us for lunch; perhaps we can get acquainted there." He stepped over to the nurse. "I will be in touch soon. I trust it was acceptable to have flowers delivered? I have an account with Leading Floral. Are there any medical restrictions? I can have them contact you if that would help."

Nurse Jensen knew instantly that this man was every bit as powerful as he appeared. "Why, that would be perfect. I have a telephone in my office. I need to stay here for lunch—the cafeteria sends our meals here, of course." She had one other patient.

"As I assumed. Thank you; you should expect a call. I'll have Brian see to it personally." He could see that the boys were waiting for him. Not what he intended, but just as well. "Shall we go, gentlemen?" he gestured to the door.

"Boy, am I glad you were here. Thanks, Mr. Swann." He was extremely happy at how that visit had gone; he had not planned to do a drawing today. Sid and Kurt took care of the decorating—the drawing was a lot more important than setting up a few fake Christmas trees.

Swann was annoyed at having lost his relative obscurity in the Troop 9 operation, but he was confident that the scoutmaster wasn't bothered. He knew him well enough to know his priorities were sound.

Ego satisfaction was not what drove the man; his example was one reason Julian's values were so sound. Still, he intended to return to the background as soon as he could. He wanted Mark to be fully in charge.

"I sure hope they figure out what's wrong. It must be awful to have to stay there all the time." The "under observation" explanation didn't help much.

Swann knew all about that. He would have his people look into it. "We were very lucky the nurse was close by." He was enormously pleased with the day and his streak of good luck with this project. He resolved to purchase the drawing from the couple for his collection and let them have it on permanent loan. Watching Julian work was an unexpected bonus, an experience he treasured already. "Thanks for allowing me to watch you draw again." What Julian had captured in their facial expressions was beyond anything a camera was able to do. He wondered if being present to see the subjects being drawn affected what he could see later—it certainly had for Kasey playing Rachmaninoff. He looked forward to Mason's response to this portrait; his eye was just as good when it came to assessing a work of art. And that is what this was. He would have Sawyer photograph it tomorrow.

"Sure… any time." He never could understand why anyone thought that was so strange. "That's the first one I've done that size. I like it a lot—perfect for half body portraits. Lots better than this!" He held up his sketchbook. He shook his head: "they need to make that place more cheerful. How do they expect people to feel good when it's all dark and gloomy?" Julian thought it was lonely and empty in there. Those flowers sure helped. "Lucky we had all the decorations," he turned his head around: "You guys did a great job; what about their apartment?"

"Pretty easy—Mr. Sanderson told us what to do… piece of cake." Sid and Kurt had plenty of time to do both while Julian was drawing.

Julian hadn't visited an infirmary before. "I sure hope they can fix whatever is wrong. Grandma Molly is a really nice person." They reminded him of his own grandparents. He was too young to visit them after they went away. "If it wasn't so far, I could visit once in a while."

306

"Dad says I can get my own car next year," Sid had been waiting to brag about that. "If you're a good boy, I might give you a lift."

Julian laughed. "Have you done a solo yet?" Sid had been practice driving all year, practically. "I get Driver's Ed last nine weeks." He wasn't in a hurry.

Swann enjoyed the boys' banter. He felt absolutely invigorated—he couldn't remember feeling better. Like everything Julian had touched recently, this facility was about to join either the upgrade or the acquisition list. A retirement facility in his portfolio might be a shrewd investment. He enjoyed surprising the financial pundits.

What he had witnessed today was totally unexpected: he had come to study the scoutmaster at work. Witnessing the creation of a work of art was a surprise bonus. The portrait from its conception to completion took less than an hour: gallery ready, a masterpiece. *those people are alive—and in pencil! preserved for all time* He shook his head. The analogy he had made a few days ago with Mozart was verified. If only there was a way to record or film the boy at work. *something to pursue... what will his output look like when he learns to work in color?*

To Julian's surprise, his mother and Geraldine were waiting in front of the retirement home when the troop was about to board the Church bus. He waved at Danny and Nick. "See ya: my mom's here." He ran over and climbed into the back seat. It was Geraldine's car—fancier than his mom's; the back seat was a lot better—more comfy and more room. She needed a fancy car for taking her clients to see the houses she had picked out.

"Hi."

"How did it go?" Geraldine was mildly impressed by this activity, as usual. Personally, she found retirement homes too dreary by half. She was smart enough to know she was in denial more than anything. The prospect of growing old and fragile was too depressing—it usually went into her "deal with later" file.

"Fun! I got to do a drawing of Grandma Molly and Grandpa Jim!" he giggled happily. That made him feel like he had done something good—made his day. "Yep. Glad we do this."

Francine understood—he had never forgotten her mother and father—they helped raise him. Their memory was etched in his mind. She enjoyed recalling Julian sitting on her father's lap while he told endless tales and read story after story.

Geraldine could see Julian in the rear view mirror. He always looked sharp in that scout uniform. She wasn't sure it appealed to the girls his age, however. "We stopped at the bank on the way, so we plan to go straight to Oglivy's. Do you have any other place on your list?"

"Depends. How much money do I have?" He took the list out of his shirt pocket.

"One thousand three hundred seventy five dollars and thirty two cents." Francine answered, maintaining a straight face.

Julian was looking out the window at an interesting tree, so it didn't register at first. He replayed that in his mind: thousand? hundred? "Umm... did I hear you right?' He sat up straight and leaned forward.

Francine handed him a copy of her receipt: "1,375.32. That's what it came to after I deposited the check Mr. Swann wrote for 'On account for services to be rendered.'" She handed him the tear off section of his check. His corporate logo was printed in the upper right corner: "Swann Enterprises."

Julian's jaw dropped. He was speechless: Mr. Swann hadn't said anything about this. The signature was very distinctive.

Francine turned; her boy's expression answered her question, though she knew without asking. "I think he plans to commission you to do a drawing." Obviously, he had not made the request yet. She exchanged glances with Geraldine. They had agreed on a strategy: see how he dealt with this without their interference for as long as possible. They waited for him to ask a question. Francine recognized that this was a unique learning opportunity—she wanted it to be managed properly.

Julian's first thought was to ask if he should accept it. Inside Guy stepped up:

You have to accept it. You know Mr. Swann, you know he probably wants you to draw his portrait. You know he would feel guilty if he didn't pay you for it.

*yeah, but a **thousand** dollars?*

For him that's easy as pie.

I better do more than one. He shook his head and looked out the window. *what should I do? how much should I spend? what should I get people?* He had never had that kind of money before.

Inside Guy was helpful: *Put yourself in their place: you want to make them feel good, not bad: you can't spend too much or they'll feel guilty because they didn't spend that much on you.*

how about five dollars for friends, and ten dollars for adults?

Inside guy was silent.

how about twenty dollars for adults?

We already made a list: Mom, Geraldine, Mark... add Mr. Swann: we hafta give him one. Inside Guy was a teammate sometimes—came in handy.

Francine and Geraldine could see him working through this. They exchanged a glance and worked to keep quiet. The car radio seemed a trifle loud, but that was just fine.

They saw Julian's eyes wow and his cheeks puff flat as he made a silent exclamation. "Oglivy's to start with, I guess." He figured he could find almost everything there. He could ask their advice along the way. *funny: Mark won't be there to help out—he'll still be at the Church. wouldn't you know it.* He shook his head. *besides, he can't go to work in his scout uniform.*

Better that way, Inside Guy observed. *That way he won't know what you got him.*

"I know!" He sat up straight: "We can go to Henderson Arts and Crafts! I can get some sheets of that large paper!" *they have everything there! wow!* He just figured it out: "That's why he gave me all that money!" *yep: he is a smart man, too. how did I get so lucky?*

A smile spread across his face: *Randall!* Randall had several negatives with Swann in them. Plenty enough for him to study… to do a surprise drawing. There was little point in spending money on Mr. Swann. A drawing would be ideal. Plenty of time before Christmas.

22   *the semester ends*

Julian sat at his drawing table staring into space, at a loss—today was the last day of the semester and he had nothing to do: all his semester exams had been taken. For the first time in months he was all caught up! He was never one to just sit around—mostly because he usually had lots to do, and getting everything done took all the time he had. The one thing he had no practice at was doing nothing. His mom was at work, so except for her radio blasting away in the kitchen, he was home alone.

> > *Yes I'm gonna take you surfin' with me* < <

"Not again!!!" *that does it!* He raced to the kitchen. *I **hate** that song!*

> > **Come along baby wait and see... surfin' safari—** < <

Sudden silence: the volume knob had been given the rapid twist to the left. *there.* Julian loved his mother dearly, but her anti-burglar system was a major pain. Victorious, he strode back to his room. He sat again, shaking his head. *does anyone actually like that song?* The Beach Boys were not welcome in his ears, even when they were turned down low. The radio was annoying more than anything, so he was always turning it down. Once in a while they played a good one, but if he had his druthers, he'd sit outside where it was quiet. *too cold out for that.* The only music he actually **liked** was Kasey's piano at that special dinner. That was a huge surprise—he was looking forward to more of that. Randall's dad played interesting music too. Julian figured he prob'ly used a fancy record player or something.

The silence was wonderful. He sat back and closed his eyes a minute to enjoy the quiet. Eventually, the sound of Grandpa's clock on the mantle in the living room filled the void. He wasn't sleepy at all, so it didn't take long for the clock to get tiresome. He shook his head: *time to get back to... where was I, anyway? oh yeah: what I'm supposed to do today.* The wall calendar read: December 18—

-make up exams

-end of Semester

Otherwise, the calendar was blank. "Big help you are!"

Well. At least he hadn't forgotten to do something. He wasn't used to a Final Exam Schedule. They didn't have those in Junior High. Having a day left over was weird. But he didn't want to spend the whole day at his table doodling. He went to the closet and pulled out the special drawing of Mr. Swann. Maybe he could figure out what to do. He wasn't happy with it. Randall's photos of the faculty meeting helped, but there was nothing for a background. Julian needed to invent something. He didn't know him well enough to know what would fit. What to do about that had eluded him. Trouble is, he didn't know anyone who he could ask for advice. He didn't know if it was a good idea to be drawing it as a surprise. Mr. Swann might have something in mind. He wasn't sure he could figure it out in time for Christmas, either. He propped it up against the window to study. *the Christmas decoration party helped a lot—especially for the clothing detail...*

At least you didn't stare at him, Inside Guy commented. *Good thing, too. You'll figure it out.* Sometimes, Inside Guy was no help at all.

He swiveled the chair around and picked up the sheet filled with leaves. Maybe he could get somewhere with that. He still couldn't figure out how to draw a breeze. Showing them falling was easy enough, but how to show them being tickled by a summer breeze while still attached happily on their branches was not. *easy if you're doing a cartoon, but...* He wasn't in the mood to draw leaves any more either.

When he needed to sort things out he had always done the same thing—Grandma's rug. Today was sort of like that. He stood, slid to the doorway, and took a calculated run/slide to the oval rug in the living room. Walking around its outside edge heel to toe had always been a good way to begin. He stretched his arms out for balance and began a favorite routine. Somehow, this always put him into a perfect frame of mind for thinking about whatever needed attention. He was a little bigger now, so it wouldn't take as long to go all the way around.

Inside Guy was waiting: *It's about time: you're overdue, y'know.*

"Yeah, I know. You gotta admit though, I've been kinda busy." Julian often talked out loud when he was alone—helped sort things out better. It had been a long time since he and Inside Guy had taken any time to look at things in general.

Where to start? Geraldine? Nothing new seemed to be going on there. *the movie date seems to have satisfied her for the time being.* Mr. Swann had her busy these days finding a place Kasey's parents could buy: that meant they were going to stay for a while. It needed to be close to the University, if possible. *she says it's hard to find anything this time of the year.*

"Oh!" He stopped a sec to think: *the number on the Calendar was **18**.* Only a week until Christmas… maybe there was something else he needed to do there. Thank goodness he had gotten all his presents squared away, early for a change—thanks to Mr. Swann… *oop: gotta go around Mom's chair…* That was a special combination of steps; he had developed special rules for how to get back to the outside row on the other side of the furniture… hard to do now, because his feet were so much larger; he had to make a few allowances. Moving anything was against the rules.

You look pretty silly, y'know. You need to come up with another way to do this. Inside Guy was good at pointing out the obvious.

yeah, yeah. one of these days… He continued his routine anyway, assuming that Inside Guy would get to work on it.

Okay—next topic: Randall. The good news there was Andy… *looks like he's taken the boyfriend job. he's in the Troop and Mark approves of him.* That meant Randall and he were still friends—what could be better?

> > giggle < < Andy's in for a surprise: Randall's an Initiate!

He had reached the chair again. *hmm… this is silly.* Beyond silly: it was stupid. He sat on the ottoman. At long last, he had come to a realization: *I have outgrown this.* With a what's-the-use shrug, he stood and returned to his chair at the drawing table. Once in a while he was aware that growing up was underway. Sometimes that felt good—but sometimes it meant giving up something that he kind of liked. Grandma's rug was in that category—it was sort of basic. That furniture and the rug it sat on had been there for as long as he could remember.

The to do list from last week was peeking out from under the sheet of leaves—maybe it was worth checking. The Christmas list was marked done; two things were left.

2: Second semester—health class and Driver's ed

Kasey

3: Geraldine and Girls

Good old Inside Guy had added number three, his usual two bits of worthless advice.

He scratched his head on the Kasey one... he didn't know what his job would be exactly. They had some classes together, but not Geometry, not Concert Band. Kasey would be taking advanced Algebra. *hum. I guess we'll find out when the time comes.* They were supposed to arrive and get settled in real soon... tomorrow or the next day. Mr. Swann said he wanted them to be squared away before Christmas.

Julian thought about that. What would it be like to move to a new town just before Christmas? *thanks, but no thanks* He wondered if Mr. Swann was organizing a welcome party or anything. Julian was looking forward to seeing him, actually. He seemed kind of shy, but who wouldn't? *if you think about it he's got a big job ahead of him* Julian wasn't worried: he would have a whole scout troop standing behind him *besides, once the school has a chance to meet him, they'll like him... why wouldn't they?*

He looked at the last item in the list—that was the toughest one of all. He liked girls as people... at least he wasn't thinking about them day and night like so many guys his age. He had lucked out there for sure. What with Kasey and all, the pressure might be off for a while, but... *say, wait a minute...* What about Kasey and girls? *ooo-ee!!* He didn't know if Kasey even liked girls. But he figured they could be a problem: what if a girl like Rita had her eyes on him? He could be in big trouble...

Better ask Mark about that. Inside Guy agreed with him on that one.

He put the sheet down. He was back to square one.

it's different, all quiet like this. No wisecracks from Inside Guy, so…

> > ***ring-ring! ring-ring!*** < <

The telephone! With the radio turned down, it seemed super loud. He could think about that later. He set out for the kitchen. Somehow, he wasn't worried about Kasey finding a girlfriend. He didn't have Geraldine on his case, for one thing.

who could be calling? his first thought was Sid, oddly enough— he used to call all the time. *prob'ly Mom…* she knew he was home today; nobody else ever called anyway. If he knew who it was he could answer it with a wise saying or something—that's what Sid always did. He raced to the kitchen, shaking his head. The Christmas list must have made him think of that. He was starting to feel guilty about having ignored Sid and Jeremy all year. *and Justin too! who else have I forgotten about?!*

He glanced at the kitchen clock as he reached for the phone— *nine thirty already. wow.*

—⟶w⟵—

As the rest of the school tidied up the loose ends of the first semester, the Cardinal staff was going full speed ahead on the second semester special newspaper. Frederick Swann, true to his word, was there in person to help steer and assist where needed. He was enormously encouraged by the intelligence and creativity on hand at Jackson High School. It enabled his enterprise to proceed several months sooner than he had thought possible. The school paper was an unexpected ally and vehicle in ways that he had not foreseen. His ability to recognize the opportune had led to his success in business—it was likely to be useful in this project as well.

315

Mr. L was enormously enthusiastic about the special edition. The goal was to have it ready to distribute at the kick off assembly in January. It would help start the first day of the second semester. The Cardinal had never produced a starting day paper: it meant asking his crew, not to mention his family, to give up some precious vacation time. After today work on it would be "off the books" so to speak, but this was a good bunch—a great deal could be done today and tomorrow. Swann had helped enormously by making sure press time was guaranteed. The nice surprise was how well he related to the students. They liked Swann's idea: do it with style. Instead of introducing the first Black at Jackson quietly, as if hoping to slip him in without getting caught, they were doing it with a splash—they were welcoming a celebrity. This put an entirely different and unanticipated advantage in play. Swann's point was that there was really no way to do it quietly, and trying to would likely cause a backlash that made matters worse. It was Andy's enthusiasm that had sold the others—he and Randall had actually met the boy.

Mr. L stood at the blackboard reviewing the mockup: each page was blocked in, providing a visual dimension to the planning. Swann had sent two from his staff to Boston—Mason and Snyder had supplied enough material to fill a full page.

"It still needs something," Paula had an intuitive, global grasp. "Something light, something to smile about." She was as good a student editor as Ladendorff had ever had—she would be missed next year.

"That's it! A fun limerick—or a maybe a cartoon." Shirley was Feature Editor. Most of her space had been taken up by the Department Chairmen interviews; there wasn't a way to plug humor into those. The other staff members were already on assignment.

Swann had a thought—he checked the report from Mason. *yes. here it is...* "Can we get Julian Forrest in on this? I see here that he has drawn a cartoon about Kasey—I'll wager he has a copy in his sketchbook." The portrait was already slated to occupy a significant part of page three.

"That's right!" Andy nudged Randall. "We watched him draw it at Sparky's, remember?"

Randall nodded. "Pretty funny, too."

316

"As a matter of fact," Swann added, "we need to be sure his role as Kasey's official guide and "buddy" is explained. I don't see that indicated anywhere," he gestured to the blackboard. "Randall, did you get a shot of him introducing Kasey to the faculty?"

Randall pulled out the folder of contact sheets. He had made a few prints for Julian from this roll. "I know I did—the parents too." He found the sheet and took the loupe magnifier out of his pocket. He spotted the first one in the series—there appeared to be five. He passed the sheet and loupe to Mr. L.

"Perfect!" Mr. L had been looking for a way to get him involved. *he still has my New Yorker.* "Frames 27 and 28 are good." He passed the contact sheet and loupe to Swann. "Unless he's taking a make up exam, he's probably home today; we can try calling him."

Swann pointed at the phone on the teacher's desk. "Is that an outside line?"

"It is—it goes straight out, not through the office switchboard." Without it, ad sales would be impossible. He frowned— "I don't have his phone number—but it's probably in the phone book." He stepped over to the desk.

Swann examined the contact sheet. The snapshot of Julian tugging Kasey into the room was perfect. He put the sheet and loupe down and picked up his calendar.

"Let's see… Forrest…" Mr. L flipped through the directory.

"Yes—on Birch Street, I believe…" Swann checked his calendar notes. "1012 NE Birch, to be exact," he stepped over to pick up the receiver. He dialed as Mr. L read the number aloud.

"ALpine 3-2627"

After four rings, an unmistakable cheerful voice answered:

> > *Hello-hello-hello! If you're looking for Julian, you're in luck! He just happens to be talking to you on the phone!* < <

Swann broke into a smile. "Well, I'm glad, since it just happens you're the very person I wanted to speak to!"

> > **Neato!!** *Hiya, Mr. Swann!* < <

317

"Good morning, Julian. I'm here at school in Mr. L's room with some of your friends. We're hoping that you can join us for a while. Can you spare a few minutes of your time?"

> > *Wow, sure. umm… now?* < <

"That would be ideal. We're working on a special issue of the paper for next Semester. Your ideas about how to welcome Kasey would help a great deal."

> > *ooo-eee! Good idea! I'll come right away. I can be there in about half an hour; Mom's at work, so I hafta ride my bicycle.* < <

This was ideal—Swann recognized the opportunity instantly. "Why don't I come pick you up instead?"

> > *Really? Super!* < <

"Bundle up anyway, it's nasty out today. I'll be there in a little while."

> > *Boy-o-boy! See ya when you get here!* < <

Swann could hear him doing one of his hops. "See you in a few minutes!" He broke into another involuntary smile. "Is he always bubbling over?"

"Kasey said it all on Monday," Randall quipped, pointing to the contact sheet. "The irresistible force!"

Mr. L laughed and looked at his editor: "You need to work that into your copy—might make a good sub head."

Paula and Shirley looked at each other then at Mr. L—they seemed to be the only ones that did not know who Julian was—an unusual circumstance, considering they were supposed to write about him.

"I can go after him if you want," Andy offered, although he and Randall were supposed to meet the wrestling coach in ten minutes. He thought it might be more important for Swann to stay here.

"Thanks, but I want to do this myself. You two are needed here—there are a lot of spaces you two need to fill." He gestured to the mockup on the blackboard. "This is your paper, not mine. Don't let me forget that!" He stood. "We'll be back in plenty of time for lunch. I take it the cafeteria is open today?"

"Oh, I'm sure it is. They always have a lunch, even on teacher work days." That was one battle Middleton had won. "We still have students taking final exams."

"Good." Having lunch with this group would be enjoyable. "See you in a while," he bowed deferentially to the editors: "Ladies," and headed for the door.

As Swann closed the door, Paula addressed Mr. L with an annoyed expression: "Well? **Who** is Julian?"

"Oh my gosh! That's right!" he had just realized the problem: "I apologize. You don't know Julian yet!" The rest of the Cardinal staff had not been in the room when Julian was here.

"What lunch do you have?" Randall asked.

"First, of course." Shirley gestured to Paula. "We're in here a couple days a week, working on the Cardinal."

"That explains it," Andy took over. "He's the sophomore that draws portraits during second lunch: you know, Li'l Abner!" He gave them the up and down flashing Groucho eyebrow.

Paula gasped and put her hands over her mouth. This was stunning news. She and Shirley had been at the Sadie Hawkins Dance. They had heard about the portraits; they had seen Theresa's—but no one had connected it with the Li'l Abner winner.

Shirley had thought to pick up the contact sheet and loupe when Swann had gone over to the phone. She scanned the sheet and found what she was looking for: *it's true!* She passed the sheet to Paula; her eyes betrayed what she felt.

Fortunately, they were able to contain themselves. The clock: plenty of time to get presentable. Their enthusiasm for this project had just doubled. Paula was eager to write the story—conducting the interview, especially. She turned to Shirley: "you get to do the article on his lunchtime portraits—that's on page one." How they had not thought of that until this minute was embarrassing, considering. They needed to

319

make sure the second lunch half of the student body was represented. This was the perfect lead for the page three feature.

"You do have pictures of him drawing in the cafeteria, don't you?" Shirley needed to have a visual element.

"Dozens," Randall reached for his three-ring binder. "I have everything you'll need." He opened his proof sheet reference. Like Julian and his sketch book, he had begun to carry his binder wherever he went. "Look though these contact sheets and jot down the page and frame numbers you want me to print." Finally, a way to do something for Julian had come his way.

Fortunately, the office was only two doors away. Swann went there directly and with a nod to the Secretary, stepped into the Administration center; he tapped on the first doorframe. "Got a minute?"

Barnes looked up: "Certainly." This was unexpected, but not a surprise. He knew that Mason was on assignment in Boston. He stood and extended his hand.

Swann closed the door; this chat was confidential. Before fetching Julian, he needed information—basic information. He sat across from Barnes with the calculated and practiced manner that had proven itself over the years when he needed candor and trust. "First of all, I need to satisfy myself about something: how did you discover Julian Forrest?"

Barnes paused a minute. He hadn't planned for this, but it wasn't a surprise that Swann was interested. Awkward as it was, this required being open and honest. He spoke quietly, even though the door was closed. "You aren't going to believe this: it was Dumb Luck. Pure Dumb Luck. We're as amazed as anyone. We had no idea what we had found. We're **still** finding out. We'd had half a dozen secret search committees looking everywhere and screening for weeks. The need for secrecy defined what we could and couldn't do, of course. We had found no one: we were desperate. We had given up and come to the conclusion that Kirk, the Student Body President, would have to carry the ball by himself and hope for the best. That was true right up to the week we were to meet the Wood family. We called a last minute committee meeting to meet Julian and his mother—just before going to the university." He paused to reflect a minute about where to start. He was used to dealing with Mason. Meeting with Swann directly was new.

"We had a last minute break: by coincidence, I happened to be on lunch duty—it was the day after Veteran's Day, a four day week. That was one very lucky assignment, scheduled months ago; it could have gone to anyone—thanks to Destiny, it went to me. It was the first day Julian had ever eaten lunch in the cafeteria. I had never seen him before." He shrugged. "Eventually, I meet all the boys of course—but his name hadn't come up yet. I'm not sure when it would have.

"Well, that was also the day he drew the first lunchroom portrait. You probably don't know about those." He paused.

lunchroom portraits?   Swann sat up straight and looked at Barnes eagerly… this might explain what had been nagging at him.

"Every day during lunch he draws a portrait. The first one was a completely impromptu act. For Julian it was of no consequence whatever." He looked at Swann directly: "He tosses them off as if they're a scribbled note. He doesn't seem to realize how gifted he is—or how his work affects people who see it. Those girls are **ecstatic** when they see what he has drawn. In two days he had a waiting list. Now it's so long they've developed a system for drawing names!" Barnes threw his hands up. "I've never seen anything like it. They barely give him time to eat his lunch. A crowd forms to watch while he draws the portrait. It's always the same: he asks them a few questions and then tells them how to sit—in ten or fifteen minutes, bingo! the portrait is finished." He sat forward: "You saw it yourself! You remember, after the banquet: he drew that sketch of Kasey at the piano? Same thing, exactly, except that he signs it, tears it out of the sketchbook and gives it to them on the spot. He and Randall barely escape the cluster of girls that gather for a close look."

Swann was thrilled by this: it helped explain what he had seen himself—he had carefully watched Julian draw Kasey as he played the Rachmaninoff piece. Perched atop that chair back! *not one erasure.* That too was about fifteen or twenty minutes. He had never seen that before. He did the same thing at the retirement home last weekend—under terrible conditions, he produced a 12 by 18 masterpiece in minutes—45 minutes, to be exact: and his subjects, even though they were seated, were constantly in motion. The boy artist had captured every line and wrinkle, every fold, even the wedding ring and it's unique mounting—it was as if he had a photograph to go by. The only camera was inside his head.

"He's happy to oblige. His pal Randall helps one of the girls do the organizing. He isn't bothered in the least by people watching; he chats amiably while he draws—he's able to answer questions—no trace of an artistic temperament—if you want to see any quirky idiosyncrasies, you're out of luck. What amazes me as much as anything is how selfless it is: it's not an ego trip. I've never seen his like, and I deal with several hundred boys a year. He could well be the least egocentric student in the school."

Swann was fascinated; this information verified what he had seen himself. It helped explain why it had seemed so routine to him—Swann hadn't thought about that: it was routine! He resolved to take a look at those sketchbooks. He was curious about what caught Julian's eye, what he chose to draw. "Are the sketchbooks filled with portraits?" He might have been perfecting that skill.

"Not the one I looked through. He showed me the drawing that had triggered the cafeteria activity—it was the only portrait in the notebook—it was a full figure drawing, not a head and shoulders sketch. No, it has all sorts of things—potted plants, stairwells—he even has a very detailed study of a shoe. Whatever strikes his fancy, I guess." At a loss to explain it, he threw up his hands. "I'd like to look through them all—I doubt if he would object. As I said, he doesn't see anything special about them—it's as if he was practicing his penmanship."

"Anyway—back to that first day in the cafeteria: he had a group of students so captivated that it caught my eye. It was so out of sync with what we're used to: I thought I'd better look into it. After all, how could a sophomore boy—so obviously a sophomore, have the social Who's Who of the Junior and Senior class so... so **enraptured**? Those are the very students that worry us the most." He didn't need to mention that it was their parents that worried them more than anything.

322

"So on a hunch, I tracked him down. Middleton agreed to take a first hand approach—on Thursday we rounded up his teachers to observe what went on in the cafeteria; afterward, they met with the steering committee. That was Stanley's bottom line: the Committee needed to give the go-ahead. He had to have their support—without it, he planned to go with Kirk and hope for the best. Until Friday after school, the **same** afternoon we were scheduled to meet the Wood family, we had not had a chance to talk to Julian or his mother. We almost didn't proceed: it was so **late**. To do so seemed too big a gamble. It was promising, but still a completely blind risk. Of course, we had no idea what we had—as I said, to be perfectly frank, we still don't. Well, he impressed everyone so much Stanley decided to take the leap—he almost had to. It's very fortunate Mason was able to take my call, by the way—he was able to make the last minute arrangements. Hats off to him: he made it happen smoothly. We went straight to the banquet from that meeting. I have never cut anything that close. I don't think Stanley has either." He paused to emphasize the embarrassing fact that they had come perilously close to not taking Julian to that banquet; they very nearly didn't.

"And that, Mr. Swann, is the raw, red-faced blushing truth." He didn't know if they had a tiger by the tail or what—all he knew was they had to hang on and pay attention.

Swann frowned. This was more than a quandary. "I appreciate your candor. It helps to know things like this." He pondered Barnes' words for a moment. The unknown was much bigger than he found comfortable. Hopefully, this would not prove to have been too hasty a start. It verified his assessment that this stage required his direct attention for a time—probably a few weeks; fortunately, he had been able to free his calendar up. His hunch about stopping here for a little information before going after Julian was a better idea than he thought. It had identified where to start. "Tell me: do you know why he had been avoiding the Cafeteria?" He assumed all the students took lunch there.

"I didn't ask, but the sketch books tell the story: he brown bags lunch so he can draw on location—that's what those sketch books are: his lunchtime 'doodles,' if you will. I take it you've seen those. That's why no one knew who he was. The entire time since school began, he's been parked somewhere or other on campus drawing in his sketchbook."

323

He thought for a moment... "interestingly, he's not anti-social in the least, from what I can tell. That's what boy scouts takes care of, evidently. But at school, drawing is a higher priority than socializing. He is unusually self-assured. The scoutmaster takes a lot of credit for that I'm sure, and his mother.

Swann paused. He'd watched Kasey and Kirk go through those sketchbooks after the banquet. "I haven't actually looked through them." *of course! the first draft of the Kasey portrait was done in one of those spiral bound sketchbooks...*

"You need to do that, believe me; so do I. I was able to thumb through the first one on Friday before he met with the committee. He's now half way to filling the **fourth**. That's why he's been so invisible—he's a good student, he's not shy or anti-social, but all he wants to do is draw, evidently." He turned to the vertical file behind his desk. Julian's folder was still there. "Take a look—here's everything we have—since the **first** grade. **Zip!**" He passed the folder across the desk. He wasn't worried about Swann's discretion—there wasn't anything to disclose; confidentiality was not an issue.

Solving puzzles or mysteries was not a particularly attractive pastime; Swann usually delegated that sort of thing. But this had to have an explanation; he opened the folder, confident that he'd spot something.

Aside from a perfect attendance record, there was nothing... one comment about his fondness for boy scouts. *hmmm...* "Frankly, I'm a bit surprised. I thought teachers made anecdotal comments of some kind. There's nothing; evidently, he never had so much as a runny nose." All the required inoculations were marked as taken.

"They often do—hobbies, friends, anything behavioral. We don't have a copy of what they write on the report card unless the teacher makes a point of having something on file. His mother probably has those tucked away safely—most mothers do. This is as blank a file as any I have seen." He reflected. "Other than that meeting, I haven't spent any time with her. She seemed very open; it might be worth your time to get acquainted—and with the scoutmaster: he is a key figure. They seemed very supportive; I sensed nothing negative." He frowned. "The shortcoming of these files is they tend to record only problems." He didn't have any idea how to change that; he still needed to schedule his standard counselor meeting with the boy—he had nothing else to share.

The implication was obvious: he needed to get acquainted with both of them. Like it or not, he had a little detective work to do. He needed to take care… be sure he didn't inadvertently say or do anything that would do any harm. Nor so engaging that it would detract from his **first** priority: what he needed from Lewis and Helgar. But something beyond curiosity about this lad had grabbed a hold on him—this was something he could not delegate. But it was very different from doing an executive search: he had never worked with teenagers—with anyone much under thirty, for that matter. He flipped back to the front of the file for a second look. He stopped short: *what's this?* "I didn't notice this before: he was born in New York City." He stared at Barnes intently. This was a clue, surely. "I had assumed he was a local boy."

"They moved here when he was in the first grade. His mother mentioned that in the interview." He reached for another folder. "I thought she said Chicago. She and Geraldine Smathers were college friends—Geraldine owns Worthington Realty; she offered her a position—that's right!" he flipped through to the interview page. "Joliet. She and Julian were living with her parents in Joliet. She talked about a Black family that lived nearby. Julian was a regular there with one of the children. I recall now—both her parents had passed on. She didn't go into any other area of their background. I don't know if she is widowed or divorced. New York never came up." He shrugged. *likely a divorce—an unpleasant one, or she would have said something.* That was fairly common.

Swann stood. "Thanks Roy—I appreciate your support. Be assured, I will move with caution. We have a responsibility as well as an opportunity. I am optimistic. We're off and running—farther along than I had imagined possible." He stepped to the door: "I'll be in touch." He headed for the Packard. Playing chauffeur would be a bit of fun.

New York… That needed to be explored.

Swann's ruminations continued as he drove to the Forrest home on Birch Street. Driving himself was a welcome break from routine. *it might do me good to give Mason a few more holidays*. He felt free, in a happy nostalgic way. Being waited on had its advantages, but being on his own was refreshing. He pulled into the driveway—the Packard was a bit too ostentatious to be parked unattended on the street.

The simple single story bungalow was well maintained—as were all the homes in this neighborhood. Nothing stood out; the covered porch felt friendly and hospitable, old fashioned perhaps, but sound. He pressed the doorbell. The basic two-tone chime was simple and audible; knocking would not be required. He stood back and took a deep breath of air: refreshing. This was an adventure as much as anything—it felt good to be 'on the loose.'

"So it **is** you!" the happy face at the door exclaimed. "After I hung up the phone I figured you meant Mason would come after me. Wow… come on in. I hafta put on my shoes and get my jacket," he opened the door wide and stepped back.

and so, the surprises begin, Swann thought to himself as he stepped inside. He had not speculated on what he would find when he entered this home, so he wasn't surprised, precisely; putting aside the fact that Julian would need to put on a pair of trousers as well as a pair of shoes, there was an unexpected sense of having been here before— long, long ago. This was like stepping into his grandmother's house. The only missing element was doilies on the furniture.

"Maybe I should put on a shirt too," Julian apologized as he shut the door. The cold air had reminded him that he needed more than a T-shirt if he was going to leave the house today.

It just occurred to Swann that he'd best observe protocol. "Does your mother know I'm playing school bus today?" He decided to allow the lad to remember the pants on his own. He himself was known to hang around in his underwear and bathrobe when home alone, so he could relate.

"Oo-ee, no. I better call and tell her. Thanks for reminding me: she likes to know where I am. umm…" he wasn't sure what to do here; he gestured to the chair by the ottoman. "You can have a seat or come along—the phone's in the kitchen."

"Go ahead—I'll tag along. No need to fuss."

"Okay!" With a hop and a giggle, Julian led the way. Without thinking, he did his standard skip and slide, coming to a precision stop at the telephone mounted on the wall just inside on the right.

Swann was entertained by the youth's spontaneity. He had noticed that characteristic at the banquet; skating on a hardwood floor in his socks was something that he had never seen or thought of doing when he was a boy. He glanced at the tidy living room as he followed along—it began to make sense: this was like walking into a Norman Rockwell painting. The tousled blond haired boy bouncing in front of him could have sprung right off a Saturday Evening Post cover. Add the doilies and it would be the 1940s here. This was the boy's private playground. An only child himself, he related to that. As he stepped into the well-scrubbed kitchen, Julian had nearly finished dialing. Here too it was in the living past: dish rack on the counter next to the sink instead of a dishwasher, café curtains in the window…

"Hi, Mom," Julian exclaimed happily. "Guess what!? Mr. Swann is here! He's gonna give me a ride to the school. They want me to help with the paper!"

Swann waited briefly, then gestured for the receiver.

"Yeah… he wants to talk to you: here he is…" he handed the receiver over with a grin.

"My apologies, Mrs. Forrest—I should have called before driving over. I have no excuse, really—I've grown too used to having Mason take care of details like that. I'm on my own for a few days while he's helping Kasey and his parents."

Julian was uncertain—should he wait, or zip into his room? He felt a little silly for waiting so long to get dressed. He got sidetracked by Mother Nature after Mr. Swann called from school. At least he remembered to put the unfinished drawing away. He wasn't ready for him to see it yet: he wanted it to be a surprise.

Better wait: Mom might have something to say. Inside Guy was on hand with some common sense.

"I'm not sure, but I doubt if he'll be late for supper. If it gets more involved, I'll give you a call. I plan to bring him back here as soon as we're through. They have a terrific start already." He winked at Julian. "Thank you, yes. Here he is—" He passed the receiver back.

"Hi— Yeah, I think I know: they want me to draw a cartoon, I think. Easy as pie," he nodded. "Okay—see ya... 'bye." He looked at Mr. Swann with a knowing grin as he hung up the phone. "She had to remind me to turn the radio up before we leave," he pointed to the countertop where it occupied the end, next to the refrigerator. He shook his head. "She thinks that thing scares off burglars. See what I mean about mothers? If I was a burglar, I'd hafta be pretty stupid to be fooled by that. I'd prob'ly figure it was a good bet nobody was home. People don't play their kitchen radios up high for hours on end—unless they're deaf or something." He gave a 'what's a guy gonna do' shrug and headed for his room.

You shoulda known to turn it up before you called her, Inside Guy scolded.

yeah, yeah, sure: what would Mr. Swann think about that, mister smarty pants? Inside guy didn't have an answer. Once in a while, Julian got the last word. He would turn the radio up on the way out.

Swann suppressed a response. He assumed he was welcome to follow along without being invited: ceremony was not Julian's thing. Just as well. This confidence reminded him of the parental heads-up Julian had provided at the Hallstrom's dinner party: he was on a fact-finding errand as well as a taxi run. His mother's fear of burglary was interesting—he doubted if the problem existed in this town to begin with. Like the furniture in the living room, an artifact from their life in Joliet.

Julian headed straight to his closet for a shirt. "Wednesday is green day."

Swann tilted his head as if asking why.

"Geraldine. She figures out what I should wear," he shrugged. "To be honest, what I wear is **not** a big deal—whatever I need to keep warm is all that matters to me." He paused. "Y'see, she and my mom have this idea that if I dress right, I'll have scads of girls lined up waiting to go on dates with me. It's like that radio. I just nod my head and do what I have to. When you think about it, keeping them happy is my main job; I learned that a long time ago. They think that since I'm in high school now I need to have a girlfriend. Or two. Geraldine would just as soon I had one for every day of the week!" He shook his head. "I mean, what's the big hurry?" He shrugged. "So I smile and do what I have to do to keep them happy." He pulled on the shirt. He was about to tuck it in when he noticed. "Oops," he giggled. "Almost forgot my pants!" He reached into the closet for his jeans. "Since I'm not going to class today, I'll put on my Levis: I like to reserve my suntans if I can— that way they last longer." He pointed to his head: "I learned a long time ago to hang things up. If I don't, my mom pitches it in the laundry whether it needs it or not." He shook his head, "that machine is a lot harder on my clothes than I ever will be." He shrugged again. "I just leave my pants hanging in the closet until I'm going somewhere. Besides, I'd just end up taking them off: pants are annoying. Why put 'em on if I don't need to?"

This narrative was as instructive as it was diverting. The fact that Geraldine determined his wardrobe was curious. She seemed to be more than his mother's employer: unique, at the very least. Swann's eyes wandered to the left: the drawing table drew his attention: a Christmas list was underway... a tour of the packed bulletin board would be nice... this room was a surprise. He had no preconceived notions about it, but this was not a typical fifteen year-old boy's room surely... no pennants or posters, no sports heroes or movie stars. Well, this was not a typical fifteen-year old boy, if there was such a thing. Not being preoccupied with girls was understandable—his interest was developing his artistic skill. Swann certainly supported that—and Julian was correct: he had plenty of time. Swann knew artists well: romance often played second fiddle.

"So, this is where you do your drawing." He noticed several studies and a drawing board. A few pencils... amazingly Spartan here. Like everything else he had seen, everything was neat and tidy. This was not the archetypical artist's nest. Two 12x18 drawings occupied a major portion of the bulletin board—a sailboat and a fascinating piece of driftwood; the letter grade and handwritten comment on the lower right corner identified them as schoolwork. He looked closely... *ah, he mentioned a teacher... fifth grade as I recall... why on earth didn't she write on the back!* It did not come as a surprise that Julian's talent was evident in the fifth grade. At some point he would find a way to study these more closely. Perhaps there were other treasures tucked away somewhere. His eyes returned to the worktable.

329

"May I ask what these are?" He pointed to the studies—some leaves on one sheet.

"**OO**, yeah!" He just remembered that Mr. Swann knew lots about art. "I'm trying to figure out how to make it look alive, like it's moving. I want to see the wind, I want to hear the leaves. All the time I have trouble with that—like at the lake, all those ripples, the splashes—I want to see them moving." He tilted his head. "Maybe it's silly, but I'm working on that." *maybe Mr. Swann knows how to show that.* He slipped on his Levis.

That rang a bell for Swann. "I'm not an artist, as you know, but I think I know what you mean. I wanted to ask you about that very thing, in a way. Do you mind talking about it?"

"Heck no!" He grinned eagerly. *wowee!* Besides Mr. van Horn, nobody else knew anything. He could use all the help he could get. And it might help him figure out what to do to the unfinished drawing in his closet: a few good closeup details would help. A fresh look at his eyes would be nice. He gestured to the study chair where Randall usually sat, and he took his regular chair.

Swann paused—he needed to proceed with care here. "I want to ask about the portrait you drew of Kasey. Do you mind indulging my curiosity?"

Julian wasn't sure what indulging meant, but it sounded okay. Besides, Mr. Swann was a nice man, a good man. *no reason to worry.* He sat back and waited to hear what Mr. Swann wanted to know.

"I watched you draw that sketch in your tablet as Kasey was playing. You gave him a larger version the next day, correct?"

"Sure. I like to draw a big one—you can show so much more in a large drawing. I really like it when I can do that. If I could, I'd always use large paper." He frowned. "Trouble is, it's not very practical to carry my drawing board around, y'know? So I do a sketch in my tablet and make a big one later, if I can. I try to put down what I need to remember when I make the big one. I'm getting better at remembering. I can do a **lot** nicer job if it's big." He pondered that a minute and added, "It feels **better**, it feels **right**, drawing it big—like I'm part of it. That sounds funny, but I don't know how else to describe it."

Swann understood immediately. "You feel more involved. Is that what you mean?"

"Yeah! **Involved**. That's perfect," he nodded vigorously. "That's it, **exactly!**" He almost hopped up and down he was so pleased. No one else understood that.

"Have you still got the small one, the first one?"

"Sure—it's in my tablet." He reached for it—all his tablets were there on the worktable; that one was on top. He flipped it open—Kasey's university sketch and address were the last things before the cartoon. He passed it to Swann.

Swann examined at it carefully—it was just as he had seen it that night—a perfect cameo. He wasn't sure, but he sensed it all the same: a hint of what he had experienced when he saw the large, finished version. "Do you still have that photo Randall gave you?" He was referring to the 8x10 of the large portrait.

Julian paused. "I think so, somewhere." *where did I put that?* He thought back... *that was just before we went to the airport.* "My 3-Ring Binder!" He pointed to the upper left corner of the desk. "I think it's in there."

Swann opened the binder cover—sure enough, it was right on top, still in its envelope. This was ideal. He put the two side by side on the table. Though far more detailed, the 8 by 10 was slightly smaller than the cameo. Incredibly, the composition and line elements were nearly identical. He squinted at the photograph, attempting to imagine it full size. This reaffirmed what he had surmised. "When I look at this, I can swear I hear Kasey playing the Rachmaninoff."

A light came on instantly in Julian's eyes—he smiled in satisfaction. He took a minute before responding. "That's really neat. I was hoping someone else would hear. I tried real hard to do that—harder than ever before." He exhaled. The fact that Mr. Swann heard it meant a great deal. It meant that he had been right.

Swann was stunned. "You **meant** to do that?" Julian's face revealed a depth he had not suspected; he felt slightly embarrassed for having prejudged this boy—as if he was just a boy. Clearly, appearances notwithstanding, this was not just a bubbly kid. This was the second time he had seen that special but momentary expression on his face—it seemed to peek out or from between the folds of joyful ebullience. This boy was intriguing indeed.

"Yeah—I always try to do that when I draw the large ones. With Kasey it was easier in a way, because of the music. I could hear it while I was drawing, y'see. It was **part** of what I was drawing." He pointed to the sketch—his forefinger following the line of the right arm as if it was in motion, his torso subtly twisting as he spoke, replicating Kasey's movement. "Usually what I'm drawing is quiet and sitting still. Makes it tricky to show what I feel, and what the person is feeling. That's what I like about the large ones—I can show feeling a lot better…" He nodded: "**Involved.** I can be involved when it's big. **Lots** more fun to do." He tilted his head and gestured with his arm: "I want to feel his arms rising, his fingers causing the beautiful sound when they touch the keys." He pointed to the studies on the table. "It's sort of like those leaves—I want to see them moving in the wind." He pointed to Kasey's hair: "Can you see it moving? Squint your eyes and listen…" he watched Swann carefully… he had never talked to anyone about this because he figured it would sound crazy. Something told him that Mr. Swann might understand. The combination of elements had to be just right: that's why he could do it better if it was big. The lines and composition had to be coordinated just right to suggest the unique movement being remembered precisely.

Swann did as Julian instructed. There was a pause. Gradually, the sound of the mantle clock dimmed… it was replaced by music—or what seemed like music; more akin to an aroma, it was **remembered** sound, produced inside his recall system—it felt almost like he was watching the performance. He was inside his memory! He was almost reliving what had happened at the Hallstrom's when Kasey and Randall first showed the full sized portrait. On that occasion, he was awed by a similar, but stronger sensation. He could have sworn he had seen Kasey's head lunge forward, the hair following, as if rushing to keep up. The surprise was how powerful the portrait was—an odd sensation, beyond surprise but akin to something he had felt before. When studying certain masterpieces he felt an emotional force—something in addition to the purely visual. This was in that realm, it shared that characteristic. This was beyond anything he had anticipated when he had looked at the sketch. Briefly, the large drawing had transported him back to the reception room at the university: the performing Kasey replaced the drawing, sound and all. Like all great masterpieces, the longer one studied the work, the more it spoke to you directly.

"How many of these large ones have you done?"

"Not very many," Julian said regretfully. "They were at camp last summer, mostly. That's where I got the idea. Uncle Max had these large sheets of paper. He gave me ten of them! I used the last one for Kasey, actually." He stopped, realizing that he had skipped over something important. "Thanks to you, I have some more now." He looked at Swann gratefully. "After we finished the Christmas decorations, my mom told me about your check. I was surprised. She said you probably wanted to commission me to do a drawing." He paused. "I didn't know what to think—nobody ever did that before. Then I figured it out: that's what you do: you help people. You prob'ly know that my mom and I don't have a lot of extra money to spend on art supplies. So I used part of it to get a few things." He pointed to the floor under his bed; the package of 24x36 paper was located for easy access. Next to it was a ream of the 12x18, the size he had used at the retirement home. He didn't want to ask if it was okay, because he knew it was. Even so, he was concerned. "Thank you. I didn't know how to say that, exactly," he shrugged with a smile, greatly relieved.

Swann felt goose bumps form and hoped his blush wasn't visible. Blatant honesty was something he never encountered. Its force and power were enormous. He shouldn't have been surprised. But he was, and he was humiliated and elated at the same time, and that was new. He paused momentarily, hoping that he was up to the challenge. "Thank you, Julian. I mean that sincerely. I need to be honest with you, too: I gave it to your mother instead of you, because I didn't know what to say. I am thrilled you understood anyway. Thank you again. I do indeed plan to commission you to do a portrait—possibly more. When I do, I will make it a request, not an obligation. And what I pay will be a lot closer to its value. You are to use the money I gave your mother for whatever you or she needs. You should not hesitate to ask for more if it is needed." He paused. "And that's between you and me. Okay?"

Julian grinned. He was right about Mr. Swann. "Deal." He did the zipped lips gesture. The neat thing was, this conversation had shown him how to finish that drawing. Looking him straight in the face for that long was perfect—something he wasn't able to do, usually. Mr. Swann was going to get that for free: it was a Christmas present. He needed to get back to his story. "Can I finish telling you about the first big one? It's kind of important."

"Please. I'd like to know about that."

"Y'see, the camp director let me draw a picture in the first aid room. This scout named Geoff had almost chopped off his toe with a machete. Wowee: did it look **awful**. I thought it would be interesting to draw for the Troop 9 Scrapbook. Mr. Jorgensen asked if I could draw it for the camp to keep—I think he wanted it to show how important it was to be careful when you use a machete."

Swann was fascinated by Julian's ingenuous account. If only he could record it somehow. He hadn't intended to take so much time here, but he needed to hear the rest. A few minutes more wouldn't hurt.

"So when the medic made Geoff lay down and rest, we went out into the hallway. He wanted to see what I had done. I was just part way along naturally—by then I could tell it wouldn't turn out very good—it was too complicated. I was worried: having the medic and Geoff, **and** Mr. Jorgensen all in one drawing—it was so teeny you couldn't see much detail. The chopped foot was only yea big." He held his thumb and forefinger up to show a half-inch space. "So I asked if the camp had anything larger I could draw it on—I thought they might have a roll of butcher paper or something... I wanted to do a good job.

"So we went to the warehouse to see. We were in luck! The neat old guy in charge—they call him Sarge—had a whole stack of these drawing boards!" He pointed to the drawing board on his table: "and packages of this huge paper—the same size as the drawing board. They were left over from something a long time ago." He remembered the Sarge telling his motto: "So he says, 'Never throw out something that might come in handy one day, Boy. That's my motto!'"

> > hee-hee! < <

Julian enjoyed imitating the way Uncle Max talked. "He's so funny. I really like him. He always calls me Boy." He pointed to the sketch at the far left of his bulletin board. "That's him on his motorcycle. He gave me a ride in that. Bumpy, but fun anyway. He calls it Bessie. I call him Uncle Max... fits better than Sarge. His real name is Maximilian."

The very cartoonlike sketch boded well for the school paper—Swann hadn't brought that up yet. He was taken by Julian's emotional connection to the man called Sarge; it helped to have an image of the man he was talking about. This all seemed to fit a pattern: it was that way at the retirement home; another quality was its instinctive nature—he recalled seeing it at the banquet: Julian took an instant liking to Kasey. He had felt it himself at the Hallstrom's, now that he thought about it. *remarkable... he accepts people on sight.* Was it simple naïveté, or something else? Julian wasn't stupid or slow witted. Swann was puzzled... he had never seen this characteristic before. It was as if the boy had a special ability.

"So anyway, Uncle Max gave me a drawing board and ten sheets of that big paper! He put them in one of those tubes to keep safe." He paused to offer an aside—"He has scads of stuff back there. And he knows exactly where everything is! Anyway, I skipped swimming and spent the afternoon in the dining hall making the large one. Mrs. Connor showed us how to do that in the fifth grade... pretty easy, really. Handy to know. Anyway: when I enlarged it I discovered I could show more than I expected—way more. I never knew that before." He paused to think—he had not analyzed this exactly until now. "Each one seems to get better or stronger... and to show me more." He shook his head and frowned. "I don't know how to tell what I mean." He really hated being so stupid. "It's different with the big ones. I can do a better job, that's all."

Swann chose not to interrupt his commentary—but this area needed to be explored when the time was opportune. That's why he had given his mother a check—incredibly, Julian had grasped that at once. He appreciated the problem they faced. He planned to explore ways to deal with the family income. He realized now why this house seemed so tidy and nostalgic: everything had to last—disposable income was absent, by and large—every penny counted. He had all but forgotten what that was like. That explained the high concern about burglars.

"So that was the first big one I did. Then I decided to do some big ones from my Troop 9 sketch book—you know, the one I used for the Scrapbook. Y'see, I had one of those for Assistant Scribe, and another for drawings to put in the Scrapbook." He pointed to the thick binder with a handcrafted wood and leather binding on his dresser next to the window. "I drew one of Leonard—he's the camp waterfront director—I really like him. Then Mark let me draw him—when he saw the one of Leonard he decided it would be okay." He paused. "I had wanted to do that for a **long** time—but I was afraid to ask, you know? I mean, who wants to just sit there and let someone stare at you for a while?" He pursed his lips: "kinda weird when you think about it…" He sat up straight: "Anyway, I made large ones of those later at the table in the cabin and in the cafeteria instead of going to Free Swimming." He tapped on the drawing board. "This makes it so easy. I just make a sketch, then enlarge it later. No big deal. I drew one of Uncle Max," he grinned wide, "That one was really fun. Then Mark let me draw a second one of him, since the first one turned out so well—I wanted to draw one of him standing. He paused. "I did that one after the campfire—right on the drawing board; I didn't have to enlarge that one." He tilted his head: "that's best of all, really, if you can: like the one I did of Grandpa Jim and Grandma Molly last Saturday. Thing is, you can't be carrying a big drawing board around everywhere."

He decided not to tell about the two he did of Randall—he had promised to keep them secret. "Luckily, I had one sheet left—and I used it for Kasey. Those large sheets are better paper—**way** better. You can do lots more detail if you have good paper."

"So you did them all the same way?" Swann realized something: *he gives away the finished drawing… does he keep the cameo?*

"Sure. If I don't have my drawing board, I draw it in my sketchbook first, then make the big one later at the table—this table is bigger than the one in the cabin. The light is lots better here too—that helps." He opened the right desk drawer and pulled out the camp sketchbook—most of its content had been removed for the scrapbook, but several pages were still there. "I still have the small ones. I always give the big ones away, o' course." He flipped open to the first aid drawing and handed it to Swann. "See what I mean about teeny? You can hardly find room to show the bandage on his foot!" He watched Swann study drawing carefully. "Mr. Jorgensen liked it. He had Uncle Max frame it, I guess. Mark said he has it on the wall in his office.

Kinda neat." The very first time he had been asked to draw something... *boy, do I miss camp!*

Swann saw instantly what Julian was talking about; there was enough in this sketch to fill a mural. He turned the page—clearly several pages had been removed. "You must have given several away." He flipped through the remaining pages: sure enough, the portraits were there. Those he would look at later.

"No—only one—I did a cartoon one and gave it to Jeremy, since I had used his face in it. He really thought it was neat, so I gave it to him and did another one for the Scrapbook. That's where the rest of the drawings are—they were done to put in the Troop 9 Scrapbook—that's what this tablet was for." He pointed across the room again; both scrapbooks were on top of his dresser.

Swann had watched him show that to Kasey and Kirk: something else he needed to have a look at.

> > *ding-ding, ding-ding...< <*

The Westminster chimes rang out softly in the living room. Grandpa's mantle clock had begun to toll the eleven o'clock hour.

"Oh-oh," Swann exclaimed. "I have gotten carried away! We should get going. You need to find your shoes!"

Julian giggled. "Sorry, I can talk away for hours." He leapt to his feet and scurried to the foot of his bed—he always tucked his shoes under there when he was at home.

Swann had another hunch. "I want to talk with you a little more about your art when I can find the time; to do you think you could do that?"

"Sure!" Julian exclaimed. Mr. Swann knew things; it would be stupid to pass that up. *he told Mr. van Horn he had a gallery! think of that!*

"Randall said you drew a cartoon about Kasey." Swann's guess was that the original was still in his sketchbook.

Julian giggled. "That was a fun idea I had after school." He pointed to the sketchbook he had given to Swann. "It's still there—it's the last one in the sketchbook." He bent down to deal with his shoes.

Swann flipped to the cartoon—he burst into laughter instantly. "This is perfect! You'll be glad to hear that Kasey has given his approval. I'm sure they'll want to use it in the special paper." Just then his eyes fell on the stack of spiral bound sketchbooks—it came to him instantly. *could I be that lucky?* As Julian finished tying his shoelaces he took a huge risk. "Could you spare those for a day or two?" he pointed to the sketchbooks. "I'd like to see what you have done."

"Sure, I don't mind; I don't use them very much, actually; I know you'll keep them safe—keep 'em as long as you want." He thought a second. "'Cept I promised Randall's dad he could see them, is all. Randall is going to photograph some of them, I think." He gave a go-figure shrug. "Seems like a lot of trouble, actually. I think Mr. Hallstrom wants to have a better idea of the school or something. No big deal. When you're through, maybe you could give them to Randall." He moved the stack of notebooks to the front of the table where Mr. Swann could get them easily, then skipped over to the dresser for the Troop 9 Scrapbook. Randall's Dad wanted to see that too. "I need this back before the next Troop 9 meeting—hafta put in the page I'm gonna do about the Christmas Decoration party."

Swann pulled a card from his pocket holder and put it on the table. "Thank you, Julian. If anything comes up and you need any of them returned, here's my phone number." He wasn't surprised that Hallstrom wanted to study these; he was a discerning person; he and his wife were on the right page. All the same, Swann resolved to do something about this lad's disregard for his own work. Barnes' remark about scribbles came to mind. How much of his work goes into a wastebasket? Julian didn't seem to be an ordinary perfectionist, one that was likely to destroy a lot of very good art—or waste any paper. At some point, he needed find out precisely how this boy worked. Self directed and taught, by and large—assumptions would be most unwise. He was forming a list in his mind about what to ask his mother. And, the scoutmaster. He stood as Julian poked a couple of pencils into his shirt pocket.

"All ready," Julian grabbed the jacket from the back of his chair. *what else do I need?* He wouldn't need his three ring binder... *Mr. Swann has my sketchbook...* "Radio!" *can't forget that...*

Don't forget your lunch, Dum-Dum. Inside Guy popped out of nowhere.

right. His mom had made his lunch as usual. He followed Mr. Swann out, but headed for the kitchen.

Sure enough, his sack lunch was on the main refrigerator shelf. *thanks Mom...* "I hafta let the burglars know nobody's home," he announced over his shoulder. He turned the volume knob to the right; an unintelligible blare filled the room:

> > *That's Matilda she take all me Money...* < <

Julian shook his head and grimaced. "They get worse and worse all the time."

The expression on Julian's face was priceless—Swann kept a straight face as he put his stack of "homework" on the kitchen table and held up his hand: "May I suggest something?"

> > *That's woman she ain't no good...* < <

Julian stopped in his tracks. "Sure." He watched Mr. Swann approach the radio; he flipped the bandwidth lever to the left and the music changed instantly.

"Whoah!" Julian exclaimed. "What did you do?" The music had changed completely.

Swann turned the volume down slightly. "Don't you ever listen to FM?" The puzzled expression answered his question. He gestured for Julian to approach. He pointed to the lever. "See this switch?" When Julian nodded, he flipped it to the right—at once the Jimmy Soul song replaced the soft melodious FM. Swann flipped it back again quickly. A look of wonder transformed Julian's face—the face he remembered seeing at the banquet. Julian's countenance was completely disarming when he was encountering something new—a mix of joy and wonder, it was infectious.

"Wow... I never knew you could do that." He was puzzled. "Effem?" That sounded familiar, sort of...

"It's meant for listening to music. It's higher quality than AM—most radio stations use AM because it has a longer range—the station can be heard miles farther away.

"Oh." Julian tended to ignore technical stuff. "I never listen to radio, really." He shrugged. "Mom's practically an addict though. Me, I usually shut it off—it's mostly noise to me."

"You don't like music?"

"Well, yeah, some kinds I guess. But most of it is…" he frowned. "Some is just noise. I'm always turning it down or off. The words especially, when you can figure out what they are." He shook his head. That was one of his pet peeves; the words were usually silly or plain stupid. He brightened: "But I like what Kasey plays. And Randall too, now that I finally got to hear him play. But you don't hear that on the radio."

"You can on FM: that's what it's for."

The difference was hard to believe. *wow.* "Effem?" *funny word*

"Yes—it's for higher quality sound: they call it High Fidelity. Good music sounds much better." The fact that this was new to Julian explained a great deal: hi-fi cost more—much more. He had been taught to make do, live within the family budget, and be content with what he had. *remarkable.* That helped explain why this room, why everything was so plain.

"Thanks, Mr. Swann." He tilted his head; he just realized that he could just flip that switch when his Mom wasn't home. He grinned wide: "Yeah." *neato!!* With a skip he headed for the door. Mr. Swann was a nice man—and then some.

You forgot something… Inside Guy made him stop in his tracks.

"Oops!" Julian turned around. "Mr. L's magazine!"

Fortunately, Swann was several steps behind with his stack of notebooks; he barely avoided a collision.

"'Scuse me—I forgot something—be right back." He scurried back to get the New Yorker. He was supposed to take that back on Monday. He had a good excuse: he was taking his final exams for the last two days and didn't think about anything else.

Swann watched with a mix of feelings; the agility and zest of a fifteen year old was long gone, and sorely missed. The nearly continuous cheerfulness and effervescence of this boy was so

340

completely disarming it made taking him seriously awkward if not difficult. But after seeing his work, and now, having talked with him, taking him seriously—very seriously—had become a priority. He had some research to do. He had not heard of a child prodigy in art, but he had found one; now he had an idea of what it must have been like to talk with the fifteen year old Mozart. Fortunately, Julian's mother was not an exploitive impresario like Leopold was. She appeared to be the very opposite: she seems to have helped preserve his childhood.

He didn't have to wait by the door long—the eager face emerged from the bedroom with a happy bounce.

"I hafta give this back to Mr. L," Julian waved the magazine in the air. "He lent me this last Friday. He wants me to learn about cartoons."

The subtle change of expression was enough to alert Swann that this was worth Ladendorff's attention: the cartoon of Kasey was proof of that. "Well, that's a good place to start—I always skip through those before reading any articles. I've been enjoying those for a long time." He stepped out onto the porch.

"Really?" Julian was intrigued. "Do you like the cartoons?"

Swan grinned. "Once in a while. I have to admit that I don't subscribe to the magazine for those." It didn't surprise Swann that Julian didn't find them entertaining. They were from a very different world. "If you read every issue you might see an artist you enjoy; that's what I do. I skip over most of them."

Julian found that very reassuring: it was okay not to like all those things after all. Mr. Swann's opinions deserved his attention. *maybe I'm not so stupid after all.*

On the drive back to the school, Swann took the opportunity to explore a bit further. "Tell me, would you do all your drawings large if you could?"

Julian had not asked himself this one. He tilted his head. After a minute he frowned. "Prob'ly not. That would take too long... couldn't do as many, for one thing. Lots of drawings are practice mostly. They make it easier to study special things and get better—make it possible to

341

do better on the big ones." He paused. "Yeah. Thanks. I never thought about that before. More than anything, I always try to do better. I bought some of that 12x18 too—I like that size."

"What do you like about it?"

"It was perfect for Grandpa Jim—a big one would have made them too big unless I drew all of them, clear down to the toes." He shook his head. "That would be kind of boring—make it hard to concentrate on what was important to them: how they felt." He tilted his head. "That was neat, showing that." That was what made him feel good. "Thanks to you and Mr. Witherspoon, I found out something new: ones that size don't need to be enlarged to show what's important. All I need is a way to have that size handy."

That made an image flash into Swann's view: *a travel portfolio that size is a standard item.* Several other tools came to mind, now that he had seen Julian's work center. One area of concern remained:

"Do you ever throw any away and start over?"

"No. I hate to waste any paper: I hafta pay attention and do it right to begin with. I did start over a couple of times at camp—but those were ones I was making up, not ones I was drawing of what I was looking at. Making them up is a lot harder to do."

"Why is that?"

"Well, you hafta picture it in your head so's you can draw it. If you can't picture it very well, you can't draw it very well either... at least I can't." *I need to practice that.* That's why he was having trouble with the one he had started of Mr. Swann. If it was right there, drawing it was pretty easy, really. He thought a bit more about the first question Mr. Swann had asked. "No—it's more than that."

Witnessing Julian's analysis was a surprise bonus—Swann was delighted; "More?" It was apparent that he had not yet thought about this—another sign of how instinct and native talent determined and defined his work.

"I mean the big ones: beside the ones I've done in school—the sailboat and driftwood on my bulletin board: I did those in the fifth grade for Mrs. Connor." He smiled at the memory of drawing for her. "She was a really good teacher," he nodded. "I was lucky there, for sure." He grinned: my mom and Sid's took us on a field trip one time when we were in Cubs—I saw those and made a little sketch for the Wolf Den Scrapbook. I kinda liked 'em, so I drew the big ones at school."

Swann resolved to look at those more closely.

"Anyway, I've only done nine of the real big ones—I used up one sheet for the Troop Scrapbook. Big ones are different from the others. I **wanted** to do those ones big. I **had** to." he bounced happily. "See, what I discovered was that when they're big, you can show way more about how they feel inside. They aren't finished until you do." He reflected on that comment briefly. "I just figured that out!" *and show what I feel.* He didn't say that out loud; he was curious about that, actually: he hoped that Mr. Swann would mention if a drawing showed that too much. *the drawings of Mark especially.*

Swann was puzzled: "What they feel?"

"Yeah, that's what I always try to do when I draw people: I try to show more than a camera does: what's inside as well as outside... like the one I drew of Kasey: I tried to show how **he** felt. That music helped a lot. The other big ones didn't have that advantage."

"So the fact that he was playing the music didn't make it harder?"

"No! Just the opposite—it helped: maybe because he was playing it, he was making the sound: it was part of him—I didn't think about that until now." He stopped to catch up with himself, the pleasure of making that kind of discovery usually took longer. "It was the same on Saturday: Grandma Molly and Grandpa Jim sitting there talking about past Christmases helped me figure out how to show what they felt like, looking at those ornaments. Lots better than just sitting there like a couple of rocks; and doing it on larger paper was a lot better than enlarging it later," he nodded vigorously. "They're right there, so you don't hafta guess about anything you don't remember so well later." They were so happy he couldn't help but capture that in the drawing.

"I hope you don't mind talking about your drawings—I don't want to make you uncomfortable."

"No, no! That would be pretty silly: I don't mind at all. You **know** about stuff. Just asking questions helps me think about things—it helps me a lot: your questions do, anyway. Most people don't do that—they just say nice things."

"Does that bother you?"

"No. I'm glad they like it—nice to know that," he didn't want to be ungrateful. "But that doesn't help me do better on the next one. I mean, they don't know any better, so I can't complain. No big deal. I'm glad they like them—that's what I wanted to do: I like making people happy by showing them how interesting they are to look at." He pondered. *maybe that's what I'm meant to do.* He was grateful to Mr. Swann for helping him figure that out. "The big ones especially."

Swann resolved to see the other large drawings. If they were like the one of Kasey—and he suspected they were—he had discovered far more than he had dared to imagine.

"I really like this car." This was the second time he had ridden in the front seat of the Packard. *why did they stop making these, anyway?* "Maybe someday I can draw it up: that would be fun." He had several possible views in mind. He looked at everything closely with his special "camera eyes." That helped him remember better—he had been thinking about drawing one of Mason driving along, looking so important. He needed to remember what it looked like here… *probably be a horizontal…* He planned to do a rough sketch after lunch.

23 *outfitting the photo studio*

"It's funny, y'know. I've known Julian for almost three years, what with scouts, and his Troop Scrapbook. But I never thought he'd be important like this. I doubt if he did, either." Andy had always thought of him as that cute little blond kid in the Wolf Patrol. He was happy and pleased, all the same. He doubted if Julian had any idea what he was in for. The way Mr. L and Mr. Swann talked about him, it must be something out of the ordinary. He glanced at his watch: *5 minutes late…* He increased their pace. Coach Switcher was a good guy; this was a teacher work day—the teachers had to get their report cards done: extra time was something they didn't have.

Randall agreed heartily. "Kasey is very lucky!" Speaking as an outsider that was taken by the hand and pulled out of the cold into the Sunny world of Julian by Julian, he doubted if Andy had any idea just how well he could vouch for that. His entire life was transformed from the moment he saw him on his first day at Jackson. The luckiest thing in his life was being put in the same second period history class. Now, somehow, he realized that Julian approved of his new relationship with Andy even though they had not talked about it. That too was amazing. "Don't let me forget to get a few snapshots of his car." Julian wanted a few reference shots for a drawing he wanted to do.

"Sure glad we didn't have to go get him—we're on a tight schedule." One thing was clear enough: when a guy like Mr. Swann wants to pick him up in person, you know something is up. *he even called him on the phone*.

"I still don't see how we're going to do this without a trailer or something." Randall remembered that mountainous stack of mats the coach showed them.

"It's going to be a little tricky—what we need is a pickup." He wished his faded '48 had a rack on top—no such luck. At least it wasn't raining today. This particular photo shoot was special—he wanted to see if he was right about Kenny and Scott. If he was, this was going to be the best photo session yet—perfect way to finish the semester!

Coach Switcher was waiting with the two wrestlers, the famous J&J—140 pound weight class, juniors at Jackson High. They would do the heavy lifting as well as the action photo session in the photo studio—Randall would be able to experiment and try special lighting effects that he would never be able to get in the gym. Having a simulated wrestling venue was like having a movie set, for all practical purposes. Fortunately, the room over the garage had lots of open space.

"Hey, Coach, we did it: we get a full page in the special issue! The entire last page is a Wrestling Special!"

"Wow. How did you swing that!?" *a whole page?*

"They need it, actually, because it's a six pager, thanks to Mr. Swann and the extra ads he helped us line up. The paper will actually make a little on this issue. If we do a good job, we should be able to have a picture or story in every issue as long as the season runs. Basketball will get first call, but Mr. L wants every sport to get some space. We just have to sell enough ads."

Switcher nodded, "There's always a catch."

"I think we can, after hearing Mr. Swann talk about it; that guy knows his stuff. I don't know how rich he is, but it doesn't surprise me that he's rich. He spent the morning with us and man alive is he ever smart. He gets it done fast and moves right on to whatever is next. And he's really nice about things—not bossy at all." Frederick Swann had caused Andy to reassess his opinion about adults in general.

The coach opened the storage room. "Here you go: keep them for as long as you want, no one else is likely to call. Are you sure you don't need them all?" He wished he could just give them away.

"Six of these will gobble up most of the space I've got. I take it you aren't supposed to double the thickness."

"No, they need to be firm. Technically, they are too thick by nearly an inch for use in competition as is." He squeezed the corner of one. "That's what is required." His fingers felt oily. "You might want to wipe 'em down good before using them though. Be a good thing to do that every time. We don't need any infections." *s.o.p. before all matches at Jackson.*

Andy just had a thought: "Guys, do we need to come back here?" He was worried that they might run out of time—there was no way to predict how long this session would run. "You guys gonna need anything in your locker?"

"Nope." Scott nudged Kenny. "We just need to get his car. It's locked, so we're good."

"I'll tell the office—but if you have the permit sticker in your window, they won't tow it away. The school will be locked up at 5 as usual. No activities tonight." The coach tapped the dolly: "just make sure you return this to the custodian's office before you take off. If you need me I'll be in my cubicle until 4 or 4:30 doing grades." He gave a wave. "Thanks boys." He almost said see you next year, but that seemed a bit frivolous, even if it was the case. He had no plans to be around here until January 3, 1963.

It took two trips to the car: three 5x5 sections were all the crew of four could handle: one to push the dolly, two to keep the floppy load upright, and Andy to open doors and supervise. "Last load, men!" He tried to add a touch of humor to what had turned out to be a real chore: these units were awkward and heavy, and they had to be secured to the top of his car with rope—more work than fun, for sure. He didn't look forward to returning these. He had a hunch he wouldn't need to—the coach said that they were not likely to ever be used by the school again anyway—they were too worn and hard to work with, and all they did was occupy storage space. Hand-me-downs, they had been replaced nearly five years ago by new rubber rollouts.

"Why did they keep these, anyway?" Kenny Johnson wondered. "Not that I'm complaining, o'course." His dad must not have been around this project. He was famous for pitching things out.

"Yeah, well," Scott countered, "Some of us are used to making thing go as far as they can; besides, these aren't that shot. I'll bet they cost a bunch."

347

"The new interscholastic rules make these obsolete anyway—they have to be one piece now, like a big padded rug—you roll 'em up when you're done." Coach Switcher had told Andy that last week. It did save a lot of time and hassle, and the custodians took care of it now, which was huge. He wondered how they were going to deal with them when the calendar project was finished. They would gobble up half of the studio, at least. Randall didn't seem to be worried. *so be it.*

"They make an interesting image atop your car," Randall offered, taking another snapshot. He hoped to sneak one of these into the calendar somewhere. "I just remembered! I need to photograph the Packard for Julian. Drive around there and pick me up on the way out." He took off running to the other end of the parking lot.

The Packard was almost out of sight by the music annex. Mr. Swann was smart—parking in front of the school for very long wasn't a very good idea. He had to shoot through the windows to get the dashboard, but it would do. Photographing the outside was no problem—fortunately, the weather was overcast but not raining. Andy pulled up just as he was taking his last shot. He had to be sure to put this roll in front of the wrestling series when they began printing later.

"Classy car," Scott observed.

"That is a Packard—pre World War Two." Kenny knew classic cars. "I'd guess 1935 or 36. Check out those white sidewalls!"

"What's it doing here?" Scott wasn't into cars.

"Don't know," Randall said, exchanging looks with Andy: they knew but were sworn to keep it secret. No one was supposed to know until after vacation.

Fortunately, J&J were focused on their objective for the day; the antique automobile by the Music wing was only mildly interesting; dwelling on it was pointless. Kenny presumed there was probably going to be an auto show during the vacation—the student lot would be a good spot for that.

"Gotta hand it to Mark: the training he gave us in securing a load on top of his rig made this possible." Andy thought it wise to change the subject. "It isn't pretty, but it will hold." He would see to it that Mark saw one of Randall's photos; might as well show off a little.

He just hoped the seals along the top of his doors weren't shot as a result. The car doors had to be open when they roped up. The rope didn't seem to mind being squeezed tight like that.

Fortunately, they made the trip without incident. Two miles wasn't far.

After almost an hour, the mats were in place—invasive to say the least. Instead of half the room, they covered nearly three fourths. Fortunately, the additional lights, diffusion panels and reflectors Mr. Swann had donated made the entire area available. The idea was to enable live action as well as posed shots. Except for the seven foot six ceiling, they had a lot of room in which to play. With a shallow depth of field, these photographs would look like they had been taken on location in the gym, but with a professional artistic polish.

J&J, shorthand for Jensen and Johnson, was a team inside joke of sorts—it suggested they were trademarked, like their team's first aid kit. The two were fast friends and as close to identical physically as fraternal twins would be, and they truly enjoyed wrestling with each other. Nothing was rumored about their sexual preference; if there was more than met the eye, it was well concealed—they both dated, so nothing was ever said one way or another. Winning for them was secondary, and when possible, they wanted to share it: neither wanted to be better or more successful than the other. Some swore they had a secret agreement to take turns winning, whether in competition or practice. They were students of the sport as well as participants, and were given to quote statistics and facts at random—Kenny was a walking reference book on wrestling. His father was a history professor, and had been a big help. J&J had their own reasons for volunteering to be featured in Andy's Calendar project.

"You do know what the word "gymnasium" means, don't you?" He was confident that he was about to enlighten someone who ought to know but didn't.

Randall did know, but he didn't want to disappoint an about to be photographed subject: an attitude of invincibility was a part of his preprogramming as a subject. "Where the gymnasts practice?" He thought that would be half right, and evoke a satisfied look and a detailed supplement. He was correct: **doubly** correct, as it turned out.

"Yes, but there's more: it was a **restricted** area. Gumnos is the ancient Greek word for nude or naked: **no clothes allowed**, a place reserved for athletes to **gumnadzo**: train naked for competition, which was also done naked. Only their coaches or assistants could wear street clothing." Kenny delighted in sharing this information. "The original gymnasiums were open arenas on the outside edge of town, with a carefully prepared flat earth surface: no stone. The only participants in the ancient Olympics allowed to wear anything were Persians—their religion required a loincloth. Since the contests were created primarily as a substitute for war between the city states, the Greek Olympic League allowed them an exception. One primary reason for naked competition was good hygiene; secondary was religious—the games were held in honor of Zeus. Of course, it was men and boys only— unmarried females were allowed to watch the competition, but the women had their own games, where men were not allowed. The Goddess Hera oversaw those."

Randall exchanged a glance with Andy. They had a history professor wrestler on their hands. That was unexpected.

Little did he know: more would be disclosed before the day was over—a great deal more.

While Kenny had been delivering his mini-lecture, Scott was in the center of the new space doing some calculating. "No over-the-head tosses." He pointed to the ceiling.

"You're right, although a suplex full body pickup would work— we could do that in the second set, the Greco Roman."

"True enough. We can flip for it." Scott reconsidered: "We'll both do one."

Randall and Andy were amazed. All the previous photo sessions had begun by being asked what to do. These two knew exactly what they wanted to have photographed. Randall shrugged. *might as well do it their way.*

Scott held out his left hand and extended three fingers: "We'd like to do three sets: a Freestyle, a Greco Roman, and a classical Greek set. We'll do a demo of each so that you can decide where to shoot from. Then, when we do the move, we will do the full move and freeze when you say to, or when we know the hold is perfect." He had been told that Randall had a lot of film. "I figured that we could do one roll of each—that way you can get more than one view—a high angle low angle, that kind of thing."

Kenny turned to Andy: "We need you to help keep track of which one of us has the winning hold, and in what color—we have both here, the home meet and the away meet colors. We need to swap them so that we're even overall." He unzipped his duffel bag and pulled out a list. "Here's what we worked out. If you need to add anything, just let us know, okay?"

Andy took the list and stepped over to Randall.

Randall was delighted. This took care of all the organizing he always had to do later. "Man, you guys are terrific." He scanned down the list. "See anything?" he thought Andy might have something to add—he was the writer.

Andy shook his head. "Can we get all this done today?" He was only half joking.

"Don't know why not," Scott said. "No school tomorrow, so we can stay at it until bedtime, if we need to. How long does it take to develop and print?"

"I never though about that," Randall admitted. "I have to send the color out; the black and white we can develop and make contact sheets tonight... maybe a few prints.

Scott frowned. He did not expect the color film problem. "Do you use two cameras, or how does that work?"

"Good news there: I have three cameras now, so I don't need to reload all as often. I have one camera for maximum detail, that's the 12 per roll camera, and two 35mm—one for color, one for black and white. That has 40 shots a roll—36 if it's color film." Thanks to Mr. Swann, his turnaround time for black and white was now slightly more than an hour with Andy assisting. "We can do a lot of the black and white tonight. Color will take a week, probably. Depends on how busy they are."

Scott and Kenny looked at each other, as if able to communicate directly—they had talked about this before. They shrugged and took their duffel bags to the side of the mat and started to disrobe. They were ready and eager to do their thing.

Andy gulped and gave Randall a wide-eyed expression that said the same thing he saw on Randall's face: they were dealing with experts here; first on the list Kenny had given him was: 'Freestyle starting position first round.'

He had to stop and watch for a minute: two very attractive 140 pound wrestlers were standing there buck naked, pulling on their spandex singletons—one white with red trim, the other red with white trim. As usual, neither was wearing a jock strap. They hadn't encountered anyone on the team that did. That suited Andy just fine. He was curious to see how long it would take for the center of interest to register its appreciation of the activity it was being forced to engage in. So far, all the wrestlers had proven to have the same tendency. Usually, after 15 or 20 minutes, they had risen to and by the occasion very nicely. He had learned to allow time after the photo session for "relief" before returning them to the school or home. Without exception, they had all wanted a "special photographic memento." Wrestlers, these at least, seemed keen on how they looked physically; getting photos of themselves was an opportunity they couldn't pass up—lots of photographs. Randall had been assembling a very impressive private portfolio; he was fussing with his tripods and missed the preview.

Randall stepped closer as J&J took crouched positions on the mat, their feet carefully placed, as if about to begin a freestyle match. "Is there anything in particular you want this shot to include?"

Kenny stood: "Good question! As a matter of fact, yes: make sure you show where our feet are positioned."

"And our heads," Scott added.

"Might as well take one from a couple of angles."

Randall agreed; "I plan to take whole figure shots—I can zoom in for most any close-up frames we want in the darkroom. What I'm not sure about is which ones need to be in color." He wanted Andy's opinion.

352

"The color pages will be the front and back covers, both sides, the 12 month pages, and one extra page of color in front, black and white on the other side and the same in back. We haven't decided what will go there—some competition shots, presumably. Four extra pages in all—it's based on one the Fire department put out last year." He skipped over to the desk to fetch it.

J&J had not seen that before. They needed to look at it closely.

Andy sensed a problem. "So, what's up?"

Scott and Kenny looked at each other: "Well, we sort of hoped there would be some leftovers we could use for a little project we've been working on." He pointed to the list he had given to Andy. "We want to make a small pocket handbook for beginning wrestlers. There is nothing out there. We figure it could make a few bucks—help out with college. With illustrations it would be perfect."

Andy grinned. "Great idea you guys." He saw what to do at once: "Tell you what: we'll take the snapshots you need, maybe a few extras, and then pick a few out of the batch for the calendar." He almost offered to put an ad in the calendar, but realized he needed to run that by the coach. He might consider talking to Mr. Swann about promoting this pocket handbook. That had promise.

The first series took about an hour and a half—it established a routine. Everything was shot in black and white with his new Nikon. When a shot looked really good, Randall shot it again in color; if it was super special, with his Yashica 120 medium format camera—those had poster size potential. All the basic holds were captured on film—half nelsons, headlocks scissors, throws—a dozen in all.

Randall was most amazed by the periodic pause to swap singlets: they wanted an equal number of exposures wearing red or white. Being as identical as they could be was their main concern; he did not inquire why. Watching them exchange was diverting: they had brought one of each color, not two. Intriguing, to say the least. They would both be wearing the same singlets. He did not inquire about that either—Kenny and Scott were the same size, so it made no difference visually.

Toward the end of that set, the issue of what to do about their erections had to be faced at last. Randall interrupted to ask the question.

353

"Y'know, we can't use anything in the paper that shows—at least not when it's as big as you guys are." He shrugged.

Kenny looked at Scott and himself. "I s'pose you're right." He looked more closely: Scott was up a little more. *odd... we're usually the same.*

"Don't know why you're so pokey today," Scott joked, and grabbed a handful.

"Illegal hold!" Kenny scolded. He pushed his hips forward briefly and turned his head to Andy. "Show me the list: how are doing there?"

They huddled around Andy, who wanted to photograph the illegal hold, still being held. Randall was amused and delighted by how offhand they were about what for anyone else would be an embarrassment of the first order. Just for fun, he took a shot of the illegal hold.

The only move on the list not marked was the double grapevine.

"Odd man for top?" Scott felt lucky.

Kenny did the odd man response. Scott was right: he won. That meant that Kenny would get the first Greco Roman pin. He turned to Randall. "We can do this one so these guys don't show. Then we need to shrink them back down. Harder to hide them in Greco Roman." He freed himself from Scott's illegal hold—now they were both up full.

Andy enjoyed fantasizing as he watched... he'd prefer to be the loser in the double grapevine: although, he doubted if Scott's legs were long enough—these guys were almost four inches shorter than he was. Still, having Scott stretched out full length on top of him would be very nice, considering what would be pressing against him. He had a very good idea of what these two might like about this particular hold, especially if they were allowed to hold it for very long. They were so evenly matched, that they took the full two minutes before Scott declared the pin. Two minutes allowed Randall to get several excellent shots. They were not posing, but demonstrating—that was hugely different.

The two bounced up and bumped elbows happily. Kenny turned to Andy, who he regarded as the one in charge. "There are two ways to

deal with this: one is we take a cold shower and take a break." He gestured to Scott.

"The other way is to sit down and do a quick pull. That's the quickest and surest way."

Randall was stunned; Andy, who was trying not to laugh, looked down at his own problem. "Is this contagious or something?"

Scott laughed, "I never though of that. You might be onto something!"

Kenny could see the wall clock—they didn't need a break. But the supper issue had not been discussed, nor whether to stay after that or what. "Well, I figure once we get this out of the way, we'll be able to get through the other two sets by five."

Randall was glad to hear that. "Excellent. That's when my mom insists on my presence. Can you guys stay for supper? Then we could do the lab work right after."

Scott was surprised by the offer—he assumed they'd order pizza.

"Listen you guys—it's not a problem. She orders out all the time—and she really likes to meet my friends from school."

"That's for sure!" Andy agreed. "Make her day to have this many. Besides, you guys **have** to meet his Dad," he winked at Randall.

"I need to let her know: you guys in? Do you need to call home?" He pointed to the desk: "I have a phone up here now."

"No sweat—we can do that later," Kenny checked with Scott, then said, "We're in. And, we're ready." He pointed downward. "You guys can watch or join in, your choice." He stepped over to the travel bag and pulled out a hand towel. He stepped over opposite Scott. They took off their singlets, sat down on the spot, loosened their scrotums and took themselves in hand.

Andy chuckled at Randall. Obviously, they had to join in. They had already taken off their shoes, so he attacked his Levis—the fly emitted its friendly p-p-p-p-p sound and the pants fell to the floor. He wondered if J would do J or the other way around. If they did, he and Randall could do a proper job.

355

Randall had seen that button routine before—this time he unzipped and followed Andy's lead. Andy chose to sit an arm's reach from Scott, to his left, almost as if he had done this before. He hadn't, but sensed that it would be a good idea in the long run. Randall sat next to Kenny.

From above it resembled a dinghy with four oarsmen facing each other rather than the stern, operating hand pumps rather than pulling an oar. Just to fit in, Andy shed his shirt; Randall did the same. They left their socks on.

Neither Randall nor Andy had ever 'taken care of the problem' this way, so they paid attention to J&J; it would seem J&J did this on a regular basis. The next surprise was exchanging hands—not from right to left, but straight across. For a time they stroked each other, then, as if a timer had sounded, they put their left hand atop and around the extended hand, as if to guide and regulate its grip.

That's when it got serious: they could tell from the facial expressions that this was a major improvement. Andy nodded at Randall, and they followed. Wow did it make a difference: doubled the pleasure at once. It was slightly awkward to watch and perform at the same time, and eventually, Randall focused on how his left hand helped. He missed the momentary hold that Kenny had given Scott's hand—the signal that he was close.

When Scott gave Kenny the hold signal, Kenny loosened and allowed Scott to continue, and they both started a very slow pace, identical intervals. The goal was to reach the apex at the same time, then alternate pulls until both had ejected their full load. They usually had the same number of emissions. It was well controlled: what little spilled hit the towel, making cleanup easy and efficient. They gave each other thumbs up and turned to watch Randall and Andy. This was the first time they had guests join their special 'ceremony.'

Randall felt an odd moment of déjà-vu: in an odd way, this was like being initiated in Hayden Park—these two guys were so ceremonial about everything.

The second set of photographs went very efficiently—many of its moves were similar, but leg holds were not allowed; most of the rules

356

had to do with areas that photography couldn't document. As a result, the Greco Roman set was done in half the time.

The third set, the classical Olympic, was very different—and neither Andy nor Randall were prepared. When the two wrestlers had taken off their singlets, instead of swapping them, they tucked them into the duffle bags and took out two small containers of olive oil. They proceeded to coat themselves and each other completely, head to toe with oil.

Randall and Andy stared open-mouthed, awaiting an explanation. The historian, seeing their puzzled faces, explained.

"Y'see, in ancient Greece, they had to wrestle in the dirt, basically. So they coated themselves in oil to seal all the pores. Then they dusted themselves with a fine powder so they wouldn't be slippery. Of course, they wrestled in the nude. The rules were like the Greco Roman, mostly, although it was a lot rougher—people got broken arms and legs even. You didn't have to pin to win—but you had to stay inside the official area—it wasn't a circle. You could win by making your opponent step out of bounds. And there wasn't a time limit. It was a lot rougher; you didn't have to weigh the same or be the same age." He stooped to fetch the container of talcum powder. He sprinkled Scott all over and handed him the container. Soon, both were oiled and dusted, ready to perform for the camera.

As he watched and took a few candid shots, Randall was furious with himself: he had not photographed the "ceremony." How to remedy that would nag at him for months.

Photographing the session was interesting, to be sure. It began by the two standing about three feet apart leaning toward each other until their foreheads touched. "Now!" Scott gave the signal to start, since they didn't have a referee.

Occasionally, Kenny provided a narration to explain what they were doing, and what they were not doing, since they did not want to cause an injury. He had begun by explaining that to be truly authentic, they would have a flute player on hand—matches as well as practices were always accompanied with a flute. Randall realized later that he could have offered to play his clarinet, but he was busy with the cameras. Kenny didn't offer any hints about what the music would have sounded like. A flute playing at a contemporary wrestling match seemed like a bad fit. Very bad. This mini match had been vaguely dancelike, but Randall thought that was coincidental, since they were performing for the camera. Though not truly competing, they put in a full vigorous effort, not simply posing—they were sweating up a storm.

Aside from the curious visual texture the oil and talcum created, the free swinging manhood found a stable stage, somewhere between a quarter to a third—enough to avoid flaccid flips and flops, but not enough to suggest any danger of going full—the pause at the end of the first set had satisfied the physical need. The erotic element had become an aesthetic value, probably as much as it was to the ancients. Preserved on film, it might invoke a variety of responses—whatever the eye of the beholder brought to the experience. That was the question that tugged at Randall: who was going to see these? He had always insisted on keeping all his negatives. Maybe these would be the exception. He hoped these guys would help do the prints—he would need to get more paper soon, that was obvious.

Kenny concluded the sequence with a very successful full body lift and throw. He went to the duffle bag and pulled out a saucer and scraper blade. After catching his breath, his professorial narrative kicked in once again: "One way the wrestlers earned a little extra was by selling their scrapings." He held the scraper against a rivulet that was running down Scott's chest, caught it, and scraped most of it onto the saucer. "They carried a little urn to collect this, and sold it to the medical practitioners. It was supposed to be good for various things—curing warts, helping sore muscles," he shrugged. "I don't know if modern medicine has tried to verify whether it was any good; I sort of doubt it." He wanted a snapshot of the scraping anyway. "At the end of the match, they would scrape themselves down completely before bathing. They cleaned off all the remaining oil and powder with a sponge bath."

Neither Kenny nor Scott explained why they wanted the third set of photos taken. Randall doubted if any of them could be used in the calendar—or in the potential handbook, but he was intrigued by these students of the sport. He couldn't stand it any longer: "Do you guys do this a lot?" If they did, he wondered where as well as why.

"No. We've just talked a lot about it and studied it," Kenny replied.

358

"Thanks to you guys, we got a chance to see what it was actually like." Scott added, clearly grateful.

"You can't say you know what it's like unless you've actually done it, can you?"

"Think of it this way: you are among the few people who have ever seen it performed. That's one reason we wanted a few snapshots—we've never seen it either." Scott shrugged: "o'course, we didn't do it outside on the bare ground, so it wasn't perfect."

"Today, probably, they wouldn't need the oil and powder, with a mat like this—although, those might have had a religious purpose. You gotta remember that originally this was a tribute to Zeus: it was supposed to be done according to strict rules. They didn't mess around when it came to following the rules: there were no jails. You were banished or exiled: that was as good as a death sentence in most cases."

"Or you could become a slave sometimes, depending." Scott added.

"So where is the shower?" Kenny wasn't interested in a sponge bath. He snagged the towels from the duffle bag—they had come fully prepared.

Randall showed them over to the bathroom at the other end of the apartment. It came as no surprise to see them enter the shower together.

Randall rounded up all the film and prepared to take it downstairs to the darkroom.

> > *Hello up there—You guys hungry?* < < Helgar's deep baritone voice filled the room.

"Hi Dad! We're on our way!" He grinned at Andy—he seemed to be just as ready to take a break as he was. "Perfect timing!"

Andy was glad to have the interruption. He wasn't quite ready to discuss the day's activity with Randall yet. He was strangely unsettled by the photo session. He didn't understand why, either. He hoped that somehow the supper and Randall's giant of a man father would inspire him; he really liked him for some reason. *hard to believe he's a college professor…*

359

The pair in the back seat of the faded 48 were tired, but very pleased with the day—long, but they got more done than they had thought possible. It was too dark in the car to look at the prints—plenty of time for that later. Kenny thought back to the supper—that was really interesting. "Have you seen any of your dad's Track and Field photos? He must have some amazing things." He assumed that was one reason Randall was so good at taking athletic photos.

"A long time ago, when I was in grade school. He never made a point of showing those around." Randall had almost forgotten about them and his father's collegiate and high school pastimes. "We spend all our time hiking and camping, and mountain climbing." Randall was as surprised as these guys were about his father's athletic honors. His dad never brought them up.

"I'll bet he looked great—he's still very fit. He must work out."

Other than walking to work, Randall didn't know of anything special there. It just occurred to him: he didn't really know what his father did with his days other than lecture and play in the microbiology lab. His father had never tried to encourage a father-son team approach to anything other than camping trips. That was a new observation... that was food for thought.

Kenny and Scott exchanged a glance. They weren't surprised—Randall was obviously not an athlete—he was the opposite. His dad was smart enough to know that. That impressed them almost as much.

"Your mom sure knows how to feed a hungry outfit." Scott was more than pleased by that. Ribs were a rare treat on his family's table. "Potato salad was sure good."

"She's a great cook, but she uses Sharple's a lot too." His father expected both quality and quantity.

"Beat's Shakey's, for sure" Kenny had been paying attention to nutrition for some time now. He had been saving a final historical tidbit. "By the way, do you know why we say Jim-nasium instead of Goom-nasium?

Andy grinned at Randall. "Goomnasium? You've got us on that one." These guys were something else.

"Nobody does: blame it on the monks who translated the Greek manuscripts into English. Some Greek letters are different: Greek U is same as the English letter Y. And since the Latin letter for U was the same as the English letter V, they flipped a coin and used Y instead of V—they were more used to writing in Latin than English, but they knew that Gvnasium wouldn't be any good." He grinned. "Besides, the Greek letter for G is an upside down L… it's all messed up. He found great satisfaction in springing little facts like that on people.

"Goomnasium? Really?" Andy couldn't imagine anyone using that word.

"Yep. That sounds closer to Greek U than Gum; they pronounced U like we do in **flute**." *no uhs in Greek probably…* He had not taken a class in Greek—probably never would.

"Why didn't they just use U?"

"Dunno. You had to be there I guess." Kenny never got that either. *I need to ask Dad about that.*

They were at the school at last. "How do you like your Ford?" Andy was getting ready to change horses—the Dodge was showing signs that it was about to cost a bunch to keep running. He needed it to last for the rest of the year, at least.

"No complaints. Mileage is fair. I kinda like the Mustang— might get one of those next." *beats a Chevy, for sure.* Kenny's father took care of that. He opened his door. "Yours is doing pretty good, considering." His family had never had a Dodge.

"Okay guys—thanks." Andy gave a thumbs up.

"I don't expect the color for a week," Randall added. "Do you want me to call, or wait until school starts after vacation?"

"If it's no problem, give me a buzz. We'd like to see those, for sure!" Kenny wanted to see the double grapevine in particular. He hoped that one would make the calendar.

Andy gave the horn a short toot, and they left J&J and the school parking lot. Andy had a plan, of sorts—that's why he had asked Randall to ride along. Before taking him back home, he needed to talk. About six blocks away, he turned right at a side street, drove a block and pulled over—it was fairly private and safe along here—the large oak provided a partial canopy and filtered the streetlight—a nice coincidence.

There was a long pause. Andy thought he was ready, but somehow, his brain had frozen and his mouth would not cooperate. Fortunately, Randall had the correct instinct, and he reached out for Andy's hand. Even though was dark, they could see what they both desperately wanted to see, what they needed to see.

"We need to do something besides develop pictures," Andy finally blurted out.

Randall squeezed his hand. He had an urge to lunge at once and kiss Andy on the mouth, but he had never kissed anyone—he was so afraid he'd foul it up. But the emotion was there, boiling over.

Andy saw the tear form and Randall starting to bite his lip. He turned and reached out both hands to hold Randall's head. He leaned forward and kissed very gently.

Randall sighed, then lunged into a desperate embrace.

They did that for a while. The 1948 Dodge had a bench seat in front; once Andy was out from behind he steering wheel, he was able to do what was needed. He sat back at last. "Wow."

Randall didn't have a better word. From the first, they seemed able to sense what they wanted to say better than they could verbalize it. Then it came to him: "Want to go camping?"

Andy was thrilled. "Brilliant! That would be perfect."

"Hayden Park!" they said in unison. They broke out laughing.

"Maybe we caught something from J&J!" Andy quipped.

"Maybe we did," Randall said, serious as a stone. "Or maybe we already had it."

"Okay: when?" It would have to be after Christmas, Andy knew that right off. He'd need to get a sub to do his paper route.

"I need to see what's going on—my guess is a day or two after Christmas… then we hafta decide how long, all that stuff." Randall just

362

realized he was talking like Julian all of a sudden. He had to smile at that. It sort of validated how he felt.

Andy thought about it. "Tell you what: think things through, and we can talk about it tomorrow after we're done at the Cardinal. Remember, we're supposed to be there at 9 o'clock to show what we have for the last page."

No problem. "I can do that tonight." He chuckled briefly.

"What?"

"Goomnasium. I kind of like that, actually." That's what Randall would use when he needed to refer to the special Calendar setup.

The real world had reestablished itself, and they were ready to proceed. They had passed over or through or whatever it was: they had answered a basic question—the details could be sorted out later. They still had a job ahead; getting ready for their new world needed to be done with care.

Helgar looked up from his book—he sensed something. Sure enough, it was Randall. He was standing in the doorway. Odd: he was just standing there, eyes unfocused… didn't seem to be in any kind of trouble or discomfort. As if clearing his throat he made a small noise… enough to attract his wife's attention.

Helgar's eyes alerted her to look toward the doorway. The Mozart playing softly in the background masked any other sound, so she had not heard him say anything. She too saw her boy's face. She closed her book and looked more closely. Something had happened.

Randall focused his eyes, looked at his mother, then his father. He did not have the words he needed, but he had the need and the sentiment. He had to let them know, somehow, that he was in a new place, a wonderful place. He smiled at his mother and blinked. Then at his father: he nodded. "G'night." He turned and went to his room.

Instinctively, both parents stood and went to the doorway—they watched him go down the hallway to his room.

Eloise held her husband around the waist and hugged. "You were so wise, dear." Helgar had insisted that Randall would be able to find his way unassisted—that it was essential that he be allowed to do that.

Helgar held her tight, lest he give in. He wanted to cheer, and he wanted to cry—but he had to remain quiet. That was his assignment. "So, my dear, were you." They kissed lightly, and prepared to call it a night. Getting back to their respective books could wait until tomorrow. They both approved of Andy, which helped a great deal.

24   *rise and shine*

>> mnmnmnmn... <<

The alarm clock started its telltale warning hum: it was about to shatter the silence less than a foot from a blissfully asleep tussled blond head.

"Oh, no you don't!" Julian awoke at once and reached behind: he needed to grab the clock before it could go off. He had developed this skill at Camp Walker, where the cabin's wind-up Big Ben was ten times as bad as his small electric Westclox; it was as quiet as a mouse compared to Big Ben. He could hear that warning click clear across the cabin.

He sat up at once, pleased that he had caught it in time. At least it wouldn't wake up his mom. He was kind of surprised, actually. Usually it got him when he was sound asleep. Well, today was special—that must be why: instead of going to school, he was going to surprise Mark and join him on his morning run. He had not done that in a long time. The clock dial—the only source of light in the room, showed 6:15.

>> yawn <<

He shook his head. *an hour before sunrise!* The problem was, Mark always took his run before work, not after. Well, he had 15 minutes to get dressed—plenty of time; Mark usually started at 6:30. *OO! first things first! gotta go...*

He tiptoed to the bathroom and closed the door quietly, chuckling to himself. He just now remembered Uncle Max's voice from last summer. After Julian had been drawing his picture for a while, he stood up from his stool: he had to go all of a sudden. "Be back in two shakes, Boy: gotta go pour the water off the spuds."

Once in a while he thought of that when he had to go in a hurry... 'cept he usually had to do more than two shakes afterward. Sometimes, like today, he had to wait for Little J to wilt a little bit first. Shaking too much or too soon was risky: Little J had his own rules about that—especially when, like today, it had been a while since he'd been allowed to play Little J's favorite game. He'd stayed up too late doing the Scrapbook page, and fell asleep instead. *not enough time now...* He'd satisfy Little J after his mom went to work.

Mark was delighted when he saw Julian hop down the steps. It had been a long time since he had joined the morning run. "Hey, you're up bright and early."

"Hiya!" Julian scurried down the steps grinning wide. "I figured that since I don't have PE during vacation, this would be a fun thing to do." The truth was, he wanted to have some time with Mark. He couldn't say that out loud, of course. It felt good to get moving at last— he'd been waiting several minutes. "Kinda chilly this morning."

"Yes, it is; they call it December. I'm glad you're joining me today. We never seem to find time to get caught up like we did at Camp Walker. It's about time, too."

Those words were better than perfect! "Yeah, I really miss that. There's so much going on now. I didn't think high school would be so busy!"

Mark laughed: "I have news for you: it's only going to get worse." He had been through the same thing, in a way—though he wasn't as talented. Julian would have more to contend with; he was going to be very popular soon. He was thankful his boyhood had been simpler.

Julian wasn't surprised to hear this—everyone else said pretty much the same thing about high school. "Geraldine tried to warn me, I guess." The thing that annoyed him the most was that Geraldine was usually right.

Mark glanced across as they jogged across the street. As intended, the bright and harsh light over the intersection emphasized things in motion; the change in Julian's height since the last time they jogged was a surprise—as was the pronounced bulge swinging below his waistline. It was evident that he did not wear anything under his sweatpants. He forced his eyes to look ahead—he had a similar problem with Roger this morning, one that he did not want to encourage—Julian was off limits regardless of the increased visual appeal. The sweatshirt and pants were doing a fair job of containing the exquisite cloud of pheromones that always radiated from him; in a closed room, they could be almost as toxic as catnip. Nonetheless, he was secretly pleased that Julian had an aversion to deodorants and scented camouflages—a mixed blessing. He was coming of age so rapidly—at least his voice wasn't cracking like Arnie's.

"So, how are things going? Any problems?"

Julian thought about the question for a second or two. "No problems, I don't think... too busy to notice if there are... all I seem to do any more is draw people. Kinda weird."

"I thought you enjoyed doing that."

"I do. I really do. I never thought about it much until lately: what else am I s'posed to be learning? Shouldn't I know how to do other things too? Before last summer, all I drew was things for the Scrapbook. It's different now... portraits are **way** different." He had no idea how many of those he had done. He thought a minute about whether he should ask about this. "It started when I drew the big picture of Leonard—maybe a little before, when I did the first big one of Geoff's chopped toe. What you told me in the cabin was right—it's more like that all the time."

"You mean what I said about the ones you drew of me?"

"Yeah: you said they were powerful. Mr. Swann said the same thing about the one I drew of Kasey," he tilted his head thoughtfully. "He **knows** stuff, you know? He's the first one—'cept you, o' course, that understands what I'm trying to do when I draw people. So I'm trying to figure it out—the one I did of Grandma Molly and Grandpa Jim at the decoration party on Saturday helped out."

367

"How did it do that?" Mark was impressed that Julian was so introspective. He had seen Saturday's drawing, but didn't look at it carefully.

"I tried to pay attention to what I felt as I drew them, and how I always try to show how the people I draw are feeling inside. It was kinda easy, in a way: they couldn't help it: they were looking at all their Christmas ornaments, the ones they had in their box. All their past Christmases got told about, 'cause the ornaments were so special that year. Made it easy to draw how happy they were, seeing and hearing them talk—it's in the drawing. If they'd sat still and been quiet, I wouldn't have seen and heard that. Like the one of Kasey: his music helped me draw him better."

He made a funny face. "Weird, that's all." He was discovering this as he went along: it wasn't being taught to him. He wondered if other artists did that. *Mr. Swann seemed to say that the other day when he stopped by to pick me up.*

You should ask Mark about him—he's the one who can tell. Inside guy was awake all of a sudden.

Julian was glad for the nudge: "It's Mr. Swann, I guess that I wonder about."

"Oh?" That came as a surprise.

"I mean, he's everywhere lately." He paused. "Geraldine says that if something's too good to be true it usually means you better watch out or you'll get a nasty surprise. Mr. Swann is kinda like that: too good to be true. Thing is, he's so nice and so generous—I really like him, y'know?" He hoped Mark could put his mind at rest. "Not because he's so rich, either: he seems to be a good person, a really **good** man." Julian wondered whether to tell him about the thousand dollars. He decided to wait; seemed like a bad idea to talk about that.

"I see your point. Maybe you should know a little more about him—I had not heard of him before that special dinner either. Randall's father explained it to me later. You should know this too, I guess—but you need to be very careful about it: do you know why he has hired Randall and Kasey's fathers?"

Julian thought that was obvious: "probably because they are the best ones for the job."

"Exactly. Mr. Swann has a very strange and rare disorder—something to do with his blood. Something he has to get fixed or he won't be around much longer. He has hired those two to lead the research for finding a cure."

Julian didn't know that, but somehow it didn't surprise him. "How long do they have?"

"I think he said two years; they don't know for sure."

whoah. that's not long... "Boy... I sure hope they can do it."

"Me too. I think we all feel that way—not just because we should: he is helping a lot of people right now—we would just as soon that didn't stop either." His support of the Troop's Christmas project was just the beginning—of that he was certain. He'd shown that by adding five thousand dollars to the Troop bank account.

"How rich is he, anyway?"

"I have no idea, but it must be a lot of money: he's more than just a millionaire, I think. Great wealth is a mystery to me too."

"Yesterday he bought everyone's lunch in the cafeteria—I mean, **everyone**, even the cooks! He did the same thing at School on Wednesday; at the work party for the school paper—he asked the lady in charge to figure out what everything cost to present the lunch that day, including the electricity."

Mark wasn't surprised. "Not to mention the truckload of decorations he bought for the retirement home on Saturday." *sure made Newberry's day...*

"Then he talked me into drawing the Cardinal editors. He likes to watch me draw I guess." *he watched on Saturday too...* "Oh: he said Kasey and his folks are supposed to arrive in town today—I guess that helped wake me up early." Julian figured he'd be needed sooner or later. He was a little worried about them. He'd heard a few whispers. Maybe everyone wasn't as willing to help out as he thought at first.

"Yes—the weather seems to have behaved this year—everyone's lucky." December wasn't a good time of the year to move an entire household.

"So I'm ready if they need me to help. I finished the Scrapbook page on the retirement home yesterday—soon as Mr. Swann is through looking at the Scrapbook, I can put it in." He puffed out a little steam. *why do we puff out a teeny cloud when we run?* He wondered if he could draw that. He had already formed an image of Mark puffing a little cloud while he was jogging—*the sweatband looks so cool.* His sweat pants were a little tight—that too was nice. Julian had a favorite memory of what was causing that. The effect of jogging several blocks had also had the other effect he liked: he could enjoy that smell—the Mark smell he had gotten so used to last summer. Little J liked it too. He made a point of puffing some extra steam to get his mind off that. "Why do we puff out little clouds that vanish? I never did understand that."

If Mark had known the technical explanation, it had been crowded into a corner somewhere. "I guess it's a reminder that we need to go back inside where it's warm when we're done. I forgot the scientific reason." He grinned at Julian, delighted that he still had little boy questions... reassured, actually. "Time to start back, I guess; let's turn around at the end of this block."

Mark wasn't willingly deluded by the little boy persona—it was real enough. Yet it was partly subterfuge, developed at camp last summer: Julian regarded it as his greatest achievement so far, top secret between himself and Inside Guy: **Job One** was not scaring Mark away. **Goal One** remained the same: when he became 18, Mark would be available. He had to make sure not to do anything that would foul that up. That was the main reason for not jogging with Mark **every** day. He needed to seem harmless. Like his drawing, no one could teach him these things; he could tell that Inside guy was nodding his head in agreement.

They stepped to the side to let the paperboy go by. He needed space so he could hit people's porches as he rode by on his bicycle. "I s'pose this is the busiest time of the year at the store." Julian was surprised Mark didn't have to be there on Saturday.

370

"Just about—we have other busy times, but Christmas keeps us busy both before and after—it's a double dose."

"Nice of them to let you work with the Troop on Saturday. They must be a good company."

"They are, but that was one of my conditions when they asked me to be Assistant Manager. They had to guarantee me that day every year, and let me have my summer vacation coincide with summer camp. What's so nice about that is it's one of the reasons they wanted me to take that promotion. They are good people. I'm lucky to work there."

"Mom and Geraldine took me Christmas shopping after the decoration project, so I'm all ready." Julian wondered about inviting Mark to Christmas supper. "I s'pose you hafta work up to the last minute."

"Oglivy's always closes at noon on Christmas eve, so it's not bad. Pat and I alternate between our parents: even years we go to her parents, odd year's to mine," Mark chuckled. "We don't dare do anything else now—it's our punishment for not providing them with any grandchildren." He held a finger to his lips: "That's a secret, by the way."

Julian nodded; made sense, actually. *oh well...* He decided not to ask about a camping trip during vacation: his job at the store would rule that out. He wasn't super eager to go camping in cold weather anyway, to be honest.

Inside Guy had an inspired thought: *Maybe spring vacation; we could try that.* Friday or Saturday after work they could go to Hayden Woods for an overnight if the weather was good enough.

Julian took another glance—this time with his photographic eye for detail. He had a few ideas he needed to sketch when he got the chance. The approaching sunrise had made it a lot easier to see. Good thing, too: they were getting close to his house already. Maybe Little J would get his way sooner than later—he was sending his usual signal.

Mark took a deep breath through his nose—he wanted another whiff of the off limits treasure running at his left. *oh boy...* he forced himself to look up. Julian's wag was undiminished after jogging for nearly a mile. Roger was pounding at his door again too. He needed to make sure that Julian didn't notice anything—*not going to be easy*. The motion of jogging had a predictable effect: the soft cotton lining of sweatpants repeatedly swiping across Roger was pleasurable—more so as Roger's appreciation grew. Mark had not worn anything else down there either. Thinking about it only made it worse.

Julian desperately wanted to give Mark a hug before going inside, but knew better. "Wow!" he giggled as they reached the walk in front of his house. "Thanks for letting me run with you. I see why you do this—makes you feel great—roarin' ready to face the day!"

"Any time: I mean that." he stopped and offered his hand for the official Troop Handshake. That was safe, if a little sneaky. He held it as long as he dared and looked him in the eye. "It just occurred to me: if Mr. Swann wants to see the drawings you did of me last summer, you have my permission to let him. He's a man I trust." He didn't want Julian to feel guilty if he was asked about them.

Julian was thrilled. "Wow. Umm, sure. Thanks." He watched Mark take off for his house halfway up the block. He held his hand up to his nose and inhaled, hoping it would smell like Mark... *too bad... oh well...*

He looked up, aghast: *I almost forgot!* "Merry Christmas!" he jumped up and down waving frantically. *darn!* Mark hadn't heard: *I didn't shout loud enough. how could I forget that!*

He looked down, disappointed; afraid of waking people up, he had not been heard. He stamped his right foot, mad at himself: here it was, Christmas Eve, and he **forgot?!**

He did not see Mark stop in his tracks and turn around. He also didn't see him jog back.

"Hey..." Mark reached out and held Julian by the shoulders. With head tilted, he smiled kindly. "Don't be mad at yourself: I forgot too. Merry Christmas, Julian." he looked at him a moment then gave him a huge hug and a pat on the back. He stood back, tilted his head the other way, smiled wide again and placed his forefingers on either side of Julian's surprised mouth, and forced a smile. "That's better." He stood back. "Be sure to give my Merry Christmas to Kasey when you see him." With a wave he jogged back to his house. He was tempted to do a Julian hop, but caught himself in time.

372

Julian waited to watch him go back inside. When Mark looked back, he waved. Eyes wowed, he did an instant hop and scurried up the steps. As he approached the front door, Little J was starting to holler—good thing he didn't have a voice: the gigantic hug had an unexpected bonus: Little J and Roger had bumped heads—and then some. Even though there were two layers of sweatpants in between, they got more than a simple bump—they got a pretty solid howdy. That was a first. Accidental, but a first.

His Mom was probably up by now making her morning pot of coffee. Before going inside, he needed to make an adjustment. He pulled the top of his sweats out and reached in to deal with Little J, who was roaring ready. He needed to be positioned so he wouldn't show as much. Too bad he had not put on any skivvies today. Unconsciously, he took a whiff of his hand—it didn't smell like Mark: but it sure did smell like Little J!

He liked that smell too, actually. *especially after running a mile! whoo!* He grabbed the morning paper and zipped into the house.

25   *Geoff and Jack pay a visit*

"There's a street map on the little shelf," Geoff pointed with his right hand. Unfortunately, his 'Vette didn't have a glove box: not very stylish, glove boxes. He decided not to buy the kit—it wasn't very stylish either.

Jack flipped through the small accumulation of items on the small ledge where a glove box ought to be. "Robin said it was easy to spot… right off the main drag."

The four hour drive from Atlanta wasn't as bad as either had expected, but they were ready to crash for a few minutes. Long distance travel was not why one bought a sports car. Geoff's new Corvette was more snug than cozy; it took a while to adjust to being so close to the ground going at 60 and 70 miles an hour—especially when passing a huge truck on a two lane highway. The new freeway ought to help considerably.

"Should we get a bite?" Geoff was ready.

"Let's call Robin first—he might want to join us." He pulled out the letter. "He says it's on the other side of the main downtown area up on the hillside, so it really stands out: Lumberjack Inn and Roadhouse, 4020 Mill Road."

Geoff agreed. Checking in first made sense. They could call from the room. Compared to Atlanta, the traffic here was nothing. Lots of trees everywhere.

Pleasantly surprised at how much lower the room rates were in this town, he stood out on the balcony while Jack called Robin; a room like this would cost twice as much in Atlanta. The view was nice enough; proximity to the mountains was a plus. Memories of Camp Walker began to form—the foliage was similar. Not like the Sierras, of course; hereabouts the leaves on half the trees were gone for the winter. Now that he had graduated from high school, he needed to focus on things like where to live and what to do: might as well see what it was like in a small town. The college here is supposed to be a good one. Jack wants to go to it—made sense to tag along at least. Atlanta was trying to become another La La Land; it had a way to go: another two million, give or take. He had a few months to play around before he needed to get serious. The only decision he had made was not to go into the television station business. He still harbored fantasies about being a certain person's houseboy in Burbank. He wasn't ready to abandon all hope, but Ronnie was not much of a correspondent. Geoff wasn't either.

When Jack suggested this little jaunt, it was the ideal opportunity: the timing was perfect. After all, he did have an invitation of sorts—Jack didn't know about that—no one did. With any luck, it might actually still be good. He'd likely have the element of surprise, whatever that was worth. Unconsciously, he squirmed and adjusted his eager, ready, and neglected man toy. Thanks to Robin, Jack had lost interest in playing around. That's why they were here. He was keen to see Robin again himself—he had certainly conquered the unconquerable: until last summer, Jack was famous for playing but never staying.

The patio door slid open: "He's on his way—he says his car might come in handy if we all want to go somewhere." Jack failed to hide the effect of the short chat with Robin: he wasn't sure they could wait until after lunch. "He says the café here is as good a place as any—we might not have to go out at all."

Geoff had had his fill of fresh air—he stepped back into the room and slid the door closed. The sun didn't help much; it would duck behind the hill eventually anyway. December was cold regardless, unless you were in Miami or Palm Beach. The altitude here made a difference. "Can you guys hold off your 'reunion' long enough to allow for a little planning? I don't fancy the idea of waiting around in the lobby; it's too cold to sit in the car." Geoff knew if it was he and Ronnie, anything remotely sane and sensible would have to wait until tomorrow morning. But he hadn't seen Ronnie for almost three years.

Jack laughed. "We talked about that. He said he'd call Tom and see if he could show you the town for a while," he poked Geoff in the ribs. "Robin isn't interested in a group event—being watched isn't his thing either." Robin wasn't likely to want to play in one of their special poker games.

"Let's wait for him in the lobby." Geoff didn't know Robin well at all, but if he had been waiting for six months, his first thought wouldn't be to sit at a restaurant table and talk about how nice the weather was, or anything else. If they were to wait for him in the room, in all likelihood he'd have the dubious pleasure of being pushed aside while they headed straight for the first bed.

it will be fun to see Tom... most likely, he would bring Nick. Those two had made the summer special—one of his best.

—⁓⁓—

Randall had almost recovered, but he had a way to go yet. Sitting next to his father while he drove the Lincoln downtown was itself something he had never experienced, certainly never expected. He had always loved his father, and missed going on camping and climbing trips—but they were always in the Rover. Now, there were no mountains to speak of, and settling into this new town was all either of them had time to do. His photography "hobby" had exploded into a full time enterprise almost. Thanks to both his parents' support and Mr. Swann's generosity, his career path seemed certain.

So when his father suggested they go to the after Christmas sale at Oglivy's Outdoor Recreation Center, he was caught by surprise. He thought they already had everything they needed. He sensed that his father had another reason—he never went to discount sales: something was up. Christmas went well as usual, so it wasn't that. They had never held one of those standard father-son talks; because they had spent so much time together, it wasn't really needed. They had learned to sense things rather than talk about them—one of the reasons he was so proud of his father. He didn't talk down or insult his intelligence with patronizing rationalizations because he "wasn't old enough." So that didn't seem likely at this stage. That didn't explain why they were in the Lincoln; the Rover needed to be driven too: it hadn't been out of the garage since they moved here in August. Randall took pride in being able to anticipate if not forecast what his father was up to: not today.

So far, Helgar was amused slightly by this outing. He was of two minds—its surprise element especially: his son's expression when he suggested taking the Lincoln was one he treasured already. His boy was so intelligent that seeing him stumped or confused was rare and quite delicious. On the other hand, he felt a real need to be in touch with Randall's self-discovery in a personal, conscious and open way. That he had always avoided. He and Eloise had agreed years ago to be hands off for the most part. The last thing they wanted was to be controlling, or be perceived as such. They had been "watering and protecting the garden," so to speak. They wanted Randall to own who he was from the start. Depending on a trauma to discover later that he had been wrong was theoretically the natural way of growing up or becoming an adult, but it was clumsy and the pain and potential damage were unnecessary. They believed it was possible to get it right from the beginning. They didn't want to force their son to suffer needlessly, nor to have to forgive them for being negligent or cowardly as parents. In addition, one day he would need to learn who his father was. Eloise thought the time had come to deal with that as well. Wise woman that she was, she insisted that he do that directly rather than delegate it to her. It was the only honest thing to do—that's why it would be difficult. Helgar always paid his dues, and the time had arrived.

"When do you take the Driving Class?" Helgar had decided some time ago that he wanted Randall to have his own car at the end of the school year.

"Last quarter—it alternates with Health Class every other day for a month." An unexpected question… Randall thought his father knew that already.

"Well, I'd like you to do a little research in your spare time. You need to select a car. You will learn faster and better if you practice with your own vehicle." This was fun: he glanced at Randall briefly—he

378

wanted to see another facial reaction. "Maybe Andy can help you with that—he knows what to look for."

Randall thought he had turned white with shock, but the rush he felt was what happened when he turned solid red. His mouth had nearly dropped open. Randall knew his father's way of putting things—he was never ambiguous. He had just been informed that his father was buying him a car sometime soon—very soon: before the end of the 9 week grading period that was about to begin. That was out-of-the-blue stunning. By the end of the second semester, he would be driving his own car.

"Thank you, Randall."

Randall's head snapped to the left—he stared at his father. "Thanks?!" *I should be the one saying thanks.*

"Yes: for being surprised. It confirms what I have always believed of you: you don't presume or assume. I daresay most boys in your situation expect to be provided a car, regardless." He looked his son in the eye: "you have rewarded your mother and me by not falling into that behavior—so easy when you are fortunate to be in a family that is well provided for. I daresay you are not the typical 'rich kid' at school either. You have earned your place as well as being born into it. So when you and Andy do your search, I want you to do that with the knowledge that you are to get what you need and what you yourself prefer. What it costs is of no concern: it is paid for in full." He waited for that to sink in. "Personally, I'd prefer it to be new. But that too is your decision." Helgar was confident it would be a sound choice.

Randall's ears were still bright red. His mind was racing—all of this was so unexpected. The notion getting a car depended on his getting a 4-point GPA had vanished. It was wonderful… but why?

"Feel free to comment or ask anything; one way conversations are a little awkward." He reached across and patted Randall's thigh. "Take a deep breath and unload anytime."

Randall shook his head. "Rich kid? I don't think of myself as a rich kid." That was confusing, actually. He knew they were better off than a lot of people, naturally, but rich?

"Yes, I know you don't; thanks again." he looked at his son warmly. "But you need to take a fresh look: that that was then. By most standards, you are indeed a 'rich kid.' It is important that you learn what that is and what it means—**especially** because of Andy." He was sure Andy had a fairly good idea of how well off his young lover was. It wouldn't take long for that to become a problem if it wasn't handled properly. His son needed to realize that he had been living in a bubble of sorts. That illusion that had run its course and no longer suited his needs.

Andy's name being mentioned got his attention instantly. Somehow Randall knew his parents were okay with his relationship, but had no idea of how or when or if he would ever talk about it. He thought to close his mouth before looking at his father: he wasn't ready to ask anything yet. He had been avoiding this until later. Obviously, later was here already.

"Your mother and I like Andy, and approve of your relationship: you have no need to fear anything unfavorable. Whether or not it becomes long term is for you and Andy to determine, not anyone else— and you will always have our support and love. If it lasts, we will have to find a way to include his family in our lives as well. That is a complete unknown for us at this point. It may be the most difficult part of your challenge."

> > gulp < <

This was the most difficult challenge in his life right now: he needed to get up to speed with his father—he had never had to deal with anything remotely like this. He exhaled loudly and looked at him directly: "You don't beat around the bush, do you?!?!"

Helgar leaned back and roared with laughter. "Too true; I don't generally dance around the issue: I'd look pretty ridiculous wearing tights and ballet slippers. I'm more of a caulk booted lumberjack—or to look at me, a marauding Viking." His son was considerably more delicate and would likely always remain at least six inches shorter, even with his shoes on: "genetics is a mysterious thing; one day, we'll understand what's going on—that's part of my work."

Randall shook his head. "You'll have to be patient while I catch up: you think a lot faster than I do."

"Maybe, a little. In my line of work that's a given. But you inherited more than just my nose. I'll try to be complete at least. I haven't planned this precisely—as you know, I am given to follow hunches. That is partly at fault here. When you came home the other night and paused before going to your room, we knew it was time. We were expecting it would be Julian." Helgar glanced at the dashboard clock: he realized at once that this was not where to start the conversation—he'd have to interrupt it when they got to Oglivy's: bad idea. He pulled into the parking lot they were approaching. "How about we grab a milkshake?" Sparky's Drive-in reminded him of his teenage years. He'd had a yen to drop in here for several weeks. He pulled into the third slot—that was far enough out to provide a semblance of privacy. This was ideal—no need to go inside. They deserved his patronage—most of these drive-ins had been replaced with drive thru windows.

—m—

Julian was in his element today—he had the whole day to himself and all he had to do was work on the special drawing of Mr. Swann. He wanted to finish it today if he could. He wasn't sure when he'd see him next, but he wanted this to be ready. He had this hot idea—without knowing it, Mr. Swann had set him to thinking about things. So far, all his big portraits were like simplified photographs—they depended on where whoever he was drawing was sitting or standing—that was part of the drawing. What if they were freed from having to be in a time or place? What if he could show who a person is no matter where they happened to be?

It had come to him in a dream—he actually saw the drawing as if it had been done a while ago and was framed already, hanging on a wall. He had forgotten the rest of the dream, but the image of the drawing had been so strong, he could still see it in his head. The odd thing was how different it was from his other drawings—it wasn't only in pencil. It had color, and it had strong black lines. He couldn't remember a dream like that ever happening before. He had often seen vivid colors in his dreams, but never thought about drawing anything because he had dreamed it. This was different—as if he was being shown what he was supposed to do. So he had started over—he tucked the first one under the bed so it wouldn't be in the way.

He was in luck: because he knew some of what Mr. van Horn was planning to teach in art class next term, he had bought more than paper when they shopped at Henderson's. Now he had a bottle of India ink and a pen set, some charcoal sticks, a box of pastels, and a bottle of fixative. He knew how to use charcoal already, and ink—but not pastels. He had bought a set of colored pencils as well, but somehow they weren't right for this drawing. The color needed to be dense.

He opened the left drawer of his table—plenty of room for these things. He got this table easel too: it made working on this a lot easier. He got a regular easel, but there wasn't enough space in his room now that he had the tall stool; he could use it later; when it got warmer, he might do some drawing on the back porch. He did get a smaller size drawing board though; he hadn't figured out a way to carry it yet.

Inside Guy had scolded him a couple of times for being too chicken to try anything different. Experimenting was something he had not done, so he was taking a chance. He was used to drawing it in his head first, then transferring that to the tablet. He figured that if it wasn't any good, no one but Inside Guy would know, so why not try? Mr. Swann deserved something special. Mr. van Horn wouldn't mind if he started to learn about pastels ahead of time.

Besides, if you think about it, pastels are just colored charcoal, only square instead of round. Inside Guy was unusually attentive today. He was like that sometimes.

He had almost finished the figure part—face and hands. Mr. Swann was standing by an open door inviting him to come with him on a trip somewhere. The outside was going to be bright and colorful and interesting; in the distance he was planning to draw the Packard with Mason standing by the open door gesturing to the back seat. There would be a bright blue sky with puffy clouds, a happy maple tree, and a lawn. He might add other things as he went along... birds maybe. The blue sky was what he remembered most—that might be tricky. It was a very special blue... connected with the eyes; Mr. Swann had blue eyes. He had some of that tape that peels off real easy without ruining the paper—Mr. van Horn used that sometimes. Very carefully, he covered the part that he didn't want to have any color—he figured it would be impossible to erase later. One reason this paper was so great to use was its ability to accept what was used on it—erasing was its primary shortcoming. Luckily, Julian rarely needed to do that.

The idea was to show that this kind generous man was inviting him to come out of the house and see what an interesting world awaited—it wanted him in particular; that's why he was depicted looking directly at the person looking at the drawing. Sort of corny maybe, but it was how he saw Mr. Swann. Like a dream, the drawing sort of blurred as it reached the edge of the paper—he had never done that either. He could tell that he needed to learn how to do water colors—they were good at doing that. Up to now, all his big drawings had gone clear to the edge of the paper; that's pretty much how he knew he was finished. That's what had been tugging at him: how to make it look alive instead of finished.

He squinted as he tried to remember what the door in his dream looked like. He had drawn one like he used every day when he left the house. He hadn't decided yet what lines would be in ink, so he drew it very light; he could erase it later if he needed to.

He was glad he had decided to do a vertical drawing—otherwise, he'd have to make half the drawing show the room, and Mr. Swann's head would be way too small. Also a first was depicting him from the waist up. That way his face was almost as big as a regular portrait. That was important: after all, Mr. Swann was the subject. His visit the other day had made it possible to study his facial features closely. Julian's memory was good at capturing important details. The eyes, especially: this time, they were staring straight at the person looking at the portrait... gave him goose bumps, actually, to see him stare right back while he was still drawing him. Usually he had his subjects looking off to the side somewhere. Mr. Swann often looked him in the eye when he was talking—that helped a lot. Julian could tell he was really interested in what he was going to say. The question was, should he make the eyes blue too?

—⁓—

The sunglasses didn't disguise Robin—Jack spotted him the minute he pulled into the drive thru on the way to the parking area. He thought he was ready, but now he couldn't decide if he should stay put and wait, or run out to meet him.

"Let him sneak up on you from behind." Geoff grinned. "That way he gets to surprise you, and you can be properly thrilled." Geoff was practiced at creating scenarios.

Jack was doubtful.

"Makes it acceptable to hug in public," he glanced around to be sure no one was listening. "Better hold off on the kissing and all the other fun stuff until you go upstairs though."

Jack knew from experience that Geoff was a genius at this art, and decided to take his advice. He had turned to face away from the door a minute or so when he was hugged from behind. Robin had found a close-in parking slot and sprinted. Like a wilting flower getting a sudden splash of cool water, Jack could feel the energy soaring throughout his body—and his conscious mind seemed to pulsate.

Geoff pretended not to see Robin approach. And the glow on Jack's face proved his prediction—it put him into a reverie... he had done the same thing once to evoke a hug from Ronnie. That was a particularly precious memory. So precious, he was too preoccupied to see Tom and Nick sneak up a few seconds later. Tom tickled under his left arm, Nick his right.

"Hey, Ace!" Tom chuckled.

"Tickie-tickie!" Nick echoed.

Geoff's decision to sit at a table instead of a booth had made this happen correctly, of course. "So, shall we get a booth?" he asked rhetorically. Booths afforded a degree of privacy. A booth would improve the chances that Robin and Jack could be coerced into joining in for a while: the day needed to be planned, and they needed to participate.

"This way, men!" Nick led the way with a Mark command—he had been here before. He knew where they would have a lot of freedom—the regular lunch crowd had gone, so several booths were open.

384

Robin and Jack slid in on the side facing the exit; the other three occupied the side facing the kitchen. It was all Robin could do to not stare at Jack—he looked even better than he expected. His mind was barely able to function, he was so relieved: he sensed that Jack still felt the same, that nothing had gone wrong.

"Ask him about the wreath," Jack pointed to the pin on Geoff's polo shirt to deflect their attention; he felt a need to protect Robin. Why he felt that way was a mystery—everyone here was a friend. His left hand had just begun to explore under the table when it was met with Robin's right. Their minds had always had the same action or thought— one of them was always finishing the other's sentence. They seemed to complete each other. Their eyes blurred momentarily as the physical connection triggered a flood of emotion and hormonal energy.

The pin was kind of classy. "So is this a secret club, or what?" Tom pushed on the inch square pin—it was ceramic on metal, embossed: a laurel leaf wreath with 1963 in the center.

Geoff looked down at his shirt; he had forgotten to leave the pin at home. "Eat your hearts out: it's my early graduation pin." He grinned smugly. "If you're a good boy, I'll give you a ride in my graduation present." He dangled his set of keys; the special leather Corvette fob with the crossed flag logo was very classy. His father had gotten a bargain—saved over a thousand dollars. The new model was about to arrive, and the dealer was eager to move the '62s out.

"Whoah! I saw that in the parking lot!" Tom was impressed. Geoff's Dad must be pretty well off. He reached out—he wanted to look at it closely. Buz had a 56 'Vette; he used to bring his brother Charlie home in it. Now they lived up in Boston. Going for a ride in that was one of his special memories—his brother was lucky to have a guy like Buz. Nick was like Buz in a lot of ways. He leaned close so they both could see it up close.

After the usual banter and niceties, Geoff posed the relevant question: "What is there to do around here during the winter break? You aren't close enough to any ski slopes." Geoff wasn't a ski slope fan anyway. Jack and Robin's attention was on finding a way to head upstairs, and he needed to postpone that a little while longer.

"Bowling or movies, mostly; camping for the hardy types," Tom shrugged. Actually, the ski resort was only thirty miles away or so, but he wasn't a ski fan—too expensive. "We're lucky there: we have our own mini-wilderness park inside the city limits."

Jack and Geoff were surprised: "In town?" Geoff guessed it was likely a Chamber of Commerce gimmick more than anything.

"Hayden Woods! Perfect!" Robin's eyes revealed his excitement at the prospect: a pup tent for him and Jack was a perfect place to spend a day or two. He had the ideal sleeping bag. He turned an eager glowing face to his 'guest' from Atlanta. "It's true: eight miles long by five miles wide. A network of trails—dozens of campsites, ready made: no vehicles allowed." The message was strong and clear: this was indeed made to order for what they had in mind.

"We were planning to stop by Oglivy's today, actually. The after Christmas sale is always worth the trip—Mark makes sure the scouting and Outdoor Departments have lots of bargains." A campout always began with getting supplies there.

Geoff's antenna caught the name instantly: "Mark?"

"Our scoutmaster—he's the store manager there now!"

Fate. Geoff had just become a believer. He hadn't even needed to inquire. He knew something these guys didn't. That one-on-one mini lesson in close order drill in the Camp Walker HQ lunchroom was so-o-o-o nice! Gave a whole new meaning to the word salute.

"So the question is when: tomorrow morning?" Robin wanted to get things moving. Sitting next to Jack much longer was not so easy—especially with his leg pressed so close. His half mast was about to go full.

Tom shrugged. "What's the matter with tonight? Plenty of time to set up camp by dark if we hop to." It was only two o'clock. Hayden Woods was his old playground: he knew it as well as his own back yard. All they needed to do was get supplies and load up. He looked at Jack. "You in?"

Jack looked at Robin: obviously, he was.

"I have everything Jack and I need ready to go." Any scout in Troop 9 was ready to go—readiness was a Troop thing. "How about you guys go to Oglivy's and get the usual stuff—we can meet you at the Woods in what—an hour?"

"Tight," Jack hated to hurry what was about to happen upstairs, but— "It would be nice to hike in with some daylight left… make it an hour and a half. How long a hike is it?"

"Pick a number between a hundred feet and four and a half miles—that's the nifty part. This time of year, we could have it to ourselves." Tom would bet on it.

Geoff was interested, but he didn't have a tent mate—or a tent. The prospect of being a third wheel wasn't very inviting. Nick was likely to see his problem without having to be asked. "I didn't bring anything along—no boots, no heavy coat…"

Nick understood at once. "There has to be a way. Why not ride along with us to the store—we'll figure it out. Maybe Mark can help out." He was confident he could find another troop member if all else failed. Tom would know who to call. "You don't need boots. The trails are good enough to go barefoot." Years of well-packed sawdust had achieved that. A new layer was added every year.

Geoff nodded. Not much else he could do, really. He doubted if Mark would be free to go camping; in any case, he wouldn't be interested in playing around with his scouts anywhere close by. Then it hit him: with Jack out camping, he would have the room all to himself! *keep your cool*, he told himself. The scouts were his passport into the store—his job was figuring how to make the "special arrangements." *if there's a will, there's a way…*

"What will it be?" The waitress had shown up finally.

They ordered cokes and Fritos—that would help speed things along. Robin and Jack could finish their refreshments in the room: they didn't have a lot of time. After a quick romp, they would stop at Robin's house to pick up his tent and sleeping bag. Geoff put the tab on the room account.

—⟋m⟍—

Grateful for a break, Randall took a sip of his milkshake—the pause had provided a way to recover somewhat before continuing the most wonderful and yet scariest conversation he had ever had in his life. "I had a lime shake here once with Julian and his friends from the scout troop." That was right after that bizarre Initiation incident—he wasn't about to tell his father about that.

"Ah—speaking of Julian, how are things with him? We don't see much of him lately. I still want to look at those sketchbooks. Have you had a chance to photograph them yet?" He hoped there hadn't been a rift. He looked at Randall closely.

"I am so lucky, Dad. Would you believe it? He actually approves of Andy and me—he even said so." He stared out the window a minute. He shook his head.

"Excellent. I must say I am not surprised. I am more than pleased."

Randall was **very** surprised. "I thought you would be disappointed. You do like him, don't you?"

"Yes, I do—I do indeed. Very much. I am not surprised, because I had seen enough in his sketchbooks to tell me that he was ahead of you in a major way: he has known who he is for a very long time: it shows in his art. Especially strong in that drawing of Kasey he did at the University. You weren't there, of course. Your mother and I were privileged to watch him do the original sketch. You photographed the finished version for Frederick Swann." He didn't tell Randall what else those sketches revealed: Julian was already committed to someone. Who was a mystery, but that also was none of his business. Whoever, he was fortunate indeed. Frederick's response to that drawing revealed that he had seen the same thing.

Randall was in awe of his father: suddenly he was discovering so much about him that he had never guessed. *how could he know these things? and Mom too...*

"I want to talk a little about Andy and shopping for a car. Okay with you?"

"For sure."

388

"You need to understand some things in advance. First, Andy knows very well that you are a 'Rich Kid,' for want of a better term. He's also older—who knows what his experience is, or if he has had any previous commitments. My sense is that you are his first serious relationship, but that is only a hunch. He comes from a larger family and is used to sharing—I don't know if he is, but he behaves and thinks like an older brother. So are you, but the age difference between you and Marietta is so wide, you are closer to being an only child, like Julian. Those things may or may not become an issue. You may have to make allowances."

Helgar stopped to enjoy a bit of his chocolate shake; he had to remember to pace this chat: dealing with these matters openly and directly was a new task for Randall—very new. He—saw a frown appear. "What I'm saying is that if he seems to treat you like a little brother at times, give him the benefit of the doubt: it will be instinctive—you should let him figure it out for himself," he paused to allow Randall a chance to break in. "There may be times when it's smart to be a "little brother." Eventually, you and he will learn how to be equals. Because he is older, it could take a while—the gap will shrink gradually; this is just a heads-up." He leaned forward: "the biggest danger you'll have is allowing him to feel that compared to you, he's rather stupid. He is not at all stupid—but there's little doubt in my mind—or in his, that you are a good deal more intelligent. That's not a problem unless you let it become one."

He let that point sink in. "One suggestion comes to mind: let him think of what to do once in a while, even if you have it calculated already: let him be first once in a while: but—and this is important: don't let him know that you are doing that on purpose."

Randall had already done that a couple of times instinctively. It was very helpful to have that approved. "So that's not being dishonest?"

Helgar raised an eyebrow: "It's being smart. Intelligence is one thing, smart is another. You need to have both. As long as you understand that, you can make the right call; that way you can avoid doing or causing harm that can't be undone."

Randall understood—having that verified was huge.

"Please feel free to consult with me or your mother should anything come along that you are uncertain about. We are able and willing to be of support and help: we do have a bank of experience that is available to you—the only requirement is that you ask or seek it: we will not impose anything. It is **your** life: our role is to support, not govern." He looked at his son soberly: "we do that consciously and take it very seriously. It is our **first** priority: **you** are in charge of your life. That's the primary reason we have been waiting until now to have this conversation."

Randall nodded again and forced his eyes to avert briefly, lest he stare at his father like an idiot, which he felt he was. *well, not idiot— how about clueless…* The point his father had just made about Andy became crystal clear. His eyes wowed: his father's wisdom was much deeper than he would have imagined; he had never had occasion to consider such a subject even: he had been in a self-created bubble most of his life. He was uncertain whether he felt naked or free—maybe it was both.

"Reality check here: your dad needs to know if you need to say something or clarify anything. How are you doing?" He looked at Randall, hoping that he hadn't messed up—he was new at this too, after all.

Randall made an audible exhale, relieved to get a pause. He tilted his head. His father had, in fact, clarified a great deal—some things he had wondered about, and others that he hadn't even thought about. He turned to look at his father. "I'm feeling a lot better about it now, actually. I appreciate you asking that—I needed to ask myself the same question." He nodded an affirmation. "Yes. I have to hand it to you: I was ready for this and had no idea that itself was an issue. I expect a question or two will form after this has settled in some." He grinned. "Takes a while for a pair of new shoes to feel comfortable, I expect. But they're the right size." He could look at his father eye to eye in a new way, a confident way. It would take a while to realize that, and to understand what it meant.

Helgar was extremely pleased: his son's metaphor was more sophisticated than he expected. Eloise was correct, as usual. "Good; I'll complete the 'lesson,' with a review, to insert a metaphor of my own. Because of your intelligence, you need to be alert to Andy's needs as well as yours: he will have a big brother attitude as well as a need to be his own man, which your wealth will challenge if not threaten. How you deal with this is crucial for you both, and by and large you have to do it on your own. You will have to decide what to share and what not to reveal. You are probably a level above him in the intelligence department. That could cause resentment if you mishandle it; he is smart enough to realize this himself, which may or may not be helpful." He stopped to look at Randall closely. "Am I going too fast, or skipping anything?"

"Umm… I don't think so—Some of this I sort of figured out already." He took a deep breath. "It's helpful to hear you say these things, actually—it verifies a lot. I think we're okay so far."

"Good. I needed to be sure. The important thing is to learn how to communicate with each other, and to be open and honest. If you do that, you have a good chance of succeeding. But you need to be aware that there are other dangers—ones you don't expect."

"What would they be?"

"The outside world; other people may have personal issues that cross your path: a lot of people think they know what's best for you, and will behave as if they had a right to insist you play by their rules, like it or not."

Randall knew about that already. The bullies in Pullman had taught him a great deal.

"I don't know anything about Andy's family either: he may have difficulties there, real or imagined." He paused. "Most of us try to pre figure or pre judge what others think rather than risk asking. Andy may or may not know what his family members think—my guess is, so far, you are a secret. Maybe you can help him with that. You want to be accepted and included, not tolerated or worse." He patted his son's forearm gently. "Just be slow and thorough, and don't make any assumptions. You will discover that there are a lot of friends out there as well. You are not a freak, but you **are** an exception. Exceptions are often thought of as a threat. Make yourself as open and available as you can, and useful. People who are useful become needed eventually. Keep as low a profile as you can, but don't apologize for yourself or for being who you are—ever." He reached out to touch his shoulder: "Model your own page after your friend Julian's. That's the page in his book that allows him to approve and delight in your relationship with Andy."

Randall felt his eyes begin to fill. He couldn't help it. A wave of emotion had welled up. He was so grateful, so proud all of a sudden. *how can I be so lucky?*

Helgar saw it and nearly joined his boy; he did not expect this to happen. He needed to corral it. He reached down for Randall's left hand. "I think it's time to hold up the 'to be continued' sign and resume our field trip to Oglivy's—what do you think?" He waited to see Randall's face.

Randall wiped the tears away with his right hand while he clenched his father's with his left. "Thanks, Dad," he glanced at him sheepishly. "I don't know how I can be so lucky."

"I wish I could answer that; let's just say it runs in the family, okay?" He squeezed Randall's hand. "When we get back home, we can grab a good hug. I trust you will indulge me?"

Randall laughed. "For sure." *more than one* He looked at his father and exhaled. "I feel so... so **free** all of a sudden!"

"Excellent. This has gone well, son. I'm just as new at this as you are." He thought to look at the dashboard: "Oh-oh! Hand me your empty cup and I'll put it on the tray." He pushed the window button.

"Oh-oh?"

"The time: we're running a little late: Andy has been waiting for us for about ten minutes. Shopping for camping supplies was his suggestion, actually," he gave his son a wink.

Yet another jaw dropper. Randall gave his father a wry grin. His claim to be objective and non-directive might be true in general terms, but he wasn't absent—and he didn't hesitate when an opportunity happened along. Most of all, he relished the opportunity to surprise. That had always been true. He giggled softly—he had just pegged his father good. Now he felt in charge of himself as well as free. He reached out his left arm and gave a friendly punch in the shoulder with the back of his fist. He had never done that before. They were pals again... but on a new level.

Helgar felt enormously proud, but guilty in a way—Eloise deserved to be here. Well, he'd make up for it soon enough. This chat had energized him enormously. He was very ready to play.

—⁓—

Andy shook the new canteen absent mindedly, as if checking to see if it had anything in it. He didn't need a new canteen and probably wouldn't buy this one, even though it was on sale. Everything in the scout department was on sale for another five hours. He was just killing time waiting for Randall and his father to show—evidently he wanted to buy something special here. He was a little surprised by the call—he said not to tell Randall. Maybe it was part of his Christmas present.

A lot of cub scouts and their parents had already come and gone—Mark had shown them around and helped the salesman. Mark was very busy—he was in charge of the whole store, on the move from department to department; he was glad to hear that Randall and his father were coming to shop—he wanted to pay his respects and see that they were able to get everything they needed. Andy was supposed to say hello and flag him to come over or find him. Mark had seen a lot of their climbing photos from out west. Randall showed some of those at one of the Troop 9 meetings.

Suddenly, he felt a very rude and familiar sensation at his 'back door.' "Hello to you too, Tony." He turned around fast—not fast enough.

Laughing, Tony pulled back at the waist quickly so that Andy couldn't grab his crotch. These two went way back and knew each other very well. Goosing Andy when he wasn't expecting it had always been a favorite trick. It had been a while—he belonged to Danny now.

Andy grinned at Danny. "I see you haven't been able to do anything with him yet. Not surprising." He squirmed a little—he had a very pleasurable aftergoose sensation—Tony was very good at those—they were usually meant to tempt, not offend. "I tried to return the favor, but didn't grab fast enough this time. You might have learned to do that already." His sack usually tickled afterward, expecting a nice massage—those were not approved at Oglivy's, probably. Fortunately, no other shoppers were close by. "What are you guys looking for?" He declined the urge to encourage or respond to the tingles that had begun to intensify; the sensation that accompanied expansion amidships was a favorite. That had begun as usual without needing to be encouraged— but he didn't want to be sporting anything visible when Randall and his father arrived. Hopefully, that could be avoided.

Danny slapped Tony's hand quickly—it had started to slide across his upper thigh. Tony habitually played around—Danny knew that if he didn't slap him away, he'd just keep going, no matter where they were. "I need a new sleeping bag." He elbowed Tony in the ribs. "Mysteriously, mine developed a few tears last summer in Barr's Meadow."

Tony covered his mouth and looked up at the ceiling, feigning innocence.

Andy pointed to a shelf section. "Mummy or regular? They have both."

Tony cupped his hand and whispered: "Standard, please." He winked: "More room."

Andy was not surprised. *in other words, room for two.*

Suddenly, their attention was captured by a familiar voice:

"Look who's here!" Geoff exclaimed, rushing past Tom and Nick.

Tony swiveled in place—squealing in delight, his arms flew open wide. An unrehearsed theatrical hug and twirl threatened to topple the others, forcing them to move fast. He stood back, holding Geoff by the shoulders: "Where have you **been**?! It's been months!" He counted them out: "five, to be exact."

One of Geoff's Poker Club inductees, Tony had a special connection. His appearance was a huge surprise. If he was here for long, Christmas vacation could take a very different direction. His antic streak made him one of Geoff's favorites.

Tony flashed his eyes at Danny—Danny and Geoff were camp delivery boys together—probably a little more. Maybe they could have a special party!

At that point Randall and Helgar entered Oglivy's. Merriment at their left was attracting other shoppers' attention. An overhead sign pointed in that direction: **Outdoor Store**. A few steps in and they saw the boisterous cluster standing near the large scout logo—Andy was in the middle of whatever it was. "Looks like some boys from Mark's outfit."

"Yes—I recognize a couple of them." Tony especially—and Danny. They had joined the tour of Julian's back yard clubhouse after waving at them from Danny's upstairs window—shirtless. That was last September.

Mark was on the way to see what all the noise was about when he saw Randall and his father going in that direction. He hailed at once: "Helgar!" He hopped forward to catch up.

Helgar turned: with a broad grin he extended his hand. "Just the man we need!" he winked at Randall. In fact, he had a second motive for this visit: he was still on the lookout for any sign that Mark was at all available for a little 'side activity.' He had no reason to hope—still, the man was devilishly tempting.

"Looks like we're headed in the same direction," Mark chuckled. "I heard a few of the boys whooping it up... from the Housewares Department, it sounded a little overboard. What brings you in today?"

"We need to get some supplies—possibly a new sleeping bag or two—we need to ensure we are prepared for an East Coast outing. I'm counting on you and your boys to make sure we're covered." He wanted Randall and Andy to have the best equipment available and induce them to spend a day or two in the woods, free of the usual restraints and cautions, including being worried about himself and Eloise. The session with Randall had made it possible for his son to build his foundation properly—an overnight in the forest was the ideal place for that. He didn't want them to wait for spring. He had heard about the local park. Since Andy had his own car, it should be simple to arrange.

"You have come to the right place. What do you say we go and redirect some boy energy at the same time?" He figured Helgar's massive six foot four Nordic appearance would settle them down real fast.

Helgar grinned: "I have just the thing—with your approval, naturally: would a Viking war cry serve?" The Scottish tartan pattern of his wool coat was wrong, and he didn't have a battle axe either—but it would be amusing anyway.

"Hah!" Mark was delighted. "Fist raised high!"

They approached unnoticed and caught the crew by surprise.

Helgar's battle cry voice, even unrehearsed, was an event to remember.

"Óðinn á yðr alla!!" he roared, right fist raised high above his head.

The group froze and turned to face whatever had made that sound. The entire store must have heard it. Helgar would never need a microphone; his voice was solid, a clear authoritative operatic basso, capable of raising the hair on the back of a foe's neck. The war cry was practiced, in fact—researched and developed with the help of a colleague in the Foreign Language Department at Washington State. In lieu of a firearm, it was instantly ready in the event a mountain lion or bear posed a problem—always possible in the Cascades.

Randall couldn't keep a straight face—he broke up instantly. His dad liked to do that in the mountains; he enjoyed testing to see how strong an echo he could cause. It was eerie to hear it bounce back when they were in a box canyon. Randall's attempts were birdlike in comparison—too embarrassing to talk about.

Geoff was transfixed at the sight of this giant—and by the fact that he was standing next to the scoutmaster of his fantasy life who was wearing the most flattering slacks imaginable. They refreshed a memory that didn't need refreshing.

The big grin on the man's face relieved the boys and allowed them to notice Randall and Mark on either side laughing it up.

Geoff's eyes returned to the giant. His scan of the man's torso was automatic and skilled—Geoff had perfected that as a beach urchin when he lived in Honolulu. In seconds he could calculate what was hanging between a man's thighs and estimate what it would be like in its full glory. The Viking in front of them had a weapon that matched his voice. He did not notice that the man had caught him in the act and done exactly the same thing.

Helgar was very surprised to see a semi-Asian in the group. They were always fascinating— *always look years younger than they are.* He had learned to guestimate their age by behaviors instead of appearance. This one was of age certainly, even if he did appear to be fifteen or sixteen. Innocent he was not: of that Helgar was convinced. He waited for the standard second look, and made certain that noticing it was seen. Their eyes met and the age-old connection was automatic. Both had a what–do-you-know moment; Geoff smirked slightly, Helgar tilted his head. Both were enormously surprised and intrigued, and likely to find a way if there was one.

Geoff had presumed he would stay at the Motel while Jack and Robin played scouts in the park. But that changed the instant he made eye contact. He had no idea who this man was, but he would remedy that soon himself if someone else didn't. He had been around the block more than once and knew the giant blond masterpiece was of a like mind: if he was staying in town, Geoff had the perfect location. If he was one of what was starting to look like an expedition, he was ready to include himself if he wasn't invited. It was obvious that the scoutmaster would likely be an after work quickie if anything, and he had no working knowledge—he wore a wedding ring; Geoff had no reason to think it wasn't real.

Helgar had not planned to go camping, but there was no reason he couldn't. His calendar was open all week, as a matter of fact. Eloise wouldn't have a problem. The only thing was Randall—they hadn't gotten to the subject in their father-son session. Helgar intended to do that—Eloise had specifically asked him to. Somehow, he would find a way if it was needed. Were all of these boys going on a camp-out? If so, he could facilitate a large group chow line operation easily. One of his talents was projecting possibilities—that's why he was a success in the laboratory. It applied here automatically, because of his own appetites and because of his plans for Randall.

That's where his mind was when he heard what appeared to be the answer to his question.

"We're going on a campout in Hayden Woods tonight." Tom wanted to get things organized quickly so they could get the tents up before dark. "There's six of us—Robin and Jack are gonna meet us there. I plan to stop at Piggly Wiggly to get fresh stuff, but we'll need the usual things from here too."

"Wow! Can we come along?" Andy checked to see if it was okay with Randall.

Indeed it was: "Perfect. I need to get my camera and stuff..." Randall nudged his father gently. He had pretended not to know Tony and Danny—or about Hayden Woods. He and Julian had spent two nights there already.

Helgar and Geoff's eyes met: they were on the same page. Geoff hoped that the nudge he saw was... he noticed their noses. *yes! father and son!*

Helgar set the stage. "I have a six man tent but that's not big enough." He shrugged. "Randall and I each have a two man, of course...

Geoff chimed in. "I have an idea—I'm kind of an odd man out here: I could tag along and be your assistant cook!" He bounced on his toes happily.

"Far out!" Nick was enthusiastic. He turned to Randall's father: "You can show us how to climb Littel Capitan!"

"Yeah!" the others chimed in.

Mark was envious of the opportunity—he'd love to be in on the campout himself—until he heard the voice: he did not realize Geoff was in the group. Instantly, he remembered the conversation he had along the trail that night about halfway up the ridge behind Barr's Meadow. He had to carry Geoff back to his camp because he had sprained his ankle. He kept a straight face, assuming—**hoping**—that Geoff's presence was coincidental: "Hello! I'm sorry, I didn't see you." He gestured to Helgar. Let me introduce you to Helgar Hallstrom. He's from the far west too— he's a climbing expert from Washington State.

"The Cascades! I used to live in California! I've done some climbing in the Sierras! My name is Geoff. Geoff Staples." He reached out to shake hands. His original plan to connect with Mark had been summarily pushed to the side, so he behaved as if there was nothing special to remember. He knew all these guys—he felt right at home already.

"Well met!" Helgar shook his hand. The deal had been made; he liked the grip—handshakes were one of his yardsticks, and this one was right up where he wanted it to be. With care, no one would know what was going on. "You can help me teach this bunch how to repel down…" he looked at Nick for a repeat of the name.

"Littel Capitan!"

"Littel Capitan." He was confident that whatever that was, he could deal with it. "What, exactly, is Littel Capitan?"

"A man-made mountain the Elks put up," Tom explained. "About fifty feet high. Named after the big one out west." His face revealed that it was a challenge, even at fifty feet.

"El Capitan!" Geoff was doubtful. "Yosemite National Park— I've been there." His eyes wowed. That was a serious technical climb.

Mark broke in: "Boys, I have a store to run. Can you help Helgar and Randall round up what they need?"

"No sweat." Tom took charge. "Okay, men, we have a job to do and the day is gonna run out on us if we don't get organized." He lowered his voice and turned to Mark: "we'll try to keep it down." He reached out to shake Helgar's hand. "Tom Dawson. I'm Mark's Assistant Scoutmaster. Pleased to meet you."

"Indeed." Helgar liked this one. He gave Mark a thumbs up. "Thanks. I'll be in touch." He was giving Mark a graceful exit. He did have a big job to do here, at that.

Mark gave a hand signal to Bob to handle the sale and made a hasty retreat. His memory of that fireman's carry up the ridge in the moonlight had not dimmed in the slightest. *another boy from Atlanta is with him—Helgar seems to have come to the recue.* Having something else to do right now was a blessing.

Helgar glanced at the Asian—the quick thinking Asian. Most interesting and intriguing. He had never actually played with an Oriental, whole or half: he was delighted by this turn of events. This one looked very hungry. That suited Helgar just fine—it had been a long time since he and Walter had last occupied the two-man on the shore of Lake Chelan. It's ideal when two in need can solve their mutual problem so deftly.

Something told him to proceed with caution—he was sure Randall wasn't ready to deal with this quite yet: he had a full list already with Andy. In any case, this was unlikely to go anywhere—he was from out of town. On the other hand, he would make a point of finding out how far away that happened to be. So far, the prospect of finding a replacement for Walter had seemed remote; he might have found one after all.

Tom had been counting heads: "We're up to ten!" He turned to Helgar. Maybe that was too many.

"Outstanding!" Helgar beamed at his son. "With a crew this size, we can bring the Weber." He looked at Tom: "I take it we'll go in as a group?"

The planning would not take very long: everyone had done this before—generally speaking. Helgar was about to call on Eloise's catering favorite for a few extras.

26 *the great winter campout*

"You were right," Nick observed as they pulled into the parking area. "Nobody here." One car at the far end was it: they had no problem—finding a cluster of adjacent campsites would be easy.

Tom and Nick were the first to arrive—the south entrance to Hayden Woods was created primarily for overnight campers. The Ranger's pavilion office was closed until May first, but an information kiosk served campers in the off-season. The honor system was sufficient for most purposes. Campsite reservations were simple: a large map board doubled as a self-serve system. Each campsite had a number and an empty hook—campers simply took a ring from the basket and put it on the hook. Thus, a glance at the map revealed what campsites were in use. People were always conscientious about returning the ring to the basket on their way out. No paper work, no fee. In the spring and summer the Ranger's office issued the ring along with a five dollar registration fee.

Tom had grown up playing in this park with his older brothers— he knew it well. The West entrance was designed to serve hikers; all the hiking trails began and ended there. The east entrance featured a vast parking area to accommodate large group activities: baseball and softball fields, a concert amphitheater and picnic facilities for groups large and small. Having Frederick Swann on the Board of Directors had made a significant difference in that part of the park.

Tom studied the campsite locations carefully: two or three ways of handling this group came to mind. He thought it best to wait until everyone was here since he wasn't in charge—no one was. It wasn't a Troop 9 activity. Patrol campouts were usually 6, no bigger than 8. The addition of Randall and Andy had changed things significantly—

especially with Randall's father and Geoff along. He grimaced: *I'm not sure about that…* he wouldn't put it past Geoff to sneak a feel during the night. He shrugged; that man could take care of Geoff easy if he got out of line—probably give him a good spanking.

✳✳

Hayden Park

Hayden Park, a vast plot of woodland five miles wide and eight miles long, was a combination City/County operation honeycombed with trails, picnic areas, and overnight camping sites. Arranged and spaced to assure privacy but not isolation, campfires were allowed in season with a permit. If nothing remained in the community firewood cache (fire crews deposited underbrush, blowdowns and tree snags there), campers were allowed to provide their own fuel to use in the designated campfire rings. A few single lane safety roads made maintenance and fire control possible. These were not open to the public; no motorized vehicles were allowed. It was possible to spend a weekend remote from civilization virtually in the middle of town—the only missing ingredient was a mountain stream: campers had to pack in their own water. Outdoor chemical toilets were located strategically along the access roads. Attempts to connect the camps to city water and sewer had failed twice at the ballot box; water and restrooms were available in the parking areas. All public access to park offerings was from one of those entrances.

In 1886 Joshua Hayden deeded a section of land he called Hayden Woods to the city and county with the stipulation that it be developed for recreation only; it was never to be sold, divided or logged. It came with a private Trust Fund dedicated to assure its maintenance; even during the Depression the Fund prospered. Thus, other than providing a Sheriff's safety patrol, the Park cost the taxpayers nothing. The part time Ranger in the summer was funded by various permits and fees. The community took pride in keeping it safe and clean; it had always operated on the honor system. Originally located at the north edge of town, by 1950 it was almost surrounded by suburbs. No commercial activity was allowed in the park itself; over time, small clusters of suburban retail stores evolved opposite the south and east entrances.

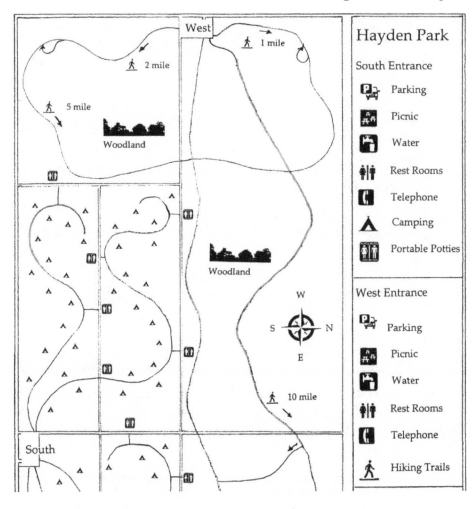

Hayden Park

South Entrance

🅿️ Parking

🏕 Picnic

🚰 Water

🚻 Rest Rooms

☎ Telephone

⛺ Camping

🚻 Portable Potties

West Entrance

🅿️ Parking

🏕 Picnic

🚰 Water

🚻 Rest Rooms

☎ Telephone

🚶 Hiking Trails

※※

"What's so funny?"

"I just had a picture flash in my head—Randall's father holding Geoff over his knees giving him a good tanning for unapproved after dark exploration in the tent."

Shocked, Nick held his hand over his mouth: "Do you think Geoff would try something?" He had not even thought of that. On second thought, he realized it was possible. Geoff had told about his secret romance out in California. Geoff had sworn him to secrecy—the guy was more than ten years older.

They turned to see who had just driven in: Danny and Tony. "I've been wondering what it's going to be like with Tony and Geoff in the same campout." Nick gave Tom a nudge. "Tony's a member of the Poker Club too, remember." They were both members of Brian and Geoff's club—so was Jack.

It struck them at the same time: what if Geoff brought that deck of cards?

Tom shook his head: "I doubt if anyone wants to play strip poker when it's this cold outside." He watched Tony park his car. *too many guys*.

Nick nodded. *probably not.* It would be in the low 40s tonight.

"They're Brian's cards." Tom doubted if he ever lent them out. "Too many guys anyway." Anything over four was a pain.

Tony bounced over, rubbing his hands: "Where is everybody?" He was ready to party—it was getting late.

"X marks the spot!" Danny snuck up and got him from behind.

Tony spun around fast enough to grab Danny by the balls just as Robin and Jack drove in. Tom checked his watch: sunset was still a solid hour and a half away; they were probably okay. *the others should be here any minute.*

Robin had his mother's car, as usual. Luckily, she wasn't planning to use it all week. "Gonna be a little chilly tonight. At least there's no rain in the forecast."

"Or snow. I thought you got snow in the winter." Jack was glad the weather was halfway decent—a tent certainly beat worrying about the people in the next room at the motel. He and Robin could get carried away—he didn't want anyone tapping on the motel wall—or door: he didn't need Geoff poking around either.

"Once in a while snow gets down this low; usually it stays above four thousand feet. We're only half that." Robin looked back at the entrance—no Rover. "Where are they?"

"They got caught by that red light a ways back—you barely made it."

"Andy knows how to get here." Danny and Tony were romping around as usual. Robin grabbed Jack's hand. "I haven't camped out here since I was a Cub Scout. This is gonna be wild!" They skipped over to see what the guys were talking about.

Jack gave Tom a thumbs up greeting. He had a very high opinion of Tom—he was the best Assistant Scoutmaster at Camp Walker, hands down. He knew how to handle Geoff too.

The red light was a nuisance, but Helgar wasn't bothered. They weren't about to get lost: he had a native on board. He was in top form this afternoon—loading up for this outing was more than fun: this trip might be just like old times—with a special twist or two. Enormously impressed by Geoff's deftness and quick thinking, he was certain that neither Randall nor Andy had any notion of what he and Geoff had in mind. That was **essential** of course—he wouldn't get a chance to square away his tent partner until after everyone had settled in for the night. That might be tricky, depending on how the tents were located. According to their leader, several campsites could be used; if so, that would help.

He looked forward to seeing this park—it did sound too good to be true. Assuming that this outing was going to be more like camping in the back yard than a respectable climb, he had given Eloise's caterer a call—they were famous for being able to whip together an order on short notice; eating out of a can didn't appeal. He had two chests full of surprises—the Rover had lots of room: Expedition was its middle name. The boys had helped assemble the climbing gear just in case this 'Littel Capitan' proved to be a challenge. The exercise alone would make the effort worthwhile—all he'd been able to do for the last six months was walk to work and back.

Geoff was happy with himself; maneuvering to get this ride had paid off—much better than looking over Jack's shoulder from the back seat of Robin's 2-door Comet… back seat had zero legroom. Meanwhile, his 'Vette was safe at the motel.

The front seat of this English rig was very butch, especially with the Great White Hunter behind the wheel. The man was full of surprises. Geoff wondered if he was aware of his son's interest in Andy. Geoff had not met Andy before—the only one of Tom's group that he didn't get to know last summer. He still marveled at how many in that troop were into playing with each other.

Andy had never ridden in a Land Rover—the back seat benches reminded him of a crew bus of some kind—facing each other. What had him going was Randall's face—an expression or something he had never seen had appeared. Something told him not to ask. He could wait until tonight. The idea of his father coming along was kind of wild—but he was a very interesting man. Andy wanted to know him better anyway. He and Randall just needed to be cool; he wasn't worried.

Randall wanted to hold Andy's hand, but that would be spotted instantly in the Rover. He was still euphoric from the talk at Sparky's. His Father had certainly pulled the biggest surprise ever, and that was saying something: surprises were his thing. His dad would be disappointed if he didn't keep his cool. Disappointing his father was the last thing he wanted to be guilty of. Looking at him from behind on the Rover bench was different now... he was so much bigger, for want of a better word—he couldn't find another. His dad had always seemed larger than life at times. Blasting out that war cry in the store—that was so funny. He could not believe how lucky he was. He could hardly wait to tell Andy about getting a car. He had no idea about that—he had never even thought about owning a car. Life was wonderful but it was weird.

"This is where Hayden Woods begins," Andy leaned forward to explain. Robin's car was long gone. "A year ago they installed the fence—there are only three entrances now. They had too much trouble keeping it clean and tidy. Too many pets and strays I guess—and the deer kept wandering into people's yards."

"They have deer in the park?" Helgar was surprised to hear that. *how do they control them?* "Do they allow hunting?" He wasn't eager to compete for space with a hunter and his firearms.

"They have a special two week season for bow hunting—they have a sign up and permit system—only a few are allowed to enter. I don't know that much about it—they don't do it every year. They have to close the park. Firearms are banned all year. So are fireworks."

The ten foot high cyclone fence was well maintained. The long straight line appeared to go forever. "How long is this park?"

"Eight miles. We're headed for the south entrance—it's half way. All the camp sites have to use this entrance."

Helgar was impressed. *some back yard!* He appeared to have been a bit hasty in his judgment. Randall had shown him a few photos he took here a few months ago, but he hadn't gone into detail about the park itself. *eight miles! that's several times the size of Central Park! equivalent to half a dozen housing developments, at least. this property is worth a fortune.*

Randall kept a straight face as they drove along the park fence; he didn't want Andy to know about the two-night stay he and Julian had here. With any luck, his dad wouldn't mention it. The Initiation was still a very confusing experience. He had not expected to camp out here ever again.

The six scouts gathered near the kiosk had been hearing that unusual sound for a minute or two; it became louder when its source turned into the parking area. The sound waves generated by Helgar's Land Rover were distinctive and unique—undertones similar to a distant helicopter, it was apparent that the vehicle had a lot of power. The boys watched wide-eyed as it came to an abrupt stop next to Tom's '56 Ford.

whoa! Tom had never seen one of these for real: *right out of National Geographic.* Some kids called his car a gunboat—the Rover made it seem more like a rowboat. The dark olive green rig was high centered, off-road capable—he could see that at once. Geoff riding shotgun was a surprise; he'd expected Randall to sit up front with his father.

When Helgar hopped out from the driver's seat it made sense: the man simply drove something his own size. Even so, one of these had never been seen in this town, and like the battle cry in Oglivy's, it stopped the boys cold. His fur lined parka and Davy Crockett cap were odd enough to be comical, but no one laughed. Geoff's face gave no indication in particular—he was a master at keeping a straight face; his borrowed parka matched. Randall and Andy followed them over to the map kiosk.

Helgar saw a minor problem: he had never had the experience of leading a group of boy scouts, and he didn't particularly want to start such a challenge tonight. Moreover, his son was in the group. Randall had no experience with scouts either—yet he and his father were probably more experienced at camping and climbing than any of these boys. Apart from that, this was a particularly important night for Randall. Rather than assume leadership by deference to his age, he marched right up to Tom and gave him a salute. "How do you like my new hat?" He flipped the tail a couple of times. "An afterthought at Oglivy's." He had intended it to evoke laughter. "I read somewhere that it was invented in these hills."

That triggered the laugh that he wanted. It took him off whatever pedestal there was. Now he could be an expert advisor. This was a fun trip, not a serious climb. He took it off and handed it to the right, expecting it to be passed around. "Try it on—see if it makes you feel extra brave."

He turned to Tom: "I have everything we'll need and a little more," he winked. "I must admit that I am more than surprised by this," he swept his arm wide at the forest. "Randall and I are ready to follow your lead—this is your turf."

Randall nodded enthusiastically. The nifty thing tonight was having Andy all to himself in their own tent. Back home in Washington, he had either been in his father's tent, or if Walter was along, by himself in his pup tent. His father always made him go to bed a little early. Sometimes he and Walter talked for hours about chemistry and other things.

While the boys had fun with the hat, Helgar stepped over to Tom. "You are the expert—what do you want us to do? Do we unload and pack in from here?" The map board and hooks caught his attention. "Looks well engineered." He stepped closer. "What campsite do you recommend?"

Tom was flattered as well as pleased. "First off," he reached for his billfold. "I have some change for you."

408

Helgar stopped his arm. "Keep it for your gas tank; we're square. This is between you and me," he added softly and pointed to the map. "You were saying?"

Tom was blindsided by the gesture: it was over thirty dollars! Somehow he was able to hold a straight face. "A lot of possibilities—as you can see, only one camp is occupied tonight. It depends on what we want to do: the best camp group is here." He touched the end of inner south trail. "Littel Capitan is here," he put his fingertip on the feature. "That's about two and a half to three miles in from the west parking area." He put his finger on the map board.

"Two and a half..." he frowned. "This map to scale?"

Tom did a hand gesture that indicated so-so, or roughly.

Helgar was a skilled map reader. This wasn't a USGS topog map for sure, but he was able to take Tom's guesstimate and convert it. He pulled back—he could see a big problem. He pointed to the south parking where they were. "Correct me if I'm wrong, but that campsite has to be a four or five mile hike from this parking lot." He ran his finger up the map board. "Half our hike-in will be in the dark."

Tom turned to the map: "You're right about that. As an alternative, we could camp close-in tonight, then hike farther in and set up camp for the second night; or, we could drive around to the West entrance in the morning. The hike to Littel Capitan is about a mile and a half from that parking lot."

Helgar frowned. He didn't want to break camp first thing in the morning. He took another look at the map. *hmm...* he pointed to the west entrance: "Why not park there tonight?"

Tom tilted his head, seeing the advantage; he pointed to the camp he wanted—it was closest to the west entrance and ran his finger along the service road. "Technically, this road is for service vehicles, not hikers—but it's not against the rules to walk or hike on it. It's about two and a half mile hike in if we use the service road as a trail," he pointed to the rest room icon. "All the outhouses are on a service road—that way they can be maintained without requiring a pack in—they have to be kept sanitary—keeps people from going behind a bush in the woods."

Helgar looked at his watch. "That still gets us there in the dark." He saw another possibility: he had a perfectly good vehicle that could go almost anywhere—more than he would need here. These service roads wouldn't be a problem. He put his finger on the map. "Why don't we just drive there?" That would allow plenty of time to put up the tents before dark—and enable them to save a great deal of effort packing in all the gear and supplies he had on board.

Tom hiked his shoulders in resignation and pointed to the steel pipe gate across the service road entrance.

Helgar saw a familiar impediment—he gave Tom a wry smile and turned to see where Randall was. The group had finished having fun with the coonskin cap and handed it to Randall; he'd put it on backwards so he could demonstrate his ability to look cross-eyed at the tail. Helgar gave a hearty laugh. "We have an old friend to deal with, Randall." he pointed to the gate. "Have at it."

Randall had been given this duty often in the Cascades, usually on a Forest Service logging road somewhere where padlocks were rarely used. He turned the cap around and skipped over to the gate. In two seconds, he had lifted the sleeve and swung it wide open.

Tom's jaw dropped. He had never looked at the gate closely. He looked to see if Nick had been watching. "I thought those were locked!"

"Locks are a bad idea if rapid access is needed. A suppression crew can't wait around for someone with a key." He pointed at the gate: that road may service the outhouses, but their main purpose is fire control." He slapped Tom on the back. "I doubt if there will be a need for either tonight."

"Or tomorrow," Nick observed.

He, like the others, did not read the small notice on the Do Not Enter sign that cautioned violators about the consequence for unauthorized entry. Penalty: five hundred dollars.

In less than 5 minutes they had determined how to proceed. Three cars would remain in the parking lot; Tom and Helgar would drive their cars in. With a trunk load of brush from the public stash, Tom would drive in his Ford with Nick in front, Robin and Jack in the back seat. Danny and Tony and their gear would ride in the Rover along with Andy and Randall. The Rover's rooftop carrier had more than enough room for all the tents and sleeping bags.

Tom put rings on the last four campsite hooks of the inner camp string—that way, if anyone reported seeing smoke from their campfire, the sheriff patrol would check the board and see the rings; an all-clear would be reported.

The service road was more accommodating than anyone anticipated. The outhouses required turnaround capability for the park service truck as well as a loading area for the brush crew that routinely policed the forest—reducing or eliminating natural fire hazards was an ongoing process. Some of the built-ins were supplemented with portable units. Parking space for both the Rover and Ford was ready made—not only would they not be blocking the road, they would be out of sight. Unloading was convenient and speedy. Tom knew these camps well— they were used less because they were at the end of the campsite string, almost four miles from the trailhead at the parking lot. He and his brothers had spent a week here when he was in the sixth grade, but they had hiked all the way. Robin and Jack took the end camp, Helgar and Geoff took the next one—the largest, a family size camp. The group meals and campfire would be there. Andy and Randall's camp was the first on the east side of the outhouse exit, Tom and Nick came next. It was open enough for two tents. Danny and Tony could have set up there as well, but Tony wanted more "space," so he and Danny took a fifth camp. Tom was happy about that—at night Tony could be a real nuisance. The campsites were separated by an eighth of a mile or more of trail.

The shopping list had been planned before they left Oglivy's; Tom, Nick, Tony and Danny had taken care of that at Piggly Wiggly while Andy had gone home to assemble his gear. Randall and Helgar followed Geoff to the motel. He needed to roust Jack and Robin, get them up to speed, and secure his car. He rode in the Lincoln to assist in

411

getting the Rover loaded and ready—all his camping gear needs were easily met out of the Hallstrom stockpile.

While Randall and Geoff assembled the usual camping utensils and tools in the garage, Helgar stepped into the house to brief Eloise on the conversation with Randall and the plan for the overnight—it sped their timetable, and he wanted her input. She was thrilled by the opportunity. On the way back to the garage, he stopped in the kitchen to call her favorite caterer. He was given the usual premier service; within an hour, two portable chest units were delivered—one with hot food, another with cold. Like the Weber barbecue, the units had their own wheels and a telescoping pull handle. Helgar decided to take the Weber barbecue and a bag of charcoal briquettes just in case—the image of a standard city park had prevailed in his thinking—he saw no need to do without. He sent the boys to the shed for a couple of armloads of dry firewood: so, for all practical purposes, once the decision to drive in was made, his image of the camp as a big back yard campout was right on target.

Unloading the Rover was a team effort: after Randall took a couple of group photos, the unloading began. The pre-chopped firewood, as well as all the tents, sleeping bags and air mattresses were unloaded first. Next, all the provisions Tom had bought at Piggly Wiggly, and the special catering service chests Helgar had ordered from Sharples'. Everyone was an experienced camper—setting up tents was speedy and efficient; about fifty minutes of daylight remained. Tom had designated the headquarter camp on the kiosk map, so they knew where to go. The trail was wide and flat; years of use and maintenance had made it safe and rock free; years of chip and sawdust layers had elevated it so much that rainwater never pooled. It was almost too soft. Aside from some minor off season litter and debris delivered by the wind, it was clear.

Tom did a double take at the chests and barbecue unit, but limited his response to a wide-eyed look at Nick. This was going to be a different campout—very different. Thanks to Helgar's derring-do approach to problem solving, the steel gate problem had been eliminated without any effort; they were able to transport the chests as well as their contents right to the campsite in under fifteen minutes.

Tom clapped his hands a few times to get everyone's attention—he continued to serve as group leader. "Okay guys, here's the plan: this is the main camp: as soon as you have your tents up and your sleeping bags squared away, come back here. Mr. Hallstrom and I will do the cooking; Geoff and Randall are in charge of the fire and barbecue."

Randall raised his hand: "I brought our family mini-pumps," he hiked his shoulders apologetically, "but we only had four." He held up a hand pump.

"I brought mine too," Danny raised a hand. Several in the troop had one—those simplified things on an overnight big time.

"Excellent. That gives us one in each camp. So, as soon as you have your mattresses inflated, get back here as quick as you can. We have gigantic hot dogs to cook over the fire—just like the ones we had last summer." He checked the sky: "it's close to sundown, so break out your flashlights. Pretty easy to trip on a fallen branch. The trails are fairly clear, but they don't keep them brushed during the winter."

The family size camp could seat a dozen at the long table as well as on log rounds around the stone ringed fire pit. Before setting up their own tent, Randall and Andy got the campfire started while Geoff helped Helgar start the Weber barbecue unit—probably the only instance of one being used in a Hayden Park campsite. Thanks to Eloise and her bridge group, Helgar had three to choose from. Once the briquettes were given a good blast from his propane torch, he and Geoff set up his 2-man tent. He did not bring the large tent—he wanted Randall and Andy to be **separate**, in their own tent. When he discovered they would have their own campsite he was delighted. Their "assignment" was to break in the new two-man he purchased at Oglivy's. It would most likely remain a special possession for Randall; that's what Helgar had in mind from the start. He had no idea the special occasion would present itself so soon—the timing couldn't be better.

To all the scouts save Geoff, Helgar was the wonderful supportive parent who had come along to assist and entertain; he might as well have been Mark. Geoff, a known party boy, would be out of circulation during the night—a subterfuge of convenience that worked because it fit everyone's needs, not just Geoff and Helgar's. The distance between camps was a bit of good fortune that he had not expected.

Fortunately, Geoff was very savvy; the prospect of having a six foot three or four mountain man take him during the night was a dream come true. He preferred older men, and he thrived on being held and cuddled, and swallowed up. The fondest memories he had were sitting in Ronnie's lap. His ability to mask his purpose was so successful, both Nick and Tom had put what concern they had out of mind. Overall, the impact of having Helgar there was to put any excesses out of consideration for Tony, who was the only one apt to get carried away. None in the group were beer drinkers to begin with, so no one was doing without because a parent was on board. Helgar chose not to bring any wine, or his evening pipe. Everything was very wholesome and ecologically respectful, ready for memorializing: Randall's camera outfit was ready to go—he had already taken half a dozen shots.

"Man alive, these are good!" Tom finished off another rib. He leaned forward to spoon more baked beans onto his platter. Randall's father had brought these huge oval sectional outdoor supper plates that held a mountain of grub.

"My wife gets the credit there—she found the best deli in the country, I swear: they had this all ready prepared when I placed the call. All they had to do was serve it up for delivery; it was brought right to the house just as we were finishing up loading." Helgar added another bone to the stack. "These must have been slow cooked for a while, too."

A modest belch from Tony went unnoticed. He sat back, shaking his head. "I'm sure glad you didn't get those gigantic buns for the hot dogs."

"Me too—they're pretty expensive for one thing. Besides, we never use those on a pack in: too bulky." Tom didn't like them much anyway.

Randall had eaten his without a bun—these plates made it easy to coat them with goop and just use a fork. Randall was proud of his

414

father, but his idea of a campout meal was somewhat embarrassing. He knew Tom and his friends had gone shopping for the same meals at the supermarket. He shook his head in amazement—his father had calculated the possibilities and likelihood, and acted accordingly, as usual. *same thing with the tent and sleeping bags for Andy and me.* It was almost as if he could predict the future. All day long he'd been seeing his father in a completely different light. His bravado façade was brilliant: these guys had no idea it was an act. At home, he was a professor reading quietly in the study while listening to string quartets.

"That tripod is pretty nifty—how heavy are those, anyway?" Tom might pick one up—he didn't think Oglivy's had anything like that. The lantern was high up, enough to light to the whole area.

"Not very—I bought half a dozen of those to use in back—Eloise likes to do an outdoor event once in a while. The outdoor furniture people have those. We have some kerosene lanterns that hang down from the center; luckily, it's sturdy enough to hold a Coleman. They're stainless steel, not aluminum." He consumed another spoonful of beans.

Randall, sitting next to his father, amazed Robin. *if it wasn't for his nose, Randall could never be thought of as related... not even close.* Same with behavior— *Randall is a typical nerd type, really. his dad is a star fullback. their western accent is the same...*

"Oboy—" Tony put his platter to the side and scurried away from the circle.

> > brump < <

A few giggles could not be suppressed, but Helgar fixed that quickly: "Speak up, we can hardly hear you!" he kept a straight face.

The group laughed heartily—what little tension there was had just been wiped away. Randall about doubled over he was so tickled.

"Have another bean or two." he winked at Nick. "Word to the wise: does a lot of good to clear the pipes before a climb." He winked at Tom. "Vertical rock climbs are single file: only one person is in front." He helped himself to another scoop. He had bought enough for both nights; the crock was still a little over half full.

A short delay while the boys translated his observation. The laughter was tempered somewhat; they exchanged looks: this guy was cool and a little crazy. This was going to be some campout.

"So tell me: what kind of night critters have you got around here—we don't need any curious bears." It was too warm for hibernating.

"No bears. Lots of coons; possums, squirrels. The cardinals can be a problem if you want to sleep in." Tom didn't remember being bothered at all.

Andy pointed at the small sign by the trail. "Most people know better than to feed the animals. They're still wild. They don't expect to be fed."

"If you stay on trail, you don't have any problems. Once in a while a bunch of turkeys can hold you up."

Helgar chuckled. "No wild boars or anything, I take it."

That drew a laugh. "I heard there was a bobcat seen over by Littel Capitan," Robin would like to see it if they got a chance.

"Coyotes, don't forget the coyotes." Andy had heard they strayed out once in a while to snag a pet dog or cat.

Helgar was satisfied they would have no problems—it was too cold to have any insects to worry about. He wasn't convinced the raccoons wouldn't do some sniffing around. He intended to have a solution for that, regardless.

Tony stood and bent over to grab his flashlight. "Did we bring any TP along, I hope?"

"Ah! So it was an announcement of coming attractions!" Helgar winked. "I took the liberty of putting a roll inside the facility." He had a couple more in the Rover. He looked around the circle: most were about finished. "The cold chest has ice cream if any one's interested. I didn't think of marshmallows."

"I think we're about ready to call it a day," Tom glanced around to see if there was anyone who disagreed. It was too cold to do much—it would be fun to do something, but he didn't have any ideas. "What time do you want to get started?

416

"When is sunup? No point in hurrying—we have what, a mile and a half to hike?"

Tom nodded. "Close, yeah."

"Well, when this is secure, I intend to take a hike up to that junction I saw on the map. Going straight to bed on a full stomach is a bad idea. Everyone's invited."

"Now that's a great idea!" Tom was ready now. "Maybe I'll have a scoop of ice cream when we get back." He stretched and patted his stomach a few times.

Though it was the only sound, a helicopter rapidly descending several hundred feet toward the airport was too faint to attract any special notice: it was ten miles to the south.

27   *five mini camps*

a Helgar and Geoff   b Andy and Randall   c Tom and Nick
d Jack and Robin   e Tony and Danny

a   Helgar and Geoff

The rigorous pace set by Helgar had done an excellent job of putting the groups' digestive tracts into high gear. Tom was the only one who was able to keep up; Helgar's long legs required Danny and Randall to jog periodically to catch up. Since they were on a road instead of a trail, they didn't have to walk in a line. As a consequence of the roughly 1.2 mile round trip to the service road junction, the likelihood any would need to relieve themselves during the night had all but vanished: a line formed to make that important stop before returning to camp.

Helgar broke into song a couple of times—a rousing **Heigh-Ho to Work We Go** on the way, and **Danny Boy** on the way back. None of the boys were able to join in—they couldn't do that and hike full out at the same time. Helgar's energy and lung capacity was Olympian.

Huddling around the campfire was not on anyone's wish list. While Randall, Andy and Geoff secured the provisions from nocturnal inspection by curious creatures in the night, the other boys took off to their tents to settle in. Helgar was able to shut down the Coleman lantern at last—the hissing roar had become tedious; silence was welcome, although the complete darkness was not—unfortunately, that lantern had only two positions: super blinding bright on, or off. As he turned to deal with the remnants of the campfire, Randall became faintly visible. As he approached, he turned off his flashlight and placed it on one of the log rounds; he stepped close and looked at his father gratefully. Words were

419

not needed—years of companionship had enabled them to have this moment.

Helgar paused briefly, then opened his arms: they got that hug in at last. It was just as well that it was so dark—it enabled Randall to stare at his father directly for a very long minute. He simply could not find the words he needed. "Thanks, Dad," he said at last, and hugged a second time—as hard and tight as he could. "G'night."

This time Helgar was grateful for the dark—it obscured the tears that were pooling; the approaching flashlight provided the perfect excuse to stand apart at last and call it a day. He couldn't see his boy skip happily as he stepped toward his trail, but he could hear—"Good night, Son." He took a deep breath and exhaled. That had made his day.

His attention turned to the ring of large river stones. These spoke well for the management—and the budget—of this operation: they were not gathered on site by volunteers; rocks like this were at least 25 pounds; some were twice that. The campfire had consumed most of its fuel—the dry wood that he had brought from his shed had performed well—another advantage of having the Land Rover. He spread the embers apart gently to speed their demise; the glowing remnants in front of him were the only light source in the camp. With the top down, the Weber kettle grill took care of itself.

"Everything is safe for the night," Geoff reported, turning off his flashlight. He had paused briefly to allow Randall and his father to have what seemed to be an important private moment. He had returned from helping Randall and Andy make an attractive pile of sparerib bones well away from camp—several hundred feet down the access road; everything else was securely sealed in the Rover. He was glad he had stopped to water a tuft of grass along the way. He allowed a minute or two to pass before appearing. "I've never heard of using a scent shield before; does it work?"

Helgar was grateful for the opportunity to change his focus. "A Forest Service ranger gave me that tip. They don't promote it, since toxic chemicals can be so harmful if not used properly. It not only masks the scent of your provisions, it can interfere with the animal's ability to smell for a while. That's a matter of survival in the wild." Discarded chemical containers were a major no-no. "A few squirts around your rig's door openings keeps the bears and raccoons away for days. It's far more reliable than putting down a bead of ground pepper." With everything in the Rover, there wasn't anything left in the camp to attract interest. The sparerib bones would lure scavengers away and keep them busy all night. He stood back for a final look. "I believe we're ready to hit the sack." Fortunately, no wind or breeze had penetrated the forest canopy—*don't need to waste any water on this.* "Getting a bit chilly." He could barely make out Geoff's face it was so dark.

Conveniently or not, tonight was a new moon, and overcast; the cloud layer blocked virtually all starlight. That meant no frost in the morning, a big plus. To an experienced camper the outline of the tent was faintly discernible nonetheless—enough to enable them to proceed without the flashlight. Ordinarily, this would have been annoying. But since Helgar and Geoff had not been "introduced" sufficiently, the darkness was an asset—it allowed them to bypass the usual awkwardness of disrobing in front of a stranger, albeit one that was about to become a bedmate. It heightened curiosity and suspense in a positive way, and made pro forma platitudes and banter unnecessary. Just as well, considering the unusual and unlikely pairing that only they knew was in the works.

Up to now, all either one had to go on was a momentary wink of recognition about six hours ago in a crowded department store. Both were smart enough and sufficiently skilled to maintain a flawless façade until now. Being in the dark literally as well seemed to help. And, since it was so cold, it made sense to snuggle into the sleeping bags as rapidly as possible. Even though Helgar had zipped the tent closed, it would not warm appreciably before it was time to rise and shine.

Prudence required Helgar to begin with caution: "So, here we are at last. Before anything else, I need a little information. It was clear from your eyes that you are not a spring chicken, to use a euphemism—your appearance notwithstanding. I need to be assured that you are of age." He didn't want any doubt about that; his phrasing and choice of words was deliberate and sober; he was not about to exploit or take advantage.

Geoff was expecting this, and was prepared. "I am grateful you asked that first—I thought you would, but I needed the assurance that question provided—thank you for that. I have always looked younger than my friends by at least a year or two."

421

Helgar was surprised—he had not expected a response at that level from someone who looked so young and unexposed.

"My mother is Cambodian, my father is British. Since I was born in Hong Kong, I am British too, although my parents had me naturalized as an American when they moved to Hawaii. I was five at the time, so I lost my father's accent. We moved to Burbank when I was twelve. My father is a television producer and manager. We moved to Atlanta three years ago, where I turned 18. My birthday is Pearl Harbor Day. You saw my shiny red birthday present at the motel. I have been legal for two whole weeks!" Geoff had been smart enough to move it back a month. He would turn 18 in nine days. He was confident that his little fib would go undiscovered. He would make sure no one had a chance to look closely at his driver's license.

"British!" That explained his syntax. "Interesting. Very interesting." If he didn't know better, that introduction could have come from a grad student. Most promising indeed. That he would get a birthday present like that red Corvette told him what he needed to know about his parents. One hurdle remained.

"You are too polite to ask about my other 'qualifications'," Geoff continued. Conversing with an intelligent adult felt wonderful— he had missed that as much as anything. Peers were fun to play with, but conversing required patience if not indulgence. "I learned my way around long before we moved to Los Angeles. You'd be amazed at what possibilities there are for a cute little beach urchin in Honolulu if he has the inclination and the talent." He reached out, poised to take Helgar's hand. He didn't expect it to take very long.

Geoff continued his narrative: "Shortly after we settled into our condo in Burbank, I had the good fortune to met someone who knew just what I wanted and needed; he was twelve years older. Age difference was not an issue for either of us. If my father had not taken the position in Atlanta, I would still be his boy."

Helgar needed a minute to deal with what he had just heard. The frankness and honestly was unexpected—its spontaneous delivery convinced him that it was authentic and not contrived or scripted; it presented possibilities as well as cautions.

422

"Thanks for your openness; I am impressed. Now that you have graduated and have your own car, what is your plan?" Helgar presumed he was about to head for California.

Geoff improvised—he had not made any plans. "I'm undecided about that. I have not had contact with my friends in California for a while; I can't assume my father would support me financially were I to go back. He's a generous man, but tends to be old school when coming of age is at issue. Fortunately, he doesn't insist that I go into broadcasting. I do need to settle on a career path. That's what I'll be doing for the next few months. I thought that as long as I was here, I would take a look at continuing my education at this University as well as others closer to home. My parents aren't in a rush to be rid of me—I am their only offspring."

Helgar was uncertain how to frame his remaining question. Fortunately, Geoff took care of that next.

"As I indicated, I have always preferred older men—unusual I expect. You are probably older than anyone I have played with, but from what I have seen so far, that doesn't seem to be a problem. You seem as fit as you were ten or more years ago: I see no midriff bulge, at least. I am not experienced enough to judge, but I don't get the impression you've even begun to go to seed—especially after that after dinner stroll. The fact that I'm only a couple years older than Randall is probably more than awkward. I think it would be best to keep him in the dark, so to speak. That's up to you, of course. Otherwise, I doubt that there is much you could teach me that I don't know already, but I like surprises."

The discretion hurdle had just been swept away, and then some. Helgar reached out of the side of his sleeping bag—he was pleased to find Geoff's hand waiting. "I believe it's time to finish setting this up: have you ever used conjoined sleeping bags?"

"Ooo!" Geoff cooed. "I'm a quick learner!" he giggled.

The two sleeping bags had been placed separately, but opened facing one another. By design, they could zip open on either side or be zipped into one unit. Helgar had purchased a pair long ago to facilitate his "recreational requirements." Geoff had deduced as much when they were setting up camp. This set was brand new. He had never used one of these, but had heard of them. Connecting the two bags was accomplished with ease even in the dark—Helgar had done this many times. He had crafted a means of snapping the air mattresses together as well, which allowed more security should nighttime activity become at all vigorous.

In minutes, Geoff was curled up as if it was where he had always belonged. This man was more like Hercules than Apollo, but he didn't mind—it had been a long time.

—ɯ—

b   Randall and Andy

It took several minutes for Randall and Andy to get their sleeping bags connected and adjusted just right—the prospect of spending the night together had grown more daunting by the minute. Figuring out how they zipped together wasn't easy in the dark—the flashlight helped, for sure.

"I wish we had done this when we set up the tent." Randall was in too big a hurry to help his dad organize the camp kitchen. He wiggled briefly, glad to be under cover at last—it was cold out there. *it certainly warms up fast.*

"I was surprised your father suggested this kind of sleeping bag." *how could we be this lucky?* Andy had not expected to be in bed with Randall so soon—being "ahead of schedule" was awkward. It felt right, but he had expected to "get there" at a slower pace; he had not even thought about doing this yet. It sure solved a lot of problems. He sensed that Randall needed to talk about it for a while—Andy did not disagree. Being two years older, he was always afraid of taking advantage. Randall had no way of knowing that he and Tony had been more than playmates for quite a while—there wasn't much they hadn't done.

Randall was surprised about the sleeping bags too, for a while. "I've been itching to talk about things like that all day: this double bag is like frosting on a cake." He wasn't sure where to start. "First off, you need to know one thing about my dad: he doesn't suggest, ever. When

424

he frames anything as a suggestion, it means he has considered the alternatives and determined that it's the best solution and is committed to supporting whatever would be needed to bring it about."

"Reminds me of my grandmother. In her case, it's a question that is supposed to be answered the way she wants it to be, even though she can't force it. So it's not really a question at all: it's a guilt trip if you answer the wrong way." He still hadn't figured a way to get around her on those.

"Dad never does that. Even so, I have a lot to talk about, all at the same time. This has been the craziest day of my life, and probably the best day too. It began this morning when out of the blue, he asked me to come along with him on a special trip to that department store. I knew something was up when he told me we'd be using my mother's car. He almost never drives the Lincoln. Only when he and my mom are going to a social event or something—then he takes the wheel." He shook his head. "In town he either walks or takes his bicycle. The Rover is for camping trips."

Andy was interested of course, but he was hoping they'd focus pretty soon on what was starting to happen halfway down the sleeping bag. Its engineering was superior—he was all warm and ready.

"First off, I'd like to know what he said when he called you about meeting us at that store. Are you at liberty to tell about that?"

"Sure. He wanted me to meet you guys there to help pick something out—he wasn't exact, but since it was at the Outdoor Store, he wanted me and Mark to be in on it. I assumed it was a part of a Christmas present or something. He mentioned the after Christmas sale."

"That's all?"

"Yeah. I didn't think it was a big deal—although I was really glad he called me." He stroked Randall's arm unconsciously. "I've been a little worried about what he thinks of me, actually. Felt good to talk with him like that."

Randall chuckled: "Well, hold on to your hat then. The first thing he said to me on the way to the store was a total surprise: he advised me to get your help in picking out a car to use in Driver's Ed next term."

"The school uses their own car for the class."

"Right. He says I'll need my own for practice... that I'll do better if I have my own car. I'm supposed to pick whatever I want." He grabbed Andy's hand. "He said if it were his decision, he'd get a new one, but I needed to decide that, with your advice. He expects it to be a good, reliable car, and your advice is sufficient: he thinks highly of your judgment, or he would not advise me to rely on it. Price is no object: whatever we pick will be paid for in full."

"Wow." Andy did not know what to say.

"That's what I mean about his "suggestions." They are conclusions. He thrives on solving problems before they arise." *that's one reason he's such a good research scientist.* "This is where to hold on to your hat: it's not just the car. He told me that both he and my mother approve of you and of our relationship. He used that word: relationship. He said they had been expecting it!"

Andy's heartbeat just doubled. He didn't know whether to laugh or cry, or what. "How..." he couldn't even frame a question.

Randall exhaled and took a deep breath. He was worried that he might be going too fast, but he saw no alternative; he pressed on:

"He took me to the store to get this set of sleeping bags for you and me: for **us**. He wasn't expecting them be used this soon, but obviously, he thought it was perfect timing; it's about the only thing he didn't plan or predict." Randall paused. "My job... **our** job, I guess... is to live up to his expectation. He is always a chapter or two ahead." He'd heard that expression somewhere recently—it fit his father perfectly.

whoah... Under most circumstances, Andy would not take well to being hurried into something—especially something as serious as this. He still hadn't come to grips with what he felt about Randall and where it would lead. An understanding family was not something he had, he didn't think—he had no reason to count on it, at least. He didn't fully understand why he was "different," either. He just knew that he was, and had learned how to get away with it up to now. His "late bloomer" cover wouldn't last forever. Like it or not, Randall's father had opened the barn door.

The long pause scared Randall: had he ruined everything? *what if I have been wrong? have I scared Andy away?* He had no experience,

426

nothing practical to guide him. *should I have saved some of this for later?*

Andy's instinct came to the rescue. He felt Randall's fear: his big brother nature forced him to reach out; he stroked the back of Randall's head gently with his right hand. He hadn't found the right words yet, but his caress was sufficient.

Randall relaxed at once, flooded with emotion unlike anything he had ever experienced. Andy's touch was perfect—it was a gesture of acceptance. He pressed his hand against Andy's and the tension, like a stretched rubber band being released, vanished. He wilted; for the first time in his life, he shivered—with a deep but brief whimper, he sobbed in relief.

Andy grabbed him with his other arm and pulled him tight. "Hey, hey…" he shushed softly, tenderly. At once he realized how vulnerable Randall was… and how essential it was for him to be where he was and be who Randall thought he was. He felt so many things at once it was hard to sort it out but he knew that he would, he could, he must. He let Randall hug him tightly and gently rocked back and forth while he regained control. He took Randall's head into his hands at last and rubbed noses briefly before placing a light kiss on his lips.

"I'm s-sorry…"

"What for? You haven't done anything wrong."

"I don't know… I was so scared suddenly—"

"Shh… shh…" Andy shushed, and kissed his forehead. "That's my fault… it took me too long to take in what you said. You warned me it was coming. You were right—boy-o-boy were you. **Double** right. I'm still working on it." He stroked Randall's hair unconsciously. "I'll bet you are too."

"I feel so stupid." His nose was runny; he tried to wipe it away.

Andy laughed kindly. "No, no. That's one thing you are not. You are human. Humans cry. It's required sometimes." Andy felt a rush… a new kind of rush: he felt needed, and he felt thrilled to be filling that need. He belonged here.

Andy's words were so comforting—Randall felt a glow—like the one he felt that night in Andy's car. He began to comprehend a little what his father had alluded to when he said he and mom knew what had happened. They had gone through this themselves. He began to understand how truly lucky he was.

The embrace became total: Andy rolled onto his back and pulled Randall on top so they could embrace and touch as much of their bodies as they could. They would talk some more later. Mother Nature had written this program long ago, and they were ready.

—m—

c   Tom and Nick

"Man, I am stuffed!" Tom complained, reaching out to Nick at last. They kissed gently; it had been a long day.

Nick worked his left leg into position between Tom's thighs and wiggled into their favorite position. The air mattresses were so much better than the feather beds in Barr's Meadow. Otherwise, they had this set up the same way, only with an extra blanket. Finding an opportunity to spend an entire night together had proven almost impossible since camp last summer. He chuckled. "I think Randall's father has you there. He must have a hollow leg."

"You ain't kiddin! **Two** hollow legs! I'd like to be there when he cuts the first one in that tent: I doubt if Geoff knows what he's in for." The baked beans and onion combination reminded him of the barbecue last summer. Randall's father must have eaten almost two cups. "I think that deli uses molasses—that stuff didn't come out of a can."

"Reminds me of Brad. By the way—fair warning: I had a big helping myself. Those were really good—everything was."

"It's weird: he paid for all the stuff I got at Piggly Wiggly, then ordered extra from that deli. I think we could hold out a week. Those takeout chests hold a lot. I've never seen those before. Tomorrow night we get T-bone steak on top of our good old mac and cheese! We have to cook 'em; no problem there."

428

"They must throw a lot of parties; Andy says their place is quite a spread."

"Mark sure likes him."

Nick cuddled a little closer. "Do we have any rules tonight?"

"Rules?"

"Yeah—rules. We're a long way from Mark's farting post." Nick had plenty of beans too—self defense if nothing else.

"Oooh yeah… I didn't think about that." He had twice as many beans tonight as he did last summer. "Kinda cold out there."

They both thought about it a while.

"I s'pose it wouldn't do any good to poke our butts out long enough to sing their song then cover up real quick…"

"Wouldn't do much good," Tom had tried that in the past. "Some always sneaks in anyway."

Nick was stumped. "I guess we have to plug our noses tonight and keep track of whose are worst."

Tom reached around and tickled Nick under the arms. "I'll pretend yours are sweet as roses." He planted a kiss on Nick's nose. He was ready to play.

Nick laughed.

"What?"

"Roses. Between us we'll have enough for a **bouquet**."

Tom didn't get it.

"Bouquet—it has two meanings."

Tom still didn't get it. "So explain it." It had to be tricky—Nick was such a smarty pants. "A bouquet of roses is a bunch of roses. So?…"

"Bouquet also means any kind of fragrance—wine especially. The experts always talk about a wine's bouquet. Some kinds are super expensive because of their bouquet."

"Huh." Tom had heard that. He wasn't a wine drinker, so he'd never taken a whiff. "Smarty pants. How do you know about things like that, anyway?" his hand wandered south while he nuzzled under Nick's ear.

"I have an uncle who spends a lot of money on wine... my mom is always scolding him about it." He felt Tom's exploring fingers. "My word, whatever are you doing?"

"Testing." He gave Nick's crotch a solid rub. He was pleased to discover that Nick was up for a little recreation.

Nick assumed Tom was referring to his elevated status. He was mistaken. Tom pulled his hand up and sniffed his forefinger as loudly as he could, then ran it under Nick's nose. "Checking on your flower patch's bouquet. Pretty good tonight. What do you think?"

Tom got a massive tickle under the arm attack. It was worth it— he didn't get a chance to pull one on Nick very often.

—m—

d   Jack and Robin

Eight thirty going on nine was early in the evening, usually—in this camp, that was not the case: it was too cold to sit around the campfire telling stories or sing songs or whatever a bunch of randy boys did when one of their parents was part of the mix. It had been a rigorous active day for both Robin and Jack, including a passionate reunion romp in the motel about six hours ago. That, and the massive barbecue meal recently concluded made hitting the hay very attractive. After all, that's why they were here. This was better than a motel room. With Robin's sleeping bag tucked into the one Randall lent them, it was almost a double wide. The cover blanket kept the top layer in place; it was more than double thick—plenty to keep out the cold air. Climbing in was a little awkward, but otherwise it was a cuddler's dream come true.

They had only spent the night together once before—their highly illegal night under a full moon by Lake Walker. No one else knew about that night, either. Whispering Oaks was the name Robin gave the

430

clearing that had become their special private place—clandestine trysts became a daily priority the second week of camp. They had both shared Robin's sleeping bag—what a sublime experience it had been. It had enabled them to commit themselves to each other for life—both were convinced of that. They had been fantasizing about this night since then—separated by over three hundred miles.

Jack's second purpose for this trip was to lay the groundwork for going to school here in the fall—since he was a year ahead of Robin, he saw no alternative. He was already in line for two scholarships, and his school counselor was hopeful another was on the way. He planned to visit the campus before Geoff and he had to return to Atlanta. He was eager to talk about it—he had good news to share. At the motel they were too busy—he had planned to deal with that at the motel after they had a chance to romp a little, but this camping trip had intervened. Now maybe he could get a word or two in.

"Where were we?" He wanted a clever opening, but didn't want to spend any more time thinking one up. He began by walking his fingers up Robin's arm.

Robin's mind was elsewhere—he inhaled deeply through his nose, then exhaled. "Oh, did I ever miss that!" He nuzzled behind Jack's left ear.

Jack squinted happily, "That tickles... miss what?"

"Your smell. I wish I could bottle it."

Jack laughed, "That's right, I almost forgot." Robin often said that at camp. "Did the after dinner walk improve it any?" He worked up a minor sweat trying to keep up with the blond giant.

"How could anything improve what's already perfect? Let me check." He inched down and nuzzled under his arm. He zipped back and rubbed noses. "See? still perfect."

Jack was still giggling happily—he was more ticklish under his arms. He took the opportunity to pucker his lips. Obviously, Robin was in the mood to play. The subject of finding a place to stay next year would have to wait until tomorrow. "Well, when those beans kick in, you may have to revise your opinion." He just remembered—the platter was handed to him already dished up. Potato salad, spare ribs and

431

beans—all he had to do was take the hot dog off the stick and add ketchup. He ate everything, **especially** the beans. He even had seconds.

Robin giggled, "If it wasn't so cold, we could have a little fun seeing what color they are."

"Color?!"

"You never can tell, according to Brad. How long since you had pepperoni pizza?"

Pepperoni pizza?! All of a sudden Robin was not making any sense. "Quite a while—I don't have pizza very often. What's that got to do with anything?"

"You don't know Brad. He's a Tiger—one of our patrols. He's an expert in setting farts on fire. He showed us all about it last summer after our Troop barbecue. He's a little weird, but I have to admit it was a lot of fun. Anyway, he says that Pepperoni pizza causes blue farts."

Jack burst into laughter "You've got to be kidding!"

Robin giggled. "No, no! I didn't believe it either at first; I set off two oranges and a light green myself."

Jack was at a loss: the sharpest troop at the camp sets farts on fire after their barbecue. "Orange and green farts?!" This was crazy. "I'll bet your scoutmaster wasn't in on the party."

Robin laughed, "You're right about that—but he had to know something was going on—that camp is in an open meadow—you can hear what's going on anywhere and everywhere if it's very loud. I was expecting him to come down and break it up any time, but he didn't. He's pretty cool, actually. He lets boys be boys." He thought back—that camp was full of great memories. "I know! you can ask Tony! He was there—he's a Tiger too. He was really good at it—he did it in his skivvies!"

Jack was amazed—he knew Tony—he's a Poker Club member. A real clown, too; it didn't come as a surprise. Jack shook his head. He had trouble picturing it. "Does someone stand behind and wait until you to cut one, then light a match?"

"No that would never work. You have to do it yourself—it's a little tricky: you have to hold the match in just the right place or it won't catch. You lie on your back and reach around your leg. It's best to leave your pants on though—they can be really hot."

"It's not something you can do in a sleeping bag then."

Robin thought a minute. "If you want to hold the flashlight I could show you, I guess. I'd have to put my pants on though—don't want to burn anything down there."

"Aha! Pants on fire. Now I get it." Jack was ready to change the subject. He reached for Robin's hand and placed it on his now receding tool: seven and half inches had become about six: not good. "He doesn't want to talk about farts any more. Your assistance is required to restore him to full size."

Robin zoomed down to nuzzle. "MMmm!!" Better than perfect smell: more intense. He puckered his lips and stuck out his tongue. "Thought so..." He did a full length suck, and enjoyed keeping it in place until it was firm. He sat up to report his findings: "Smell test: double perfect. Taste test: too early to tell." He rubbed noses again.

Jack grabbed him into an embrace, laughing: "You are too much!" he smothered him with a long kiss. He emerged to take a breath. "**That's** where we were! How could I forget?"

Robin was ready.

—⟋⟍—

e   Tony and Danny

"Didn't one of these come with a set of instructions?!" Tony was about out of patience with this conjoined sleeping bag thingamajig.

"We should have done this before it got dark. It can't be that hard. Randall's dad bought two sets—I heard him tell Mark he'd been using them for a long time out west where they came from." He just thought about that a sec: *instructions*. "Where did you put the cover—you know, the carrying bag they came in. I think there was something sewn onto that."

Tony lifted up their coats: sure enough, they were there, all wadded up. He shook one out and smoothed it flat. "Aim the light over here a minute." The patch had an illustration of the special conjoining zipper being engaged. "So **that's** how they do it!" He felt a little sheepish. *why the heck don't they make the special zipper a different color!* "Okay: here's what we do. First spread them flat like we did before, only upside down. Then we find this starting point, zip it down all the way to the bottom… then we flip it over and pull it up on the front side. We get in and out on the side using one or the other of those zippers; the other two get covered up instead of being used.

"Huh. The opposite of a mummy bag, kind of."

"Maybe that's why Randall's dad likes these—he's way too big to fit in a mummy bag, for sure." Tony giggled naughtily. "Be fun to see if he and Geoff set theirs up like this." He was half sorry he couldn't figure a way for Geoff to stay here and have a threesome. On the other hand, he didn't want to share Danny with anyone. He was through doing that kind of thing; that's one thing Danny had caused. Poor Geoff would have to sleep alone.

The bags conjoined at last, Danny and Tony lifted the cover blanket and crawled in. The tent flap was zipped closed, so they were all set! The bag took no time at all to reflect their body heat inward. Tony's toes connected with a pant leg—he scooted it to the side. Any scout knew well the wisdom of going to bed with their clothes inside the sleeping bag. Cold clammy clothes were not a good way to meet the new day.

Danny laughed. "If only Randall's dad knew what Geoff could do!" Danny thought Geoff could handle about anyone—he took care of Tom big time. *he's almost as tall as Randall's dad.* Were all tall guys two handers?

Tony hadn't checked him out. Geoff was about average size— one hand size; Tom was a two—odds were that Randall's dad was a two. "He's pretty cool for a dad, when you think about it."

Danny giggled. "Sure is." *never guess Randall was his kid.* "How did Julian find him, anyway? I never did figure that one out. He just showed up with him at a troop meeting that time."

434

"Must have a class together or something. Other than being about the same height, they're way different." Tony thought Andy was a better match anyway. Randall was more his type. "Come to think about it, how come Julian isn't on this campout? I thought he and Randall were total buddies."

"Say, that's right!" After all, Both Julian and Randall were in the Initiation—Danny remembered that well enough. Andy might be in for a surprise tonight. He froze.

"What?" Tony could tell Danny was on to something.

"The Initiation! Remember?"

"Well, duh! How could I forget? I got you guys into that."

Danny was a step ahead for a change. "Why do you suppose I got this kind of new sleeping bag instead of one like I had at camp?"

Tony thought that was pretty obvious—he was there. "Because Randall's dad said..." it dawned. "Do you think he did that on purpose?!" *could he tell we would use it like this?*

"I thought he was just replacing the one he and Randall's mom used. They go on family trips in the summer, I think."

"Why would he want Randall to have a set though?" Tony did think that was strange.

"Maybe when they go on a high mountain trip they hafta go in pairs—makes sense to sleep huddled together—like in those Mount Everest climbs. That way nobody gets frostbite while they're asleep at night or hiding out in a blizzard."

"I don't think they do anything **that** crazy. Those pictures he showed at the troop meeting didn't have tons of ice and snow everywhere." Tony didn't see anything he couldn't handle if he was there.

"Yeah. You're right. I thought for a minute he knew Andy and Randall might want to put them together like this." Randall's dad couldn't be **that** cool.

435

Tony thought about that. "Andy's too smart—I doubt if he knows what's going on—**if** there is anything going on. He said these were as good a single bag as you could get too."

Danny had not spent any time watching Andy and Randall. They were both on the school paper. That must be it. "Say, by the way: did you know about Robin and Jack?" Danny had never met Jack before.

Tony thought about that... "No, now that you mention it. He's a friend of Geoff's—he must have been at camp; maybe he's in the same troop."

"No, he's a friend of Tom's too... I think he's an Assistant Scoutmaster like Geoff and Tom are." Danny was impressed by how he and Robin were so committed to each other. They wanted to hold hands and be together every second... like he and Tony, in a way.

Tony fondled Danny's curly locks absentmindedly. Unlike the others, spending the night together wasn't that special. Tony had stayed overnight several times—six or seven, he didn't keep count; Danny's upstairs room was perfect. There was no problem after school either, usually. "What do you want to do first?" It had been a couple of weeks since they had spent the whole night together. Without thinking, he cut a small fart.

"Thanks a lot!"

"Sorry—it just slipped out. I forgot." Tony was used to farting openly—it was a Tiger Patrol thing, thanks to Brad.

Danny sniffed: "how come I don't smell anything?"

"It was just a little one... they don't always smell, actually, unless you're nose is close in: you can check it out closer in if you want—I don't mind."

"Maybe later." Tony is such fun all the time. Danny thought he was just about the luckiest kid in town. Never a dull moment. He broke into giggles and quoted: "Speak up, I can hardly hear you!"

Tony laughed aloud. "I'm gonna use that first time Brad lets one go." *he's always cutting the cheese*—"he doesn't need beans."

They held hands a while, each waiting for the other to decide where to start—neither could remember whose turn it was.

436

"I know," Danny broke the silence. "Since you're the expert, tell me this: is it possible to cut one if you have a stiffy?"

Tony laughed. That was a new one. He honestly did not know, come to think about it. "Huh. You got me there."

Danny decided to run a test. "Let's find out!" He ducked down to get started; he was ready to play. He didn't notice any difference in the aroma down here—the other one left no traces, at least not in front. After several minutes he surfaced. He needed to get a breath of fresh air.

"I was a good boy," Tony complained.

"Thanks—it's way too warm down there!" He fanned his face.

Tony ducked down to check for himself. After a few minutes, he surfaced. "Whoo! You are right! These bags are **too** good."

It took a while to figure out how to get around the problem, but they were good scouts. No hurry, anyway.

28   *at Kasey's overnight*

Kasey was not accustomed to using a telephone—for one reason or another, he had always been given the handset to take a call that had already been answered. Belmont dorm rooms did not have telephones, and he didn't have any "pals" to speak of in Boston, so using a telephone to call anyone had never played a part in his life. Nonetheless, his mother had insisted that he make this call himself. The mechanics of the dial were simple enough—he couldn't remember exactly when or where, but he thought he had done this once before—long ago, before his Belmont days. Perhaps he had just seen it done. This particular instrument appeared to be brand new—very smooth and quiet. Dialing had triggered a curious electronic sequence: the background tone had been replaced by brief periodic pulses—he focused on the unfamiliar sound; it was being sent somehow, and several miles away that pulse was being translated into a ringing sound… he was uncertain about how many times it would ring before it would be answered. He had not thought to keep a count… the buzzing sound stopped abruptly—

> > *Hello, hello hello! I sure hope you're calling Julian, 'cause he's the only one here right now.* < < A pause on the line indicated that the caller wasn't expecting a weird answer like that, so he continued—

> > *or maybe you called a wrong number; that happens sometimes… hello? anyone there?* < <

"Sorry," Kasey laughed, "but it took me a minute to figure out how to respond."

> > *Kasey!! Neato!!* < < Julian recognized the voice and accent at once.

"I didn't expect anyone to answer the telephone like that." He shook his head and with a chuckle, grinned at his mother. Unexpectedly, he felt a surge of emotion—Julian was just the same. More than reassured, he felt welcome. He gave his mother a happy grin as Julian continued. She must have known he would feel like this.

> > *Sorry about that... I never know what to say, so I make it up on the way to the phone. Plain old hello is kinda boring. You sound close: are you moved in yet?* < <

He sat and shifted the receiver to his left hand. This wasn't so bad, at that. Using a telephone was likely to become a part of his new life 'down south,' to use Wyatt's terminology.

> > *or maybe you could use a hand unloading stuff. I can probably round up a few guys to help out...* < <

Kasey frowned. Unfortunately, everything had been done by the movers; the perfect chance to meet Julian's friends was eliminated. "Thanks, but all that was taken care of. Besides calling to say hello, I'm calling to invite you to drop in. My mother would like both you and your mother to visit." He felt very awkward about this—understandable, since he'd never been in a situation like this before.

> > *Wow-ee! I'd like that. Mom's at work. I can call and see.* < < He thought a second... > > *I could ride my bicycle over now...* < <

"I don't think that's a good idea—it's several miles out in the country."

> > *Oh...* < < He had to think a minute. > > *Tell you what: give me your phone number. That way I can call you back. I hafta call my mom. Maybe she can get permission or something.* < <

He covered the handset briefly: "He has to call his mother—she's at work."

> > *She and Geraldine have been looking for a place for your folks, I know that much.* < <

Julian thought for a second. Something wasn't right.

> > *But it was s'posed to be close to the university, not out in the country.* < <

"We're staying in Mr. Swann's guest house for the time being. It's out past the airport somewhere." He had seen a sign on the way. He looked at the dial on the phone and covered the handset again: "is this the phone number?" he pointed at the center of the dial. When she nodded, he read it aloud: "ALpine 4-3245."

> > *Ooo-eee! Wait a sec: I hafta go get pencil and paper. Numbers are too slippery for my brain; they go right out the other ear.* < <

Kasey shook his head and giggled. "He's going for a pencil." He looked at his mother happily. Julian's way of expressing himself was… he searched for a word that fit. It took a minute. *original.* For now, that would have to do.

The instantaneous change in her son's demeanor was precisely what Candace Wood sought; it confirmed her conviction that this move was a godsend for her son—that unusual boy was the perfect solution. She continued with her needlepoint as usual—that was her way of keeping busy when there wasn't much else to do—it allowed her to pay close attention to her son without seeming to—a fiction that didn't fool him: he used it as well—it made it easy to avoid being annoyed by her 'mothering.' Needlepoint connected her to her own mother; those connections meant a great deal to her; one day they would be important to her son as well.

Ike raised his head and looked at his young master: his tail wagged, revealing that he sensed young master was suddenly happy. The family dog was getting on in years; but he was always ready for a scratch under the chin and a gentle pat on the head.

Now that Julian had grown too big to sit in front comfortably, he was able to appreciate the advantages of sitting in the back seat. It allowed him to focus on the scenery a lot more. Geraldine always insisted in taking her car when she was taking him and his mom somewhere, which was nice since her car was a lot fancier. He wasn't surprised—Geraldine almost always took charge. Well, in this case, it made sense, since she was trying to find them a house. They didn't usually both leave the office at the same time though, so this was special.

He had only been in this part of town once before; that was when Mr. Swann was taking Kasey and his folks to the airport, so he didn't see much—he was too busy talking and looking at all the neat things inside that ritzy car.

One thing that caught his eye now was how different it looked in this part of town—the houses were closer together and not as fancy. Then he figured it out: several Blacks had driven by—this must be the Black part of town. He had been over here a couple of times: last summer with Ed; they had to pick up Zeke on the way to work. This trip was lucky—he should find out more about this part of town, especially since his new job at school was to help Kasey fit in. He felt sort of stupid, actually. He had lived here almost all his life and almost never saw Black people other than the guys on Geraldine's crew. He had probably seen others and not thought anything about it. He was not aware that there was a requirement about where people lived. There wasn't—custom and tradition were just as effective.

Social and political issues had never interested him; he was oblivious to the social unrest and changes taking place. As far as race was concerned, he figured that people were people, no matter what color they were: that's the way God wanted it. It would be boring if everyone looked the same. That's the way God worked—there were different colored everythings: dogs, cats, trees—you name it. It was like those parallelograms: they were all sizes, but still the same thing; with people, same deal, only people were in 3-D and moved around.

The Black population was real low here from what he had heard… prob'ly just as many Cherokees. Until now, whatever affected him or his mom was all that got his attention. Nowadays, whatever he was drawing occupied his mind whether he was working on it directly or not. He liked his drawing of Mr. Swann mostly, but was still not satisfied. He might have to do more with the pen… it sort of stood out… made the pencil look pale. *how do you shade things with a pen? might have to start all over, actually—or finish the first one. the blue part turned out just fine…*

442

Now there were lots of drab industrial buildings and parking lots... *that one's a cannery... nothing interesting to draw.* Kasey was right—riding his bicycle would have taken a long time. Too cold outside for it to be any fun. The scenery became rural now—large open fields or pasture land, Julian wasn't sure which. A signpost announcing the airport was a mile ahead just rushed by—Geraldine was driving faster, now that they were out of the city limits. He watched carefully—maybe... *nope... looks like Mr. Swann's airplane is put away for now.*

The driveway to the Swann guesthouse was similar to the one at Randall's, only the house stood all by itself in a bunch of trees; no neighbors. *like a park or something.* Julian hopped out quick and opened the door for his mother. Inside Guy had poked him about that just after they passed the airport. He was supposed to remember things like that now; he didn't mind... this was fun too: he took his mother's arm and jauntily led her to the house.

Francine looked at Geraldine with a smirk; her almost-a-gentleman boy was as comical as he was gentlemanly—but she was charmed anyway. Geraldine masked her amusement well, but was pleased that something had stuck in his head—she was never certain about what would take and last beyond a week or two. She took a quick visual survey of the area—she was unfamiliar with this property —she concluded that it must be within the Swann Estate: no neighbors anywhere close. It wasn't within the gated portion—this was still a county road with a standard address—it had development potential.

> > *klannng- - - klannnng!* < <

The chimes rang out clearly; Julian thought they must be awful loud inside; sounded huge—like big bells.

Kasey had been on the lookout; when he saw the car turn into the driveway, he called his mother. They were waiting when Julian pushed the doorbell; he opened the door, delighted. The school jacket was a welcome sight.

In his eagerness to see Kasey, Julian was standing very close to the door: a wall of intense deep blue wool met his eyes first off—the arresting color of the shaggy sweater startled him—he had forgotten that Kasey's head was a little farther up. "We're here at last!" he bounced

443

happily. Kasey's countenance was reassuring—the eyes especially radiated welcome. He gestured to his left: "You remember my Mom—and Geraldine, o'course." He stood back so they could enter first.

Unaccustomed to greeting guests, Kasey was slightly awkward. "Umm... of course. Welcome. Won't you come in?" He stepped back to reveal his mother, standing back a few feet. Greeting was still awkward for her as well. As a young girl she had been trained to receive visitors as they were presented while she was seated in a parlor. All in her family were trained from an early age to display their royal heritage when anyone but family was present. Nearly twenty years in America had been unable to erase that completely; she seemed aloof and distant as a result, and forming social friendships was difficult. Most of her connections in Back Bay were a byproduct of Lewis' colleagues at the University. Race was not a factor in Cambridge. They had no other contacts or connections; the other inhabitants in the brownstone were cordial and friendly with one and another, but the apartments were more efficient than flexible; space was at a premium.

"We are so pleased you could pay us a call," she began. Sensing these ladies preferred informality, she gestured to the kitchen area. Now that Mason had returned to his regular duties, she was on her own. She rather looked forward to that, but it was certain to be a challenge in this open pastoral setting. Space was new: she was accustomed to having neighbors close by.

Julian grinned wide, assuming that Kasey would take the hint and spirit them away—he wasn't eager to sit in on a bunch of lady talk. He'd done enough of that already, times ten. When Kasey hesitated, he was quick on his feet:

"So show me around this place. Pretty fancy. I bet you have a nice bedroom."

Kasey's mother had given him permission with her usual nod. He had never had a guest of his own—this was thrilling, but a little frightening. He was uncertain, but followed Julian's suggestion. "Take off your jacket," he pointed to the coat hooks along the wall by the front door. "Then I'll give you the grand tour—I'll save my room for last."

Julian took off his coat quickly, glad that Kasey had taken his suggestion. Obviously, he needed to share a few secrets about how to

444

deal with mothers and their friends—Kasey wasn't used to them being around all the time. He hopped over. "Lead the way." The faster they got away the better—Geraldine might want them to hang around; he didn't need to hear again about how hard it is to find a house anywhere close to the university—especially in the winter time. He had heard all about that more than once already. Boring: **very** boring.

While the boys disappeared down the hallway, Candace assisted her guests in taking off their coats, grateful Kasey had thought of that. As she led them into the kitchen, she began by apologizing.

"I regret that all I can offer is tea," she gestured to the oval shaped table.

It was high quality, as was everything here; the room looked like an illustration for a high-end furniture store—it did not look lived in. Understandable, since they had just moved in.

"Whatever is easiest, Candace, please. We have been drinking coffee all morning at the office." Geraldine pulled out a chair. "There's no hurry."

Francine had a hunch. As she sat, she pulled out the chair closest to her. "Yes, unless you need something yourself, please sit and tell us how it's going—you haven't had time to settle in yet. We are so pleased you called." She patted the chair. "It must be difficult." She had taken note of the teakettle on the stove; no coffee pot in sight.

Candace sat, thankful for Francine's thoughtfulness; her tone of voice was comforting—at once she saw where her boy's open acceptance and friendliness had come from. It was unique in her experience, and genuine: precisely what she needed—now more than ever. It was a lifeline, evoking a facial expression that rarely found its way to the surface.

"Tell me: you haven't had a chance to go shopping, have you?"

The look of fear and anxiety said it all. She shook her head slightly. "I have no idea where to go or how. I've ordered deliveries so far." *Lewis uses the car to go to the campus—he has an office to move into.*

I thought so… Francine looked at Geraldine with her rarely used expression of decisiveness and authority. "We are going to fix that, here and now." She turned to Candace: "you can't run a household on take-out orders." This house was like a life raft: she and Geraldine needed to help get it ashore. She pulled the small spiral notebook out of her purse. "We are going to do first things first: I'll be secretary. You and Geraldine will tell me what to put down. Then we are going shopping. All three of us." She looked at Geraldine, determined. "IPA or Piggly Wiggly? You'll need to set up an account for her to use."

Geraldine sat up, wide eyed; she had to agree. "IPA, I think— better personal attention." She had forgotten that her 'protégé' could take command like that—she didn't have the occasion very often. As usual, Francine was completely right. Practical experience from having to raise a child and keep a husband happily fed: Geraldine had done neither, but she understood the value and the wisdom Francine had gained from experience. She could talk with Lewis about property later.

—◊◊—

The first stop on the tour was the living room; oversized, like everything in the guesthouse, the crew had left some of Swann's furnishings in place here and in the dining room. They needed to augment the furnishings from the Brownstone, where they had been living in about a fourth the space. Julian's drawing occupied a prominent position on the wall opposite the concert grand. Kasey did not point it out, assuming Julian would see it first thing.

Julian had never seen a drawing of his framed and hung on the wall—he didn't recognize it and his eyes didn't stop to look—framed paintings were not where his eyes stopped. His mind was doing a courteous tour that would end in Kasey's room, which is what his mind was readying itself to address: his new friend's room—that's what was important. Aside from Randall's, this was the only fancy new house he had been in. He figured this place would be the same; he had never been in Randall's room though.

Kasey was puzzled when Julian didn't say anything; he stepped over to a floor lamp.

446

Julian turned to see why he had turned on the lamp—"Whoah!" at once he saw: the lamp had been positioned to draw attention to the space. His reaction was complex: at first he did not realize it was his drawing. He had seen it briefly in the faculty meeting after it had been framed; his double take brought that image forward. Hanging on a wall changed its character significantly. He had not anticipated that; he didn't know what to say—he stared at it wide-eyed, unable to speak a word.

This is not the reaction Kasey expected. "Is something wrong?"

Julian was stuck: he had just gotten a dose of his own medicine, strangely enough, but didn't know it; it would take a while to understand that. "No, I guess not... I didn't expect it to look like this." It helped to talk about it, a little.

Kasey was surprised—like he was by virtually everything Julian said and did, but this was not comical.

"I've never seen one of my drawings framed and hung on a wall before." He stared at it briefly. It looked so different. Why would that be?

"What did you expect?"

Julian took his time. He shrugged: "I didn't. I never thought about that." He looked Kasey in the eye. "I guess that's kind of stupid, isn't it?" He gave his typical Charlie Brown clueless grin. "I always try to show who I'm drawing how interesting they are. Once they see it, that's that. Unless they want something fixed, of course." That hadn't happened yet.

"You've never seen one of you drawings framed?" Kasey found that hard to believe.

Julian shrugged. "No. Mostly I put them into the Scrapbook. I haven't drawn very many big ones like this. I'm kinda new at that. I guess Uncle Max framed the first one I did... that was at Camp last summer. I drew that for Mr. Jorgensen." He could tell Kasey wouldn't know about that. "See, this kid hurt himself real bad: he almost cut off his toe using a machete. So I asked if I could draw a picture of the medic bandaging it up. I was gonna put it in the scrapbook, but Mr. Jorgensen asked me to do one for the camp. I think he wanted to use it to tell about being careful when you use a machete. So Uncle Max found this large paper for me so I could do a big one. Well, with three people in the drawing, my sketchbook wasn't much good. So anyway, he gave me ten sheets of that big paper." He pointed at the drawing of Kasey: "Your drawing is on the last sheet!" he bounced happily. "That's on Camp Walker paper!" He gave the Groucho eyebrow lift.

Kasey was faced with a phenomenon that defied all: Julian seemed to value the paper more than the drawing. He was aware suddenly that he had a responsibility and a duty: while Julian was his helper in getting squared away at the new school, he would be Julian's helper in return. Somehow, Julian needed to realize what his art meant to others. Obviously, that's one thing his art class had not addressed. Having a purpose like that was at once thrilling and exciting: he had a mission at last. After he got a nod from Julian, he turned off the floor lamp so they could get on with the tour.

It didn't take long to run out of things to show and talk about—they took a quick peek at the patio from the room his dad planned to use for a study—it was too cold to spend any time out there. Next came the garage workshop; he had no idea what that was used for. The house was huge and mostly empty; he didn't show the three guest rooms on the far side of the two car garage. Both he and his sister had their own rooms, and his parents' master bedroom—he did not show those. The faint "woof" at his sister's door needed explaining: "That was Ike—our family dog. He is assigned to stand guard for my sister. He's very old now—probably hasn't much time left. You'll get to meet him later—and my sister, naturally—she's four years old as of last week." She was tucked away as usual—that's one of the ancient family customs his mother saw to: little girls especially were never seen or heard by visitors. He didn't want to spend any time here.

His room at last: as he opened the door he was somewhat embarrassed: even with his red chair from Belmont it looked empty; it contained his desk, bookcase and study chair from the Boston brownstone apartment, along with his double deck bunk bed in the corner; the room seemed to be waiting for more—table tennis and indoor exercise equipment would fit nicely... maybe a chess table. The room looked half empty because it was.

"Neato!!" Julian exclaimed, seeing the bunk beds. "What's it like? Do you sleep on the top one or bottom? You could trade off if you wanted." He skipped over to take a closer look. *Danny has one of these.* He had never seen it but heard him talk about it once. He saw the ladder on the end and turned eagerly: "Okay if I climb up?"

Kasey wasn't about to say no. "I guess so—I never use it. I think it's safe." He watched Julian climb up. Fortunately, the ceiling was a full 8 feet.

With a giggle he stepped up the ladder—he had always wanted to climb up onto one of these beds. He was about to crawl on and test it out, but stopped in time. "Oop! I almost hopped on—forgot about these!" He shook his right shoe, then climbed back down. He looked around the room. "Where's your closet?"

Kasey pointed to the walk-in door.

"Oh. Stupid me," he shrugged. "I thought that was another room."

"Well, I suppose it is." He stepped over and opened the door.

Julian zipped over: it was a combined walk-in closet and dressing room. *whoah...*

"It's just like my parents' room, only doesn't have a bathroom on the other side." Its extravagance was embarrassing.

Julian was at a loss to say anything; he was glad Sid wasn't here—he would have a wisecrack about this, for sure. *look at all the mirrors!* He didn't want Kasey to feel bad. "Well, I s'pose Mr. Swann has to be prepared for anything; this is his place, right?" *looks like a movie star's room in here.*

Just as Kasey turned off the light, they heard Geraldine call out:

"Julian... Kasey: your presence is required in the kitchen."

When Kasey peeked out into the hallway, she added, "bring your sister too, if you would, please," and returned to the kitchen.

He looked at Julian, hoping for an explanation.

Julian shook his head, resigned. *figures.* "Geraldine always takes over," he shrugged. "You'll get used to it eventually. The odd thing is she's usually right. Drives me crazy sometimes." He gave a 'what's a guy gonna do?' shrug. "That reminds me: when we get a chance, I'll fill you in on a few things—you're no longer safe from them: this isn't a boys' school, y'know." He recognized Geraldine's tone of voice: they were in for it for sure. He reached out to grab Kasey's belt but got a handful of wool sweater. "Oh—sorry." He looked at it closely… "Feels nice. Where'd you get this?"

"My mother made it. She likes to knit things." She was always working on something.

"Wow: she's really good. I've never seen one like this." He felt the texture. "Put this on your school clothes list." He tugged anyway: "We'd better scoot: second calls from Geraldine are a no-no." He looked at the sweater again. "You might wear that the first day, if you can." He had a hunch that would make a very good first impression. Inside Guy gave him a silent pat on the back—clothes were usually the last thing he thought about.

"I hate to say this, but it's too bad you don't have a radio." Julian used to hate radio pretty much until Mr. Swann showed him how to tune in Effem stations. "But I'm almost done." He had talked Kasey into letting him draw another sketch—this time sitting in his red chair—a good frontal angle. He was doing the usual tablet size drawing of course, since that was all he had—he always had his sketchbook along. He hadn't decided yet whether or not to make a big one of this. They had run out of things to do—too early to go to bed. Besides, after another one of those big suppers, going to bed early wasn't any fun. His folks were watching the TV. Neither of them wanted to do that anyway. They played with the dog for a while, but he was too old to do very much; they took him for a walk so he could go potty. He always spent the night with the little girl. *made sense*.

"Take as long as you want—I'm always comfortable in this chair." He missed the record player in the common room. It made studying possible with several guys hanging out. It had not occurred to him to ask for one of his own; he usually filled space like this with music of his own making—oboe or piano. His oboe was in the closet; the piano was in the living room—he didn't feel like going there after supper; he hadn't tried it out. His sheet music was still in a box. He was delighted when Julian suggested going to his room to do this. His red chair was good for reading and relaxing—and recuperating from stuffing himself at another epic meal dished up by that catering service. He was enjoying himself, actually, reviewing one of the most terrific days of his life—bizarre, and busy. He could write a book about it. The supper was only the second chapter: the shopping spree was the first. He was in his 'Rodin' position, as usual—the one he usually assumed in this chair to let his mind float wherever it wanted to—an assignment, a piece of music... and now a shopping spree in a supermarket, of all things.

Julian's mom and her friend—or employer, to be more accurate—had taken his mother shopping for groceries and supplies. He, Zeyla and Julian sat in the back seat. They had never gone shopping as a family—his mother usually did that by herself. He and Julian were the worker ants who fetched this and that. They had **boxes** full when it was over—the other lady, Mrs. Hallstrom showed up as well—the one who hosted that fancy meal with Mr. Swann. Each had a large cart full by the time they were done. He and Julian ended up loading all the provisions into her Lincoln; its pale lavender color had impressed both he and his mother. Her daughter was assigned to play with Zeyla while everyone else shopped. What a wild time! Especially with Julian's commentary. *I ought to jot those comments down... nobody else talks like that—they are unintentional and spontaneous, completely unpredictable.* Julian saw the world through special lenses or filters. Kasey felt privileged to witness it—it elevated him and reminded him how wonderful it was to be alive, to be here: everything was so fresh!

"I'm thirsty," Julian licked his lips. At home, he'd whip into the kitchen and pour himself a glass of water. He tucked the pencil into the spiral of his sketchbook and stepped over to Kasey. "Done for now." He handed it to him for a look-see—it was similar to the ones at school, slightly more detailed. "Sorry, I had to cut off your legs—need a bigger sheet for those," he joked. He stretched and yawned. He was kinda sleepy, actually.

Kasey fully expected to be stunned by this—he had seen what Julian could do. He looked at it closely... stunned was inadequate to

451

describe what he felt. It made him think of Belmont of all things: *this is what they saw.* At once he comprehended how they felt about him and his leaving; being reminded took his breath away. How could a simple pencil sketch do that? *this was done in such a short time!* He checked his watch and looked at Julian in amazement.

"What?"

"Fifteen minutes. You did this in fifteen minutes."

Julian shrugged. "Sorry about that. Didn't want you to get bored just sitting there—left out a lot of detail." He had several things in mind to do when he was back at his drawing table. "I always add that later."

His matter-of-factness was equally stunning. It was hard to believe—but he was witnessing it, living it as he sat here. It was not an act.

"It usually takes about that long; lunch hour is long enough; sometimes I don't take as long—ten or twelve minutes is usually plenty."

Kasey looked at him in wonder. After the revelation in the living room about never seeing his drawings framed, he didn't know what to think—how could he be so anonymous? So undiscovered?

"I thought it would be a good idea if you knew ahead of time—I do one of these every noon hour at school." He shook his head. "The girls go crazy over them for some reason," he shrugged. "You may want to bring a book. Lunch period is the same as any class for time." Actually, he was secretly hoping the piano would be moved somehow so that Kasey could play it once in a while. He didn't want to say anything about it until Mr. Barnes said to. He gestured to the tablet: "see anything that needs fixing?"

Kasey was not given to sarcasm, but he was sorely tempted. He sensed Julian's weak point: incredibly, that was an honest question. He seemed to have no idea how talented he was. Somehow, it came to him: that was one area where he might be of some use as a friend. *I might actually be needed someday to stand witness.*

"Okay if we go for a glass of water?"

452

Kasey snapped out of it and stood. "Yes! Great idea." He was thirsty himself. He looked at the drawing again. "Is it possible to show this to my parents?" He presumed they were still in the study watching television—his dad was fond of doing that in the evening.

"Sure. Good idea." Maybe they had a suggestion—he wasn't completely satisfied with it—needed something. Sometimes it helped to let it sit overnight and look at it with fresh eyes the next morning; sometimes a question or comment made him see the problem instantly. Mark was good at doing that for the Troop 9 Scrapbook drawings.

"Man, that hit the spot!" Julian licked his lips. He thought for a sec: "why would I be so thirsty?" he scratched his head. "Especially after a big supper like that. I had plenty to drink."

Kasey shrugged. "Can't say. I was thirsty too." He led the way to the study. "Something we ate must be dehydrating as it works its way down."

Julian had heard that word; Geraldine used it from time to time. Sometimes they used powdered milk on campouts; the box used that word; he figured it out: *just add water to un-dehydrate.* He had just un-dehydrated.

Their timing was perfect: a Phillip Morris commercial had just started. "Before saying good night I thought you'd enjoy seeing what Julian did a few minutes ago. This is one of his fifteen minute sketches." He masked his smirk—he was curious to see their reaction. As usual, they were on their cozy loveseat—that had always been where they sat to watch television.

"How thoughtful of you," Kasey's mother said before joining her husband in taking a look—after doing a double take, he was wide eyed and glued.

After a rather significant pause waiting for them to finish with his sketchbook, Julian felt a familiar urge: Mother Nature was calling—the drink of water must have woken her up. He crossed his legs: "Let me know if you think anything needs fixing." He gave Kasey his Cheshire cat grin, hoping that he would get the hint.

Lewis understood at once what Helgar was talking about—he had seen this sketchbook and went on about it for several minutes not long ago. "This is excellent work, Julian." He assumed he and his wife would be allowed to spend some time with it. He looked at his son: "Did you say fifteen minute—" he stopped in mid sentence when he saw Kasey's nod and facial expression. He was about to ask when Candace did what she **never** did:

"May we keep this a while, Julian? It deserves our full attention. Perhaps we can return it in the morning—unless of course, you were going to work on it some more tonight."

Candace knew how to phrase things—Julian heard his own mother asking the question. "Sure. No big deal." He remembered his mother's instructions just in time: "thanks again for inviting me to stay over." He grinned wide: "I get to sleep on the top bed! I never did that before." he bounced on his toes happily.

Lewis tore his eyes away from the drawing: he saw at once what his wife was so pleased about: this was a fundamentally happy boy. His son needed the opportunity to get away from the distorted world of pretentiousness and cynicism of a boarding school. The real world could be a happy place as well as dangerous. This lad was the perfect companion. The fact that he was an artistic prodigy was a coincidence. He couldn't remember ever meeting a more natural, normal, unassuming boy. He envied his son's good fortune. He resolved to let Frederick know how grateful they were. *we are going to find a cure: we have to. it's the least we can do.*

"Thank you, young man—you are welcome to stay in our home at any time. Sleep well." He reached up for a handshake.

Julian realized that Kasey's dad was being complimentary, but he didn't know how to react, so he just smiled. He wasn't sure what being a young man required, actually. At least he wasn't a little kid in his eyes—some progress there anyway. He reached out to take Kasey's mom's hand too—he thought he was supposed to. Geraldine forgot about this in her what-you're-supposed-to-do lesson, so he guessed. Obviously, moms weren't used to shaking hands.

At last, they were in the hallway. "Gotta scoot! Mother Nature called a little while ago!" Julian took off pumping his arms, doing a Barney short step shuffle—he knew where the bathroom was—this place had lots of them.

Kasey was delighted by the comedic exaggeration—he felt the urge now himself. "See you in my room!" he took off in the other direction—the small WC next to the kitchen was close.

Julian took longer than Kasey—not only had he accomplished a major delivery—he wouldn't need to do any visits in the middle of the night. An effort to brush his teeth without a toothbrush came next—a fingertip rub followed by a thorough rinse. *might as well...* He looked at himself in the vast mirror lit with fluorescent bulbs on all sides. Like everything here, the mirror was King Size. The hand soap was regular at least; the air wick bottle on the tank relieved his concern about what the next customer would have to deal with.

When he got to the room, Kasey was in bed already. His clip-on reading lamp was turned on, but he didn't have a book.

"Go ahead and turn off the overhead light—my bed lamp should be enough." That would save a trip over there.

oo—eee... Julian was a little surprised, but it made sense—he didn't have his tablet, and there wasn't anything to do but talk—might as well do that in bed. He was ready. He turned off the light. "Should I close the door?" He always did at home.

"Yes, thanks." That would protect him from Ike's good morning rise and shine wakeup lick across his face.

Julian shut the door and stepped over to the foot of the ladder. "This is gonna be fun: I've never slept in a top bunk!" he loosened his shoe laces. "That's better!" he remarked to himself aloud.

"What's better?"

oop... "Sorry—I talk to myself sometimes without thinking: taking my shoes off. I go around in my socks at home." He took his socks off next. "You might want to put on your sunglasses." He wanted to set Kasey at ease; being a little silly ought to do that.

"I'll bite: why sunglasses?"

"Cuts down the glare when I expose my totally white rear end. That part didn't get a tan last summer." The front didn't either, of course, but he didn't need to point that out. He pulled off his Levi jeans and laid them flat next to the shoes; he usually hung them up. Same with his shirt—since it was Friday, it was the coral Strad. There was so much space he could lay everything flat. His T-shirt and skivvies were next— he plonked those on top of his socks. With a giggle, he stepped over to the foot of the ladder and stepped on the bottom rung... *oh...* the rung was the about same circumference as a broom handle: it felt very different without shoes on: not the fun part. *too bad...*

It happened so fast it took Kasey by surprise. He had not offered to lend a pair of pajamas because they would have been far too large; he assumed Julian would sleep in his underwear. The last thing he expected was to discover that he slept in Nature's Own. No problem, of course— he had seen naked boys frequently over the years at Belmont. Even so, he never expected to see one in his own bedroom. This one was very white in the middle—he had seen that before; one of his housemates always spent the summer poolside. He tilted his head: a Julian phrase had popped up: *no big deal.* It fit the situation perfectly. He was tempted to do a Julian giggle: that matched perfectly as well. Unconsciously, a new worldview was beginning to form.

Julian crawled onto the bed and gave it a test bounce... *not bad. better than an army cot.* He knee walked toward the pillow.

Kasey had never seen knee bulges moving overhead—the mattress must not be very thick. He had not anticipated that. He heard another giggle—that seemed to be as much habit as anything, though it was interesting—Julian obviously found everything interesting—and fun; that was refreshing—and instructive.

Julian tugged at the bedspread to free up the pillow—it had been made up by the moving crew, and was more for appearance than function—the pillow flew into the air and hit the ceiling, then promptly fell to the carpet.

> > plop < <

"Oopsie!" Julian exclaimed. "Watch what you're doing, dum-dum!"

456

An upside down face appeared at Kasey's upper left.

"Sorry… I'm new at this. Can you do me a favor?"

Kasey was highly amused: an upside down grin looked incredibly bizarre. Chapter three of the day was underway: an upside down Cheshire cat grin with bouncing blond hair underneath was a perfect beginning for the next chapter—a perfect way to follow the comical hustle to the bathroom.

He had no idea where this chapter would go; he wasn't worried—he was thoroughly entertained—and happier than he ever remembered being. Glad to oblige, he flung back his covers and swung around. The pillow was just out of reach—he got out of bed and fetched it. He handed it up. "Any time." He noticed how dark it was up there. "Sorry there's no reading light up there." Julian was the first person to use the bed.

"'Sokay, actually—I don't have a book to read anyway." He rarely read in bed—always fell asleep. He squinted and looked closely at the PJs. "What are those?" he pointed.

Kasey looked down at his chest—he didn't see anything.

"On your PJ's. They're too small to make out from up here."

He looked at his pajama sleeve: "Oh! Little Pooh Bears." He extended an arm so Julian could see one up close; he hiked his shoulders and arms into a not-my-fault nothing-I-can-do-about-it.

"I know what you mean. Mothers. I **hated** those things… always got tangled up at night." He had a pair of Pooh Bear jammies when he was little. "I finally got my way on that. My mom let me sleep in my skivvies instead. She doesn't know I quit doing that yet—that's one thing I learned at camp last summer: it's the best way, hands down. You have to promise to keep it a secret, okay?" He had undressed so automatically he forgot all about leaving his skivvies on. *o well…*

The confidence delighted Kasey; needless to say, Julian's secret was safe… back to bed. He was halfway there when it struck him: *why not?!* He made a snap decision. In a flash he stood back up, removed his pajamas and returned to his usual place under the covers. His eyes batted back and forth unconsciously… busily assessing the new sensation: he was amazed at how different it felt; he had not expected that. The full length of his body seemed to be reporting in.

Julian was busily settling in, unaware that a momentous event had just taken place: he had inspired a mini revolution without knowing it. He propped himself up as if to read and sat with his hands folded in his lap. This wasn't anywhere close to being as comfortable as his own bed, but he wasn't fussy—he was used to sleeping on bear grass, leaves, and broken off branches, and now army cots. If he was sleepy, all he had to do was curl up and fade into dreamland, wherever he was. The problem now was simple enough: he wasn't sleepy any more. Besides, he had a few things he wanted to talk about.

"I really like your mom and dad."

?? Kasey couldn't quite hear. "What?"

Julian spoke a little louder: "I said I really like your mom and dad."

He still had trouble understanding—something about Dad… "Sorry, still not loud enough."

The upside down head reappeared: "I said I really like your mom and dad."

Kasey felt warm and flattered. "Thanks. I do too." The head disappeared. There was a pause—it was his turn to say something. "Your mom is nice too—and so is Geraldine." It felt odd to call her by her first name, but he didn't know her last name. *no one calls her by anything else.*

> > plop < < a soft sound to his left almost went unnoticed.

However, the overhead knee bulges going the other direction made a unique stretching sound: that stood out. So did the ghostlike figure with the pale midriff coming down the ladder at the foot of his bed: it had blond hair.

Julian snagged his pillow and pulled back the covers: "Scoot over a little." He propped his pillow against Kasey's headboard and jumped in, much as he had forced his way onto the piano bench at the university. "There. We don't need your folks thinking we're arguing or anything. Since we don't have walkie-talkies, I figured this was the best thing to do. I want to talk about stuff for a while. Okay with you?" It didn't occur to him to ask permission in advance.

Kasey gulped, almost unable to speak. "Um, sure." *pretty lame* "I don't mind." He was at a loss as to what Julian needed to talk about, but he was probably right about talking too loud. It felt strange to feel his bare upper leg and torso touching Julian's, but there wasn't room to leave a space. Complaining was out of the question—it felt all right—a little warm. *I'll get used to it.*

"Good. I mean, when else are we gonna have a chance like this? Nobody's gonna interrupt or take us off to do this or that this late. Besides, we need to get to know each other a little. And I promised to tell you about that movie. It's too complicated to write about—that would take weeks." Julian wanted to know about a lot of things— *quicksand, especially... and that one guy that kept saying 'it was written.' what was that about, anyway?!*

This was so unusual and so wonderful that Kasey had trouble figuring out how to respond or what to ask. Unlike Julian, he had not had a regular childhood playmate that he crawled under the covers with to take naps: he had a puppy and a devoted mother. As a result, he had no negative bias whatever—and the sheer power of Julian's positivity was irresistible. He was keenly aware that tomorrow he would be kicking himself for failing to think of what to ask or talk about.

Luckily, Julian had mentioned a good starting point: that movie date he talked about in his letter. "Movie... that's right. You talked about how the scout patrol solved your problem."

"Boy oh boy. I owe them big. I would never have found a date on my own—" He exhaled an exaggerated sigh of relief.

"So she was okay then?" He didn't know exactly what to ask, since he had never gone on a date himself.

"Yeah. She sure went through a lot of popcorn: over three buckets! It would take me a week to eat that much." He looked at Kasey with a grimace: "She had two dippers of hot butter sauce poured over each one! Bleah!"

Presumably she was a good sized girl. "I've never tried that." Popcorn had not played a large part in his life.

459

"Don't bother—makes your fingers all greasy; doesn't taste all that great either. Anyway: I wanted to ask you about that guy Lawrence of Arabia. I had never heard of him before going to that movie. I figure that you must know about him." He looked at him directly again: "I don't suppose you saw the movie, did you?"

"Almost. Dad was going to take us—my mom really wanted to see it. She comes from that area, you know. But the move here changed everything. We plan to see it when it comes around on its second run. Evidently that's a sure thing. The guys at Belmont were talking about it too."

"Huh." Julian was glad to hear that. "Ask your dad if I can tag along. I really want to see it again." *maybe he knows what was written.*

Kasey was curious about Julian and girls—he realized that he would face that problem one day himself. But something didn't compute: a little while ago, he said he drew a picture of a girl every day during lunch. He could understand why they were thrilled to have themselves drawn—he knew the feeling! Learning that he shared that feeling with lots of girls gave him pause. He must like girls… why else would he be drawing their portraits?

"I was wondering just now about your date: why didn't you ask one of those girls—you know, the ones you draw portraits of every day.

"Eew. No thanks! That's the **last** thing I'd want to do! You don't know those girls! They'd be scrapping and pulling each other's hair out trying to be the first, they'd all want a movie date—all I'd be doing would be going on movie dates. Geraldine would love it—she'd even pay for them." He nudged with his elbow: "she'd have to: they cost a lot of money! Over ten dollars when you add in all the candy and drinks!" He shook his head: "She's been trying all year to trap me into I don't know what. We need to talk about that some day: you don't want her to be your mom's boss the way she's my mom's boss. No sir-ee!" He fluffed the blankets up and down to let some air get in. "Getting too warm in here." He fluffed a little more.

Both boys looked down automatically—not intending to notice what was underway. Since the reading light was still on, they could see both laps and what occupied their center; the one on the left was particularly visible: not only was it white, the paucity of pubic hair

460

insured that the occupant, one Little J, was entirely visible—flatteringly so. Both were slowly enlarging, but neither had reached the point of making their control center aware of it: it was the body heat more than anything.

By way of apologizing, Julian put the blame on the usual suspect. He let the blankets cover them again. "Thanks... feels lots better. Body heat does that, you know. Little J gets out of line when it gets too warm down there." He shrugged "One of those things." He figured Kasey would agree.

"Little J?"

"Yeah. You know," he pointed to his chest: "I'm Big J." He pointed to his crotch: "He's Little J."

Kasey's jaw dropped.

Julian pointed to Kasey's chest: "You're Big K, he's Little K." He had used his "No Big Deal" tone of voice.

Whether it was his matter-of-fact-ness or the construct itself or both, Kasey exploded in hysterics. After a day full of Julian's witticisms and originality, this broke the dam.

At first it was startling—Julian had never evoked a reaction like that. After watching and listening a while, it became infectious and he started giggling too.

At long last, Kasey ran out of whatever had driven that sustained outburst, a complete total anomaly. His nose was running and his eyes watering—he didn't have a handkerchief handy, so he leaned forward and used the bedspread.

"Oh boy, Julian." He took a couple of deep breaths. "Sorry, but that took the cake!"

Julian was amazed and sympathetic. Somehow, he understood how sheltered and inexperienced Kasey was. It widened his sense of responsibility and purpose... that felt good. They were about the same age, but Kasey was both a little brother and a big brother. Julian was in the middle: exactly where he was needed.

In control at last, he looked at Julian with an accusatory grin and flipped the covers back. "Just look at what you did: you woke him up!"

461

All the hysterics and laughing had thrown a switch, and Little K was almost standing tall.

Julian looked down. This time he was drop-jawed: "Say! What happened to your PJ's?" He had not realized they had been taken off. *when did he do that?*

"I removed them before you came down here, of course. I wasn't expecting you to notice—or to come down. After your question about Pooh Bear, I wondered what it was like. You were still settling in."

"Neato!! See what I mean?"

"Yes I do. I don't know if I can get away with it though."

"Sure you can. You can always go to bed in your undies and take 'em off in bed." He sat forward. "Mind if I look?" He had never seen a dark one before. He didn't wait for permission—somehow he knew it was okay. "Not as big as Tom, but plenty big enough." He looked as closely as he could without touching. "These guys are really interesting. Hard to figure out sometimes though… man, you have a lot more hair down here than I do." He sat back. He would like to have felt it, maybe see how it worked—maybe stroke it like he had Tom's, but he figured that would be going too far. "I learned a lot about them last summer at camp," he said that off handedly: he did not plan to go into detail. He frowned. "I just realized something: there were no Blacks." He looked at Kasey, concerned. "I wonder if they are allowed. I never thought about that. Mark said they have a Black Troop. He tried to get permission to have a Black join Troop 9, but they wouldn't let him because of that." He frowned. "That's wrong. Plain wrong."

Kasey didn't disagree; he had not been discriminated against directly, but he had known all his life that the world was not a welcoming place for anyone with dark skin. He didn't relate to the term Black, personally. Focusing on that issue was more than difficult: he still had not recovered from the shock—the novelty—of having someone looking closely at… *aha! now I get it!* at his Little K, as if it was an exotic plant or whatever. In his own bed…

A new problem, an unexpected one: unplanned for, a complication had 'arisen.' Little K, his newly named pecker, was demanding attention. With Julian here, that posed a problem. They were still uncovered, very much on display.

462

Julian noticed the glance just given to Little K and understood at once. He nodded knowingly, "There he goes. They do that all the time." He looked Kasey in the face. "That's one reason it helps to give him a name: he has a mind of his own—they all do. It helps to have a name to use when he forces you to pay attention. How else are you gonna be in charge?" He looked down again. "At least he isn't drooling yet. Once he does, you're cooked... won't let you alone until you give him what he wants. Until you do, he's in charge."

They both watched it pulse a few times.

"Why isn't Little J..." Kasey had difficulty—his active vocabulary did not have the appropriate term on file. He couldn't remember what any of his roomies would say—he usually ignored their crude wisecracks about each other's anatomical features.

"Ready to play?" Julian offered an ending to his inquiry. "Who knows. See what I mean? These guys have a mind of heir own; they do whatever they want whether you like it or not, no matter where you are, no matter what time of day or night. I've been trying to figure out Little J for over a year. Tell you what though: I've been saving up my questions for that Health class we have coming up. I figure they'll know." He glanced at Kasey sympathetically.

Their peripheral view picked up a major pulse in Kasey's lap. Automatically, they looked down: a glistening bead emerged, twinkling happily thanks to the very bright reading lamp; in this location, its 60 watt bulb seemed like 100.

"Oh-oh," Julian warned. They looked down to see more and discovered that Little J was on the move—a sympathetic response more than anything. Julian offered an aside: "sometimes I think they can talk to each other—some kind of silent signal or code."

Kasey suppressed an urge to laugh—this entire episode, or whatever it was, defied description.

"They're pretty sneaky—they make it feel good to keep you interested; they gradually increase the pressure until you hafta give in."

Little J was up full now. Julian pulsed him to see how ready he was. "See? He's trying to catch up with Little K." *...darn it, Little J...* Julian realized where this would have to go. His job was to do his best to make it a positive experience—he didn't want Kasey to feel guilty or taken advantage of. He sensed that making it fun was essential. He needed it to be "no big deal" when he knew it was probably a very big deal. His Inside Guy had been of no help so far. He continued his matter of fact narrative.

"I learned a lot about these little guys last summer." He turned to Kasey again: "If you ever get the chance to go to a boys only camp, you should take it. I never expected it to be a big help, but it was. Makes sense—a whole camp full of guys with the same question and problem—you swap information, and learn lots of ways to handle these guys—no way to learn all that on your own. Besides, it was lots of fun." He nudged with his elbow: "I just figured it out! That's one reason why they have those camps, I bet! That way they don't have to talk to us about that stuff! They let us figure it out for ourselves! Yeah! Why else would they put us in tents out in the wild for a couple of weeks without any grownups around?" He shook his head, sadly. "Sometimes it takes me a while to figure things like that out."

This situation was growing awkward—Kasey was fast getting to a point of no return; a casual discussion no longer fit his need. So far everything Julian had said made perfect sense, and was useful and good to know—but what was he going to do now? "Umm... you're quite right, of course... but..." he looked down at his lap again. "I think I have reached that point you talked about."

"Yikes. You are right: now is the time." he looked at Little J. "I will too in a minute. We'd better get it over with. There's a lot of ways to take care of these guys—you learn a lot about that at camp. I can show you one or two, if you're interested." He tilted his head. "Or, if you want, I can climb back upstairs. This bed is well built—it can handle it, I think."

It had never occurred to Kasey that there was more than one way to take care of this.

"Either way, we're going to need to clean up afterward. Do you have a box of Kleenex handy? Or a hand towel?" he lifted his right arm to flash the scout salute. "Be prepared. Good advice."

464

"I don't know… there might be something in that dressing room… or I could get something in the bathroom…" he put his hand over his mouth. "I think my parents are still watching TV though."

Julian swung his legs out. "Let's go see." He headed for the closet.

Kasey was right behind. He reached over Julian's hand to flip on the switch—Julian was off by several inches. The light was blinding; he had not searched any of these drawers—there might be something. Julian started on the other end. It didn't take long—empty, all of them. They looked at each other, disappointed. At the same time they glanced to the side and behold: there they were, in nature's own, staffs of life wagging patiently.

"Wow…" Julian was fascinated. The contrast was almost comical: tall and short, dark and light. It was a sight that neither expected and both found very interesting—they had to stop a minute and look. It was unlikely to ever occur again, and both wanted to remember it—neither understood why, nor cared. It was not an erotic event, oddly enough, for either boy. It was interesting and kind of fun. Julian was surprised at how long his suntan had lasted. He'd never been this tan; working for Geraldine made this happen. He swung his hips back and forth. "Little J wants to wave at those silly kids in the mirror."

Kasey wagged his hips too. His giggle was lower—he was a baritone while Julian was a tenor. A droplet flew to the left and landed under Julian's right arm, evoking a laugh.

"We better hurry!" Julian scurried out to the bedroom door. He waited for Kasey: they needed to be super careful. He opened the door a crack and put his ear against the opening. Kasey put his ear up higher. "Hear anything?" Julian whispered.

They listened carefully: nothing. Slowly, Julian pulled the door open… he inched back a little and bumped into Little K accidentally—he knew that, because it was wet. "Sorry…"

Kasey wasn't—it felt good. He didn't mention that, largely because it hadn't registered in his head yet—the chain of events tonight was too fast paced to assimilate—a waiting line had formed—sorting it out would have to be done later.

Julian listened carefully, then poked his head out to look down the hallway to the den—or family room, where the TV set was. The light was still on, door open... a faint sound—music background of some kind. It was one of those movies that didn't have loud noises... still going. He pulled his head back. "I think we're okay; you lead the way."

Kasey poked his head out and listened... Julian was right. He swung the door open wide and tiptoed hurriedly across the hallway to the bathroom. Julian was right behind. The door was open, fortunately. He waited for Julian to be in the room before he turned on the light. He closed the door quietly.

"Perfect!" Julian whispered. He knew exactly what to do: they had stocked this up after the shopping trip. Thanks to that, a lower cupboard was full of toilet paper rolls. He snagged one and handed it to Kasey. He opened an upper cupboard: sure enough, a stack of bath towels. He grabbed two of those as well. He grinned: "we can use these in the morning after we take a shower!" Kasey nodded back eagerly. Julian turned to the mirror and waved. "Better wave our thank yous." The refection was similar to the one in the dressing room—it was funny this time. Their staffs were still up full—Julian wagged again. "Let's wave back together!"

They stood side-by-side and wagged. "I need a stool to stand on," he shrugged, then covered his mouth. "I forgot to whisper! Sorry. You lead the way, okay?"

Kasey felt like he was in a movie: *this does not happen in real life.* He stepped to the door and turned off the light. He opened the door quietly. They did the listen test again: all clear.

Halfway to the room, a clearly audible fanfare broke the silence: the movie had just ended! They stepped on the gas. Julian closed the door the second he was in the room. They had made it!

"Whew!" Kasey was relieved.

Julian was on task already. "Let's go over by the bed." He spread out a bath towel. "Side by side, or across from each other?"

Kasey had no idea; this was so far from anything he ever imagined it was all he could do to pay attention, let alone keep up.

466

"Let's sit across from each other—easier that way, I think." His session with Danny and the sun cream came to mind—*that was a good one*. He spread the other towel so that they were end to end, about an inch apart. He turned to Kasey. "You take this one—get on your knees. This thick carpet is perfect... more room down here. Besides, on your bunk everything would be too bouncy. Unwrap that TP and put it on one side—we might need to grab it quick." Kasey hadn't moved yet. "Makes it easy to clean up—we flush the evidence down the drain!" he grinned.

Kasey still hadn't caught up—he hadn't been here before. Like the banquet where he met Julian, this was another game! His wide-eyed stare revealed that he was probably able, but stepping over to that towel seemed... he didn't understand why he hadn't moved.

Julian, not thinking too clearly himself, reached over and gave Little K a tug. "Tell Big K to get a move on. Little J wants to get started."

Julian had said that to Little K, but it broke through above. Kasey stepped over in a single stride—long legs helped. He unwrapped the roll of tissue and put it on the right, next to the open space. *Julian is right about the carpet.*

"So: the first question is do you want a dry one or a wet one?"

Another wide-eyed look. "Wet one?"

"Yeah. I learned two ways: dry is like this—" he mimed an up-down with his empty hand. "Or wet—with saliva and the stuff oozing out the top—it feels a lot more intense... I like it better, myself. You prob'ly know some of this already."

Kasey shook his head slowly. "I don't think so..."

"That's okay—it isn't hard. You'll catch on real fast—I sure did. The second question is whether to do it to yourself, or to the guy across from you. You pro'bly haven't done that before. It's just as easy, actually.

how can I decide such a thing?! Kasey glanced down at Little K: he had just emitted another droplet—a big one that spilled over—like a dripping candle. His voice was unsteady: "Y-you decide."

"You sure?"

He nodded. He trusted Julian.

"Okay: sit up straight and reach out with both hands, then hold onto my shoulders." Julian sat up straight. "Good. It's important—you need to steady yourself, especially at the finish line." He cupped his right hand and filled it with saliva. Simultaneously, he held the base of Little K with his left thumb and forefinger, and took the tip into his right hand and gave the top three inches a good coat by twisting his hand back and forth—enough to assure that it was well coated with a mix of saliva and natural drip. Like glycerin, it was smooth and slippery. He estimated that Little K was slightly larger than Little D, but not as large as Little T—or Not-so-little T: Tom had the biggest he had ever seen or played with.

"OH!" The sensation was immediate and profound: Kasey had never had this kind of sensation: it was ten times what he knew. His simple one-handed masturbations were learned a couple of years ago at Belmont when he had stumbled onto a circle jerk by mistake. This was an order above that—two or three orders.

Julian proceeded, including the entire shaft. He was very good at this, thanks to several episodes at Camp Walker. He was certain that Kasey was unable to do a mutual one—that would have to happen later if at all. "Now, when you want, slowly push forward and pull back a few times—see how that feels… that's it. Perfect. You can keep doing that until the end if you want—if you do, that's when you hafta hold on tight. I'll hold my hand in one place. You can close your eyes, or watch." Julian braced himself—Kasey was a lot taller and stronger—enough to tip both of them over. Needless to say, he intended to watch every minute. He figured this was a one-time event—he had to make it as good as he could. Besides, he really enjoyed doing this.

Fortunately, Kasey didn't spoil the occasion for himself by firing too soon. He was able to get 'a good one.' He delivered a huge load, at a substantial velocity, striking just above Julian's stomach. Not a drop went astray—the carpet and towel were spared. "UNH!!!" the last thrust was full force—he held the position several seconds before sitting back on his haunches.

Julian was very pleased at how that had gone—he had done well. He needed to let Kasey rest a minute; he looked at the expression on his face happily. He thought it best not to make his usual wisecrack and spoil the moment. After a minute the sensation of liquid rolling down toward Little J drew his attention. He reached over and tore off a little tissue.

That broke the afterglow spell perfectly. "Wow." Kasey shook his head. "I don't know what to say, Julian." At a loss, he shrugged. "Thank you hardly covers how I feel."

"Yeah. I know what you mean. Especially since it was your first time." He enjoyed sharing the moment with his friend. "I'm glad it was a good one." He reconsidered that. "Actually, they're all pretty good. The first one is special though, I hafta agree." He paused briefly. "Some guys do it a lot, I guess. You can both do it at once when you get the hang of it." He didn't go into detail—it was time to deal with Little J. He sat up and grinned wide: "now you get to do it!"

Kasey's eyes opened wide. He had not paid sufficient attention to the instructions—or to the implications: **it was his turn!** He had never touched anyone else down there. He gulped and took a deep breath: this was a test as well as a game, and he intended to pass it. He sat up and waited for Julian to hold him by the shoulders. He looked down: Little J was there, all right, and ready: he had drooled at least a couple of times. He looked at Julian in the eyes—he wasn't sure why. He saw trust and confidence, and… he saw a friend. He cupped his hand and filled it with saliva—and with his left thumb and forefinger, held Little J by the base and pressed. His right hand followed the same steps Julian had, as if he knew what to do. The difference was real: his fingers were much longer. They were pianist fingers. They knew all about touch—Julian was in for a new twist. Even though Kasey had not done this before, his fingers had learned what Little K liked—that would have to do.

He alternated watching Little J and Julian's face—the tip of his tongue peeked out from one side, lending a childlike charm. He had not studied Julian's face closely until now. It was remarkably clear and fair—and quite handsome. The clown was quiet for the time being… he felt honored and privileged.

Kasey was concerned momentarily: Julian's eyes were still closed. Had he done this well enough? He'd sat back with a big smile, but that was a while ago. *what should I do? oh...* He reached for the roll... *wait...* he held his forefinger under one of the larger splotches on his stomach to stop it from sliding any farther; he examined a swipe of it close-up. *looks just like mine...* he tasted it... *hmm...* with a shrug, sucked his fingertip clean. *just the same.* He tore off some toilet paper.

Julian opened his eyes. "Sorry... sometimes I do that—I try to make it last as long as I can. Gotta hand it to Mother nature: she rewards you if you do what she wants—or what Little J wants... same thing, I s'pose."

Relieved, Kasey nodded emphatically. He didn't know how to articulate what he was feeling.

"Thanks. You did a good job." He looked down at the resting but not yet flaccid problem children. "Boy." He didn't know what to say. "What a surprise. I didn't exactly plan on this; I bet you didn't either."

That was an understatement. Kasey nodded twice.

"I expect you're all tuckered out—I sure am."

Kasey wasn't, especially

"But before we call it a night, I think it's important to talk a little."

Kasey tilted his head: *now what?*

"See, the thing is, I don't want you to feel bad about this tomorrow. Things always look different the next day. That can be good, or bad. I don't want you to feel like we did something wrong or anything. I want to be your friend, your pal as well as your 'Buddy' at school. I'd hate it if I wrecked that because Little J took over.

"No, no! Don't even think that!" The intense brown eyes staring at him were proof of Julian's concern and his honesty.

"Thanks, but it's really important. This has to be a secret—I never did this exact thing before. I'm glad I did, don't get me wrong. But I don't plan on making a habit of it or anything. I'm not planning to jump on your bones every time we're alone in the dark."

Kasey had to giggle at that—Julian's terminology was special. He had never had a chat like this—it was a surprise like everything else

470

connected with Julian. He didn't want to foul everything up by saying something stupid or hasty—he stuck to his inclination to keep his mouth shut unless he knew what he was talking about.

Julian had an afterthought: "and I don't want you to think anything's wrong if I **don't** 'jump on your bones.'" He remembered Sid last summer—he thought Kurt was mad at him when exactly the opposite was true. "If anything is wrong, I want you to promise you'll say so—no matter how hard it is. That's super important. The minute you assume something without checking, you start to mess everything up for yourself."

Kasey was amazed at Julian's clear headed thinking.

"Last summer I had a pal at camp that did that—luckily, I got a friend to help him out. I was right, too: it turned out the opposite of what he thought was true."

He wondered if Julian was talking about himself.

"That's another thing: I'm not going to mention any names— you'll prob'ly meet these guys eventually. I learned a long time ago how bad it is to tell anyone's name when you're talking about them when they aren't around. Unless you have their permission, o'course. It doesn't take long for things to spread around. It can really hurt people. I figure I can talk about the what if it's important, but not the who."

Kasey felt a lump in his throat—his emotional level just went off the chart. This was twice as strong as the one that hit him as he left Belmont. He actually missed those guys—but he would be devastated if he had to go back. Julian was the first person, aside from his parents, who actually connected with him **personally, directly**. Others included him, or allowed him: Julian connected directly. It was so wonderful, so powerful. Now he understood what Professor Marchbank was talking about in that lecture about Plato and Alexander the Great. It gave him a rush. He doubted if Julian knew about that—he came by it naturally— just like his artistic talent: it was pure, it was inborn.

Julian was afraid he was going too fast—Kasey wasn't saying anything. He looked at him closely: "Are you okay?"

Kasey's eyes bulged: "Are you kidding?! I've never been so okay in my life, thanks to you!" He reached out, grabbed one of Julian's

471

hands and squeezed hard. "I'm sorry I haven't said much—I feel like I arrived late and need to pay attention so I won't make a fool of myself. So far, you have been filling the blanks perfectly. I'm not as smart as you think—I get extra credit for keeping my mouth shut."

Julian laughed. "I know what you mean—me too." They had that in common. "I'm glad we talked a little. We have lots of things coming up; neither one of us knows what or how. School most of all, but only half of that is classes. There's all kinds of stuff..." he shrugged. "There's Geraldine, there's **girls**—**everyone** will want you to be on the basketball team o'course. And other friends... you're gonna need to know more guys than just me. You gotta figure out what you're gonna be when you grow up..." He paused. "My job is to help make it fun. That's about the only thing I'm any good at, now that I think about it."

Kasey laughed. "You **are** good at that," he shook his head. "You forgot to mention that you are a great artist. You're going to be famous someday." He had overheard Mr. Swann tell his father that.

Julian blushed. "Thanks... but I'm not so sure I can do that for a living. Geraldine says I need to find something I can count on when I'm out of high school. She's always right about that kind of thing. Besides, I only started that serious drawing at camp last summer. Before, all I did was the Troop 9 Scrapbook. I kinda spread out from there." He was just starting to understand it, thanks to Mr. Swann. "I do like it—no, I **really** like it. But I'm just a beginner. That's why I like the Art Class so much: it shows me about other stuff. Otherwise, all I know how to do is use a pencil; I do okay there. I'm getting better all the time." He grinned, "I can draw elbows now!"

Kasey laughed, "You are..." he hated to be corny, but it fit: "you are too much." *elbows!*

Julian yawned and shook his head. He was a little thirsty. He decided not to go get a drink—it would mean waking up under pressure, probably with a stiffy. He glanced down—still not all the way limp. It usually took a long time after one of those good ones. Sometimes Little J wanted a second one. That was probably not a good idea.

Kasey got a kick out of seeing him shake his golden locks. The puppy in him leapt into view. He was reminded of the first time he saw Julian—he thought he looked like Alexander when he was fifteen. He still did, in a way—*a little on the scrawny side.* Alexander of Macedon was an athlete and a scholar.

"I spose we ought to talk about tomorrow morning—do we flip a coin for who takes a shower first? or does your dad take one in the morning?" *Mark always likes to take his in the morning.*

"They have a shower and bathroom of their own—it's part of the bedroom!"

"Wow—I think Randall's folks do too." Julian wondered why some people wanted all these bathrooms everywhere.

"It's a double shower too, just like the one across the hall."

"Double shower?"

"Yes—made so two or even three can use it at the same time."

"Huh. I've never seen one of those." *perfect for me and Mark... good to know.*

"We might be able to do that after breakfast—I think Mr. Swann will be here around ten to take you home."

"Oo. I almost forgot about that!" He sat up: "Maybe I'll get to ride in that neat car again. Maybe Mason will be driving again!" He grinned wide.

Kasey enjoyed watching Julian talk—he was always so animated.

"Kind of handy, actually—I drew a picture of him for Christmas. Now I can give it to him." He put his finger on his lips. "Don't tell... I want it to be a surprise."

"My lips are sealed."

Julian giggled and did the zipped lip swipe. "That's what we do in scouts: we give the zipped lip promise." His day was about done—he blocked an urge to nod off—he did that sometimes when he was tired. "I'm done for. If it's okay with you, I'll climb back up." He shrugged: "I'd like to cuddle up with you, but your bed is a little too narrow. I'd prob'ly fall out in the night... 'sides, I don't trust Little J: I wouldn't put it past him to poke you a good one. He really likes a second round." He stood. Little J was still slightly puffy. Julian wagged him a couple of times: "see what I mean?"

Kasey got an instant pulse from Little K. He opened his eyes wide: *they **do** talk to each other!* He looked down in disbelief.

Unlike several of his scout friends, Julian had never slept overnight with anyone. He had not thought about doing that at all—probably because his mind had settled the matter of who he wanted to sleep with long ago: Mark. Until that could happen, sleeping over with anyone was unlikely. Unless someone else tried to engineer it, even being considered was unlikely. Randall would have leapt at the chance, but he was not sufficiently forward, nor cunning enough to contemplate or daydream about it. Short of being trapped together in a blizzard, it wouldn't happen. For Julian, the only purpose for going to bed was to get some sleep.

If Kasey's bed had been as wide as his was, he might have yawned, said good night and turned on his side and fallen asleep at once. Instead, he yawned and announced: "Mr. Sandman is here," and pointed to the top bunk. Julian stooped across to fetch his pillow, causing Little J to come within an inch of Kasey's nose.

It didn't connect, but the pheromones certainly did, in considerable concentration. That was yet another first: an aroma that Kasey had never encountered: pungent, yet sweet. It happened so fast that it took a while to register. The fact that it would linger for several minutes made slipping off into dreamland slightly difficult: Little K was trying to compete for attention. Kasey prevailed for the rest of the night, finally. But just like Little J, Little K had put it on his unseen calendar.

29 *Littel Capitan*

Because it had grown colder—or, to be more accurate, seemed to be colder because of the increase in humidity and surface wind, Helgar deemed it wise to begin the day with a two mile hike to the West parking lot on the way rather than head straight for the climbing opportunity called Littel Capitan. It was a bad day for a climb of any kind, particularly one that required roping up—especially with a party of ten, all but three without any climbing experience. He suggested as much to Tom as they enjoyed a third sausage link and a coffee refill; his presumption that Tom would agree was correct—he still preferred that Tom remain the titular leader of this expedition. They took all the gear along just in case.

The rather hefty breakfast took some time—they weren't in a hurry—no one was eager to crawl out of their sleeping bags anyway, and their objective was relatively close by. They had waited until well after sunrise, since there was no need to do otherwise. No one wanted to suggest a change of plans though: they had provisions for a second super supper—and, of course, looked forward to a second night in the tent. Unless the weather turned really bad, everyone was looking forward to that more than anything. They weren't expected home until Monday morning. No one was planning on a big New Year's Eve party, so there was no hurry. No storms had been predicted; it was supposed to be storm free for several days. Helgar hoped the wind would die down in an hour or two when the sun was a little higher. The cloud ceiling had insulated them during the night, but now it blocked the sun. It might open up for a while like it had yesterday—that could add fifteen or twenty degrees—that would make a huge difference.

Well, it was late December, after all… the change in conditions would not be problematic in town, but at the base of Littel Capitan, the difference was considerable. The installation was in an open meadow without trees of any size to shield it from the prevailing wind. Helgar was an experienced climber, and even at this altitude, knew it was a no go without any open sun. A five to ten mile an hour wind on a rope was not going to be any fun when it was forty degrees out—the wind chill took it closer to freezing than most realized. Only four of them had a pair of gloves to begin with—and regular gloves were less than ideal on a rope anyway—they could slip off easily, usually at the worst possible minute. Heavy duty boots weren't the best thing either, though this particular climb wouldn't be a problem.

They had done a complete tour around the base—it was a terrific training site, with pre-bolted routes for both adults and minors, ready for carabiners and figure 8s—pitons would not be needed. Both vertical and lateral routes were well plotted as well as a full top to bottom chimney; a few cracks, slits, toe perches and handholds were on both the front vertical face and the overhangs on the back side. It was a recreational installation as well; a sign outlining proper procedures and dangers was posted: it was not for use without a qualified instructor present, and its hours were regulated. Technically, it was not open off-season—use was supposed to be scheduled at one of the Park Guard stations. Climbers were required to check in and out, lest someone fall or need assistance; there was no way to call for help. Nonetheless, it was wide open. Helgar thought a summertime visit would be fun and worth the effort for both him and Randall, and Andy too. At only fifty feet high, it was a half day project at most, weather permitting.

On the reverse side a narrow stairway with a woven steel cable guardrail served the hardy and adventurous tourist who wanted to see what the view from the top was like. A six foot wide platform occupied the center twelve feet. Four foot high four inch by four inch hardware cloth fencing reinforced with galvanized pipe every eighteen inches made it safe, but At Your Own Risk danger signs were visible from every approach and vantage point.

The boys were curious enough, disappointed enough, and young enough to undertake the challenge; their egos required it. With Randall's camera along, they would be able to prove they had been on top. With all the gear along as well, they might be able to get away with pretending they had come up the other side. The load was heavy by the time they reached the top, but that was a small price. The wind was on the other side, so the climb up the stairway wasn't bad at all. Posing for a few photographs was all they wanted to do: it was not nice up there, and the view was not particularly interesting. Helgar valued the exercise, and was pleased to discover it was relatively effortless—he was still in passable shape after all. He treated them to his hearty Viking battle cry when they reached the top. No echo—Randall was disappointed. They waited up there while Randall descended to get a shot of them waving from the top.

In spite of the miserable weather and the disappointments, they were in high spirits when they returned to camp. Thanks to the stash in the Rover, dry firewood was on hand—they had plenty left from the late breakfast; the campfire was up and roaring in no time: they were ready for that! And, for the T-Bone steak and baked potato supper—not to mention the baked beans. They were able to start feasting in a little over half an hour; about forty minutes of daylight remained. Ordinarily, this would be early. But they had earned this meal, and their metabolism was prepared to tackle it, regardless. They had skipped lunch, opting for a few strips of jerky.

Tom decided not to make the macaroni and cheese—it wasn't in demand anyway; it could stay in the boxes until summer. He supervised cooking the T-bone steaks over the open fire while Helgar completed the baked potato operation, another Sharples' specialty the Weber made possible. Wrapped in foil, the medium size russets had been pre-baked and prepped to have Lucian's special warm-up kit applied: after being split lengthwise and pinched to make them more absorptive, a hefty square of butter was inserted; the potatoes were then rewarmed on the Weber grill for fifteen minutes while the other 'condiments' were prepared: in lieu of bacon bits, a six inch length of pepperoni had been diced and crisp fried; two large sweet onions were chopped into quarter inch chunks and both were stirred into a pint of sour cream: two or three heaping tablespoons of this were then plopped into the re-warmed potato: sprinkled with coarse black pepper, and voila! a gastronomic delight to sit along side a freshly cooked T-bone steak and a cup of baked beans. Helgar did not sprinkle them with Tabasco sauce, but the small bottle was put on the table for the adventuresome, alongside the A1 steak sauce. To the scouts all this would have seemed like campout heresy, but the cold weather and the physical activity dismissed any reservations—they were readying themselves for another night of hibernatory cuddling. Besides, it wasn't a scout outing anyway.

Robin paused a minute to comment on the potato: "Man, I wasn't that big on potatoes before!" he looked at Helgar. "You get these often?"

Helgar tipped his head—"No, these are a recent discovery. I had a short chat with the head chef—we use their service frequently—my wife's favorite. I tried them once before, and thought they'd be just the ticket here. They aren't an everyday dish. Calorie count is way too high. Eat these for a week and you will put on a few pounds." He did not mention the peculiar 'side effect.'

Tony had a hunch about that very thing when he got a whiff of the goop spooned on top. It reminded him of what Brad said last summer about pepperoni pizza. Inspired by the thought, he lifted his right heel and tipped to the left:

> > *braaap!!* < <

"That's better," Helgar observed with an approving grin. He hadn't expected results this fast, but he was pleased. This set the right 'tone' for the occasion. When the laughter and feigned protests had settled down, he added a footnote: "As my college roommate liked to say, 'Keep talkin', sweet lips, I'll find ye in the dark!'"

Another roar of laughter and exchange of disbelieving looks. Helgar had said this in complete deadpan, adding to its impact.

Helgar directed an observation to Andy: "when you take Freshman Literature, you'll run across that most likely. It was written about five hundred years ago—one of the earliest campfire stories ever recorded, as far as I know." He winked at Geoff. "You'll have to read the original to see why it's really very funny."

"Any hints?" Randall knew some of his father's literary references, but this one was new.

"Hmm. Do you know Romeo and Juliet?"

"Everybody knows that—it was one of the school plays last year." Danny kind of liked that one. Swords were nifty.

"Remember the balcony scene?"

478

Everyone was intrigued.

"That's the same scene, written a couple hundred years later, give or take."

They looked at each other, mystified.

"End of hints. You have to wait for Freshman Lit class or check out a copy of Canterbury Tales; your school library might have an uncensored copy." He whispered, "look for The Miller's Tale," and helped himself to a spoonful of beans. "Anyone?" He passed the crock to Tony: "Might as well top up…"

While diverting and humorous, literary allusions invariably serve as a reminder that a significant generational and educational gap is present: like it or not, the gigantic "buddy" had become a parent again. Tony was about to suggest having a little fun torching farts, but now… *maybe not such a hot idea.* He had a bunch on the way, too. Danny was in for it, for sure. Tony hoped Danny would have a few to fight back with.

With that menu, no one would be a bystander this night: everything was a known 'gastronomic' culprit. Nothing had been left to chance—Helgar, a lifelong prankster, was already enjoying himself—he correctly assumed none of the boys would figure out they had been lured into a bombastic night. That it was winter verged on being a little mean, but…

a Helgar and Geoff

Helgar had not spent any time thinking about Geoff during the day. That in itself was telling: if he had been the long sought replacement for Walter, he would likely have spent time making plans. He was good, he was experienced, knew everything in the book and then some more than likely, but Helgar couldn't quite deal with his impossibly young appearance—especially when he was so much on his son's wavelength. His name was annoying—he did not look like a

Geoffrey ought to look. That wasn't being fair, of course—the boy didn't pick his name, his parents did.

Helgar was happy to enjoy a second night, of course, but for the time being he would defer any plans for the future. Geoff would be 'in reserve' so to speak. Maybe his need for a playmate was reduced these days—he was preoccupied much of the time with his new research regimen with Lewis. Eventually, that would become his full time assignment—possibly as early as Summer Term.

Geoff wasted no time cuddling up. He wasn't in the mood for a hugely active night, but would go wherever his Sugar Daddy wanted. He knew that was where this relationship would go, in any case. Helgar was too massive and muscular, too Herculean to allow anything else. Ronnie was a graceful prince—Helgar would never compare. For Geoff, he was a fun night or two, likely a one time event. Geoff wouldn't rule out another romp, but he wouldn't go out of his way; he sensed that the feeling was mutual. He wanted to part friends.

He was reconsidering his father's offer to set up an apprenticeship at the TV station—they were talking about a huge expansion in the new CATV industry—it showed great promise. His dad was usually ahead of the rest of the pack. Helgar had made him rethink things a little, and Jack's example reminded him that leaving the nest was impending, and he did not have a plan.

"This is nice," Geoff wiggled slightly to ease over one of the air mattress ridges—it had been slightly overinflated. He truly enjoyed being cupped in a grown man's embrace—his back against a warm furry chest was a favorite. "Mind if I say something?"

"Not at all, not at all…" Helgar couldn't find the right word to call him other than his name—'my boy' would seem patronizing.

"You are an interesting man. I have never met anyone like you. You are very complex. I enjoy knowing you—and this of course," he squirmed slightly rather than select a word or phrase. "But what impresses me the most is what a good father you are."

Helgar did not expect to hear that—it took him completely by surprise—for once, he was unable to find any way to respond.

"I hope that doesn't offend you—it is sort of personal."

480

Helgar broke out laughing, grateful to have been given a way to reply. "Excuse me for laughing, Geoff. I am quite fond of irony, and you have just scored a good one. Thank you for that—and thank you for the compliment: I couldn't have gotten a better one. You have been astute enough to perceive he is of extreme importance to me. And to his mother, I might add. One day you should meet her: she gets equal credit. We are very pleased at how he has turned out."

Geoff chuckled. "You and my father would get along fine. My name tells all about that: as a way of proving a point to several persons of privilege, he named me after the Archbishop of Canterbury. He says it was to secure my citizenship in the British Empire in case there was any doubt. Evidently there were ways to get around doing that. It seems I did not look at all English when I arrived at Queen Mary Hospital in Hong Kong.

Helgar laughed heartily—he liked the man already. "You don't look very English now, actually... not that it matters. You got a better deal, as far as I'm concerned."

"That's nice... thank you. I have to admit that I take advantage of it once in a while. I expect as I age that will fade."

"You have plenty of time, my boy, plenty of time." There was a pause. "I want you to know you have gained a friend. You should not hesitate to use me as a reference should you have need. In some quarters it might be worth a good deal—depends on where you're headed of course." There was a pause while both thought about what had been said and about the events of the day. Helgar broke the silence by raising a warning flag: a storm was on the way.

"Unless, of course you select biochemistry. I am well known there, particularly where I am employed. And you might be able to get a creative start by observing tonight's concert. I can't say I am well-read in that specialty, but I have a hunch it's a wide open field." Helgar was enjoying himself.

Geoff was smart enough to know he was being set up, but he played dumb—he didn't want to spoil Helgar's plan. "Umm... concert?"

"Yes: the Duo Concertante for meth horn and meth trumpet—it's just now getting underway." He had released a minor one, not yet noticed, still under wraps, so to speak. "Unless I am mistaken, you will be playing trumpet, and I'll be playing horn."

Geoff got it at once and it tickled him so much that the first trumpet note was felt and heard. Since he was cuddled up in Helgar's arms, Helgar's still asleep battering ram was hit directly, thus starting that process.

Helgar's involuntary flex triggered the fist audible horn tone. That triggered more laughter... the concert had begun.

—m—

b Andy and Randall

"I'll say one thing for your dad, he sure is right about these sleeping bags!" Andy remarked enthusiastically as he pulled Randall into a close embrace.

Randall chuckled, tempted to add another item to what was a very long list. He thought better of it—bragging about his father seemed a tad immature.

"I really like him—the way he handled Tony!" he laughed. "'**That's better!**' How cool is that, anyway! then he helps himself to another spoonful of beans!"

Randall chuckled. "Yeah—he's always had fun with that; on our campouts in the Cascades he always took enough beans and onions to guarantee he'd be able to have some fun—Walter was an expert on them; he called it a professional interest as a microbiologist."

"Who's Walter?"

One of Dad's grad students. He was great—he taught us a lot about climbing. Most of our two or three night trips, Walter was along— he had already climbed a lot of those—he belonged to a club that climbs everywhere. They do a lot of technical climbs."

"Technical?"

"Mm-hm. Like the real El Capitan: vertical, straight up climbs, or descents. Those guys even spend the night halfway up the thing in a cocoon." He shook his head. "No thanks." He pondered a little. "What I still don't understand is how he knew about... about you and me."

Andy was less surprised. "Well, two and two is four: we spend a lot of time together in that lab—and upstairs." he pulled Randall closer, indicating what went on up there.

Randall continued his narrative. "Dad and Walter used to have bizarre competitions: who would fart first and last were always noted. Each trip they came up with a trip special category—loudest, worst smelling, high note low note, three or more in a row... I was afraid for a minute he would suggest that our group have a contest after supper." Randall was never able to compete.

Andy laughed. "Tony would have loved that! He's a Tiger! So am I."

Randall assumed that was a scout thing.

"The Tiger Patrol is called the Fart Patrol by some of the guys— the Panthers use it against us whenever they can. We pulled one at camp last summer—Brad showed us how to torch farts—we had a ball. The whole meadow could hear us. I don't know why we weren't busted— Mark had to hear us."

"Y'know, those guys were boys once: we didn't invent torching farts—I'll bet Mark and my dad were doing things like that when they were our age. They just grew up." Randall wasn't especially impressed that he had just discovered an old as history fact of life.

Andy nodded, "Good point." Then it dawned on him: *is that why he seems so savvy about me and Randall?* He decided not to ask that aloud. Randall might not want to think about that. Andy still felt insecure about this relationship—he did not want to cause any problems; he didn't know how sensitive Randall was, and he did not want to take any chances. He was almost ready to believe he had found what he needed and wanted—it had come along too easily. He had always believed that important things took work—a lot of work. This had almost come walking through the door looking for him. That wasn't supposed to happen, was it? *do first ones ever last?* He could see that Robin and Jack were in a very special place—same with Tom and

Nick… maybe even Tony and Danny. Geoff he didn't know yet. He hadn't heard anything.

Randall decided to take a risk: "I sure hope my father is right about us," he said softly. He had developed a predictable problem, as had Andy—neither had made any comment about it yet.

thank you, Randall!! Andy needed the prod and a signal: "So do I." He puckered and made a kissy-kissy sound.

Randall clung tight and they had a very long kiss—both were still new at it. They relaxed at last—they had both needed to do that: further progress depended on it.

Randall sighed—both because he was very satisfied with the kiss, but because he had just done the math. "Another thing about my father you should know: he not only loves to surprise, he loves to play pranks—especially if they aren't expected. Since you guys don't know him, you would never expect this one—it is a whopper."

Andy took a while on this—his logic circuits were lower voltage than Randall's. "But you have figured it out anyway…"

"MM-hm. You will too in a minute. The meal tonight was planned while you and Geoff and I were loading the Rover: he made that phone call to Sharples'. Except for the ice cream, everything they supplied is known to cause intestinal gas—in abundance."

Andy thought of Brad at once—he had gone on about that last summer… he must have read up on it somewhere. He was a fanatic, for sure.

Randall pushed gently on Andy's abdomen: "Do you feel the pressure yet? I've been holding one back for a couple of minutes."

Andy broke into laughter. He realized that all five tents were about to erupt.

How does one explore the delights and mysteries of the night under these conditions? That was the prank.

—m—

c *Tom and Nick*

"You know, I could get used to this," Tom remarked as Nick cuddled up. "Seems like only yesterday we were stuck doing this."

Nick chuckled. "I agree… must be habit forming."

"You think Andy and Randall have discovered what we have?" Tom was surprised at that actually—Andy and Tony used to be two peas in a pod.

"I think so, though they're pretty cool about it." He thought a little longer about them as a couple. "I'm a little surprised—I thought Randall was stuck on Julian."

"That's right!" Tom agreed. He remembered the meeting at Sparky's—the Patrol came to the rescue and got Julian a movie date. Andy was there too…

"Come to think about it, why isn't Julian on this campout—he talked about it at the last Troop meeting."

"Dunno," Tom hadn't thought about that. "Maybe something came up—he's usually raring to go when it comes to campouts." Tom knew that Julian was sort of limited—his mom was a little on the protective side.

oh wait… Nick just thought of something: *that guy at the retirement home.* "Something's up—I remember now: he told me it was top secret. Mark is going to talk about it at the next Troop meeting."

"Oh, yeah…" Mark had told him about the special program he was planning for the troop after school started back up.

"You remember that guy that bought all those artificial Christmas trees and lights for the front?"

Tom hadn't been introduced, but he had seen him. "Yeah—that must have cost a pretty penny, too."

"It has something to do with him. Julian swore me to secrecy. I don't know why—he seemed to think it was a good thing though." He felt a sudden intestinal pressure, not very big…

> > *purt* < <

"I wondered when that would happen—I thought I would have be first one. Did we decide who won last night?"

"No. You conked out on me. You had the biggest one, no contest there!"

Tom agreed; he was reluctant to give Nick credit for having the worst smelling. "I think we tied on the smell." He poked his forefinger into Nick's left hand. "My turn: pull a little."

Nick encircled the finger and gave it a gentle tug.

> > **BWOMP!!** < <

"Oops. I didn't mean to pull that hard."

"Plenty more where that came from... I took a second helping of beans."

—m—

d *Jack and Robin*

"How's your shin?" Jack wasn't worried, really, but it was a little scary.

"Still smarts a little—good thing I was wearing long pants, that's for sure." Robin gave Jack a grateful mini-kiss. "I wasn't worried—my hero was there. He always comes through!"

"Yeah, well, he was scared shitless today, that's for sure too. He needs to kiss it better again." Jack dove down and placed a gentle kiss on Robin's right shin. He took advantage of the opportunity and did a series of those all the way to Robin's crotch where he paused to be a little more thorough—and yet a bit more... "YUM!"

The sound was muffled, but that didn't matter. "mmmm..." When Jack surfaced, he continued. "You are so good at that." He kissed back. "I'm all better now." The only thing about this tent that annoyed him was its ability to keep it dark inside: he wanted to look into Jack's eyes some more.

486

"I'm glad. I'll do it again after a while—they wear off you know, those kisses."

"So true," Robin giggled.

"Anyway—we need to report to someone about that stairway: too easy to slip forward off the steps. They need a stop on the back edge."

Robin didn't disagree, but he needed to be more careful and watch where he was going. He wanted to get back to last night's main topic. "Anyway: I didn't tell you about the special petting room they have there—I think you'll like that! They have a special deal with the Humane Society, I think." He wanted to get back on task to plan for next fall. Jack was preparing to enroll in the Animal Husbandry school.

"Yeah—I talked Geoff into coming along—I hope that's okay—he is my transportation. I'll be a couple days late for school, but it's not a problem for him—he's a graduate now."

"What's he plan to do? Maybe he could enroll there for the winter term!"

"I doubt that… it takes a while to get admitted into college—especially if you're from out of state. I don't know what he wants to do."

"When will you find out about those scholarships?"

"I need to check. If I'm lucky, I won't have to find a job." He ran his hand over the top of Robin's head a few times. "Nice… very nice."

"Thanks." That was something new; Jack had never done that before.

Jack did it again, but stroked down the neck and over to the shoulder. "I can't tell in the dark: are you a puppy or a kitten?" The petting room had given him the idea.

Robin thought a second; either one was okay. "Puppy?" He guessed that's what Jack liked best.

Jack rubbed noses. "I thought puppies had wet noses." He rubbed again… still dry.

"Puppy. Definitely a puppy."

Jack wet kissed his nose then rubbed again. "Thought so."

The puppy wiggled down, sniffing all the way to the crotch and lapped one way, then the other, and tip-of-the-tongue touched the tip and sniffed. He wiggled back up and nuzzled behind Jack's ear.

"Yep," Jack held his head between his hands and kissed softly. "Good Puppy."

They could deal with the trip to the campus tomorrow. Robin planned to tag along.

—m—

e Tony and Danny

"Brrr-brrr! Man, am I glad this is already set up!" Tony was averse to cold air; too bad there wasn't a way to warm it up in here.

Danny giggled. "After a supper like that, it won't take long to fill this with hot air!"

"You're right. I thought it would be worse last night. I expected it to wreck things good." He cuddled up close. "I'm kind of cold tonight for some reason," he rubbed Danny's buns. Danny reciprocated. "Mmm, that's better..." they wiggled front sides too, just to get ready. After last night, neither was super needy. "Ever since we were on top of that weird Capitan thing I've had the chills."

"Darn. I was hopin' you'd demonstrate how to do that torch thing."

"Huh." That surprised Tony for some reason. "Weird."

"What's weird?" He rubbed Tony's backside some more.

"I was just about to suggest everybody do that after I cut that one after supper—y'know, when Randall's dad patted me on the back for 'speaking up.' All of a sudden, I felt kinda stupid, so I didn't." *don't want to be another Brad... that's his thing.*

Danny laughed. "I'd like to see him torch a fart!" That would be something.

"I guess that's why I kept my mouth shut. I doubt if he would have. I figured I'd be wrecking things good, so I shut up. It's too cold out anyway—I don't think it would be that much fun." Tony had just put two and two together: now he understood why Mark didn't schedule any campouts in the winter months.

Torching farts is a summer sport… no adults allowed.

30   *Swann on tour*

Frederick Swann's office suite occupied the northwest corner at the top of his 16 floor headquarters building. Ten years old, the building was the tallest in the business center, and likely would be for several years. From its vantage point, three fourths of the city could be seen, including the south end of Hayden Woods, one of his many pet projects. It was the only building in the business center with a helipad. Used only occasionally, it was enormously helpful if time was a critical factor, or if discretion was an issue—there was no way for the media or anyone to see who was arriving or departing. The local television station had been given permission to use it a few times, and it was available for any emergency operation that might need it; it was not staffed. Swann preferred to keep a low profile whenever possible—he disliked public showcasing. He was not a recluse, but he went to great lengths to avoid publicity; he had no tolerance whatever for sycophants, and his personal private life was unknown by everyone except his butler and sole confidant, Mason. Essentially, his business was his family. Anyone in business, banking or investments knew him or wanted to.

The arrival of his Bell 205 went unnoticed by most, primarily because it had come in from Atlanta at a high altitude; its touchdown had been direct and efficient. His aircraft had been modified in several ways, including specially designed mufflers and an executive cabin that accommodated four. This trip included himself and Sawyer, his research specialist—invaluable because of his knack for organizing detail and connecting ostensibly trivial information to the area or project most likely to find it useful. His photographic skills frequently saved time and removed the need for a second on site visit. He had been filling in for Mason more lately, as Mason was needed in town temporarily until the

Wood family finished settling in. That as much as anything attested to its importance to Swann.

"Bring plenty of film along tomorrow—I have a hunch we'll need to take a few aerial shots as well."

"Color?"

"Your choice—I doubt if it matters, with all the snow we'll be encountering. I'll want the proofs as soon as it's convenient, but it isn't urgent. Whatever is in the pipeline." Swann always preferred color, but he deferred to this pro's judgment.

Sawyer was always able to provide what was required. "Departure time?"

"Early—plan for 8:30, unless I call. Keep a close eye on the weather—winds especially. If we have a visibility problem, let me know. I'd like to be back by dark. Mason will meet us at the airport." He turned to wave at the pilot as the Bell lifted off; it would refuel and return for tomorrow's trip to the mountains. He and Sawyer ducked into the rooftop entrance pod in time to miss most of the rotor wash.

Swann's calendar was complex and variable, and subject to change at any time, which required his office manager and reception personnel to be alert and efficient. There was no 'routine' as such, only likely or preferred practice. They always knew his whereabouts; he made it a point to keep them informed about where he would need to be at least 48 hours in advance. He rarely traveled by land if any distance was involved—his time was too valuable. His occasional flights to New York and Geneva usually used Atlanta as the point of origin. The local airport served as base for his air rental business.

In excess of 500 full time employees worked for Swann Enterprises, a mix of wholly owned subsidiaries and what he preferred, limited partnerships. He knew most of his employees by name and made it his business to see that their needs were met; their work was rewarded, whether he saw it in person or not. Most of his enterprise was elsewhere—local projects and partnerships were more sentimental than central to his operations, though to the locals he was regarded as essential and fundamental to their success. Few realized how many people and businesses were affiliated with Swann Enterprises; he preferred that the name be a footnote rather than a headline. He owned anywhere from ten to thirty percent of a dozen or more local firms. Most had returned his investment two or threefold.

Several had become very wealthy by welcoming Swann Enterprises to be their company's 'Junior Partner.' Among these was Avery Oglivy, the son of Simon Oglivy, founder of the town's first department store—the store that now occupied the first three floors of the Swann Enterprises building. Oglivy's signs were how the building was known and seen—the Big O. The fact that Oglivy's was a tenant was not generally known. Swann's corporate name was above the side entrance that provided access to the elevator, and on the entrances from the adjacent parking tower. The town knew the building simply as Oglivy's. Swann had invested in them for that as much as anything—and in return provided the capital the department store needed to expand—nearly doubling their size and market. Their former two floor store had been razed to provide space for the ten story parking structure that served building tenants and customers as well as nearby merchants—it made parking downtown simple and convenient.

In addition to his corporate telephone lines, a separate personal phone enabled him to connect independently when he needed to, or for simple convenience: it was quicker. These calls were not logged; it allowed him to call Avery directly, off the record. In this instance that was preferable: it prevented speculation. Office buzz could be useful or a nuisance, and when he called it inevitably became a subject of conversation. Some numbers required no directory assistance; Swann dialed this one without having to look it up. A cheerful voice answered on the third ring.

> > *Good afternoon, Frederick! I trust you are well.* < < Avery Oglivy's voice sounded full and confident, reflecting the good sales figures that he was reviewing.

"Indeed, I am happy to say that I've never felt better. I hope I'm not catching you in the middle of anything important. Have you got a minute?"

> > *Of course, my friend. I'm able to share the good news a little early: sales this year are more robust than I had projected. The year-end sale is only two days in, and it's above last year by almost*

ten percent already. We have four more days—I expect it to be a new company record! < <

"Excellent. I'm especially glad to hear that, because I need a small favor, and the timing is probably a little awkward. I am hoping that you are able to accommodate me on this."

Oglivy was able to mask his concern—he realized at once that it could be problematic or Frederick wouldn't be placing a direct personal call. It went without saying that whatever Frederick wanted, Frederick got.

"I need to borrow one of your employees for a day. I'm hoping you can provide a substitute to fill in for him. I can supply someone if you need, but that would not be as satisfactory as using one from your own staff—that would be your decision, of course."

Avery thought about that briefly; he couldn't think of anyone that couldn't be replaced for a day—that didn't seem to be a problem at all.

> > Glad to be of assistance—any time, of course. I presume you need a specific individual: ask away. Who is the fortunate fellow? < <

"Mark Schaeffer." Swann knew this could be problematic. "Rest assured, Avery, it's just for the day—this isn't a personnel raid." He knew that would be his first concern. It should be, too.

It took Avery a moment to frame his response.

> > I am relieved to hear that. I'm just now reading his report on the day's activity and sales. He's the least expendable man in the store. < <

"That comes as no surprise. The remaining question is whether you would prefer to tell him yourself, or do you want me to call him. I think it wise to inform him tonight. That will allow him to prepare properly; I see no advantage in surprising him in the morning—I'll want him to report directly to my office."

> > I appreciate that—I'll give him a call in a few minutes— I'm sure he has locked up for the day—he handed me this report

almost fifteen minutes ago. He's likely on the road at the moment. By the way: do you want a copy of this sent up? < <

"That's an idea—can you attach a comparable from last year?" Swann didn't know if he needed it, but he liked to be complete. Last year's figures would simplify assessing the new ones.

> > *Of course—Bonnie is still here. She keeps all that straight.* < < He chuckled, > > *She is **not** available, should you be interested.* < <

"Understood," Swann grinned. "You have my word. Oh—by the way, he has no idea this is coming. Tell him, if you would, it has to do with his scoutmaster activities, including summer camp." *that should set everyone's mind at rest.*

Swann did not hear the sigh of relief on the other end.

> > *Delighted. Anything else I can help with?* < <

"Not today. Be sure to give my best to Martha. Over and out." He hung up the phone, pleased with how that had gone. He wasn't surprised that Avery was suspicious of his motive; any good manager would be. That's one reason he had invested so much in his department store—it didn't need baby sitting.

He turned to his in-basket; a few things to finish up remained. He planned to stay over in the apartment—Mason wouldn't need to come after him tonight. Sawyer was in one of the staff apartments, ready for tomorrow's trip. He looked forward to this one—it had an adventure element, like everything connected to his new "Project." Everything that lad touched had that element. *most refreshing.* He could hardly wait to see those drawings. He pulled out the credenza drawer—a peek at the miniature originals was always a pleasure: seeing the enlargements tomorrow would be the high point of the week; after the excursion just completed he was deserving, certainly. He wrote himself a note:

inquire about photostats of Julian's scrapbook.

why not check that now? He picked up his house phone—it connected to Sawyer's room directly. *those might be done.* He wanted to return the original to the boy as soon as possible. After the trip tomorrow would be perfect.

—‑ᴍ‑—

> > *Klik!* < <

The sound of the bolt engaging was reassuring and welcome: the workday had ended at last. Locking the door on his way out was like turning off the lights when leaving the room. Mark was already thinking about a hefty glass of wine when he got home. All in all, he was pleased: the after Christmas sale had gone very well today—a record had been set. Though he would get most of the credit, he didn't do it by himself; any bonuses would be passed along.

He and Carl made the short walk to his car in the tower—this level was reserved for Oglivy employees, and his was the number two slot, right next to the boss.

"I appreciate the lift, Mark." Carl's car was in the shop for a few days.

"Hey, you're due a lot more." Until Mark had bought the station wagon, Carl had given him a lift home on Fridays—Mark hadn't kept a count, but it was a few dozen at least. "You had a pretty good day."

"Sure did. Sold out of a few things: that doesn't happen very often. Other than a few swaps for wrong sizes, we had no returns."

Mark was pleased: the secret there was stocking the right items to start with. His replacement in purchasing was proving to be a terrific asset. Mark had trained him himself, much as he was training Carl—he enjoyed that part of the job as much as anything.

"This is quite a car." Carl was surprised he had chosen a huge unit like this. It was on the posh side as cars go. It seemed to handle nicely.

"Yep. We call it The General," he patted the dashboard proudly. "The boys picked the name by vote—it honors the memory of the scoutmaster I followed. Finally, I have a rig big enough for a weekend camping trip." And, he no longer had to depend on a volunteer.

Carl chuckled. "I got a kick out of your boys today." The outdoor store and scout supplies must have had a good day. Thanks to Mark, The Men's Store department was now adjacent.

Regrettably, his promotion to Manager had made it impossible to go on their campout. He hadn't come up with a solution for that.

"Who was the tall adult in the Macintosh tartan coat?" Carl had never seen him before.

Mark laughed. "One of the parents, believe it or not. His son had on a matching coat. A professor at the university," he shook his head "New this year—he's from the Pacific Northwest. A genuine mountain climber to boot." *quite a character.* "Did you hear his Viking battle cry?"

"Who didn't!" Carl hadn't done anything about it, since Mark was at his side.

"It quieted the boys down at least. That's why I allowed it. I've been wondering whether or not it was a good idea."

"It did settle the boys down; I didn't see a mass exit—but then you were there.

Mark nodded.

"Anyway, their purchases offset the noise, for sure."

Mark agreed with a chuckle—he had never seen that many sleeping bags go out the door at the same time. Bob had circled it on the sales report.

The drive to Carl's house wasn't far—only a few blocks beyond Mark's house on Birch Street. He was glad about that—he needed to put his feet up and relax tonight; he planned to spend some time with his new color television set. One side benefit of his promotion was being able to pick that up at cost. The jump in his salary didn't hurt either. As he was pulling into the driveway, his thoughts returned to the camping trip. He was just as happy he wasn't there tonight—it was supposed to be very cold tonight. Not to mention that precocious boy from Atlanta: Mark did not want to deal with him, ever again, even if he was probably of age now. He chuckled. *Maybe he'll try to seduce Helgar.* Mark wasn't worried; Tom and Nick would be able to take care of him.

He parked behind Pat's car as usual. These days they left the house at the same time; that helped.

"I'm home dear," he called out in jest.

Pat put down the book she was reading. She was happy to hear the announcement—an indicator that he had had a good day. She stood and turned to greet him as he entered. "You seem chipper enough after such a long day." She turned her cheek to accept his kiss—they were pro forma, but genuine. She had mastered the after work protocol long ago; when she was off duty, she enjoyed playing the domestic partner's role. Though platonic, their affection for each other was genuine and deep. She didn't deliver the message until he had a minute to shed his coat and pour himself a glass of wine. "Would you like me to fix anything?"

"A few crackers, maybe... slice of cheese. I had a good supper snack at the store—the new commissary makes a huge difference. They have hot soup now!"

She paused on her way. "Pour me a glass, will you? Before you settle down for the duration, you need to call Mr. Oglivy. He called about five minutes ago. He said it was important to call as soon as you came home. He's still at the store."

That was out of nowhere! Mark couldn't imagine why he would call.

"He sounded jovial as usual—I didn't sense anything catastrophic."

Mark headed for his bedroom—he needed to get into something more comfortable: watching TV in his work outfit was no way to end the week. *must be something in the daily report...*

As Mark put the handset into its cradle, Pat looked at him expectantly: the puzzled frown on his face needed an explanation.

"So much for sleeping in tomorrow: I have to be there early." He couldn't relax quite yet. "It seems that Mr. Swann requires my presence. I have to be there by 8 o'clock."

Pat sat up, expecting more.

"All he said was it had to do with scouts and Camp Walker." *why would he need me all day?* He was reminded of the letter from Jorgenson. *best take a look at that tonight. he's been after me to put on a workshop of some kind.* It seemed unlikely that Swann had anything to do with that. Mark didn't know him very well—he was surprised and delighted that he helped with the holiday decoration project. That was thanks to Julian, evidently. *good thing I gave Carl some tips today...*

Mark was not particularly curious about the 'ruling class,' such as it was. He was middle class: always had been, and always would be as far as he knew—he was not an ambitious man. He was a natural born leader, but did not think in those terms. He was who he was and where he was as much by accident and circumstance as anything. His advancement was not the result of ambition and goal setting, but of innate ability and personal values being recognized and put to use. He had no idea that Frederick Swann owned over a third of Oglivy's and of Sharples' Deli and Catering, among other things, nor that he was in negotiations to acquire the retirement home that his boys had been decorating for years. He had no idea that Frederick Swann was about to become a benefactor of Troop 9 and the entire Council—possibly their greatest in a long history of benefactors. Nor did he know he was a recent addition to the list of people and enterprises to keep an eye on that Swann kept in his confidential file.

Slightly amazed, Mark gazed at the reflection of himself and the two men on his right. The high gloss surface on the panels in the Swann Enterprises elevator was almost a mirror. He had never expected to be one of three men wearing a fur lined parka with matching cap and snow boots—top of the line items from Oglivy's Men's store; Mr. Swann had taken the scout motto seriously: they were more than prepared. They were dressed to survive a blizzard. The three outfits were Carl's first sale this morning, likely making him the top salesman of the day—as well as being his substitute. That didn't begin to compete with his own surprise this morning when he answered the doorbell—Swann's butler Mason was there to pick him up—he did not have to drive to the store as usual. He had given the keys to Pat so she could move it out of the way or make use of it herself.

Swann was not a stranger, by any measure. He had met Swann on three previous occasions, the decoration project being the most recent. He had also been present at the special banquet at the university, and the dinner at Helgar's, so he did have a speaking acquaintance—but Mark had never had an extended conversation with him. Today, that changed dramatically. As of 8:15 this morning, he had been the focus of Swann's attention. After a brief conversation, he and a Swann employee were 'invited' to join him in a ride down the elevator to Oglivy's to be outfitted for todays trip to Camp Walker. Now they were riding the elevator back up to the roof: he was about to experience his first helicopter ride.

"I failed to inquire earlier: am I correct in assuming you do not get air or sea sick?"

"Not so far. I've never been in a helicopter, but I don't think I'll have a problem.

"Good—I'm not sure what we're apt to run into—I've not had occasion to take a journey into mountainous terrain before now. I'm told that wind currents can be problematic. My crew is skilled and practiced, so I'm not concerned, but there is always an element of risk." He didn't want to force anyone who was truly reluctant to fly against their wishes.

"I doubt if we'll have any trouble—the terrain around Lake Walker isn't particularly rugged."

"Thank you. I am encouraged by that—I am looking forward to your assistance in guiding our aerial tour."

why in the world does he want an aerial tour of Camp Walker? Mark was highly puzzled—he assumed it was because of Julian, somehow.

The elevator reached the top. The three filled the small rooftop pod that served as an exit/entrance to the helipad: the helicopter was ready and waiting; Mark was fascinated and thrilled, now that he saw it: it wasn't one of those glass bubble units at all—those always resembled a giant mosquito. This one looked like one of the military or Red Cross evacuation Hueys he had seen in the television news, only customized to fit Swann's executive air service—evidently he had more than one.

The pilot waited until everyone was buckled in before starting the engine; considered good safety procedure, he said it allowed the passengers to avoid the propeller downdraft, which could be considerable.

The flight to Lake Walker took nearly two hours, but Swann did not waste a minute. For the first hour he met with his research man— evidently he had been meeting with an architect about a house he was having built. He had a small portfolio with photographs and blueprints. Mark didn't want to be nosy, so he entertained himself looking out the window for the most part; it was fascinating, even in the winter. The overcast was high, well above six thousand feet—no rain was forecast— or blizzards.

About halfway, Swann directed his attention to Mark. "I appreciate your patience—I needed to get that cleared up so that Sawyer could get prepared to photograph the area we're headed for. That leads to my first question: would it be possible to do that before we land, or do you think it best to have John along?"

It took a second to deduce who John was—Mark was not on a first name basis with the Camp Director. "Oh— Um, well it depends on what you need to know. How much detail you want as you are seeing it—some camps may be hard to see—most are half in the trees; a couple are likely to be snowed in. I'm sure we'll be able to see the trail system—it's well brushed. I don't know how big his winter crew is. I know they open the camp to various outside groups for recreation and training. It's an important revenue source. Survival training, hunting parties... I have no experience with any of that. Some troops have a winter campout there if the road is open. It is a little over four thousand feet. I don't know what the snow level is this year."

Swann opened the manila folder he had just pulled out of his satchel. "Here's the map John sent." He spread it out on the small conference table. "It would save considerable time if we didn't have to land and pick him up. Do you think with this you could guide Sawyer such that he could photograph the area with some accuracy?"

Seeing the map helped. He took a minute to review it. "You know, I think so—I have been to every part of the camp at one time or another, either as a scout or a scoutmaster—I've been here every summer since '51. It's not very complicated, really. It is widespread and comprehensive—I'm sure Jorgensen has a number of photographs on file that would fill in any blanks. The main concern I would have is whether or not he needs to see it from above—or if it would please him, for that matter. It might make his day, you never know. I doubt if he has ever had a tour from above."

The answer told Swann precisely what he wanted to know—both about the camp, and about Mark. His concern for the Camp Director was key: that defined the man. He was enormously pleased—he was not surprised.

For the next twenty minutes, Mark responded to questions about the camp and its activities and some details about his experiences as a scoutmaster. Swann had never been a scout as a boy—it was something he had missed, and Julian's scrapbook was terrific reading.

"I understand John wants you to conduct some kind of training session—can you describe what you have in mind?" He glanced at Mark's new satchel—Swann had bought both him and Sawyer one along with the one he got for himself—high quality and weatherproof. Mark pulled out his scoutmaster's notebook—a three ring binder he maintained—the one item his troop management relied on: it had everything he needed. He passed it to Swann.

"This is my notebook. I'd be lost without it. What I plan to do is walk Jorgenson through it and let him pick out what he thinks the guys need." He shrugged. "Some of them are a little short on training for one reason or another. Jorgensen is probably the best one to make that call—he's got another ten or fifteen years of experience. He's a good man." He pointed to the notebook: "I can't claim all this—I took over from a highly experienced man—he was my scoutmaster when I was a boy. He was the best. I have tried to imitate him more than anything."

502

Swan was very pleased. He pulled the Troop 9 Scrapbook out of his satchel. "This is the reason I wanted to visit the camp in person. I presume you have been curious about that."

"Ah, now I understand," Mark smiled wide: this book made him more proud than anything in his life. He looked at Swann expectantly. He understood precisely why he wanted to visit Camp Walker. "My favorite book."

"To be frank, I couldn't wait until the weather improved. It's a safe bet that I will want to revisit it one day, preferably when the Camp is in session. This scrapbook is more of a travel adventure book— scrapbook is an inadequate word."

"You're right—but it's Julian's call—this is his invention, completely—he did not take this over. No one will be able to take it on after he moves on." He looked at Swann sadly: "They all move on at some point." He shook his head. "One of those bittersweet facts of life." He paused, then unaccountably surprised himself and looked at Swann in the eye: "I've never told anyone this before: it's the most important thing I do. And I don't get paid a dime to do it. You have met Julian: you know that already. I have nearly fifty of these boys—Julian is special of course—but they all are, in their own way. It may be corny to say this, but I consider myself the luckiest man in the world." He took a deep breath. He noticed Swann sitting back and looking at him strangely.

"Thanks for giving me a nudge—I usually don't expound like that; I hadn't articulated that before—either aloud or to myself." He shrugged. "Felt good to get it off my chest!" he chuckled.

Swann's brain was going a hundred miles an hour: this man would be of enormous value—what for was to be determined—and carefully prepared for.

"I'll be returning this to Julian soon; could I persuade you to walk me through it—we have a few minutes left, I think." He did not reveal his plans for Julian yet. That occasion needed to be prepared for as well.

"My pleasure!" he sat forward and opened the bulging binder. "He needs to start volume two."

Jorgensen was more than a little nervous—that helicopter had been flying back and forth for the better part of fifteen minutes. He and Sarge had come back inside—too blasted cold out there to just stand around. They must be doing a mini survey or something. *Swann said they might take a few photos… must be taking a few extras.*

"Refill?" Sarge stood and lifted his coffee mug. He'd been on a chopper a few times, just before leaving active duty. This one sounded different—they'd improved some since his day.

The sound grew louder—it was about to land. They put their coats back on and hurried to the door—they stopped cold: the prop wash had caused a mini blizzard… best to let it slow down before walking out.

Unintended consequences: the prop wash had caused a minor snowdrift a few feet from the entrance—neither had their snow boots on.

"We can wait here—no point in wading through that." The platform was clear, so Jorgensen stood where he could be seen and waved a welcome; that would have to do.

Sarge shrugged; his rig out back could handle this later. *after they leave I'll take care of it.*

Jorgensen did a weather check—they were okay. *good thing they came today.* The sleek dark blue helicopter was very impressive—a sight he never expected to see. *pilot knows his business…* The wide door slid open as the huge blades slowed to a stop. Three men dressed in fur trimmed gear stepped out onto bare ground—landing had blown nearly six inches of snow away, creating an 18 inch deep ring of chunky snow—the permanent winter layer had packed somewhat over the last month.

Jorgensen broke into a broad smile: Mark was the tallest of the three—stood out. Otherwise the trio was a little foreboding—two had identical satchels, one a shoulder bag.

Sarge was impressed in spite of his inclination to dismiss visits by 'higher ups,' which this looked like. Executive types more often than not were up to something. That fella on the end looked familiar…

Jorgensen waited for them all to enter before opening the door to the large meeting hall. Once welcoming handshakes were out of he way, he led the visitors into the cafeteria/meeting room and over to the serving counter where the coffee was ready. His office couldn't accommodate this many people. HQ had no Visitor's Lounge or greeting area—no need for one until now. The echo and cold air were not very welcoming.

"We keep this closed up in the winter, usually—there is no central heating. Between my small portable and Sarge's wood stove in the shop, we're cozy enough until spring—the sun takes care of us just fine most of the year."

Swann noticed the healthy bursts of steam issuing from everyone as they walked into the large room—appeared to be large enough to seat between five and seven hundred. He was disappointed in himself for not anticipating this. He had just started his list: a new physical plant. Obviously such a thing was out of reach for this organization. That was doable—he had seen to that before. The Scrapbook narrative had talked about the air conditioning problem in this room, and the large diesel generators out back. The place was overdue for attention: those things were much easier to arrange these days.

Fortunately, Sarge had used the thirty-cup percolator. *maybe should've used the hundred...* there were five visitors. Everyone took seat—he had set up a table and eight chairs—one extra.

"Excellent!" Swann exclaimed after sitting down with his steaming mug; he removed a glove and took his first sip. "Most welcome—after two hours in the air, most welcome indeed. You must be Sarge—or may I call you Uncle Max?" He recognized him at once from Julian's sketch.

Sarge was taken aback: *the Boy!* Only the Boy called him that.

"I feel like we've met; Julian speaks fondly of you—I bring his personal greetings."

Mark was almost as startled.

"You are one of the reasons for this visit," he said cheerfully, and reached into his satchel. He pulled out Julian's well-worn sketchbook—

505

the one with most of the pages torn out for the Troop Scrapbook. "I have come to see the finished work." he flipped it open to the original sketch.

Sarge looked at the sketchbook wide eyed—he recognized it at once: "Haw!" He held out his open hand—he wanted to see it up close. It was almost like having the Boy here, seeing that.

Jorgensen and Mark exchanged surprised glances—before their eyes, the gruff curmudgeon they knew as Sarge had transformed into the very mellow and grandfatherly Uncle Max.

Grinning wide he looked up at Swann: "He drew that sitting on the floor by my workbench!" he chuckled. "Never seen anything like it. Took him all of fifteen or twenty minutes!" he shook his head. "Came back the next day to do some last minute touches to the big one— wouldn't let me fetch a chair."

Mark and Jorgensen looked at each other, surprised. Mark had seen the large one, but not the notebook sketch. He remembered the occasion well—one of the better before lights-out conferences.

Uncle Max gazed at it fondly. He had tucked the big one away after framing it. He looked at Swann gratefully. Swann had been accepted; Sarge saw no reason to hesitate: *the Boy trusts this fella—good enough for me.* "I keep it in a safe place back in the shop. Should I fetch it, or do you want to come on back to see where the Boy drew it?"

Swann stood: "Lead the way!" he gestured to Sawyer and the flight crew. "Gentlemen, you are welcome to tag along if you wish." He was very pleased that they weren't wasting any time "After Sawyer documents this, I'd like to see the other one—the one in the medic's room." If all went smoothly, they could do Atlanta as well.

"Easier to cut through the kitchen. Follow me—it's pretty well shut down for the winter… don't rent it out any more." He didn't rub it in. That's one battle he had won.

The pilot shrugged at his second in command. *better tag along… no telling when the boss will come up with something—it's still early.* Swann was inclined to 'invite' when he meant it was expected— he rarely phrased his wishes as a command. It was one of his performance yardsticks. Besides, it was cold in here.

Sawyer made mental notes as they passed through the kitchen—that was routine—his primary function was to record information and organize it for future access—his employer rarely travelled randomly. His job was to make a second visit unnecessary. As far as he knew, this facility was on the upgrade or acquisition list—or both.

Sarge strode proudly through the dormant kitchen—he didn't need to turn on the lights—plenty of windows. The door to his workshop had a 24x30 inch window, enough to light the passageway between the cooler and the dishwashing work area. The group followed through the door and around to the left—his workbench and stool were straight ahead. The temperature changed instantly from around 40 to 65. It seemed even warmer. A small wood stove next to a closed delivery entrance made the space quite livable.

"Might as well take off your coats." Sarge assumed they would prefer to stay here a while. "You can put 'em over there on the worktable. He headed for a tall cupboard door. "Help yourselves to a folding chair," he gestured to his stash of army surplus chairs; he had a closet full.

Mark recognized these at once and stepped forward. "These are very clever, if you've never seen them," he grabbed one for Swann and helped himself to another. He demonstrated how they opened. "Remarkably comfortable, and sturdy."

Sarge grinned, recalling last summer. "War surplus. Can't get 'em any more." he shook his head and unbuttoned his coat as he walked to his workbench. After moving the stool aside he extracted the frame tucked behind the table—it faced the wall. He placed it atop the stool and leaned it against the workbench table, then stood back and flashed his eyes. His most prized possession. He bounced on his toes. Everyone but the photographer had opened a folding chair and followed Jorgensen's lead—he knew more or less where Sarge would place the drawing—nothing else made sense—the area was fairly well defined.

Of course, everyone, including the flight crew, was taken by surprise; even Mark, who had seen it right after it was drawn. He looked closely: *ah! more tools on the hanging rack—* he grinned. He had suggested that.

Swann was so surprised, his jaw dropped. He had opened the tablet to the original, expecting to do a comparison much like he had done with the drawing of Kasey. This was hugely different: the original was a head and shoulders drawing. The large version was a full-length figure, filled with additional detail.

Swann showed Mark the drawing in the tablet.

It took a minute for it to register: "I don't remember seeing the sketch—I saw the full size one in the cabin—he wanted to know if I saw anything that needed fixing—he always asks that—and it's an honest question, believe it or not."

Sarge and Jorgensen stepped close to see what they were talking about. After a minute, they all understood: The head and shoulders, in great detail, were identical to the large drawing except in size—and without a torso, legs, and all the rest of the apparatus in the large one. The small one resembled a peep-hole view. The large one was with the door thrown wide open, viewed from within the room. Indeed, they could see some of the artifacts for themselves, since they were now in that very same room. Even though it was in pencil, it was so skillfully done, the eye filled in areas automatically, making it appear even more real.

"I just realized: the one he did of me is the same: full size."

Swann flipped through to the drawing of Mark's head.

"Yep. Same thing. I remember him showing that to me—when I saw the full sized one, I... I have to be honest: I almost lost my balance and tipped over—it was like a jolt of energy, or something." He looked at Swann, revealing his confused state of mind: "I still don't understand it."

Swann flipped back to the drawing of Leonard's head and showed it to Mark.

"Yes! He showed me that: that's why I let him draw one of me! I had no idea the full size one would be anything other than an enlargement."

Swann beckoned to Sawyer. "Take a close look." When he saw Sawyer's wordless response, he turned to Sarge: "Can you describe how

508

he drew your picture—I assume you remember—it wasn't terribly long ago—six months about, if I am not mistaken."

Sarge pointed to the wall next to the man who had asked. "That's where he sat, the whole time, right on the cement floor!" he shook his head, "Legs crossed Injun style... wouldn't take a chair—he liked the angle. I was fixin' one of those white gas lanterns. Didn't even know he was there until I got up to get a refill—quiet as a mouse, he was." He tilted his head and looked at the detail. "Liked my whiskers," he chuckled quietly.

Swann listened carefully to this—he was busily associating the man with the drawing as he stood to the side. He had never had an opportunity to see the subject and his portrait so close together, aside from the drawing of Lewis' boy after that dinner. This was similar... this is where Julian had developed that... he had not found the exact word he needed—it was a unique quality, but quality was a poor word; this was something much stronger. He expected the Atlanta drawing to have the same whatever it was; Julian mentioned it specifically as the one that triggered the process, whatever it was—he said the two of the scoutmaster were like that as well—this was done after those three. He flashed a glance at Sawyer, directing him to capture the moment: the subject and the drawing together was special.

True to his assignment as usual, Sawyer had refit his camera to take medium and close in shots while everyone was getting a cup of coffee. He had made certain the rise in temperature hadn't caused any condensation by changing in a new roll of film. He stuck with Tri-X; indoors, it allowed much greater flexibility—no flash unit would be required.

"I am making a study of Julian's art. I am assuming you have no objections to my taking a few photographs." Swann gave Sarge a grateful nod and turned to Jorgensen. "I need to see the first one—the medic at work. I understand that is in your office."

"Of course! Happy to help in any way—do you want to see it there, or should I bring it here?

A nod from Sawyer confirmed his hunch. "The lighting is better here, I should think... Let's ask the expert." He gestured to Sawyer.

"Yes—this is a bright room—the high windows light the area perfectly—I don't need to compensate or use a flash. I would like to have it more vertical. With your permission, I'd like to see to that before taking a final photograph."

"I'm sure Sarge can help with that," he turned to Swann: "Why don't you supervise while Mark and I go after the drawing hanging on my wall."

"Excellent," Swann's opinion about Jorgenson was verified. Mark filling him in a little would facilitate things considerably.

It wasn't far to Jorgensen's office. The moment they were out of earshot he inquired softly, "I was under the impression we were going to talk about a workshop. Can you clear this up a little?"

Mark looked over his shoulder. "I'm almost as surprised as you—I knew he was interested in Julian's work, of course. This is more than interested. I know he plans for you and me to talk about training—we talked about it on the flight—he looked at all my materials—I have my Scoutmaster notebook along."

Jorgensen turned on the light as they entered his office. "Well, he is unique. He seems to have the boy's best interests in mind, that comes through loud and clear. And you have confidence in him?" The District Office was impressed that he was planning a visit—they advised handling him with care—evidently someone knew him or about him. He stepped over to the east wall. "Give me a hand—Sarge's frame is anything but lightweight." The drawing was four feet above the floor—the subjects were at eye level. At first glance, it looked like an open window. It took a minute to realize it was in pencil and had no color—it didn't seem to need it.

"Oof! You're right. Let me carry it."

When they reentered the shop, they saw a rapt Swann studying the drawing of Sarge intently—Mark had not seen that level of focus ever—except maybe Julian at work. Swann was on the same frequency or something; the two pilots were on stepladders holding large panels of cardboard. They waited for Swann to rejoin their world.

510

After a moment, Swann stood back quietly. "Thank you, gentlemen, for indulging me—this has affected me more strongly than I expected." He smiled at Sarge: "I suspect you know the feeling." He turned to the aircrew. "One more to go, gentlemen." Turning back to Mark, "if you and Sarge can swap those drawings, we can photograph the other one." He wanted Jorgensen to understand what he had hanging on his office wall: "This is a particularly important piece; Julian described it to me in some detail. This is where it began."

Jorgensen and Mark looked at each other wide eyed: Swann had not explained what "it" was. They stayed tuned.

As Sawyer and the airmen set to work, Mark saw what they were up to: they were blocking direct light so that the glass had no reflections. That eliminated the need to remove it from the frame. Sawyer knew his craft. The shot was made rapidly. Sawyer signaled, and they climbed down and handed the cardboard to Sarge and returned the ladders to their place along the south wall—Sarge had half a dozen as well as several extension ladders. Everything loose was returned here for the winter.

Swann had approached the drawing to examine it carefully—he had studied the cameo closely before the flight—his eyes darted back and forth rapidly—he stopped abruptly. "I need the sketch. Sawyer, can you hand it to me? It's on the chair." He stood straight. "This is thanks to you, entirely, Uncle Max: when you gave him that paper and drawing board, you opened the door: you made this possible—and you got your special name: he truly thinks of you as family, you know." Swann paused to let the man have a moment to appreciate how special he was in Julian's eyes. "He would have discovered his ability to portray others eventually, I am sure; but this was vastly better: it made it his own... he wasn't shown. That is one thing that makes this so special. That is what the great ones do: DaVinci, Michelangelo, Van Gogh... most artists are their offspring. Like them, this boy has invented something entirely new. I'm sure that comes as a surprise—you didn't realize what it meant or would mean: no one would have. But you and you alone get the credit— deservedly. I am in your debt."

Sarge blushed—for the second time in less than an hour. He knew to keep his mouth shut—he remained blank faced—he would have to talk with John after this man flew away. He wasn't sure what he was talking about, exactly.

Sawyer handed him the sketchbook; Swann opened it and stood about five feet away—just far enough for it to fill his field of vision. He held the sketch about a foot away and rapidly scanned the two in what appeared to be a systematic way. "You are welcome to share this experience, gentlemen. Feel free to stand beside me."

Mark and Jorgensen glanced at each other and stepped close, one on each side, and tried to do what Swann was—it was interesting—fascinating… but they had no idea what to do other than compare a small drawing with its enlargement. It was remarkable, certainly.

"Sawyer, come close and look."

The photographer did so.

"Do you see what I see?"

Sawyer had spent many hours in a darkroom: He knew all about enlarging and zooming. He studied it briefly. "I doubt if I could do any better." He shook his head.

Jorgensen frowned: *what are they **talking** about?!* He looked at Mark.

"Julian has a camera lens in each eye—he even says that—he looks with his 'camera eye.' I thought he was talking about his memory. That's only half if it. The large one is a perfect blow up—in perfect focus."

"Thank you, Mark. That is spot on. I know of no other artist that does this—or that could if he chose to. He tilted his head: "I'm not sure it's entirely a good thing."

"Why? What could be bad about it?"

"I'm not sure… it could be limiting. An artist needs to be free." Swann paused, then looked at Mark: "I will never say that to him, of course."

Mark waited for an explanation.

"It's far more important for him to continue as he has done: remain uninfluenced by other's values and prejudices. He has done superbly on his own up to now—it would be criminal to intervene. He is almost entirely self–taught. If he needs help, he will ask for it. It would be a shame to jeopardize that ability. He is still a work in progress. I intend to support that, to foster it..." he nodded forcefully. "To **protect** it. I am sure you agree. I wouldn't be so open with you if I thought otherwise. You all know this anyway—you practice that policy yourselves. That's one reason we see this—" he gestured toward the drawing. "He has been supported, not pushed."

Swann would have spent longer studying it, but realized that sawyer could make full sized replicas quite easily in the lab. That was the obvious route to take with this one—it was far more complex than he expected. He closed the notebook and handed it to Sawyer. "Thank you. John, for allowing me this—I remain indebted. I intend to return the favor. Now then—I suggest that you and Mark return this to its proper location and have a chat about that workshop. Sawyer and I will enjoy a guided tour of this facility in the meantime. I'll join you after the tour—I may want to borrow your telephone before we take our leave."

Sarge's tour took slightly over an hour; having such an intelligent and interested person to show off what they did here was a delightful surprise—he enjoyed doing it and would have gladly taken him on a ride in his sidecar to see other camp highlights if he had been asked to, snow or no snow. That photographer went through a second roll of film. Even the pilots came along. Luckily, he had cleared the path to the outbuildings this morning, so he was able to show off Bessie, his pride and joy. The Boy had shown him that cartoon!

When they reached Jorgensen's office, Mark and the Camp Director had finished their exploration of training opportunities and needs, and were reminiscing about various camp experiences they had enjoyed over the years; as a result, they had become better acquainted and could call each other friends—a complete plus.

They had stopped to refill their coffee mugs on the way. "It seems our timing is about right," Swann began. "Perhaps I can pay a call

513

again, when the snow has gone—I'd enjoy seeing some of the activity areas."

John and Mark stood. "That would be a pleasure. Yes, Mark and I have had a good talk. Scheduling remains—lots of work to do before we can set a date. I'm more than pleased."

"Sit, sit, please." Swann took one of the side chairs. "I am happy with how this has gone. I have to pause at this point to inquire about our itinerary. One more drawing remains to be seen—unfortunately, it is in Atlanta. I need to know whether that can be arranged today, or if it requires a separate trip. It's up to you, Mark: a side trip to do that will add a couple of hours to our day. It means arriving home after the sun has set—I'd estimate around six, but it could be later. We haven't talked about lunch or dinner, either." he gestured to the clock. It's time for lunch already. Your thoughts?"

This took Mark by surprise. He had not seen the large drawing of Leonard, so he was very interested. He had not been thinking of anything beside having lunch and flying back home; he had assumed everything had been planned. Being asked for input was totally unexpected—from what he had seen, Swann usually had things pre-arranged. "Well, getting home a little late is no problem—Pat is very flexible. Nothing special is planned. Weekends are usually very casual. She is used to proceeding without me," he explained. "She's the one in charge around there when she isn't on duty at the hospital. She knows where I am, so…"

"I am glad to hear that." He turned to Jorgensen. We have brought a picnic basket of sorts, prepared with the assistance of my friend Lucian. I asked him to accommodate everyone," he gestured to Sarge and the Director. "With your permission, I'll have the crew bring it in—or, if you prefer, we can feast while we're on our way."

They had not planned anything. Sarge was expecting to open a couple of cans of soup. "Picnic is fine with me!" He liked this fella.

"I presume the cafeteria table will do," he looked hopefully at Sarge—"unless you can set up something in your workshop."

Sarge stood. "Your boys are fit—they can help me set up a table back there—plenty of room in front of my woodstove." The chairs were already set up.

"Excellent." The crew was standing by in the hallway. Sawyer led the way to their coats: it was still below thirty out there.

"Next, John, if you would, please place a call to Leonard in Atlanta. He is expecting to hear from you, I believe."

Another surprise. Jorgensen pulled his Rolodex over—he had all his data there.

After four rings, Leonard picked up his receiver.

> > *This is Leonard—May I ask who is calling?* < <

"Good afternoon, Leonard. It's John Jorgensen. I trust all is well with you—that you had a happy Christmas."

> > *Why, yes, thank you.* < <

"I have a guest that wishes to speak to you. Here he is…" he stood and handed Swann the handset. He traded places.

Swann covered the handset and gestured for the others to remain—this was not a confidential call. "Hello, again Leonard—I hope I'm not interrupting your lunch."

> > *No, thank you—I have been waiting for your call. I'll do that afterward. I'm free all afternoon.* < <

"I am so pleased to hear that. I am here with Mark Schaeffer. I trust that you are still able to meet us along with your special drawing. We have just been looking at the two here."

> > *Of course. I have it here in its cardboard tube, safe and sound.* < <

"Excellent. Here's what I suggest:" he checked his wristwatch. "After you have a bite to eat, you should expect to receive a call to make final arrangements. My service will transport you to the airport—I use a conference room there from time to time. I have a standing reservation in the Red Carpet room. That's in the lobby that serves United. They will be expecting you; you will be admitted without any problem. All you need to do is press the buzzer and give your name. That's where we will visit and have a look at your drawing. Afterward, the service will take you home—or anywhere else you might need to go. We should be there in a little over an hour."

> > *That's pretty painless! I'm glad I don't have to find a place to park! That alone takes an hour, at least—that is one busy place!* < <

"That's doubtless true. Well, I have another call to place. Do you have any questions or concerns?"

> > *Don't think so—just stay by the phone? No need to call anyone?* < <

"That's it. Thanks so much, Leonard. This means a great deal to me. We'll be seeing you soon!" He hung up the receiver. "I trust I have leave to make another call? I'll be sure to leave a quarter or two in your phone kitty."

"Of course." It was fascinating to watch this man in action.

Swann dialed a number without looking it up. "This won't take long… Hello—is Marie available please? This is Frederick Swann." He pulled a miniature scratch pad from his shirt pocket, just in case. "Hello, Marie; good to hear your voice again. I need two things—first, reserve the conference room—I'll need it for about an hour, but my arrival time is not exact. So block it in for two, say, two to four o'clock. I'll need the usual, service for four. Then call Henry and give him a message to call this number to arrange the car—he is expecting the call." He recited Leonard's phone number from memory, though it was on the Rolodex a few inches away. "The name is Leonard."

Two wide-eyed men watched in awe: they had never seen anyone operate at this level of efficiency—it seemed so effortless.

"Thanks, Marie… see you soon." He put the receiver in its cradle. "Mark tells me you may have a file of camp photographs—perhaps we could browse through those while we grab a quick lunch." He stood, and returned the small pad to his shirt pocket.

John fetched a file from his filing cabinet and led the way to the workshop—Sarge and the others had set up the table; Sarge was feeding the firebox in his small woodstove—a Sharples' baked bean crock was on top, rewarming. The crew was setting out the other contents of the Sharples' Catering cart—very like the ones to be employed in Hayden Woods in an hour or two—this one divided into cold and warm sections. It contained the usual fare—potato and macaroni salads, assorted sliced

516

fruit, and a variety of cold sandwiches. Utensils were included, removing the need to do dishes later.

Swann enjoyed exposing the unsuspecting to Sharple's treat: "Lucian knows how to prepare a meal. You are to keep any leftovers, by the way—but I do need to take the bean crock home. He usually includes more than can be consumed in a single meal... a flaw that I encourage: they are irresistible. You are welcome to transfer the leftovers to a container of your own," he sat and pulled up a plate. "Time to dig in!"

The folder of photos gave Sarge an idea; he pulled open a drawer at the worktable, removed his prize possession and took it over to Swann. "Figure you'd get a kick out of this too," he winked at John. Both had read Julian's letter several times.

Fortunately, it was not peak arrival time; the new terminal had improved things considerably. Swann's company had a working relationship with Prestige, the hometown Atlanta charter service. His Limousine Express had full access, making the run to the public concourse simple and convenient; their stopover here would be shortened considerably; it was perfect for refueling and servicing for the final leg—three and a half hours back to the home base at Jennings Field.

ATL, short identifier for Atlanta Municipal Airport, was already the busiest airport in the world. Many airlines used it as their major hub. As a Lifetime Red Carpet Club member and a frequent traveller, Frederick Swann was well known and welcome. Here, as in other places, he had identified a key employee who he retained—for a very handsome fee—to be an on site representative and agent on the side, off the books. The new Red Carpet Room was lavish and convenient to the business traveller, occupying the prime location before entering the long concourse leading to the United gates, saving its members considerable inconvenience and time. Golf cart service for Club Members removed the need to hand carry luggage or walk long distances. Members like Swann used the RC room as a meeting site, saving a trip into town or to the Sheraton Airport Hotel. This instance saved him an hour easily.

Leonard was waiting inside when Swann, Mark and Sawyer arrived—it had taken longer to get a landing clearance than they had expected. The tower was used to his Lockheed JetStar—the Huey had to be verified.

"Thanks for your patience, Leonard—I am sorry it took us a little longer than usual. I see that Marie has taken care of you nicely," Swann extended his hand. He noted the empty gin and tonic glass on the small table, and the mailing tube by his side. "Let's get set up in the conference room;" he gestured to the door marked 'Reserved.'

Mark reached out, "Good to see you, Leonard."

"Hi." Leonard liked Mark; he was one of the best scoutmasters— his kids always entertained—always behaved. He was slightly embarrassed about Mark seeing this… he wasn't sure it was a good idea. He followed Swann into the conference room. Mark and a photographer followed behind.

Swann went directly to the far end of the conference table; a large marker board occupied one corner of the room; it was there for use as a screen or display area. A small cupboard below contained various supplies, including dry erase markers and mounting tape. He selected a roll of blue tape and placed it on the table. He gestured for Sawyer to approach.

"Allow me to introduce Sawyer, Leonard—he is my specialist for occasions such as this. If you would be so kind as to bring your precious work of art over here, he will assist in mounting it temporarily—we don't want it to be wrinkled or harmed in any way. I'm sorry to say I failed to bring along any gloves—we will avoid touching it as much as possible."

Sawyer promptly pulled two pair of gloves out of his case—he always carried a set or two with his camera equipment. He handed Leonard a pair.

Swann looked at Leonard, proud of his assistant. "I should have remembered. Thank you, Sawyer."

Leonard was amazed. Any hesitation had just vanished—he didn't take this kind of caution ever.

518

Swann pulled a business card out of the special pocket in his wallet and handed it to Leonard. "At your first convenience, give Maynard a call. He will be expecting it. I will call him later to make the arrangements for you to have his gallery frame this properly. You should keep the tube for emergency use, of course. As long as you keep this out of direct sunlight or any bright light, it shouldn't yellow or fade. Maynard has the finest materials available. I insist on paying for this, by the way. It's the least I can do in return."

Leonard looked at Mark wide-eyed. *this is really happening!*

Mark winked back with a grin. He sat back to enjoy the fun—he did look forward to this, but he had assumed it would be much the same as the other two drawings. When he saw the picture unroll he realized at once that was **not** true—the scrapbook sketch was very simple—almost a start, and it focused primarily on the hands and face. He recalled that, because that sketch was largely what had allowed him to grant Julian's wish to pose for him. It was after Julian had shown him the early, rather primitive sketches he had been doing in secret from memory. Julian had torn them out of the sketchbook and tucked them away in his footlocker. Presumably, they had been tossed out.

Now he was looking at a fully detailed portrait; it was like the drawing of Sarge they had been studying an hour and a half ago: a photo that had been transferred onto a large 24x30 inch piece of paper.

There was a long pause as everyone admired the drawing—the lighting in the room was very supportive; pin spots from three angles were designed for that purpose. On a dimmer circuit, Swann was able to make a careful adjustment from the presenter's control panel. All it needed was background music.

Leonard gasped audibly. "I… I had no idea." He had never troubled to think of it as a work of art; he felt like clod all of a sudden; in this setting, the erotic elements that had preoccupied him seemed trivial. It was a miracle that it had survived intact, considering how often it had been in and out of that cardboard tube.

Swann assumed Leonard would be surprised. Indeed, it was more than a minor discovery: this one conveyed a stronger sense than the drawing of Uncle Max—a younger sense… Again, Julian had portrayed an inner quality of the person as well as an outward image. It

519

seemed to greet the viewer, to invite him. Remarkable—especially with Leonard staring back at it in awe.

He glanced at Sawyer with his standard silent cue: he wanted to capture this encounter while it was in progress. The other portrait had done this as well, but Sarge was an older man; this one had the power of a young man in his prime: Julian seemed to link or connect the viewer with an inner energy, or life force. The only word Swann could come up with was power—an inner power, unique to the subject being depicted. It was almost like a soundtrack. He was uncertain if everyone could see—or feel it. This was a new thing—the kernel, the genius. Ordinary language wasn't equipped. Perhaps Aristotle would provide what he was after. This is what the portrait of Kasey had shown him—what had begun this quest or obsession. It had captured him totally. Now, it was his responsibility to protect and nurture whatever it was this boy had. The world saw a cute teenager, a good boy scout: Swann saw a great deal more. How much more was yet to be understood. His gut instinct told him it would be beyond his expectation. Already, the boy had shown that pencil was a far more capable media than he had imagined possible—simplicity was as much an advantage as a limitation.

Mark saw some of this, but did not know how to articulate it—it was very like the drawings Julian had done of him, in a way. It was very different at the same time: the power was recognizably different. His own had made his knees buckle, it was so potent. This one didn't; Leonard didn't seem to react quite as strongly… interesting. He glanced at Swann. He seemed to understand what was going on more than anyone. Mark decided to pay very close attention from here on.

"Can you describe how he drew this?" Swann was ready to talk about it.

"That's what is so hard to believe—he sat on the dock, leaning against the lifeguard tower the entire time. He sat cross-legged, and worked non stop… about thirty to 45 minutes! He was very particular about how I sat. He got up and put my right foot exactly where he wanted it: he was composing it, evidently—he had pre-drawn the table and chair before I sat down! He was very concerned for my comfort— told me to 'scootch' around to get as comfy as possible." He thought a minute—"I **was** comfortable, amazingly, once I put down the binoculars." Leonard sat forward: "it was charming, in a way, to see him concentrate—the tip of his tongue appears gradually from one corner of his mouth. He would glance up once in a while, look briefly, then get back to work." He shrugged. "He didn't seem to look at me directly for any length of time whatever."

Swann handed him the notebook cameo. "Did he show you this?"

"Yes! That's the very one! He asked if I saw anything that needed to be fixed!" he chuckled. "I mean, really! What could be fixed?! It was perfect as it was." He looked at it again. "It still is!" He looked at Swann, confused. "Julian didn't think so, for some reason. He came back the next day with that drawing board… said he needed to make a few finishing touches. Ten minutes later, he gave it back to me to trade for the one he had drawn of Sarge—he wanted me to see if anything needed fixing in that one too!" He shook his head. "I had forgotten about the smaller one. Fortunately, it was a light day at the lake—fewer scouts swimming—many were away on an overnight hike. Good thing—no splashes or stray drops of lake water."

Swann pulled back. "It's time for Sawyer to do his work. We need to give him full clearance." He noticed a curious expression on Mark's face.

"This is the first time I have seen this—It must have been under the drawing of Sarge. He did this in the cabin or in the cafeteria; he worked on more than one at a time—he kept one face down under the one he was working on to protect it, I suppose. You can see what he means by his camera eye: he draws most of it later. Then, when he's satisfied, signs it and gives it to the person he's drawn. That was automatic—a given. He does that to this day."

"He was a fanatic once he had that large paper to work with— that made all the difference in the world to him. You are quite right about that—Sarge gets the credit. No one had any idea what it would unleash—Julian included. It was a spontaneous reaction. I thought it appealed to his perfectionism—he was always complaining about the problem in the scrapbook drawings—he couldn't 'put everything in.' Always annoyed him—he's continually sharpening his pencil so he can be faithful to detail—most are missed by everyone else anyway." He shrugged. "I know nothing about art or drawing—I just stood back and stayed out of the way, mostly—I had lots to do anyway, so I was happy as a clam—he set me free to pay attention to the other boys—stupidly, I didn't pay attention, really—had no idea what was going on—probably just as well. I could have kept him occupied doing any number of things, but I didn't need to. A scoutmaster is busy looking for problems to head off or solve—unending, that."

Swann appreciated the effort to avoid taking credit, but he wasn't buying. "Don't sell yourself short: your support and flexibility were—and are—precisely what these boys need—and they thrive on it. I saw that myself at the retirement home. John sees it as well. Fate was in Julian's corner when you entered the picture. I suspect—and this only a guess—but I suspect you may be the reason he found this other quality that neither of us can define or pin down." He hoped he wasn't making a mistake to tell Mark that: he didn't want to change how he functioned as a supervisor. It was instinctive and clear of artifice. A rare phenomenon, particularly in the for-profit society they had to operate in.

"That should take care of it," Sawyer announced. "You need to look at it any longer, or should we put it back into the tube?"

Swann stood. "Thank you Leonard for allowing us to see this, and to document it properly. I shall be forever in your debt. Alas, we do have a long flight ahead. Is there anything else I can say or provide before we take our leave?" He extended his hand.

"Gosh—I can't think of anything—this has been an eye opener for me too. Thank you for that! Thank you very much."

"I regret that I forgot to order in—I had intended to have refreshments brought, but it slipped my mind. I hope you will overlook my inattention."

"Just as well," he patted his stomach. "Gotta stay in shape!"

Sawyer took care of the drawing with ease—he handed the tube to Leonard with a slight bow. He was ready to run interference. "Shall I have them make the call?" The limo to pick them up needed to be summoned—Marie would do that.

Swann nodded. Sawyer left the room; he knew where Marie was located when she wasn't at the reception desk.

"If you don't mind Leonard, you can ride with us to the helicopter; the driver will then take you wherever you direct—he is yours for the evening, if you have any other way to use his services."

"Wow. Thanks!"

"First, I have a call to place. If you don't mind, of course."

Mark picked up on that: "Sure—let's wait in the lounge, Leonard." He gave Swann a thumbs up. If he had wanted them to stay, he would have said so. He was learning how Swann functioned. The reaction he saw out of the corner of his eye confirmed his hunch.

Swann was on a roll—he had to arrange to see the remaining two portraits. He wanted to do that tomorrow, if he could. He needed to arrange it now—it would be too late after they got home. He had not decided yet whether to do that with Mark present. He would decide that on the flight. He still didn't know enough about this man. The flight home should take care of that. Mark was just as important as Julian was—Julian's allegiance and regard for him was central—that much was beyond question.

31   *watching for bubbles*

Even though it was winter and still dark out, Julian was wide awake all of a sudden. He didn't know why, or how early it was, because he was in the top bunk of Kasey's double decker, and there was no clock to look at that he knew of. He generally arose when Mother Nature thought it was time, no matter what his clock thought. She had a personal representative make the announcement: he had a full tank, and Little J was on duty keeping the floodgate closed. The problem was, of course, LJ had only one way to do that, and his patience was limited. Julian threw back the covers and leaned over the side to see if Kasey was awake: too dark to see. *o well…* he swung around and knee walked to the ladder. The room temperature was noticeably higher than he was used to—his mom always turned the heat way down at night.

Julian had never heard of a house that had a thermostat in every room to control radiant heat built into the ceiling—it was a warm dry summer night in the top bunk. He didn't notice that the temperature lowered at the same time he descended; it was still warmer than it would have been at home. It wouldn't take long for the air to mix once people started to move around.

Even though it was still dark, enough light from the approaching dawn and the security lights outside came through the window. He could see where it was safe to step; no problem finding his way down the ladder.

Likewise, Kasey had no trouble seeing a figure descending from above. Wagging a stiff one: some way to start the day! It was comical, in a way, and he had to giggle. He had not slept at all well, but the sound of the knee walk was enough to return him to a conscious state—the sound of bare feet on the ladder brought him current, as if he had just turned his reading lamp off—the events of last night flooded back: the dream was up and running again. It was a dream, wasn't it? "Good morning." He was sure the ghostlike figure would reply.

"Hey, Kasey! You awake?"

That's a silly question. Inside Guy observed; he was on duty early today.

Kasey yawned. "I don't know why, but I am."

"What time is it?" Julian looked around… still no clock.

Kasey lifted his wristwatch and yawned again. "Almost seven," he shook his head—half of him wanted to go back to sleep. He just realized that he had the same problem: full tank. Conversing directly with a very erect Little J bouncing a couple of feet away was a novel way to begin the day, to say the least. Again, he felt like he was a spectator… that he would wake up and all this would vanish.

seven… Julian figured as much—that's pretty much when he usually woke up at home—late if it was a school day. He plucked up one of the bath towels and wrapped it around his waist; they were still there from last night. If Little J wasn't so obnoxious, he might have hopped in with Kasey like last night just to be friendly. Anyway, it wasn't cold out here—no need. These bunks were kinda narrow. "What time do your folks get up on Saturday morning?"

"I don't know for sure—this is the first one in this house, come to think about it." He thought about it. "At home… I mean in Boston… they slept in sometimes, if they watched the late-late movie—I didn't pay attention last night. I don't know if you have those here."

"Well, I had this hot idea last night: how about us kids making them breakfast for a surprise?"

Kasey had never imagined such a thing. "Wow."

Julian sat on the edge of the bed. "Unless your mom is one of those ladies that doesn't allow anybody else in her kitchen… Jeremy's mom is that way… Boy! with her you hafta get permission to get a glass of water!" He tilted his head. "My mom really likes it when I make her a cup of coffee and take it into her room." Ever since camp he had been doing that; Inside Guy usually reminded him. "Saturday is the only day she sleeps in. Only day she can, 'cept Sundays—if we go to the late service."

"I think we're okay…" He didn't really know the routine, because he was at Belmont most of the time—he went home on some weekends; either he caught a ride or took the bus in; only took an hour or so. On Sundays, his mom often went to the early service all by herself—it was brief; back home by nine, easily.

"This is the first time I ever stayed overnight at a friend's, so I don't know what's happening today." No matter: Julian had to go—they could talk about this in a minute or two. "I could't tell last night: are the pipes loud in this house?"

? pipes? "Huh? What pipes?"

"You know, water pipes. Will flushing the toilet wake them up?" Julian didn't want to wake them up if he didn't have to.

"I haven't the foggiest, to quote Professor Marchbank," he chuckled. This was the kind of question that would evoke that response.

"Well, we hafta flush—otherwise we might forget. Moms hate to run across unflushed toilets—I bet your mom is like mine there." He poked Kasey in the side. "Get up—we can go together. That way we only hafta flush once. I gotta go: I bet you do too." He stood and picked up the other towel for Kasey.

Kasey shook his head: it was one surprise after another! Chapter four—or was it five? was underway. He flipped back the covers. Now that he understood what Julian was talking about, he agreed completely.

Tiptoeing across the hallway went just like it had last night, with the addition of modesty towels: no problem. When the door closed silently, Julian flipped on the light and they stepped toward the closed lid—it was just as he had left it last night. "Be good, Little J, we're almost there," he whispered. He raised the lid and seat. "Might as well go together, unless you want to take turns." He let the towel fall to the floor: this took both hands when Little J was puffy—he had gone down quite a bit.

Kasey was under more stress—Little K was still at 45 degrees, threatening to stand tall again.

The problem with this toilet was it had a wide body of water—you couldn't hit the side of the bowl without some splash landing outside: you had to aim at the center and make a lot of noise; Julian frowned and aimed for the center of the pool. His mom had made a big fuss over his splashes. He closed his eyes and concentrated... he didn't want Little J to start up again... amazing how loud a stream like that was in a mostly empty bathroom at seven in the morning, even when it wasn't full strength.

"He always takes longer when he's puffy," he apologized. Julian didn't hear a second stream—he opened one eye, then looked at Kasey's face. "Close your eyes and concentrate; he's prob'ly trying to impress Little J."

Trying not to laugh helped. Little K began to wilt finally.

Through the wall they heard a faint "woof."

"I expect he wants to go out," Julian guessed. "I bet he woke up your sister... does she use this potty too?" *we'd better scoot.*

"You're right!" Kasey thought rapidly: "let's let him out—he can follow us until we get dressed. We can take him out the same as last night. By the time we come back in, she'll be done in here." He looked at Julian to see if that made sense.

"Good thinking." He put his left hand on the lever: "Ready?"

Kasey did a last squirt: > > *ssp... plp!* < < "Yep."

Fortunately, the flush itself was nearly silent. Julian tilted his head, listening intently for the telltale whine of water rushing to refill the tank. He nodded his approval. *these new ones are a lot quieter...*

Insulated pipes running under the house didn't hurt any either; the house was barely five years old. Swann had acquired it after Paramount was finished shooting a mini-series in the area—the price was very attractive, and it bordered on his property.

Julian had forgotten about taking a shower—he was replaying the breakfast plan he had cooked up last night just before he went to sleep. He waited for Kasey to flip off the light—he hurried out the door and headed straight for the bedroom next door; he got set to open it a crack. He wasn't worried—the dog knew who he was. He put his ear against the door—he could hear it sniffing at the crack. *amazing thing how they know when someone's there.* Sid's dog was like that. Julian had always wanted a dog. "You want to open the door?"

"Go ahead." He had heard Ike do a sniff-puff at the crack. "I don't want him to start scratching to get out."

528

Julian opened the door slowly so the dog wouldn't jump on him. Ike nosed it open anyway and wiggled out, intent on finding out what that smell was: he rammed his nose right into Julian's towel—it promptly fell to the floor, exposing a bouncing and still puffy Little J and company—it was company and the surrounding area that Ike's olfactory system sought to investigate: his long snout was the perfect tool.

"Ooo-eee!" Julian pulled back quickly. A cold wet nose down there was not what he had in mind. The problem: Ike was a German shepherd: even though he was old, he was still strong and very large—well over seventy pounds: enough to tip Julian over if he wasn't Jack-be-nimble!

Kasey caught the door in time to stop it from slamming open. He peeked in to see if Zeyla was awake. He couldn't tell one way or another—it was dark in there—night light was off for some reason. He closed the door softly and picked up Julian's towel. He and Ike were headed for his room: yet another memorable picture. *if only I had a movie camera built into my head!* He thought of Huck Finn and Tom Sawyer up to a prank of some kind—this was fun, actually.

Before going to sleep last night, Julian had spent some time ruminating about Kasey and what he was facing. Between summer camp and Randall, he had learned some useful things. At camp, he had learned a great deal from Danny: not only how to fix breakfasts, but why: it was a sign he was growing up—he had to prove that he wasn't a little kid any more—he didn't have to depend on Mom for everything: one sign he was doing his share was fixing breakfast once in a while. Then along came Randall. He had revealed what it was like to have a complete family: he had a little sister; he and his family ate their meals together and took bicycle rides together: that was special.

Other than doing the dishes, he and his mom didn't do much together; half the time they had to do whatever Geraldine wanted. But Geraldine wasn't a father: that was hugely different. Julian figured his job, or part of it, was to help Kasey adjust to life at home—at Jackson

High, he'd be surrounded by kids that were used to that. It was bound to be a lot different from a boarding school.

Another thing was learning what it was like to have a little sister and a dad around—he wanted to get a peek at that. He wasn't complaining—he and his mom did fine, really—he didn't have any complaints at all. But he was curious; that's one reason he thought it was neat to include his little sister—he wasn't sure when girls became a problem... but Zeyla was kind of cute, for a girl. He always felt a little sorry for Randall's little sister—she was always around at supper... otherwise you'd never guess she was there. Randall got all the attention as far as he could see.

They had a big advantage this morning, thanks to Mom and Geraldine: they had helped put stuff away after the shopping trip! They knew where everything was. Once they had watered the dog and brought Zeyla into the kitchen, they were good to go. She was eager to join whatever was going on.

After assembling all the ingredients they would need, Julian put on his best pretend-I'm-Danny frame of mind: he would do what Danny did last summer in the Flaming Arrow camp—real easy, because the stove in this kitchen had those teeny blue flames.

"First thing you do is make the coffee." He paused. "Maybe you know this already...

Kasey shook his head.

"Real easy: my mom and Geraldine do this all the time—they finally taught me how—it's almost like at camp, 'cept here you don't hafta use the stove—you just plug in into the wall." He gave a wink. "You get lots of points for doing this one. Don't ask me why—personally, I don't like the stuff. Bleah." He opened the can.

> > *whis-s-shhh!* < < The room filled with the pungent odor of freshly ground coffee.

"See what I mean?!" he plugged his nose and looked at Zeyla with a grimace.

She giggled and plugged her nose too. Zeyla was very shy, but Julian fascinated her: she stared at his blond hair—she wanted to fluff it with her fingers to see what it felt like; she was too shy to ask.

Starting the percolator was easy. He talked to Zeyla, knowing that Kasey was paying attention as well: "You know it's done when it stops making the bubbly noise." He shrugged. "It doesn't smell that bad after it's done."

He handed her a big stirring spoon. Your first job is gonna be stirring stuff together: okay?"

Wide eyed, she nodded eagerly.

Julian wondered if she ever talked. He glanced at Kasey, figuring he would alert him to any problems.

Before long, everything having gone smoothly, the pancake batter was ready, and the big iron frying pan warming; Zeyla took the first cup of coffee to the bedroom, giving Julian a chance to confer with her big brother. They got the juice poured, the cantaloupe cut and sliced, the oven set on low, and the sausage links started while she was gone.

Kasey had no complaints whatever, or suggestions: Julian was showing him how to relate to her, something he had not even thought about. Julian was presenting a whole new side of his personality, and Kasey was truly amazed.

The sound of an excited four year-old girl running from the master bedroom caused Julian to turn. "You're back already! Was she happy?" He squatted down so he could look at her straight on—instinctively, he didn't want to be looking down on her when he was talking to her. It made a huge difference: she spoke at last.

"She gave it to Daddy." She grinned wide.

"Was he surprised?" Julian opened his eyes wide.

"Yeah!" she was so happy. "He gave me a big hug!"

"I'm glad. I thought he would. Your daddy is a good man. He deserves a good cup of coffee first thing."

She nodded back eagerly.

"Okay! Now you get to help make pancakes! Are you ready?"

She nodded again, glowing.

He stood and handed her the spatula. "Come over between Kasey and me—while Kasey and I cook the sausage links and eggs, you can do bubble duty. It's pretty easy, but real important!"

531

"Okay." She looked at Kasey happily. Standing by him would be nice—she didn't get to do that usually—he was way too tall.

"First, we do a test one. Now watch carefully: this is the batter you helped make. This is what pancakes are made of—it's magical. Maybe you have seen this before…"

She wasn't sure. "Not up close. I'm not 'posta touch the stove."

"Oo yeah, you don't want to do that!" He looked at Kasey, hoping this wasn't a bad idea after all." Kasey's shrug indicated he was okay. "Okay: watch real close…" he put a spoonful of batter in the center of the frying pan. It rose instantly, making a faint sizzle—he had added plenty of oil.

Her eyes opened wide.

"Watch now: pretty soon you'll see the bubbles."

Sure enough they appeared—small at first, they grew in size.

"Here's what you get to do: when they start to pop open, you get to poke me with the spatula. I'll use it to turn the pancake over so it won't burn. Okay?"

She nodded.

"Peek inside after they pop: you'll see all these teeny spokes… kinda neat." When half of them had popped open, he pointed: "See? This is when you hand me the spatula." He held out his hand.

She stood tiptoe to watch, though she was tall enough to see it: she was keenly interested.

Julian flipped it over—the sizzle combined with the sudden rise and doubling of thickness was thrilling to a first time viewer—even Kasey was impressed—he had never seen this up close either. The soft pff-pff sound seemed to invite being eaten: so did the aroma.

"Hand me a saucer…"

Kasey pulled one out of the cupboard.

"Now watch close…" he lifted the test cake onto the saucer and handed it to her. "There…" He tore it in half and turned up the edge: "See? All done! Ready for butter and syrup! Careful, it's still kind of hot."

She looked at it up close: no runny batter left. "Wow," she grinned wide at her big brother.

Soon the routine was established; the pan was large enough to do three at a time. That proceeding as planned, Julian had instructions for Kasey: they needed to get the sausages into the oven and the eggs started.

Kasey brought the egg carton over from the refrigerator. He handed Julian an egg.

"The thing is, you don't want any shell fragments to get in here. You can crack them all open into a bowl first, or do it right over the pan." He shrugged. "I like doing it over the pan—saves having another dish to wash. But you hafta do it sort of fast." He broke the first egg and emptied it toward his side of the pan." Now you do one," he pointed to the other side. "You do six, I'll do six. When the clear stuff turns white, we pop the yokes and stir... okay?"

Kasey had never broken an egg before. He was surprised at how strong the shell was.

Julian put his empty shell back into the carton and reached for another. They had worked this out well; they alternated, each egg being placed in its own space on the grill. A couple more and they would be ready for some salt and pepper...

Sudden input from a pleasantly surprised Little J intruded: the scrambled egg project was upstaged instantly.

"OOPsie!" Julian exclaimed and took a step back. He looked at Zeyla and thought fast: "His door came open by accident!"

He had put on his Levis too fast—he did a poor job of buttoning—the bottom two buttons had come open—he had skipped the bottom one as usual, since it was always hard to do anyway; the one above it resisted being inserted completely into the button slit—the pants were still new enough; thus, it had worked loose—that had happened before—he usually caught it after sitting down.

Little J was being frisky this morning—he usually was the day after a Good One, and his bulging point was clearly visible: reaching back and forth past Kasey to get another egg opened the door considerably. Working on his feet allowed LJ to swing freely, providing frequent contact with the soft cotton—more than satisfactory as far as LJ was concerned—his relatively healthy state this morning took it as a reward for doing such a fine job the night before; he sensed that a state of readiness was expected—no problem. Little J had always been fond of this stage: too soon to announce, but on standby.

Any typical four year old that had been standing close by on pancake bubble watch duty for several minutes couldn't help noticing something move around in there: it was almost a straight ahead view. Luckily, Julian was wearing his skivvies, and they were new enough to remain closed in front. Still, it seemed to invite a curious four year old's forefinger to give it a poke. Little J, of course, enjoyed the attention and was eager to respond: she had connected at the ideal angle: she had to feel its healthy and instant reaction, not unlike kitty-kat pushing up when rubbed at the base of her tail. Zeyla would have used two fingers, but the boy pulled away too quick.

"Sorry about that—" he turned slightly and buttoned it shut quickly, glancing at Kasey, who was watching wide eyed, not knowing what to do: his little sister had begun to peek into Julian's fly!

Julian crouched down so he could look her square in the eye. "See, the thing is, you aren't supposed to know he's in there—he's not allowed to talk to little girls. It's against the rules. I shouldn't have put on my pants so quick. Don't worry, I caught it in time—he can't get out now. I promise not to tell. You won't be in any trouble." He did the zipped lip gesture. "Okay?" She looked at him open eyed, still processing. Julian didn't want to say anything that would make her cry. He smiled gently: "Okay? You hafta promise too." He zipped his lips again and did the Groucho eyebrow bit.

Zeyla zipped her lips and nodded.

"Good girl!" He gave her a thumbs up and a wide grin. He stood and gave Kasey a roll of the eyes. Fortunately, she didn't ask any questions.

Kasey looked down to see if Little K was at all visible. He had not realized that a little sister could be curious. He shook his head. Julian was a genius! He was correct in assuming that she had never seen what occupied the space between a boy's legs; later the event did cause her to glance down there secretly at odd times. She wondered who—or what—

534

stayed down there; it was smaller than a squirrel. Maybe she'd get a secret peek one day.

Fortunately, the pancake duty had another five or ten minutes to go. Julian took the spatula and stirred the eggs slowly as if nothing had happened. They looked better with more egg white visible than usual. However, he had a job of it for a while trying to discourage an eager Little J—he didn't succeed completely for almost an hour. It was a good poke: LJ wanted another—**expected** another.

Soon, it was time for Zeyla to fetch her parents.

Lewis and Candace had been hearing activity off an on, and were curious; Zeyla had told them to wait until she came to get them: they had a surprise, but it wasn't ready yet! She had skipped happily out of the room, delighting them at once. That was another first. The extended cuddle was nice—with their own private bathroom, what else could they wish for? When Zeyla returned, Lewis was ready for a second cup. They were in their bathrobes, ready to be surprised. They had never seen her this animated. She had grabbed the empty cup and skipped out of the room urging them to hurry into the kitchen. She had to refill the cup and put it on the table.

After the blessing, everyone was eager to have a bite of the fresh pancakes—the bountiful supply of cakes in the center of the table, flanked by scrambled eggs, link sausages and cantaloupe wedges looked just as tasty and inviting as one of Sharples' meals, only freshly cooked.

They were a few bites into a pancake when the peal of long brass tubes being struck by an unseen hammer filled the entry foyer.

> > *klannng- - - klannnng!* < <

The doorbell chimes were considerably louder inside the house, as Julian had suspected they would be when he pushed the button yesterday morning. He looked quickly at Kasey: opening the door was his job: the parents were their special guests for breakfast—besides, on purpose, they were still in their bathrobes.

Kasey remembered Julian's admonition, and stood at once, gesturing to his parents to remain seated: he would handle this. He decided to employ his little sister as an assistant; she could be an alternate when he was not at home. This would be her first training session: no time like the present: simulating Julian's approach, he opened his eyes wide: "Would you like to help me answer the door?"

To everyone's surprise, she responded at once with an affirmative nod. She presumed it was a serious question, and she answered it seriously by backing her chair up a few inches and holding out her hand: big people always wanted to hold onto it when they went someplace. She seemed to know it was important to do it quickly, since it was wrong to keep anyone waiting—especially when it was cold outside.

Julian was as surprised as the parents... they watched wide-eyed as Ike, the always faithful companion and security escort, followed behind. Lewis and Candace had never seen Kasey and his little sister do anything together, hand in hand or otherwise. They almost missed the smile on Julian's face.

Kasey opened the door, as focused on Zeyla as on seeing who was at he door; he was somewhat surprised to see Mason, but it wasn't unusual—for the past few days he had come and gone frequently, helping everyone get settled in.

"Good morning, Master Kasey... and Miss Zeyla. I am here this morning to assist Mister Swann." He moved to one side: Frederick Swann stood directly behind. He was here to take Julian home after stopping for a brief visit.

He had arrived exactly an hour earlier than expected—the message had been misunderstood somewhere along the line—either Francine had been mistaken, or Candace had misunderstood... whatever the cause, Kasey had to deal with it as well as he could—with all the breakfast activity, both he and Julian had forgotten about Mr. Swann being expected, or anything else. Their attention had been on doing a great job without making a huge mess while they were at it, and they were having a ball doing it. Julian had no idea that Mr. Swann had a plan for the day.

Swann was enchanted at once, especially with the little girl, who paid as much attention to what her brother was doing as she did to what they had been sent to do—she tried to mimic his facial expressions and

536

nodded in agreement to whatever he said. She didn't go so far as to speak aloud.

Kasey was untrained in etiquette, though he had been surrounded by it all his life. That was just as well, since he didn't think to show Mr. Swann into the living room to wait for his parents to make themselves "presentable." Instead, he followed his instinct, and did what he assumed Julian would do: invite them to join the party—in this case, share: he happened to know there was plenty to go around, Mason included. His parents had guests once in a while in Boston, but he was seldom present—he was accustomed to staying out of sight.

"Good morning," he smiled wide and stepped back: "Won't you join us? We're all in the kitchen." He stopped there—his mother would decide whether or not to invite him.

"Why, thank you!" He bowed slightly to the little girl and stepped inside. The aromas betrayed what was taking place or just finishing in the kitchen. He motioned for Mason to come along—he saw no point in his having to wait in the Packard. He held out his hand for the dog to sniff—they had met before; Swann knew the rules. The dog was old and near sighted, but his nose was as good as ever. The wagging tail indicated that he had passed the inspection and was welcome to enter. He waited for Mason to be approved before following Kasey into the kitchen.

"Mr. Swann and Mason are here," he announced, leading them into the room.

"Neato!!" Julian exclaimed, jumping up and hurrying over to shake their hands. He had figured out who was at the door and had formed a plan. "You're just in time!" He wanted to hug them both, but controlled himself. "This is perfect. I clean forgot you were coming! Naughty me! Kasey and I can grab a couple of chairs from the dining room!" he headed in that direction. He didn't frame it as an invitation—there wasn't a graceful way for Swann or Mason to decline or for the Woods to apologize—nor time: Zeyla knew these men and reached for Mason's hand: she wanted him to sit next to her. She was eager to tell him all about the bubbles.

When Mason looked for a command, Swann gestured for him to join the gathering rather than sit in the next room. The domestic picture he and his man had entered was a wonderful surprise. He knew at once it was Julian's doing—he intended to let it play out. He would have to call Avery again, and Mark. He could find a way to do that. As if this had been planned, he addressed Candace:

"Thank you for your hospitality. Mason and I are happy to join you. We are pleasantly surprised." He bowed slightly to the little girl— her name escaped him. "And thank you, young lady, for your wonderful greeting at the door." He winked at Lewis.

Lewis was unable to respond to his wife's need to have her hand squeezed—a wink would have to do; his nod to Swann was inadequate, but all he was able to do for the time being. He intended to give Swann a quick look at the drawing Julian had done last night—the sketchbook was sill in their bedroom.

Julian and Kasey arrived with the chairs rapidly, so the pause was only momentary. The table was large enough; getting settled in was not difficult. Julian and Kasey were quick to provide the plates and flatware. Julian moved his plate around to the other side, next to Zeyla so that Swann and Mason had that side of the table: it had worked out perfectly.

Swann had had his toast and marmalade this morning and a cup of Sanka. Fortunately, he had set aside the entire day. He had planned to call Mark on the way into town, so he could spend a few minutes here— clearly, it would mean a great deal to Lewis—the other reason he had come to the door. It had been a while since he had been inside this house. He had no reason to think it needed his personal attention, but it never hurt to have a first hand glimpse occasionally. He looked at the table: he didn't need to eat, but the occasion seemed to require him to participate—fortunately, he had not overdone—it was a couple of hours ago.

32   *the two Marks*

Shortly after it registered in Julian's head that Mr. Swann was here to take him home, he realized he was in a bind: how to say 'thank you for your hospitality' properly was only one thing he had to figure out: it was not covered in any of the etiquette lessons Geraldine and his mom had given him. He had never stayed overnight at a friend's house before—his mom didn't approve of it—or didn't use to. When Kasey's mom did the inviting, she thought it was a fine idea. *go figure.*

People were almost done eating! There were dishes to do: what about that? He wasn't in a hurry to leave—they were having fun. Of course there wasn't much to do except the dishes—it just seemed wrong to hurry off… besides, they didn't even talk about school yet… got sidetracked last night, thanks to Little J. But then he had a thought: *why would Mr. Swann go out of his way to take me home in the first place?*

Maybe it isn't out of his way. Inside Guy had some ideas about this.

Julian nodded—this was close to his house, sort of. Kasey said it wasn't visible from here; he had not seen it himself, but Mason said it was close—*he lives there.*

Remember, you have a present for him… Inside Guy was good at reminding him of things.

ooo… yeah. Another problem: *which one should I give to him?*

One of Frederick Swann's skills was the ability to observe and analyze simultaneously—and to do so without drawing any attention to himself—he was able to become a passive object, something that was so taken for granted he was automatically skipped over, should anyone be looking. For several days, his goal had been to study and learn as much as he could about this unique boy. Julian had been under his scrutiny from the minute he arrived. When he noticed that Julian was preoccupied by something, he realized it was time to take the wheel. It was time to get the day underway, lest after breakfast table talk take control. He lifted his napkin with his right hand.

Mason was a master—not only did he take note of the gentle patting around the mouth, but when his employer used his right hand instead of his left, he knew what he had been instructed to do. It was simple in this instance, since they had been seated directly opposite the three cooks—the parents were at opposite table ends, still in their bathrobes. "Mr. Swann would like to compliment the person who made these excellent pancakes."

Julian and Zeyla broke into big smiles and pointed at each other.

"And the eggs?"

Zeyla pointed at Kasey and Julian, Julian and Kasey pointed at each other. No words had been spoken, which evoked a smile from Swann and a giggle from Zeyla and the boys. The parents were enormously pleased by the camaraderie: it was new and unexpected. They were ready to have Julian stay indefinitely.

"My thanks to you all—it was a fine breakfast." Swann winked at Zeyla, then turned to Candace. "I appreciate your hospitality, of course, but I do have things to do today, so I fear I must steal away at last; and I need to take one of your cooks along—I have need of his service for a while today." He saw the disappointed look on Zeyla and Kasey's faces. "I'm sure he will be visiting again."

"We certainly hope so," Lewis said, smiling at his wife.

"Thank you, Julian. You are always welcome." Glancing at the trio, she added "Perhaps next time you will show me your special way of making pancakes. These were **very** special."

Julian tried not to blush—he wasn't used to compliments; his quandary about how to deal with departing had been taken care of: he was being shown the door as well. "Um, sure—but..." he put his hand on Zeyla's back: "I bet Zeyla can show you—" he cupped his hand, pretending to make an aside, "be sure to remember the oil."

Zeyla nodded somberly, grateful for the reminder. She was not very vocal, but she was as intelligent as her brother, and fully engaged.

Mason detected an impending problem—he addressed Zeyla directly: "if you put on your coat, you can come along to see him off—I'm sure Master Julian would enjoy your company as we go to the car." He scooted his chair back and looked at Kasey, making a silent invitation to him as well.

Kasey nodded in the affirmative, unable to completely mask his tendency to see offers like this with a degree of skepticism.

As Kasey and Zeyla ran to get their coats, Swann whispered something to Mason. Candace turned to Julian: "Thank you, Julian, for everything. I am truly serious: you are welcome at any time." She would save her full appreciation for his mother. She and her boy had completely changed her point of view about many things—and in a seemingly effortless way. "You appear to have acquired an addition to your fan club. Thank you again—I hope Zeyla wasn't in the way."

fan club?! He chuckled. "What an idea! Fan club! Zeyla is fun!" He lowered his voice. "No, she seemed kinda shy—I don't have a little sister, but I have friends who do. I figured Kasey needed a way to… well, since he's gonna be around now instead of being away at school, he hasta be a big brother all the time: it's part of his job now. I figured he could use a way to do that without being bossy. I hope you like surprise breakfasts once in a while," he shrugged, and flashed his eyebrows up and down. He whispered, "I didn't tell him that—he's smart enough to figure it out for himself." He put his fingers on his lips.

She tipped her head thoughtfully—she had not given him sufficient credit—she had not suspected he had a purpose. There was a thoughtful boy inside as well as a happy one. Francine and her friend had done very well.

Meanwhile, Lewis had signaled Swann to stay put: he hurried to retrieve the sketchbook from his bedside table. He returned just as Julian was about to put on his jacket. Lewis handed it to Swann and spoke quietly: "he drew this last night after supper. I thought you'd appreciate a glimpse before I return it. Kasey said it took **fifteen** minutes to draw." He looked at Swann, still incredulous. "Helgar told me about this sketchbook." He pointed to the sketch. "He is certainly worth your time.

541

But you, of all people, don't need to be told that." He waited for Swann to return it.

Swann looked closely: like the other drawings, this had an unseen tone or quality that imposed itself; it was different from the others, but there—unmistakably there. Elusive... this was almost like a sampler. He closed his eyes for a second and looked again. *remarkable*... he closed and handed it back. "Thank you Lewis; I appreciate this—the timing couldn't be better. That is what this little trip is about, in fact. I am in your debt." He stepped toward the door— Mason was leading the entourage of breakfast cooks out. He donned his new parka without assistance.

They paused at the threshold to watch as the trio and Mason approached the Packard. It was far enough away to make hearing what was being said impossible.

"Wait..." Candace wanted to watch the interaction between the three—Kasey had picked Zeyla up so she could see what Mason was pointing to—evidently Julian wanted him to tell them something about the front seat. She had never seen Kasey pick her up like Lewis often did—obviously he was strong enough: he was seven inches taller than his father.

Mason had finished talking about the special features of the front seat; the brief pause provided Zeyla with the chance she had been hoping for.

"Can I..." she was afraid to ask right out, but it was right there in front of her...

"Can you what?" Julian grinned happily.

"Can I feel your hair?"

Kasey was mortified—but Julian surprised him again—

"Sure!" He tipped his head toward her—his mom's friends used to do this all the time when he was Zeyla's age.

Carefully she reached out with her forefinger and poked tentatively—it was so soft she could hardly feel a thing!

"Give it good fluffing up!" He shook it back and forth vigorously: "use both hands!"

Giggling happily, she fluffed it up with both hands.

After a minute she stopped, and he looked at her with a big grin: "Thanks. I needed that." He shook his head again. "And thanks for asking permission," he winked. "Shows you are a good girl. Besides, if you don't ask, how are you going to find out?" He asked her eagerly: "Can I fluff your hair too?"

She nodded happily.

He gave it a gentle stroke—it was about as opposite as it could be to his. It had been fashioned as her mother's, in a very traditional elegant and simple short well brushed wool coat slightly more than an inch long, common to the Ethiopian upper class in the thirties and forties. "Huh. I never thought about doing that until now. Thanks to you, I found out something new!"

"How come you have brown eyes?" She thought they were supposed to be blue.

"I'm an oddball: I got them from my mom—she has brown eyes. How come you and Kasey have blue eyes?"

"My momma…" she grinned proudly.

"See? You and Kasey are oddballs too! Personally, I like to be an oddball: more fun. "On you, blue eyes are special—look a lot better on you than on me, I bet." He winked at Kasey. "Us oddballs hafta stick together, okay?"

Kasey and Zeyla laughed, looking at each other happily.

Lewis handed the notebook back to Swann. "He'll think of it after you have left, more than likely."

"That boy is a blessing, Mr. Swann." She cuddled close to her husband. "We'll wait here to see you off, if you don't mind."

"Of course." He shook Lewis' hand. "I'll be seeing you soon— Sawyer has shown me the plans. It will take a couple of months, I'm sorry to say—but with your approval I will select a builder. We intend for you to be involved all the way—I don't want anything to interfere."

543

He paused to look at the siblings; Mason had just opened the rear door for Julian. "This morning was a very nice surprise—I don't get many of those." He nodded toward the car. "Although, they seem to follow in his wake... they pop up like wildflowers." He paused. "In a way, I hope he never grows up completely. Well, then: I'll be in touch." He had just remembered Mark's wistful observation about his scouts having to move on.

Julian felt all warm and fuzzy inside: little Zeyla ran back to hug her mother—obviously thrilled at having fluffed up his hair. He giggled unintentionally and turned to Mr. Swann happily. "She wanted to fluff up my hair!" He shook his head. "I used to get that a lot when I was little—my mother's friends always did that. Never could figure out why." He shrugged. "Must be a girl thing." He sat back, ready to turn the page. "Thanks for giving me a ride—saves my mom making the trip."

"You must have had a good visit."

"Mm-hmm... sure did. Kind of a surprise—Kasey's mom thought of it. Good idea, actually. I didn't really know them yet—and with school about to start up and everything, I figure the better I know them, the better job I can do.

"Lewis asked me to return this," Swann handed the sketchbook to Julian— "he appreciated having some time to look at it."

"OO-eee!" he was aghast. "Thanks!" He frowned: *how could I forget this?!* annoyed with himself, he held it tight.

Word choice was one of Swann's yardsticks. "Job?" He regarded Julian carefully, hoping for a clarification. When it wasn't forthcoming he nudged a little: "You referred to having a job to do."

Julian was puzzled. *job?* It took a minute to replay what he had said "Oh! Well, yeah. Maybe there's a better word; I'm not so hot with words—Randall's better there. Mr. Middleton said he needed my help. As a scout it's my job to do that—to help out; any good scout knows that." He paused. "Actually, it's Kasey and his folks that need help." He turned to Swann: "See, I try to make it fun at the same time if I can. But if it needs to be done, then it's a job: a job needs to be done, one way or another. Better if it's fun, though. Especially if it's for nice people like

Kasey and his family. Same for Grandpa Sanderson and the retired folks. Nice people deserve it. Besides, it helps me too: makes me feel worthwhile; I always make a new friend." He thought about that a minute. "Yeah…I never thought about that before. It **is** like a job, kind of: you have to do it, because it needs to be done—simple as that. There's no pay in the usual sense, but a new friend is worth a lot—better than money—way better. I figured that out a long time ago." He paused and added an afterthought. "I usually say 'no big deal' when I think something is obvious; but in this case it **is** a big deal." He chuckled: "see what I mean? I just now figured **that** out!"

Swann and Mason exchanged glances in the driver's mirror. Swann was grateful he had someone he could share this with—no one was better at understanding than Mason. This boy seemed capricious and free spirited, but he was purposeful underneath—a native trait and ability—like his art, untrained and pure. He reached into his executive travel case and pulled out the original, the first spiral bound sketchbook. "This has been my guidebook today. I have just returned from visiting with Leonard, Mr. Jorgensen and your dear friend, Uncle Max. They send their greetings, and hope to see you in June." He did not return the sketchbook—not yet.

"Wow!" He looked at Swann eagerly. "Neato neato neato!! **Neee…toe!!!** How are they?" he bounced up and down on the seat.

Julian's enthusiasm was a little startling at close range, but engaging; clearly genuine, an example of what he had just observed: he had not met those men before going to that camp—now they were as close as any friend. Truly remarkable. Swann wondered if it was a vulnerability. "I am pleased to report that they are well—I'm not sure I would be, after spending a winter up there."

Julian had not thought about that: he imagined seeing HQ under six feet of snow. He was amazed: did he have to use snowshoes and everything? He didn't want to ask a stupid question like that…

"They were most kind and accommodating. You see, I had travelled there to see the final versions of your drawings. This afternoon, I am looking forward to seeing the other one—Mark tells me you have it in safekeeping along with another." He was pleased with himself for finding a way to bring it up.

545

Julian sat up, surprised: no one knew about those. Except Mark, of course. "Mark said it would be okay for you to look at them." He tilted his head. *I forgot about that...*

It's okay, Inside Guy advised. *Just tell him you didn't want them to be curly permanently because of that tube.*

He nodded to himself... he didn't need to give Mr. Swann the main reason. He needed to be sure to keep the ones of Randall out of sight—he had promised. He'd just as soon Mr. Swann didn't see those anyway... or Mark. He was kind of proud of them. He learned a lot drawing those. They were the only drawings he had never given away.

Swann had learned to recognize when Julian was mulling things over in his mind—thinking what to say or not say, or take into consideration before opening his mouth or doing anything hastily. It was very like his own process, but the boy had not learned to mask it completely. At this point, Swann was happy to take advantage of that insight. It might help him proceed more effectively—he was aware that the clock was always running, and he was not at all sure how long he had. It would not be enough, most likely; efficiency was important, but haste was stupid and invariably more expensive. He needed to spring Mark free for another hour or two—he wanted him to be there—seeing the subject interact with their drawing was enormously instructive—and he doubted he had the ability to see that—at least not fully—without Mark there in the room. Sawyer was very good at capturing that.

"I hafta admit I was surprised he gave his okay," Julian said finally—he hoped it didn't matter if he took his time about explaining those drawings in particular—they were very special for a lot of reasons. "See, Mark is real touchy about things like that—he doesn't want them hanging on his wall—he's one guy who doesn't like to show off who he is—how good looking or important. That's one reason he wants us to call him by his first name: he hates to put himself above anyone else—'specially us scouts." Julian shifted in his chair. "I feel the same way. I think of myself as an ordinary kid, no better, no worse than anybody else." He shrugged—"kinda weird, maybe, but..." He looked at Mr. Swann: "You know what I mean: you know how to stand behind other people better than anybody I ever met." He giggled. "Kind of hard when you go around in a car like this! I gotta hand it to you."

Mason couldn't control himself completely after hearing that; it was a good thing he was fully occupied.

Swann couldn't hold it against him; he had to cross his legs to create place to put his elbow while he covered his mouth. The boy had no idea his observation was filled with ironic wit—it was an honest and accurate observation, but very humorous.

"I don't like being in the front row, especially, either," Julian continued. Too many kids get all puffed up about how cute they are, or how neat they look or how popular they are—they get so full of themselves they aren't much good for anything else. Each to his own, I guess. Me, I'd rather draw something interesting. Or someone—I guess I've been drawing people lately more than anything. No two are alike."

Julian really enjoyed riding back here with Mr. Swann. He could see now why he liked this car: you could relax and think about things. Their talk had made him think about how little time there was before they had to be back in school. *I need to call Nick and Tom...*   they could help him figure out what to do on the first day. Nobody had said much about that. Flaming Arrow to the rescue! He scooched appreciatively: "I sure like your car."

Swann was able to keep a straight face; he gave the silent command to Mason via the mirror—he wanted Mark to arrive at about the same: it was time to make the call. Sawyer was standing by. Francine and Geraldine were enjoying a lunch at Amanda and June's. He thought it best to get this taken care of before they appeared.

"Thank you, Julian. Is there anything in particular that pleases you?"

"Yes. Besides being comfy, it's super quiet. Helps me think about stuff... I just figured that out!" he grinned wide and turned to Mr. Swann to explain. "Sometimes I notice when I have figured something out. Usually it's no big deal—people do that all the time..." He felt a little sheepish. "I useta think I was a little on the stupid side, y'know. I figure I'm just a little slow 'cause my brain is too busy doing something else; it gets around to it later, is all." It was time to think about the first day at school: he still had to figure out what to do.

Swann wished there was a way to peek into Julian's thoughts—but he had it exactly right—being a good place to think without being distracted was exactly what he treasured most about this back seat. What could this wunderkind be thinking about now? He thought it wise to let him have a few minutes. He could use the time to review his plan for the rest of the day.

When the Packard approached Julian's house, an unfamiliar car was parked in front. "Oh-oh… we have company today." *strange… mom's car is gone… no Geraldine either… must be working…* He sat up and looked carefully—two guys dressed in big fur lined parkas were getting out… parkas like Mr. Swann was wearing!

"Excellent! They are here. You haven't met Sawyer yet, Julian. He accompanied Mark and me to Camp Walker yesterday."

Julian's eyes opened wide: "Mark?" he looked again closely: "It's Mark! Wow!" He grinned at Mr. Swann happily. He was always glad to see Mark! He almost opened the door and hopped out. *oop…* He turned to Mr. Swann: "Excuse me, but I've been meaning to ask: am I s'posed to wait for Mason to open the door, or is it okay to just hop out? I mean, I don't want Mason to look bad 'cause I goof it up." That had been bothering him ever since the drive to the airport. Opening and closing those doors was part of his job.

"Thank you, Julian, for being so thoughtful." He decided to take some time with this—he owed it to Mason; he gave him a silent signal to stay put. "You are correct to be concerned. Like many things, there is more than one answer—it can depend on where you are or have been. If it's a formal event, it's proper to allow Mason to do that—it is his job to present his passengers in the best light. Assisting them to get in and out of the car is a part of that. If it isn't a special event, then it's fine to open the door yourself, as long as you tell him that you would like to do that first. That way, you are being polite to him as well as considerate. If he thinks you should wait for him to do it, he will say so. Today, that would be the best way, I think.

"Thanks. That's been bothering me. All fixed!" He leaned toward the open window between the front and back seats: "Okay with you if I hop out?" he grinned wide.

"Yes, Master Julian. Thank you for asking." He tapped the visor on his chauffeur cap, maintaining his deadpan perfectly. Moments like this were what made working for Swann so special. It was a privilege.

With a giggle, Julian hopped out and ran to greet Mark. He was unable to stop himself: all his effort to look grown up and not a little kid any more vanished: he ran to greet Mark with a big hug. Sometimes he just seemed to boil over he was so happy. "Mr. Swann told me you were at the Camp to visit Uncle Max!"

Mark was not expecting such an effusive greeting—he knew Julian well enough to realize he was in unusually high spirits. "You must have had a great weekend yourself!"

"Oo, yeah!" he hopped up and down: "Mom let me stay overnight at Kasey's! We took them shopping yesterday and everything. They're staying in this huge house—bathrooms everywhere," he giggled. "How is Uncle Max?" Julian was worried about all the snow. "Must be hard to get around up there with all the snow." He didn't think it was a good idea for him to be up there all winter long.

Swann stood back with Mason to watch for a moment. He spoke quietly to his servant/confidant: "watching this boy is like having another taste of boyhood myself, in a way. I don't think mine was anywhere close to being so full of fun."

Sawyer gazed open-eyed in wonder: **this** is the artist who's work he had been photographing? He looked at Swann: both he and Mason nodded confirmation. Now he understood why Swann was so preoccupied—he hadn't really been paying close attention. The school jacket emphasized how young he was—it was a little too large.

Julian dug into his pocket for the house key he always carried. He knew at once his mother wasn't home—she would have invited Mark and his friend in. *wait... friend*: "Hello, I'm Julian. You must be a photographer. I have a friend who has a case like yours. He has a **Nikon**!" he added proudly. "He even has a photo lab."

"Pleased to make your acquaintance, Julian. My name is Sawyer." He knew about Randall and the lab—he had selected several items to upgrade its capabilities. He had not seen it yet himself. He had thought that boy was older as well.

"Neato! I like Buz Sawyer!" Julian exclaimed. "I don't s'pose you're related or anything," he giggled… "Gosh! No point in standing around outside! Come on in, everyone!" he ran up the steps and unlocked the door. Sure enough, he could hear the radio blasting away—he needed to shut that off quick!

While Julian hurried ahead Mark showed everyone in—he felt quite at home in this house. "Francine is very frugal," he said quietly to Swann. "It doesn't take long for the furnace to kick in."

Julian emerged from the kitchen having just flipped the radio to Effem and turning it down. "Y'know, the best coat rack is prob'ly the kitchen chairs." Those parkas would never fit in the hall closet—it was almost full anyway—Mom and Geraldine's always filled it tight. He had another thought: he needed to play host, with his mom gone. He led the way. "Maybe you would like a cup of coffee…"

Discreetly, everyone but Mark looked around at the very plain and simple homespun room. Swann had been here before, but his staff had not. They were at a loss—it was immaculate, but very humble and almost museum like. Sawyer, given to an occasional witticism wondered where Aunt Maude slept; he expected her to appear any minute, rimless spectacles and all, crochet basket in hand.

Julian was in luck: his mother had the coffee pot all ready—all he had to do was plug it in. While the others entered the room, he realized he needed to take off his school Jacket. He pointed at the four chairs around the kitchen table. "See what I mean? Perfect coat rack." He took his off: "be right back…" he assumed Mark would take over.

Julian hurried to his room and quickly flopped his coat on the back of his chair; he stood a second: his room was too small—that was obvious… he hurried back into the kitchen. *gosh*… he had no idea what to do.

Swann could see that Julian was utterly helpless. "I suspect your room is a bit small for what I have in mind. I think the living room would serve best, don't you?"

Julian nodded.

"Let's go in there—Sawyer is an expert at these things."

"Neato!!" Julian was enormously relieved. He looked at Mark to see if he agreed. The nod took care of his concern. He had not realized before now how important it was to have a mom do all this stuff.

They filed into the living room after Sawyer; Mason remained standing by the kitchen entrance.

"If you would take that chair, Mr. Swann, I'll stand where I think the drawing will be best seen, given this light. The widow will provide most of what we'll need—I may want to supplement it." He turned to Julian: "Do you have an easel?"

Julian hopped eagerly. "A big one and a small one!" He ran to get them both—*might as well.*

Sawyer looked at Swann: "Once I have the first one in place, you will need to determine where you want Mark to be." He had become well enough acquainted to call him Mark, which is what he preferred anyway.

Julian entered with both easels. "I thought you might want this little one too." He looked at Mark, apologetically. "I hope you don't mind, but I couldn't stand leaving them in that tube—that curl is real hard to get rid of. Last summer, the guys on the yard crew helped me get some big pieces of cardboard out of a dumpster—so I taped them flat—and I keep them in the back of my closet. Nobody knows they're there—Mom and Geraldine included... should I go get them now?" They were Mark's drawings, after all.

"The seated one was drawn first, I take it?" Swann inquired. Julian had told him about these—there was no small version of the second one—it was apt to be of most interest.

Julian nodded.

"Bring that one first—I think it best to look at them one at a time."

Mark gave consent without betraying his underlying concern—he remembered seeing these two side by side on the floor of the cabin. He had tried to block it out but gave up finally. He needed to confront this demon once and for all. He did not understand why these drawings caused him to respond so viscerally. Oddly enough, he thought having a crowd around improved his chances. His eyes had blurred while he ruminated—he did not realize Julian had brought it in already and

551

placed it on the easel. Coincidentally, he was sitting in almost the same pose in Francine's other wing chair—he half expected to see Julian on the floor by the ottoman staring at him—a pose he remembered well, after three years.

Julian was a little worried; the last time Mark looked at these drawings he nearly cried—he was both happy and sad at the same time. Julian still didn't understand that at all.

Swann had turned toward the easel—like the Leonard and Uncle Max, they were full length figures. The impact was enormous and immediate—stronger than he had expected—and it wasn't even properly positioned. This one was the most powerful yet: it nearly shouted at him. He took a deep breath. "I'm curious about something, never having done this myself: how long did you sit for this?"

Mark appreciated the question—it freed him somehow, enabled him to look away: "Let's see—it was after the troop campfire, between that and lights out, wasn't it?" Unconsciously, he wiped away the tear that had formed in his right eye.

"Sort of. Remember, I had it figured out ahead of time before you came in: I spent about five minutes roughing in the table and chair—I was trying to do one like I did of Leonard at the lake that day. So you had to sit about twelve or fifteen minutes I think before the lights out call; you let me have another five minutes to finish drawing your shoes. Then I did the big one next day during Free Swimming. That takes about an hour or so, usually. You let me do some last minute fixups after campfire the next night—another five or ten minutes." He noted an important difference: "Not as long as I spent on the first big one, o'course—that one had three people in it!" His attention returned to the Mark portrait—he was tempted to do a couple of fixups but didn't—not without asking Mark. "This was the second big one, actually—then I did the big ones of Leonard and Uncle Max."

Swann noticed that both Sawyer and Mason were staring at the drawing in disbelief, mouths open: they had both done the math. The boy couldn't have spent two hours on it all told. It was hard to believe—but he had seen him do the very same thing at the retirement home in less than half that. Now he was debating with himself between continuing this discussion as they were, or to have Mark sit next to the large drawing. He decided to postpone that for the photo session. "So you weren't uncomfortable staying in place for that long?

"No, as a matter of fact—Julian was very helpful—he made sure I was okay before starting," he recalled fondly, "he told me to scooch around until I was comfortable; it worked. The only problem was the humidity—it was awful both nights—sweat running down under your arm is ticklish—makes it hard to sit still. Julian allowed me to take off my shirt. That helped considerably. I was able to give him another ten minutes the next night on the large version."

Now the big question: "What do you think about when you have to sit still for fifteen minutes?" He was hoping to get something that explained what was screaming at him when he studied this—especially the large one.

Mark took some time... "My mind wandered some, I think—I was worried about the water polo team... a couple of issues in the patrols... Tony and his Patrol Leader were at odds again..." he enjoyed revisiting the moment; "one of the boys was mentoring another after seeing the camp chef teach a crew how to peel potatoes..." He turned to Swann: "I always take a final walk-by of all the patrols before lights out," he touched his temple: "smart—problems are easier to fix if you catch them early. I gave Jorgensen that tip yesterday," he shrugged. "Not rocket science."

Swann frowned; he had not heard anything to explain why he got such a jolt from this drawing.

Mark saw his troubled expression. "So you see it too."

Swann looked at him eagerly, relieved that Mark felt it. "Yes." He shook his head; "they all have it to some degree—each is different, yet there. This one is the most powerful yet."

Julian perked up: *that's what Mark said in the cabin! Leonard said it too—Kasey sort of said it.* "I don't get it."

Everyone looked at him, surprised and a little embarrassed—he was the creator, after all.

"I mean, all I do is draw what I see, what I feel, inside. What I hear, what I smell—or what who I am drawing feels—it's why they look the way they do—it's why I like to draw people—everyone's different." He looked at them, frustrated. "Am I doing something wrong?"

"No, no, Julian. It's anything but wrong. It's... it's something new. Somehow, you capture and synthesize these things like no one has ever done before—you seem to hear things we miss or aren't able to hear—if hear is the right word.

Mark's eyes opened wide: "that's it... **that's it**." He leaned back. "That's what looking at this does: it shows me how I felt inside, emotionally when this was drawn: looking at it takes me back there instantly." He whispered: "that's who I was that night." He looked sad, and he looked happy. He looked at Swann, amazed that he could see it too.

"Years ago I lost someone. That haunted me for a very long time. I think I have gotten past it now..." He gestured to the drawing: "I hadn't when this was drawn." He hoped he didn't need to go into detail—especially with Julian here. He turned to him: "I know you didn't intend this—but like I told you in the cabin: your drawings are powerful. I think they are good powerful, not bad powerful. I feel blessed to have this—it reminds me of a happy time as well as a sad time." He reached out—he did not want the tears he feared were on the way.

Julian leapt forward to take Mark's hand. He didn't know what to do, exactly.

"Thank you again, Julian." He squeezed his hand, fighting the urge to embrace him. "This and the other one—**especially** the other one, are precious to me. More precious than I am able to say." He released his hand.

Swann was enormously touched—but the expression on Julian's face confirmed his underlying suspicion. It was an expression of pure love and devotion. Well hidden usually, obviously by design. He was certain Mark did not see it. Not yet. But this explained the maturity of all Julian's work. That was an irrevocable state: Julian was committed. Was that why he was able to read or hear Mark so well? Of that he wasn't sure—probably not: all the drawings had that quality.

"If you don't mind, I think I would like to see the other one now, Julian." He sensed that Mark agreed.

"Yes. Thank you—I would rather have that one to look at." Now that he had deduced what Julian was doing, he realized that the second drawing portrayed a happy man—a free man: the man he had become.

554

Julian ran to his room; determined to see what they were talking about—he still didn't see what they did. *weird, that's all...* He had propped it against the side of his bed. He was a little concerned about this one; the cardboard backing had been handled a lot, actually. He hurried back and traded it for the first one. He handed that to Mr. Sawyer, then sat cross legged by the ottoman.

Everyone was fascinated. Swann sat forward: he and Mark both nodded slowly, almost together—they saw it at once. It was just as powerful, but since they were anticipating it, it was almost fulfilling as opposed to jarring.

Mark broke the silence. "The last time I saw this, they were side by side." He reflected briefly. "I almost couldn't handle it—it was like a tug of war inside my head... my heart." He shook his head, relieved. He owed Swann. "Thank you for helping me sort this out." He still didn't want them hanging on his wall in plain sight. Somewhere else would be suitable. He didn't want to get stuck explaining them to any and all. *Pat should see them probably...*

Julian saw it through different eyes: he was better at drawing now—he saw things to fix. He turned to Mr. Swann: he would know. "I think I know the answer to this, but I still want to know: is it wrong to do any fixing up later? I sort of thought that was against the rules—but I don't know what the rules are, or if there are any."

Swann looked at Julian, amazed yet again. "Fix? What could you possibly do to fix this, Julian? It's magnificent as it is." He had trouble masking his horror at the idea of changing anything.

Julian shrugged. "Nothing big... there's always something that can be just a little better." He tilted his head. "See, for this one I didn't use my camera eye as much—didn't need to, 'cause I did most of it while Mark was standing right there.

"I always try to show what I see and what I hear—sometimes they are the same thing; and I try to show what they feel inside... kinda tricky—some are harder than others. It's easier to remember if I have the small one—I use my camera eye when I do those—makes drawing the big one later easier. I'm getting better at it overall—it helps if they talk about something or to somebody. I try to see what they look like from different sides—helps make it better. Sometimes I leave things out on purpose." He looked at it again. "Crickets. The crickets were real loud that night. It was real muggy—that's the night we had a thunderstorm, I think."

"I sure remember that. I had forgotten about the crickets."

Swann was fascinated: omission—a major clue: what isn't drawn is important as well—he had noticed that in the sketchbooks. This "camera eye" seems to be the key... the sound of Sawyer's camera reminded him. "I don't suppose you had time to make any proofs..."

Sawyer had a hunch he would want these ASAP. He walked over to his camera bag. They were in a side pocket.

"I assume you have no objections to my having these framed properly." He had addressed that to Julian, who was squinting at the drawing critically, still trying to find fault with one of the most perfect pencil works ever done in the Western World. He turned to accept the 8x10s and loupe from Sawyer.

"Julian?" Mark thought he had not heard the question.

"Hm?"

"Didn't you hear Mr. Swann's question?"

Julian frowned.

"He asked if it would be all right to have these framed."

"Sure," Julian shrugged. "Okay by me: they're your drawings. Up to you, not me." Otherwise he'd be working on those toes. He couldn't believe how bad they were.

Swann and Mark looked at each other, amazed. Swann had never met an artist that didn't always harbor a sense of ownership of his work; Julian seemed to be the exception again. He resolved to provide Julian a full set of 8x10 prints anyway. He planned to have Sawyer make a full set of actual size blowups for his personal collection.

Mason returned from the kitchen—he had taken the liberty of pouring a cup of coffee for Swann and Mark.

'Thank you, Mason! Your timing is perfect, as usual."

"Amen to that!" Mark took the cup at once.

"I think you will agree, Sawyer: we can take the final exposures at the gallery just before they are framed. Better lighting conditions."

556

"Or at our lab. I think it best to leave them as is until then... we can transport them face to face."

Mark had a thought suddenly—he felt so much better about these. "I'd like to check something first, if you don't mind: I'd like to see them side by side one more time."

Sawyer retrieved the first one—he had propped it up against the wall by the kitchen entryway.

Mark got up and moved them into position—each against an easel leg.

"Huh." Julian was pleasantly surprised.

This helped Swann clarify his thinking: the eyes and facial elements were key: they set a direction, for the want of a better word, that governed the rest of the drawing; that was true for several major art works. Side by side, the difference was quite clear if one was looking for it. Mark's comment had explained it perfectly. "How many days apart were these drawn, Julian?" Swann was intrigued—all these large drawing had been done within the same week. That alone defied explanation. Anyone would expect a work of this caliber to have taken a long time—a very long time.

Julian tilted his head, trying to remember... "Two?" He nodded: he had done Leonard and Uncle Max before the second Mark.

"Close... couldn't have been more. Camp was almost over, I think." The bottom corners caught his attention. "You didn't sign these."

"Oh yeah... I forgot!" he looked at Mr. Swann, expecting to be told if it was okay to add one later.

Swann had not noticed. "Well. That's interesting." He recalled the other three—all were signed. Julian's inquiring face was also interesting—it was a reminder to answer with care. "A few artists sign their work on the back or on the frame. Some forget all together: there is no fixed rule—one of the lower corners is probably the most common way, the most expected. I prefer that—it depends a little on the subject—it's best not to do it on top of anything important. I'd recommend a simple signature, not too close to the edge. Framing sometimes covers a narrow strip." Swann thought it best not to inquire

557

about the fact that they were still unsigned. He wasn't sure if that was significant or circumstantial. It was worth a revisit.

Julian frowned: *cardboard... lousy backing—too soft.* He pointed to the spiral sketchbook in Mr. Swann's hand. "Can I borrow that a sec?"

"Of course. I need to return it to you now anyway." He glanced at Sawyer: he needed to capture this.

Julian knee walked to the foot of the easel and pulled the first one over and laid it flat on Grandma's braided rug. Carefully, he peeled the lower right corner free and slipped the sketchbook cover underneath. He grabbed one of the pencils out of his shirt pocket and checked the point... *looks okay... not too sharp.* The tip wouldn't break on him. Carefully, he wrote his name in cursive, almost elegant in its simplicity. "I s'pose one of these days I oughtta come up with a special autograph, one that's hard to figure out," he giggled. "Am I s'posed to date it?"

Swann was so charmed by this lad. "I would, but that's me. You should decide that. The month and year would be helpful to the viewer. Some artists include the day and hour.

"**That's** pretty silly..." There was room enough for June 1962. He didn't want a comma for some reason. He plugged the year in and looked at Mark: "Okay?"

"Perfect. Thank you, Julian;" he glanced at Swann as Julian signed the second drawing—sharing this was nice. His opinion of Swann had risen considerably—he was almost a colleague where Julian was concerned. He felt strengthened and supported. He had not thought in those terms before. It began to dawn on him that before long, Julian would benefit greatly from the man—he wasn't passing the baton by any means, but Swann would provide what he would never be able to. The timing for him to enter Julian's life was ideal.

Swann regarded him closely. "Do you want to look at them again before we take them away? And where should we return them? Here or..."

"How about my office?" That had just popped into his head. That way, he could plan how to share these with Pat.

Julian, meanwhile, was saying goodbye to his secret friends. He knew this day would come, eventually. He wasn't worried: he had

558

already planned on drawing a special secret reserved set that no one would know about, ever. He had a library of images on file in his head: time for a few of those to get onto paper. It would be two years and six months before he would be eligible for anything else.

He froze: Inside Guy had just poked him a good one: his Christmas present! His eyes moved from Mark to Mr. Swann and back, alarmed.

Mason picked up on it instantly and flashed a signal to his employer. Swann looked at Julian at once: he could see why Mason had acted so abruptly.

"Is something wrong, Julian?"

Mark looked at him: what had happened?

Julian frowned. "I almost forgot. I feel kind of stupid—I made a present for you. Now I'm wondering if it's such a good idea..." he gestured at the Mark drawings. "I didn't ask permission. Always before, I asked permission... I wanted it to be a surprise." he shrugged. "I thought of it while I was drawing Grandpa and Grandma Samuelson— you were so interested and all... I did it from memory though." He thought about it. "It's kinda different from these—I had to make it up. I never did that before." He gestured to the Mark drawings and shook his head. "They're not like these—'cept for size. I tried one the usual way, but I didn't like it much... then I did a different one—I would have shown them to Mr. van Horn, but school was out by the time I was done." He paused. "I didn't want to throw them away... but... after hearing you and Mark talk about these, I... I just don't know. I don't think they're good enough." He slumped, muttering, "prob'ly shoulda kept my mouth shut..."

Swann's eyes betrayed the shock and joy and surprise—a combination quite new to him—he braced himself on the arms of Francine's living room chair and took a very deep breath. "I'm very touched, Julian, and surprised, of course. I must apologize—I have been very selfish today. You should not feel sorry—I just took over. I see that now. I don't usually do that—at least not first thing." He winked at Mason. "You didn't have a chance. I hope you can forgive me. It is entirely my fault."

Julian smiled. "You didn't do anything wrong," he looked at Mark. "He's always so nice—trying to take the blame all the time," he shook his head. "But thanks."

Mark stepped in: "Julian, do you remember what I told you that night in the cabin after you showed me those drawings?" he paused. "I was on my way to take a shower: I remember it well."

Julian thought back to that night… it took a minute, but it came to him. He raised his head: "You said to never apologize for my work. You said if anyone didn't like it, it was their problem—they weren't worth my time." He smiled at Mark, the slump had vanished. Mark's words always cleared his head and pointed to what was true. He stood and went to his room. The drawings were on his worktable, just as he had left them when Kasey called: face down, the experimental one was still mounted on the drawing board. He snagged an unused panel of corrugated cardboard from his closet stash to use for the first one. He put a small piece of masking tape on the upper corners to prevent the paper from falling to the floor. *wish me luck*…

You'll do fine. Inside Guy had been paying attention all along, of course. This had turned into one of those Important Days.

Still, Julian was not at all comfortable: he hated to show off: there was a **room** full out there, not just Mr. Swann. And Mark: that's who counted most of all. He didn't know what he would do with himself if Mark was disappointed.

Swann watched with forced calm as Julian entered. He placed what appeared to be several layers on the easel… about twelve feet away from both of the chairs—coincidence, but ideal, in away. He was ready—he had a hand on each arm of the chair, ready to grip tight.

Julian stood to the side and the full-length pencil drawing appeared. It was different from all the others in that it did not fill the entire space: it seemed to float, giving it a dreamlike quality; it seemed free, as opposed to unfinished.

well… He was certainly surprised: he wasn't hit with a gale force of emotional energy, but a fresh spring breeze—he could swear he smelled lilacs! He gasped… of course! There was a bow of lilac blossoms in the flower arrangement that he had ordered for the Sandersons! Well out of season, they were very special—and very expensive… they were not visible in the drawing. *why do I smell them?*

Julian's troubled countenance had transformed into a beaming grin—Mark turned to look at Swann and understood why. The expression on his face was fabulous too—he glanced at Sawyer—yes! He got the snapshot. Mark resolved to get a print somehow.

"My, Julian. This is wonderful. I think this makes me feel as good as the fellow in the drawing! I recognize his stick pin!" he sat back, smiling and pointed to his right eye. "I think your camera eye was on duty that day."

Julian beamed. Mr. Swann really meant it: he liked it—actually liked it! He bounced on his toes and grinned at Mason. He was smiling too.

"May I see it up close?"

oo! Julian grabbed it along with the cardboard and took it across the room.

Swann examined it closely: "You have the Packard down perfectly... he has you too, Mason—down to the cuff of your pants!" His own face was so **detailed**... how could anyone do this from memory?

"Remember that time you stopped by to pick me up to work on the school paper? I got a super good look at your face that time. You're fun to draw, actually. Someday I'd like to do a good one."

Swann broke into a hearty laugh. "I don't see how you could do any better than this!" He really believed that. It was a little disconcerting to being stared at by himself—this is the first drawing of Julian's to have the subject appear to be looking directly at the viewer.

Mark wanted to say 'just wait, you'll see.' He sat on it for the time being: they still had not seen the other one. He fully expected it to be a surprise: he knew... he had been there.

Swann held it up for Mason to look closely at how well Julian had captured his chauffeur persona. "I think we are ready to see your second thoughts about this," he gestured to the drawing board, still on the easel.

here goes... Julian stepped over to flip it *oop* it was upside down... he fixed that and stepped out of the way so that everyone could see it.

Like the sun coming out from behind a cloud, the burst of color evoked a choir of French horns punctuated with a flurry of harps pronouncing a new hallelujah… this one had a good solid blast, not a breeze. It was a good thing he was sitting down. Swann gasped, inarticulate.

It was the very same drawing, yet entirely different: the intense splash of color and the sharp dense black lines of India ink were employed with superb simplicity, doubling their impact—making it visible at twice the distance at least. In a gallery it would dominate an entire exhibit. The all pencil drawing beckoned him: this one drew him like a magnet. At the same time, he was looking into a mirror: the man in the drawing was staring straight at him—beyond hypnotic. Those twinkling blue eyes evoked a compelling feeling of trust. *evidently, this is who Julian sees when I look at him.* It took his breath away. Julian had found a way to blend pen and ink with pencil very effectively; he was reminded of Dali… and Picasso. But most of all, he was made aware of the breadth and scope of his responsibility—the number of people who depended on him and who trusted him. It did not weigh on him: it verified—it removed any burden. It was so personal.

Mark enjoyed a private told-you-so moment. He was glad he had kept it to himself. This one stunned him almost as much as his own.

Sawyer realized that he was witnessing an important moment: he had the privilege of being present and the responsibility to document it. He would not disappoint.

"Oops." Julian whispered. He shook his head. "Didn't sign either one… couldn't tell if I was done or not." Obviously, Mr. Swann liked them. He went to his room to fetch the blue pastel stick.

33   *the Flaming Arrows plus*

The thing about Mr. Swann, Julian finally realized, was that he made him think about things—not just art and drawing, but other things too: especially Kasey. Ever since getting home from church yesterday, he'd been thinking about the last couple of days: the overnight at Kasey's, and giving Mr. Swann the special drawings... Mark and him talking about the large drawings... it was kind of weird—almost as if he wasn't in the room, the way they went on.

But what Inside Guy wouldn't leave him alone about was how little time was left before school started up again: he had a homework assignment, and he hadn't even thought about it. So as soon as his mom left for work, he started the day by opening his three ring binder and getting a blank piece of paper. He needed to write out what he would say to introduce Kasey at that assembly. He didn't have a chance before the faculty meeting. That went okay, but he could have done a lot better.

He'd been staring at this blank piece of paper for almost fifteen minutes before he figured it out: he had never given a speech before. He had all kinds of things he could say about Kasey now, but nothing he could tell the entire student body of Jackson High School. Nothing Mr. Swann or Mark talked about was of any help at all. He felt like a total dummy.

Why not call Nick? He's an expert on everything.   Inside Guy was good at thinking of obvious things—especially if they were right in front of him.

Julian paused... technically, he wasn't supposed to talk about Kasey until the Troop meeting. Trouble was, the next meeting would be too late: it was a week after school started. On the other hand, Nick could keep a secret—and he was super smart. He opened the Troop 9 tab: it had a troop list and everyone's phone number.

> > *klack!* < <

He removed the list and headed for the kitchen. Nick told him to call if he ever needed help. Inside Guy was right about this.

Tom was getting more P. O.'d by the minute: after Julian had filled him and Nick in about what was coming up, he couldn't believe they would dump a load like that in anyone's lap, let alone a kid as clueless as Julian. There might just be something missing here. Before coming up with a plan, they needed to get some info from Kirk. He would know what was going on if anyone did. *sure hope he's home...* the phone was on it third ring—

> > *Fox residence, this is Kirk* < <

"Hey, Kirk: Dawson here. How's it hangin'?" There was a slight pause.

> > *Just fine, thanks... what's up?* < <

"We gotta talk. I'm here with Julian—Julian Forrest. He just filled me in on what's coming down when school starts up. I figure you must know, since you're going to introduce him at the assembly he's been telling me about."

Julian was amused by Tom's approach—jock talk seemed to be required if you're a big football star; Tom didn't usually talk that way. He was lucky to know a guy like Tom, actually. He gave Nick a grateful nod. *boy, am I glad I called him...*

After another pause, Kirk had decided how to reply... it so happened, he was working on his speech.

> > *It's a big deal all right. What do you want to know?* < <

"Enough to make sure my bud Julian isn't gonna be left holding a bag of trouble he doesn't deserve. Can you come over here and bring us up to speed?"

oh-oh... > > *I suppose, yeah. Where's here?* < <

"A dozen blocks or so from Sparky's—Tenth and Birch"

> > *Who all is there?* < <

"Besides Julian, there's Nick—Norman and Frankie are on the way. Why?"

> > *Well, it's supposed to be secret ahead of time—they don't want a lot of talk and rumors going around. We don't want a bunch of protesters screwing things up.* < <

"We're with you all the way on that. This has become an official project of Troop 9 now—and we don't want to foul anything up either. That's why I want you here—we are planning what we need to do."

> > *Whoah... okay. I didn't know about that... okay... I can be there in ten minutes.* < <

"Thanks... see ya in a bit." Tom smirked at Nick on the way back to the kitchen table. "That shook him up," he chuckled. "He's on the way."

"I kinda like him," Julian said. "We had a lotta fun at that big dinner." Kirk was a fellow blond.

"I wish we had known about this sooner." Nick wondered if they should call Mark. "Mark was there too?"

"Good thing, too. I didn't know what was going on at first; I'm not so worried now, with you guys here."

"We need to get Danny over here. This is a Flaming Arrow Project as of this minute. What about the new kid? He ought to be in on this too, don't you think?" *I sure would be.* It didn't make sense to dump it all in his lap either. Tom shook his head. He couldn't believe how stupid adults could be sometimes. Mark had filled him in on that a long time back. They forget the most important thing half the time because they don't remember what it was like to be 'just a kid.'

"We can holler across the fence in back—Danny's room is right there."

"I'll do that while you get hold of... what's his name again?"

"Kasey."

Tom checked his watch. "You know his number?" He was intrigued; meeting the new kid would be interesting, actually.

Julian thought a sec: *he'll need a ride.*

Call Mason. That's who will hafta bring him, you know. Inside Guy was handy with a good idea sometimes.

oo yeah… he headed for his room: he had pinned the card Mr. Swann gave him on the bulletin board. It had Mason's name as who to call. *made sense* He figured Mr. Swann might want to know, but Mason decided that kind of thing; Mr. Swann was a very busy man.

Julian did not know that very few people were given that particular card: it was the direct pipeline to Swann. All other calls went to the central switchboard for screening.

It was New Year's Eve day, and, as it happened, only Frankie and Kirk were planning to celebrate New Year's Eve: that didn't complicate things much, but Tom pressed forward regardless. Before long, the impromptu and unlikely meeting at Julian's house would grow from three to a very awkward and unwieldy dozen.

First to join Tom, Nick and Julian were Danny and Tony. They were trying to play a game of **Sorry!** when someone shouting from Julian's back porch interrupted. Danny hopped over to lift the sash of his second floor window: it had a perfect view of Julian's back porch—*it's Tom!* "Hey, Tom. What are you doin' at Julian's?"

"Emergency meeting of the Flaming Arrow; put on your shoes and come on over."

Tony popped up by Danny's side. "Hey, Tom: what's up?" The campout had more than satisfied their need to get out of the house, but a gathering at Julian's would be more fun than this stupid board game.

"Flaming Arrow Meeting—you can come along too if you want. You just have to swear to keep your mouth shut—it's top secret until next week."

"Oh. School starts next week. Is Mark there too?"

"No, he's at work, I think. We might call him tho—dunno yet. I still need to call Frankie and Norman."

"Norman?!" *he's a Wolf… something is up for sure.* "Who else is gonna be there?"

566

"Kirk Fox." He thought a sec... "that's secret too. Anyway—it's cold out here—put your pants back on and get over here before I change my mind." He didn't think they were goofing around after that campout, but with Tony, you could never tell.

Danny pulled down the sash quickly—it was darn cold out there. He turned to Tony with a feigned look of innocence: "how did he know you don't have your pants on?"

While Tom and Danny were hollering back and forth over the back fence, Julian dialed the phone number on Mr. Swann's card. It was answered on the third ring:

> > *Good morning, this is Mason; how may I be of assistance?* < <

"Hiya, Mason! Neato! Mr. Swann gave me this card. I sorta need your help, I think..."

Mason recognized the voice at once.

> > *How good of you to call, Master Julian. I am your servant: what, may I ask, do you need?* < <

He pushed the alert button on his desk; this allowed his employer to listen in if he chose to.

"See, we're here at my house trying to figure out what I'm s'posed to say about Kasey when I introduce him at the assembly. Tom thinks he ought to be here to help out. I think he's right—he usually is. So I'm calling to see if you can bring him over—his mom doesn't have a car. I haven't called him yet, but I'm pretty sure he's at home." There was a brief pause on the line.

> > *Just a moment—I need to check my calendar; may I put you on hold temporarily?* < <

"Sure." He held his hand on the mouthpiece. "He's checking his calendar," he nodded at Nick, still seated at the kitchen table. "You haven't met him—he's really..." Julian's vocabulary didn't have a good word to describe Mason... "really a good guy, for a butler." Butlers were people too, after all. After a couple of minutes, Mason was back.

567

> > *Hello again. Can you tell me who Tom is? I do not know that name. < <*

"Sure: he's my Troop's Assistant Scoutmaster. He's head of my Patrol, the Flaming Arrow. See, we always pitch in to help a patrol member who's in a jam. So the Patrol is gonna help me figure out how to do a good job: it's a real important thing—I don't want to mess it up, y'know? Mr. Swann knows him, I think—he was in charge of the Christmas decoration project. Mr. Swann helped us out a lot. I think you were helping Kasey get moved."

> > *I see. I am sure I can be of assistance. I trust it is permissible for me to remain nearby... I will need to return him home, of course. And, should you need any other assistance, I will be available. Can you give me a guess about how long the meeting will last? < <*

"Gosh... let me ask. I didn't think about that!" he turned to Nick. "He needs to know how long the meeting will last... what do you think?"

"I should have thought of that—well, it will take an hour or two at least, once everyone's here—then there's the time it takes to get him here... better allow for three or four. We should be done by supper time, I think."

"Nick thinks we'll be done by supper time—prob'ly four hours or so."

> > *I see... who, may I ask, is Nick? < <*

"Oh, he's the Troop Scribe—I'm his assistant. He does the minutes and the Troop 9 Newsletter. You'll really like him. He's the smartest one in the troop, for sure!" Julian bounced on his toes. He didn't mind Nick overhearing that.

> > *Is Master Kasey expecting me? < <*

"OO—ee! No. I still hafta call him—I called you first to see if you could bring him. It would be a lot better than us going after him. Tom can always take him home if you want. I have Kasey's phone number though—I was gonna call him next anyway."

> >   Let me take care of that for you — I will need to speak to his mother.   If there is a problem I will call you back.   Otherwise, we will be there as quickly as possible. < <

"Wow, thanks Mason. Oh! almost forgot: tell Zeyla hello for me," he giggled. "Tell her I would have invited her too, but girls aren't allowed at boy scout meetings."

As he slipped on his pants, Tony did some thinking about this meeting. He'd heard something on the campout about the school paper that rang a bell; he figured he'd better call Andy about this: something about a special issue they were going to pass out. When Tom said Kirk Fox was in on it, he assumed Andy would want to know. He and Randall might come in handy anyway. Tony had the special phone number to call at the photolab—he and Randall were making some prints of the campout today.

Back at Julian's, while Tom was calling Norman and Frankie, Julian went to fetch his sketchbook. He wanted to show Nick what he had drawn for the Christmas decoration party—he might need something for the newsletter. He had just started when the doorbell rang. "Be right back…"

Julian did his skip and slide to the arch, then a major one to the front door: he could do that in one slide now. *not good for the socks, but…* it was Danny. "Come on in. We're in the kitchen. Boy, you got here quick!" He looked past Danny's shoulder. "Where's Tony?"

"He's coming—he had to call Andy." He stepped in fast—it was super cold out there.

Julian peeked out: Tony was just coming around the corner. He closed the door and waited. "They're in the kitchen. Go on in—I'll let Tony in… put your coat on my bed; door's open."

There wasn't room enough at the kitchen table now, so the meeting moved into the living room. Tom liked it better—the winged armchair was more comfortable, and its location was ready made for running a meeting. Nick took the other winged armchair, while Danny and Tony claimed the ottoman.

Just as Julian was getting settled in his customary cross-legged position on Grandma's braided rug, the doorbell rang again: it was Andy and Randall. It turned out they knew about this assembly, since they had been at that faculty meeting. Before they hopped into the Dodge, Randall had assembled his camera gear along with all the prints he had done of the campout. The group got sidetracked instantly. Julian hadn't even heard of the trip—just as well, since he was at Kasey's place.

Julian was on his knees looking at a photo of Littel Capitan when the doorbell rang again; he handed the photo back to Andy. Randall was fussing with his camera—he had taken it upon himself to 'cover' this meeting as an exercise in his role as the Cardinal's new staff photographer.

"Hi Julian! Good to see you again! Sorry it took me so long." Kirk had never been here before—he was a little surprised. He had assumed that Julian lived in a more affluent neighborhood.

Kirk had parked in Julian's mother's space. That brought the number to eight. "C'mon in. Everyone's tossing his coat on my bed; follow me. Some guys aren't here yet." Julian fetched a couple of chairs from the kitchen.

Randall, always on the alert, began taking snapshots, just in case. He was the only one who knew this house was the worst possible place to hold a meeting, but mentioning that didn't occur to him until later.

The doorbell rang again: Frankie had arrived with Norman; Rhonda, his steady, wanted to come along too—she wasn't about to let him go off with the boys today, of all days: she had a big party planned, and knew better than to let him get loose for a minute. Thus, he had a time limit: if he didn't report back in half an hour, he would be toast.

Julian thought it was funny—he was used to girls taking charge and was curious to see if Rhonda was anything like Geraldine. He had wondered about that after having so much fun with Kasey's sister. When and how girls learned to take over would be good to know. He was just as glad Rhonda wasn't here; she's the one who lined him up with Brenda for that double date.

With the chairs and stool from his bedroom, the living room was packed. Ten people filled the space. They had just finished getting settled when the doorbell rang yet again: Julian raced to the door. It was Mason and Kasey

"Good day, Master Julian. It is good to see you again." Kasey was directly behind him, but visible over his head smiling wide, obviously delighted to be visiting his new friend at his house.

"Hiya Mason, Hi Kasey! Wow, come on in!" He opened the door wide and stood back.

The sound of Mason's voice was so unusual and impressive, everyone looked toward the door and immediately stood.

Mason entered first, as was customary—normally, he would have announced his charge's name, but for this occasion he thought it wise to simply show Kasey in. The packed room was a surprise, to say the least. Ten people seemed like fifteen in a room that was full with four, and crowded with six.

Kasey stepped in, suppressing an urge to do something chummy—they had not developed a way to do anything routine—Julian usually poked or pulled him by the belt. Today, he was startled by the sight: a crowd of standing guys—probably boy scouts; none in uniform. Fortunately, the 'politician' was present.

"Kasey, welcome!" Kirk nodded at Mason with a friendly bow and stepped forward to shake Kasey's hand. "It's great to see you again. You're looking good."

Kasey had glanced around at the assemblage, slightly nonplussed; he saw someone as tall as he was and exchanged a look: boys of that altitude felt an instant kinship of sorts—not necessarily friendly, but looking other people straight in the eye was not an everyday experience. In this instance, the first impression was distinctly positive for both.

Norman was strangely thrilled; now he understood why he had been invited: as Captain of the varsity basketball team, he was the obvious person to think of—Kasey was taller than anyone on the team. He broke into a smile; nodding straight ahead at someone his own height was unusual and special. Kasey's blue eyes were a complete surprise.

"Julian, why don't you introduce Kasey to everyone while I show Mason where to put his coat?" Kirk assumed it should be added to the mountain of coats atop Julian's bed; evidently there wasn't any place else.

Kasey was bemused already—this was another chapter in the series of unusual comical features created in Julian's wake, to continue the metaphor he had come up with during the visit on Friday and Saturday. He handed his coat to Kirk. "Thank you. Good to see you again." He expected Julian to lead the way. He was still adjusting to the simplicity—he had assumed, incorrectly, that Julian was from a higher income family, like his friend Randall, who had just waved at him.

"Gosh—sorry it's so crowded you guys. I never had company before. If it was summer, we could go out in the back yard; oh well." He scratched his head: "What if I say your name and you raise your hand. I'll save Tom for last: he's gonna run things, because he's good at that… okay?"

Lots of nods, no other suggestions. "Okay then. First, there's Randall, star photographer—you prob'ly remember him: we had supper at his place and had fun in his photolab. Next is Andy, he's the star reporter for the school paper—he was at that faculty meeting. Nick is the Troop Scribe, my boss in Troop 9. He's the brains; next is Danny, he's my other boss in the troop—he's the guy that taught me how to fix breakfast; Tony is his pal, here by special invitation on account of he was hanging out at Danny's when we called. Next is Tom, who I'm skipping over for now. Norman is the new leader of the Wolf Patrol, where I used to be before Mark moved me to the Flaming Arrow. He's the one who showed me the ropes at Camp last summer. Like you, he's a story taller than everyone else in the room. He's the Captain of the basketball team too. Next, there's Frankie Ferris: he's the Troop Bugler…" He stopped to take a breath. "Last there's Kirk, who you know, and me, the one you hafta watch out for. Last, but not least, is Tom, our Patrol Leader and Assistant Scoutmaster, and Star Football Player—I forget what he plays, I'm kinda dumb when it comes to sports." He bounced on his toes, proudly.

"Let's hear it for Julian," Tony applauded. "Almost in one breath!"

Everyone laughed and applauded. Kasey was overwhelmed.

Tom stepped forward to shake hands. "Hi, Kasey. Great to meet you; as you probably know, a friend of Julian's is a friend of everyone in Troop 9. We're going to make sure you are welcome at Jackson High. Your job is to speak up and let us know if we have forgotten anything, or anything else is needed. Starting at a new school in the middle of the year isn't easy for anybody. And since you will be the first non-white to attend Jackson, we will be on hand to handle whatever comes along. I'm not worried, but better to be prepared than surprised. Might as well keep that in mind from the start, right?"

The other scouts were very surprised and proud of Tom. They didn't see the pleased look on Nick's face: he had done a good job of getting Tom focused on what the Troop was facing.

Tom had the leadership skill to carry the ball over the finish line. "Sit down, everyone—it's cozy, but so what?" They didn't need to waste any more time getting squared away.

Fortunately, Julian was happy to sit cross-legged on the floor by Kasey; Mason was content to stand by the door and 'disappear.' The front lawn had become a parking spot for the Packard; he was under instructions to monitor and report, and if he deemed it necessary, be of assistance—and to ensure Swann's name be kept out of the discussion.

Tom continued: "First, I want Kirk to fill us in on what the plan is, so that we can fix it."

"How do you know it needs to be fixed?" Danny was honestly curious about that.

Tom looked at him directly: "Think about it: have you ever gone to an assembly put on by the principal and faculty that wasn't totally boring? One where everyone wasn't looking at the clock wondering when it would be over so they could get out of there to take care of their sore butts after sitting on those bleachers?

Danny nodded. "Yeah… guess you're right about that."

"Right." Tom gestured to Kirk: "You're on. What's the plan? I figure you probably know the schedule—they're not completely stupid."

Kirk was very surprised at Tom's cynical view, and his forceful manner—he was glad he had not run against him for office. He cleared his throat. "Thanks, Tom. I'm glad you invited me. I want to do whatever I can to make it interesting. I don't want them all looking at the clock either. Here's what they have planned: everyone reports to their first period class for roll call and announcements. They will allow 15 minutes for that, then the PA will call everyone to the gym, beginning with the seniors as usual. The band and rally squad will be there for roll call—that way the band will be playing the Alma Mater while the kids come in; after the Alma Mater, they'll play the school fight song, and the cheerleaders will lead everyone in a few yells. By that time the sophomores should all be seated in the top section—that's the plan, at least; they can do an extra yell if they need to." He looked around to see if anyone was bothered so far.

No surprises there; Tom had it figured right.

"When the cheers die down, I'm supposed to present Mr. Middleton to speak. He will ask everyone to stand while the band plays the National Anthem, and to stay standing to give the Pledge of Allegiance to the Flag. After everyone sits down again, Mr. Middleton will introduce the Superintendent. He will give a speech about the Brown Decision that is being put into action, and that the assembly is honoring. He will introduce the members of the school board. They wanted to invite the mayor and Congressman Duffy, but decided against it—they didn't want the TV and radio stations to get wind of what was going on—they don't want to stir up the usual types." He glanced around—with Kasey right there he didn't want to say anything offensive or controversial.

"You mean the Purebloods and the Holy Roller sign carriers? Might as well be honest about it." Tom was annoyed.

"They don't expect any problems, but they are doing everything they can **not** to invite them."

Tom nodded. *kind of chickenshit, but better than nothing.* He glanced at Kasey to see if he was okay: Tom liked what he saw.

"Next, Mr. Middleton will say a few words about the second semester and some other things the faculty is doing, then he will turn it back to me. My job is to give an official welcome to the new student by introducing Julian. Then Julian comes out and takes a bow and waits for all the upper class girls to calm down..." he winked at Julian: "sorry, I had to toss that in—that's going to happen whether you like it or not."

"Huh?!"

"You have one of the biggest fan clubs going, you know." He looked at Kasey—"to them, he's the new Li'l Abner. My girlfriend can't shut up about him." He fired a pantomime pistol shot. "I'm supposed to pull strings to get her in line for your first portrait last nine weeks—she has first lunch... deal?"

Julian nodded, grinning. Kirk was a good guy, really. Praise and flattery about his good looks had always bored him more than anything—when he was little, all those gushing and cooing ladies his mom and Geraldine had around with their stinky perfume and nylon socks had made him so immune he ignored it. It didn't occur to him that this was any different.

Kasey was not surprised in the least to hear that Julian was popular among the girls. His looks alone would guarantee that—and having been drawn by him, he knew what Kirk's girlfriend was after. Julian's indifference about being popular was evident in this group as well. Like everything with Julian, this was an adventure so different from anything in his experience, he half believed he was watching a movie. Being welcomed by this group without question or reservation was something he had not considered possible: but here he was—not only allowed, but welcome.

Looking at Kasey, Kirk returned to the assembly topic: "then Julian introduces you and your parents. Mr. Barnes will escort you in from the hallway behind the platform. Then you—or your father, I'm not sure which, will say your hellos and whatever you want. After the applause, I'm supposed to dismiss everyone to go back to their first period class." He looked at the group. "That's about it."

"Figures." Tom sat forward: "so who is left holding the bag for a totally boring assembly? Two guys: Julian and Kasey. As if it was their idea!" He shook his head in disgust. He looked at Kirk. "We are gonna change that: we are gonna send those kids back to class eager and all pumped up—happy and wanting to meet Kasey personally if they can, or be allowed... same for Julian." He pointed his right forefinger: "Your job, Student Body President, is to make darn sure we can. It's gonna add time, unless they are willing to hold off on some of those really interesting speeches they have planned."

Nick enjoyed this immensely—Tom had assimilated more than he expected.

Kirk sat back, very surprised. "How are you going to do that?"

Tom looked at him as if he was a third grader: "That is what this meeting is for. We have a room full of smart and talented guys. We are going to pitch ideas out and figure out which ones are good, and what we'll need to get it done. We have two and a half days to get it ready. There are a hundred or more other Jackson kids just sitting around— getting help is not gonna be a problem." He looked at Kirk somberly. "Right?"

"Right." This was new territory for Kirk. He was unsure why, but he trusted Tom. It was not hard to join in his program... he was relieved, in a way. He had to agree with everything Tom said so far—it was as if he had turned on the overhead light, making the entire room visible. It was a bigger room than he thought.

Nick cleared his throat, his standard ploy to get attention. "Before we get going, Tom, I think we need to take something else into consideration. This is a very small room—and I doubt if Julian is in a position to supply us with refreshments, unless he has come up with a lot of money lately." He gave Julian a friendly wink.

Julian shrugged with a nod; Nick was right. He had not even thought about that.

"I suggest that we hop into our cars and drive up the street to Sparky's. They have a sizeable corner booth that will take care of the seating problem, and I'll bet that at this time of day they will be empty and eager to have a customer or two." The place was mostly empty during vacations.

Tom grinned wide: "All in favor?" He raised his hand. He could always count on Nick to figure things like that out. Everyone except Kasey raised a hand eagerly. Tom noticed, of course. He waited for an explanation.

Kasey hesitated, and looked at Mason. Mason's nod was all he needed: the idea of going to a teen hangout with Julian and his friends was wonderful—like everything associated with him was. "I'd like that very much. I must alert you to the fact that I have never been to an

576

establishment like you suggest this one is, but I am willing to give it a try. I assume someone will tell me if I am doing anything wrong."

This was the first solid dose of his Boston accent they had heard and it took everyone but Kirk and Julian by surprise.

Julian giggled and nudged Kasey's leg with his elbow—he had scooted closer to lean against his legs. "I forgot to tell you guys he talked like the President. They come from the same town, I think, or close by. You get used to it pretty quick."

That made everyone laugh.

Tom had a hunch: "Kasey, I'd like you and Norman to sit close by me when we get there. Who has pencil and paper?" Kirk, Andy and Julian raised a hand. He looked at Julian: "Bring extra, okay? Why don't you ride with Kasey." That covered everything. "Okay guys, let's head out!" Nick motioned him to come close when everyone went to get his coat.

Nick whispered something short—no one else heard.

"I'm dead!" Frankie exclaimed, and looked at Kirk in desperation: "You gotta back me up: I'm supposed to call Rhonda five minutes ago!"

Julian pointed: "Phone's in the kitchen."

Kirk followed Frankie into the kitchen; he knew Rhonda well. Tom went directly to Mason, who was standing by the door. He offered his hand. "Howdy. I'm Tom Dawson. I need to know if there are any special rules." He didn't know who he was, other than being an escort of some kind.

"Hello Tom. I am Mason. I appreciate your question and commend your thoughtfulness. As you probably surmised, I am here to assist Master Kasey in any way he requires. So far, I am impressed with your leadership in this matter. It is inappropriate for me to join your group, but I do require being present. May I add that I am instructed to take care of any and all your expenses, should there be any—that includes the refreshments these boys will doubtless require during your meeting. If you would be so good as to ask the waiter or waitress to put everything on one bill, I will take care of it. You need not worry about repaying it later." He paused, briefly. "I am not at liberty to say who employs me, but Master Julian can vouch for my service, should you have need. I presume he will be riding with Master Kasey."

Tom was, to put it mildly, blown away. What had Julian gotten them into here? It was even bigger than he thought. He gave Mason a thumbs up.

Andy's '48 Dodge was the first to arrive at Sparky's. He, Randall, Tony and Danny hopped out and hurried in to get dibs on the inside corner—it was considered the best place. It wasn't often that a guy got to sit in that booth anyway, and sitting in the choicest seat was a good brag to have on file.

Tony was well known there; he entered the empty restaurant with a flourish: "We're here to save the day, Georgia! There's gonna be twelve of us: wake up the cooks!" He and Andy ran for the corner booth: two ways around the table were ready and waiting. They plopped on opposite benches and scooted on their butts all the way to the corner. Oops: there were two corner seats—one faced the kitchen, the other the door to the west parking lot—the one the carhop served. What they failed to notice in time was that the same table space served both seats— it was a 45 degree corner: a tight fit for two sets of legs. Neither had ever sat here before; they soon discovered that they had been tricked: instead of the best seat, it was the worst; fortunately, they didn't mind being squeezed together.

Frankie's Chevy was next to arrive—he and Norman followed Andy by half a block, and were disembarking as Tom and Nick were pulling in. Last was the Packard, with Kasey and Julian. Mason had purposely let the other cars have a significant lead; he needed to park as unobtrusively as possible. As it turned out, there was no way to do that very well—it was an open design. After driving all the way around the building to see where the corner seat was situated, he parked where he would be able to keep the Packard in sight. Tom and Nick waited at the door so they could all enter at the same time. He wanted the waitress to be serving the others when he entered with Kasey. He checked to see if Mason was at all worried. They exchanged glances: they were on the same page. He nodded to Norman to follow him in. Kasey and Julian were next, followed by Nick and Mason.

Georgia had brought everyone a glass of water, napkins, and a few extra menu stands; the boys helped by scooting everything into place for the ones who were coming. Tony had said twelve, and twelve glasses were brought. She was standing by, eager to take orders—this many people meant a very nice tip. She grinned at once when she turned: her favorite regulars Nick and Tom were leading the others in. The smile began to fade when she saw the three that followed: one of them had remarkable blue eyes—she had never seen that bright a blue; it took a moment to realize that they appeared so unusually exotic and bright because the face around them was so dark. *oh...* It registered: it was so dark because... she glanced at his hair: *black.* They had entered so confidently that she didn't react. She hesitated too long... they had taken their seats already! The Black was between the blond boy and another tall one wearing a Cardinal Basketball patch on his jacket—obviously a player on Jackson's team. She didn't know what to do; this had never happened before—she looked toward the kitchen. The fry cook was staring in disbelief, jaw hanging wide open. The manager was in his office, out of sight. What was she going to do? She had been told when they hired her that no Blacks were to be served at a table. Take-out only was allowed. At least Tom was on the outside—she could talk to him. She stared at him, waiting.

"Hi, Georgia. We have a hungry bunch for ya!" he smiled as if nothing was wrong—he could tell by the look on her face that his fear was correct. He had a job to do, but he was ready. He waited for her to say something, but she seemed to be stuck. "Where's your friendly smile? Is something wrong?"

"Umm... I'm not supposed to serve anyone... any... any Negroes inside. Takeout only." She had almost whispered it, but everyone heard.

"Oh? Why is that? I don't see any signs saying that." It wouldn't have made any difference if there were, of course—but that fact was very helpful. There weren't any signs because there had never been any question about it. This had not come up until now. The restaurant had begun as a roadside eatery in 1935; successive expansions and remodels had occurred, but racial signage had never been added, because it wasn't needed.

Everyone paid attention, opened eyed, and in suspense. No one had thought to bring this up at the meeting—the group did not realize they were about to witness, let alone be involved in a very significant event. Fortunately, Tom and Nick did; as usual, Nick had advised Tom briefly—but he had learned much of how to deal with this from his oldest brother.

"Umm... Because that's what the manager says. I just work here."

"So if the manager says it's okay, then you will serve my friend?"

She nodded eagerly.

"Well, I hope he is here. Would you ask him to come over? I'd like to talk to him for a minute."

Georgia nodded, white faced. She looked at the others: obviously, they were all agreed about this. She walked carefully to the opening at the end of the counter and headed for the office.

Tom helped himself to a big gulp of water. It felt very strange to realize that everyone was staring at him in silence. "It's cool. Talk it up, guys. This won't take long." He turned to Kasey. "Sorry about this. It won't happen again." He looked at Kirk, man to man, as if to say 'you better back me up.'

Kirk nodded, wide eyed in shock and admiration. The determination in Norman's eyes also impressed. He could hardly wait to tell Mr. Barnes about this.

Randall reached into his case and pulled out a bunch of photos. "Here, you guys—be looking at these." Tom confirmed it was the right thing to do and mimed snapping a photo: he wanted this on film. When the manager showed up, everyone was occupied as if nothing unusual was going on.

"What seems to be the problem?" The manager had appeared, annoyed but patient. His waitress stood a few feet away.

"Oh, hello," Tom said, amiably. "Are you the manager?"

"I most certainly am. Oscar Olson." He bounced on his toes. The Friar Tuck hairdo went perfectly with his very affluent tummy. The bow tie and red carnation in his lapel looked very Rotary Club, although that was lost on Tom and the boys around the table. Some of them looked familiar; he presumed they were regular customers.

"Glad to meet you, Mr. Olson. I am Tom Dawson, a senior at Jackson High. You might have heard of me—I played running back on this year's winning team. We had quite a party here after the last game. You have the best burger basket in town; best shakes, too."

Olson was pleasantly surprised in spite of what was going on. "Thanks... we aim to please," he quoted the slogan printed on all their advertising without thinking.

"Glad to hear it," Tom continued. "Let me introduce our Student Body President Kirk Fox, and the captain of this year's varsity basketball team, Norman Miller. The other boys are in my scout troop, Troop 9. We are taking a break in our meeting for lunch. Georgia tells me that she is not allowed to serve our guest without your permission. We need you to give that so that we can all order lunch."

Olson was in a spot he never suspected could occur. He was in an impossible position. He really had no choice: he had to give in for now. He needed to make a few calls to see what to do. He dared not pause longer. "Well, your request has been made so politely, I will give my permission today." He smiled thinly—no one was here—he had covered himself for now.

"Today?" Tom smiled apologetically. "I'm sorry, I must not have asked that the right way: your permission needs to be permanent, no exceptions. We'd like to keep coming here. Not everyone likes pizza. And Shakey's milkshakes?" He shook his head. "I'll have to get a coke. I don't like cokes that much."

Olson had turned ash white. "What do you mean?" he sputtered helplessly.

"It's pretty simple, really. Jackson High students won't hang out in any restaurant that won't serve our friend here, or any of his friends, or their families." He looked at Olson straight in the eye. "When the school assembly meets on Wednesday morning, we were hoping to pass out a special discount coupon to everyone to use here... here only. I'd

581

hate to change that to a pizza discount; like I said, I'd a lot rather get your double burger basket." He glanced at Kirk.

"Good point, Tom. I'm glad you mentioned that." Kirk nodded vigorously.

The boys all raised their glass in a toast.

"You don't need to make a big deal about it or spend any money announcing a change—unless you want to," he shrugged. "Word will get around on its own." he extended his hand. "Do we have lunch here?" He continued to look him straight in the eye.

Olson was dumbfounded. The sound of a camera clicking had sealed his fate. He shook Tom's hand. "We aim to please. Please enjoy your lunch." His lips smiled, but not his eyes. With a nod, he retreated into his office.

"Georgia: I need a double burger basket and a chocolate shake." Tom grinned at the guys: "Order up! Whatever you want—it's been paid for already." He winked at Mason and got a nod in return. He turned to Georgia: "Put everything on one bill." He winked at her too.

Mason was seated in the next booth. He flagged Georgia to stop at his table briefly—he informed her that he would be paying for the boys' meal. He ordered a tuna salad sandwich and cup of coffee for himself and gave her a five-dollar bill folded in half as a pre-tip and told her to tuck it away quickly. He inquired about the availability of a secure telephone he could use after the boys were served.

—m—

Promotion to Sales Manager came with one perk that Mark had not fully appreciated until now: his own private office. Oglivy's was closed at last, the daily receipts had been submitted; as far as he knew, other than the janitorial crew, he was the only one left in the store. Maybe, just maybe, he could sort out what had been gnawing at him since returning from the 'viewing' at Francine's house yesterday. Until now, he had not used this space for any personal purpose. It was the perfect place to reflect: the switchboard was closed for the night—no one could call or interrupt.

Delivered by courier just before closing, the framed drawings were standing against the wall by the door, still wrapped. Presumably, they had been given first-rate treatment by Swann's people. The question now was what to do with them. *do I want to look at them again? then what do I do? I feel an obligation to let Pat see them—she is the only one who knows what they represent or reflect. on the other hand, is it fair to her to show them? hmmm… why wouldn't it be? still, I don't want them hanging on the wall where I'll be running into them day and night.*

That made him feel guilty—they were truly fine works of art that ought to be seen… Swann had convinced him of that. Maybe, in time. Luckily, Julian didn't care about that. For Julian, they were a greeting card, essentially, drawn for the person being portrayed. The prospect of being exhibited for the public to see did not enter his mind. He could tuck them away in a closet or whatever he wanted and Julian would never know. He did not intend to do that, certainly.

He felt lighter, oddly enough—as if a burden had been removed. That was new, unexpected. The conversation with Swann yesterday had helped enormously. Seeing the drawings again was much less traumatic than he had expected—he owed Swann for that. Actually, it wasn't traumatic at all… it seemed to finish a chapter somehow. Waiting six months had been enough, evidently; Eric now seemed a treasured memory, not an amputation. He had reached that level last summer—the short talk with Julian had enabled that, hadn't it? That's what he learned yesterday. Between Swann's keen eye and Julian's openness, the pieces fell into place at last. The second drawing was done the evening after that very special talk.

He'd had a nightmare—the usual nightmare—and he'd left the cabin to calm down. He couldn't very well pace around the cabin without waking Julian. For the better part of an hour he sat on that stump wrapped in the Ladies' Auxiliary quilt—had a good cry, as usual… that had always helped. But when he returned to the cabin, Julian was sitting atop his cot wrapped in his cover blanket, waiting.

obviously, he had seen me on the stump—it's only a hundred yards from the cabin. I didn't ask how long he had been waiting… but it was long enough. I knew at once that he realized I was dealing with a personal problem. Julian wasn't about to pry—but he wanted to help.

I had given him a good scare, yet his only concern was for my happiness. he could feel my pain and agony—it was reflected on his face and in the tears he quietly shed. he was so selfless, so giving—I was the child and he was the adult. I felt so guilty... I was responsible for his pain.

Mark paused a moment: he had just grasped something important: *I did not realize it then—I have just figured it out: the scare I had caused him was not his concern at all. he was trying to remove my pain: he wanted to take it away, to absorb it. he seemed to know what it was, even though he couldn't have—only Pat knew about Eric.*

I had to tell him about my grief over losing someone—I owed him that much—though I did not identify who it was. oddly, he understood instantly, or seemed to... he didn't say a word.

why did I think he understood? was I reading that in to satisfy my conscience?

Mark was unaccustomed to self-analysis—until now he had avoided it rather successfully, rather deftly. He took a deep breath—self-discipline was one of his assets; he was employing it now, all hands on deck. It wasn't half as hard as he had expected it to be. The immediate problem was a parched mouth: he had failed to provide anything to quench his thirst: this office did not include any water features. The water cooler was only a few feet down the hall. He continued his train of thought on the way...

I need to be honest with myself: that's what did it! Julian's sympathy gave me permission to say goodbye to that recurring agony—sharing it with Julian is what set me free.

That's what the second drawing captured: a man freed from the torture of his past. Wounded, of course, but healing. The second portrait was drawn about 20 hours later that evening, just before lights out. Mark shook his head in disgust: *I promised to leave a note if I ever had to leave in the night again. I promptly broke the promise the very next night when I had to take Geoff back to his camp.* Julian had forgiven him, of course.

What Mark did not realize was how the release from his agony worked: his severed heartstrings had reattached to a live person. It was unconscious—and would remain unperceived for a considerable length of time—the need to protect his young charge overrode everything else—it forbade any personal relationship. In any case, he was incapable of exploiting anyone regardless of age. He was not the active type—he was the passive, the willing, the follower: Eric was his anchor. For six years now he had to do without until another came along. What he did not understand, at least not yet, was that Julian was not simply standing by, ready to serve as that anchor: it had already begun without either being aware of it when they were sitting side by side on that cot. Mark stood and gave Julian his signature pinch on the shoulder—meant to be paternal, that night it was a direct two way conduit.

That is what Swann saw revealed in Julian's face, and what he understood. It reinforced his decision to support both of these extraordinary individuals.

Mark's mental sorting continued. Paternal: that line of thought brought Pat's observations to mind—and her efforts to alleviate his loneliness. He had not felt lonely for some time now—several weeks. His unruly libido—if that's what it was, seemed to be on vacation as well. Roger had not been a problem; he had turned down two opportunities to go out with Peter—the Pompeii experience had told him what not to bother with, evidently. Another discovery: Peter was not, nor ever could be his anchor. It was pointless to pursue that course. His libido was an annoyance lately, nothing more. He could manage on his own—he had no choice. His brief, but very deep legacy with Eric would have to do in the interim—no matter how long. He was not looking for anyone.

Those drawings—particularly the second one—had brought Mark to his senses. Julian seemed to see inside him—that's what the drawings demonstrated—but how? *how could he possibly know what I had gone through, let alone relate to it, or preserve it in a pencil drawing? he wasn't even fifteen years old... he has to be unaware of what he's recording or reporting or celebrating... it was a combination of all three. was it meant for only me to see?* All of Julian's portraits were drawn for their subjects, not for the public. *they aren't intended to be private, necessarily—that's up to the subject to decide.*

He glanced at the package by the door, still wrapped with string reinforcement. He didn't particularly want to open it; not because he was afraid, or uneasy, but this little escape in his office had already succeeded in stripping him bare—he didn't need to see it depicted as well.

That's what it felt like, though, looking at those... exposed, as if he was standing in front of a mirror totally undressed; what did Swann and the others see? Did they see something else? The drawings of Leonard and Sarge had a similar quality, though not as strong—and the double drawings of Swann did too—he could almost hear them.

Pinning this down was frustrating... *is there another sense?* An emotional sense maybe... *that must be what fascinates Swann.*

One quality in Swann's portraits was similar to Mark's second portrait. Mark was responsible for 47 boys—they were what mattered. Swann had a larger 'troop.' Julian's drawing made it clear that they were what mattered to Swann—several hundred or more. Both drawings revealed that inner character trait. Mark could not identify what or how he saw it in the drawings—it had to be visual—yet he couldn't isolate it, whatever it was. It was in the eyes, and in the confident stance.

That 'viewing' at Francine's, on top of the trip to Camp Walker, had awakened him—his boys, all forty-seven of them, were filling whatever it was he thought he needed—companionship? He had done without a sex partner for so long now, he was used to doing without. Self-analysis and introspection had never been his cup of tea, and that remained the case—yet this afternoon, his mind seemed able to take a look at things. Had he arrived at his place in this world, this life? Something in him said no—he was, like his boys, a work in progress. And that seemed to be okay. He wasn't hiding out in his purchasing agent cubbyhole any longer, either literally or figuratively. He sensed that this executive office was not a final destination, but a step or a stage.

He had learned a great deal from Julian today. The second drawing helped him see who he was: a free, an open man—ready to meet the day. The drawing of Swann next to his this afternoon was a happy coincidence. Julian had captured Swann's strength and generosity, his greatness as a human being as well as his role as a provider and guide—a hint of that quality was in the second portrait that Julian had drawn in the cabin: he had not appreciated or understood how leadership was seen by a boy of fifteen, which is what Julian had become six months ago. Because he was an artist, Julian saw a good deal more.

Thanks to Julian, and to recent events, Mark felt comfortable in his own skin: he could look at himself in the mirror now, if he wanted to. One of these days, he would give that a test. Curiously, he did not take note of the erotic implications of either drawing—he hadn't noticed that in the Leonard drawing either—an indicator that his libido was not active these days; the subject did not come up.

And what about his feelings for Julian? They remained hidden by and large in his unconscious mind. He could not go there, and would not if he could. Fortunately, Julian was behaving himself. The greeting as he leapt out of Swann's car before the viewing was a reminder that Julian was still a boy in many ways. Mark's unconscious mind, however, had stored another very different perception—equally central to his thinking: after the early morning jog several days ago, the hug of reassurance about wishing Merry Christmas was a fond memory of a very different sort—not a memory of a little boy at all: it was of a bigger boy, very nearly ready: he was taller, stronger… and little boys did not exude exquisite aromas, nor deliver inadvertent bumps below that were awkwardly pleasant.

Mark stepped over to the string reinforced package. He would take these home as is. Pat could decide what came next for these drawings.

34 *the grand entrance*

"Thank you, Cindy," Miss St. Johns was pleased at how well that had gone—asking her to move over a chair was asking a great deal now that Julian had become a such a celebrity among the girls. A place for the new student had to be arranged in advance. "You can leave your books here, Julian. You need to report to Mr. Barnes right away. You and Kasey will come directly here after the assembly." Once he had gone, she would explain to the class what was about to happen: this class would have the new student every day first period. She was determined to see that it would always be a good start to his school day. Fortunately, no one was absent this morning.

"Oo, yeah!" It was time already; the assembly was at a special time—usually they were just before lunch or at the end of the day. *makes sense...* "Thanks, Miss St. Johns." He was ready—outfitted in his new maroon pullover sweater Geraldine had given him for Christmas. She thought it would be perfect with the coral shirt he always wore on Fridays. He appreciated the difference it made in the cold weather, but it covered up his shirt pockets. He had to figure a way to get around that problem. Covering up his pencil holders was not good at all. The pencil point always broke off when he used his pants pockets. For once, he would have to leave his sketchbook behind, so it didn't matter for now.

Funny way to start a term: a two-day week. Personally, he would have waited until next Monday to start things off. But he was ready—the run through yesterday went perfectly. He walked to the door, oblivious to the surprised stares; the other students in his English class did not know what he knew: this special assembly was more special than they would ever guess, and he had a special job: introduce Kasey. Surprisingly, he looked forward to it. Yesterday's rehearsal made a huge difference: thanks to the Flaming Arrow guys, this time he knew what was needed and what was expected. That was a good feeling—a terrific feeling.

The office aide saw him approaching the door. She couldn't believe she had been given this assignment. She had only seen him from a distance, but had heard that he was friendly.

"Hi, I'm Julian," he said brightly—he knew why she was there. That's one thing that never changed around here: you either had a hall pass or an escort. He didn't mind; it was a good way to meet someone new. "What's your name?"

"Oh! I'm Gail." She had not expected to be asked. "Mr. Barnes sent me: we need to hurry." She was so thrilled with herself! She had done that without any mistakes. He was every bit as handsome as she thought he would be—and so **nice**—*just like everyone says! he even invited me to lead the way!*

"Hi, Gail! Do we get to run?" He knew that was a no-no inside the building. He walked alongside and set a quick pace. He took a second look. He was sure glad he wasn't a girl—she wore a nice wool skirt, but her legs were bare. He figured girls must have a special built in heaters or something. *maybe that's why their legs are so big around.* One nice thing about being a boy: you got to wear full length pants when it was cold out.

"Is it fun to be an office assistant?" He had never talked to one about that before... might as well be friendly.

She had not expected to be asked a question. She blushed at once, not only because she had never thought about it being fun or not—but the last thing she expected was this boy to be interested enough to ask her anything. She wasn't ready—all she wanted to do was look at him. He was so good looking it was hard to believe he was real.

Julian sensed that she was too shy to respond, so he offered her a way to answer. "Must be interesting to go all over the school and meet lots of new people." He shrugged: "A big school like this? So far I barely know my way around—way bigger than Wallace, for sure." He glanced at her again. "Which Junior Hi did you go to?"

She didn't have time to answer; the intercom broke the silence as they were approaching the second floor turn in the stairway:

>> *Your attention please, attention...* <<

Miss Watkins, the official voice-from-the-office began to order the transfer of students to the boys' gym—the only facility large enough to accommodate the entire student body at one time. Her voice could penetrate anything.

"Oo-ee! We **gotta** scoot, now!" Julian began to skip every other step. In a second, the halls would be filled wall to wall with students headed for the boys' gym. Seniors always got to go first. Gail would have to keep up the best she could.

—ᴍ—

Kasey found himself in an odd frame of mind—he seemed to be detached from his body, watching what was happening from the safety of a suspended booth somewhere. He'd had dreams like this—as if he was watching a movie being made—sort of a halfway state of suspended action—like he was backstage awaiting his cue to walk out and make a long awaited concert debut. The problem, of course, was uncertainty about what it was like to play for an audience—any audience. He wasn't exactly starting small: there would be well over twelve hundred this morning, most of them students. His piano fingers were ready. Fortunately, his part in the program was very minor.

He restudied the complex grain in the hardwood burl from which the trim around the windows of Frederick Swann's Packard had been made, as if he might discover a hidden pattern that explained why it looked like it had been cooked and poured into a mold rather than grown, harvested and hand shaped by a craftsman in the 1930s. He needed something to occupy his mind while he and his parents awaited Mason's return. Any minute, he would appear to escort them into the building for the all school assembly—he was about to enter Jackson High School with his parents at his side; he had Julian's letter—now his most precious possession—in his breast pocket for good luck. So he wasn't in a complete panic. He liked his new blazer—it was almost the right color. He wasn't sure about it; he had expected to be outfitted in a school jacket like Julian's.

The last few days had made a huge difference—he now had more friends than he had ever had in his life, thanks to Julian, the boy wonder—including two girls! Watching Julian rehearse dancing was something he never expected—he seemed to be having so much fun. After lunch on Monday, they had gone to Randall's house to rehearse everything they had planned at that drive-in restaurant. Their party room was perfect—piano and all, dance floor—everything. Julian's friends were really into this project—so was Randall's mother. All this was so foreign to him it was hard to believe it was his new world—poles different from life at Belmont. If it weren't for Julian's constant support, he might well have asked his father to reconsider. Julian's eagerness and amusing behavior, combined with his genuine affection was extremely powerful, unlike anything he had ever known. Remembering the last few days was a good way to occupy his mind while waiting for Mason to return and escort them into the building.

Yesterday, Mr. Swann and his company had set up the gymnasium—it looked as if a Hollywood crew was setting things in place for one of those rock band concerts. He and the others in Julian's group couldn't watch what they were up to because they were too busy rehearsing. After the Baldwin was delivered and tuned properly, they asked him to give it a good test—he played the Joplin especially for Mr. Swann. The piano was wonderful—*what a pleasure to play...* the acoustics of a huge gymnasium was quite a shock. *what will it be like filled with people?*

Lewis Wood and his wife thought it wise to allow their son to focus on his immediate challenge—they understood the stress he was feeling—it was a huge test. They were confident he could handle it, but were grateful to be at his side.

The Packard was parked in front of the school this time, not tucked out of sight behind the building. They would be entering by the front door in full public view. Kasey thought there might be reporters here—at least no protesters had surrounded the campus.

He had no way of knowing that Mr. Swann had persuaded the Superintendent to discuss this event with the Board in their routine executive session dealing with personnel—the media was not allowed to attend those, so the Times reporter did not know there was anything unusual happening this morning. As a result, Swann would be able to supply information as he saw fit. A calculated risk, but after what that boy had achieved at the drive in restaurant, he felt even safer. Especially fortunate, since it was a slow news day at the Times-Herald—he would discover that they had devoted their energies to weather news, comparing the local history of snowstorms with the record breaking blizzard underway in England. Incredibly, no one had leaked a word.

Kasey had never been a student in a school this large. Private schools were a different thing entirely: instead of continuing to row a skiff around Walden Pond, he expected to be leaving New Bedford aboard the Pequod or its like. It was easy to think of Julian as a blond Ishmael and himself as Queequeg without the tattoos; fortunately, Mr. Middleton wasn't a Captain Ahab—he was headed for Bermuda and calm seas. North Carolina was half way there. Still, it was winter, not summer... a squall or two would likely come along eventually. In any case he doubted if very many Jackson students had read any Melville. The way Tom took care of the restaurant manager still took his breath away—Tom had smiled the entire time!

Not many students walked by—this was not the main route for foot traffic. Bicycles for the most part had come this way. The curious glances at the Packard were not a problem: tinted glass made seeing who was inside impossible. Kasey wondered how he would be getting here every day—that was a new problem. He was used to living on campus. Swann's guest house was miles away. Awkward, to say the least. Probably a new assignment for Mason.

"It must take a while to get things organized," Candace Wood patted her son's thigh—she sensed that he was growing uneasy.

"Lots of Administrivia," Lewis chuckled. He had gone to a high school twice this size. "New semester, attendance, announcements, getting everyone herded to the gym... we could be here a while longer."

Kasey smiled at his father, gratefully. "We get to miss all the fun speeches out here. Still, it's a little strange to be the surprise at a surprise party."

Lewis chuckled. His son's wry sense of humor was reassuring. He was up to the challenge. And it was a considerable challenge. But Swann's precautions had been extensive. He didn't think there was any danger. He gave his wife a nudge: all was well.

Kasey took a deep breath and sat back. Fortunately, the back seat of a 1936 Packard was very comfortable, even for a gangly six foot four kid from Boston. It was a sunny day, but in the low 40s—not much different than Boston would be, oddly enough. The angle of the sun might be different... his mind drifted back a week and a half to those last minutes at Belmont. They were special—to his great surprise...

farewell, Angus Murray House

"We're all loaded, I guess." Kasey had just done a final nook and cranny check, just to be safe—he wasn't a packrat, so there wasn't anything to find, even after four years in this room.

Mason suppressed a smile. "We need to touch base in the common room before going to the car." He had been given the privilege of doing this himself; his employer was busy at Kasey's new school. Usually all he did was set things in place. Having Snyder along helped considerably. This enabled the boy's parents to supervise the moving crew in Boston. The goal was to have the Wood family installed in the guest house in time for Christmas.

Kasey had a brief twang of regret—leaving Angus Murray House was leaving home, in a way. Another thing that was unusual: *Mr. Swann seems just as interested in my needs* as *my father's... not the average boss.* He didn't have a camera, but Mr. Swann's assistant had taken several snapshots. Kasey was enough of a history buff to realize the value of having a visual record; he was very grateful. He might not be returning here ever again. Not a happy thought particularly, but realistic nonetheless.

The second they stepped out of Kasey's room, the 'sentry' ducked out of sight.

Kasey had intended to take a last look at the common room before leaving—it was where he spent more time than anywhere, and was probably what he would miss most: especially his chair. That chair was made with him in mind.

"For he's a jolly good fellow," a dozen people burst into song the moment he turned into the room. Kasey was stunned—he couldn't step back because Mason was right behind. He was shocked and helpless—unable to do anything but accept the glass of punch that was forced into his right hand and step forward because 'Saint Joe' was pulling at his left elbow. In seconds he was in the center of the room, surrounded by a singing circle of well-wishers.

The song ended with a cheer, and the Headmaster took charge: "Be seated, everyone." He gestured to the circle of chairs—the room had been rearranged; several folding chairs had been brought in to accommodate the extra people. Kasey noticed at once that all his professors were here as well as a few other staff members.

"This is irregular, of course, but so is anyone departing mid-year. None of us are pleased that you are, in fact, departing. We wanted you to know that you will be missed, and that we wish you to succeed wherever Fate decides that will be." He raised his glass, and everyone else did the same. "We know that you can't stay for a proper farewell party, but Mason has been very helpful in advising what is possible." He raised his glass again and deferred to the current Head Boy of Angus Murray House.

Hayden was ready. He stepped forward with an oversized envelope. "On behalf of the six remaining inmates of Murray House, we are seeing to it that justice is served." He handed Kasey the envelope, trading it for the glass of punch.

Kasey pulled out an 8x10 certificate—signed by all six of his housemates, it read: "Be it known by all present and interested, that the red leather chair is now and forever the property of one Kasey Wood." It was suitable for being framed.

Kasey blushed—so surprised and moved, he was unable to utter a word. Where the chair should be, by the window overlooking the quad, a small cabinet stood instead!

"Thanks to your benefactor, we now have a new record player to substitute for our dear departing live piano player." Hayden shrugged, inferring that it was second best, but better than nothing.

"Where's...."

"On its way to Boston with the rest of your things," Mason gestured toward the door. This had gone well, but they needed to be on their way. His employer was going to be very pleased at how this had turned out.

"Best of luck, Kasey," Professor Marchbanks stood and extended his hand. "Stay in touch—feel free to send news or ask a question—any time. I truly mean that."

Kasey shook his hand, thrilled.

"Yeah: 'be sure to write if you get work,'" Edison added. He always had a Bob and Ray or Stan Freburg line handy.

Awkwardly, Hayden gave him a farewell hug. He was surprised at himself: for once he had no words—or was too choked up to get them out. That made a hug or handshake from all the boys possible and mandatory.

Kasey had not expected anything like this, and was at a loss how to respond—it was largely impromptu and genuine. He felt a sense of loss himself, and that too was unexpected.

"Hold that pose and look this way, everyone." Sawyer was there with his camera to document the occasion.

He was able to mutter Merry Christmas…

∽⧉∾

"Here comes Mason." His reverie was interrupted: his mother had just tapped his arm. The moment had arrived: it was time to say goodbye to Belmont and hello to Jackson.

—⧓—

Frederick Swann's media team had spent the better part of yesterday setting up; a full crew was deployed, as if they were doing a complete 30 minute infomercial. Based in Atlanta, the full three truck Bantam Media fleet was on site at the back of the building. They had done their usual installation of film and video cameras and sound yesterday—the site was easy to cover, including high angle and overhead. Lights were not needed; the gymnasium was well lit: no shadow problems whatever. The installation was appropriately masked—aside from a few cables taped to the floor, most people didn't realize it was there. No mobile cameras were in use, but they could zoom from four of the six camera angles. The entire event would be filmed and recorded, directed remotely from the control van. A two-man crew was stationed out of sight behind the platform in case one of the remotes developed a problem. Setting all this up in one day was an achievement, but easily within their capability. Everything passed the technical check this morning with flying colors. The new wireless mikes worked superbly.

Julian and Student Body President Kirk Fox were sitting by the side door to the main gym, awaiting their cue to enter. The Cardinal team entered from this door to play home games. A bunch of hoopla would precede their entrance this morning. Unknown to all but a few, this was a carefully crafted event. Unlike most schools' official first day of integration, it was tailored to fit a single student rather than several hundred—that would take place in the fall.

Four other chairs awaited; presumably, they were about to be joined by Kasey and his parents.

"You'll do okay; it's not so hard once you get started." Kirk advised. "Just take a deep breath first, and make sure you hold the microphone right in front of your mouth—if they can't hear you, you're dead for sure." He shook his head. That had happened to him once... getting attention after that was a toughie. "I always take it off the stand and move around while I talk," he patted Julian reassuringly. "That way you know it will be in the right place. You get used to it pretty quick... saves you from having to fuss with adjusting the stand." At least they would be on the main floor, not on the platform. Having multiple mikes was a big help—Mr. Swann's tech crew was out of sight, but knew their business.

The band was playing now, setting the mood or something. Julian didn't mind band music—a bit loud, but that was okay for this kind of event. It was kind of hard to understand what the speaker was saying—sort of echo-like here in the passageway. He tilted his head trying to tune it in.

597

"He has to introduce everyone," Kirk explained. "The School Board and all the department chairmen. Luckily, they don't have to give a speech, or we'd be here all day." He was glad that Mr. Barnes agreed with the revision he asked for. Now he didn't have to start the assembly off. Tom was right about that.

Julian didn't exactly feel cheated, being offstage during that stuff; lucky was a better word. *oo!* footsteps from behind, around the corner: sure enough, it was Mason leading Kasey and his parents this way.

"Hi, Kasey!" he jumped up and waved happily. "Hi, Mrs. Wood, Professor Wood," he bounced on his toes. "We saved you a seat!" he pointed to the empty chairs. "Can't see a thing from here, but you can hear, sort of." he giggled. He waved at Mason happily.

"Hello, Julian," Lewis Wood was delighted to see him. This boy was able to elevate the occasion instantly as if he had a magic wand: beyond fortunate.

"Good morning Julian," Candace Wood smiled openly. Julian seemed to lighten things—she usually remained silent, but he charmed his way straight through her decorum shield without any effort; she could almost feel the stress wrinkles vanish.

Mason stepped over to consult with Kirk briefly.

"So, you holding up okay?" Julian gave Kasey his typical poke in the tummy. He looked up at his face and grinned: Kasey seemed to be fine, and ready.

Julian's magic always worked. He had no idea what being Kasey's 'Buddy' meant to Kasey: Julian was his Rock of Gibraltar. Instantly, Kasey was back with a lifelong pal.

A sudden burst of music interrupted the conversation. "Yow!" Julian jumped: the Star Spangled Banner just preempted everything. Even off stage, they felt compelled to stand. That was not usually played at an assembly—it meant that this event was more than a pep rally— being first thing in the day instead of last was proof of that. Kirk stood by the door; Mason was on duty to keep it open far enough to see and hear when the time was at hand. Kirk would enter first to give his speech and then introduce Julian.

This was strange, a little. Usually, it would be Kirk out there starting things. Julian remembered: it was Tom's idea to change that. *when all the bigwigs are here, that's different. shows who is in charge I s'pose... made sense.* They couldn't rehearse all this stuff yesterday. He gave Kasey a friendly bump with his elbow as the National Anthem came to a finish. A rousing cheer followed—gave him a goose bump, actually. *feels kinda weird, being backstage...*

Inside the gym, the sophomores filled the upper tier of bleachers, accessed directly from the second floor. The juniors and seniors occupied the main floor, and were divided roughly in half, vertically: the seniors on the north, juniors the south; it was not a fixed line. As the year progressed it gradually dissolved; more sophomores invaded as they became steadies with upper class members. This was a social tradition, not in the rulebook. But social rules were sometimes harder to get around than official policy. The unofficial rules were what the administration and board were worried about most, and what they were counting on Julian to navigate for Kasey. It was their hope that he could open the door wide first thing. Once the social elite was on board, the others would surely follow—they always had in the past.

Little did they know that the objective had been partially achieved already—the grapevine buzz yesterday had put the important figures on the alert, set up effectively by Rhonda and Theresa after the rehearsal. Phones were humming all last evening. Julian's unofficial fan club was ready and waiting. The dignitaries were about to get a huge surprise: few had attended a pep assembly lately, and this was going to surpass most of those by a wide margin.

Opposite the bleachers, the speaker's platform had been expanded to provide room for the seven member Board of Directors, the Superintendent and his Deputy, and special guest Frederick Swann; the Jackson Administration and Department Chairmen on the speaker's left along with some special guests, there because Swann wanted them: Mark, Julian's mother, and Randall's parents as well as Geraldine. Two chairs were reserved for Kasey's parents. They would be seated after being introduced. The band was arranged concert style in the center of the court. They were not called on to do any marching, but the rally and dance teams were present to do a warm up routine and lead a yell or two. Getting the students into a patriotic frame of mind with a festive upbeat tone would typically have been at the end of the day, just before an interscholastic game. Thanks to Kirk and Tom, this was going to be a pep rally on steroids: a most unusual way to start the school day and a new semester.

"Please be seated," the Principal had returned to the microphone. "I want to thank the Superintendent for his kind words and the Board for their support during the exciting changes we will be seeing this year and next. But now the time has come: to kick things off, here is your Student Body President, Kirk Fox!" Middleton made a sweeping gesture to his left: the yell King and rally squad leapt to their feet and led the student body in a rousing cheer as Kirk burst out of the side door and skipped forward to the floor mike in front of the platform. Kirk was very popular, having been in leadership roles all through school. The cheers went a little longer than Kirk had expected, and he had to get them calmed down. Finally, a few shush gestures worked.

"Thanks. Thanks a lot. First thing I want to do is congratulate Terry and Coach Brodie, and Tom Dawson of course, for the big win that ended the season."

He had to wait for the cheers to die down again. Even though the game was a couple of weeks ago, it remained a topic of discussion, since the conference championship game was not far off.

"Now it's time for everybody to stand behind Norman and Coach Hopper and the greatest basketball team in the conference!" he gestured for them to stand.

"Go Team!" he added, then took a pause, walking slowly to the right until the crowd was silent. He had learned how to get their attention: he was obviously about to say something important. Walking back to the center, he spoke in a new, serious tone.

"I needed to mention Coach Brodie and the team a minute ago for a couple of reasons: first, to apologize for not being at that game." There was a moment of absolute silence—it was not generally known that he had missed the game.

"Sometimes, you have to be two places at the same time, and that night was one of those. It turned out to be one of those times that you're just plain lucky to be there. Mr. Middleton and I had to be at the

600

university that night to meet someone very special, someone who you are about to meet—and who, as of today, is Jackson High School's newest student." He paused for a moment, to make sure they were all tuned in. "To introduce him, I have invited another very special student to do the honors. He was there that night too, and that's one reason I was so lucky—until then, I had not known him. Thanks to Mr. Middleton and Mr. Barnes—somehow they knew he'd be perfect for the assignment to make our new student feel welcome and at home. They were so right: no one could do that better than this kid. Most of you know him or about him already. So it is my pleasure to invite him to say a few words: the pride of the Jackson High Sophomore Class, Julian Forrest—better known to most of us as this year's Li'l Abner! Come on out here, Julian!"

A roaring cheer: the sophomores stood automatically, flattered and duty bound; the junior and senior girls from second lunch, scattered across the main bank of bleachers gave their predictable squeal of delight—the boys figured they had better join in as well. It was infectious: Julian skipped happily across the gym to greet a huge cheering crowd, and gave Kirk a friendly fist bump. His light blond hair flopping happily, he was instantly recognized, and the cheer increased in enthusiasm. A few whistles were added by those who always whistled no matter what was going on. Julian's welcome was just as enthusiastic as Kirk's had been. They were already hyped up, and for most, this beat being in class—might as well take advantage of the opportunity. Kirk knew that and counted on it. He gave Mr. Swann a secret grin. It took a while to calm down; Julian assumed it was Kirk that was being cheered most of all.

"Wow! You guys!" He giggled. Kirk's applauding with them was a nice surprise. "Thanks, everyone." He looked like a celebrity, and his positive unassuming nature made stage presence seem like his native state.

The cheering continued; he didn't know what to do—this wasn't rehearsed. "You guys!! Come on!" He hopped a little and waved merrily at everyone generally, then at each class. He bowed a couple of times as if he had done something—they seemed to demand it. He looked over at Kirk and shrugged—he was still applauding too. One more bow, then he stopped to stare them down with a smile; eventually it calmed to silence, their pent up energy had run out at last. The expanse of eager faces was completely unexpected; he didn't deserve all this, but he didn't let it deflect his purpose. Instinct cut in, and he got started.

"Thanks again." He didn't know what else to say, so he waded right in: "Here's the thing, you guys—oh: and girls too, for sure!" he giggled apologetically. "Think about this a sec: what are you gonna do if all of a sudden your dad gets hired to do an important job miles and miles away, hundreds of miles away. Because he could be there a while, he wants to have his family around too—especially since he may be there a long time, maybe a year or two years even, who knows." He paused to give them a minute to think.

"Figure it out: you can't expect him to do a good job for long if his family is hundreds of miles away every time he comes home from work." He shrugged with arms open to emphasize the obvious. "So they hafta move too. It's only right."

"That's what's going on here: it's not Kasey's fault his dad is a famous scientist and the best man for the job—so even if you like your school and classes just fine the way they are, truth is, you need to stay with your mom, and your baby sister and your dad." He threw his hands open, resigned. "Kasey isn't the kind of kid who's gonna mess that up." He paused and stared at them doing a slow sweep across the width of the stands while it sank in.

"So: what do you do if all of a sudden you are all alone in a strange school and don't know anybody?" He stared at them briefly, giving them time to think. "There's nothing you **can** do! It isn't fair." He stamped with his right foot. "They don't know you from Adam, and why should they care, anyway?" He paused again.

"So, put yourself in the new kid's place, and you can see what I mean. That's where I come in—where all of us come in, really.

"It's like in scouts: we always have a buddy along. If you go swimming, you always have a buddy with you, just in case you get in trouble and need help—or you need to be his help. Last summer, Norman was assigned to be my swimming buddy at the lake." He scanned the crowd, expecting to spot Norman—sure enough, there he was. He pointed: "You can usually spot Norman, y'know... he's a little taller than most." He gestured toward Norman to take a bow just for the fun of it. Norman was used to Julian's way of talking. The crowd laughed and gave a short cheer to the captain of the basketball team.

Frederick Swann was ecstatic: he had no idea Julian was an ex tempore speaking talent as well as an artist.

"Norman did a super job of getting me squared away at Lake Walker. So that's what I decided to do: be Kasey's Buddy at Jackson High. Why not? You never know, your buddy might be someone you like and that your friends will like too. Easy as pie, problem fixed." He paused for effect and took a few steps. "Only this time, I'm the lucky one. Kasey is fun and interesting—and boy-o-boy can he ever play the piano!" He paused and turned.

"But hold the phone: there's something else you need to keep in mind—and this is true whether or not you're a Buddy: sometimes people have a special difference that you need to know about and make allowances for, something that they can't change even if they wanted to. Otherwise, they're just like you and me. I have a friend that was born on Halloween—all his life, people want to dress up as a ghost or a witch or something for his birthday party. Not his fault, but he's stuck with it. He hates his own birthday! I have another pal that was born on Christmas— he doesn't get a birthday party on his birthday at all. Some people are born to be short, some tall. Some are left-handed. They don't have a choice. Kasey is just like you and me, but he has the same problem Norman has: he's kinda tall." He paused, and looked at Norman with an exaggerated nod. He cupped his hand around the mike as if to whisper a secret fact: he hiked his shoulders and grimaced, "I think he might be a little taller," He stepped a few feet to his right while the audience reacted. He continued that topic—he had discovered how to work a positive house and gave them more with ease. He was able to use facial expressions and gestures as if he had been trained.

"If you're six and a half feet tall, people sometimes look at you kinda funny—just ask Norman." He pointed to the proof: "it's hard to duck out of sight." Remembering what Arnie said at summer camp, he paused to let them laugh. This was kinda fun... When they were ready, he continued: "So: to be fair, you hafta make allowances and be glad you don't have that problem yourself at least."

Norman stood and applauded that sentiment, and the students laughed and applauded again. Julian took advantage of the moment and let it run its course. When they were watching him again, he spoke to a happy, receptive crowd:

"Before I invite him out here, I hafta warn you about one other thing: when he talks you know right away he's not from around here: he sounds just like the President. He's from Boston, y'see, and that's the way they talk up there. No big deal; you get used to it." He turned and added an aside: "Runs in the family—his mom is from England, and she sounds just like the Queen!" Again, he grinned happily and waited for the laughter to quiet down.

"Anyway: I hit the jackpot, 'cause I really like them and they are my friends as well as my Buddies. So here they are, Kasey Wood and his folks." He opened his left arm toward the entrance he had used; quickly he returned the mike to its stand so he could applaud with the crowd. The dignitaries and guests on the platform applauded as well.

Mason served as usher and led them to the microphone stand, then stood behind a few feet, ready to escort the parents to the platform with the other guests. His beige chauffeur's cap was a surprise, as was the tall dark skinned boy wearing a red blazer. The boy's mother was particularly striking—her elegant demeanor and striking formal dress looked regal and exotic. His father looked like a professor wearing a classy three-piece suit.

Kasey stood with his parents for as long as he could stand it; he reached out for Julian to join him at the microphone. He had never addressed an audience, let alone have over a thousand people greet him with enthusiastic applause: but Julian's presence was all he required. He placed his left hand on Julian's shoulder, and pulled the mike free from the stand:

"Thank you, Julian—" he looked at the sea of faces, a sight he had not expected to see, ever. Fortunately, they were sufficiently distant to remain anonymous. He spoke to them directly. "I'm tempted to say that he is a tough act to follow, but he is not an act: he is the real thing." He paused briefly so that could sink in. "I don't have a speech to give, but my parents and I are glad to be here, and are grateful for your welcome." He turned to Julian: "as I said to the teachers when I met them, you are an irresistible force. Thanks for being my Buddy—and my friend." He returned the mike and reached out for a fist bump.

The audience applauded: what else could they do? They were touched by his sentiment, and stunned by his extraordinary stature—not to mention his brilliant blue eyes, quite visible to most of the audience since they contrasted so sharply with his very dark skin. He did not look negroid, but he was as dark as most Blacks any of them had seen. And he did sound like President Kennedy. He had been sold, and without reservation. Everyone wanted to meet him in person sooner or later.

Julian hopped in delight and gestured to the band teacher. He and a student went for the new grand that had been placed by the back of the platform. They moved it to the center, behind the band while Mason escorted Kasey's parents to the platform, where the Principal greeted them and showed them to the awaiting chairs next to the Hallstroms.

Julian took the mike along: "Now, time for a surprise! just wait 'till you hear this guy play the piano!" he tugged Kasey by the belt. He decided not to mention that Mr. Swann had donated that to the school yesterday.

"He's going to play three things: one for all the teen boppers out there, one for everyone else in the world, big kids and teachers especially—then, a surprise one he doesn't expect. Now here's what you get to do: you get to vote on which one comes first—you hafta hear all three. Okay? Kirk gets to pick the winner." He didn't give them time to think: "All those in favor of the Teen Bop one first, raise your hand!"

Kirk stepped next to him and took the mike while he and Julian assessed the raised arms. "Okay, all those who want the one for big kids and teachers first?"

As expected, the Teen Bopper selection won the vote. "Okay. Teen Bopper it is! Will Frankie, Rhonda, Theresa come on over? And from the band, Freddie and Stu." He took the mike stand over by the piano while the other students hurried across the gym to join him and Julian. The trumpet and drum duo stepped over behind the mike, and Kirk gestured to Kasey to sit at the piano. The setup was fast and efficient, so well rehearsed and planned it created interest and raised expectations; in less than two minutes, the performers were in position. The students were wide eyed, on the edge of their bleacher seats.

605

With a formidable downbeat, Kasey began a special version of Elvis Presley's **You ain't nothin' but a hound dog**. It had been carefully tweaked to feature the piano instead of a guitar. Kirk did more than a passable job of singing the lyrics. Immediately, Frankie and Rhonda, Julian and Theresa broke into dance—Frankie and Rhonda did their very elaborate bop routine complete with overhead tosses, while Julian did his standard two step with Theresa—a reprise of their three song turn at The Sadie Hawkins Day dance. He enjoyed dancing, and it showed—his movement was lyrical, poetic, and mildly suggestive; his fluffy, light golden hair and dark eyelashes made him look like a prince—his well-shaped body, though clothed, was teasingly evident. Theresa was a good dancer and a second turn with Julian placed her at the top of the social ladder. Fortunately, her boyfriend Teddy was okay with it. Now all the girls the school had seen him dance, and most wanted an opportunity, somehow, themselves. For many, it upstaged Kasey's piano and Kirk's gyrations at the microphone. The rehearsal had lent Julian confidence and enabled him to more than live up to the mythical reputation that had followed his crowning at the Sadie Hawkins dance. The same follow spot was in use, but it was aimed at Kasey and Kirk. With Frankie and Rhonda and their flamboyant and gymnastic prowess, the triple action areas made it look as if American Bandstand had come to town.

Everyone was wowed of course, including the adults. Geraldine was ecstatic. Swann could hardly wait to see what his crew had captured on film. At song's end, the dancing pairs bowed to each other and to the screaming and standing crowd in the bleachers. Julian stood still, waiting for Kirk to bring the mike over. Frankie went to stand by the drummer while the girls obviously thrilled and proud to have been selected, returned to the bleachers.

Randall, who had been photographing everything, re-appeared, having unobtrusively traded his camera for the clarinet tucked behind the platform along with Frankie's cornet. The rehearsal yesterday enabled them to guess quite accurately that the crowd would take that long to quiet down. Kirk handed Julian the mike.

"Okay, everybody, now you get to sit still for a minute or two. Wait 'til you hear this!" He and Kirk retreated to the platform and sat on the edge.

606

The audience grew absolutely silent—Kasey appeared remarkably elegant and refined seated at the piano; anyone seeing him had to pause and take note. The follow spot narrowed, enabling the audience to focus on him; the reduced area intensified the light appreciably: he looked like a concert pianist. When he began the Rachmaninoff Rhapsody on a Theme of Paganini, jaws dropped open. Sound filled the room; the full meaning of the name Grand Piano became clear in an instant. He knew the work well, and had modified it slightly to allow some of the orchestral material to be carried nicely by the clarinet, trumpet and cornet combination. With mutes, they did a passable job replacing violins. They supported rather than competed; several had heard the theme before—it had been used in a recent movie. Lasting almost six minutes, everyone wanted to hear more—but they applauded respectfully. Someone stood and soon everyone followed. Though the score was on the rack above the keyboard, he had not looked at it. He had it memorized; that too was noticed.

Kasey insisted that Randall and Frankie join him to take a bow. The applause grew and with the support of those on the platform, everyone stood.

Julian had waited patiently during the performance, but was in considerable discomfort—he used the applause break to take off the sweater. After dancing with Theresa, he was overheated. Fortunately, Kirk ran into this problem often, and gave him a hand—soon the arms were tied below his neck like a scarf, the rest draped down his back like a cape. He rolled both sleeves half way up the forearms, and with a few shakes, his hair was back where it felt best—just as the trio took their fifth bow.

He stepped forward with mike in hand and waited for the audience to sit. He paused and opened his arms wide: "See what I mean?" He waited for the laugh and applause to quiet down. The rolled up sleeves doubled his sex appeal.

"Now for the surprise!" he handed the mike to Kirk and with a hop, skipped over to the piano and sat on the right half of the bench. He gestured to Kasey and pointed to the left side.

Obvious to all, Kasey was taken by surprise. He broke into a big grin and sat; he nodded to Julian to begin. They played a perfect stanza of Chopsticks.

The audience broke into laughter and applause.

Kasey and Julian stood when they finished, shook hands, and bowed to the audience. Julian gestured to Kirk to take over. The applause and laughter had to be given a few minutes; Julian and Kasey were obviously pleased with themselves and each other. Kirk had a good sense of when to wrap things up.

"An announcement or two before we go back to class..." he paused briefly. "Can everyone hear me?" he asked rhetorically, and waited. The quiet returned. "Two announcements. First lunchers, you will get your chance soon: Julian will have First Lunch the last nine weeks. So if you want to get in a Julian portrait, you have time to get ready." A mixed reaction: the second lunch people were not pleased.

"Second thing: be sure to grab a copy of the special issue of The Cardinal—it has more coverage of the last game and all about Kasey." He waved one in the air. "It has a coupon for Sparky's too. Cheers to the Cardinal staff for getting this ready over the vacation!" He checked with Middleton to verify that he was to dismiss and send everyone back to class.

"Okay, everyone: First Period begins in ten minutes!" He cued the band director, and they struck up a reprise of the school fight song. The student body rose and began the exodus back to class.

Kirk, Julian and Kasey went to the platform to shake a few hands and get a bit of positive feedback.

"Hang on a sec, Kasey," Julian stepped over to say hello to Mr. Swann. He was surprised to see Geraldine sitting by him, smiling proudly. At once, he realized why: Mark was sitting next to his mom. Before talking to Mr. Swann, he grinned wide and bounced on his toes; he flopped the arms to show off the Christmas sweater she had given him. "Got too warm," he shrugged. Without hesitation, he accepted her proud hug.

"The sweater looks perfect that way... we were so **proud** of you out there!" Most of all, she felt vindicated: seeing all those girls screaming in delight when he was introduced had made her day.

"Thanks, Aunt Geraldine, he hugged. Her praise was unexpected and made him feel very good. He was grateful; he could tell she had bought a new outfit for this—he had not seen this one, and he had seen most of her outfits at one time or another. He turned to Mr. Swann—

"Hi... Um... I didn't know if I was s'posed to mention you or not." He was worried, a little. He didn't want to seem ungrateful.

Swann was very pleased. "You did that perfectly, Julian. It's best that my name not be used. I'm glad you didn't, actually. Thank you for that, and thank you for the wonderful way you introduced Kasey." He took the liberty to hold him by the shoulders. "Kasey will do well here; after being presented by you and your friends, he is already on first base. Well done." With a wink he added, "Don't forget your promise to make some room for me on your busy schedule. I'll be getting in touch about that one of these days—soon, I hope." Thanks to Mason, he knew the names of the two boys who were responsible for this. They too would be hearing from him.

"Ooo, yeah. I'd like that." Mr. Swann knew lots about art. "Well, gotta get to class. Thanks," he smiled and gave a short bow to the other people there—he didn't know who they were exactly, but he figured they must be important. He went to the other side of the platform to get a hug from his mom—and a handshake from Mark.

Francine, entirely pleased and amazed by her boy, was able to remain composed but only just. His hug was what she needed, and it was just as loving and energy filled as ever—but he was a bigger boy now, so it was a surprise as well. It would take a while to recover from it, just like seeing him hold the entire audience listening raptly to his simple homespun words would. Fortunately, she'd had time to dry the tears that had erupted after he had finished speaking. His appearance and ability to speak to a huge audience so well was so unexpected, she had trouble believing her eyes. "You were wonderful, Julian." She felt inadequate suddenly, but she knew that he wasn't looking for praise or profound statements. The look into his eyes reported, as usual, that he knew how she felt, and that was all he needed and all he wanted. She blinked happily, releasing him to thank Mark, his idol.

Mark held him by both outstretched arms, enormously proud and pleased. "You did that very well, Julian. I'm very proud of you." He had to resist the urge to hug him close. "We all are." He looked him in the eyes, quite amazed.

Julian locked eyes with him briefly: his camera eyes. Mark's smile was genuine and from the heart: no one more important could have uttered those words. They were almost as good as that special squeeze on his shoulder that he really hoped was on the way. What Julian didn't know was that his camera eye had developed a new capability—it could send as well record images: this time when the squeeze was applied, the signal was carried back to its sender—far more subtle, but with the same salutary effect, reaching particularly well into the subconscious realm.

After a hug from his parents, Kasey remained a discreet distance for Julian to finish touching base; he paid close attention. It reinforced everything he felt about Julian and the decision to move here. As luck would have it, a student passing out copies of the school paper approached just then; he asked for one—the student gave him several and moved on. When Julian turned, he handed him a copy, and passed the extras to Mark. "You may want to get an extra copy or two of this." It had a picture of the drawing as well as an article about his lunch hour activity.

"Oh, yeah... thanks," he was about to lead the way off the platform, but caught himself just in time and stepped over to Kasey's parents. He shook hands with his dad first. He didn't know what to say, but thought it was important. He looked him in the eye with confidence, as if to say that Kasey was in good hands. Julian's smile was magical, as always. He turned to Kasey's mom: "Say hi to Zeyla and give her my hug!" He leaned forward, as if Candace was his own mother.

Candace was unaccustomed to hugging, but this was so natural and effortless, it was over before she knew it had happened. She would treasure the moment for a very long time; it was reassuring and

610

genuine—she now knew how her boy felt: special. She and his father watched as he tugged at their son's belt and led him off to class.

"We have a long walk, y'know. First period class is up on the third floor at the other end of the building. My books are already there. I can share things today, if that's okay."

"Good. I don't have a thing. I assume we can deal with that tomorrow."

"Yep. Good idea." He hopped merrily: "you're gonna like Miss St. Johns."

Soon they were swallowed up in the throng. Because Kasey's head was a foot or more above everyone, the eager ones elbowed their way close to say Hi and be able to say they had talked to one or the other of them. Both were so unusual, everyone wanted a close look. The red blazer and maroon sweater stood out. At the foot of the stairwell, a particularly eager girl pleaded for their autographs. Several of her friends were ready to be next.

They were going to be just a little tardy.

34.1 *the thing is,*

as Julian would say, this book is too long already; it went over the conventional limit a long way back. You deserve a break. So the Muse is allowing the telling of Julian's saga to pause at this point.

The new semester is poised to begin: this is a handy place for an intermission. The three chapter "surprise party" at Margo's house will have to wait, along with a lot of other fun and frolic. Valentine's Day, Spring Vacation, buying cars, and Health class… the list of possibilities is varied and tantalizing. Both Julian and Kasey are celebrities now—a status that has a dynamic all its own, one that neither one is prepared for. And what about Frederick Swann?

The author hopes it won't take as long to get the next volume ready—hopefully it will finish the sophomore year. If the demands of the outside world will recede for a while that is, pandemic and politics included—and if the Muse allows.

Supplementary Materials

A word about the style

Appendix: Candace Wood

Glossary

Music

Index of names and Places

A word about the author

A word about the Julian books

Reviews

a word from Eldot about the style...

While writing *Julian's Private Scrapbook*, I became annoyed by the cumbersome conventions employed by standard fiction. Experimentation followed, and a quest of sorts evolved: access the intimacy of the first person point of view within a third person point of view perspective. I tinkered until I found an approach that worked. It required mixing verb tenses in a new way and abandoning conventional rules of punctuation and paragraphing.

By "worked," I mean it freed the reader from the burden of having to translate what they read as they were reading. For example, the standard by-the-rules approach would read:

> The Sun was up already. If he were seen, it would mean failure. He ran as fast as he could, but it was too late. They'd seen him coming and shoved off. They were well downstream already.

This places present action in the past tense; it is ungainly and archaic—and worse, it keeps the reader at a distance rather than inside the character.

What if I do this:

> *the Sun is up already. if I'm seen, I'm out of luck...* He ran as fast as he could, but he was too late. *rats! they saw me coming.* They had shoved off and were well downstream.

Here the reader jumps in and out of the character's point of view with ease, and between present and past. It's unusual and unexpected at first, but it achieves something new. It lends a first person intimacy and involvement to material that is essentially passive when in the third person. It helps remove the dulling effect of using the narrative past tense "was" to a vivid alive "is," and it does so without the weight and clutter of grammatical helpers. It requires reserving the *italic* typeface for first person point of view, and **boldface** for stress and emphasis. Not capitalizing the letter at the beginning of a sentence alerts the reader that they are "inside" the character.

This novel continues Julian's story, so it employs the same stylistic device. The print versions are able to employ several fonts to refine the narrative even further. [see the symbol key following the Table of Contents.] This technique is utilized in varying degrees. In many places it is not used at all, in others it is extensive. The goal always is to get the reader into the character's perception to the maximum extent—unwashed grammar and all—while retaining the ability to see things from the outside.

So when you run across this phenomenon, that is what's going on—it's not a typo. I hope it makes the experience of following Julian more fun; a few of my old English teachers might be appalled, but others would grin.

Candace Wood and the Queen of Sheba

Editorial note: This book should not be cited as a source for historical information; it is not a scholarly treatise, but a work of fiction. The author has done some selective cutting and pasting from various sources, including the Internet. The goal has been to assemble a plausible basis for what the story relies on for its setting and its characters. This has been done to lend verisimilitude and plausibility to various characters' backstories. Nothing is being offered as a report of historical fact. Since this is fiction, the conventions of citing authorities and permissions have not been followed. It is supplemental, not required to follow or understand the story.

The Queen of Sheba (romanized: Al-Malikah Balqīs) is mentioned in the *Bible*, the *Quran* and the Ethiopian *Kabra Nagast.* In the original story, she brings a caravan of valuable gifts for the Israelite King Solomon. This tale has undergone extensive Jewish, Islamic, and Ethiopian elaborations, and has long been one of the most widespread and fertile legends in the Orient.

Genetic research suggests Ethiopians mixed with Egyptian, Israeli and Syrian populations about 3,000 years ago. This is the time the queen, mentioned in great religious works, is said to have ruled the kingdom of Sheba. According to fossil evidence, human history goes back longer in Ethiopia than anywhere else in the world. But little has been known until now about the human genetics of Ethiopians.

The research, published in The American Journal of Human Genetics, also sheds light on human migration out of Africa 60,000 years ago.

Sheba was a rich kingdom that prospered through trade with Jerusalem and the Roman Empire, and spanned modern day Ethiopia and Yemen. Some texts record that she had a son with King Solomon.

Christian

Christian scriptures mention a queen of the South who came from the uttermost parts of the earth to hear the wisdom of Solomon. She was the Queen of Sheba, who is assumed to have been Ethiopian.

The bride of the Canticles is assumed to have been Black due to a passage in Song of Songs 1:5, which translates as "I am very dark, but comely", while the New Revised Standard Version reads, "I am black and beautiful."

The story of Solomon and the queen was popular among Copts, as shown by fragments of a Coptic legend preserved in a Berlin papyrus. The queen, having been subdued by deceit, gives Solomon a pillar on which all earthly science is inscribed. Solomon sends one of his demons to fetch the pillar from Ethiopia, whence it instantly arrives. In a Coptic poem, queen Yesaba of Cush asks riddles of Solomon.

Ethiopian

A 17th-century painting of the Queen of Sheba from a church in Lalibela, Ethiopia is now in the National Museum of Ethiopia in Addis Ababa.

The fullest and most significant version of the legend appears in the *Kebra Nagast* (Glory of the Kings), the Ethiopian national saga. Here Menelik I is the child of Solomon and Makeda (the Ethiopic name for the queen of Sheba) from whom the Ethiopian dynasty claims descent to the present day.

In the Gospels of Matthew (12:42) and Luke (11:31), the "queen of the South" is claimed to be the queen of Ethiopia. In those times, King

Solomon sought merchants from all over the world, in order to buy materials for the building of the Temple. Among them was Tamrin, great merchant of Queen Makeda of Ethiopia. Having returned to Ethiopia, Tamrin told the queen of the wonderful things he had seen in Jerusalem, and of Solomon's wisdom and generosity, whereupon she decided to visit Solomon. She was warmly welcomed, given a palace for dwelling, and received great gifts every day.

Solomon and Makeda spoke with great wisdom, and instructed by him, she converted to Judaism. Before she left, there was a great feast in the king's palace. Makeda stayed in the palace overnight, after Solomon had sworn that he would not do her any harm, while she swore in return that she would not steal from him. As the meals had been spicy, Makeda awoke thirsty at night, and went to drink some water, when Solomon appeared, reminding her of her oath. She answered: "Ignore your oath, just let me drink water." That same night, Solomon had a dream about the sun rising over Israel, but being mistreated and despised by the Jews, the sun moved to shine over Ethiopia and Rome (i.e. the Byzantine empire). Solomon gave Makeda a ring as a token of faith, and then she left. On her way home, she gave birth to a son, whom she named Baina-lehkem (i.e. bin al-ḥakīm, "Son of the Wise Man", later called Menilek). After the boy had grown up in Ethiopia, he went to Jerusalem carrying the ring, and was received with great honors. The king and the people tried in vain to persuade him to stay. Solomon gathered his nobles and announced that he would send his first-born son to Ethiopia together with their first-borns. He added that he was expecting a third son, who would marry the king of Rome's daughter and reign over Rome, so that the entire world would be ruled by David's descendants.

Then Baina-lehkem was anointed king by Zadok the high priest, and he took the name David. The first-born nobles who followed him are named, and even today some Ethiopian families claim their ancestry from them. Prior to leaving, the priests' sons had stolen the Ark of the Covenant, after their leader Azaryas had offered a sacrifice as

620

commanded by one God's angel. With much wailing, the procession left Jerusalem on a wind cart lead and carried by the archangel Michael. Having arrived at the Red Sea, Azaryas revealed to the people that the Ark is with them. David prayed to the Ark and the people rejoiced, singing, dancing, blowing horns and flutes, and beating drums. The Ark showed its miraculous powers during the crossing of the stormy Sea, and all arrived unscathed. When Solomon learned that the Ark had been stolen, he sent a horseman after the thieves, and even gave chase himself, but neither could catch them. Solomon returned to Jerusalem, and gave orders to the priests to remain silent about the theft and to place a copy of the Ark in the Temple, so foreign nations could not say that Israel had lost its fame.

According to some sources, Queen Makeda was part of the dynasty founded by Za Besi Angabo in 1370 B.C., with her grandfather and father being the last male rulers of the royal line. The family's intended choice to rule Aksum was Makeda's brother, Prince Nourad, but his early death led to her succession to the throne. She apparently ruled the Ethiopian kingdom for more than 50 years.

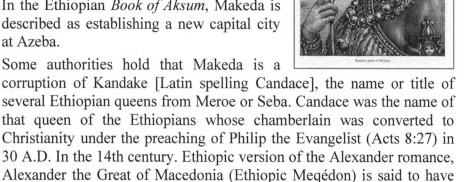

Candace, queen of Ethiopia.

In the Ethiopian *Book of Aksum*, Makeda is described as establishing a new capital city at Azeba.

Some authorities hold that Makeda is a corruption of Kandake [Latin spelling Candace], the name or title of several Ethiopian queens from Meroe or Seba. Candace was the name of that queen of the Ethiopians whose chamberlain was converted to Christianity under the preaching of Philip the Evangelist (Acts 8:27) in 30 A.D. In the 14th century. Ethiopic version of the Alexander romance, Alexander the Great of Macedonia (Ethiopic Meqédon) is said to have met a queen Kandake of Nubia.

Historians believe that the Solomonic dynasty actually began in 1270 with the emperor Yekuno Amlak, who, with the support of the Ethiopian Church, overthrew the Zagwe Dynasty, which had ruled Ethiopia since sometime during the 10th century. The link to King Solomon provided a strong foundation for Ethiopian national unity. "Ethiopians see their country as God's chosen country, the final resting place that he chose for

621

the Ark – and Sheba and her son were the means by which it came there." Despite the fact that the dynasty officially ended in 1769 with Emperor Iyoas, Ethiopian rulers continued to trace their connection to it, right up to the last 20th-century emperor, Haile Selassie.

According to one tradition, the Ethiopian Jews (Beta Israel, "Falashas") also trace their ancestry to Menelik I, son of King Solomon and the Queen of Sheba. An opinion that appears more historical is that the Falashas descend from those Jews who settled in Egypt after the first exile, and who, upon the fall of the Persian domination (539–333 B.C.) on the borders of the Nile, penetrated into the Sudan, whence they went into the western parts of Abyssinia.

Menelik II

According to the medieval African book of the *Kebra Nagast*, Ibn Al-Hakim, "Son of the Wise." Menelik was conceived when his father Solomon tricked his visiting mother, the Queen of Sheba, into sleeping with him. His mother raised him as a Jew in Ethiopia and he only traveled to Jerusalem to meet his father for the first time when he was in his twenties. While his father begged Menelik to stay and rule over Israel, Menelik told him that he wanted to return to Ethiopia. So, Solomon sent many Israelites with him, to aid him in ruling according to biblical standards, and they, aggrieved at being exiled forever, plotted to and then stole the Ark of the Covenant, taking it to Ethiopia. God allowed this theft because he wished to transfer the power of the Israelites to his new chosen people of God, the Ethiopians. Menelik then became king of Ethiopia, upon the death of his mother.

According to legend, Menelik I founded the Solomonic dynasty of Ethiopia that ruled Ethiopia with few interruptions for close to three thousand years. This ended 225 generations later, with the deposition of Emperor Haile Selassie in 1974. However, historical records show that the Solomonic dynasty began in 1262, when Yekuno Amlak, who claimed descent from the Kings of Aksum and Solomon and Sheba, overthrew the last ruler of the Zagwe dynasty, dismissing them as not of

Haile Selassie,
son of Menelik II

"the house of Israel" (i.e., of Solomon). To date, there is no evidence that the people of highland Ethiopia were Jews before the fourth century.

This is all somewhat speculative, connecting facts and accounts that may be corrupted or conjectured—or 'educated guesses.' The royal Ethiopian refugee party that found sanctuary in England was large and organized in haste; it included a mix of family and servants and their families and retainers. Candace Wood was never certain who her father was; her mother was one of the personal family servants. All the children were reared together, regardless of their parentage. It is likely that no one stepped forward. As matter of family honor, she was considered a part of the family, and the opportunity to marry an American solved a problem—she was granted a full dowry, and took a new name. She had been given her royal name at birth, and that stood.

The blue eyes are probably not a part of the royal bloodline. Several sub groups in East Africa and the Middle East have blue eyes. All stem from a genetic flaw or aberration, as do all blue eyes; it gets passed on. Kassa and Zeyla inherited them from Candace, who inherited them from a grandparent in Ethiopia. The gallery below shows several examples. Kassa actually bore a resemblance to one of the Selassie sons, and to the unnamed Black with the goatee and horn rim glasses.

624

Glossary for Julian's Sophomore Year, Part 2

This section is provided for readers who are not familiar with the United States in the 1960s, and who have not read The Julian's Private Scrapbook series. Rather than bog down the novel with explanations, the text assumes the reader knows what is being referred to. For those who don't, this should help. Many of these entries are still contemporary.

64 dollar question: [1] the essential or ultimate question. One of the most popular radio quiz shows during the 1940s was *Take It or Leave It* in which contestants strived to answer question after question until they reached the top prize of sixty-four silver dollars. The questions increased in difficulty, and at any point contestants could choose to stop and keep the amount of money they had won to that point. The phrase "64 dollar question" became a catchword and eventually became the program's name. Soon, people applied the phrase to any very important question or matter.

Even more popular was the 1950s television spinoff, *The $64,000 Question.*

Still in use, the silver dollar coin was in wide circulation until the 1960s. Today, aside from casino and slot machines, most are for special occasions and collectors.

1948 Dodge Custom: [4, 5, 7, 8, 10, 19, 23, 33] a full-size car produced by Dodge from 1946 to early 1949. The Custom model featured special interior trim, seats, dual electric windshield wipers and chrome exterior beading around the windows. It was offered in 5 models. All models

were powered by a 230 hp inline six cylinder engine. A three-speed manual transmission was standard while a "Fluid Drive" option provided no metal-to-metal contact between the power source and drive.

Dodge shared market with Pontiac Silverstreak, Oldsmobile 66,

Studebaker Champion, Hudson Commodore and Nash Ambassador. Andy's car had been the family car until his father replaced it with a '58 DeSoto. He kept the Dodge as a second car, presuming Andy would inherit it when he was old enough to drive. It had oxidized badly and had several scratches and minor dents—it looked its age.

'57 Chevy: [20] Frankie's car is an auto icon. Introduced in September 1956 for the 1957 model year, it was available in three series models: the upscale Bel Air, the mid-range Two-Ten, and the One-Fifty. A two-door station wagon, the Nomad,  was produced as a Bel Air model. An upscale trim option called the Delray was available for Two-Ten 2-door sedans. It is a popular and sought after classic car. These vehicles are often restored to their original condition and sometimes modified. The car's image has been frequently used in toys, graphics, music, movies, and television.

The Alamo: [10] By 1945 John Wayne had decided to make a movie about the 1836 Battle of the Alamo. He hired James Edward Grant as scriptwriter, and the two began researching the battle and preparing a draft script. Wayne and producer Robert Fellows formed their own production company, Batjac. As Wayne developed his vision of what a

movie about the Alamo should be, he concluded he did not want to risk seeing that vision changed; he would produce and direct the movie himself. In 1956, he signed with United Artists; UA would contribute $2.5 million to the movie's development and serve as distributor. In exchange, Batjac was to contribute an additional $1.5–2.5 million, and Wayne would star in the movie. Wayne secured the remainder of the financing from wealthy Texans who insisted the movie be shot in Texas.

The movie set, later known as Alamo Village, was constructed near Brackettville, Texas, on the ranch of James T. Shahan. Chatto Rodriquez, the general contractor of the set, built 14 miles of tarred roads for access to the set from Brackettville. His men sank six wells to provide 12,000 gallons of water each day, and laid miles of sewage and water lines. They also built 5,000 horse corrals.

Historians Randy Roberts and James Olson describe it as "the most authentic set in the history of the movies." Over a million and a quarter adobe bricks were formed by hand to create the walls of the former Alamo Mission. The set was an extensive three quarter-scale replica of the mission, and has since been used in 100 other westerns, including other depictions of the battle. It took more than two years to construct.

The film does little to explain the causes of the Texas Revolution or why the battle took place. Alamo historian Timothy Todish said "there is not

a single scene in The Alamo which corresponds to a historically verifiable incident." Historians James Frank Dobie and Lon Tinkle demanded their names be removed as historical advisors.

Alexander: [5, 7, 9, 28] king of Macedon, an ancient Greek kingdom. Born in Pella in 356 BC, he was raised like other noble Macedonian youths, learning to read, play the lyre, ride, fight, and hunt. Tutored by Aristotle until age 16, he became king at 20 after his father Philip II was assassinated in 336 BC. After finishing his father's military campaign, he pressed on, consolidating the entire Greek peninsula. Most of his ruling years were spent on a military campaign through Asia and northeast Africa; by the age of thirty he had created one of the largest empires of the ancient world, stretching from Greece to northwestern India and south to Egypt. Undefeated in battle, he is one of history's most successful military commanders. He founded twenty cities, including Alexandria, Egypt. Among the most influential people in history, he died in 323 BC at the age of 32 in Babylon, the city that he planned to establish as his capital. His death was caused by poisoned wine—who was responsible remains unclear; political intrigue was likely.

Aristotle taught Alexander and his companions medicine, philosophy, morals, religion, logic, and art. He had a passion for Homer's Iliad; he identified with Achilles. Aristotle gave him the annotated copy he carried on his military campaigns.

Alexander and Hephaistion's lifelong relationship began in Aristoltle's

academy. They were often compared to Achilles and Patroklos in the Trojan War; they were idolized as a couple as well as heroes. Plutarch reported that Alexander asked his Persian eunuch Bagoas to fill in whenever Hephaistion was away on a diplomatic mission or military campaign.

Kasey's response to seeing Julian the first time was due to an intense study of Alexander then underway in his history class at Belmont. Professor Marchbank's lectures and the assigned readings had formed strong vivid images in his mind—he was familiar with many of the ancient sculptures; Lysippos, retained by Alexander, did several busts and full figure statues [*page 627*] to serve as his symbolic presence in conquered countries. Others were done by sculptors who had actually seen him—his well documented physical beauty was lifelong. Though he could not have seen the 2004 Oliver Stone film, Kasey had read the Mary Renault trilogy on which it was largely based. The photo at the right is a close approximation of what he saw

walking toward him; Mark did not have a beard, and aside from her hair, Francine did not resemble Angelina Jolie—nonetheless, in his mind's eye, Kasey saw Alexander and his parents, Olympias and Philip being escorted directly to his table.

 **Alfred Pennyworth:** [7] full name Alfred Thaddeus Crane Pennyworth, also known by his other alias Christopher Miller, a fictional character appearing in DC Comics, most commonly in association with the superhero Batman. Alfred serves as the loyal butler of Bruce Wayne/Batman. Pennyworth is Bruce Wayne's loyal and tireless butler, housekeeper, legal guardian, best friend, aide-de-camp, and surrogate father figure following the murders of Thomas and Martha Wayne. He serves as Bruce's moral anchor while providing comic relief with his sarcastic and cynical attitude which often adds humor to dialogue with Batman. In Television and film, the character has been portrayed by several noted actors. Alan Napier played the role in the original 1966 TV series. Michael Caine played Alfred in the recent Dark Knight films. In 1962, Batman was still a comic book hero.

Artful Dodger: [Chapter 2] Jack Dawkins, better known as the Artful Dodger, is a character in the Charles Dickens novel Oliver Twist. The Dodger is a pickpocket, so called for his skill and cunning. He is the leader of the gang of child criminals, trained by the elderly Fagin. A century later, the nickname was often applied to anyone able to get away with something without being caught.

Baby moon hubcaps: [4] chromed highly polished solid Stainless Steel baby moons are center caps made to fit standard steel wheels of older Pre-1990 American cars and trucks 11-7/8" (12 inch) were available singly or in sets of four.

Bell 204 and 205: [30] civilian versions of the UH-1 Iroquois single-engine military helicopter of the Huey family of helicopters, used in a wide variety of applications, including crop dusting, cargo lifting and aerial firefighting.

The UH-1 Iroquois (nicknamed "Huey") utility military helicopter is powered by a single turboshaft engine, with two-bladed main and tail rotors. Developed by Bell to meet a 1952 US Army requirement for a medical evacuation and utility helicopter, it first flew in 1956. The first turbine-powered helicopter produced for the United States military, more than 16,000 have been built since 1960.

The Iroquois first saw service during the Vietnam War, with around 7,000 helicopters. The Bell 204 and 205 are versions developed for the civilian market.

Benny Goodman: [3, 14] Benjamin David Goodman (May 30, 1909 – June 13, 1986) an American jazz clarinetist and bandleader known as the "King of Swing."

In the mid-1930s, Goodman led one of the most popular musical groups in the United States. His concert at Carnegie Hall in New York City on January 16, 1938 is described as the single most important jazz or popular music concert in history: jazz's 'coming out' party to the world of 'respectable' music.

Goodman's bands started the careers of many jazz musicians. During an era of racial segregation, he led one of the first integrated jazz groups. He performed nearly to the end of his life, exploring an interest in classical music.

In 1942 he recorded Gershwin's Rhapsody in Blue under Toscanini for V-disc distribution to the troops via Armed Forces Radio. That recording was Kasey's favorite.

Big Plan: [1] When Julian discovered that his goal to win Mark as his life love partner could not be achieved during the two-week summer camp, he regrouped and did some serious planning. He realizes that he has to grow into the position—literally and figuratively. His new goal is to win Mark for his eighteenth birthday. All his dealings with Mark are calculated to achieve that goal. He will not confide that information to anyone.

630

Brown Decision: [1] Brown v. Board of Education of Topeka, 347 U.S. 483 (1954), Supreme Court of the United States Argued December 9, 1952, Re-argued December 8, 1953 Decided May 17, 1954.

The landmark decision of the U.S. Supreme Court in which the Court ruled that American state laws establishing racial segregation in public

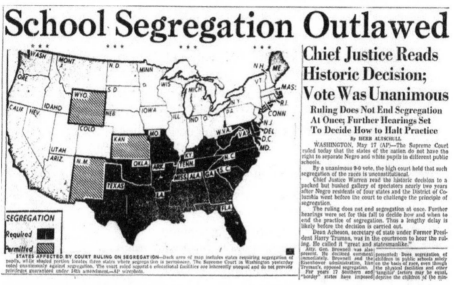

School Segregation Outlawed

Chief Justice Reads Historic Decision; Vote Was Unanimous

Ruling Does Not End Segregation At Once; Further Hearings Set To Decide How to Halt Practice

By HERB ALTSCHULL

WASHINGTON, May 17 (AP)—The Supreme Court ruled today that the states of the nation do not have the right to separate Negro and white pupils in different public schools.

By a unanimous 9-0 vote, the high court held that such segregation of the races is unconstitutional.

Chief Justice Warren read the historic decision to a packed but hushed gallery of spectators nearly two years after Negro residents of four states and the District of Columbia went before the court to challenge the principle of segregation.

The ruling does not end segregation at once. Further hearings were set for this fall to decide how and when to end the practice of segregation. Thus a lengthy delay is likely before the decision is carried out.

Dean Acheson, secretary of state under Former President Harry Truman, was in the courtroom to hear the ruling. He called it "great and statesmanlike."

Atty. Gen. Brownell was also present. He declined comment presently. Brownell and the Eisenhower administration, like Truman's, opposed segregation. For years 17 Southern and "border" states have imposed...

SEGREGATION Required ▇ Permitted ▨

STATES AFFECTED BY COURT RULING ON SEGREGATION—Each area of map includes states requiring segregation of pupils, while shaded portion locates three states where segregation is permissive. The Supreme Court in Washington yesterday voted unanimously against segregation. The court ruled separate educational facilities are inherently unequal and do not provide privileges guaranteed under 14th amendment.—AP wirephoto.

...Does segregation of children in public schools solely on the basis of race, even though the physical facilities and other "tangible" factors may be equal, deprive the children of the min-

schools are unconstitutional, even if the segregated schools are otherwise equal in quality. Handed down on May 17, 1954, the Court's unanimous (9–0) decision stated that "separate educational facilities are inherently unequal," and therefore violate the Equal Protection Clause of the Fourteenth Amendment of the U.S. Constitution. However, the decision's 14 pages did not spell out any sort of method for ending racial segregation in schools, and the Court's second decision in Brown II (349 U.S. 294) added, "with all deliberate speed."

The case originated in Topeka, Kansas, where the public school district had implemented a segregated school system for its elementary schools. In 1951, the district refused to enroll the daughter of local resident Oliver Brown at the school closest to their home, instead requiring her to ride a bus to a segregated black elementary school further away. The Browns and twelve other black Topeka families then filed a class action lawsuit in U.S. federal court against the Topeka Board of Education, alleging that the school district's segregation policy was unconstitutional. A three-judge panel of the U.S. District Court for the District of Kansas

631

rendered a verdict against the Browns based on the Supreme Court's precedent in the 1896 case Plessy v. Ferguson, in which the Court had ruled that racial segregation was not in itself a violation of the Fourteenth Amendment's Equal Protection Clause if the facilities in question were otherwise equal, a doctrine that had come to be known as "separate but equal". The Browns, represented by NAACP chief counsel Thurgood Marshall, appealed to the Supreme Court, which agreed to hear the case.

Many Southern governmental and political leaders embraced a plan known as "Massive Resistance", created by Virginia Senator Harry F. Byrd, in order to frustrate attempts to force them to de-segregate their school systems. Four years later, in the case of Cooper v. Aaron, the Court reaffirmed its ruling in Brown, and explicitly stated that state officials and legislators had no power to nullify its ruling.

Café curtains: short curtain sliding on a horizontal rod so as to cover the lower and sometimes upper portions of a window.

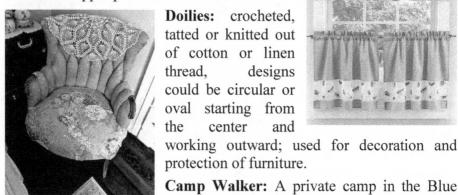

Doilies: crocheted, tatted or knitted out of cotton or linen thread, designs could be circular or oval starting from the center and working outward; used for decoration and protection of furniture.

Camp Walker: A private camp in the Blue Ridge Mountains near the Nantahala National Forest in western North Carolina, formerly Cherokee tribal land. Each troop in the local Council could reserve a campsite for the annual two week summer camp. Trails to the sites radiated out from the central headquarter building. Each camp session averaged between five and eight hundred scouts, or up to seventeen troops. Nearly a hundred miles of internal trails connect the camps and provide training and hiking activity.

South of the HQ areas for large multi-troop assemblies, recreational fields, were set aside with over a mile of lakeshore. When not in use by the scouts, parts of the facility were leased to outside groups. Prior to

632

Affirmative Action in 1970, the camp observed the late nineteenth and early twentieth century custom of nude swimming at segregated sites. Women were not allowed to enter the camp.

Cardinal: Official mascot of Jackson High School from its founding in the 19th century, North Carolina designated the northern cardinal (Cardinalis cardinalis) as official state bird in 1943. One of America's favorite backyard birds, cardinals are distinctive in appearance and song, known for their "cheer cheer cheer," "whit-chew whit-chew" and "purty purty purty" whistles.

Charlie Brown: [20] A "lovable loser," Charlie Brown is  one of the great American archetypes and a popular and widely recognized cartoon character: the principal character of the Peanuts comic strip, syndicated in daily and Sunday newspapers all over the world. Charlie is the only character to have been a part of the strip throughout its 50-year run. He shows both pessimistic and optimistic attitudes: on some days, he is reluctant to go out because his day might just be spoiled, but on others, he hopes for the best and tries as much as he can to accomplish things. Julian identified with him because of his blond hair and signature zig-zag striped T-shirt.

Charles M. Schulz, The character's creator, said he was a caricature of the average person. "Most of us are much more acquainted with losing than winning." Charlie Brown does not always suffer; he experienced some happy moments and victories through the years, and he has sometimes uncharacteristically shown self-assertiveness despite his frequent nervousness. Schulz also said: "I like to have Charlie Brown eventually be the focal point of almost every story."

 **Cheshire Cat:** [1, 7, 9, 14, 17, 21, 28] A character in *Alice in Wonderland*. The animated film version featured a wide closed tooth open lipped smile. Julian adopted the smile as his own and used it frequently.

Chopsticks: [9, 34] was written in 1877 by Euphemia Allen, a 16 year old English schoolgirl, with the title "The Celebrated Chop Waltz." Her intent was that the upper two-note melody be played by the two little

fingers while holding both hands rigidly upright, as if they were cleaver blades chopping on a cutting board.

Chrysler Ghia Crown Imperial [5] The Imperial name had been used since 1926, but was never a separate make, just the top-of-the-line Chrysler. In 1955 the company decided to spin Imperial off as its own division to better compete with its North American rivals, Lincoln and Cadillac. Imperial introduced new or modified body styles every two to three years, all with V8 engines and automatic transmissions, as well as technologies that would filter down to Chrysler Corporation's other models. For 1957 through 1965, long-wheelbase Imperial Crown cars would be finished by Ghia in Italy. Each took a month to build and carried a high price for the time ($18,500 in 1963-64). A total of 132 were manufactured by Ghia from 1957-65. All 1961 models used the 1960 styling front and rear. At about 6,200–6,300 lb curb weight, the 1957-65 Ghia built Imperial Crowns are the heaviest standard production cars sold by an American firm since the 1930s.

Throughout her husband's term as President, Jacqueline Kennedy's personal car was a Ghia built 1961 Imperial Crown with 1960 model year styling. The car figured prominently in her various duties as First Lady. In President John F. Kennedy's funeral procession on November 25, 1963, near the front of the motorcade, carrying Jackie and her children, was her Imperial Crown.

New York governor and heir to the Standard Oil fortune Nelson Rockefeller, later Vice President of the U.S. during the term of President Gerald Ford, also owned a 1960 Imperial Crown. It is one of 17 limousines made by Ghia in that year, and the only one with blind rear quarter treatment.

In the 1974 movie The Godfather Part II, a black Ghia built 1958 Imperial Crown was used by Michael Corleone (played by Al Pacino) while at the family compound near Lake Tahoe, Nevada.

Ethiopa: [7, 32] a country in the northeastern part of Africa, known as the 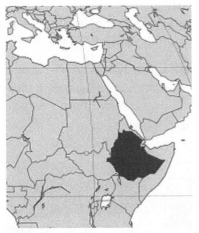 Horn of Africa. Currently, it borders Eritrea to the north, Djibouti to the northeast, the de facto state of Somaliland and Somalia to the east, Kenya to the south, South Sudan to the west and Sudan to the northwest. Ethiopia is the most populous landlocked country in the world and the second-most populous nation on the African continent with a total area of 420,000 sq. miles. Capital and largest city is Addis Ababa, a few miles west of the East African Rift that splits the country into the Nubian and Somali tectonic plates.

[see **Appendix** below.]

Ford Country Squire 9 passenger station wagon: [5, 16] a full-size station wagon built from 1950 to 1991, encompass-sing seven model generations. It was the premium station wagon model in Ford's full-size car range. The Country Squire was initially built as a full "woodie," using real wood.

After the mid-1950s the rear body used fiberglass covered by a vinyl appliqué printed to simulate wood. Fourth generation (1960–1964):

The passenger capacity enabled Mark to transport an entire patrol.

Flaming Arrow: [4, 15, 17, 18, 20, 21, 31, 32, 33] The leadership patrol of Troop Nine, an executive council. Includes the Junior Assistant Scoutmaster, Senior Patrol Leader, Scribe and Bugler. Julian was promoted to the patrol a year early.

Geoff's Poker Club: [25] The boys from Atlanta formed a special club for playing strip poker. It provided a game master that decreed what sexual acts were to be performed and by whom at the end of the game.

Great Scott! [4] The Oxford Dictionary of English labels the expression as "dated" and simply identifies it as an "arbitrary euphemism for Great God!" It was widely used in the 19th century, possibly because Mark Twain used it to poke fun at author Sir Walter Scott. Helgar was a Mark Twain fan.

Gymnasium: [29] The gymnasium (Greek: γυμνάσιον or gumnasion) in Ancient Greece functioned as a training facility for competitors in public

games. It was also a place for socializing and engaging in intellectual pursuits. The name comes from the Ancient Greek term gymnós meaning "naked".

636

Groucho Marx: [5, 7, 10, 14, 20], 21, 22] of the Marx Brothers hosted *You Bet*

Your Life with announcer and assistant George Fenneman. The quiz show aired on both radio and television. The show debuted on ABC Radio in October 1947, then moved to CBS Radio in September 1949 before making the transition to NBC-TV in October 1950. In 1960, the show was renamed *The Groucho Show* and ran a further year.

Groucho's signature eyebrow raise became a common nonverbal form of facial expression to signify being pleasantly surprised.

Hayden Park: [10, 18, 19, 23, 25, 26, 30] A nature reserve near the high school in Troop 9's town. Hiking trails, campsites, park benches and picnic areas make the five acre park a favorite. (*see map, page 403*)

Joseph Rainey: [1] (June 21, 1832 – August 1, 1887) the first black person to serve in the United States House of Representatives, the second black person (after Hiram Revels) to serve in the United States Congress and the first black presiding officer of the House of Representatives. Born into slavery in South Carolina, he was freed in the 1840s by his father who purchased the freedom of his entire family.

Junior Assistant: Highest position for a scout in the troop.

Junior High School: Grades 7-9. Before the reforms of the 1970s, High School was a three year program, grades 10-12.

Lawrence of Arabia: [20, 21, 28] 1962 British epic historical drama film based on the life of T. E. Lawrence, directed by David Lean. Screenplay by Robert Bolt and Michael Wilson, Peter O'Toole played the title role. The film  depicts Lawrence's experiences in the Ottoman Empire's provinces of Hejaz and Greater Syria during World War I, in particular his attacks on Aqaba and Damascus and his involvement in the Arab National Council. Its themes include Lawrence's emotional struggles with the personal violence inherent in war, his own identity, and his divided allegiance between his native Britain and its army, and his new-found comrades within the Arabian desert tribes. The film also stars Alec Guinness, Jack Hawkins, Anthony Quinn, Omar Sharif, Anthony Quayle, Claude Rains and Arthur Kennedy.

 Nominated for ten Oscars at the 35th Academy Awards in 1963, it won seven, including Best Picture and Best Director. In the years since, it has been recognized as one of the greatest and most influential films in the history of cinema. The dramatic score by Maurice Jarre and the Super Panavision 70 cinematography by Freddie Young are also highly acclaimed. In 1991 the film was deemed "culturally, historically, or aesthetically significant" and selected for preservation in the US Library of Congress National Film Registry.

It is written: *Maktub* is an arabic word which literally means it is written. It means fate or destiny. From mystical point of view, it points to the fact that whatever happens is already known to the One. It signifies that Destiny exists, and that everything is already known to God. Lawrence confronts this belief

more than once in the film, always dramatically, involving life and death, frustrating Julian—it is assumed that the viewer understands the meaning. In this scene he has just said, "Nothing is written..." after rescuing a man in the desert who had been left behind by the expedition, presumably to die because he couldn't keep up.

Leave It to Beaver: [4] a black-and-white television sitcom broadcast between 1957 and 1963 about an inquisitive and often naïve boy, Theodore "Beaver" Cleaver (portrayed by Jerry Mathers), and his adventures at home, school, and around his suburban neighborhood. The show also starred Barbara Billingsley and Hugh Beaumont as Beaver's parents, June and Ward Cleaver, and Tony Dow as Beaver's brother Wally. The show attained an iconic status in the United States, the Cleavers exemplifying the idealized suburban family of the mid-20th century.

Li'l Abner and Daisy Mae: [1, 14, 22] Li'l Abner was a satirical American comic strip featuring a fictional clan of hillbillies in the impoverished mountain village of Dogpatch, Arkansas, the first strip based in the South. The Al Capp strip ran for 43 years. Comic strips typically dealt with northern urban experiences. Julian won the best Li'l Abner contest at the annual Sadie Hawkins Day dance, and his date won Best Daisy Mae.

Lincoln Continental: [4, 25, 26, 27, 28] Eloise Hallstrom's car; Introduced in 1939 as a personal vehicle of Edsel Ford, the coachbuilt Lincoln Zephyr competed with Packard and

Cadillac, featured European "continental" styling elements, including a rear mounted spare tire. Produced for 55 years across nearly eight decades, there are ten generations of the Lincoln Continental. The Continental was the progenitor of an entirely new automotive segment, the personal luxury car. Following World War II, the segment evolved into coupes and convertibles larger than sports cars and grand touring cars with an emphasis on luxury and style over handling.

Living Color: [4] NBC made history with the first live national broadcast in "living color" over a 22-city network hastily constructed by AT&T on New Year's Day, 1954. The Tournament of Roses Parade in Pasadena, was tailor-made to show off RCA's brand new color television technology.

Only a few thousand people actually saw the parade in color that day. For the occasion, RCA built a special run of only 200 color sets designated the Model 5 (for prototype #5) for the NBC affiliates and RCA Victor TV retail distributors.

The first consumer color television receivers hit the market a few weeks later, with 5,000 units rolling off the RCA assembly line in Bloomington, Ind., in March 1954.

Even with these special broadcasts, it would be a long time before most Americans experienced color television in their living rooms. Those indelible images from the Kennedy assassination in November 1963, 10 years after the Rose parade colorcast, were still in black and white. The RCA Model CT-100 had a 12-inch diagonal screen and cost a whopping $1,000 (well over $6,000 by today's standards).

Since only 31 stations in the United States had color capability, there wasn't much to watch. In fact, any color program broadcast in the 1950s was a big event.

The tide began to turn in the early '60s, after about half a million color sets had been sold. Walt Disney's Wonderful World of Color began in 1961. The first color cartoons, the Flintstones and the Jetsons, began in the fall of 1962. However, to baby boomers and their parents, one show would come to define the move to color television. The first episode of Bonanza aired in color on Sept. 12, 1959.

Lockheed JetStar: [15] is a business jet produced from the early 1960s to

the 1970s. The JetStar was the first dedicated business jet to enter service. It was also one of the largest aircraft in the class for many years, seating ten plus two crew. It is distinguishable from other small jets by its four engines, mounted on the rear of the fuselage, and the "slipper"style fuel tanks fixed to the wing.

Miles   Davis: [3]   (1926-1991)   American   jazz trumpeter, bandleader and composer was among the most   influential   and acclaimed figures in the history of jazz and 20th-century   music.   Davis adopted   a   variety   of musical directions in a five-decade   career   in   the forefront of many major stylistic developments in jazz.

641

Loupe: [22] a small magnifying glass used by jewelers, watchmakers and photographers.

Mount Mitchell: [6] highest peak of the Appalachian Mountains and mainland eastern North America, located near Burnsville in Yancey County, North Carolina. In the Black Mountain subrange of the Appalachians, it is about 19 miles northeast of Asheville. It is protected by Mount Mitchell State Park and surrounded by the Pisgah National Forest. Elevation is 6,684 feet (2,037 m) above sea level.

The mountain was named in honor of Dr. Elisha Mitchell, an educator and scientist from Chapel Hill, who died while climbing the mountain in 1857 in his effort to prove it was the highest peak in eastern North America. The grave of Dr. Mitchell lies next to the observation deck.

Mount Mitchell State Park contains extensive spruce-fir forest, an ecosystem that is common in northern climes, but which is only found in a narrow band in the Appalachian Mountains. This natural community is characterized by evergreens, particularly red spruce and Fraser fir. The Park offers numerous hiking trails as well as a museum, restaurant, concession stand and gift shop. A new observation deck, accessible by wheelchair, offers breathtaking panoramic views.

Nantahala National Forest: With over a half million acres, the Nantahala is the largest of the four national forests in the mountains and valleys of southwestern North Carolina. Elevations range from 5,800 feet at Lone Bald in Jackson County to 1,200 feet below Appalachian Lake Dam. A ranger manages Cheoah, Tusquitee,

Wayah, and Highlands districts.

"Nantahala" is Cherokee for "land of the noon day sun," a fitting name for the Nantahala Gorge, where the sun reaches to the valley floor at midday.

Established in 1920, the 1911 Weeks Act provided authority to acquire lands for national forests to protect watersheds, provide timber, and regulate the flow of navigable streams.

The forest offers a wide variety of recreational activities, from off-highway vehicle riding to camping, whitewater rafting, mountain biking, and hiking on over 600 miles of trail. Three long-distance trails cross the forest: Appalachian, Bartram, and Mountain-to-Sea.

Odin: [25, 29] a god in Germanic mythology. Norse mythology associates Odin with wisdom, healing, death, royalty, the gallows, knowledge, war, battle, victory, sorcery, poetry, frenzy, and the runic alphabet, and portrays him as the husband of the goddess Frigg. In wider Germanic mythology and paganism, the god was known in Old English as Wōden, and in Old High German as Wuotan. *Óðinn á yðr alla!!* Loosely translates as 'you're all Odin's'

Odin was a prominent god throughout the recorded history of Europe, from the Roman occupation of regions of Germania from 12 BC through the Viking Age [8th to 11th centuries AD]. In the modern period the rural folklore of Germanic Europe continued to acknowledge Odin. References to him appear in place names throughout regions historically inhabited by the ancient Germanic peoples, and the day of the week Wednesday bears his name in many Germanic languages, including English.

Packard 12 Cabriolet: [5, 7, 14, 15, 16, 17, 22, 23, 25, 31, 32, 33, 34] The Packard Twelve was a series of V12-engined luxury automobiles built by the Packard Motor Car Company in Detroit, Michigan, built from 1933 until 1939 as a successor to the twelve-cylinder Twin Six. In addition to production bodies

and chassis sent for custom coachwork, Packard cataloged a number of styles from the major coachbuilders, among them Dietrich, LeBaron, Rollston and Brunn. One of the distinctive styles of the late 30s, the cabriolet was a seven-passenger semi-enclosed type built either as the All Weather style, with removable roof over the chauffeur compartment, or Touring Cabriolet with a fixed roof and clerestory windows over the windshield. Either could be had as a collapsible cabriolet, in which the rear roof of the passenger compartment retracted, or non-collapsible, with solid rear quarters and landau irons.

Many were actually Dietrich semi-customs: Packard-made bodies with special touches. In October 1935, President Franklin D. Roosevelt gave Joseph Stalin an armored Packard Twelve, the dictator's favorite vehicle for many years.

Pogo: [Chapter 15] the title and central character of a long-running daily

American comic strip, created by cartoonist Walt Kelly (1913–1973) and distributed by the Post-Hall Syndicate. Set in the Okefenokee Swamp of the southeastern United States, the strip often engaged in social and political satire through the adventures of its anthropomorphic funny animal characters. Pogo combined both sophisticated wit and slapstick physical comedy mixing allegory, Irish poetry, literary whimsy, puns and wordplay, lushly detailed artwork and broad burlesque humor.

Push processing: [Chapter 8] a developing technique that increases the effective sensitivity of the film being processed. The film is developed for more time, possibly in combination with a higher temperature. This overdevelops the film, compensating for underexposure in the camera. This allows capturing images under lighting conditions that would ordinarily be too low. This technique alters the visual characteristics of the film: higher contrast, increased grain and lower resolution. **Pull processing** involves overexposure and underdevelopment, effectively decreasing the sensitivity of the processed film by developing the film for a shorter time, possibly at a lower temperature. Pull processing displays the opposite change in visual characteristics. This may be deliberately exploited for artistic effect. Digital photography cannot use these techniques; some of the effects can be imitated by various computer programs such as Photoshop.

Pythagoras of Samos: [1] (c. 570 – c. 495 BC an ancient Ionian Greek philosopher and founder of Pythagoreanism. His political and religious teachings were well known and influenced the 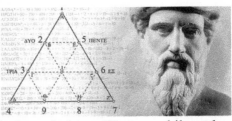 philosophies of Plato, Aristotle, and, through them, Western philosophy. Plato's dialogues, especially his Timaeus, exhibit Pythagorean teachings. Pythagorean ideas on mathematical perfection also impacted ancient Greek art; his philosophy had a major impact on scientists such as Nicolaus Copernicus, Johannes Kepler, and Isaac Newton. Pythagoras was credited with devising the tetractys, the triangular figure of four rows which add up to the perfect number, ten—regarded as a symbol of utmost mystical importance.

Quicksand: [20, 21, 28] In *Lawrence of Arabia*, Lawrence has two young servant boys, Daud and Farraj. Daud falls into quicksand; Lawrence and Farraj try to save him, but fail. In real life, Daud died of hypothermia. Quicksand is a trope of adventure fiction, particularly in film, where it is typically and unrealistically depicted with a suction effect that causes

people or animals that walk into it to sink and risk drowning. This gimmick had its heyday in the 1960s, when almost 3% of all films showed characters sinking in clay, mud, or sand.

Rip Kirby: [15] was a popular comic strip featuring the adventures of the lead character, a private detective created by Alex Raymond in 1946. Displaying the talents of more than a dozen writers and illustrators, the strip had a long run, spanning five decades. After World War II, Raymond did not return to work on any of his previous successful comic strips (Flash Gordon, Jungle Jim, Secret Agent X-9) but  began the new strip in which ex-Marine Rip Kirby returns from WWII and goes to work as a private detective, sometimes accompanied by his girlfriend, fashion model Judith Lynne "Honey" Dorian. The artistic merits were of special interest to Julian.

Rock Climbing terms [25, 26, 27, 29]

Carabiner—Metal loop (usually aluminum) with a spring-loaded gate on one side used for connecting various parts of a climbing system. May be oval, pear- or D-shaped.

Chimney—Wide, vertical crack large enough for a climber to fit inside and climb. A move done inside the chimney by using opposing force with the feet and the body.

Figure 8 knot or stopper—either a manual knot or metal fixture for roping to a climbing partner.

 **Piton**—a metal spike (usually steel) driven into a crack or seam in the climbing surface with a climbing hammer, which acts as an anchor to either protect the climber against the consequences of a fall or to assist progress in aid climbing. Pitons are equipped with an eye hole or a ring to which a carabiner is attached; the carabiner can then be directly or indirectly attached to a climbing rope.

Rappel—To descend a cliff or other height by lowering oneself on a fixed rope, with feet against the wall. Friction is placed on the rope, usually with a belay device, to keep the descent slow and controlled.

646

Rover: [4, 18, 25, 26, 27, 29] Helgar Hallstrom's recreational vehicle. Started in

1947 by Maurice Wilks, it was simply called Land Rover. The design was influenced by the American Willy's Jeep, developed during World War II. The prototype was built on a Jeep chassis and axles. The early color was dictated by military surplus supplies of aircraft cockpit paint, so early vehicles only came in various shades of light green. All models until recently feature sturdy box section ladder-frame chassis. It has become the most reliable and hardy off road vehicle.

Schwinn: [4] The Schwinn Bicycle Company was founded by German-born mechanical engineer Ignaz Schwinn (1860–1945) in Chicago in 1895. The dominant manufacturer of American bicycles through most of the 20th century. Prior to the interest in racing bikes in the 1960s, wide wheel Schwinn's were the most popular. Like the auto industry, they upgraded and

introduced new models every year. Randall's father had bought a new "family fleet" shortly after they settled into their new home.

Sherlock Holmes: [4] *Deerstalker Cap:* A deerstalker is a type of cap

that is typically worn in rural areas, often for hunting, especially deer stalking. Because of the cap's popular association with Sherlock Holmes, it has become stereotypical headgear for a detective, especially in comical drawings or cartoons along with farcical plays and film. *Ulster Coat:* a Victorian working daytime overcoat, with a cape and sleeves. It is often seen in period productions of Victorian novels, such as those of Charles Dickens and Sir Arthur Conan Doyle's Sherlock Holmes stories.

Siren's song: [7] the song of the siren, dangerous creatures in Greek mythology that lured sailors with their hypnotic music and voices to shipwreck on a rocky island.

Strad: [1] Stradivari men's shirts, the classic postwar gab shirt, were a gabardine sport shirt, usually with long sleeves, slightly fitted sides, straight hem,

pearl button front and cuffs, two patch chest pockets with tapered open tops, and long pointed collar. A fashion item, some years they offered a special limited edition color or fabric.

The Twilight Zone: [5] an American television series created by Rod Serling. Episodes are in various genres, including fantasy, science

fiction, suspense, horror, and psychological thriller, often concluding with a macabre or unexpected twist, and usually with a moral. A popular and critical success, the series, shot entirely in black and white, ran on CBS for five seasons 1959 to 1964.

USGS Topog map: [26] general-use maps at medium scales that present elevation (contour lines), hydrography, geographic place names, and a

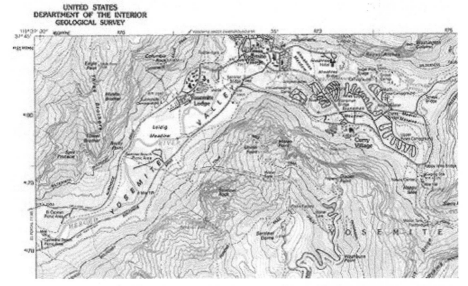

variety of cultural features. Current generation topographic maps are created from digital GIS databases, and are branded "US Topo." Historic maps originally published as paper documents in the period 1884-2006 are available as scanned images.

Wizard of Oz witch: [1] Miss Gulch (Margaret Hamilton) is the real life counterpart to The Wicked Witch of the West. She does not return for Toto at the end of this film, being the tornado's victim; instead, she was transformed, and became The Wicked Witch of the East.

Song and music Credits

The music referenced in the text are described briefly in alphabetical order.

Beach Boys Surfin' Safari: [22] debut album by American rock band the Beach Boys, released on October 1, 1962 on Capitol Records. The official production credit went to Nick Venet, though it was Brian Wilson with his father Murry who contributed substantially to the album's production; Brian also wrote or co-wrote nine of its 12 tracks.[2] The album peaked at No. 32 in its 37-week run on the US charts.

The album was preceded by two singles: "Surfin'" and "Surfin' Safari", which charted at Nos. 75 and 14, respectively. The success of "Surfin' Safari" helped secure a full album for the group while an additional single, "Ten Little Indians", was issued, charting at No. 49.

Beethoven Für Elise: [15] Bagatelle No. 25 in A minor for solo piano, is one of Ludwig van Beethoven's most popular compositions, discovered 40 years after his death. Composed: April 27, 1810. Published: 1867.

Danny Boy: [27] is a ballad written by English songwriter Frederic Weatherly in 1913, and set to the traditional Irish melody, *Londonderry Air*.

Harry James: [3] an American musician best known as a trumpet-playing band leader who led a big band from 1939 to 1946. He broke up his band for a short period in 1947 but reorganized and was active again from then until his death in 1983. He was especially known for his technical proficiency as well as his tone, and was influential on new trumpet players from the late 1930s into the 1940s. He was also an actor in a number of films that usually featured his band.

Heigh-Ho: [27] song from Walt Disney's 1937 animated film Snow White and the Seven Dwarfs, written by Frank Churchill and Larry Morey. It is sung by the group of seven dwarfs as they work at a mine with diamonds and rubies, and is one of the best-known songs in the film. It is also the

650

first appearance of the seven dwarfs.

The expression "heigh-ho" was first recorded in 1553 and is defined as an expression of "yawning, sighing, languor, weariness, disappointment". Eventually, it blended meanings with the similarly spelled "hey-ho". The phrase "hey-ho" first appeared in print in 1471, according to the Oxford English Dictionary, which says its nautical origin marked the rhythm of movement in heaving or hauling.

Hound Dog: [34] has been recorded more than 250 times. The best-known version is the July 1956 recording by Elvis Presley, which is ranked number 19 on Rolling Stone magazine's list of the 500 Greatest Songs of All Time; it is also one of the best-selling singles of all time. Presley's version, which sold about 10 million copies globally, was his best-selling song and an emblem of the rock 'n' roll revolution. It was simultaneously  number one on the US pop, country, and R&B charts in 1956, and it topped the pop chart for 11 weeks—a record that stood for 36 years. Presley's 1956 RCA recording was inducted into the Grammy Hall of Fame in 1988, and it is listed as one of the Rock and Roll Hall of Fame's 500 Songs That Shaped Rock and Roll.

Jimmy Soul: [22] Born in Weldon, North Carolina, James Louis McCleese became a preacher at the age of seven and performed gospel music as a teenager. He acquired his performing name, "Soul," from his congregation. Soul toured the southern United States as a member of various gospel groups. During this time he became popular around the Norfolk, Virginia area. There Soul was scouted by Frank Guida and 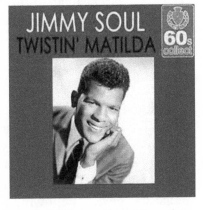 recruited to sing songs handpicked for one of Guida's other hit artists, Gary U.S. Bonds.

Leopold Mozart: [22] Johann Georg Leopold Mozart (1719–1787)

German composer, conductor, music teacher, and violinist, best known today as the father and teacher of Wolfgang Amadeus Mozart, and for his violin textbook *A Treatise on the Fundamental Principles of Violin Playing*—referred to simply as the Violinschule.

Miles Davis: [3] an American jazz trumpeter, bandleader, and composer. He is among the most influential and acclaimed figures in the history of jazz and 20th century music. Davis adopted a variety of musical directions in a five-decade career that kept him at the forefront of many major stylistic developments in jazz.

Sketches Of Spain can be placed in the 'most melodic' era of Miles Davis's work, being one of his most accessible and less improvisational albums which broke out of the constraints of Jazz as a genre. It was one of the four albums where Miles and Gil Evans collaborated with a small orchestra of horns and percussion.

Mozart Sonata in C major K 545: [14] described by Mozart himself in his own thematic catalogue as "for beginners". Mozart added the work to his catalogue on June 26, 1788, the same date as his Symphony No. 39. The exact circumstances of the work's composition are not known. Although the piece is well known today, it was not published in Mozart's lifetime and first appeared in print in 1805. A typical performance takes about 14 minutes.

Rachmaninoff, Sergei: [9, 14, 18, 21, 22, 34] 1873–1943; Russian-American composer, virtuoso pianist, and conductor; a personal style notable for song-like melodicism, expressiveness and rich orchestral colors. He took up the piano at the age of four. He graduated from the Moscow Conservatory in 1892, having already composed several piano and orchestral pieces. Following the Russian Revolution, Rachmaninoff and his family settled in the United States, first in New York City. With his main source of income coming from piano and conducting performances, demanding tour schedules led to a reduction in his time for composition;

between 1918 and 1943, he completed just six works, including Rhapsody on a Theme of Paganini, Symphony No. 3, and Symphonic Dances. By 1942, his failing health led to his relocation to Beverly Hills, California. One month before his death, Rachmaninoff was granted American citizenship.

Saint-Saëns: [3] The Carnival of the Animals is a humorous musical suite of fourteen movements by the French Romantic composer Camille Saint-Saëns. The work was written for private performance by an ad hoc ensemble of two pianos and other instruments, and lasts around 25 minutes.

The Swan, (Le Cygne) Written for Solo Oboe and piano, duration 3 minutes. A staple of the cello repertoire, this is one of the most well-known movements of the suite, usually in the version for cello with solo piano which was the only publication of this work in his lifetime. More than twenty other arrangements of this movement have also been published, with solo instruments ranging from flute to alto saxophone

Scott Joplin [9, 34] (November 24, 1868 – April 1, 1917) an American composer and pianist. Joplin achieved fame for his ragtime compositions and was dubbed the King of Ragtime. During his brief career, he wrote over 100 original ragtime pieces, one ragtime ballet, and two operas. *The Entertainer* written in 1902 was sold first as sheet music, and in the 1910s as piano rolls that would play on player pianos. It returned to interna-tional prominence as part of the ragtime revival in the 1970s, when it was used as the theme music for the 1973 Oscar-winning film The Sting. The Recording Industry Association of America ranked it

#10 on its Songs of the Century list.

Somewhere over the Rainbow: [9] "Over the Rainbow" is a ballad composed by Harold Arlen with lyrics by Yip Harburg for the 1939 film The Wizard of Oz and was sung by actress Judy Garland in her starring role as Dorothy Gale. It won the Academy Award for Best Original Song and became Garland's signature song.

Index of Names and Places

*(This index provides a quick assist to readers who would like to identify a particular **character**, or place, to see their relative importance at a glance. Numbers in italics indicate the name is not used, but mentioned or referred to. Many were featured in previous books about Julian. Place or business names are fictional)*

Name   Brief description   [chapter]

Brodie, Larry: Coach of the Cardinal Football team. [6, 8, 10, 11, 13, 17, 34]

Buz: Charlie Dawson's lover, mentioned only. [25]

Camp Walker [1, 15. 21, 24, 25, 27, 28, 30, 32, 34]

Cardinal: school mascot and school newspaper [1, 17, 34]

Carl: Men's Clothing salesman at Oglivy's Emporium; mentioned only. [30]

Casey Snyder: Life scout in the Wolf patrol; mentioned only. [17]

Charlie Dawson: Tom's older brother. [25]

Connor, Florence: Julian's fifth grade teacher, significant influence in Julian's artistic development. [14, 22]

Danny Laskey: Life scout, Senior Patrol Leader of Troop 9. He lives across the fence from Julian. At the end of camp he and Tony connected and became lovers. [4, 20, 21, 25, 26, 27, 29, 33]

Doris: Coach Les Switcher's wife; mentioned only. [2]

Dr. Janus: colleague of Pat Schaefer at the hospital; mentioned only. [14]

Dr. Overstreet: Francine's and Julian's family doctor; mentioned only [12]

Ed: one of Geraldine's yard crew; half Cherokee, mentioned only. [3, 12, 28]

Edison Howell: one of Kasey's housemates at Belmont. [18, 34]

Erik: Mark's first love, killed in an airplane crash when Mark was a college Junior. He has been Mark's only romantic partner. [5, 32]

Fernbrook Manor: Retirement home. [21]

Flaming Arrow: the leadership patrol within Troop 9. [4, 17, 18, 33]

Forrest, Francine: Julian's mother; estranged and divorced from her husband while Julian was an infant, she has made a new life in a new state in her friend's Real Estate firm. [*1*, 3, 5, 7, 9, 11, 12, *15*, 18, 20, 21, 22, 28, 32, 33, 34]

Frank Ferris: (Frankie) Troop 9 Bugler, Flaming Arrow patrol. He has been a sexual playmate of Danny's for fun, not romance; he is known as a 'ladies man.' [1, 4, 17, 20, 21, 33, 34]

Frankel, Art: Biology teacher; astute and progressive. [1, 15, 17]

Franklin: steward on Swann's private jet. [16]

Freddie's Shooting Gallery: an unauthorized diversion at summer camp. [19]

Freeman, Elliott, PhD: Dean of the School of Pharmacy; he and his wife Elizabeth are introduced at the banquet; mentioned only. [7]

Gail: office aide that escorts Julian to the opening Assembly. [34]

Geoff Staples: A scout from Atlanta that had a significant impact on several Troop 9 members and on Mark as well when they were at summer camp. [22, 25, 26, 27, 29, 30]

Georgia: Waitress at Sparky's Drive-In. [17, 18, 33]

Grandma Mattson: Julian's Grandmother. [18, 22]

Grandma Molly Sanderson: [21, 22, 24]

Grandpa Jim Sanderson: [21, 22, 24, 32]

Hallstrom, Eloise: Randall's mother; a bridge player and campus social figure, from a wealthy New England family that owns a "cottage" on Greenwich Bay. [1, 4, 6, 7, 9, 10, *13*, 14, *17, 19*, 23, 25, 26, 34]

Hallstrom, Helgar, PhD: Randall's Father, Associate Professor of Biology, and mountain climber, recently from Washington State University. [4, 6, 7, 9, 10, 11, 14, 21, 22, 23, 25, 26, 27, 28, 29, *30, 34*]

Harold's: a cocktail bar not far from the High School. [15]

Harvey Jennings: Sophomore sits next to Julian in Geometry, last class of the day. [1]

Hayden Caruthers: one of Kasey's housemates at Belmont. [18, 34]

Hayden Park: [19, 23, 25, 26, 27]

Hazel: A neighbor that visits Francine and Julian from time to time, usually with homemade cookies or a freshly baked pie. She's the unofficial news bureau of the neighborhood. Mentioned only. [18]

Henderson, "Baldy": Retired Journalism teacher—mentioned only. [2]

Henderson, Mary: Exec Secretary to University President Wayne Selfridge. [5, 7]

Henderson's Art supplies store. [21, 25]

Hopper, Eldon: Basketball coach, history teacher. ; mentioned only [34]

Ike: Woods family German Shepherd dog. [28, 31]

Initiate, Initiation: In Part 1, an overnight camp 'experience' in Hayden Woods that Tony induced Julian and Randall to 'enjoy.' [10, 22, 27]

Inside Guy: An internal monitor Julian created when he was a child. Originally a companion when he was home alone, he is now there to help solve problems. The device helped keep his thinking balanced, and often saved him from jumping to conclusions. [1, 3, 7, 12, 14, 15, 16, 17, 18, 20, 21, 22, 24, 25, 28, 31, 32, 33]

Jack: Captain of the visiting Coyotes football team. [6]

Jack Haley: from Atlanta; became Robin's lover at Camp Walker. [25, 26, 27, 29]

Jake: Black worker on Geraldine's yard crew; mentioned only. [3, 5]

Janet: Sherri's friend; mentioned only. [1]

Jennings Field: Airport near Swann's estate. [30

Jeremy Baker: Julian's friend, Star scout in the Wolf patrol; a Cub Scout with Julian. Mentioned only. [21, 22, 31]

Joe McDougal: "St Joseph" housemate at Belmont. [18, 34]

Jorgensen, John: Camp Director at Lake Walker. [14, 30]

Joseph Rainey: Black High School. [1]

Julian Forrest: Star scout, main protagonist. An only child, unaware that he has inherited extraordinary artistic talent from his father, a Greenwich Village sculptor whom he has never known. His goal is to turn his six year crush on Mark into a full romance. At summer camp, Sarge, the Camp Quartermaster, gave Julian a drawing board and large sheets of drawing paper; this diversion from his personal goal was transformative. He retains his secret goal to win Mark. [1, 2, 3, 4, 5, 6, 7, 9, 10, 11, M, 12, 13, 14, 15, 16, 17, 18, 19, 20, 21, 22, 23, 24, 25, 27, 28, 29, 30, 31, 32, 33, 34]

Justin Blake: Member of Zebra Patrol, Troop 9. Mentioned only. [3]

Kasey Wood (Kassa): Son of Lewis and Candace Wood of Boston. Kassa is an ancient Ethiopian name that originally meant "gift from God." In the Anglo American world, is sounded like the nickname sub for the initials K.C., or the given Anglo Saxon name Casey, which meant watchful or vigilant, a clue about its origin, probably an occupational or function descriptor for the one who kept watch. It also has seen use as a nickname for Cassandra [Kassandra] the Greek name possibly related to the central European Casey, a royal family name in medieval Hungary. Kassandra was the famous prophetess daughter of King Priam of Troy who correctly predicted the outcome of the Trojan war of Iliad fame. Kasey Wood was content with the compromise to Kasey. It retained his ancestral identity sufficiently. *{see Appendix for ore background}* [3, 5, 7. 9, 11, M, 12, 14, 15, 16, 17, 18, 20, 21, 22, 23, 24, 28, 30, 31, 32, 33, 34]

Kenny Johnson: Wrestler, one of the J&J pair who pose for the calendar. [23]

Kirk Fox: Student Body president. [1, 5, 7, 9, 11, 13, 15, 22, 33, 34]

Kurt Davis: Life scout in the Zebra Patrol. An encounter at camp with Sid was the beginning of a personal relationship. [21]

Ladendorff, Earnest: "Mr. L" Journalism Advisor, Modern Problems teacher. [2, 6, 13, 15, 16, 17, 18, 21, 22]

Lanny: First wrestler photographed for the calendar. [19]

Larry Sinclair: "Sir Lawrence," Belmont housemate. [18, 34]

Leo Bernardi: "King Leo the Lionhearted" housemate at Belmont. [18, 34]

Leonard Stafford: Camp Walker waterfront director. [21]

Little Joe: Julian's kindergarten friend in Joliet; son of Big Joe Biggs, a local jazz musician. [1, 3]

Marchbank, Benjamin: Professor of History, Belmont. [3, 5, 7, 9, 18, 31, 34]

Marcie: Theresa's friend in the cafeteria; Julian draws her portrait first. [1]

Mark Schaefer: Scoutmaster of Troop Nine. Major protagonist. He is a retail purchasing agent and manager. When he was a senior in college, he was asked to replace his former scoutmaster who died from a heart attack. This and his marriage of convenience have helped him to cope with a devastating personal loss [see Erik, above]. He devotes all his personal time to scouting. He is unaware that his self-imposed celibate mourning period is coming to an end. His personal demeanor is changing as a result, making him attractive to several of the older boys. An overt seduction attempt by a scout at summer camp caught him unprepared. He was sorely tempted but able to refuse. The encounter was traumatic, nevertheless—and continues to haunt him. [1,2,3,4,5, 7, 9, 10, 11, M, 13, 14, 17, 18, 20, 21, 23, 24, 25, 27, 28, 29, 30, 31, 32, 33, 34]

Marietta Hallstrom: Randall's eight year old sister; mentioned only. [4, 28]

Martha: Avery Oglivy's wife; mentioned only. [30]

Mason Davis: Swann's Butler and chauffeur. [7, 9, 11, M, 14, 15, 16, 18, 21, 22, 28, 30, 31, 32, 33, 34]

Middleton, Stanley J. Phd: Principal of Jackson High School. [1, 3, 5, 7, 9, 11, 15, 16, 22, 32, 33, 34]

Neville, Rev. Charles: Dean and Rector at the Abby of Bath during WW II. Facilitated the wartime romance of Lewis and Candace; mentioned only. [15]

Nick Harrison: Eagle Scout, Troop Scribe, member of the Flaming Arrow patrol. Appointed to mentor Julian as a troop journalist; at camp he and Tom felt compelled to sleep together in the troop supply tent. He confided in Julian about his romance. [1, 14, 15, 16, 17, 20, 21, 25, 26, 27, 29, 32, 33]

Norman Miller: Life scout, Patrol Leader, Wolf patrol. basketball team captain. [5, 17, 33, 34]

Nurse Jensen: Administers the infirmary at Fernbrook Manor. [21]

Paula Smith: Editor of The Cardinal school paper. [21]

Peter Gustafson: RN, colleague of Pat Schaeffer. [32]

Quimby, Alistair: Julian's World History teacher. [15]

Randall Hallstrom: Recently moved from Pullman Washington. Sophomore, in Julian's World History class. [1, 2,3,4, 6, 7, 8, 10, 11, M, 12, 13, 14,15, 16, 17, 18, 19, 21, 22, 23, 24, 25, 26, 27, 28, 29, 31, 33, 34]

Neville, Rev. Charles: Dean and Rector at the Abby of Bath during WW II. [15]

Rhonda: Frankie's girlfriend on the double date. [17, 20, 33, 34]

Rita Mitchell: Buxom daughter of an attorney, very bright and sexually precocious. Member of the Girl's Dance Team, she has been one of the social elite all through school. [1, 12, 17, 20]

Robin Simmons: Life scout in the Lynx patrol. [25, 26, 27, 29]

Rodney: usher at Orpheum. [20]

Roger: Mark's personification of his *membrum virile*. [24, 32]

Ronnie Johnson: wrestler on Jackson team. [19]

Roscoe: Assistant coach of Coyotes; mentioned only. [6]

Rosso, Joe: Choir and Vocal Music Director, Jackson High School; mentioned only. [11, 16]

Sammy: Barbara's's date in Part 1; mentioned only. [12]

Samuels: Swann employee who heads research and security matters; mentioned only. [9]

Samuelson: music teacher at Belmont; mentioned only. [3]

Sanderson: Grandpa Jim at retirement home. [21]

Sandy: Football player for the Cardinals. [8]

Sandy Rayburn: Friend of Andy's; mentioned only. [4]

Sawyer: researcher for Swann. [M, 30, 32]

Scott Jensen: Wrestler, one of the J&J duo Randall photographs. [23]

Selfridge, Dr. Wayne, Phd: President of the University. [5, 7, 9, 11]

Schaefer, Pat: Mark's wife; a Registered Nurse, studying to become an M.D. Their marriage is one of mutual convenience, not romance. They have been friends since high school. [2, 14, 30, 32]

Shakey's: a pizza parlor and teen hangout. [20]

Sharples, Lucian: Owner of Sharples' Delicatessen and Catering; semi-retired, was a well known gourmet chef before he developed his highly successful business. [M, 14, 15, 29]

Sharples' Deli. [4, 14, 18, 19, 26, 29, 30 14, 15]

Spenser, Scott: coach of the visiting Coyote Football team. [6]

Sherri Smith: Junior at JHS, is a sixth period office aide assigned by Roy Barnes to escort Julian to his office. [1]

Shirley Sawyer: Feature editor of the Cardinal. []

Sid Thomas: Star Class scout in the Wolf patrol. Julian's friend from school and Cub Scouts. He is known for his prankster sense of humor and his extremely skinny physique. [5, 7, 5, 17, 21]

Smathers, Geraldine: Real Estate Agent, friend and employer of Francine Forrest. She has adopted Francine and her son as family—she has no other. [1, 3, 5, 11, 12, 14, 15, 17, 18, 20, 21, 22, 24, 28, 31, 32, 33]

Snead, Archie: Boys' P.E. teacher. [15]

St. John, Lillian: Julian's English teacher. [15]

Stan: Center, Cardinal football team. [1, 11]

Stu Jenkins, drum player. [34]

Steve: JV coach, Cardinal football; mentioned only. [6]

Swann, Frederick: Multi-billionaire. [5, 7, 9, 11, M, 12, 14, 15, 16, 17, 18, 19, 21, 22, 23, 24, 25, 26, 28, 30, 31, 32, 33, 34]

Snyder, Gary: Research specialist for Swann. [21]

Switcher, Les: Wrestling coach. [2, 17, 18, 19, 23]

Ted: Cardinal football player; mentioned only. [8]

Teddy: Theresa's date at the Sadie Hawkins dance; mentioned only. [20]

Terry Marshall: Captain Cardinal HS Football team. [6, 34]

The General: Mark's 1962 Ford Country Squire station wagon. [5, 30]

Theresa: Friend of Rita; swaps a dance and teaches Julian the Mashed Potato. Invites him to join her for lunch. [1, 34]

Thompson, Robert: Superintendent of Schools. [15, 16, 34]

Times-Herald hometown Newspaper. [6, 8, 10, 17, 18, 20, 34]

Tom Dawson: Junior Assistant Scoutmaster of Troop 9 and Eagle
Scout. A star swimmer and football player; he relies heavily on
the analytic ability of Nick Harrison, his protégé and lover. [1, 4,
6, 8, 13, 14, 15, 16, 17, 19, 20, 21, 25, 26, 27, 28, 29, 33]

Tony Johnson: Star scout in the Tiger patrol. Talented, comical, and
usually in need of points; frequently penalized for simple
infractions and oversights. He is the troop's most talented actor
and clown. At the end of summer camp, he fell in love with
Danny, causing a major change in his behavior. [4, 25, 26, 27,
29, 32, 33]

Trish: Kirk Fox's girlfriend; mentioned only. [1]

Uncle Max: Julian's name for Sarge Oliver, Camp
Ranger/Quartermaster, retired Army Sergeant. Oversees all
maintenance at Camp Walker. At camp Julian brought out the
generous heart of the inner man and transformed his outlook on
life. [12, 14, 15, 20, 21, 22, 30, 32]

van Horn Ralph: Art Teacher at Jackson High School. [1, 2, 11, 12, 14,
15, 16, 17, 20, 22, 25, 32]

Wallace Jr. High: Julian attended there. [1]

Wally Hughes: Sophomore on the football team. The benchwarmer. [6,
8]

Walter: Grad Student of Helgar's at WSU. [26, 29]

Watkins, Gladys: School Secretary. [1, 2, 34]

Whispering Oaks: Secret space on the shore of Lake Walker. [27]

Wilson, Father Thomas: Rector at St Bartholomew's; mentioned only.
[14, 15]

Withers, Bernard: Teaches Geometry and advanced Algebra at
Jackson High School. [1, 12]

Witherspoon, Milton: [21] Retiree at Fernbrook Manor; teaches an art
class.

Wood, Lewis Phd, MD: Kasey Wood's father, a Bostonian. WW II
veteran, and Surgeon and Professor of Microbiology at Harvard
Medical School. [3, 5, 7, 9, 11, M, 14, 15, 16, 22, 28, 29, 30, 31,
32, 34]

Wood, Candace: Kasey's mother{*nee Kandake Selassie*}. [3, 5, 7, 9, 11,
M, 15, 16, *18,* 28, 31, 32, *33,* 34]

Worthington Realty: Geraldine's Real Estate business. [22]

662

Wyatt Wilson: "Big Dubbya" housemate at Belmont. [18]

Zack Peters: Black worker on Geraldine's yard crew; gives Julian an issue of Playboy Magazine on instructions from Geraldine. Julian adopts Zack's expression "no big deal" as his own. [3, 5, 7, 12]

Zeke: Black worker on Geraldine's yard crew; mentioned only. [3, 5, 28]

Zeyla Wood: Kasey's three year old sister. [14, 28, 31, 32, 33]

a word about the author

Eldot is a simple cipher: the author's first initial followed by a period, spelled phonetically [L. = Eldot]   Why? When his first novel was published in 2008, the subject matter was more sensitive and controversial than it is today. Lest relatives, friends or former colleagues be inconvenienced or victimized, the nom de plume was adopted as a shield.   Secondly, the author didn't want media opportunism to distort what the book was seeking to achieve. Media treatment of the subject was the major motivation to write Julian's side of the story in the first place.

All the Julian books received positive critical reviews. Twelve years later, the potential for controversy still exists, but the extremist groups have lost their clout—society has evolved rapidly: social media and the cell phone have changed the landscape; the Julian novels are made more topical than ever. By 2018 the subject matter had become relevant and openly discussed; a movie on the same theme was a contender for the 2018 Best Picture of the year. For this reason and to satisfy readers' response, the six books were revised in 2019, updated, and re-issued. *He's kinda tall* is the next chapter in the Julian-Mark story.

A pen name isn't easy or wise to remove, but it's appropriate to let the reader get a peek behind the curtain. Eldot has lived in the Pacific Northwest for most of his life. In order to dodge the draft and avoid the Viet Nam war, he took an occupational deferment to teach high school Drama and English. The interminable nature of the war and the draft lottery kept him in that occupation so long that the refuge morphed into a successful career. Why change a good thing? He became a local and state leader in his profession. After thirty terrific years as an educator, he retired. In his seventies he took up writing. As Julian would say, "might as well." Now in his eighties, he's still healthy and going strong. The novels are not autobiographical.

Leland Alan Hall

Publications:

1960: Emperor Commodus Prompt Book: Use of Masks in Drama
[*Honors Thesis, a translation from the Greek, housed at
U of O Library*]

1979-81: Editorials, *Oregon Education*

2011: *Little J and Roger* [eBook only]

2012: *Barr's Meadow*
The Poker Club
The Shooting Gallery
Thunder and Lightning

2013: *The Champions*
Inside Eldot's World: a literary gazetteer [eBook only]

2015: *You're in High School Now, Julian's Sophomore Year Part 1*

2016: *'56 Scrapbook* [PDF and spiral bound]

2018-19: *Julian's Private Scrapbook, books 1 thru 5 Revised Edition*

2019: *You're in **high school** now*, Revised Edition

2020: *He's kinda tall, Julian's Sophomore Year, Part 2*

Author Website Link: http://www.diphra.com

Facebook: https://www.facebook.com/AuthorEldot/
Twitter: https://twitter.com/AuthorEldot

about the Julian novels

Julian's Sophomore Year was to have been the title of one book. Alas, it has grown into two and it's still not finished—a side effect of the author's approach to composition: organic as opposed to pre-determined outline. Allowing the narrative to develop intuitively leads to unanticipated expansion; as long as that serves the story, it has been allowed.

At about chapter 20 of the first part it became clear that it would be impossible to tell all that's important about Julian's sophomore year within a single volume. Finding a good place to pause was required—that proved to be an artistic challenge. It took another five chapters to find a suitable point in the action.

Thus, the original title has been reassigned to serve as a series title. There will be at least one more "sequel" to get through rest of the sophomore year.

That's what happened with the first Julian novel—in that instance, a two-week timespan at a summer camp became a series of five novels entitled **Julian's Private Scrapbook**. *You're in **high school** now* covers a little over four months. *He's kinda tall* covers a little more than two.

An extensive discussion of this phenomenon is discussed in *Inside Eldot's World,* available to download free in a deluxe interactive PDF version   at http://www.diphra.com/Gazetteer.html].

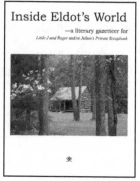

Inside Eldot's World
—a literary gazetteer for
Little J and Roger and/or *Julian's Private Scrapbook*

That book also goes into detail about the controversial aspects of the content as well as a number of literary topics.

Julian's story is fictional; it is an attempt to address the failure of society and the media to deal honestly with the problems that many young people face when it comes to sexual identity and development. It rises from years of observation and experience, and frustration. The vehicle chosen is unusual, if not unique: romantic comedy. The perspective is from within the characters: it is what they see, think, and feel—the view that is generally never allowed a voice. That, of course, is what can lead to controversy.

The "system" fails to recognize or remember that individual human beings under the age of 18 are conscious beings: learning, setting goals, and making life direction decisions at every turn. That is the world readers enter in these pages.

He's kinda tall is not dependent on the previous Julian novels; reading them is not a requirement. But it is continuing story: many of the characters are the same; their memories include what has gone on before, and are factors in their behavior. Anything that the reader needs to know is explained within the new segment, so referring to the earlier books is not necessary. However, for any who are not acquainted with the previous books, a listing is below:

The Julian's Private Scrapbook series

The two week summer camp of 1962 is the setting. The story is divided into five parts, roughly equal in length. Each part is written as if it were a stand alone, and has its own title. They are meant to be read in sequence, however, for a full and complete reading experience. The eBooks appeared in 2008-9.

Barr's Meadow: 300 pages; revised edition 2018 [first edition November, 2011]
The Poker Club: 334 pages; revised edition 2019 [first edition December, 2011]
The Shooting Gallery: 350 pages; revised edition 2019 [first edition February 2012]
Thunder and Lightning: 362 pages; revised edition 2019 [first edition March, 2012]
The Champions: 428 pages; revised edition 2019 [first edition May, 2012]

All are available in hardcover, paperback, and eBook versions at any bookstore and online at Barnes & Noble and Amazon.

He's kinda tall is the second in the *Julian's Sophomore Year* series

Independent Reviews of all seven books follow

Reviews

He's kinda tall

a romantic comedy
by Eldot

Julian's Sophomore Year, Part 2

KIRKUS

Another overly busy but nonetheless memorable snapshot of LGBTQ+ high school life in a bygone era.

HE'S KINDA TALL

BY Eldot · Pages: 664
ISBN: 9781732880566

The continuing saga of a resilient gay high schooler's adolescent adventures.

Prolific author Eldot picks up where You're in High School Now (2015) left off, with young North Carolina high school sophomore Julian Forrest facing new feelings and challenges in late 1962. The author again succeeds in establishing the era in which his protagonist's youth plays out amid themes of inclusivity, friendship, burgeoning sexuality, and the precarious state of race relations during the school desegregation movement of the mid-20th century. Eldot imparts many life lessons over the course of the narrative; the first is that focused dedication to one's schoolwork will not only garner one good grades, but also beneficial recognition from instructors when one least expects it. Julian's consistently pleasant demeanor, personal flair, and conscientious, hard work make his teachers think of him as a model student. His rare, enviable qualities draw the attention of several teachers who believe he would make an ideal helper for an incoming Black student named Kassa "Kasey" Wood. The son of a prominent Boston scientist, Kasey is a polite, friendly, and impressively talented young pianist who comes to appreciate the time that Julian devotes to helping him adjust to a new town, a new school, and new classmates; in a compelling sequence, Julian even insists on racial equality at a segregated "whites-only" diner. The relationship between these two characters would be sufficient to carry the entire novel, but Eldot has grander visions in mind, carried out by a parade of peripheral teenage characters who take their turns marching through the novel.

Their storylines—some fleeting, some with greater staying power—definitely add some panache to the tale and enliven what becomes a rather overlong tome, as it extends to nearly 600 pages in length. Readers will likely want Julian, a budding artist, and pianist extraordinaire Kasey to remain at center stage, and they often do. However, they're upstaged much too often by other scenes concerned with randy camping adventures, fart jokes, or extended family melodrama. The omniscient third-person narration is often dryly humorous, but the book also explores Julian and Kasey's friendship through the eyes of folks who know very little about them. This narrative twist affords readers a look at what it's like to be observed and blindly judged by casual strangers. As with the other books in this series, the author doesn't ever shy away from the nuances of sexual attraction, which plays a particularly substantial role in Julian's young life. The teens' flirtations and overt physical carnality are portrayed as unashamed and innocently exploratory; they show the characters to be primarily concerned with mutual, guiltless pleasure, but also fully aware of the necessity of social discretion in that time and place. Although the narrative does feel extravagantly expository at times, its overall sense of social consciousness is remarkable. A concluding, expansive glossary, filled with historical references to the 1960s, will be helpful for newcomers to the setting.

Another overly busy but nonetheless memorable snapshot of LGBTQ+ high school life in a bygone era.

He's kinda tall

a romantic comedy
by Eldot

Julian's Sophomore Year, Part 2

He's kinda tall:
Julian's Sophomore Year, Part 2

Eldot
Publisher: Diphra Enterprises **Pages:** 582 **Price:** (paperback) $19.95 **ISBN:** 9781732880566
Reviewed: September, 2020

He's Kinda Tall is author Eldot's latest installment of the adventures of Julian, a gay boy growing up in small-town North Carolina during the early 1960's.

Picking up from the last novel, it follows the rest of Julian's first semester in high school, as he's chosen to help Kasey, a Black boy who will be the first to integrate Julian's school next semester. Kasey's family is moving from Boston so that Kasey's scientist father can help develop a cure for a man named Swann's medical condition. As Swann, a millionaire, helps ensure an easy transition for the family and community, he comes to know Julian and his incredible skill at drawing.

Julian immediately befriends Kasey, knowing from his Boy Scout days that "everyone needs a buddy." His friends support him, helping plan the school assembly to introduce Kasey and eating with him at a whites-only restaurant. Julian brings Kasey out of his isolation, joyfully teaching him how to make pancakes at a sleepover.

The sex scenes display a spirit of playfulness and tenderness, employing boyish humor. When some of Julian's friends take a weekend camping trip, they mix sex with tickles and fart jokes. Eldot skillfully combines innocence and experience within the boys, showing both their eagerness for exploration and sensitivity concerning relationships. They have no guilt about sex, just an awareness of the need for discretion.

While all the books in the series can stand alone, several sub-plots here are interesting enough to inspire titles of their own.

The narrative contains one minor distraction: Since Eldot explains in a prefatory note that he tried to "lessen or sidestep the offense inflicted by" 60's racial terms, it's jarring that some characters think of Kasey as "negro," although the word is never spoken aloud or used pejoratively.

Nonetheless, with its well-drawn characters and detailed, nuanced understanding of how boys think, this novel will appeal to readers interested in coming-of-age scenarios told from a gay perspective.

Barr's Meadow: Julian's Private Scrapbook, Part One

Eldot
Publisher: Xlibris Pages: 281 Price: (paperback) $15.99 ISBN:
9781469145129
Reviewed: January, 2014
Author Website: http://www.diphra.com

Pleasant, nostalgic and ingenuous, *Barr's Meadow* is set at a Boy Scout camp in the early '60s, the fictional story of a gay young man named Julian.

Julian, nearly 13, is handsome, enthusiastic and affable, as well as a skilled artist. Julian has a crush on Scoutmaster Mark. Mark — who, while married, has been open to same-gender sex in the past — has resolved to confront this with sensitivity and fraternal affection, realizing that Julian's trusting nature could make him the victim of more predatory scouts.

Author Eldot (who writes under one name) explores the daily activities of scout camp and the politics of sex between teenage boys. The author focuses mostly on the gay characters and Julian's sexual thoughts, but this is not really gay erotica (although the back cover warns: "Not for sale to persons under 18"). With the exception of two somewhat explicit (though not heightened) passages, it reflects on same-gender, male sexuality while generally avoiding the salacious.

Eldot gets inside the heads of the characters, including Julian and Mark, as in: "Mark stepped around to the other side of the bed and watched Julian hustle. He bounced on his toes unconsciously. He had faced the unknown here and it had gone very well. I was right about this."

Barr's Meadow is comparable to other teenage boy coming-of-age narratives, such as The Last Picture Show, minus the cynicism, sophistication or relative depth. This doesn't mean that it's poorly crafted; only that Eldot's prose is simple, direct and seeks to examine the lives and thoughts of guys who are only beginning to view the world with introspection. Eldot walks the precarious line between making the boys evolved and depicting them as saints. He allows them moments of tenderness and nurturing without suggesting their virility has been tainted.

Barr's Meadow, the first in a series, never breaks through to the transcendent realms of literary brilliance, but it is intelligent, moving, well-grounded and memorable.

Also available in hardcover and ebook.

Author's Current Residence
Portland, Oregon

KIRKUS
REVIEWS

TITLE INFORMATION

BARR'S MEADOW
Eldot
Diphra Enterprises LLC (283 pp.) ISBN: 978-0-9966325-5-3

BOOK REVIEW

A debut novel tells the story of a young gay Scout's sexual awakening at camp. Twelve-year-old Julian Forrest has been raised by his single mother, never knowing his father. He loves drawing and being a Cub Scout. He has even made a Scouting journal full of drawings of his activities. He has recently become aware of his sexual desire, which is wound up in his habit of watching a neighbor, the adult Mark Schaefer, come home from work every day. When Mark comes over to the house to invite Julian to join his Scouting troop, the youngster can barely contain his excitement—or hide his erection.

Two years later, Julian gets to attend the annual two-week Scouting summer camp at Walker Lake. By this point, Mark is aware of Julian's crush, though he is unsure how to proceed: "What bothered Mark—a little, not a lot—was that Julian had become a presence in his thoughts...*at this point it's only a presence...but it's something new*...it felt pleasant, it made him feel light." The first two days at Walker Lake will prove transformative for many people, including Nick Harrison and Tom Dawson, members of the troop's leadership patrol. In the all-male environment of a Scouting camp, Julian quickly discovers some of the rules of his new masculinity—and a few things about his burgeoning sexuality as well.

Set in the 1960s, this series opener deftly depicts feelings of childhood nostalgia, as evidenced in Eldot's wistful prose: "At last the sausage patties and pancakes were ready and waiting in the oven. Julian helped Danny put out the OJ and milk. *oh! a bubbling sound— the coffee!* He rushed over to the stove to watch." But the author dwells heavily on the sexual thoughts of several characters, including the teenage Julian. While these aren't necessarily erotic, there is an undeniable romanticism to them. This will likely make many readers decidedly uncomfortable, particularly those scenes that deal with the attraction between minors and adults. Eldot may argue that he's depicting an experience common to young gay men, but if this book isn't crossing a line, it's walking right up to it.

An uneven coming-of-age tale.

professional reviews of independently published books

The Poker Club: Julian's Private Scrapbook, Part Two

Eldot

Publisher: Xlibris **Pages:** 279 **Price:** (paperback) $15.99 **ISBN:** 9781477118344

Reviewed: March, 2014

Author Website: http://www.diphra.com

This unusual novel is sure to cause controversy for its subject matter. The second in a projected five-novel series, the book takes place at a scout camp during the summer of 1962, and follows several groups of boys as they form friendships, learn new skills, and fall in love. Much of the book concerns their various sexual explorations; indeed, the "Poker Club" of the title refers to one group's method of beginning such activities – and the author is careful to note on the back cover that the book "is meant for mature readers."

In between the sex, several plotlines start to form. Julian, who has a crush on his scoutmaster Mark, learns more about life matters while interacting with his fellow scouts. Tom, an older boy who has been with many other boys, finds himself falling for Nick, one of his earlier conquests and now a friend. Geoff, a co-founder of the Poker Club, recruits other scouts to join in the fun, including Tom and Nick.

While the extensive explicit sex scenes can feel somewhat exploitative, generally they are handled well, combining experience with innocence in an endearing way. Julian in particular, while certainly experienced in some sexual matters, still has much to learn. His sweet, innocent looks make Mark and the other scouts want to protect him from such things, so that, for instance, while a remark about "choice buns" makes Julian curious about what that means, he doesn't learn the answer until nearly the end of the book.

The developing relationship between Tom and Nick is also fascinating; in the previous book, Tom hoped to seduce Julian but now only wants to be with Nick and feels guilty for his earlier pursuits.

The author includes a summary of the first novel along with maps of all locations. If readers are open to the subject matter, they will find intriguing insights into the complex world of boys in this unique novel.

Also available in hardcover and ebook.

Author's Current Residence
Portland, Oregon

The Poker Club: Julian's Private Scrapbook, Book 2
Eldot
Diphra Enterprises [perfect bound] 15.95
106,286 words   350 pages
ISBN 978-0-9966325-6-0

Reviewed December, 2018

Quality
Review
Service

Second in Eldot's Julian's Private Scrapbook (a summer fantasy) series: *The Poker Club* details Julian's ongoing adventures during a two-week stay at Boy Scout Camp. Julian (like many teenage boys) lacks a father figure in his life, and has a mancrush on Mark, the scoutmaster who invites him to stay in his cabin at camp. Julian already knows Mark, they're neighbors back at home. Mark senses Julian's ache for the presence of a caring dad in his life, and is happy to provide that, as he can. Julian is an ingenue in the true sense of the word. He's guileless, gifted, sweet-natured, gung-ho and quick with a searching and curious mind. Like the older scouts, Mark feels very protective of Julian, and tries to acquaint him with the convivial (but sometimes risky) world of maleness, with its jovial mischief, code of behavior, and amped up libido that tortured us as adolescents. Mark tries to answer all Julian's questions about sex, with admirable frankness and discretion. Julian is somewhat overwhelmed by his feelings for Mark (it's all so much to process) but there's great warmth in their platonic connection.

Like the other scouts, Julian has his goals: learning new skills, earning merit badges, improving his swimming technique, depicting experiences in his artist's notebook. Julian's sophisticated technique is impressive and puts him much in demand. Other key characters include Danny, Tom, Nick, Geoff, Bruce and Sid. There are all kinds of activities to master. Archery, riflery, backpacking, planning skit night, to name a few. Lots of the boys enjoy swimming the cold, exhilarating lake, exploring underwater breathing, speed, rescue and distance. Like the YMCA and other all-male gatherings, they happily and casually swim naked, often without a second thought. This sets Julian's interests in motion, but no more so than other guys.

The Poker Game referenced in the title is a diversion for the older, more intrepid scouts (Tom, Geoff, Jack, Brian) where slyly introduced removal of clothing leads to avid sexual experimentation and fulfillment. This is 1962, and the world outside may not be quite so understanding of such behavior, so the guys must be discreet and careful. Eldot recognizes that teenage boys (consider *Spring Awakening*, *The Last Picture Show*) have an impetuous, profoundly intense need to actualize the rush of male hormones that runs through their veins. Not all the guys are headed for a life of same-gender coupling, but they want to express their manhood, and enjoy each other's company, in a zillion different ways. They are giddy, game and secretive, but never disrespectful or brutal. They are kind and gradual, never foisting themselves. Eldot imbues these passages with a kind of celebratory energy while avoiding hyperbole. Julian gladly helps his friend Danny by rubbing lotion on his painful, sunburned "buns". What follows is spontaneous, friendly, and mutually pleasurable.

I struggle to explain the balancing act that Eldot manages in Julian's Private Scrapbook series. Eroticism between guys is a part of the tapestry, to be sure. But by creating a rich, layered context of male companionship and clustering, it takes on a different hue. Eldot confides the goofy, ridiculous, sweet, hilarious, imperative and earnest world of boy scout camp with its all-male milieu. Julian's previous lack of closeness with other boys serves as a springboard for discovering what it means to connect and bond. Male Fart Culture, silly skits, learning to shoot dive, cook for the other guys, it's all in there. There's a kind of spirited, military feel, with none of the negative implications that so often accompany that experience. Erotic enjoyment is described in plain, forthright, unflinching language that is neither inflated or suffused with salacious intent. What makes *The Poker Club* so effective is Eldot's mastery at evincing that sexuality is simply one aspect of a vast, full, contented life. He convincingly shares the rowdy, raucous joys of maleness, in all its boisterous and sometimes nuanced mystery.

QRS Highest recommendation

The Shooting Gallery: Julian's Private Scrapbook, Book 3

Eldot

Diphra Enterprises [perfect bound] 15.95
350 pages ISBN 978-0-9966325-7-7

Reviewed January, 2019

In part three of Julian's private scrapbook, 15 year-old Julian Forrest's odyssey continues. As suggested by the extended title, it is indeed a homoerotic fantasia, with a crucial difference. It is set within the detailed context of Camp Walker, a boy scout camp, with simple, exhilarating, all-male joys. Swimming naked, canoeing, archery, hiking, forestry; earning merit badges and enjoying the camaraderie of buddies, with a noteworthy absence of toxic pissing contests. Like similar, benign, men-only communities, they do inspections and dutifully make their beds, cook for each other, and plan funny skits. They help each other with skills sets like holding a bow properly, how to navigate a canoe across a lake, adjusting their uniforms just so, and plenty of banter and unabashed sharing to boot. They giggle and shake hands and josh and fart as if nothing could be more hilarious. It's really very touching, maybe because they can be themselves, without girls to impress. (Hey, I can't get the hang of this life vest. - No worries, man, it's easy-peasy. Here.) Eldot has a vivid feel for the energy and chemistry of guys enjoying the company of guys. And, yes, sometimes impulsively engaging with other blokes to appease a spontaneous boner.

Julian is crushing pretty hard on Scoutmaster Mark Schaefer, but he's too sweet and deferential to push or be inappropriate. Mark is well aware of Julian's attempts to catch a glimpse of him naked, and takes it all in stride. After all, many boys, straight or gay, are curious about other guys, and Mark gets it. Right away Mark realizes the extent of Julian's naivete, and insists that they share his cabin, lest Julian fall prey. Mark genuinely cares for Julian, and would never exploit Julian's feelings. He addresses Julian as a scoutmaster and a friend, answering his questions honestly. Keeping him safe, while encouraging him. Mark understands boys and men, and never shames Julian for his curiosity or intrepid desire to understand his burgeoning sexuality. When he gives Julian a talk about using careful judgment in certain circumstances, Julian gets the gravitas while feeling empowered to learn and grow. None of this, or anything else in Eldot's novels, is tongue in cheek. Not really. He never indulges in the winking, or salacious nudging so common in queer erotica.

And Eldot doesn't neglect the supporting cast. Nick and Tom discover unexpected intimacy in their sexual capers. Sid and Julian catch Doug and Paul getting oral skinny, and Kurt the muscle guy, find impulsive joy by experimenting on each other. Eldot introduces Geoff Staples, a beautiful Hawaiian boy, who is not at all shy (though discreet) when it comes to his desires and demonstrating formidable skill. In a delightful episode, Andy and Tony catch up with Tom on the trail and engage in some gorgeous, adventurous ways of sparking ecstasy. Throughout all of this, Julian brings such utter kindness and unpretentiousness, that he earns the affection and respect of all the guys. His impulsive bravado gets them jazzed; fills them with sublime glee. It's important to note here, the friendly, playful group dynamic that Eldot creates. It is a sad fact that when The Barr Meadow series is set (the early 60's) intolerance and persecution of the Gay Community was prevalent. Ruined lives wasn't the worst of it. It's also a disgrace that though it's gotten better, ignorance and abuse persist to this day. Eldot's halcyon gathering, where straight and gay chaps rock their mutual sexuality in't far off the mark. It's not exactly front page news that teenage guys have rampant libidos. Even after the age of majority, many men, given the right circumstances (often the absence of women) have no problem with same gender sexuality. Wherever they take it, they can move ahead without shame.

Eldot embraces the unspoken truth that guys can explore each other's eroticism without humiliation or self-loathing, if they know how; especially when surrounded by enlightened buddies. Eldot's prose is measured and down-to-earth, without the purple, hyperbolic descriptions that too often define man to man queer erotic literature. We go inside the character's heads and learn about their boldness, their reasoning, their graciousness, their insecurities, their eagerness to find the sybaritic realm of pleasuring. The encounters are plain-spoken and enjoyable, set within a plausible context, and not too formal to discuss the first time you connect, with amazing results. The Shooting Gallery culminates in a funny, randy, circle jerk competition; fifteen guys, glorying in bouncing erections, go off like rockets, if you'll excuse a flight of fancy.

QRS Highest recommendation

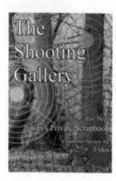
The Shooting Gallery: Julian's Private Scrapbook, Part Three

Eldot

Publisher: Xlibris **Pages:** 302 **Price:** (paperback) $15.99 **ISBN:** 9781477149867

Reviewed: May, 2014

Author Website: http://www.diphra.com

The Shooting Gallery is the third in Eldot's five-part series: "Julian's Private Scrapbook." We find ourselves in a Boy Scout Camp, where our pubescent hero, Julian Forrest, comes of age in June 1962.

Julian is a prodigy when it comes to drawing, a talent that garners many accolades. As we might expect, there are other skills to be mastered at camp: swimming, canoeing, archery, cooking — and, in this case, sex. In *Barr's Meadow* (Part 1) readers came to appreciate Julian's beauty, exuberance, affability and guilelessness. There, Eldot laid out the rituals and routines of scout camp: inspection and clean-up, naked swimming and campfire sing-alongs. In the midst of this cheery beehive, Julian had his first sexual experience with another scout; another encounter involved two older, more experienced boys.

In *The Shooting Gallery*, the author again presents the everyday activities we might expect, but now, sexual behavior is more frequent. While this kind of intimacy is often explored in fiction, it's much rarer to find it imbued with positive, canny eroticism, as it is here. In The Shooting Gallery, the tone is somewhat Utopian; the characters are not influenced by the usual shame or taboos society places on sex between males. Boy Scout Camp becomes a refuge where characters freely (though conscientiously) experiment with same-gender eroticism.

Eldot not only examines male-only sexual episodes, he anchors them in verisimilitude. Unlike more fantasy-driven erotica that sets up outlandish, compulsive scenarios, the sex here arises organically from the plot. The author goes inside the heads of the characters, so that we understand their bashfulness, their longing or curiosity. There is a nonchalant, playful tone that removes the stigma of queer intimacy that easily might have tormented teenaged American men in 1962.

All in all, *The Shooting Gallery* is a satisfying, intelligent story, notable for its warmth and credibility. It's perfect for those who appreciate homoerotic content without the usual overblown raunch so common to the genre.

Also available in hardcover and ebook.

Author's Current Residence
Portland, Oregon

professional reviews of independently published books

Thunder and Lightning: Julian's Private Scrapbook, Part Four

Eldot

Publisher: Xlibris **Pages:** 327 **Price:** (paperback) $15.99 **ISBN:** 9781479756841
Reviewed: June, 2014
Author Website: http://www.diphra.com

This unusual novel, the fourth in a five-part series, takes place at a scout camp during the summer of 1962 and follows several groups of boys as they form friendships, learn new skills, and fall in love. Much of the novel depicts their various sexual explorations, and the author clearly alerts readers to such content. "This series is meant for mature readers," he writes on the back cover. "...This book should be stored in a place not accessible by persons under 18."

In between the sex, several plotlines progress from the earlier books. Tom, an older boy who had been with many others before committing himself to Nick, makes amends for his past treatment of Kurt, an earlier partner. Nick advises Kurt on how to overcome his fear that his past with Tom will sabotage his relationship with his current partner Sid. Julian continues to improve his artistic skills, drawing beautiful portraits of the lifeguard Leonard and his scoutmaster Mark, while taking on further responsibilities in the campground. In a new development, Geoff, another older boy, becomes attracted to Mark and devises a plan for seducing the unwitting scoutmaster. Meanwhile, Mark begins to confront his past trauma.

While the extensive sex scenes may make some readers uncomfortable, they are handled well, showing the tenderness between the boys. Their relationships are fascinating to watch, as many are now committed couples, yet their emotional bonds are strong enough to allow them to learn new positions and techniques in sessions with more knowledgeable boys. Geoff's pursuit of Mark is handled humorously, leading to a situation where both attempt to conceal their erections. The author helpfully includes summaries of the previous novels, a glossary of terms and characters and more at book's end.

Thunder and Lightning is a charming read in spite of the controversial subject matter. As it shows further growth in the series' characters and their relationships, it sets the stage for the concluding tale.

Also available in hardcover and ebook.

Author's Current Residence
Portland, Oregon

Thunder and Lightning:
Julian's Private Scrapbook, Book 4
Eldot

Diphra Enterprises [perfect bound] $15.95
362 pages ISBN 978-0-9966325-8-4

Quality Review Service

Reviewed February, 2019

Set in the summer of 1962 at Camp Walker, Thunder and Lightning: Book Four is the continuing series culled from Julian Forrest's private scrapbook. Julian is a beautiful 15-year-old, irresistible young man. He is adventurous, sweet-natured, self-deprecating, guileless, and always eager to help. Beginning with Barr's Meadow, the series has evolved into something of an ensemble cast, with any number of narratives and situations to absorb and savor. There's Nick and Tom, Julian and Mark, Kurt and Sid, Robin and Jack, Danny and Julian, Geoff and Mark, to name just a few. Bear in mind, not all these relationships are sexual. The plot is somewhat intricate (as you might expect) with sometimes planned, often spontaneous sexual episodes, arising plausibly from circumstances. Thunder and Lightning captures the complications, follies and joys of male community and interaction.

Author Eldot is always meticulous when it comes to creating context. Consider for instance Latter Days, as opposed to, for instance, an "adult" film. The intense, yet measured, lovemaking between the two young men is more erotic, because it happens within the realms of the recognizable world. So it is with Thunder and Lightning. Eldot's structure never functions merely as a tenuous skeleton to connect unprovoked eruptions of robotic sex. He provides maps, synopses, dictionaries, site descriptions, commentaries, a glossary of cultural references, all to realize the experience of attending an American scout camp in the 1960s. He wants us to get what's actually going on. Here are young men cooking French toast, corn on the cob, and mac and cheese for the others. Setting up tents and digging latrines. Stripping naked to swim or play water polo. Doing morning inspections after breakfast. Thunder and Lightning is thorough and rich in detail.

Eldot spins an unforced homoerotica. It's never compulsory or salacious. Eldot recognizes (as any man will tell you) that teenage boys are about 90% horndog. However they navigate those treacherous waters, hormones go spilling into the bloodstream, and it's nearly impossible to think about anything else. Eldot balances this burden and/or blessing with the everyday tasks and recreation you'd find at any boy's camp. A canoe excursion might inspire an opportunity for learning new techniques. A break from swimming might culminate in one pleasuring the other. Erections would seem to have an infectious or (if you will) reverse domino effect.

These rambunctious fellows concoct poker games and target practice that mix urgency with playful release. Connections always bend toward consideration and mutual consent. In a particularly moving scene, Tom makes genuine amends with Kurt for past exploitation. Julian is not averse to experimenting (he finds unappealing appealing) to enhance buddy Sid's ecstasy. Some guys feel unexpected tenderness and exhilaration for newly discovered lovers, while others are happy to just explore and learn from each other, without deception or chicanery. Even Geoff, the incorrigible schemer, is careful with partners, wielding excitement but taking it slow. What makes Thunder and Lightning such a pleasure is Eldot's sublime celebration of young adult maleness. It has all the insanity, all the hilarity, all the panic and sybaritism and casual combustion, depicted with a true affection for its cast of young men.

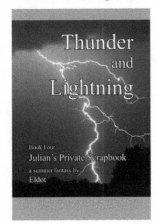

QRS Highest recommendation

The Champions:
Julian's Private Scrapbook, Book 5
Eldot

Diphra Enterprises [perfect bound] 15.95
450 pages ISBN 978-0-9966325-8-4

Reviewed March, 2019

Eldot's fifth and final book in *The Julian's Private Scrapbook Series*
The Champions follows Julian's progress as he reaches the last of his
14-day stay at Walker Boy Scout Camp. Julian is only 14 going on 15,
with all the best qualities of being that age. His gift for drawing is truly
phenomenal, yet he's humble. He's sentient and guileless and
adventurous and impulsive, but grounded by a sense of moral
responsibility and consideration for others. When he discovers two of his
friends are lovers, he's discreet and respects their privacy. Julian
intuitively, spontaneously knows how to make others feel deeply
appreciated and good about themselves. He sincerely enjoys making
others happy. In this last novel, he reveals a gift for showing the
profound beauty and character of others (like Sarge and Leonard) in
their portraiture, without realizing he's doing it. His relationship with
Mark has matured from effusive crush to one of mutual respect, deep
caring and empathy.

Anyone familiar with this series knows that Eldot explores the various
kinds of sexual attachment that happens between young men, and
sometimes, intergenerationally, as well. There are circle jerks and strip
poker, impromptu hand jobs and kissing and fellatio. There is casual
buddy sex and intense opportunities and sincere, full blown love affairs.
Often what begins as something brash and reckless evolves into
monumental emotions. Eldot could have easily turned this series into a
ridiculous, torrid caricature of queer lust, or a prolonged, insipid romp.
Instead he gives us an elaborate background of what makes boys and
men tick, when they are sharing each other's company. Attraction
emerges in various manifestations, among teenage boys and grown men
alike. No one is immune. Erections appear in all kinds of places: the
tents, the lake, the dining room, and on the trail. What makes The Julian
Series so brilliant is the absence of salaciousness. The sex is detailed,

and forthright, but not exactly graphic. It's not vague but it's not smutty. In this final volume of the series, I was overwhelmed by numerous moments of men vigilantly searching for the honorable choice—the conscientious path—and interactions marked by utterly canny warmth, devotion and tenderness. Yes, tenderness.

Just like other camps, the session culminates in contests, awards (merit badges) a banquet, promises and sad goodbyes. The scouts work out strategies for water polo and relays. Who's fastest, who shows an aptitude, who needs to be included. They practice their skits and work out seating arrangements and prepare speeches. They choose menu items and make presentations. Understanding they will soon be returning home, they try to resolve problems when and how they can. Eldot creates a very palpable, authentic sense of humanity in this gathering, weaving in occasions of humor, grace, panic, surprise and ingenuity. Situations like a scoutmaster carrying an injured young man for two miles, a cantankerous veteran transformed by genuine affection, sincere contrition expressed in the midst of adversity: all serve to imbue **The Champions** with substance and memorable experiences.

Speaking as a gay man born in the late fifties, it's hard to describe the impact this series has had on me. Psychologically, spiritually, emotionally. Being queer and teenaged (especially then) could be extremely painful, because it's a time in your life when everything seems disproportionately urgent, when you're desperate to fit in and must carry a secret that you never will. And we're not out of the woods yet.

The profound gift of this narrative is the creation of a world where same-gender sexuality isn't depicted as some grotesque violation of human goodness and desire for meaningful, physical connection. Instead, like any other aspect of mankind's identity, it's treated as an action sometimes whimsical, sometimes sloppy, sometimes exquisite, sometimes passionate, sometimes ridiculous. Eldot has the wisdom to grasp that sometimes a guy is happy to be with another guy, in that special way. And whatever comes afterward, it needn't be traumatic or vile or filled with regret.

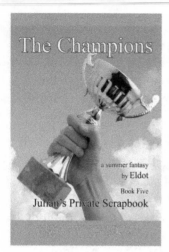

QRS Highest Recommendation

Quality Review Service

The Champions: Julian's Private Scrapbook, Part Five

Eldot

Publisher: Xlibris **Pages:** 375 **Price:** (paperback) $15.99 **ISBN:** 9781479780419
Reviewed: July, 2014
Author Website: http://www.diphra.com

The conclusion to a sexually infused five-novel series, *The Champions* takes place during the last day of a scout camp during the summer of 1962 and follows several groups of boys as they deepen their relationships, build on new skills, and ponder life after camp. Much of the novel depicts their various intimate explorations, from a final ejaculation contest known as "the Shooting Gallery" to the couples pleasuring each other on the bus ride home. In between, several plots building during the previous books reach their end.

Geoff, one of the oldest scouts, makes his move — even with his injured foot — to seduce the scoutmaster, Mark, in the middle of the night. Julian, while working on his remarkable drawings, befriends Sarge, the camp's quartermaster, and draws out the gruff retired Army man's soft side, even calling him "Uncle Max." Tom, continuing his process of maturing, learns how to get out of uncomfortable situations without the help of his lover Nick, and even becomes a confidante to other scouts worried about their relationships.

Mark comes across as one of the strongest figures in this novel, encouraging all the scouts under his care to become the best that they can be. He makes plans for Julian to receive art lessons after camp, further developing his talent. He shows his tremendous strength, both physical and moral, during his late-night encounter with Geoff. It's no surprise that his troop wins all the prizes at the last day's competitions, or that Julian has a crush on the scoutmaster.

Charming and humorous, with sex scenes that are erotic without being over the top, the novel successfully ends the series, while leaving open the possibility of further adventures. The controversial subject matter may make some readers uncomfortable, but for those interested in a sexual adventure told from a gay perspective, this is a wonderful look at boys transitioning between childhood and adulthood.

Also available in hardcover and ebook.

Author's Current Residence
Portland, Oregon

You're in *high school* now: Julian's Sophomore Year, Part 1

Eldot

Diphra Enterprises [perfect bound] 19.95
600 pages ISBN 978-0-9966325-3-9

Reviewed May, 2019

In this last (so far) of Eldot's Julian novels, we join 15 year-old Julian Forrest as he begins his first year of high school. Acclimating to the new environment of unfamiliar faces, different classes, different clothes, teenage girls, and women contrasts with the previous novels, where Julian was in Scout Camp—the female sex was nowhere in sight. A talented artist, Julian continues to sharpen his craft, evolving and perfecting his technique. He's still involved in scouts, and spends time with his scoutmaster crush, Mark, when he can.

But now there are all kinds of other experiences. Biology, Geometry, Art Class. His mother Francine, and her busybody employer Geraldine continually push him to interact romantically with girls. An especially unpleasant girl named Rita invites him to the Sadie Hawkins dance. An accidental collision in the hall results in gaining a new friend named Randall. He and Randall are invited to a campout by friends of friends; an arcane "Initiation" takes place that weekend. While sexy, it is not an altogether positive experience for the two.

In addition to Julian, Eldot explores the ruminations and lives of other characters, some more peripheral to Julian than others. We come to understand Francine's (Julian's mother) fears and hopes for her son. Her resentment of Julian's father and his absence from their life is explained. Mark's wife Pat cares for him, and encourages him to get out and find romance again. The passing of his partner Erik six years earlier is no longer a viable excuse. Her colleague Peter helps him navigate the underground opportunities in the big city to explore life of men who must keep one foot in the closet. Attention is given to Danny and Tony and Nick and Tom, Julian's friends from Scout Camp. Time is spent with Randall, his painfully shy new friend, who plays clarinet, loves photography, and aches for a sense of belonging.

Julian is gay, but consistent with the closeted 1960's, this is only known to Mark, and friends of the same orientation. Eldot manages a difficult balance in depicting Julian. He is kind and friendly, genuine, energetic, smart and phenomenally attractive to both genders. Despite this, Julian is never arrogant or full of himself. His caring impulses are intuitive and touching. He gives off a profoundly innocent vibe, but he's gung-ho when it comes to exploring his same-gender erotic impulses. Which is not to say he's cavalier or promiscuous. He's simply unencumbered by shame or guilt over sexuality. Eldot could have easily fallen back on Julian's well-established personality from the previous books. Instead, Julian continues to learn, mature and grow as a young man. His identity changes in both salient and subtle ways.

One of Eldot's strengths is his gift for imbuing the narrative with humanity. He creates a very complete, detailed world in which stereotypes (especially queer ones) are avoided, and the rare occurrence of warmth and tenderness between teenage boys is included. He carefully creates opportunities for this, and yet they feel canny, never contrived. Most of the key characters are gay males, but there's plenty of differentiation, quirkiness and nuance. Apart from their sexual identities, Eldot creates a milieu of boys who (just like the straight ones) all deal with the same problems: earning money, unwanted erections, demanding appetites, the goofy fun of nonchalant belches and sonorous farts. Also, it's a relief to find a novel that doesn't lionize jocks, alphas, prissy cheerleaders and the rest of the mindless mob. Time after time, in defiance of our expectations Eldot surprises us with his imaginative turns and events.

Having grown familiar with Eldot's treatment of sex between males, I have come to appreciate his frank, unflinching approach. It's never lascivious or hyperbolic. Never reductive or quaint. He doesn't idealize or diminish. Eldot respects naive young men as they process just exactly how homoeroticism fits into their lives, and the impact it has on their emotions. It's not unusual for men to sometimes share pleasure outside of intense heartfelt devotion, and Eldot neither ignores or condemns this. When Randall and Julian have their unfortunate involvement with older boys (and their irresponsible behavior) we grasp their mixed feelings of gratification and being wounded. You're in High School Now is an absorbing, compelling, sentient and comprehensive addition to the story of Julian Forrest, a young man who makes the world better (like George Bailey) for most every soul he touches.

QRS Highest Recommendation

You're in *high school* now

★★★★★

a romantic comedy
by Eldot

Julian's Sophomore Year, Part 1
Second Edition

QUALITY REVIEW SERVICE

You're in High School Now: Julian's Sophomore Year, Part 1

Eldot

Publisher: One Spirit Press   Pages: 610   Price: (soft cover) 15.99
ISBN: 9781893075771
Reviewed: June, 2015
Author Website: Visit »

This charming novel continues the story of Julian, from author Eldot's series Julian's Private Scrapbook. Set in the early 1960s, it follows Julian's coming of age as a gay man through the first half of his first year in high school, as he makes new friends, learns about girls, and navigates this strange but exciting new world.

The title refers to the refrain his mother and her friend continually use when explaining to Julian why he must pay attention to his clothes now and other new "rules." Julian's only real concern is his mother's interest that he take out a girl. Since he is only romantically interested in his scoutmaster Mark, that presents an obstacle. Fortunately, he attracts the attention of Rita, one of the school's prettiest girls, who invites him to the Sadie Hawkins dance. Julian's complete ignorance about Rita's intentions during the dance and the car ride afterwards (as well as his description to his mother later) provides some of the novel's funniest scenes.

Julian is certainly experienced when it comes to sex, however. He continues the explorations he discovered at scout camp the previous summer, both as an initiate in a secret society of like-minded boys, as well as with Randall, recently moved from Washington. Randall, a victim of bullying at his previous school, is instantly drawn to Julian when he sees him, and they form an immediate, deep friendship. Julian introduces Randall to his scouting troop and takes an interest in his photography, and Randall is deeply impressed by Julian's drawing skills. The two bring out the best in each other.

While not every reader will appreciate the sex scenes, they are sensitively drawn and important to the story. The only complaint this reader has is waiting for Part 2, where it seems the situation will become complicated. Well-written, with engaging, likable characters, this book skillfully presents the challenges and pleasures boys who love men face in growing up.

Also available in hardcover and ebook.

You're in *high school* now

Julian's Sophomore Year, Part 1

Reviewed by Amanda Silva, July 23, 2015

You're in *high school* now

This YA romantic comedy reflects traditional coming-of-age themes, further complicated by issues of sexuality and identity.

Eldot's romantic comedy *You're in High School Now* follows Julian, a young gay man in who is getting to know himself while creating his place in the world. This particular world is high school in 1962, a microcosm fraught with prizes and pitfalls, where bullies abound and fitting in is a constant quest. This narrative reflects traditional coming-of-age themes, further complicated by issues of sexuality and identity.

a romantic comedy
by Eldot

Julian's Sophomore Year, Part 1
Second Edition

These are sensitive topics for many readers, regardless of age, but Eldot writes with an urgency to connect with those young adult readers for whom these issues might be especially difficult. This story is an extension of Eldot's earlier series, the Julian's Private Scrapbook novels, but can be read in isolation. Readers should be aware it contains sexual content and adult themes layered throughout.

Julian is a sympathetic character, thoughtful and comical in his observations about himself and those around him. His internal struggles and interactions with his peers will likely connect with young readers, regardless of gender or sexual orientation. Self-acceptance rings as a universal desire and pursuit throughout these pages.

Although the writing is clear, the structure is not. While it is admirable for an author to experiment with a new writing style, the clarity of the work can sometimes be compromised. Eldot eventually explains—but not until the end of the book—that the narrative intentionally combines first- and third-person points of view as a means of freeing both writer and reader from "cumbersome conventions" concerning paragraph structure and punctuation. Eldot is a teacher with more than thirty years of experience; his frustration, or perhaps boredom, with convention is understandable. However, the resulting lack of clarity ultimately detracts from his work.

And this is important work. At the very outset, Eldot writes: "The grand social purpose that motivated the *Julian's Private Scrapbook* series lurks in the background, unsolved as always: social change is never as rapid as one would like. There are still bullies … So it's worth the effort to add a positive chapter or two."

Eldot's message is, indeed, as important as ever. When it comes to sharing that message through mainstream media, however, revisions in defense of convention and organization would bring these already bright and positive chapters to greater light.

FOREWORD
REVIEWS

You're in *high school* now:

Julian's Sophomore Year: Part 1

You're in *high school* now

a romantic comedy
by Eldot

Julian's Sophomore Year, Part 1

Q Press, 626 pages (paperback), 978-1-893075-77-1
Reviewed: **October, 2015**

KIRKUS REVIEW

The life and times of an adventurous, gay high school sophomore.

In the latest installment featuring Julian, the affable lead in the Julian's Private Scrapbook YA series, author Eldot (*The Champions: Julian's Private Scrapbook,* 2013, etc.) re-creates the autumn of 1962 as Julian embarks upon another school year full of books and boys at Jackson High School. Amid a backdrop of artistic inclinations and first-day jitters, Julian's romantic feelings for Mark, his Scoutmaster at Camp Walker over the past summer, continue to simmer, with their exploratory fondling lingering in his memory. But his concerned mother, Francine, encourages him to show an interest in girls. When Rita, an attractive, mischievous schoolmate, asks Julian, aka "the blond masterpiece," to the Sadie Hawkins dance, the obvious awkward clashing of orientations ensues.

Humor is one of Eldot's strong suits; he has an impressive capacity for penning farcical, innocently disastrous moments. He also builds a good supporting cast, like Mark, who is in a heterosexual marriage of convenience after his longtime partner died seven years prior; and Randall, a gay virgin and recent arrival to Jackson High. Intimate shenanigans occur at a secret society campout for randy boys, but the author takes care to handle these moments with restraint. Structurally, however, Eldot fumbles a bit. He shifts perspective awkwardly and adds too many disclaimers, style notes, and end matter that are meant to illuminate Julian but result in informational overload. Still, Eldot successfully taps into the experiences of gay youth with a believable blend of engaging characterization, humor, pathos, back story, and teenage angst.

Fun, frolicsome series with good humor and a message of unity and equality; new readers may want to start at the beginning.

KIRKUS